# TEMPEST AND SUNSHINE

### AND

## THE LAMPLIGHTER

POPULAR AMERICAN FICTION

# TEMPEST AND SUNSHINE

*Mary Jane Holmes*

AND

# THE LAMPLIGHTER

*Maria Susanna Cummins*

EDITED BY DONALD A. KOCH
*Simpson College*

THE ODYSSEY PRESS • NEW YORK

# INTRODUCTION

## 1

When Mary Jane Holmes died in 1907, *The Nation* carried a brief memorial in the October 19 issue in which the editor remarked, "It is an eternal paradox of our world of letters that the books which enjoy the largest sales are barely recognized as existing by the guardians of literary tradition." The guardians were most vigilant in the case of Mrs. Holmes. In her busy lifetime, she wrote 39 novels which sold an aggregate of more than two million copies; "yet she has not even a paragraph," continued the editor, "devoted to her life and works in the histories of American literature." To the commentator in *The Nation*, her omission from the literary histories seemed an injustice, but the very essence of her work was destined to exclude her. Mary Jane Holmes was a "popular" author, the kind that appeals to the unsophisticated taste of the masses. Nowhere in her voluminous writings did she exhibit the stamp of genius and workmanship that sets the artist apart from his fellow men. Her novels were the fustian fiber of a past social fabric, novels that now hold a greater interest for the cultural historian than the literary historian. And, as such, they are being "rediscovered."

Until quite recently, the fate of Mrs. Holmes was shared by scores of similar *sorores obscurae,* who a century ago claimed a massive audience at home and abroad. During the eighteen fifties and sixties such writers as Maria Cummins, Susan Warner, Mrs. E. D. E. N. Southworth, Caroline Lee Hentz, Marion Harland, Ann Sophia Stephens, Fanny Fern, Augusta Jane Evans Wilson, Catharine Maria Sedgwick, Mrs. H. B. Goodwin, and Emily Judson were conspicuous in the fireside idiom; today they are virtually unknown. Their novels were once devoured by an admiring public; now they quicken only the interest of those scholars who are less concerned with the impoverished literary art contained in their yellowed pages than with the prevailing attitudes and cultural standards of young America. For the few serious readers of Mary Jane Holmes and Maria Cummins who may still linger, this reprinting of *Tempest and Sunshine* and *The Lamplighter* will conjure wistful memories of the old "Sunday-school libraries," or of youthful browsing among the books in grandmother's parlor; but for those readers who are unfamiliar with such antique pleasures, it presents two rococo classics reflective of a social and literary phenomenon of a century ago.

The vogue of the sentimental domestic novel was sardonically noted as early as 1855 by Nathaniel Hawthorne while he was consul at Liverpool. A nasty English winter confined him to his dismal quarters in the consulate and he spent the better part of January and February reading the latest novels from home. Curiously, most of them were written by "bluestockings."

One in particular, by a fellow Salemite, spurred him to comment peevishly in a letter to his Boston publisher, William Tichnor:

> America is now wholly given over to a d---d mob of scribbling women, and I should have no chance of success while the public taste is occupied with their trash—and should be ashamed of myself if I did succeed. What is the mystery of these innumerable editions of the 'Lamplighter,' and other books neither better nor worse? —Worse they could not be, and better they need not be, when they sell by the 100,000. . . .

Hawthorne's query went unanswered; instead, Tichnor sent the author of *The Scarlet Letter* a favorable report on his royalties and "a box of the finest American apples." The senior partner in the distinguished house of Tichnor and Fields may have shared his friend's bewilderment over the appeal of such books as Mary Jane Holmes' *Tempest and Sunshine* and Maria Cummins' *The Lamplighter,* but their success at the book counter was no mystery to him. The masses clamored for them, kept library shelves bulging with them, and encouraged a type of feminine writing that dominated the literary scene for over a score of years. Tichnor himself contributed to the rise of the "scribbling women" by publishing Mrs. Emily Judson's *Alderbrook,* a series of "trippings through authorland," which brought both the writer (better known as "Fanny Forrester") and the publisher tidy profits on an average of three editions a year from 1847 to 1850.

The commercial value of the literary ladies was a matter of lively interest to every publisher. Assessing the book industry for the first five years of the eighteen fifties, Samuel Goodrich reported, in his *Recollections of a Lifetime,* that almost half the gross sales of $12,500,000 came principally from domestic fiction, an "advance of one hundred and twenty-five percent in ten years." He went on to observe that "the momentum of preceding periods was reinforced by the quickening impulse of a host of female writers, whose success presents a marked phenomenon in the history of our literature at this time." And he further added that "Mrs. Stowe . . . so far as the sales of her works is concerned, may be considered the most successful woman-writer ever known; Miss Warner, Fanny Fern, Mrs. Stephens, Miss Cummings (sic), Marion Harland, and others, produce books of which twenty, thirty, forty, fifty thousand are sold in a year." If the ring of the cash register moved him to exaggerate the success of Mrs. Stowe, his observation about the other ladies was authentic.

The average sale for Maria Cummins' *The Lamplighter* during the first two months after publication was 5,000 copies a week. At the end of the first year it had sold 70,000 copies. By the end of the decade Miss Cummins was the darling of every literate American household. It came as no particular surprise that, after 1858, two of her novels—*The Lamplighter* and *Mabel Vaughan*—were published in the famous Tauchnitz Library of British and American Authors. A place in this coveted collection (which numbered only 4,800 titles by 1929) was clearly a mark of international reputation. Moreover, the distinction was heightened when the darling of every literate British household, Elizabeth Cleghorn Gaskell, was asked to write the preface to

*Mabel Vaughan.* Mrs. Gaskell was also an accomplished domestic novelist, and her preface is noteworthy for its description of the *genre:*

> These American novels unconsciously reveal all the little household secrets; we see the meals as they are put on the table, we learn the dresses which those who sit down to them wear . . . we hear their kindly discourses, we enter into their home struggles, and we rejoice when they gain the victory.

It was fitting that *The Lamplighter* and *Mabel Vaughan* should be received into the Tauchnitz Library. The venerable Leipzig publishing house earned its early hallmark by specializing in Bibles and dictionaries; Miss Cummins' books were appropriately charged with piety and superlatives.

If the *genre* disgusted Hawthorne, it was not scorned by all talented intellects, then or later. Lincoln shared the mass enjoyment of the works of Harriet Beecher Stowe; Dickens did his best to advance the career of Mrs. Gaskell; the Irish novelist James Joyce acknowledged something fetching in *The Lamplighter.* The brilliant scholar George Saintsbury and the great Dutch artist Vincent Van Gogh were unashamedly enthusiastic about Susan Warner's *The Wide, Wide World.* Even the incisive critic Heywood Broun could pause momentarily in his grim pursuit of social injustices at the turn of the century to write a kindly word on the passing of the "school" of Mary Jane Holmes and Laura Jean Libby.

A poor choice of publisher resulted in a slower start for Mary Jane Holmes' *Tempest and Sunshine,* but within a few years its sales reached the quarter million mark. Even the enormous popularity of such British novelists as Dickens and Thackeray failed to limit her audience. The American sales of *Tempest and Sunshine* matched those of *Bleak House* and *The Newcomes.* It was said that her *Marian Grey* brought the firm of Street and Smith from the brink of bankruptcy to comfortable solvency by quadrupling the circulation of their *New York Weekly,* a literary paper which serialized a number of her novels. Her income from this one periodical alone was a substantial $5,000 a year. Publishers great and small competed for the services of the "scribbling women" and with good reason.

Two weeks after G. P. Putnam published Susan Warner's *The Wide, Wide World,* large orders came rolling in from Providence, Boston, and New York. The first edition was sold out in four months. Two years, half a million copies, and thirteen editions later, it set a record surpassed only by Harriet Beecher Stowe's *Uncle Tom's Cabin.* All told, Miss Warner's classic was reprinted 67 times and her *Queechy,* 34 times. About *The Wide, Wide World* an astonished reviewer in the *New York Times* exclaimed, "one book like this is not produced in an age!" His comment was merely rhetorical. Augusta Wilson's *St. Elmo* was so popular that the publishers were obliged to print special editions "limited to 100,000 copies." Mrs. Caroline Hentz's *Linda* and *Ernest Linwood* were in the hands of 90,000 readers within three years; Mrs. Southworth's *Ishmael* and *The Hidden Hand* topped 2,000,000 copies each; Mrs. Ann Sophia Stephens' *Fashion and Famine* and *The Old Homestead* earned her a sizeable fortune, besides recognition as "one of the best known of the

New York literati." She also held the distinction of writing the first "dime novel," *Malaeska*, a *genre* of quite another character, and one which is excellently discussed elsewhere in the Odyssey series.

The remarkable success of *The Lamplighter* "and other books neither better nor worse" was never really a "mystery." If occasional genius fretted over these best-sellers, the popular mind was in complete rapport with them. At a time when national life was in great turmoil, the American domestic sentimentalists produced a folk fiction with all of the appealing characteristics that distinguish a *genre*. A great part of the popularity of their novels arose from the sense of security and satisfaction they imparted. Society had just passed through a fabulous decade of unsettling events: a transition in political affairs from an old order directed by a professionally select few to a new order dominated by the rank and file; the golden promise of commerce, with all the hopes it held out to the aspiring self-made man, and all its attendant panics and disasters; the spread of maritime enterprise, which gave a new complexion to seaboard centers of population like Boston, Salem, New York, and Philadelphia; a tide of immigration which saw 5,000,000 new faces and numerous cultures altering the way of life; a geographic expansion bringing countless new names and strange places into ken. It was—as Meade Minnigerode so appropriately described it in *The Fabulous Forties*—a time of nation building when society was

> ever changing, all in motion and activity, nothing complete, the old continent pouring in her surplus to supply the loss of the eastern states, all busy as a hive, full of energy and activity.

Into the fifties this society moved anxiously and unsteadily, searching for identity while confronted with the need to turn its institutions into more "stately mansions" without adequate social blue prints to do so. It seized upon anything and everything that promised a guideline. The didactic spirit and moral tone of the domestic novels at least pointed toward perfection. In the absence of answers to larger social dilemmas, these books with their stereotyped formula and optimistic philosophy were at hand to offer a comfort. The home was the one safe haven from which the average American family could look out upon the chaotic excitement of the world. It was the sanctuary of the heart, the known quantity in an era of "billowing luxuriance of feeling." The tiniest home episodes were the stuff of the domestic novels, and their kindly homilies on family virtues together with myriad scenes of fireside domesticity were anodynes against the harsh realities of life. They allowed the readers to "embrace the common . . . and sit at the feet of the familiar." Since they seldom focused upon trying issues or great events, there was little need for the middle class audience to do more than transfer the narrative to their own lives and view the characters as normal people. For such an audience it was enough merely to "feel" the warm current of life that seemed to pulse through them and draw from it whatever interpretations were necessary to show how man behaves on simple and ordinary occasions. For the great middle class of Americans, the domestic novels were to literature what the Currier and Ives prints were to art—chaste, benign, and familiar.

2

The origin and the development of the American domestic novels are more difficult to explain than their popularity and appeal. Doubtlessly, their ancestors were the eighteenth-century English novels of sensibility. They bear an undeniable kinship to Richardson's *Pamela* and *Clarissa* in their portrayal of characters in high emotional response to actions and events, and to Sterne's novels in their efforts to raise reciprocal emotional responses in readers. But thereafter the lineage becomes cloudy. What occurred as acceptable sentimentalism in Richardson and Sterne became mawkish sentimentality in the nineteenth-century American domestic novels. Purely indigenous influences together with feeble talent and provincial literary standards produced a vastly different type of fiction by 1850. As early as 1842, William Gilmore Simms sourly described it as "a second- or third-rate imitation of a very inferior school of writings, known as the social life novel," composed chiefly of "the ordinary events of the household, or of the snug family circle."

By "social life novel" Simms obviously meant a corruption of the "novel of manners" in which the behavior and conventions of a particular social class are reflected. Such novels at their best give a detailed and accurate account of the social mores of a specific time and place. They are, perforce, realistic in manner and historically sound. But the American domestic novels were romantic, not realistic, and historically accurate only in the broadest reactionary way. The mirror they held up to the times was either concave or convex. Their hearth-side scenes have a stereopticon reality, like tableaux slightly out of focus. Whatever authenticity was mustered by the detailed descriptions of routine, daily domestic life was soon weakened by the impossible qualities and improbable adventures assigned to the characters. Their plots were frequently episodic and drawn to interminable lengths—a condition encouraged, no doubt, by the persisting techniques and demands of periodical and gift-book writing. Their characters were usually stock figures in repeated charades or postures of contrast, like Hogarth's good apprentices and bad apprentices. Just a glance at some of their titles reveals at once their altruistic purpose and their paucity of imagination: *The Lofty and the Lowly, Here and Hereafter, Keeping House and Housekeeping, Fashion and Famine, Married or Single, Charms and Counter-Charms, True Riches: or Wealth Without Wings, Spending or Saving, Blonde or Brunette, Alow and Aloft, Tempest and Sunshine, Live and Let Live, The Intemperate and the Reformed, Two Lives, Virginia and Magdalene, The Poor Rich Man and the Rich Poor Man.* Simms was right; they were second- or third-rate, inferior, and imitative. Still, they gladdened the hearts of many thousands of American readers with nostalgic pictures, exciting escape from the real world, and satisfying emotional catharsis.

Charles Dickens and the Brontë sisters cast a long shadow over mid-century American fiction. Their romantic devices were borrowed freely by the scribbling women. The underprivileged waifs, attractive rascals, suffering maidens, shrewish aunts, and elderly philanthropists came trooping through the do-

mestic novels like ghosts of their English originals. It takes no practiced eye
to recognize the American cousins of "little Nell" in Miss Cummins' Gerty,
or Miss Warner's Ellen and Fleda, or Mrs. Stowe's little Eva. The dubious
Murrays, Delafields, and other regenerated heroes are but Rochester-like
projections in native guise. The gaggle of tender-aged females, like Mrs.
Holmes' Fanny (Sunshine), who reach unspoiled adulthood after infinite
pages of suffering and tribulation, bear an unmistakable resemblance to Jane
Eyre and Catherine Linton. The Nan Grants and Uncle Trues, somewhat the
worse for Atlantic salt-brine and American salt-tears, seem to have traveled
right out of the pages of *David Copperfield* and *Oliver Twist*. Byron, Scott,
and Bulwer-Lytton were not infrequently raided for examples of wicked vil-
lains, gallant behavior, and drawing-room scenes. Mrs. Southworth was especially fond of creating characters of "high degree" and placing them in settings reminiscent of Scott. In spite of contemporaneous disclaimers to the
contrary, the domestic novels owed more to foreign genius than to native
originality.

But there were characteristics of a purely indigenous nature that set these
novels apart from other types of fiction at this time. One of the most noticeable is the pall of religiosity. Their pious tone was in part a concession to
the lingering puritan attitude that "products of fancy" were respectable only
if they offered moral instruction; in part, it was a natural response to the
mood of religious evangelism that moved a great many Americans during the
antebellum decades. In the feverish search for ways and means of turning
America into a utopia, all manner of sects and cults sprang up, most of them
with a quasi-religious foundation. The colorful Chardon Street Convention
of 1840, so graphically described by Emerson, was typical of the kind of activity going on in many corners of the country. The Millerites, Jansonites,
Owenites, Shakers, Mormons, Fourierists, Methodists, Calvinists, Amanites,
Unitarians, Spiritualists, were all stirring "the pot of national Uplift." The
air was charged with "moral electricity," and the mood spilled over into
feminine fiction. In spite of Cooper's warning that "the supreme folly of the
hour is to imagine that perfection will come before its stated time," the
domestic novelists made a noble attempt to hasten it. Every novel carried its
homiletic, almost every page its injunction. Characters were more often
vehicles of some sober-suited truth than believable persons. Religious sentiment spread through these books like the cloying odor of funeral flowers.
And the astonishing thing is that the authors were entirely sincere about it.
T. S. Arthur through his heroine, Anna, in *The Three Eras of a Woman's
Life* spoke for all the domestic novelists when he had her say, "unless our
actions are regulated by Divine laws, our morality has but a slender base to
stand upon." The avowed purpose of many of the domestic novels was to
strengthen this base.

The word "novel" disturbed Susan Warner when it was applied to *The
Wide, Wide World*. She preferred to call it "story," a term, in her mind,
closely akin to "parable." Her sister Anna claimed that Susan in all her work
lived by the motto: "Life, is to do the will of God." Mrs. Stowe humbly admitted that God wrote *Uncle Tom's Cabin*—she was merely the scribe; Eliza-

beth Stuart Phelps frankly owned that her masterpiece, *The Gates Ajar*, was written at the bidding of an angel. Mary Jane Holmes seldom resolved the sorrows and trials of her characters without ostensible lessons in humility and Christian piety. It was "providence" that enabled Edna, in Mrs. Wilson's *St. Elmo*, to work a miracle of transformation on the unsavory Murray. And little Gerty of *The Lamplighter* experiences her renascence when she learns the meaning of prayer and discovers the "religion of the heart."

Less noticeable than the religious nature, but a definite characteristic nonetheless, is the thoroughly feminine cast of the domestic novels. Shortly after Hawthorne dispatched his vituperative letter about female authors to Tichnor, he read Fanny Fern's *Ruth Hall*. In a mood of contrition he penned another note to his publisher:

> I have since been reading 'Ruth Hall'; and I must say I enjoyed it a good deal. The woman writes as if the Devil was in her; and that is the only condition under which a woman ever writes anything worth reading . . . can you tell me anything about this Fanny Fern? If you meet her, I wish you would let her know how much I admire her.

Hawthorne had no way of knowing that the "Devil" he found in Fanny Fern—nee Sarah Payson Willis—was roused directly by a particular male, her famous brother N. P. Willis, who treated her rather shabbily when she was struggling for literary recognition. It would not have mattered if he *had* known about the Willis family feud, in time he would have discovered the same satanic quality in other domestic novels. Among the numerous shadings in these novels are the umbrae of Adam and Eve in the Garden.

It is a curious fact that although students of nineteenth-century American fiction frequently mention the pious, conservative, sentimental nature of domestic novels, they seldom acknowledge the thrust these novels gave to the nineteenth-century feminist movement. The devil that Hawthorne detected was a manifestation of the feminine mystique of a hundred years ago. Domestic novels were written mainly by women, about women, for women. The few successful male writers—like T. S. Arthur, E. P. Roe, and J. G. Holland—who applied the domestic formula, either did not understand the psyche of them or were unaware that their male characters were inevitably brought to heel in one way or another by their female protagonists. Ruth Hall emerges victorious over her selfish brother and captures the affections of editor Walters in *Ruth Hall*. Gabriella gradually transforms Ernest from a small-minded person to a decent human being in Mrs. Hentz's *Ernest Linwood*. Little Gerty of *The Lamplighter* rises from sordid beginnings to angelic heights, capturing and converting male hearts—including Willie's—under the most unbelievable odds. Rosa Lee in Mrs. Holmes' *Meadow Brook* subdues the proud Richard Delafield and wins him for a husband. In novel after novel the subtle subjugation of the male is carried out. If the heroine doesn't marry the hero, she mothers him; if she doesn't charm him, she frustrates him; if she doesn't ennoble him she enfeebles him. In each case, the heroine emerges as a strong character and the hero a moulded figure whose design is nearly always determined by the female. Helen Waite Papashivily insists that the domestic novels carried a "faint bitter taste of poison," that they were "a witches' broth, a lethal draught brewed by women and used by women to destroy their common enemy man." There may be some truth in her remarks, for just about the time the floodgates of feminine fiction opened and the domestic novels began pouring on the market, the first Woman's Rights Convention, held at Seneca Falls, New York, in July 1848, came to a close on an ominous note: "We shall employ agents, circulate tracts, petition state and national legislatures and endeavor to enlist the pulpit and press in our behalf." Enlist the press they did! For the next thirty years feminine authors labored in the garden, beguiling a generation of readers with literary fruit more luscious than the apples Tichnor sent Hawthorne. The image of conspiring Eves may not be amiss, when we remember that one of the most prolific of the domestic novelists always insisted that her byline read—Mrs. E. D. E. N. Southworth.

Seldom in the domestic novels did the authors overtly propagandize for equality of the sexes. After all, the stock perspective of the day was that woman's place was in the home; it was brazen to be anything other than a clinging-vine. Woman's role was that of cook-laundress-seamstress-nurse-gardener-counselor-housekeeper. If she had talent, it was best channeled in singing, needlework, or piano playing. Bluestockings were frowned upon. Her highest purpose was to be a wife and mother. The business of politics, commerce, and reform was man's domain. She was not expected to display an interest in causes or public affairs. Nevertheless, women did commence to take part in the life of the mind during the second quarter of the century. The bolder ones became militant reformers—"crusaders in crinoline"; the more conservative wrote vapid verse and domestic novels. Such causes as temperance, abolition, and women's rights slipped into the dialogue of their novels, but always carefully obscured by a mantle of piety or innocently inserted as part of the "kitchen realism." Without resorting to the deliberate attacks and critical techniques of "cause" or "purpose" fiction, the feminine writers were highly effective as fomites, seemingly innocent instruments of contagion whose warmly sentimental stories leavened the popular mind to constructive action against a variety of social injustices. The apparent shallowness of these novels is deceptive; they were, in fact, marvels of persuasion— all fraught with countless examples of the things society strove to reform, all charged with noble precepts, all sharply tuned to the exciting emotional pitch of the times.

The domestic novels resist any precise definition. Beyond their fireside detail, freighted morality, and feminine point of view, they blend with the broad stream of American romantic fiction. They were sensational, but no more so than the Beadle and Adams dime novels. They were inspirational, but less objectively so than the manuals of self-help and the success stories of the Horatio Alger type. They were to the mid-nineteenth century middle class mind—especially the feminine segment of it—what the "hope-chest" was to the woman-in-waiting of a generation ago. Perhaps the best view of them was set forth by Professor Herbert Ross Brown in his *The Sentimental Novel in America:*

Here are to be found the compensations in fiction for the coveted values
life had failed to give them. Nowhere outside of their books could these
women have encountered a delicacy so fastidious and a poetic justice so
immutable. Nowhere beyond their pages could womanhood have survived with such glory the fiery ordeals of hot pursuit, hairbreadth escape,
and uncomplaining endurance . . . these domestic novels did succeed in
presenting ideals which were cherished. . . . Their yellowed pages reveal
the aspirations and hopes, which in its earnest moments, a generation of
readers strove to achieve.

3

*Tempest and Sunshine* and *The Lamplighter* were both published the same
year, 1854. Mary Jane Hawes Holmes was then a young matron of 29, Maria
Susanna Cummins a premature spinster two years her junior. Their careers
coincided for about a decade until October 1, 1866, when, after a long period
of illness, Maria Cummins died at her residence in Dorchester, Massachusetts.
Mrs. Holmes continued to flourish, averaging a book a year, until shortly before her death on October 6, 1907. *The Lamplighter* became a best-seller
almost immediately, while *Tempest and Sunshine* gathered readers slowly at
first but soon in such numbers that Mrs. Holmes' second novel, *The English
Orphans,* published in 1855, was virtually assured success. In 1856 a collection
of her stories, *The Homestead on the Hillside,* and what is often considered
her best novel, *Lena Rivers,* continued to add to her growing popularity.
These were followed by two more highly acclaimed novels—*Meadowbrook* in
1857 and *Dora Deane* in 1858. Thereafter each successive book proved profitable to author and publisher alike. During the sixties and early seventies no
writer, with the possible exception of E. P. Roe, had a stronger hold on the
public's affection. In 1872 the records of the largest municipal library in New
England reported that her novels circulated as widely as the durable favorites
*Ernest Linwood* (Caroline Lee Hentz), *The Hidden Hand* (Mrs. E. D. E. N.
Southworth), and the current *Barriers Burned Away* (E. P. Roe). Year after
year in cloth and in paperbacks her books maintained a steady market. They
sold especially well in more expensive bindings at the holiday season as suitable gifts for friends and family. In "cheapbacks" they were hawked in railroad stations, on trains, and wherever else light literature was sold. As late
as 1927 some of them were still in print, presumably for the same reasons
that made them good publishing ventures sixty years earlier.

Maria Cummins' fame was perhaps more brilliant, if shorter lived, than
that of Mrs. Holmes. The reputation of Mrs. Holmes was a steady accumula-
tion, Miss Cummins' a sudden bright glow. When *The Lamplighter* first appeared, it was the most talked about novel of the year. J. P. Jewett first
brought it out in Boston and within a short time Sampson, Low and Company issued it in London as an import. Other British publishers unhampered
by copyright restrictions released unauthorized editions. It soon appeared on
the Continent translated into French and German. A number of the European versions were altered, abridged, even rewritten, but it all added luster

# INTRODUCTION

to the name of Maria Cummins. There was something about the very title that roused the sentimentality of an age, something that was undiminished after the novel was read. Perhaps the frequency with which the story was pirated, parodied, and praised during its first flush of popularity hints at the kind of ingredients that gave the novel its appeal. Miss Cummins applied the cardiac formula again in 1857 with *Mabel Vaughan*. Again her light shone brightly in the literary heavens. Readers responded favorably to this new offering of "moral molasses" and especially to its warning that good old home-life could never be replaced by the new-fangled "boarding-houses" that were springing up in cities for the young women who were lured out of their village homes by the promise of high paying jobs in the urban mills and factories. This novel was followed in 1860 by *El Fureidis,* a tale of the Levant drawn purely "from imagination." Her last novel, *The Haunted Heart,* appeared in 1864. It was her poorest novel, but it had a certain intensity which may have been inspired by reflections on her personal condition. Her last years were plagued with ill health and soon after *The Haunted Heart* was published, she died.

Among the many charms that contemporary reviewers found in the domestic novels were their pictures of small town life. If anything about these novels can be called realistic, it is the authentic settings so familiarly employed by the authors. A great majority of the domestic novelists were women who were born and bred in New England. They knew intimately the bittersweet experiences of down-East rural living. Whether they grew up on some lonely farm or in some quiet village, their memories retained the physical details and the cherished ideals of the New England way of life. The ties of large families, the simple pleasures of quilting parties or husking bees, the mellow hours in the district school, and the pious hours in Sunday school marked a mode of existence common to all, a mode seriously threatened by the encroachment of growing urbanization and the rise of industrialism. Mary Jane Holmes and Maria Cummins were true daughters of New England. Their novels at times were as poignantly regional as any of the work of the later local colorists. *The Lamplighter* begins in Boston and *Tempest and Sunshine* in Versailles, Kentucky, but they meet on the common ground of New England values and experiences. A critic for *The North American Review* spoke for both novels in 1855 when he wrote "The characterization is exquisite. . . . The picture of rural and village life . . . deserves to be hung up in perpetual memory as types of humanity fast becoming extinct. . . ."

The type of "humanity" the *North American* critic had in mind may well be extinct, but New England women who write novels giving pictures of small town life are still among us—therein lies an irony. When Sarah Bowerman wrote the *Dictionary of American Biography* article on Mrs. Holmes, she concluded by saying "Long before Sinclair Lewis gave 'Main Street' a particular small town life identity, Mary Jane Holmes was writing 'Main Street' stories." A hundred years after Mrs. Holmes (in dimity and shawl) wrote her "pictures," another New England housewife (in masculine shirt and blue-jeans) gave us hers. The novel was *Peyton Place.* And about the author the

*New York Times* said, "Sinclair Lewis would no doubt have hailed Grace Metalious as a sister-in-arms." The *Denver Post* in describing *Peyton Place* used words strikingly similar to those describing *Tempest and Sunshine* in contemporary reviews: "alive-tender . . . , bittersweet, full to overflowing with human frailties mingled with human greatness." The parallel could be drawn to considerable length, but suffice it to say that both writers knew the value of the emotional and the sensational, both recognized the touching effect of oppressed womanhood, both employed the same time-tried narrative techniques. *Tempest and Sunshine* and *Peyton Place* open in autumn (there is something ecstatically melancholic about October) and then plunge immediately into the graphic detail that made them "pictures." If the cherished ideals of *Tempest and Sunshine* were tarnished in *Peyton Place,* the human concern was not, for the author intended her book to be an exposé of "the false fronts and bourgeois pretensions of allegedly respectable communities." Unfortunately, she reveled too much in the sordid and her book lost its constructive purpose. In missing its mark it yet retained its pictorial quality, for the *Denver Post* reviewer added, "it will bring a reminiscence of kind to small towners everywhere," even as *Tempest and Sunshine* did and still does. Professor Carl Bode has called attention to the "soap opera" content of the nineteenth-century domestic novels. The crowning touch to the irony occurs when we note that *Peyton Place,* notwithstanding its "sophisticated" idiom and perspective, is enjoyed today in the form of a popular television serial by countless housewives, who find in its sensational story the same "detergent" to daily cares that housewives a century ago found in the domestic novels.

## 4

Mary Jane Holmes was born in Brookfield, Massachusetts. Some confusion surrounds the date of her birth, but the *Vital Records* of Brookfield list April 5, 1825. She was the daughter of Preston and Fanny Olds Hawes, both of old New England families. Her grandfather Joel Hawes served in the militia during the Revolutionary War; his son the Reverend Joel Hawes became a well-known pulpit orator and essayist. The latter's influence contributed to the moral tone of his niece's books. The flashes of droll humor that appear in her novels may have been the inheritance of her father, Preston. Her mother Fanny was a sensitive woman who encouraged in her daughter a love of poetry and romance. At the age of three Mary Jane began her formal schooling, at six she was accomplished in English grammar, and at thirteen became a teacher herself in the district school. Before she was sixteen she published her first story. She might thereafter have settled permanently into the kind of routine spinsterhood that Mary Wilkins Freeman portrays in Louisa Ellis, the heroine of her story *A New England Nun,* but fate had other things in store for her.

In 1849 Mary Jane married a young lawyer from Brockport, New York, Daniel Holmes. She was then twenty-four and he was twenty-one. It was a good union, but childless, and in the absence of offspring she mothered

Daniel. Her husband was a frail, diminutive person who suffered from recurrent malarial attacks, but his intelligent mien, judicial top hat, and frock coat gave him a dignity that compensated for his slight stature and physical infirmities. Soon after their marriage, legal business took Daniel to Versailles, Kentucky, and Mary Jane willingly followed him. Here she gathered background material for *Tempest and Sunshine* and some of her later novels. After a year they returned to Brockport, where Daniel continued with his law practice and Mary Jane wrote *Tempest and Sunshine*.

As novel followed novel, success mounted for Mary Jane. She acquired Brown Cottage as a permanent home in Brockport and a summer residence at Oak Bluffs, Massachusetts. When not busy writing, she and her husband traveled widely to England, France, Russia, the Mediterranean, and the Far East. From these distant places she gathered curios of all kinds—statuary, paintings, furniture, tapestries—which brightened the rooms of Brown Cottage. Her elegant wardrobe and collection of fine jewelry made her one of the best-dressed women of the day. But the rewards of her success were as often shared with her friends and her public. She gave a tenth of her income to the church and with her own money built the parish house in Brockport. She paid for the education of two little Japanese girls whom she befriended during her travels. She gave aid to the needy dependents of numerous Civil War soldiers and to the veterans themselves after they returned from the war. Her time was as generously given as her fortune. She organized a local temperance society, a literary club, and a town reading room, she taught a Sunday School class, and her home was always open to groups of young girls for whom she gave talks on art and travel. During the severe depression of 1893, Mrs. Holmes could be seen daily tending the soup kitchen she maintained for the unemployed of her native city. "She loved everybody and everybody loved her," declared her housekeeper, Mrs. Jennie Stewart, who benefited from the writer's kindnesses as frequently as anyone. The tall, slightly stooped, sweet-faced mistress of Brown Cottage was indeed a favorite with all kinds of people, especially the Brockport children, who knew that a visit to the "cottage" was always good for a handful of cookies.

To her contemporaries, Mrs. Mary Jane Holmes was a good woman whose works served a good purpose and were accepted as good literature. Her style was plain and straightforward, and it reflected an ethical code equally as uncomplicated. Her virtuous characters were always lily-white, her villainous ones always double-dyed. No blended figure ever appeared to confuse a reader or cloud a moral. Her skill in recreating the familiar scenes of town and country life more than offset the comments of occasional critics who called attention to her repetitious plots and commonplace action. A sophisticated reader today would find her language wearisome, filled with trite clichés and hackneyed phrases. He would find less humor in the characterization of the bumptious "pa" Middleton in *Tempest and Sunshine* than in the artless handling of the heroine in *Dora Deane,* who on one occasion was made to exclaim in all seriousness—"I would rather die than marry a man I did not love because of his gold." But an audience who found nothing strange in novels where every hero "lights up his Havana" and every heroine "reclines on soft cushions," who found nothing disturbing when my-lady "little dreams" that males sometimes have dishonorable intentions or when things "grate harshly" on the nerves—such an audience could and did accept the novels of Mary Jane Holmes on their face value. Such an audience mourned her passing, when, after returning from her summer home at Oak Bluffs, she was stricken as her train passed through Albany, but she managed to reach Brown Cottage where she died a few days later. Her novels have gone the way of all *genres,* but in her time she was remembered because "she had ideals of life, . . . she was never vulgar, and . . . she was in dead earnest."

Maria Susanna Cummins was born in Salem, Massachusetts, on April 9, 1827. If anything, she was even more a child of New England than Mary Jane Holmes. Her father, David Cummins, was a distinguished judge, highly regarded by the townspeople of Salem for his intellectual pursuits in addition to the law. His family line goes back to earliest colonial times to Isaac Cummings (the name was then spelled with a "g"), an immigrant of Scottish extraction who settled at Ipswich shortly before 1638 and acquired large land holdings there. Maria's mother was Mehitable Cave Cummins, also a descendent of an old and prominent New England family. Maria was strongly aware of her ancient pedigree, especially through her father, with whom she enjoyed a close relationship.

Judge Cummins took special pains to insure a good education for his daughter. He personally supervised her earliest schooling at home, among his books, where he constantly placed before her the best of the world's classics. He discovered early that she was both talented and precocious. A man of cultivated literary taste himself, he encouraged Maria's inclination to write stories and poetry. After a time he sent Maria to Mrs. Charles Sedgwick's fashionable school for young ladies at Lenox. Here Maria met the famous novelist, Catharine Sedgwick, sister-in-law of Mrs. Charles Sedgwick, and was further inspired to write as she listened to the author read from her *Hope Leslie* and *A Poor Rich Man.* Most accounts of Miss Cummins' life report that after her graduation and before she was twenty she was contributing to the *Atlantic Monthly.* Since the *Atlantic Monthly* was not founded until 1857, this is incorrect. But she very likely did have some of her juvenile pieces printed in New England periodicals, perhaps anonymously, before she reached her majority.

The tie between Maria and her father finds a parallel in that of Elizabeth Barrett and again in that of Emily Dickinson. Judge Cummins dominated his daughter's life while he was alive, but it was not resented. Their mutual affection may, or may not, have resulted in Maria's remaining a spinster. Her writing seemed to compensate for an unfilled womanhood. After Judge Cummins' death, Maria moved to Dorchester, Massachusetts, where she made her permanent home. The loss of her father greatly grieved her, but she found solace in writing and in devotion to church work. Apart from these, her only other interest was her home, a charming old colonial house on Bowdoin Street adjoining an apple orchard and surrounded by pine trees and spacious gardens. Here, beside her small fishpond, amid the delightful odor of ripe apples and pine cones, she wrote the books that made her famous. Her existence was pleasant, if it wasn't exciting. The solitary life she enjoyed could find counterparts a hundredfold among New England women of the nineteenth century. Perhaps this is why some of her narrative images were more meaningful to audiences a hundred years ago than they could ever be today. Early in 1866 Miss Cummins' health failed. She lingered through the summer, and just as her beloved apple trees bowed low with their russet offerings, she died on October 1 at the still young age of thirty-nine. The following Sunday her minister announced to his congregation that the title of his text for the morning service would be "Sermon Preached in First Church, Dorchester on the Sunday Following the Decease of Maria S. Cummins." Thus the author of *The Lamplighter* was eulogized, and there were many who went misty-eyed from the church that morning, just as they had come misty-eyed from a reading of *The Lamplighter* a dozen years before.

A footnote remains for those who would discredit the tear-compeller queens of a century ago. In a recent catalog of used books, there were several by Mary Jane Holmes offered for sale. At the peak of her prominence the best editions of her novels sold for no more than $1.50 a copy. In the catalog, the 1888 editions of Mrs. Holmes' *Daisy Thornton* and *Jessie Graham* were priced at $27.50. And even more recently the library of a well-known midwestern college counted it a bargain to pay a mere $49.50 for copies of *Tempest and Sunshine* and *The Lamplighter*. For whatever reason, domestic novels still have a market of sorts—and it may be presumed they are still read.

*Simpson College*
*November 1967*

DONALD A. KOCH

# BIBLIOGRAPHICAL NOTE

The nineteenth-century American domestic novel does not lend itself to a precise definition. Its characteristics were often shared by other varieties of nineteenth-century fiction. There are numerous studies, however, which more or less effectively describe it. The best general treatment of domestic fiction to date is Herbert Ross Brown's pioneer work *The Sentimental Novel in America, 1789–1860* (Durham, N.C., 1940). Professor Brown's book is especially valuable because it traces the evolution of the domestic novel and demonstrates how it reflected the culture of its era. A more recent study, Helen Waite Papashvily's *All the Happy Endings* (New York, 1956), focuses upon the scribbling women themselves, their feminine audience, and the purposive nature of their novels. Alexander Cowie includes a brief but informative chapter on the domestic sentimentalists in his *The Rise of the American Novel* (New York, 1948). A work of broader scope is Carl Bode's panoramic view of mass culture during the antebellum years, *The Anatomy of American Popular Culture, 1840–1861* (Berkeley and Los Angeles, 1959). His analysis of the domestic novels is heavily charged with Jungian interpretations. A similar but more perfunctory discussion of them occurs in Leslie Fiedler's *Love and Death in the American Novel* (New York, 1960).

Two works which illuminate the popular appeal of the domestic novels are Frank Luther Mott's *Golden Multitudes: The Story of Best Sellers in the United States* (New York, 1947) and James D. Hart's *The Popular Book: A History of America's Literary Taste* (New York, 1950). Mott's book is rich in anecdotal material, and both books provide interesting information relating to the publishing history of the domestic novels.

Indispensable for an understanding of the times that spawned the domestic novels are Meade Minnigerode's *The Fabulous Forties, 1840–1850* (Garden City, N.Y., 1924), Fred Lewis Pattee's *The Feminine Fifties* (New York, 1940), and E. Douglas Branch's *The Sentimental Years, 1836–1860* (New York, 1934). For a sequential view of the times, Alice Felt Tyler's *Freedom's Ferment: Phases of American Social History to 1860* (Minneapolis, Minn., 1944) and Merle Curtis *The Growth of American Thought* (3rd ed., New York, 1964) are among the most perceptive.

Of course the novels themselves and contemporaneous reviews of them remain the best primary sources for impressions. The diaries, journals, letters, and autobiographies of such writers as Marion Harland, Sarah J. Hale, Susan Warner, and others provide background as well as biographical information. The most extensive biographical sketches of Mary Jane Holmes and Maria

Cummins are to be found in the *Dictionary of American Biography* (vols. II and V; New York, 1958).

The texts for *Tempest and Sunshine* and *The Lamplighter* printed here were graciously supplied by Professor C. Hugh Holman from the holdings of the University of North Carolina. The novels were often reissued under various imprints and were occasionally revised, apparently by the publishers. The 1894 issue of *Tempest and Sunshine* published by C. W. Dillingham and the 1854 first edition of *The Lamplighter* published by John P. Jewett were used for this contribution to the Odyssey "Popular American Fiction" series.

# CONTENTS

# TEMPEST AND SUNSHINE

*or*

## Life in Kentucky

## BY MARY JANE HOLMES

# Chapter I

It was the afternoon of a bright October day. The old town clock had just tolled the hour of four, when the Lexington and Frankfort daily stage was heard rattling over the stony pavement in the small town of V——, Ky. In a few moments the four panting steeds were reined up before the door of the Eagle, the principal hotel in the place. "Mine host," a middle-aged, pleasant-looking man, came bustling out to inspect the new comers, and calculate how many would do justice to his beefsteaks, strong coffee, sweet potatoes, and corn cakes, which were being prepared in the kitchen by Aunt Esther.*

This good dame divided her time between squeezing the steaks, turning the corn cake, kicking the dogs, and administering various cuffs to sundry little black urchins, who were on the lookout to snatch a bit of the "hoe cake," whenever they could elude the Argus eyes of Aunt Esther. When the rattling of the stage was heard, there ensued a general scrambling, to ascertain which should be first to see who had come. At length, by a series of somersets helped on by Aunt Esther's brawny hand, the kitchen was cleared, and Aunt Esther was "monarch of all she surveyed."

The passengers this afternoon were few and far between, for there was but one inside, and one on the box with the driver. The one inside alighted, and ordered his baggage to be carried into the hotel. The stranger was a young man, apparently about twenty-five years of age. He was tall, well proportioned, and every way prepossessing in his appearance. At least the set of idlers in the bar-room thought so, for the moment he entered, they all directed their eyes and *tobacco juice* towards him!

By the time he had uttered a dozen words, they had come to the conclusion that he was a stranger in the place and was from the East. One of the men, a Mr. Edson, was, to use his own words, "mighty skeary of Northern folks," and as soon as he became convinced that the stranger was from that way, he got up, thinking to himself, "Some confounded Abolitionist, I'll warrant. The sooner I go home and get my gang together, the better 'twill be." But upon second thought he concluded, "his gang" was safe for the present, at least; so he'd just sit down, and hear what his neighbor, Mr. Woodburn, was saying to the new comer.

The Kentuckians are as famous as the Yankees for inquisitiveness, but if they inquire into *your* history, they are equally ready to give *theirs* to you, and you cannot feel as much annoyed by the kind, confiding manner, with which a Kentuckian will draw you out, as by the cool, quizzing way with which a Yankee will *"guess"* out your affairs.

On the present occasion, Mr. Woodburn had conjectured the young

* Pronounced *"Easter."*

3

man's business, and was anxious to know who he was, and, if possible, to render him assistance. It took but a short time for the stranger to tell that he was from the East, from New York; that his name was Wilmot, and that he was in quest of a school; and in as short a time Mr. Woodburn had welcomed young Wilmot to Kentucky, but expressed his regret that he did not come sooner, for all the schools were engaged; "But," added he, "you had better remain around here awhile, and get acquainted, and then there will be no doubt of your eventually getting a situation. Meantime, as you are a stranger here, you are welcome to make my house your home."

Such kindness from an entire stranger was unlooked for by Wilmot. He knew not what to make of it;—it was so different from the cold, money-making men of the North. He tried to stammer out his thanks, when Mr. Edson interrupted him by nudging Mr. Woodburn, and saying, "Don't you mind old Middleton? He's been tarin' round after a Yankee teacher this six weeks. I reckon this chap'll suit."

Mr. Woodburn hesitated. He did not like to send Mr. Wilmot to such a place as Mr. Middleton's, for though Mr. Middleton was a very kind man, he was very rough and uncouth in his manner, and thought his money much better applied, when at interest, than when employed to make his house and family more comfortable.

At length Mr. Woodburn replied, "True, I did not think of Mr. Middleton, but I hardly like to send a stranger there. However, Mr. Wilmot, you must not judge all Kentuckians by him, for although he is very hospitable to strangers, he is extremely rough."

Mr. Wilmot thanked them for their information, and said he thought he would go to Mr. Middleton's that night.

"Lord knows how you'll get there," said Mr. Edson.

"Why, is it far?" asked Wilmot.

"Not very fur," said Mr. Edson, "little better than four miles, but a mighty mean road any time, and a heap worse since the rains. For a spell you can get on right smart, but then, again, you'll go in co-slush!"

Mr. Wilmot smiled; but said, "he thought he would try the road, if Mr. Edson would give him the direction."

Then followed a host of directions, of which the most prominent to Wilmot were, that "about two miles from the house is an old hemp factory, full of niggers, singing like all fury; then comes a piece of woods, in the middle of which is a gate on the left hand;—open that gate, and follow the road straight till you come to the mightiest mean-looking house you ever seen, I reckon; one chimbly tumbled down, and t'other trying to. That house is Middleton's."

Here Mr. Woodburn said, "that as the road was so bad, and it was getting late, Mr. Wilmot had better stay at his house that night, and the next day they would send him to Middleton's."

Before Mr. Wilmot had time to reply, Mr. Edson called out, "Halloa! just in luck, Wilmot!" Then rushing to the door, he screamed, "Ho! Jim Crow, you jackanapes, what you ridin' Prince full jump down the pike for? Say, you scapegrace, come up here!"

Mr. Wilmot looked from the window, and saw a fine-looking black boy, of about sixteen years of age, riding a beautiful horse at full speed through the street. He readily divined that the boy was the property of Mr. Edson, and as he had brought from home a little abolitionism safely packed away, he expected to see a few cuffs dealt out to the young African. But when the young hopeful, at the command of his master, wheeled his horse up to the door, gave a flourish with his rimless old hat, and a loud whistle with his pouting lips, Mr. Wilmot observed that his master gave the bystanders a knowing wink, as much as to say, "Isn't he smart?" then turning to the boy, he said, "How now, you Jim, what are you here for, riding Prince to death?"

"I begs marster's pardon berry much," said the negro, "but you see how I done toted all the taters you told me and missis she 'vise me to ride Prince a leetle, 'case he's gittin' oneasy like when Miss Carline rides him."

"Likely story," said Mr. Edson, "but for once you are in the way when I want you. You know where Mr. Middleton lives?"

"Yes, marster, reckon I does."

"Well, this young man wants to go there. Now jump down quick and help him on, do you hear?"

"Yes, marster," said the negro, and in a moment he was on the ground, holding the stirrup for Mr. Wilmot to mount.

Wilmot hesitated for two causes. The first was, he was not a good horseman, and did not like to attempt mounting the spirited animal, before so many pair of eyes. He looked wistfully at the horse-block, but did not dare propose having the horse led up to it. The second reason was, he did not know whether to accept or decline the kindness of Mr. Edson; but that man reassured him, by saying,

"Come, what you waiting for? jump up, I'd a heap rather Jim would go with you, than ride Prince to death, which he surely would."

"Yes, marster," said Jim.

Here Mr. Woodburn spoke. He knew that New York people were, comparatively speaking, inferior riders, and he readily conjectured why Mr. Wilmot hesitated; so he said,

"Here, Jim, lead the horse up to the block for the gentleman;" then turning to the bystanders said, as if apologizing for Wilmot, "you know it is so thickly settled in New York that they do not ride as much as we do, and probably the young man has always been at school."

This was satisfactory to the white portion of the audience, but not to the group of blacks, who were assembled at the corner of the house. They thought it a shame not to be a good rider, and when they saw the awkward manner in which Mr. Wilmot finally mounted the horse, and the ludicrous face of Jim Crow, as he sprang up behind him, they were, as they afterwards told Aunt Esther, "dreffully tickled, and would have larfed, sartin, if they hadn't knowed marster would have slapped their jaws."

"And sarved you right," was the rejoinder of Aunt Esther.

But to return to Mr. Edson. As soon as Mr. Wilmot, Jim, and Prince had disappeared, he felt a return of his fears concerning the "confounded Abolitionist." Thought he, "What a fool I was to let Prince and Jim Crow too, go off with that ar' chap! Thar's Prince, worth a hundred and fifty, and Jim, at the least calculation, 'll fetch eight hundred. Wall, any way, they can't get far on that dirt road, so if Jim isn't at home by nine, I'll go after 'em, that's so." Having settled the matter thus satisfactorily in his own mind, he called for his horse, and started for home.

Meantime Mr. Wilmot was slowly wending his way towards Mr. Middleton's. It took but a short time for him to ascertain that the road was fully equal to the description given of it by Mr. Edson. At times he could scarcely keep his seat, and he felt conscious too, that the black machine behind him was inwardly convulsed with laughter at his awkward attempts to guide the horse, in the best part of the road. At length he ventured a remark.

"Jim, is this animal ugly?"

"*Ugly!* Lor bless you, marster, is you blind? As handsome a creetur as thar is in the country!"

Mr. Wilmot understood that he had used the word "ugly" in its wrong sense, so he said,

"I do not mean to ask if the horse is ill-looking, but is he skittish?"

"If marster means by that, will he throw him off, I don't think he will, as long as I'm on him, but sometimes he is a leetle con*trary* like. Reckon marster ain't much use to ridin'."

By this time they had reached the gate spoken of by Mr. Edson. To Mr. Wilmot's great surprise the horse walked up to it and tried to open it with his mouth! Mr. Wilmot was so much amused, that he would not suffer Jim to get down and open the gate, as he wished to see if the horse could do it.

"Oh, yes, marster, he'll do it easy," said the negro; and sure enough, in a moment the well-trained animal lifted the latch and pushed open the gate! But it was a rickety old thing, and before Prince had got fairly through, it tumbled down, hitting his heels, and causing him to jump sideways, so as to leave Mr. Wilmot riding the gate, and Jim Crow in quiet possession of the saddle! With a great effort Jim forced down his desire to scream, and merely showed twenty-eight very large and very white teeth.

Springing from the horse he offered to assist Mr. Wilmot to mount again, but he had no inclination to do so. He preferred walking the rest of the way, he said, and as he could now easily find the house, Jim could return home. This was not what Jim wanted. He had anticipated a nice time in relating his adventures to Mr. Middleton's negroes, but as Mr. Wilmot slipped a quarter into his hand, he felt consoled for the loss of his *"yarn"*; so mounting Prince again, he gave his old palm-leaf three flourishes round his head, and with a loud whoop, started the horse at a tremendous speed down the road, and was soon out of sight, leaving Mr. Wilmot to find his way alone through the wood. This he found no difficulty in doing, for he soon came in sight of a house, which he readily took for Mr. Middleton's.

It was a large, old-fashioned, stone building, with one chimney fallen down, as Mr. Edson had said, and its companion looked likely to follow suit at the first high wind. The windows of the upper story were two thirds of them destitute of glass, but its place was supplied by *shingles,* which kept the cold out, if they did not let the light in. Scattered about the yard, which was very large, were corn cribs, hay racks, pig troughs, carts, wagons, old ploughs, horses, mules, cows, hens, chickens, turkeys, geese, negroes and dogs, the latter of which rushed ferociously at Mr. Wilmot, who was about to beat a retreat from so uninviting quarters, when one of the negroes called out, "Ho, marster, don't be feared, 'case I'll hold Tiger." So Wilmot advanced with some misgivings toward the negro and dog.

He accosted the negro, and asked if his master were at home.

"No sar, marster's done gone away, but Miss Nancy, she's at home. Jist walk right in thar, whar you see the pile of saddles in the entry."

Accordingly Mr. Wilmot "walked in where the pile of saddles were," and knocked at a side door. It was opened by a very handsome young girl, who politely asked the stranger to enter. He did so, and found within a mild-looking, middle-aged lady, whose dark eyes and hair showed her at once to be the mother of the young lady who had opened the door for him.

Mrs. Middleton, for she it was, arose, and offering her hand to the stranger, asked him to be seated in the large stuffed chair which stood before the cheerful blazing fire. In a few moments he had introduced himself, told his business, and inquired for Mr. Middleton.

"My husband is absent," said Mrs. Middleton, "but he will be at home to-night, and we shall be glad to have you remain with us till to-morrow at least, and as much longer as you like, for I think Mr. Middleton will be glad to assist you in getting a school."

Mr. Wilmot accepted the invitation, and then looked round the room to see if the interior of the house corresponded with the exterior. It did not, for the room, though large, was very comfortable. The floor was covered with a bright-colored homemade carpet. In one corner stood a bed, the counterpane of which was as white as snow, and the curtains of the windows were of the same hue. In another corner was a small bookcase, well filled with books, and on a stand near a window, were several house plants.

He concluded that the books and the plants were the property of the young lady, whom Mrs. Middleton introduced to him as her eldest daughter, Julia. She was an intelligent looking girl, and Mr. Wilmot instantly felt interested in her, but when he attempted to converse with her, she stole quietly out of the room, leaving her mother to entertain the visitor.

At last supper was brought in by old Aunt Judy, who curtsied so low to the "young marster," that she upset the coffee-pot, the contents of which fell upon a spaniel, which lay before the fire. The outcries of the dog brought Miss Julia from the kitchen, and this time she was accompanied by her younger sister, Fanny, who, together with Julia and Aunt Judy, lamented over the wounded animal.

"I didn't go to do it, sartin, Miss July," said Aunt Judy, "Lor knows I didn't."

"Who said you did, you black thing, you?" said Julia, who in her grief for her favorite, and her anger at Aunt Judy, forgot the stranger, and her bashfulness too. "You were careless, I know you were," she continued, "or you never could have tipped all the coffee over in this manner."

"Never mind, sister," said Fanny, "never mind; of course Aunt Judy didn't mean to do it, for she likes Dido as well as we do."

"Lord bless Miss Fanny's sweet face, that I do like Dido," said Aunt Judy.

"Yes, that you do," repeated Julia mockingly, "just as though *you* could like anything."

Here Mrs. Middleton interposed, and ordered Julia and Fanny to take their seats at the table, while Judy cleared away all traces of the disaster. Julia complied with an ill grace, muttering something about "the hateful negroes," while Fanny obeyed readily, and laughingly made some remark to Mr. Wilmot about their making so much ado over a dog, "but," said she, "we are silly girls, and of course do silly things. Probably we shall do better when we get old, like you,—no, not like *you,* like *mother,* I mean."

Here she stopped, blushing deeply at having called Mr. Wilmot *old,* when in fact she thought him quite young, and very handsome,—in short, "just the thing." She thought to herself, "there, I've done it now! Julia and I have both introduced ourselves to him in a pretty light, but it's just like *me,*—however, I'll not say another word to-night!"

The little incident of the coffee-pot gave Mr. Wilmot something of an insight into the character and dispositions of the two girls. And surely nothing could have been more unlike than their personal appearance, as they sat side by side at the supper table. Julia was about seventeen years of age, and was called very handsome, for there was something peculiarly fascinating in the ever-varying expression of her large black eyes. She was a brunette, but there was on her cheek so rich and changeable a color, that one forgot in looking at her, whether she was dark or light. Her disposition was something like her complexion,—dark and variable. Her father was a native of South Carolina, and from him she inherited a quick, passionate temper. At times she was gentle as a lamb, but when any thing occurred to trouble her, all her southern blood boiled up, and she was as Fanny said, "always ready to fire up at a moment's warning." Mr. Middleton called her "Tempest," while to Fanny he gave the pet name of "Sunshine," and truly, compared with her sister, Fanny's presence in the house was like a ray of sunshine.

She was two years younger than Julia, and entirely different from her, both in looks and disposition. Her face was very pale, and her bright golden hair fell in soft curls around her neck and shoulders, giving her something the appearance of a fairy. Her eyes were very large and very dark blue, and ever mirrored forth the feelings of her soul.

By the servants, Julia was feared and dreaded; but Fanny was a favorite with all. Not a man, woman, or child, on the plantation, but was ready to do anything for "darling Miss Fanny." And they thought, too, every one must love her as well as they did, for they said, "she showed by her face that she was an angel." This was the opinion of the blacks, and it was also the partially formed opinion of Mr. Wilmot before he finished his supper; and yet he could not help thinking there was something wondrously attractive in the glance of Julia's large, dark eyes.

After supper, he tried to engage the two girls in conversation, in order to ascertain which had the best mind. He found Fanny most ready to converse. She had forgotten her resolution not to talk, and before the evening was half spent, seemed perfectly well acquainted with him. She had discovered that his name was Richard, that he had a sister Kate, who called

lcome to my house—such as it is. It's mighty mean though,
"
d to Julia, who had just entered the room. Then he went
est raves and t'ars about the old house, and can hardly
d before she spends my money in fool fixins. Devil of a cent
, if she rides as high a horse as she generally does! I'll give
e'; yes, I will, she's more gentle-like and comes coaxin' round
her soft arms round my old shaggy neck, says, 'Please, pa, if
ke a nice pudding or pie of Aunt Judy, will you buy us a
ss or rocking chair?' And then 'tisn't in my natur to refuse.
e is a darling," said he, laying his hand caressingly on Fanny's
at moment showed her sunny face in the room.
fast, Mr. Middleton inquired more particularly into Mr.
and wishes, and told him there was no doubt that he could
school in that immediate neighborhood. "Your best way,"
be to write a subscription paper. The people can then see
ou write, and half the folks in Kentuck will judge you by that.
u must tell *what* you know, and what you ask to tell it to others.
st with my two gals, and give you a horse to go round with,
empest and Sunshine too, that you'll get a full school afore

art of his speech, Julia curled her lip and tried to look in-
Fanny laughingly said, "Pa, what makes you always bet sister
s though you could sell us like the horses? It's bad enough to
e blacks, I think."
you've got some free State notions already, have you?" said
. "Well, honey, you're more'n half right I reckon." So saying,
th time, passed up his coffee cup.
ing over, he took his young friend to the stable, and bade
his own use any horse he chose. Mr. Wilmot declined, saying,
not much accustomed to horses, he preferred that Mr. Middle-
ose any horse he pleased.
said Mr. Middleton; "from the accounts I have had of your
it may be improved; so I reckon I'll not give you a very
to begin with. Thar's Aleck'll just suit you. He'll not throw
te, for he doesn't trot as fast as a black ant can walk!"
Aleck was saddled and bridled, and Mr. Wilmot was soon
l, with his subscription paper safe in his pocket, was riding
cribers. He was very successful; and when, at night, he turned
eward, he had the names of fifteen scholars, and the partial
e more.
boy, what luck?" said the gruff voice of Mr. Middleton, as
d the sitting room that evening.
l success," returned Mr. Wilmot; "I am sure of fifteen scholars,
a promise for five more."
y good," said Mr. Middleton; "fifteen sartin and five unsartin.
unsartin ones?—old Thornton's?"

him *Dick*, that he was as yet possessor of his own heart, but was in great danger of losing it! The compliment Fanny very generously gave to her sister Julia, because she observed that Mr. Wilmot's eyes were often directed towards the corner where the dark beauty sat, silent and immovable.

Julia had taken but little part in the conversation, and Mr. Wilmot's efforts to "draw her out" had proved ineffectual. She felt piqued that Fanny should engross so much attention, and resolved on revenge; so she determined to show Mr. Wilmot that she could talk, but not upon such *silly* subjects as pleased Fanny. Accordingly, when *books* were mentioned, she seemed suddenly roused into life. She was really very intelligent, and a very good scholar. She had a great taste for reading, and what books she could not prevail on her father to buy, she would borrow, so she had a tolerably good knowledge of all the standard works. Mr. Wilmot was surprised and pleased to find her so well informed; and in the spirited conversation which followed, poor Fanny was entirely cast into the background.

Fanny, however, attributed it to her sister's superior knowledge of Latin, and inwardly "thanked her stars" that she knew nothing of that language, further than the verb Amo, to love. The *practical* part of that verb she understood, even if she did not its conjugation. She sat quietly listening to Mr. Wilmot and her sister, but her cogitations were far different from what Julia's had been.

Fanny was building *castles*, in all of which Mr. Wilmot and Julia were the hero and heroine. She gazed admiringly at her sister, whose face grew handsomer each moment, as she became more animated, and she thought, "What a nice-looking couple Julia and Mr. Wilmot would make! And they would be so happy too! that is, if sister didn't get angry, and I am sure she wouldn't with Mr. Wilmot. Then they would have a nicer house than this old shell, and perhaps they would let me live with them!"

Here her reverie was interrupted by Mr. Wilmot, who asked her if she had ever studied Latin. Fanny hesitated; she did not wish to confess that she had once studied it six months, but at the end of that time, she was so heartily tired of its "long-tailed verbs," as she called them, that she had thrown her grammar out of the window, and afterwards given it to Aunt Judy to light the oven with!

This story, however, was told by Julia, with many embellishments, for she delighted in making Fanny appear ridiculous. She was going on swimmingly, when she received something of a drawback from her mother, who said:

"Julia, what do you want to talk so for? You know that while Fanny studied Latin, Mr. Miller said she learned her lessons more readily than you did and recited them better, and he said too, that she was quite as good a French scholar as you!"

Julia curled her lip scornfully, and said, "she didn't know what her mother knew about Fanny's scholarship." Meantime Fanny was blushing deeply, and thinking that she had appeared to great disadvantage in Mr. Wilmot's eyes; but he very kindly changed the conversation by asking who Mr. Miller was; and was told that he was a young man from Albany, New York, who taught in their neighborhood the winter before.

The appearance of some nice red apples just then, turned the attention of the little company in another channel, and before they were aware of it, the clock struck ten. Mr. Middleton had not yet returned, and as it was doubtful whether he came home at all that night, Julia went to the kitchen for Luce, to show Mr. Wilmot to his room. She was gone some time, and when she returned, was accompanied by a bright-looking mulatto girl, who, as soon as she had conducted Mr. Wilmot into his room, commenced making excuses about "marster's old house! Things was drefful all round it, but 'twasn't Miss Julia's fault, for if she could have her way 'twould all be fixed up, sartin. She was a *born'd* lady, any body could see; so different from Miss Fanny, who cared nothing how things looked if she could get into the kitchen, and turn hoe cakes for Aunt Judy, or tend the baby!"

By this time Luce had arranged the room all it wanted arranging, and as Mr. Wilmot had no further need of her services, she left him to think of what she had said. He did not know that the bright red ribbon which appeared on Luce's neck, next morning, was the gift of Julia, who had bribed her to say what she did to him. Julia knew that she had made a favorable impression on Mr. Wilmot, and she thought to increase that impression by making him think meanly of Fanny.

What Luce said had its effect upon him too. He was accustomed to the refinements of the North, and he could not help respecting a young lady more who showed a taste for neatness. That night he dreamed that a bright pair of dark eyes was looking at him from each pane of *shingle* in the window, and that a golden-haired fairy was dancing the Polka in Aunt Judy's hoe-cake batter.

# Chapter II

Next morning before daybreak Mr. Wilmot was aroused from a sound slumber, by what he thought was the worst noise he had ever heard. He instantly concluded that the house was on fire, and springing up, endeavored to find his clothes, but in the deep darkness of the room such a thing was impossible; so he waited awhile, and tried to make out what the noise could be.

At last it assumed something of a definite form, and he found that it was the voice of a man calling out in thunder-like tones, "Ho, Jedediah! come out with ye! Do you hear? Are you coming?"

"Yes, marster, comin'."

Then followed a long catalogue of names, such as Sam, Joe, Jack, Jim,

Ike, Jerry, Nehemiah, Ezariah, Jud Phema, and at the end of each name had preceded that of Jedediah; and same response, "Yes, marster, comin'."

By this time all the hens, geese, tu joining their voices in the chorus, ma hideous with their outcries. At last the the house, and Wilmot tried to comp awoke, the sun was shining brightly himself, but felt in no hurry to see was sure, and had given such tremende his lungs.

Mr. Wilmot finally descended to the which presented itself was a man, who and large in proportion. His face was creased by a beard of at least four wee old slouched hat, from under which a as Wilmot appeared, the uncouth figure his hand, gave it a grip, which, if co crushed every bone! He began with—

"Well, so you are Mr. Wilmot, from abolitionist; but I don't care for that, if self, and not try to preach your notions

"Heard of *me*, sir!" said Mr. Wilmot, in

"Yes, of you; and why not? Thar's n judging by your looks, has had a hearing heard of you by the papers. As I was co to old man Edson's, and I seen him sw 'Ho, old man, what's the row?' 'Oh,' says h row. I've done let my best horse and nig free States, who said he's going to your h Jim not at home yet. Of course they've 'don't be a fool, Edson; if that ar chap goin' thar. I'll bet all my land and niggers somewhar. You come along with me and w on the pike, till all of a sudden we met P This looked dark, but I told Edson to say to Woodburn's fine house, and thar in th and heard the niggers larfin' like five hun tinguish Jim Crow's voice; so we crept slyl in, and sure enough, there was Jim, tellin' rode, and how you got flung on to the gat Prince, who got oneasy like, and started fo who came out, and told how he didn't go said you could find the way, and he might turned right round and said you were a likel I could for you. So that's the way I heard o

Kentuck, and w as 'Tempest' says

Here he turn on, "Yes, Temp wait till I'm dea she'll get though it all to 'Sunshi me, and puttin' I'll learn to ma new looking-gla Oh yes, Sunshin head, who at t

During brea Wilmot's plans obtain a good said he, "will what for a fist In the paper yo I'll head the li and I'll bet T night."

At the last dignant, while and me, just a bet, and sell th

"Ho! ho! s Mr. Middleton he, for the fou

Breakfast b him select for that as he was ton should ch

"Very well, horsemanship skeary horse you on the ga

Accordingl mounted, an off after subs his face hom promise of fiv

"Well, my Wilmot enter

"Very goo and have hal

"Yes, pret Who are the

Mr. Wilmot replied that he believed it was a Mr. Thornton, who had hesitated about signing.

"He'll sign," said Mr. Middleton. "I's thar after you was, and he told me you might put down five for him. *I* say for two on 'em. He lives on my premises; and if he doesn't pay up fort t'other three, why, he'll jog, that's all."

Mr. Wilmot said he hoped no one would send to school against their wishes.

"Lord, no," rejoined Mr. Middleton; "old Thornton wants to send bad enough, only he's stingy like. Let me see your paper, boy."

Mr. Wilmot handed him the paper, and he went on: "Thar's ten scholars at eight dollars—that makes eighty, then thar's five at eleven dollars, and fifty-five and eighty makes a hundred and thirty-five; then thar's five more at fifteen dollars;—five times fifteen; five times five is twenty-five—seventy-five dollars;—seventy-five and a hundred and thirty-five;—five and five is ten, one to seven is eight, eight and three is eleven—two hundred and ten dollars! Why, quite a heap! Of course you've got clothes enough to last a spell, so you can put two hundred out at interest. I'll take it, and give you ten per cent."

Mr. Wilmot smiled at seeing his money so carefully disposed of before it was earned, but he merely said, "There's my board to be deducted."

"Your *what?*" asked Middleton.

"My board, sir. I have no other means of paying it. I find I can get boarded for a dollar and a half a week."

"The deuce you can," said Mr. Middleton. "Who'll board you for that?"

Mr. Wilmot gave the name of the gentleman, to which Mr. Middleton replied, "I want to know if he will board you *so very cheap!*"

"Why, yes," said Mr. Wilmot. "Do you think I ought to pay more?"

"*Pay more!*" replied Middleton. "Don't be a fool! Why, here's this infernal old shell of a house wants filling up, and thar's heaps of horses, and niggers lounging 'round, with nothing to do: then I've plenty of potatoes, bacon, and corn meal—and such fare as *we* have you're welcome to, without a dollar and a half, or even a cent and a half."

Mr. Wilmot remonstrated against receiving so much at Mr. Middleton's hands, but that good man put an end to all further argument by saying, "Do let me act as I like. You see I've taken a liking to you, and because I see you trying to help yourself, I am willing to try and help you. They say, or Tempest says they say, I'm a rough old *bear,* and may be I am; but I'm not *all* bad; it's a streak o' fat and a streak o' lean; and if I want to do you a kindness, pray let me."

So it was settled that Mr. Wilmot should remain in Mr. Middleton's family during the winter. To Julia, this arrangement gave secret satisfaction. She had from the first liked Mr. Wilmot, and the idea of having him near her all the time, was perfectly delightful. She resolved to gain his good opinion, cost what it would. To do this, she knew she must appear to be amiable, and that she determined to do—before *him* at least. She had also seen enough of him to know that he set a great value upon talent, and she resolved to surprise him with her superior scholarship and ability to learn. She, however, felt some misgivings lest Fanny should rival her in his esteem; but she hoped, by negro bribery and various little artifices of her own, to deter him from thinking *too* highly of her sister.

The following Monday, Mr. Wilmot repaired to his school-room, where he found assembled all his pupils. It was comparatively easy to arrange them into classes, and ere the close of the day, the school was pretty generally organized. Weeks passed on, and each day the "Yankee schoolmaster" gained in the love of his scholars, and one of them, at least, gained in the affections of the teacher. Julia had adhered to her resolution of appearing amiable, and of surprising Mr. Wilmot with her wonderful powers of learning. This last she did to perfection. No lesson was so long but it was readily learned, and its substance admirably told in words of her own. She preferred reciting alone, and as she so far outstripped the others in the length of her lessons, it seemed necessary that she should do so. Mr. Wilmot often wondered at her marvellous capacity for learning so much in so short a space of time, for she never took home her books at night, as she said she had plenty of time for her lessons during school hours.

With Fanny it was just the reverse. *She* got her lessons at home, and played all day at school! Sometimes a reprimand from Mr. Wilmot would bring the tears into her eyes, and she would wonder why 'twas she could not behave, and make Mr. Wilmot like her as well as he did Julia. Then she would resolve not to make *any more faces* at that *booby*, Bill Jeffrey, for the girls to laugh at, nor to draw any more pictures on her slate of *Dame Sobriety*, as she called Julia, and lastly, not to pin any more *chalk rags* to the boys' coats. But she was a dear lover of fun, and her resolutions were soon forgotten. Her lessons, however, were generally well learned, and well recited; but she could not compete with Julia, neither did she wish to. She often wondered how her sister *could* learn so long lessons, and, secretly, she had her own suspicions on the subject, but chose to keep them to herself.

Meantime the winter was passing rapidly, and, to Mr. Wilmot, very agreeably away. He liked his boarding place much, and one of its inmates had almost, without his knowledge, wound herself strongly around his heart. For a time he struggled against it, for his first acquaintance with Julia had not left a very favorable impression on his mind. But since that night she had been perfectly pleasant before him, and had given but one demonstration of her passionate temper.

This was one evening at the supper-table. Zuba, a mulatto girl, brought in some preserves, and in passing them carelessly spilled them upon Julia's new blue merino. In the anger of the moment, Mr. Wilmot and his good opinion were forgotten. Springing up, she gave the girl a blow which sent her half across the room, and caused her to drop the dish, which was broken in twenty pieces. At the same time she exclaimed, in a loud, angry tone, "Devil take you, Zube!" The loss of the dish elicited a series of oaths from Mr. Middleton, who called his daughter such names as "lucifer match," "volcano," "powder-mill," and so forth.

For her father's swearing, Julia cared nothing, but it was the sorrowful, disappointed expression of Mr. Wilmot's face, which cooled her down. Particularly did she wish to recall what she had done, when she saw that him *Dick,* that he was as yet possessor of his own heart, but was in great danger of losing it! The compliment Fanny very generously gave to her sister Julia, because she observed that Mr. Wilmot's eyes were often directed towards the corner where the dark beauty sat, silent and immovable.

Julia had taken but little part in the conversation, and Mr. Wilmot's efforts to "draw her out" had proved ineffectual. She felt piqued that Fanny should engross so much attention, and resolved on revenge; so she determined to show Mr. Wilmot that she could talk, but not upon such *silly* subjects as pleased Fanny. Accordingly, when *books* were mentioned, she seemed suddenly roused into life. She was really very intelligent, and a very good scholar. She had a great taste for reading, and what books she could not prevail on her father to buy, she would borrow, so she had a tolerably good knowledge of all the standard works. Mr. Wilmot was surprised and pleased to find her so well informed; and in the spirited conversation which followed, poor Fanny was entirely cast into the background.

Fanny, however, attributed it to her sister's superior knowledge of Latin, and inwardly "thanked her stars" that she knew nothing of that language, further than the verb Amo, to love. The *practical* part of that verb she understood, even if she did not its conjugation. She sat quietly listening to Mr. Wilmot and her sister, but her cogitations were far different from what Julia's had been.

Fanny was building *castles,* in all of which Mr. Wilmot and Julia were the hero and heroine. She gazed admiringly at her sister, whose face grew handsomer each moment, as she became more animated, and she thought, "What a nice-looking couple Julia and Mr. Wilmot would make! And they would be so happy too! that is, if sister didn't get angry, and I am sure she wouldn't with Mr. Wilmot. Then they would have a nicer house than this old shell, and perhaps they would let me live with them!"

Here her reverie was interrupted by Mr. Wilmot, who asked her if she had ever studied Latin. Fanny hesitated; she did not wish to confess that she had once studied it six months, but at the end of that time, she was so heartily tired of its "long-tailed verbs," as she called them, that she had thrown her grammar out of the window, and afterwards given it to Aunt Judy to light the oven with!

This story, however, was told by Julia, with many embellishments, for she delighted in making Fanny appear ridiculous. She was going on swimmingly, when she received something of a drawback from her mother, who said:

"Julia, what do you want to talk so for? You know that while Fanny studied Latin, Mr. Miller said she learned her lessons more readily than you did and recited them better, and he said too, that she was quite as good a French scholar as you!"

Julia curled her lip scornfully, and said, "she didn't know what her mother knew about Fanny's scholarship." Meantime Fanny was blushing deeply, and thinking that she had appeared to great disadvantage in Mr. Wilmot's eyes; but he very kindly changed the conversation by asking who Mr. Miller was; and was told that he was a young man from Albany, New York, who taught in their neighborhood the winter before.

The appearance of some nice red apples just then, turned the attention of the little company in another channel, and before they were aware of it, the clock struck ten. Mr. Middleton had not yet returned, and as it was doubtful whether he came home at all that night, Julia went to the kitchen for Luce, to show Mr. Wilmot to his room. She was gone some time, and when she returned, was accompanied by a bright-looking mulatto girl, who, as soon as she had conducted Mr. Wilmot into his room, commenced making excuses about "marster's old house! Things was drefful all round it, but 'twasn't Miss Julia's fault, for if she could have her way 'twould all be fixed up, sartin. She was a *born'd* lady, any body could see; so different from Miss Fanny, who cared nothing how things looked if she could get into the kitchen, and turn hoe cakes for Aunt Judy, or tend the baby!"

By this time Luce had arranged the room all it wanted arranging, and as Mr. Wilmot had no further need of her services, she left him to think of what she had said. He did not know that the bright red ribbon which appeared on Luce's neck, next morning, was the gift of Julia, who had bribed her to say what she did to him. Julia knew that she had made a favorable impression on Mr. Wilmot, and she thought to increase that impression by making him think meanly of Fanny.

What Luce said had its effect upon him too. He was accustomed to the refinements of the North, and he could not help respecting a young lady more who showed a taste for neatness. That night he dreamed that a bright pair of dark eyes was looking at him from each pane of *shingle* in the window, and that a golden-haired fairy was dancing the Polka in Aunt Judy's hoe-cake batter.

# *Chapter II*

Next morning before daybreak Mr. Wilmot was aroused from a sound slumber, by what he thought was the worst noise he had ever heard. He instantly concluded that the house was on fire, and springing up, endeavored to find his clothes, but in the deep darkness of the room such a thing was impossible; so he waited awhile, and tried to make out what the noise could be.

At last it assumed something of a definite form, and he found that it was the voice of a man calling out in thunder-like tones, "Ho, Jedediah! come out with ye! Do you hear? Are you coming?"

"Yes, marster, comin'."

Then followed a long catalogue of names, such as Sam, Joe, Jack, Jim,

Ike, Jerry, Nehemiah, Ezariah, Judy, Tilda, Martha, Rachel, Luce, and Phema, and at the end of each name was the same list of questions which had preceded that of Jedediah; and ever from the negro quarters came the same response, "Yes, marster, comin'."

By this time all the hens, geese, turkeys and dogs were wide awake, and joining their voices in the chorus, made the night, or rather the morning, hideous with their outcries. At last the noise subsided. Silence settled around the house, and Wilmot tried to compose himself to sleep. When he again awoke, the sun was shining brightly into the room. He arose and dressed himself, but felt in no hurry to see "his host," who had come home, he was sure, and had given such tremendous demonstrations of the strength of his lungs.

Mr. Wilmot finally descended to the sitting-room, where the first object which presented itself was a man, who was certainly six and a half feet high, and large in proportion. His face was dark, and its natural color was increased by a beard of at least four weeks' growth! He had on his head an old slouched hat, from under which a few gray locks were visible. As soon as Wilmot appeared, the uncouth figure advanced towards him, and seizing his hand, gave it a grip, which, if continued long, would certainly have crushed every bone! He began with—

"Well, so you are Mr. Wilmot, from New York, hey? Of course a red-hot abolitionist; but I don't care for that, if you'll only keep your ideas to yourself, and not try to preach your notions to me. I've heard of *you* before."

"Heard of *me,* sir!" said Mr. Wilmot, in surprise.

"Yes, of you; and why not? Thar's many a man, not as good as *you,* judging by your looks, has had a hearing in his day; but, however, I hain't heard of you by the papers. As I was coming home last night, I got along to old man Edson's, and I seen him swarin' and tarin' round, so says I, 'Ho, old man, what's the row?' 'Oh,' says he, 'that you, Middleton? 'Nuff's the row. I've done let my best horse and nigger go off with a man from the free States, who said he's going to your house, and here 'tis after nine, and Jim not at home yet. Of course they've put for the river.' 'Now,' says I, 'don't be a fool, Edson; if that ar chap said he's goin' to my house, he's goin' thar. I'll bet all my land and niggers he's honest. Likely Jim's stopped somewhar. You come along with me and we'll find him.' So we jogged along on the pike, till all of a sudden we met Prince coming on home all alone! This looked dark, but I told Edson to say nothin' and keep on: so we came to Woodburn's fine house, and thar in the cabins we seen a bright light, and heard the niggers larfin' like five hundred, and thought we could distinguish Jim Crow's voice; so we crept slyly up to the window and looked in, and sure enough, there was Jim, tellin' a great yarn about the way you rode, and how you got flung on to the gate. It seems he didn't half hitch Prince, who got oneasy like, and started for home. Edson hollered to Jim, who came out, and told how he didn't go clear here with you, 'cause you said you could find the way, and he might go back. Then old man Edson turned right round and said you were a likely man, and he hoped I'd do all I could for you. So that's the way I heard of you; and now welcome to old

Kentuck, and welcome to my house—such as it is. It's mighty mean though, as 'Tempest' says."

Here he turned to Julia, who had just entered the room. Then he went on, "Yes, Tempest raves and t'ars about the old house, and can hardly wait till I'm dead before she spends my money in fool fixins. Devil of a cent she'll get though, if she rides as high a horse as she generally does! I'll give it all to 'Sunshine'; yes, I will, she's more gentle-like and comes coaxin' round me, and puttin' her soft arms round my old shaggy neck, says, 'Please, pa, if I'll learn to make a nice pudding or pie of Aunt Judy, will you buy us a new looking-glass or rocking chair?' And then 'tisn't in my natur to refuse. Oh yes, Sunshine is a darling," said he, laying his hand caressingly on Fanny's head, who at that moment showed her sunny face in the room.

During breakfast, Mr. Middleton inquired more particularly into Mr. Wilmot's plans and wishes, and told him there was no doubt that he could obtain a good school in that immediate neighborhood. "Your best way," said he, "will be to write a subscription paper. The people can then see what for a fist you write, and half the folks in Kentuck will judge you by that. In the paper you must tell *what* you know, and what you ask to tell it to others. I'll head the list with my two gals, and give you a horse to go round with, and I'll bet Tempest and Sunshine too, that you'll get a full school afore night."

At the last part of his speech, Julia curled her lip and tried to look indignant, while Fanny laughingly said, "Pa, what makes you always bet sister and me, just as though you could sell us like the horses? It's bad enough to bet, and sell the blacks, I think."

"Ho! ho! so you've got some free State notions already, have you?" said Mr. Middleton. "Well, honey, you're more'n half right I reckon." So saying, he, for the fourth time, passed up his coffee cup.

Breakfast being over, he took his young friend to the stable, and bade him select for his own use any horse he chose. Mr. Wilmot declined, saying, that as he was not much accustomed to horses, he preferred that Mr. Middleton should choose any horse he pleased.

"Very well," said Mr. Middleton; "from the accounts I have had of your horsemanship, it may be improved; so I reckon I'll not give you a very skeary horse to begin with. Thar's Aleck'll just suit you. He'll not throw you on the gate, for he doesn't trot as fast as a black ant can walk!"

Accordingly Aleck was saddled and bridled, and Mr. Wilmot was soon mounted, and, with his subscription paper safe in his pocket, was riding off after subscribers. He was very successful; and when, at night, he turned his face homeward, he had the names of fifteen scholars, and the partial promise of five more.

"Well, my boy, what luck?" said the gruff voice of Mr. Middleton, as Wilmot entered the sitting room that evening.

"Very good success," returned Mr. Wilmot; "I am sure of fifteen scholars, and have half a promise for five more."

"Yes, pretty good," said Mr. Middleton; "fifteen sartin and five unsartin. Who are the unsartin ones?—old Thornton's?"

Mr. Wilmot replied that he believed it was a Mr. Thornton, who had hesitated about signing.

"He'll sign," said Mr. Middleton. "I's thar after you was, and he told me you might put down five for him. *I* say for two on 'em. He lives on my premises; and if he doesn't pay up fort t'other three, why, he'll jog, that's all."

Mr. Wilmot said he hoped no one would send to school against their wishes.

"Lord, no," rejoined Mr. Middleton; "old Thornton wants to send bad enough, only he's stingy like. Let me see your paper, boy."

Mr. Wilmot handed him the paper, and he went on: "Thar's ten scholars at eight dollars—that makes eighty, then thar's five at eleven dollars, and fifty-five and eighty makes a hundred and thirty-five; then thar's five more at fifteen dollars;—five times fifteen; five times five is twenty-five—seventy-five dollars;—seventy-five and a hundred and thirty-five;—five and five is ten, one to seven is eight, eight and three is eleven—two hundred and ten dollars! Why, quite a heap! Of course you've got clothes enough to last a spell, so you can put two hundred out at interest. I'll take it, and give you ten per cent."

Mr. Wilmot smiled at seeing his money so carefully disposed of before it was earned, but he merely said, "There's my board to be deducted."

"Your *what?*" asked Middleton.

"My board, sir. I have no other means of paying it. I find I can get boarded for a dollar and a half a week."

"The deuce you can," said Mr. Middleton. "Who'll board you for that?"

Mr. Wilmot gave the name of the gentleman, to which Mr. Middleton replied, "I want to know if he will board you *so very cheap!*"

"Why, yes," said Mr. Wilmot. "Do you think I ought to pay more?"

"*Pay more!*" replied Middleton. "Don't be a fool! Why, here's this infernal old shell of a house wants filling up, and thar's heaps of horses, and niggers lounging 'round, with nothing to do: then I've plenty of potatoes, bacon, and corn meal—and such fare as *we* have you're welcome to, without a dollar and a half, or even a cent and a half."

Mr. Wilmot remonstrated against receiving so much at Mr. Middleton's hands, but that good man put an end to all further argument by saying, "Do let me act as I like. You see I've taken a liking to you, and because I see you trying to help yourself, I am willing to try and help you. They say, or Tempest says they say, I'm a rough old *bear,* and may be I am; but I'm not *all* bad; it's a streak o' fat and a streak o' lean; and if I want to do you a kindness, pray let me."

So it was settled that Mr. Wilmot should remain in Mr. Middleton's family during the winter. To Julia, this arrangement gave secret satisfaction. She had from the first liked Mr. Wilmot, and the idea of having him near her all the time, was perfectly delightful. She resolved to gain his good opinion, cost what it would. To do this, she knew she must appear to be amiable, and that she determined to do—before *him* at least. She had also seen enough of him to know that he set a great value upon talent, and she resolved to surprise him with her superior scholarship and ability to learn. She, however,

felt some misgivings lest Fanny should rival her in his esteem; but she hoped, by negro bribery and various little artifices of her own, to deter him from thinking *too* highly of her sister.

The following Monday, Mr. Wilmot repaired to his school-room, where he found assembled all his pupils. It was comparatively easy to arrange them into classes, and ere the close of the day, the school was pretty generally organized. Weeks passed on, and each day the "Yankee schoolmaster" gained in the love of his scholars, and one of them, at least, gained in the affections of the teacher. Julia had adhered to her resolution of appearing amiable, and of surprising Mr. Wilmot with her wonderful powers of learning. This last she did to perfection. No lesson was so long but it was readily learned, and its substance admirably told in words of her own. She preferred reciting alone, and as she so far outstripped the others in the length of her lessons, it seemed necessary that she should do so. Mr. Wilmot often wondered at her marvellous capacity for learning so much in so short a space of time, for she never took home her books at night, as she said she had plenty of time for her lessons during school hours.

With Fanny it was just the reverse. *She* got her lessons at home, and played all day at school! Sometimes a reprimand from Mr. Wilmot would bring the tears into her eyes, and she would wonder why 'twas she could not behave, and make Mr. Wilmot like her as well as he did Julia. Then she would resolve not to make *any more faces* at that *booby,* Bill Jeffrey, for the girls to laugh at, nor to draw any more pictures on her slate of *Dame Sobriety,* as she called Julia, and lastly, not to pin any more *chalk rags* to the boys' coats. But she was a dear lover of fun, and her resolutions were soon forgotten. Her lessons, however, were generally well learned, and well recited; but she could not compete with Julia, neither did she wish to. She often wondered how her sister *could* learn so long lessons, and, secretly, she had her own suspicions on the subject, but chose to keep them to herself.

Meantime the winter was passing rapidly, and, to Mr. Wilmot, very agreeably away. He liked his boarding place much, and one of its inmates had almost, without his knowledge, wound herself strongly around his heart. For a time he struggled against it, for his first acquaintance with Julia had not left a very favorable impression on his mind. But since that night she had been perfectly pleasant before him, and had given but one demonstration of her passionate temper.

This was one evening at the supper-table. Zuba, a mulatto girl, brought in some preserves, and in passing them carelessly spilled them upon Julia's new blue merino. In the anger of the moment, Mr. Wilmot and his good opinion were forgotten. Springing up, she gave the girl a blow which sent her half across the room, and caused her to drop the dish, which was broken in twenty pieces. At the same time she exclaimed, in a loud, angry tone, "Devil take you, Zube!" The loss of the dish elicited a series of oaths from Mr. Middleton, who called his daughter such names as "lucifer match," "volcano," "powder-mill," and so forth.

For her father's swearing, Julia cared nothing, but it was the sorrowful, disappointed expression of Mr. Wilmot's face, which cooled her down. Particularly did she wish to recall what she had done, when she saw that

Fanny also had received some of the preserves on *her* merino; but instead of raging like a fury, she arose and quietly wiped it off, and then burst into a loud laugh, which she afterwards told her mother was occasioned by the mournful look which Mr. Wilmot's face assumed, when he saw that Julia's temper was not *dead*, but merely covered up with ashes.

From this remark of Fanny's the reader will understand that she was well aware of the part her sister was playing. And she was perfectly satisfied that it should be so, for by this means *she* occasionally got a pleasant word from Julia. She however often wished that Mr. Wilmot could be constantly with her sister, for his presence in the house did not prevent her from expending her wrath upon both Fanny and the blacks.

For some days after the affair of the preserves, Mr. Wilmot was somewhat *cool* in his manner towards Julia, who had discernment enough to attribute the change to the right cause. Earnestly did she desire to win back his esteem, and she accordingly cast about for some method by which she could undo what she had done. She could think of no way, except to acknowledge her error to Mr. Wilmot, and promise to do better in future. So one evening when her father, mother, and Fanny were absent, and she was alone with him, she adroitly led the conversation to the circumstance of her spoiled merino. She acknowledged that it was very unamiable and unladylike to manifest such passionate feeling,—said she knew she had a quick temper, but she tried hard to govern it: and if Mr. Wilmot would, as her teacher and friend, aid her by his advice and influence, she was sure she should in time succeed. So nicely did she manage each part of her confession that Mr. Wilmot was thoroughly deceived. He believed her perfectly sincere, and greatly admired what he thought to be her frank, confiding disposition.

From that time she was dearer to him than ever, and Julia, again sure of his esteem, placed a double guard upon her temper, and in his presence was the very "pink" of amiability! Affairs were gliding smoothly on, when the family unexpectedly received a visit from a gentleman, whom Julia would rather not have seen. This was Mr. Miller whom we have mentioned as having taught in that neighborhood the winter before. Mr. Wilmot found him in the sitting-room, one night, on his return from school. When the young men were introduced, they regarded each other a moment in silence, then their hands were cordially extended and the words *"Richard Wilmot,"* *"Joseph Miller,"* were simultaneously uttered.

It seems that, years before, they had been roommates and warmly attached friends in the Academy of Canandaigua, New York, and now, after the lapse of ten years, they met for the first time far off in Kentucky. A long conversation followed, relative to what had occurred to each since the bright June morning, when they parted with so much regret in the old Academic halls of Canandaigua.

At length Mr. Miller said, "Richard, what has become of that sister of yours, of whose marvellous beauty you used to tell us boys such big stories?"

"My sister Kate," said Mr. Wilmot, "is at present at school in New Haven."

"And is she still as beautiful as you used to try to make us think she was?" asked Mr. Miller.

"I will show you her likeness," returned Wilmot, "and you can judge for yourself."

So saying, he drew from his pocket a richly cased daguerreotype, and handed it to Mr. Miller. It *was* a face of uncommon beauty which met Mr. Miller's eye, and he gazed enraptured on the surpassing loveliness of the picture. At last he passed it to Fanny, who was eagerly waiting for it, and then turning to Wilmot, he said, "Yes, Richard, she has the handsomest face I ever saw."

"And the handsomest face *I* ever saw with *one* exception," said Mr. Wilmot, glancing admiringly towards Julia who followed the direction of his eyes, and as he saw the beautiful face of Julia, he sighed for fear his young friend might or had already become entangled in her dark meshes.

Just then Fanny exclaimed, "Oh, how handsome; look, mother,—Julia, isn't she perfectly beautiful!" And then she added, "But, Mr. Wilmot, is she as good as she is beautiful?"

"How absurd," said Julia hastily, "just as though one cannot be handsome and good too."

"I didn't say they couldn't, sister," said Fanny, "but I thought,—yes, I'm sure she looks a little selfish!"

"Upon my word, you're very polite," said Julia. "Mr. Wilmot will doubtless feel complimented by what you say of his sister."

"Never mind, Fanny," said Mr. Wilmot, "never mind; you are more of a physiognomist than I thought you were, for Kate's great fault is being too selfish; but she will overcome that in time, I think."

"Oh, yes, I'm sure she will," said Fanny, who was anxious to do away with any unfavorable impression she might have made. So she went up to Mr. Wilmot, and laying her hand on his shoulder, said, "I am sorry if I said anything bad of your sister. She is very beautiful, and I think I should love her very much. Do you think she will ever come to Kentucky?"

"I hardly think she will," said Mr. Wilmot, "but I think you would like her, and I am sure she would love you. I often write to her about my two Kentucky sisters."

"Oh, do you," said Fanny, clapping her white, dimpled hands, "do you really call us both sisters? And do you tell her how much handsomer Julia is than I am, and how much more she knows?"

"And how much more does she know?" said Mr. Miller, who was always interested in whatever Fanny said.

"Oh, she knows a 'heap' more than I do," said Fanny. "I fear I haven't improved much since you left, for Mr. Wilmot is so very indulgent that he never scolds when my lessons are but half learned, but consoles himself, I suppose, with Julia's great long *yarns*."

"And are Julia's lessons so very long?" asked Mr. Miller.

"Yes, sir," replied Fanny. "It is the wonder of all the girls how she manages to commit so much to memory in so short a time, for she never brings home her books, and she spends two thirds of her time, during school hours, in writing something on a sheet of foolscap. We girls have our own suspicions about that paper, for when her lesson is very hard, we notice that she is unusually confined to her *notes*."

Here Julia angrily exclaimed, "Fanny, what do you mean? Do you intend to insinuate that I write my lesson down, and then read it?"

"*Fire* and *fury!*" said Mr. Middleton, who had been an attentive listener, "what's all this about? Tempest, do you write down your task? Good reason why you don't bring home your books. Speak, girl, quick,—are you guilty of such meanness?"

Julia burst into tears, and said, "No, father, I am not; and I think it too bad that I should be suspected of such a thing, when I am trying to do as well as I can."

"I think so too," said Mr. Wilmot, whose sympathies were all with Julia.

Mr. Miller thought otherwise, but he said nothing. Julia had never been a favorite with him. He understood her character perfectly well, and he felt grieved that his friend should be so deceived in her. Perhaps Julia read something of what was passing in his mind; for she felt very uneasy for fear he might tell Mr. Wilmot something unfavorable of her. Nor was she mistaken in her conjectures, for after the young men had retired for the night, their conversation naturally enough turned upon the family, and the two girls, both of whom Mr. Wilmot spoke of in the highest terms. Mr. Miller agreed with him as long as his remarks were confined to Fanny, but when he came to speak of Julia, and of her superior beauty, intellect and agreeable manners, he ventured to disagree with him.

Said he, "As to Julia's beauty, there can be but one opinion, for she is very handsome; but the interior of the casket does not correspond with the exterior; she is as *false* as fair. Then as to her intellect, I never thought it greatly superior to Fanny's. To be sure, she has a way of showing off all she does know, while Fanny is more retiring."

Here Mr. Wilmot spoke of the faculty she possessed for learning so long lessons. "Even your favorite Fanny," said he, "admitted that."

"True," returned Mr. Miller, "but have you forgotten the *notes?* Do you not think there may be something in that?"

"Is it possible," said Mr. Wilmot rather warmly,—"is it possible you think the high-souled Julia capable of such meanness? You do not know her as well as I do, if you think she would stoop to such deception. You shall go to school with me to-morrow, and then you can see for yourself."

"Yes, I will do so," said Mr. Miller, and then as he saw Mr. Wilmot seemed somewhat excited, he changed the conversation, which had been heard by other ears. Adjoining the room of Mr. Wilmot, was a long, dark closet, the door of which opened into the apartment of Julia and Fanny. This closet was used for a kind of lumber room, in which were stored promiscuously old barrels, trunks, hats, boots, and so forth. It originally had a window, but the glass had long been broken, and its place supplied by a large board, which failed to keep out the wind and rain, so that during the winter season, the closet was a cold, cheerless place.

But on the night of which we are speaking, it contained a novel piece of *lumber.* Crouched behind an old barrel, sat Julia, listening eagerly to the conversation between her teacher and Mr. Miller. When it ceased, she arose from her dark hiding-place and muttered to herself, "So you'll *see*, will you? You old torment! I wish the Old Scratch had got you, before you ever came here. If I dared to I'd——but no, I wouldn't do that, bad as I am. However, I'll cheat you for once, you hateful limb! But what shall I do?"

She indeed was in a dilemma; but she had often boasted that she never yet was in so straitened a spot that she could not devise some means of extricating herself, and she relied on the *Master she served,* to aid her in this difficulty. She never brought her books home, and, as the reader will ere this have surmised, she was in the daily habit of writing a sketch of her lesson on foolscap, and then reading it off. When school first commenced she had asked the privilege of sitting in her seat while reciting, and by this means she could hold the paper under her desk, and thus avoid Mr. Wilmot's suspicion. Her lessons for the next day were unusually long and hard, and as Mr. Miller would be present, she dared not resort to her usual artifice, particularly after what had been said about her *"notes."* She knew she never *could* learn all that long lesson in school hours, neither would she fail of having it for anything. What could she do? For some time she sat by the dying embers with her dark face buried in her hands, revolving in her mind the best scheme by which to outwit Mr. Miller.

At last she rose up, and a malicious smile of exultation passed over her features. She looked at the clock, and saw it was already half-past ten, and then stealing softly to the bedside where Fanny lay quietly sleeping, she bent down and assured herself that her sister really was unconscious of her movements. She then hastily threw on her overshoes, cloak, and hood, and stealing noiselessly down the stairs, was soon in the open air alone in the darkness of the night. Just as she shut the door of the house, the watch dog, Tiger, came bounding furiously towards her with an angry growl. She silenced the fierce animal by saying, "Down Tiger—poor Tige—don't you know me, Tiger?" After quieting the dog, she proceeded on her strange errand, which was to obtain her books from the school-house, which was more than half a mile distant.

The mud, which was very deep, was not more than half frozen, and at each step she sank into a mixture of mud, snow and ice. Still she kept fearlessly on, till at last she found herself in the midst of the thick woods. Here her courage somewhat failed her, for she called to mind all the stories she had ever heard of runaways, who were said to walk abroad at this dark hour of the night. Once she thought she saw the giant form of a negro standing in her path, but it proved to be a black stump, and she was about laughing at her fears, when her ear detected the sound of a light, rapid tread, coming towards her. Almost paralyzed with terror, she stood perfectly still, and listened for the sound to be repeated, but all was silent, and again she went on her way and soon reached the school-house.

But here a new difficulty presented itself. The house was locked, and the key was in Mr. Wilmot's pocket; but the old adage, "where there's a will, there's a way," came into her mind, so she felt round on the half frozen ground till she found a long rail, which she placed against a window; then climbing up, she raised the sash, and in a moment was in the schoolroom. The atmosphere of the room was still comfortable, and she stopped for a moment at the stove to warm her benumbed fingers, then groping her way to her desk, she easily found her books, and made her way out of the house in the same manner that she had entered.

Just as she reached the ground, a large, dark object sprang towards her, and two glittering eyes looked up into her face. She uttered a loud shriek, which was answered by a low whine, which she instantly recognized as belonging to Tiger. "Why, Tiger," she exclaimed, "how you frightened me! What did you follow me for?" It seems Tiger had thought there must be something wrong, or his mistress would not be out at this unreasonable hour, so he had followed on after her. She was noways displeased at this, for she liked not the idea of again going alone through the wood, but with Tiger for a companion, she went fearlessly on, and reached home just an hour after she had left it.

On entering her room, she struck a light, and then tried to warm her chilled limbs over the few faint coals which still glimmered on the hearth; but there was no wood in the room, and she dared not go for any, so she sat down with her cloak still around her, and for four long hours studied as she had never before done in all her life. At the end of that time, her lessons were very nearly learned, and sick with cold and fatigue, she threw aside her books, and prepared for bed.

Her movements awoke Fanny, who on seeing her sister up at that hour of the night, started with surprise, and exclaimed, "What is it, Julia! What is the matter?" Julia immediately extinguished the light, lest her sister should discover her books, and then said, "Nothing, Fanny, nothing, only I have the toothache, and I got up for the camphor, but cannot find it."

"The camphor is down stairs," said Fanny, "but I will go for it if you wish me to. Does your tooth ache very hard?"

"Yes, rather," said Julia, and her kind-hearted sister arose, and found her way in the dark, down stairs, to her mother's room.

"What in thunder's come now!" called out Mr. Middleton. " 'Pears like somebody's been tousing 'round the house all night."

"It's only I, father," said Fanny. "Julia has the toothache, and I am after the camphor bottle."

"Oh, it's you, Sunshine, is it? The camphire's on the mantletry. Be keerful and not break it, honey."

While Fanny was after the camphor, Julia arose, and seizing her books, threw them hastily into her bureau drawer. She then sprang back into bed, and when Fanny came in, she was making a very appropriate moaning on account of her aching tooth!

"How cold you are, sister," said Fanny, "let me warm my shawl and put 'round you."

"You can't warm it, for there is neither fire nor wood," said Julia; "and besides, my tooth is much better now!"

So Fanny lay down by her sister, and the two, purity and guilt, were soon fast asleep, side by side, and the angel of innocence spread his broad wing protectingly over the yellow locks of the one, while a serpent lay coiled in the dark tresses of the other.

## Chapter III

At the breakfast table next morning, Julia's pale face was noticed and commented upon.

"She had a violent toothache last night, which kept her awake," said Fanny.

"Now I think of it," said Mr. Middleton, "I wonder, Tempest, how you can have the toothache, for you are always bragging about your handsome, healthy teeth, and say you hain't a rotten fang in your head."

Julia colored, for what her father said was true, neither did she remember of ever having had the toothache in her life; but quickly recovering herself, she said, "Neither have I a decayed tooth. It was more of a face-ache, I suppose, than the genuine toothache."

"Probably you have taken some cold," said Mr. Wilmot.

"I think quite likely I have," returned Julia, and so the toothache matter was dismissed for the time. Mr. Miller, however, thought he could see in it a plan of Julia's to avoid going to school that day, and when he heard Mrs. Middleton say, "Julia, as it is so cold and chilly, perhaps you had better not go out," he was rather surprised to hear her reply, "Oh, no, mother, Mr. Miller is going with us, and I would not miss of being there for any thing."

So the party proceeded together to the school-house. When school commenced Julia took her books, and going up to Mr. Wilmot, said, loudly enough for Mr. Miller to hear, "Mr. Wilmot, do you know that you gave me a very hard lesson for to-day?"

"Yes, Julia," said he, "I know it is hard and long and as you do not seem well, I will excuse you from as much of it as you choose, or from the whole of it, if you like."

"No, no," said Julia; "Mr. Miller is here and I would like to show him that I have improved since last winter, when, as I fear, I was often sadly remiss in my studies. All I want to tell you is, that if I do not recite as well as usual, you mustn't scold a bit; now, will you?"

"Oh, certainly not," said Mr. Wilmot, and then he added in a tone so low that no one heard but Julia, "I could not scold *you,* dear Julia."

Thus flattered, the young lady took her seat, and for a time seemed very intensely occupied with her lessons. At last she opened her portfolios, and taking from it a sheet of foolscap, cast an exulting glance towards Fanny and Mr. Miller, the latter of whom was watching her movements. She then took her gold pencil and commenced scribbling something on the paper. By the time her lesson was called for, she had written one page. When asked to recite, she laid the paper on the desk, and prepared to do *honor* to herself and teacher. The moving of the paper attracted Mr. Wilmot's notice, and going towards her, he very gently said, "I presume you have no objection to letting me see what you have written here."

She at first put out her hand as if to prevent him from taking it, but at last she suffered him to do so, but tried to look interestingly confused. Mr. Wilmot read what was written, and then smilingly passed it to his friend, who looked at it, and saw that it was a piece of tolerably good blank verse.

"Is this your composition, Julia?" said Mr. Miller.

"Yes, sir," she replied.

"And have your 'notes' always been of this nature?" asked Mr. Wilmot.

"That, or something similar," said Julia. "I find no difficulty in learning my lesson by once reading, and as I am very fond of poetry, I like to employ the rest of my time in trying my powers at it!"

Mr. Wilmot looked at Mr. Miller, as much as to say, "I hope you are satisfied," and then proceeded to hear Julia's lesson, which was well learned and well recited. Julia's recitation being over, Fanny's class was called. Fanny came hesitatingly, for she knew her lesson was but poorly learned. That morning she had found under her desk a *love-letter* from Bill Jeffrey, and she and some of the other girls had spent so much time in laughing over it, and preparing its answer, that she had scarcely thought of her lesson. She got through with it, however, as well as she could, and was returning to her seat, when Mr. Miller called her to him, and said, rather reprovingly, "Fanny, why did you not have a better lesson?"

"Oh, Mr. Miller," said she, almost crying, "I did intend to, but I forgot all about your being here;" and then, as a new thought struck her, she said mischievously, "and besides, I have spent all the morning in writing an answer to Billy Jeffrey's love-letter!"

At this unlooked for speech, all the scholars burst into a laugh, and directed their eyes towards the crestfallen Bill, who seemed so painfully embarrassed, that Fanny regretted what she had said, and as soon as school was out for the morning, she went to him and told him she was sorry for so thoughtlessly exposing him to ridicule; "but," added she, "Billy, I'll tell you what, you mustn't write me any more love-letters, for 'tis not right to do such things at school; neither need you bring me any more candy nor raisins. I don't object to your giving me a nice big apple occasionally, but candy and raisins you had better give to the little children. And now to prove that I am really your friend, if you will get that old dog's-eared arithmetic of yours, I will show you how to do some of those hard sums, which trouble you so."

Billy was surprised. The butt of the school, he was accustomed to the jeers of his companions, but such kindness, and from Fanny, too, was unexpected. He, however, drew from his desk his old slate and arithmetic, and he and Fanny were soon deep in the mysteries of compound fractions. A half hour passed away, and at the end of that time Billy's sums were done.

"Now, Billy," said Fanny, rising, "see that you do not send me any more letters, and mind too, and not *wink* at me so often; will you remember?"

Bill gave the required promise, and Fanny bounded away in quest of her schoolmates, who laughed at her for taking so much pains with such a dolt as Bill Jeffrey. That afternoon Fanny resolved to retrieve her character as a scholar; so she applied herself closely to her task, and before recitation hour arrived, she had learned every word of her lesson. But alas for poor Fanny! She was always stumbling into some new difficulty, and fate, this afternoon, seemed resolved to play a sorry trick upon her.

The school-house stood at the foot of a long, steep hill, which would have been chosen for a capital sliding place by New-York boys; but in Kentucky the winters are, comparatively speaking, so mild, that the boys know but little of that rare fun, *"sliding down hill."* The winter of which we are speaking was, however, unusually severe, and the school-boys had persevered until they had succeeded in making a tolerably nice sliding place, and they had also furnished themselves with a goodly number of rather rough-looking sleds, of which Bill Jeffrey owned the largest. The girls were all anxious to try a ride down the hill, and none more so than Fanny; but the boys would not lend their sleds, and the girls would not ride with the boys, and as the latter always hid their precious sleighs, the girls had as yet never succeeded in their wishes. But on this day, Bill Jeffrey, touched by Fanny's unlooked for kindness, whispered to her just as school was commencing, that she might take his big sled at recess.

This was a treat indeed, and when recess came, Fanny, with half a dozen other girls, climbed to the top of the hill, and began piling on to Bill's old sled. It was settled that Fanny should guide the craft, and numerous were the cautions of the girls that she should "mind and steer straight."

"Oh, yes, I'll do that," said Fanny; "but wouldn't it be funny," added she, "if we should make a mistake, and go plump into the school-house!"

At last all was ready, and the vehicle got under way. At first it moved slowly, and the loud, merry laugh of the girls rang out on the clear, cold air; but each moment it increased in swiftness, and by the time it was half way down the hill, it was moving at an astonishingly rapid rate. Fanny lost her presence of mind, and with it her ability to guide the sled, so that they passed the point where they should have turned, and made directly for the school-house door, which flew open, as once did the gates for the famous John Gilpin. There was no entry way to the building, but as the sled struck the door, the jolt threw off all the girls except Fanny, who manfully kept her seat, and so made her grand entrance into the school-room, stopping not till she reached the stove, and partially upsetting it, to the great astonishment of the teacher, visitor, and boys, the latter of whom set up a loud huzza. Poor Fanny! 'Twas her *first* sled ride, and she felt sure 'twould be her last; but she resolved to make the best of it, so she looked up from under her long curls, and said very demurely, "Please, Mr. Wilmot, may I stop at this station? I do not like being so near the engine!" meaning the stove, whose proximity made her quarters a little uncomfortable.

Mr. Wilmot gave her permission to take her seat, which she readily did, wondering why it was that she always managed to do something which made her appear ridiculous, just when she wanted to appear the best. Her mishap gave secret pleasure to Julia, who delighted to have Fanny appear as badly as possible, and she felt particularly pleased when she saw that Fanny's strange ride had scattered all the ideas from her head, for the afternoon's lessons were but little better recited than the morning's, and at its close Julia gave her a look of malicious triumph, which Mr. Miller observing said, as if apologizing for Fanny, that he was sure she had every word of her lesson before recess, but 'twas no wonder she was somewhat disconcerted at the unexpected termination of her ride. Fanny smiled gratefully upon him through her tears, which she could not restrain; but her tears were like April showers—they did not last long, and that night, at the supper table, when Mr. Miller related her adventure to her father, she joined as gayly as any one in the laugh which followed.

Julia was much displeased to think that Fanny's "ridiculous conduct," as she called it, should be told of and laughed at, as though it were something amusing. She was anxious, too, that Mr. Miller should draw his visit to a close, but as he did not seem inclined to do so, she resolved to make the most of it, and give him a few new ideas. She knew that Fanny had ever been his favorite, and she very naturally supposed that the reason of his preference was because he thought she possessed a very lovely, amiable disposition. She determined to make him think otherwise, and set herself at work to execute a plan, which fully showed the heartless deception which almost always characterized her actions.

Fortune seemed to favor her, for after supper, her father and mother announced their intention of spending the evening at one of the neighbors', and soon after they left, Mr. Wilmot, who had letters to write, retired to his room, together with Mr. Miller. As soon as they were gone, Julia repaired to the negro quarters, and by dint of threats, flattery, and promises of reward, finally prevailed upon Luce to join with her in her dark plot. They then went to Julia's sleeping room, and carefully opened the closet door, so that every word of their conversation could be heard in the adjoining room.

Julia's voice was strangely like her sister's, and by means of imitating her, she hoped to deceive both Mr. Wilmot and Mr. Miller, who were startled by a loud, angry voice, exclaiming, "Come, you black imp, no more lies, you know you've stolen it, so just confess, and tell me where it is."

The young gentlemen looked at each other in surprise, for the voice was like Fanny's, and yet it was so unnatural for her to be in such a passion, that they thought it impossible. Their fears were, however, soon confirmed by Luce, who said, "Oh, Miss Fanny, Lor' knows I never tached it. Now sartin, I knows nothin' 'bout it."

"Hold your jaw, or I'll slap your mouth for you, you lying thief!" said Julia (*alias* Fanny). "Of course you've got it, for no one else has been in here, so tell where you hid it."

"Lord massy! how can I tell, when I dun know nothin' whar 'tis," said Luce.

"There, take that, to brighten up your ideas," said Fanny, and at the same time there was the sound of a blow, which was followed by an outcry from Luce, who exclaimed, "Oh—oh—oh—Miss Fanny, don't go for to whip me, case I hain't nothin' to tell; if I had, I'd tell right off. I hain't seed your hankercher 'tall. Mebbe you've done drapped it somewhar."

Just then the door opened, and Julia, again speaking naturally, was heard to say, "Why, Fanny, what are you doing just as soon as mother is gone? Luce, what is the matter?"

"Oh, Miss Julia," replied Luce, "Miss Fanny done lost her fine hankercher, and she say how I stole it, but I hain't."

"What makes you think Luce has got your handkerchief, Fanny?" asked Julia.

"Because I left it on the table, and 'tisn't there now, and no one has been in the room except Luce," replied Fanny.

"Very likely you have put it in your drawer and forgotten it; let me look," said Julia.

There was a moment's silence, and then Julia was heard to exclaim, "There it is—just as I thought. Here it is, safe in your box. I do wish, sister, you would not be quite so hasty, but stop a little before you condemn others." So saying, the party left the room.

While this scene was taking place, Fanny was quietly seated by the fire in the sitting room, getting her lesson for the next day. At last her eye chanced to fall upon a purse which Julia was knitting for her father, and which she had promised to finish that night.

"I wonder," said Fanny to herself—"I wonder where Julia is gone so long? She told father she would finish his purse this evening, and he will scold so, if 'tis not done, that I believe I'll knit on it till she returns."

Suiting the action to the word, she caught up the purse, and when Julia returned to the sitting-room, she found her sister busily engaged in knitting for her.

"Why, Julia," said Fanny, "where have you been so long? I thought you were never coming back, so I have been knitting on your purse, for I was afraid you would not get it done, and then father would scold, you know."

As Julia looked into her sister's bright, innocent face, and thought of all her kindness, her conscience smote her for the wrong she had done, but quickly hushing the faithful monitor, she thought, "Never mind, 'tis natural for me to be bad. I cannot help it."

Meantime the gentlemen above were discussing the conversation which they had overheard.

"Is it possible," said Mr. Miller, "that I have been so deceived in Fanny, and that, after all, she is as passionate as her sister?"

"As passionate as her sister," repeated Mr. Wilmot; "I think we have had good proof that she is much more so. I hope you are now convinced that Fanny is not infallible, though I will confess that I am surprised and disappointed, for I thought she was really of a very gentle nature."

Mr. Miller did not reply directly, but went on, as if speaking to himself, "Oh, Fanny, Fanny, how has my idol fallen! I never would have believed it, but for such convincing evidence."

He was indeed sorely disappointed. He had always thought of Fanny, as the embodiment of almost every female virtue, and although she was so young, hope had often whispered to him of a joyous future, when she, whom her father designated as *his* "Sunshine," should also shed a halo of sunlight around another fireside. But now the illusion was painfully dispelled, for sooner would he have taken the Egyptian asp to his bosom, than chosen for a companion one whom he knew to possess a hasty, violent temper.

Next morning he took leave of Mr. Middleton's family. When it came Fanny's turn to bid him good-bye, she noticed the absence of his accustomed cordiality, and wondered much what she had done to displease him. That night she wept herself to sleep thinking of it, while Julia, secretly exulting in her sister's uneasiness, laughed at her for her foolishness, and said, "It was probably a mere fancy; and even if it were not, what matter was it? What did she care for Mr. Miller's good or bad opinion! She mustn't expect everybody to pet and caress her just as father did, who was an *old fool* any way, and petted her and his dogs alternately." This kind of reasoning did not convince Fanny, and for many days her face wore a sad, troubled expression.

Thus the winter passed away. Spring came, and with it came an offer to Mr. Wilmot of a very lucrative situation as teacher in a school in Frankfort. At first he hesitated about accepting it, for there was, in the old rough stone house, an attraction far greater than the mere consideration of dollars and cents. Julia at last settled the matter, by requesting him to accept the offer, and then urge her father to let her go to Frankfort to school also.

"And why do you wish to go there, Julia?" said Mr. Wilmot, laying his hand affectionately on her dark, glossy hair.

"Because," she answered, "it will be so lonely here when you are gone."

"And why will it be lonely, dearest Julia?" continued he.

"Oh," said she, looking up, very *innocently* in his face, "you are the only person who understands me; by all others, whatever I do or say is construed into something bad. I wish you were my brother, for then I might have been better than I am."

"Oh, I do not wish I was your brother," said Mr. Wilmot, "for then I could not have claimed a dearer friend, which I hope now to do at some future time."

Then followed a declaration of love, which Julia had long waited most anxiously for. Most eloquently did Mr. Wilmot pour out the whole tide of his affection for the beautiful but sinful girl, who, in a very becoming and appropriate manner, murmured an acknowledgment of requited love. Thus the two were betrothed.

And truly 'twas a fitting time for such a betrothal. The air had been hot and sultry all day, and now the sky was overspread with dark clouds, while everything indicated an approaching storm. While Mr. Wilmot was yet speaking, it burst upon them with great violence. Peal after peal of thunder followed each other in rapid succession, and just as Julia whispered a promise to be Mr. Wilmot's forever, a blinding sheet of lightning lit up for a moment her dark features, and was instantly succeeded by a crash, which shook the whole house from its foundation, and drew from Julia a cry of terror, which brought Fanny to see what was the matter, and made Mr. Middleton swear, "There was noise enough from the *tempest* out doors, without the *Tempest* in the house raising such a devil of a time!"

# Chapter IV

When Mr. Middleton was spoken to, on the subject of sending Julia to Frankfort, he at first refused outright. "No," said he, "indeed she shan't go. What does she want of any more flummerdiddle notions? What she does know is a damage to her!"

"But do you not wish to give your daughters every possible advantage?" said Mr. Wilmot.

"Who's said any thing about my *daughters?*" said Mr. Middleton. "It's nobody but Tempest, and she's always kickin' up some bobbery. Now if 'twas Sunshine, why, I might,——but no, neither of 'em shall go. It's all stuff, the whole on't." So saying he turned on his heel, and walked off, while Julia burst into tears, and repaired to her own room, whither she was soon followed by her mother, who tried to console her. Said she, "Why, Julia, you don't take the right course with your father. Why do you not propose having your sister accompany you? for if *you* go she will, and you know she can always coax her father to do as she pleases."

This was rather humiliating to Julia, but she concluded 'twas her only alternative, so she dried her eyes, and seeking out her sister, very soon talked her into a strong desire to try the mysteries of a school in Frankfort, and also drew from her a promise to try her powers of argument upon her father. Accordingly that evening Fanny made an attack upon him, and as her mother had predicted, she was perfectly successful. It was settled that she and Julia should both go, and the next morning early, Mr. Middleton set off for Frankfort to find, "as smart a boarding-place for his *gals* as any body had." There was as yet no boarding house connected with the school, and he was obliged to find a place for them in some one of the numerous boarding houses with which Frankfort abounds. He at last decided upon a very genteel establishment, kept by a Mrs. Crane, who at first hesitated about receiving into her family persons who possessed so rough and shabbily looking a father.

But Mr. Middleton brought her to a decision by saying, "What the deuce you waiting for? Is it because I've got on cow-hide *stogies,* and a home-made coat? Thunder and lightning! don't you know I'm old Middleton, worth at least two hundred thousand?"

This announcement changed the current of Mrs. Crane's ideas. The daughters were not rough, if the father was, so she decided to take them, and for the very moderate sum of seven dollars per week, promised to give them all the privileges of her house. The first day of June was fixed upon for them to leave home, and at sunrise, Mr. Middleton's carriage stood at his door, waiting for the young ladies to make their appearance. Julia had long been ready, and was waiting impatiently for Fanny, who was bidding the servants an affectionate good-bye. Each one had received from her some little token of love, and now they all stood in one corner of the yard, to look at their darling as long as possible.

"Lor' bless her," said one, "Kentuck hain't many like her, nor never will have."

"No, nor Frankfort nuther," said a second. While a third added, "No, and I reckon Heaven hasn't nuther."

To which a fourth responded, "Amen."

Her old Aunt Katy, who had nursed Mr. Middleton and his children after him, hobbled up to Fanny, and laying her hard, shrivelled black hand on her young mistress's bright locks, said, "The Lord who makes the wind blow easy like on the sheared lamb, take keer of my sweet child, and bring her back agin to poor old Aunt Katy, who'll be all dark and lonesome, when Sunshine's done gone."

This was regarded as a wonderful speech by the negroes, and as none of them could hope to equal it, they contented themselves by lustily blowing their *trombones,* and wiping the same on their shirt sleeves, or the corners of their aprons. At last the good-byes all were said. Julia merely noticed the blacks with a slight nod, and then sprang nimbly into the carriage, which disappeared from view just as the negroes struck up in a loud, clear, and not unmusical tone,

> "Oh, it's lonesome now on the old plantation,
> It's lonesome now on the old plantation,
> It's lonesome now on the old plantation,
> Case Sunshine's gone away."

"Stop your yelp, can't you?" said Mr. Middleton; but his voice indicated that he would not be very much displeased even if they did not obey, so they tuned their pipes still louder, and this time the six dogs joined in the chorus, with a long mournful howl.

"Thar, that'll do," said Mr. Middleton, "now to your work, quick; and mind, the one that works best this week shall go Saturday, and carry *Miss* Crane some strabries!"

The negroes needed no other incentive to work, than the prospect before them of going to see Fanny. Never had Mr. Middleton had so much accomplished in one week. When Friday night came, it was hard telling which was the favored one. At last it was settled that Ike should go to Frankfort, and the rest should have a sort of holiday. Ike was a sprightly negro boy of seventeen, and almost idolized his young mistress Fanny. Long before "sun up" (a favorite expression in Kentucky for sunrise), he had filled his basket with strawberries, and just as the first rays of sun light streaked the eastern hills, he started on his mission, laden with numerous messages of love for "sweet Miss Fanny," and a big cranberry pie, from Aunt Judy, who "was sartin the baby wanted some of old Judy's jimcracks by this time."

Meanwhile Julia and Fanny had become tolerably well established both in school and at Mrs. Crane's. Julia was perfectly delighted with her new quarters, for she said, "every thing was in style; just as it should be," and she readily adopted all the "city notions." But poor Fanny was continually committing some blunder. She would forget to use her napkin, or persist in using her knife instead of her four-tined silver fork. These little things annoyed Julia excessively, and numerous were the lectures given in secret to Fanny, who would laugh merrily at her sister's distress, and say she really wished her father would dine some day at Mrs. Crane's table.

"Heaven forbid that he should!" said Julia. "I should be mortified to death."

"They would not mind his oddities," said Fanny, "for I overheard Mrs. Crane telling the exquisitely fashionable Mrs. Carrington, that our father was 'a quizzical old savage, but rich as a nabob, and we should undoubtedly inherit a hundred thousand dollars apiece.' And then Mrs. Carrington said, 'Oh, is it possible? one can afford to patronize them.' And then she added something else which I think I'll not tell you."

"Oh, do," said Julia. "It's too bad to raise my curiosity and not gratify it."

"Well, then," said Fanny, "Mrs. Carrington said, 'There is a rumor that the eldest Miss Middleton is engaged to Mr. Wilmot. I wonder at it, for with her extreme beauty and great fortune, she can command a more eligible match than a poor pedagogue.' "

The next morning at breakfast, Mrs. Crane informed her boarders that she expected a new arrival the next day, which was Friday. Said she, "It's a young gentleman from New Orleans. His name is Dr. Lacey. His parents were natives of Boston, Mass., but he was born in New Orleans, and will inherit from his father an immense fortune; but as he wished for a profession, he chose that of medicine. He is a graduate of Yale College, and usually spends his summers North, so this season he stops in Frankfort, and honors my house with his presence. He is very handsome and agreeable, and these young ladies must put a lock and key on their hearts."

The last part of this speech was directed to Julia, who blushed deeply, and secretly wondered if Dr. Lacey were as handsome as Mr. Wilmot. She frequently found herself thinking about him during the day, but Fanny never gave him a thought until evening, when as she and her sister were together in their room, the latter suddenly exclaimed, "I wonder if Dr. Lacey will be here at breakfast to-morrow morning."

"And if he is," said Fanny, "I suppose you want me to be very careful to use my fork, and break my egg correctly."

"I think it would be well for you always to try and show as much good breeding as possible," said Julia.

"Well," returned Fanny, "I reckon this Dr. Lacing or Dr. Lacework,—what's his name?—will never be anything to us, for I'm sure he'd never think of *me*, and you are engaged to a man who is much better than any of your New Orleans' *pill bags!*"

Little did Fanny dream how closely the "New Orleans' pill bags" were to be connected with the rest of her life. Julia said nothing, but probably thought more.

When the young ladies entered the breakfast room next morning, they noticed, seated opposite them, a tall, dark, handsome young man, whom Mrs. Carrington introduced to them as Dr. Lacey. There was something remarkably pleasing in his manner, and before breakfast was over, he had completely won Fanny's good opinion, by kindly breaking her egg for her, and when she had the misfortune to drop her fork, he drew the attention of the company from her, by relating an anecdote of himself, which was, that he was once invited to a dinner party at the Hon. Henry Clay's, and as he was trying to be very graceful and polite, he unfortunately upset his plate, the contents of which, together with his knife and fork, were deposited in his lap. This story raised such a laugh that all forgot Fanny, who gave Dr. Lacey such a look of gratitude, that after breakfast he asked Mrs. Crane, who the pale, blue-eyed girl was, and received about the same information that Mrs. Carrington had received.

That day Mr. Wilmot's eyes were not as handsome, nor his teeth as white as usual in the estimation of Julia, who often found herself wondering why he did not wear whiskers. That evening he called at Mrs. Crane's, and for the first time in her life, Julia was not much pleased to see him. He, however, rose ten per cent in her estimation when she saw the familiar and cordial manner with which Dr. Lacey treated him. They talked as though they were old and dear friends.

After Mr. Wilmot had left, Dr. Lacey said, "Why, that Wilmot is a remarkably intelligent man and very agreeable." Then turning to Mrs. Carrington, he added, "Let me see, is he a teacher?"

"Yes," said Mrs. Carrington, "and these young ladies are his pupils, and report says he looks after the *heart* of one of them as well as the head."

"Well," continued he, "whichever one is favored with his preference should feel honored, for he is a capital fellow." Just then his eye fell upon an elegant piano which stood in the room, and he asked Mrs. Carrington to favor him with some music.

"Perhaps Miss Middleton will oblige you," said Mrs. Carrington, looking at Julia.

"Thank you," said Julia, "I am just taking lessons," so Mrs. Carrington sat down to the instrument, and as Julia saw how skillfully her white, jewelled fingers touched the keys, she resolved to spare no pains to become as fine a player as Mrs. Carrington, particularly as she saw that Dr. Lacey was very fond of music, and kept calling for piece after piece till the evening was somewhat advanced.

"You ought to play, golden locks," said he to Fanny, at the same time taking one of her long yellow curls in his hand.

"I am taking lessons," said Fanny, "but I make awkward work, for my fingers are all thumbs, as you might know by my dropping that four-tined pitchfork this morning!"

Dr. Lacey laughed heartily at this speech and called her an "original little piece," at the same time saying, "You remind me of my sister Anna."

"Where does she live?" asked Fanny.

Dr. Lacey sighed as he answered, "For three years she has lived in Heaven; three long years to us, who loved her so dearly."

Fanny observed that he seemed agitated while speaking of his sister, so she dared not ask him more about her, although she wished very much to do so. Perhaps he read her wishes in her face, for he went on to tell her more of his sister, who, he said, drooped day by day, and they took her to Cuba, but she daily grew worse, and often spoke of dying and of Heaven, and then one bright summer morning, she passed away from them, and they buried her under a group of dark orange trees. That night Fanny dreamed of sweet Anna Lacey, sleeping so quietly in her lone grave, far off 'neath the orange trees of Cuba. Julia had dreams too, but of a different nature. In fancy she beheld Dr. Lacey at her feet, with his handsome person, princely fortune, and magnificent home near New Orleans, while off in the dim distance loomed up a dark coffin, in which was the cold, pale form of one whom she knew too well. Was her dream an omen of the coming future? We shall see.

Next morning just as the town clock rang out the hour of eight, a strange looking vehicle, to which was attached a remarkably poor looking horse, was seen picking its way slowly through the upper part of Main Street, Frankfort. The driver of this establishment was a negro boy, whom we readily recognize as our friend Ike. He was taking it leisurely through the town, stopping before every large "smart" looking house to reconnoitre, and see if it resembled the one his master had described.

At last he was accosted by a young African, who called out, "Ho, thar, old boy! what you keepin' yer eyes peeled, and yer mouth open for? Is you catchin' flies?"

"No, sar," replied Ike. "I's tryin' to find Miss Crane's boardin' house."

"Oh, yes; wall, it's up t'other way. You jist turn that ar old rackerbone of yourn straight round, and turn down that ar street, whar you see that steeple, and the fust house on the corner is Miss Crane's. But say, is you and that ar quadruped jist out of the ark?"

"I dun know nothin' 'bout yer ark," said Ike, whose Scripture knowledge was rather limited, "but I 'longs to Marster Josh, and I'm goin' to see Miss Fanny—and now I think of it, won't you ride?"

"Lord, no," said the negro, "I'm in a great hurry; goin' arter the Doctor for ole Miss, who's sartin she's goin' for to die this time."

"You don't seem in much of a hurry," said Ike.

"No," returned the other, "ole Miss has died a heap o' times, by spells, so I reckon she'll hang on this time till I git back, jist so she can jaw me for bein' gone so long."

So they parted, the stranger negro to go for the Doctor, and Ike to go to Mrs. Crane's, with his berries, and Aunt Judy's cranberry pie. He had often wondered during his ride whether Fanny would not give him a piece of the pie. As often as this thought entered his brain, he would turn down the white napkin, and take a peep at the tempting pastry; then he would touch it with his fingers, and finally take it up and *smell* of it just a little!

While he was making his way into Mrs. Crane's kitchen, Julia and Fanny were in their room, the windows of which were open and looked out upon a balcony, which extended entirely around the house. There was no school that day, and Fanny was just wishing she could hear from home when a servant entered the room, and said there was a boy in the kitchen, who wished to see Miss Fanny.

"A boy want to see me," said Fanny, "who can it be?"

"Reckon he's from yer home, 'case he says how he belongs to Marster Middleton," said the negro girl.

"Oh, joy!" exclaimed Fanny, "somebody from home, how glad I am! Come, Julia, won't you go down too?"

"No, indeed," said Julia scornfully, "I am not so anxious to see a greasy nigger. I hope you will not take it into your head to ask him up here."

Fanny did not answer for she was already walking down the stairs. Going to the kitchen she found Ike, and seemed as delighted to see him, as though his skin had been snowy white. Ike delivered all his messages, and then presented Aunt Judy's pie.

"Dear Aunt Judy," said Fanny, "how kind she is," then seizing a knife she cut a liberal piece for Ike, who received it with many thanks.

"Now, Ike," said she, "you must wait here until I go out and get a ribbon for Aunt Judy's cap, and some tobacco for old Aunt Katy." So saying she ran up stairs to her room.

When she entered it, Julia exclaimed, "In the name of the people, what have you got now?"

"Oh, a pie, which Aunt Judy sent me," said Fanny.

"How ridiculous," answered Julia. "I don't think Mrs. Crane would thank Aunt Judy for sending pies to her house."

"Mrs. Crane need know nothing about it, and would not care if she did," said Fanny, and then she added, "Ike is down stairs, and he says father is coming after us in two or three weeks."

"Great Heavens!" said Julia, "what is he coming for? Why does he not send a servant?"

"And why cannot father come?" asked Fanny.

"Because," answered Julia, "who wants that old codger here. A pretty figure he'd cut, I think. I should be ashamed of him, and so would you, if you knew anything."

"I know he is *odd*," said Fanny; "but he is my father, and as such I would not be ashamed of him."

"Well, I'm ashamed to own that he is my father, any way," answered Julia; "but where are you going now?" she continued, as she saw her sister putting on her bonnet.

"I am going to buy some ribbon for Aunt Judy, some tobacco for Aunt Katy, and some candy for the children," answered Fanny.

"Well, I do believe you haven't common sense," said Julia; "but where is your money to buy all these things?"

"Oh," said Fanny, "I've concluded not to go and hear Fanny Kemble tonight. I had rather spend the money for the servants; it will do them so much good."

"You certainly are a *fool*," said Julia. Fanny had been told that often, so she did not reply, but hastened down stairs, and was soon in the street. As she turned the corner, she could see the windows of her room, and the whole length of the balcony on that side of the building. Looking in that direction, she saw Dr. Lacey sitting out on the balcony, and so near her window that he must have heard all the conversation between herself and sister! She thought, "Well, he of course thinks me a little silly dunce; but I *do* like our blacks, and if I ever own any of them, I'll first teach them to read; and then send them all to Liberia." Full of this new plan, she forgot Dr. Lacey, and ere she was aware of it, had reached the store. She procured the articles she wished for, and returning to Mrs. Crane's, gave them to Ike, who was soon on his way home.

At supper that evening, the conversation turned upon Fanny Kemble and the expected entertainment. "I suppose you are all going," said Mrs. Crane to her boarders. They all answered in the affirmative except Fanny, who was about to reply, when Dr. Lacey interrupted her by saying, "Miss Fanny, will you allow me to accompany you to hear Mrs. Butler this evening?"

Fanny was amazed. Was it possible that the elegant Dr. Lacey had honored her with an invitation to accompany him to the literary treat! She was too much surprised to answer him until he said, "Do not refuse me, Miss Fanny, for I am resolved to have you go!" She then gracefully accepted his polite invitation, and at the same time glancing towards Julia and Mrs. Carrington, she saw that the former frowned darkly, while the latter looked displeased. This damped her happiness somewhat, and as soon as supper was over, she hurried to her room.

Mrs. Carrington was a gay, fashionable woman, and was just as willing to receive attention from unmarried gentlemen now as she had been in her girlish days. Her husband was an officer in the United States army, and was absent a great part of the time, but she had never cared much for him, so she managed to pass the time of his absence very happily in flirting with every handsome, wealthy young gentleman who came in her way. When Dr. Lacey appeared, she immediately appropriated him to herself. 'Tis true, she somewhat feared Julia might become a rival, but of the modest, unassuming little Fanny, she had never once thought, and was greatly surprised when Dr. Lacey offered to escort her to the Reading. She had resolved on having his company herself, and when she saw the frown on Julia's face, she flattered herself that she could yet prevent Fanny's going.

Accordingly after supper, she asked Julia to go with her for a moment to her room. Julia had become perfectly charmed with the fascinating manners of Mrs. Carrington, so she cheerfully assented, and the two proceeded together to her richly furnished apartments. When there, Mrs. Carrington said, "Miss Middleton, do you not think your sister too young to accept the attentions of any gentleman, or at least of a stranger?"

Julia well knew that the fact of Dr. Lacey's being a stranger was of no consequence in Mrs. Carrington's estimation, but she quickly answered, "Yes, I do; but what can be done now?"

"Oh," said Mrs. Carrington, "your sister is very gentle and if we go to her and state the case as it is, I am confident she will yield."

So they went to Fanny's room, where they found her sitting by the window, thinking how much pleasure she should enjoy that night.

Julia commenced operations by saying, "Fanny, what made you promise Dr. Lacey that you would go with him to-night?"

"Why," said Fanny, "was there any thing wrong in it?"

Here Mrs. Carrington's soft voice chimed in, "Nothing very wrong, dear Fanny; but it is hardly proper for a young school girl to appear in public attended by a gentleman who is not her brother or cousin."

Poor Fanny! Her heart sank, for she was afraid she would have to give up going after all; but a thought struck her, and she said, "Well then, it is not proper for Julia to go with Mr. Wilmot, and she has promised to do so."

"That is very different," said Mrs. Carrington; "Julia is engaged to Mr. Wilmot, and unless you are engaged to Dr. Lacey," continued she, sarcastically, "it will not be proper at all for you to go with him."

"But I promised I would," said Fanny.

"That you can easily remedy," answered Mrs. Carrington. "Just write him a note, and I will send it to him."

Thus beset, poor Fanny sat down and wrote as Mrs. Carrington dictated, the following note,—

"Dr. Lacey:

"Sir—Upon further reflection, I think it proper to decline your polite invitation for to-night.

"Yours very respectfully,
"Fanny Middleton."

"That will do," said Mrs. Carrington; and ringing the bell, she dispatched a servant with the note to Dr. Lacey.

"You are a good girl to submit so readily," said Mrs. Carrington, laying her white hand on Fanny's head. But Fanny's eyes were full of tears, and she did not answer; and Mrs. Carrington, sure of Dr. Lacey's attendance that evening, left the room exulting in the result of her plan. In a short time she descended to the parlor, where she found Mr. Wilmot and Julia, but no Dr. Lacey, neither did he make his appearance at all and after waiting impatiently for a time, she was at last obliged to accept the arm of the poor pedagogue, which was rather unwillingly offered, for Mr. Wilmot greatly preferred having Julia all to himself. She had become as dear to him as his own life, and in his opinion, her character was like her face—perfect. Deluded man! 'Twas well that he died before he had come to a knowledge of her sinfulness.

But to return to Fanny. After she was left alone by her sister, she threw herself upon the sofa, and burst into tears, but at length wiping them away, she arose and went down to the parlor, determined to have a nice time practising her music lesson. It was rather hard, and with untiring patience she played it over and over, until she was suddenly startled by a voice behind her saying, "Really, Miss Fanny, you are persevering." Looking up, she saw Dr. Lacey, who had entered unperceived.

"Why, Dr. Lacey," said she, "how you frightened me. Why are you not at the Reading?"

"Because," answered he, "when my lady breaks her engagement, I think I too can remain at home. But why did you change your mind, Miss Fanny? I thought you were anxious to go."

Fanny blushed painfully, and the tears came to her eyes, but she replied, "I was anxious to go, but they thought I had better not."

"And who is 'they,'" asked the Doctor; "and why did they think you had better not go?"

Fanny answered, "Mrs. Carrington and Julia said I was too young to go out with——"

"With such a bad man as I am," said Dr. Lacey, laughing.

"Oh, no," said Fanny, "they do not think you bad, they said with any gentleman."

"Too young, are you?" said Dr. Lacey. "How old are you, Fanny?"

"I was sixteen last May," she replied.

"Sixteen; just as old as Anna was when she died, and just as old as my mother was when she was married; so it seems you are not too young to die, or to be married either, if you are too young to go out with me," said Dr. Lacey.

Fanny did not reply; and he continued. "Whom would you have gone with, if you had not spent your money this morning for those old Aunts?"

Fanny started; and giving him a searching look, was about to reply, when he anticipated her by saying, "Yes, Fanny, I overheard your conversation this morning, and I cannot sufficiently admire your generous self-denial. I have heard Fanny Kemble two or three times, so I did not care to hear her again; but I decided to go, for the pleasure of having you hear her; but as you did not choose to go, I have remained here with you, and wish to have you tell me something about your parents and your home, and also wish you to ask me to go there some time."

Fanny answered hesitatingly, "I am afraid you would not like to go there, Dr. Lacey."

"Why not?" said he. "Do you not like your home?"

"Oh, yes, very much," she replied; "but father is a little odd, and you might feel inclined to laugh at him; but he is very kind, and if you could forget his roughness, you would like him."

"I know I shall like him, just because he is your father," said Dr. Lacey.

He then turned the conversation upon other subjects, and Fanny found him so agreeable that she never thought of the hour, until Mr. Wilmot, Mrs. Carrington and Julia suddenly entered the parlor.

"Upon my word," said Mrs. Carrington, "you have both stolen a march upon us. No wonder neither of you wished to go out."

"I hope you have been agreeably entertained, Dr. Lacey," said Julia, in an ironical tone.

"I assure you I have," said he warmly. "I do not remember having passed so pleasant an evening for a long, long time."

"I dare say not; Fanny is usually very interesting," was Julia's contemptuous reply, and as Mr. Wilmot just then took his leave, she very haughtily left the room, and went up stairs, muttering to herself, "Foiled for the first time in my life."

From this time nothing of particular importance occurred for two or three weeks, except that Dr. Lacey seemed each day to grow fonder of

Fanny, which greatly annoyed Mrs. Carrington and Julia, both of whom spared no pains to make Fanny appear in as bad a light as possible. But Dr. Lacey understood their manoeuvres, and whenever they were present, seemed to take delight in being very attentive to Fanny. He ardently desired to see the father of the two girls, and ere long his wish was gratified. But of this we will speak in another chapter.

# Chapter V

Julia and Fanny had been gone from home about four weeks, when Mr. Middleton suddenly determined "to go and see his gals" and bring them home. Accordingly he "fixed up right smart," as he thought, which meant that he took off his beard and put on "a bran new suit of *jeens*." He preferred driving his own carriage, so he set off alone for Frankfort.

It was Friday morning, and as his daughters were in school, he stalked into Mrs. Crane's parlor to wait for them. Spying the piano, he sat down to it, and commenced producing a series of unearthly sounds, not altogether unlike the fashionable music of the present day. Mrs. Carrington chanced to be crossing the hall, and hearing the noise from the parlor, looked in. As her eye fell upon the strange looking, giant form of Mr. Middleton, she uttered a very delicate scream, and as she just then saw Dr. Lacey entering the house, she staggered back a few paces, and tried to faint very gracefully! But the Doctor caught her in his arms just in time to restore her to consciousness!

Mr. Middleton now came towards them, exclaiming, "Lightning guns! what's to pay now? Skeered at me, are you, Madame or Miss, whichever you be? I won't hurt a har of your soft skull!"

"Ugh-u-u," said Mrs. Carrington, shrinking from him in disgust, as he advanced towards her, and laid his large hand on her head, "just to see," as he said, "if she were made of anything besides jewelry, curls and paint."

At this allusion to her brilliant color, Mrs. Carrington relieved Dr. Lacey from the delightful duty of supporting her, and disappeared up the stairs, saying in no very gentle tones, "What an old brute!"

"Fire away thar," called out Mr. Middleton. "I am an old brute, I s'pose."

"But your right name is Mr. Middleton, I conclude," said Dr. Lacey.

Mr. Middleton started and answered, "How d'ye know that? Just as you'd know his Satanic Majesty, if he should appear to you?"

"Something upon that principle," said Dr. Lacey, laughing, "but," he continued, "I am glad to see you, Mr. Middleton. I suppose you have come to visit your daughters."

"Yes, and to take them home and let their mother and the rest of the blacks see them," answered Mr. Middleton; then after a pause he added, "They'll be right glad to see me, I reckon, or at least Sunshine will."

"Who is *Sunshine?*" asked Dr. Lacey.

"Well now," said Mr. Middleton, "here you've lived with 'em four weeks, and don't know that I call one Tempest and t'other Sunshine, and if you've any wit, you'll know which is Sunshine."

Just then a voice was heard to exclaim, "There, I told you father was here. I hear him now talking about Sunshine," and Fanny rushed in, and throwing her arms around her father's neck, kissed again and again his rough cheek, while he suddenly felt the need of his red and yellow cotton handkerchief, and muttered something about the roads being so infernal *dusty* that they made a fellow's eyes smart! Then turning to Julia, who still stood in the door, he said, "Come, Tempest, none of your pranks! Come here and shake your old pap's paw. You needn't be afeared of this young spark, for he knows I'm your pap, and he hain't laughed at me neither." So Julia advanced, and shook her father's hand with a tolerably good grace.

"I'm come for you to go home and see the folks," said Mr. Middleton; "so you pick up some of your duds,—and mind not to take a cussed bandbox,—and after dinner we'll start for home."

"It wants an hour of dinner time," said Julia, "and as we are not hungry, we can start in a few moments, if you like."

"Fury-ation," said Mr. Middleton, "I wonder if we can. Well, start on then afoot, if you're in such a hurry. I shan't budge an inch till I've had my dinner; besides, I want to see Mr. Wilmot."

Julia saw that she must submit to the mortification of seeing her father at Mrs. Crane's dinner-table, and with a beating heart she heard the bell summon them to the dining-room. Mrs. Carrington did not appear;—her nerves had received too great a shock,—and for that Julia was thankful. Dr. Lacey sat by her father, and paid him every possible attention.

"Will you take soup, Mr. Middleton?" asked Mrs. Crane.

"What kind of soup? Beef soup, or mud-turkle?"

"It is vermicelli," said Mrs. Crane, hardly able to keep her face straight.

"Vermifuge—vermifuge," repeated Mr. Middleton: "that's almighty queer stuff to make soup on. No, I'm 'bleeged to you, I ain't in need of that ar medicine just now."

Julia reddened, while Fanny burst into a laugh and said, "Father isn't much used to French soups, I think."

"Use your napkin, father," softly whispered Julia.

"What shall I use that for?" said he. "My trousers are all tobarker spit now, and grease won't hurt 'em any how. Hallo! here, waiter, bring me a decent fork, for Lord knows I can't eat with this 'ere shovel, and if I take my fingers, Tempest'll raise a row de dow."

The servant looked at his mistress, who said, "Samuel, bring Mr. Middleton a steel fork."

When the dessert was brought in, Mr. Middleton again exclaimed, as he took his plate of pudding, "Now what can this be?"

"It is tapioca pudding," said Mrs. Crane.

"Tap-an-oak-ky," returned Mr. Middleton. "Well, if you don't have the queerest things to eat! You ought to come to my house. We don't have any your chicken fixin's nor little three-cornered handkerchers laid out at each plate."

At last, to Julia's great relief, dinner was over, and she got her father started for home. Suddenly Mr. Middleton exclaimed, "That ar Doctor is a mighty fine chap. Why don't you set your cap for him, Sunshine?"

"It would be of no use, father," answered Fanny.

"Wall, if I'm not mistaken, he's laid his snare for a bird and I don't care how soon you fall into it, darling," said Mr. Middleton.

"How ridiculous!" exclaimed Julia.

"Ho! now, jealous, are you, Tempest?" said her father. "What in thunder do you think he'll want of you, who are engaged to Mr. Wilmot?"

This was a truth which had troubled Julia, and she greatly regretted her engagement, for she well knew Dr. Lacey never would think of her, as long as he thought she belonged to another. She had watched with a jealous eye the growing intimacy between him and Fanny, and resolved to leave no means untried to prevent a union between them, and to secure the Doctor for herself. To do this she knew she must break her engagement with Mr. Wilmot, and also give Dr. Lacey a bad opinion of her sister. She felt sure of success, for when did *she* undertake any thing and fail? Sinful girl! She was freed from her engagement in a way she little dreamed of.

Four weeks from the time of her first visit home, word came to her one morning, just as she was starting for school, that Mr. Wilmot was sick, and would not be able to teach that day. He had been unwell for several days, and next morning it was announced that he had the typhoid fever. Fanny's first impulse was to go and see him, but Julia prevented her by saying that he would send for her when he wanted her.

That evening Dr. Lacey told Julia that Mr. Wilmot had expressed a wish to see her. She went rather unwillingly, and something in her manner must have betrayed it, for he seemed troubled, and regarded her with an anxious look. She however manifested no affection, and but very little interest for him, and inwardly resolved that when she came again, her sister should accompany her. That night he grew worse, and as there was of course no school, Julia hired some one to take herself and sister home. Earnestly did Fanny entreat her to remain and watch over Mr. Wilmot.

"I shall do no such thing," said Julia. "It would not be proper, and I should be talked about."

"Well, then," said Fanny, "*I* shall stay till mother sends for me. I do not care if I am talked about."

This rather pleased Julia, who said, "Well, you can stay if you like. I dare say you care more for him than I do, and you can tell him so, if you please."

"Oh, Julia," said Fanny, "what has changed you so towards Mr. Wilmot?"

"Nothing in particular," replied Julia. "I never liked him very much."

So Julia started for home, while Fanny took her station by the bedside of her beloved teacher. When Julia reached home, she found that her father had left the day before for Missouri. He owned land there, and as he had gone to make some improvements on it, he would probably be absent two months. Julia carelessly told her mother of Mr. Wilmot's illness, and that Fanny had staid to watch him. When Mrs. Middleton heard this, her maternal fears were roused lest her daughter should take the fever, and in a few days she went herself to Frankfort to bring Fanny home. She found Mr. Wilmot very ill, but not as yet dangerously so, and after staying a day, she announced her intention of taking Fanny home.

"Why not leave her?" said Dr. Lacey. "She seems peculiarly adapted to a sick room, and will do him more good than a dozen physicians."

"Yes, let her stay," said Mr. Wilmot; and drawing Mrs. Middleton closely to him, he whispered, "Tell Julia to come to me, will you?"

Mrs. Middleton promised that she would, but persisted in taking Fanny. When Mr. Wilmot's message was given to Julia, she said, "No, indeed. I'll not go. I could do him no good."

Ike was sent to Frankfort every day to inquire after Mr. Wilmot, and see if any thing was wanted, and each night Fanny waited anxiously for his return. As soon as she saw him enter the wood, she would run to him, and inquire for Mr. Wilmot. Julia, however, manifested no anxiety whatever. She would not have acknowledged that she hoped he would die, and yet each time that she heard he was better, her spirits sank, for fear he would yet live. At last Ike brought to Fanny the joyful intelligence that the crisis was passed, and Mr. Wilmot was out of danger.

That night, in the solitude of her chamber, Julia communed with herself as follows: "And so he'll live after all. Well, I may as well let him know at once that I will not marry him." So saying, she opened her portfolio, and wrote the following note:

"Mr. Wilmot:

"Sir:—When I became engaged to you I was very young, and am still so; consequently, you will hardly be surprised, when you learn that I have changed my mind, and wish to have our engagement dissolved.
"Yours truly, as a *friend,*
"Julia Middleton."

Ike did not go to Frankfort again for two or three days, but when he did, he was the bearer of this heartless note. Mr. Wilmot was indeed better, and when he heard Ike was in the house, he expressed a desire to see him, as he wished to send some word to Julia. When Ike was ushered into the sick room, he immediately handed his young mistress's letter to Mr. Wilmot, who eagerly took it, for he recognized the handwriting of his idol. Hastily breaking the seal, he read twice the cruel lines before he was convinced that he read aright; then the paleness on his cheek grew paler, and was succeeded by a deep flush. When Ike asked what he should tell the folks at home, Mr. Wilmot's voice was husky, as he answered, "Nothing, Ike, tell them nothing." Ike was alarmed at the change which had come over his young master, and called for assistance.

From that time Mr. Wilmot hourly grew worse. Mrs. Middleton was sent for, and a telegram was forwarded to his friends in New York, bidding them come soon if they would see him alive. Mr. Miller, who was teaching in a distant part of the county, dismissed his school to attend his dying friend. It was heart-rending to hear Mr. Wilmot, in his delirium, call for Julia to come to him—to let him look on her face, and hear her voice once more before he died. Then he would fancy himself at home, and would describe Julia to his sister in all the passionate fervor of a devoted lover; then he would think it was Julia who was sick, and would beg of those around him to save her, and not let his loved one die. At last Mrs. Middleton could bear his pleadings no longer. She resolved to go home, and persuade her hard-hearted daughter, if possible, to go to the dying man.

Just before she was ready to leave, consciousness returned to him for a few moments, and calling her to his bedside, he asked where she was going. On being told, he replied, "Mrs. Middleton, I am dying. When you return, I shall not be in this world; but I know that my Redeemer liveth, and am not afraid to die, for I feel assured of rest beyond the grave; but there is one thing I would have. Ere I go hence, I would see Julia once more. I have loved her, perhaps too well, and for this I must die. Tell, oh, tell her how I missed her when the fever scorched my brow, and bid her hasten to me, ere it be too late! but if she will not come, give her my blessing, and tell her my last prayer was for her, and that in Heaven she will be mine."

With many tears, Mrs. Middleton promised him that every word of his message should be delivered to Julia, and that she should come to him. On reaching home, her swollen eyelids attracted Fanny's attention, and excited her fears. Springing up, she exclaimed, "Mother, mother, how is Mr. Wilmot? Is he dead?"

"No," answered her mother, "he is not dead, but is dying."

Then she repeated to Julia his request, and added, "You had better go immediately, if you wish to see him alive, for he cannot live till morning. Fanny will call Ike to go with you."

Fanny arose to do her mother's bidding, but Julia stopped her by saying, "You needn't call him, Fanny."

"Why not?" said Fanny, looking wonderingly in Julia's face.

"Because I am not going," said Julia coolly.

"Not going!" exclaimed Fanny.

"Not going!" echoed Mrs. Middleton. "Why do you say so? You are going, you *must* go!"

"There is no *must* about it," answered Julia, "I do not choose to go, and I shall not go!"

"Are you in earnest, Julia?" asked Mrs. Middleton.

"As much in earnest as I ever was in my life," replied Julia.

"Well then," returned her mother, in a decided tone, "you shall go; I command you to go, and I must be obeyed!"

"I'd like to see your commands enforced, madam," said Julia, her beautiful face dark with rage. "Yes, I'd like to see any body make me go if I do not wish to. Mr. Wilmot is nothing to me, and I would hardly go to save his life."

"Oh, Julia, Julia!" said Mrs. Middleton bitterly, "has it come to this? I can see it all now!"

"What *all* can you see so distinctly?" asked Julia scornfully.

"I can understand what part you have had in causing Mr. Wilmot's death," answered Mrs. Middleton.

Julia turned ashy pale, and her mother continued—"Often in his ravings he spoke of a letter, a *cruel letter* he called it, and I heard it hinted that 'twas the receipt of that letter which brought on a relapse. Now you will tell me whether *you* wrote that letter, and if so, what were its contents?"

"I wonder how I'm expected to know what letter you mean," said Julia. "However, I did write to him and ask to be released from my engagement, and I had my reasons for so doing."

Mrs. Middleton sighed, and said, "It is as I feared; on *you*, Julia, rests in a measure the cause of his death."

"Better call me a murderer at once. But I'll not stay for more abuse," said Julia, as she left the room.

When she was gone, Mrs. Middleton buried her face in her hands, and sent forth sob after sob from her crushed heart—crushed by the sinfulness and mocking disobedience of her first-born. While she was still weeping, Fanny stole softly from the apartment, and went in quest of her sister. She found her, as she had expected, in her room, and going up to her threw her arms around her neck, and pleaded long and earnestly that she would go to Mr. Wilmot. But Julia's answer was ever the same, "No, I will not."

"And why will you not?" asked Fanny.

"Because," replied Julia, "Mr. Wilmot is nothing to me, and there is no reason why I should go to *him*, more than to any other lovesick youth, who takes a fancy to send for me. You would not feel obliged to run, if Bill Jeffrey should have the measles, or some other dire disease, and send for you!"

"Oh, stop, stop," said Fanny, "you shall not liken Bill Jeffrey to Mr. Wilmot, who is so good, so noble. You loved him once, and for the sake of that love, go to him now; it can do you no harm."

"It will seriously affect my plans for the future; and once for all I tell you, I will not go," replied Julia.

"Then *I* will," said Fanny, "and show him that I, at least, have not forgotten him."

This idea pleased Julia, and she answered, "I wish you would, for your presence will do as much good as mine."

Fanny hastily ran down stairs, and going to her mother said, "Mother, Julia will not go, but I will. I should like to very much. Will you let me?"

Mrs. Middleton was too much engrossed in her painful thoughts to give much heed to what Fanny said. She only knew that she wished for her consent to something, and she mechanically answered, "Yes, yes, go." It was then after sunset, and as the sky had all day been cloudy, darkness was fast gathering over the earth, but Fanny heeded it not. She bade Ike make haste, and in a few moments her favorite pony was saddled. Ike's horse was then got in readiness, and they were soon galloping off in the direction of Frankfort. 'Twas a long ride of twelve miles, and the darkness increased every moment, while a steady, drizzling rain commenced falling. Still Fanny kept perseveringly on, occasionally speaking an encouraging word to Ike, who pulled his old cap closely over his ears, and muttered, "Lord bless young miss. Seems like 'twas her that was done promised to young marster, a puttin' out this desput night to see him." •

But Fanny kept her thoughts to herself, and while she is making her way to Frankfort, we will precede her, and see what is taking place in the sick room. The large drops of sweat which stood upon Mr. Wilmot's high, white forehead, showed that the hour of dissolution was at hand. His mind was wandering, but still the burden of his soul was, "Julia, Julia! oh, will she not come?" Mr. Miller stood by him, and endeavored as far as possible to quiet him, and once, during a lucid interval, he asked, "If Julia does not come, what shall I tell her when I see her?"

Mr. Wilmot's eyes opened wide, and for a moment he looked wistfully at his friend, and then said mournfully, "I cannot see you, Joseph, my vision has departed for ever, and if Julia comes, I cannot now look on her loved features, but if I die ere she arrives, ask her if *she wrote that letter*."

Just then there was a noise without, and the sound of horses' feet was heard coming up the gravelled walk. Some one in the room whispered, "It must be Miss Middleton." The sound caught the dying man's ear, and he wildly exclaimed, "Has she come? oh, has she come?" Fanny was now heard speaking in the hall. We have said, that her voice was strangely like her sister's, so 'twas no wonder that Mr. Wilmot in his feverish delirium mistook it. Clasping his hands together, he exclaimed, "Thank God, she has come; she has come."

The excitement was too much for him, and for a few moments he was unconscious. When at last animation was restored, Fanny was hanging over his pillow, and Fanny's tears were upon his cheek; but he thought it was Julia, and drawing her to him, he imprinted a burning kiss upon her fair brow, saying, "God bless you for coming, precious Julia, I knew you would come; and now tell me, do you not love me as well as you always have?"

Fanny was bewildered, and looked imploringly at Mr. Miller, who said, "Richard, do you think it is Julia who is standing by you now?" The sick man gave a startled look, and almost shrieked out, "Julia? yes, is it not Julia? speak quick and tell me, isn't Julia here?" Mr. Miller's eyes filled with tears as he answered sadly, "No, Richard, Julia is not here; it is Fanny who has come." A deathly paleness passed over Mr. Wilmot's face, and a paroxysm of delirium ensued more violent than any which had preceded it. At last it partially passed off, and he became comparatively calm, but still persisted in thinking it was Julia, whose hand he held in his and whose breath was upon his cheek. "Heaven bless you for coming, beloved one," he would say. "I knew you would come, and still the dreadful thought has haunted me, that you might be false, for that was a cruel letter; but you did not write it, did you?"

Fanny answered through her tears, "No, Mr. Wilmot, I did not write it. It is Fanny who is speaking to you." But Mr. Wilmot understood only the first part of what she said, and continued, "I knew you did not, I am satisfied now to die; and yet 'tis hard to die when I am so young, and so far from home, but it is sweet to know that I have your love to the last. When I am dead, you will tell them at home how I loved them and prayed for them. My mother will weep bitterly for her son, who died so far away, but she does not love me as well as you do, does she, dearest?"

Just then Dr. Lacey entered the room. He seemed surprised to see Fanny there, and to hear the words of endearment addressed to her by Mr. Wilmot, but Mr. Miller softly told him of the mistake. This seemed to satisfy him, but he anxiously noted every change of Fanny's countenance. At last Mr. Wilmot said, "If you did not write that letter, who did? was it, could it have been your sister?"

"Oh, no! no!" said Fanny, "*I* did not write it."

"I know you did not, dearest," said he; "you would not do such a thing, but who did? I cannot think it was Fanny, who was always so gentle, so guileless."

Poor Fanny! she felt that her beloved teacher was dying with a suspicion of her innocence, and she wept most bitterly. At last a change passed over Mr. Wilmot's face, a change which showed that the last trying moment had come. It frequently occurs with dying persons, that at the last their faculties are for a moment fully restored. So it was with Mr. Wilmot. A bright smile broke over his face, and looking up at Mr. Miller, he said, "I thank my heavenly Father I can see again. Now, where is Julia? I would look on her face once more."

"I told you," said Mr. Miller, "that you were mistaken; it is not Julia."

"Not Julia!" said Mr. Wilmot, again becoming delirious. "Not Julia! It cannot be true." Then drawing Fanny towards him he looked earnestly in her face. Slowly the bitter truth broke over his mind, and he said, "Yes, I was mistaken! but I bless *you* for coming; but Julia, my too dearly loved Julia—*she* is not here. Oh, if I can never see her in this world, shall I see her in heaven?"

They were the last words he ever uttered. Falling back on his pillow, he drew Fanny's face to his, and with his last breath, kissed her quivering lips, and all was over. Sadly Mr. Miller closed the eyes of his departed friend, and smoothing the covering about him, left him to the care of the servants. A few hours after, Fanny entered the room with Dr. Lacey, again to look on the face of Mr. Wilmot. The sun was just rising, and its first red rays fell upon the marble features of the dead. There was on his face an expression so calm, and heavenly, that Fanny held her breath while looking at him, lest she should disturb his peaceful repose. At length she kissed his cold forehead, and silently left the room which contained the pale sleeper.

In the course of a few hours she returned home, bearing the sad tidings, which were received by her mother with a burst of tears; but Julia preserved the same cool indifference which she had manifested throughout all Mr. Wilmot's illness. Hard-hearted as she was, there came a time in after years, when that proud head was bowed with grief, and those dark eyes were bedimmed by tears of penitence, which could not atone for the past; for they were of no avail to bring back the dead from their silent resting-place.

## Chapter VI

Mr. Wilmot's death occurred on Tuesday morning, and the following Thursday was appointed for his burial. It was the 1st of September, and a bright, beautiful day; but its sunlight fell on many aching hearts, for though he who lay in his low coffin, so cold and still, was a "stranger in a strange land," there were many whose tears fell like summer rain for one who had thus early passed away. He had, during his lifetime, been a member of the Episcopal church, and his funeral services were to take place in Ascension Church.

The house was filled to overflowing. Mrs. Middleton, Mr. Miller, Dr. Lacey and Fanny, occupied the front seat as principal mourners for the deceased. Many searching eyes were bent upon the fair young girl, whose white forehead gleamed from under the folds of her veil, and whose eyelids, wet with tears, drooped heavily upon her pale cheek. Madam Rumor had been busy with her thousand tongues, and the scene at the death-bed had been told and re-told in twenty different forms, until at last it had become settled that on Fanny's part there was some secret attachment, or she never would have evinced so much interest in Mr. Wilmot. She, however, was ignorant of all this, and sat there wholly unconscious of the interest she was exciting.

Julia was not there. She had again defied her mother's commands, and resisted all Fanny's entreaties, that she would go to the funeral.

"You ought to see Mr. Wilmot," said Fanny. "He looks so calm, so peaceful, and," she added in a low voice, "so forgiving."

"So forgiving!" quickly repeated Julia. "I wonder what he has to forgive. If I had continued to love him 'twould not have saved his life."

Fanny sighed, and turned away from the hard-hearted girl, who was left alone with her thoughts during all the long hours of that day. But to do her justice, we must say, that after her mother and sister were gone, a feeling of sadness stole over her; her stony heart somewhat softened, and in the solitude of her chamber, she wept for a long time; but whether for Mr. Wilmot's death, her own conduct towards him, or the circumstances which surrounded her, none can tell.

Let us now return to Frankfort, and go back for a few moments in our story. Just as the funeral procession had left the house, and was proceeding towards the church, the steamboat Diana, which plies between Cincinnati and Frankfort, appeared round a bend in the river. She was loaded with passengers, who were all on the look-out, as they neared the landing-place. Just at that moment, the tolling bell rang out on the air. Its tones fell sadly on the ear of a tall, beautiful girl, who was impatiently pacing the deck, and looking anxiously in the direction of the city. The knell was repeated, and she murmured, "Oh, what if that should be for Richard!" The thought overpowered her, and sitting down on a seat near her, she burst into tears.

"Can I do anything for you?" said the Captain, who at that moment passed by her.

"Nothing, except to land me in Frankfort as soon as possible," said the young lady, whom the reader will readily suppose was Kate Wilmot.

"Are you in a great hurry?" asked the Captain.

"Yes, sir," returned Kate. "My brother is dangerously sick, and I am anxious to get to him."

"Where does your brother live?" asked the Captain.

"He boards with Mrs. Williams, on Elm street," answered Kate.

"Then," said the Captain, "if you will show me your baggage, I will see that it is sent there, for you probably will not wish to waste time in looking after it when we land."

Kate thanked him for his kindness; and when they reached the shore, the kind-hearted man called one of his boatmen, and ordered him to show Miss Wilmot the way to Mrs. Williams' residence. As Kate approached the house, she noticed the air of desertion about it, and her heart sank for fear her brother might be dead. Running hastily up the steps, she rang the bell, which was answered by a female domestic, who was too old and too infirm to attend the funeral. Kate accosted her, by saying, "Does Mr. Wilmot board here?"

The old lady replied by lifting up her hands, and exclaiming, while the tears coursed their way down her furrowed cheeks, "Lord bless me, if this isn't poor young marster's sister."

"Yes, yes," said Kate, impatiently, "I am his sister. But tell me, is he dead? Am I too late?"

The woman replied, "Not too late to see him, if you're right spry. They've carried him to the church."

"Where? What church?" asked Kate, wildly.

"Right yender; that ar brick house, with the tall steeple."

Kate waited for no more, but darted off in the direction of the church. Meanwhile the services were ended, and the friends of the deceased were taking their last leave of him. Mrs. Middleton and Mr. Miller stood on one side of the coffin, while Dr. Lacey and Fanny were on the other. Fanny gazed long and earnestly upon the face of her teacher, as if she would stamp his likeness with daguerreian accuracy upon her heart.

She was turning sadly away, when a noise at the door caused all eyes to be directed that way. A pale, lovely face was seen looking anxiously in, and then a slight female figure advanced through the crowd, which gave way for her to pass. She passed up the aisle till she reached the coffin, then bursting into a flood of tears, she wrung her hands, exclaiming, "My brother, oh, my precious brother—are you indeed dead?" She then imprinted kiss after kiss upon the cold lips of him, who never before disregarded her caresses; and as the full force of her loss came over her, she uttered a low, piercing cry of anguish, and fell fainting into the arms of Mr. Miller, who recognized in her beautiful features the original of the picture which Mr. Wilmot had shown him a few months before.

He bore her out into the open air, where he was instantly surrounded by half a dozen ladies, each insisting that the fair stranger should be taken to her house. First among these was Mrs. Crane, who saw by a glance at Kate that her presence would not be derogatory to any house, so she determined to have her taken to her own dwelling, and urged her claim so hard, that Mr. Miller at last consented, thinking that Mrs. Williams must be wearied with the recent illness of Mr. Wilmot.

Accordingly, when Kate was again restored to consciousness, she found herself in an elegantly furnished room, with a gaily dressed, handsome lady sitting by her. This was Mrs. Carrington, whose delicate nerves would not suffer her to attend a funeral. On seeing Kate move, she spoke to her, and asked if she felt better.

"Yes, much better," said Kate; "but where am I? What has happened?" And then as the recollection of what had occurred came over her, she burst into tears, and said, "My brother—they have buried him, I suppose, and I cannot see him again."

Mrs. Carrington answered, "I think they have not gone to the cemetery yet. I will dispatch a servant, and ask them to delay the burial a few moments, if you desire it."

Kate thanked her; but at that moment a messenger came from Mr. Miller. He had anticipated Kate's wishes, and sent word that a carriage was waiting to convey her to the church, where she could have another opportunity of seeing her brother. Mrs. Carrington felt constrained to offer to accompany her, and the two proceeded to the church and thence to the cemetery.

Although Mrs. Carrington had not visited Mr. Wilmot during his illness, she was by no means ignorant of Fanny's attentions. She had taken great pains to comment upon them in Dr. Lacey's presence, saying, that "she had often suspected Fanny of possessing a more than ordinary affection for Mr. Wilmot, and she had sometimes thought her affection returned. For her part, she did not blame Julia for absenting herself from him, for she had probably discovered his preference for her sister." Her object in doing this was to make Dr. Lacey think less favorably of Fanny, for with her practised eye, she had discovered that for no other female did he feel such an interest as for "Little Fanny Middleton," as she always termed her.

At the grave, she noticed Fanny's pale face and swollen eyes, and found occasion to say to her, loud enough for Dr. Lacey to hear, "I am astonished, Fanny, to see you show to the world how much you loved your sister's betrothed!"

This remark had no effect upon Fanny, except causing her to look at Mrs. Carrington in surprise, and to wonder what she meant. With Dr. Lacey it was different. Imperceptibly, "Little Fanny Middleton" had won a place in his heart, which no other one had ever possessed. At first he admired her for her frank, confiding nature, and afterwards he learned to love her for the many lovely traits of her character. He had thought it perfectly natural that she should feel a great interest in Mr. Wilmot, who was for a long time a member of her father's family; but the wrong construction which was put upon her motives, annoyed him, and even made him fearful that her heart might be more interested in Mr. Wilmot than he was willing to believe. As he stood by the open grave, into which the cold earth was heavily falling, there rested upon his brow a deeper shade of sadness than was occasioned by the mere death of his friend. Mrs. Carrington observed it, and resolved to follow up the train of thought which she saw was awakened in his mind.

After the burial, Kate returned to Mrs. Crane's, where she was treated with every possible attention which politeness or sympathy could dictate. A few days after the funeral, she one evening casually asked, "If that fair, delicate-looking girl at her brother's grave, were not Miss Middleton?"

"Yes," replied Mrs. Carrington. "Did you not think from her manner that she was a sincere mourner?"

Kate was about to reply, when Dr. Lacey prevented her by saying, "Pardon me, Mrs. Carrington; but I think you have given Miss Wilmot a wrong impression. She doubtless thinks it was Miss Julia Middleton."

"Yes," said Kate; "I think it was Miss Julia. Was I mistaken?"

Dr. Lacey replied, "That it was Fanny—Julia's younger sister;" and then he told how faithfully she had watched over Mr. Wilmot during his illness. Of Julia, he said nothing; and although Kate wished to know something concerning her, she determined not to question Dr. Lacey, but to wait and ask Mr. Miller, who, for some reason, seemed nearer to her than any other one of the strangers by whom she was surrounded. He had been solicited to take charge of the school, which was now destitute of a teacher, and as the situation pleased him, he readily accepted the offer, and selected Mrs. Crane's as his boarding-place. Perhaps one inducement which led him to do this, was the presence of the beautiful Kate, in whom he daily became more interested.

Years before, when but a boy in the boarding-school at Canandaigua, he had often fancied that the time would come, when he should both see and know the sister whom Richard Wilmot used to describe in such glowing terms. Since then, another image had filled his heart, and he had dreamed of another face—not as fair, perhaps, but quite as innocent. But now the dream was sadly over, and he had never thought of the gentle Fanny for a wife, since that night when, as he supposed, he saw the dark side of her character. He, however, could not conquer his old partiality, and always spoke of her in the highest terms. Consequently, from his description of her, Kate received a very favorable impression.

He said but little of Julia; but told Kate that he would take her to Mr. Middleton's the first fine day. He wished to go there in order to induce Mrs. Middleton to send her daughters back to school. The next Saturday was fixed upon for the visit, and at an early hour, Mr. Miller and Kate were on their way to Mr. Middleton's.

Kate Wilmot was not only very handsome, but was also very intelligent and agreeable, and by the time their ride was half completed, Mr. Miller was more than half in love, and was building air castles just as he had done months before, when Fanny was the mistress of them all.

About noon they reached Mr. Middleton's, where they were received very kindly by Mrs. Middleton, very joyfully by Fanny, and very coldly by Julia, whose face always wore a darker frown whenever Mr. Miller was present; but he apparently did not notice it, and went on conversing upon different subjects. At last he asked when Mr. Middleton was expected home.

"I am expecting him every day," said Mrs. Middleton, "and," she added in a lower tone, "I almost dread to have him come, for I do not know that he has ever heard a word of Richard's illness and death."

"Why, have you never written to him?" asked Mr. Miller.

"Yes," replied she; "but it is so uncertain as to what place he is in, or how long he will remain there, that it is doubtful whether he ever received the letter. We heard from him a few days ago. He was then in Indiana, and as he said nothing about Mr. Wilmot, I presume he has not heard of his death."

Just as she had finished speaking, the dogs set up a great barking, and the negroes uttered the joyful cry of, "Marster's come! Marster's come!" The family ran to the door to meet him; but Fanny could not wait for him to enter the house, neither could she stop to unfasten the gate, but clearing it with one bound, she was soon in the arms of her father, who uttered his usual "Ha, ha," and said, "Well done, darling; you'll do for a cirkis rider. Are you glad to see your old pap?"

The blacks then gathered round, and he shook hands with them all, saying, "How d'ye, boys? How d'ye? Have you worked right smart since I've been gone? If you have, you may have a play spell the rest of the arternoon."

So saying he entered the house, where after greeting his wife, Julia, and Mr. Miller, he was introduced to "Miss Wilmot." He took her hand, and looking at her for a moment, said, "Wilmot, Wilmot! Are you Dick's sister?"

Kate's eyes filled with tears as she answered, "Yes, sir, Richard was my brother."

"Richard *was* your brother! Great Moses! what does this mean? And you in black, and crying!" Then looking at his wife, who was also in tears, he added impatiently. "What in thun——" but instantly recollecting himself, he said more gently, "Can't any body tell me what has happened?" And the old man's cheek paled, and his voice trembled, as the dread of what might have happened stole over him.

Fanny at last went up to him, and said softly, "Father, Mr. Wilmot is dead!"

Mr. Middleton sank into the nearest chair, and covering his rough face with his hands, wept as freely as a little child. He had loved Mr. Wilmot with almost a father's love, and during his absence had not been unmindful of him. Safely stowed away in his carpet bag, were several costly books, which he had purchased as a present for Richard. He had also hoped that as Julia's husband, he would have a good influence over her, and improve her fractious disposition; and many were the plans which he had formed, as to what he would do when Richard was really his son. But now he was gone for ever. The blow was so sudden, so unexpected, that for several minutes he was stunned by its force, and wept on in silence.

At last lifting up his head, he turned to Kate and said, "You must not think me a silly old fool, child, for Lord knows old Josh Middleton hain't shed sich tears afore, since he was a little shaver and cried when they buried up his dead mother."

Kate could not reply, but from that time she felt for Mr. Middleton a respect and esteem which nothing could ever change.

After Mr. Middleton had become calm, he proceeded to enumerate to Mr. Miller the many good qualities of Mr. Wilmot; said he, "He was a capital feller; allus just so. Lively as a cricket; none of your stuck-up, fiddle-faddle notions. And then he was such a good boarder—not a bit pertikler what he et; why, he was the greatest kind of a man—eat corn bread, turnip greens, or any thing!"

At this speech Kate smiled in spite of her tears, and Mr. Middleton went on; "But he warn't as handsome as his sister, and I'll be skinned if I ever seen any body that was. Tempest can't hold a candle to her, for all she feels so crank. Why, Kit, or Kate, what's yer name, you're as handsome as a picter!"

Mr. Miller probably thought so too, if the admiring look which he gave her was any criterion. Mr. Middleton observed it, and forgetting for a moment the death of his friend he slapped Mr. Miller on his shoulder, saying, "I tell you what, my boy; it's a mighty mean wind that blows nobody any good fortin. Miss Kate warn't sent to Kentuck for nothin', and unless you're a bigger loggerhead than I think you be, you'll try to find out what she come for, and how long she's goin' to stay."

Mr. Miller smiled and said, "I hope we shall be able to keep Miss Wilmot all winter, for the people of Frankfort are wanting a music teacher and have solicited her to remain in that capacity."

"By Jove!" said Mr. Middleton, "that's just the thing. And you have taken Dick's place in school, poor boy—poor boy, to die so soon!" The tears were again moistening his immense beard, but this time he hastily brushed them away and went on, "Yes, that's a capital idea, and you want me to patternize you by sending my two gals—hey? Well, I reckon I can't do better, if they want to go. Ho! Tempest,—Sunshine,—what d'ye say? D'ye want to go back to Frankfort and board at Miss Crane's 'long of Mr. Miller, Dr. Lacey, Katy did, and that 'tother infernal *Katy didn't*, what fainted spang away at the sight of old Josh? But though she was so dreadfully skeered, the pooty color didn't leave her cheek an atom. Lightnin' spikes! let me catch my gals paintin' and I'll——'

But he was prevented from telling what he'd do by Fanny, who clapped her hands and said, "Oh, father, you are a dear good man; may we really go?"

"I thought Fanny would be pleased with the idea," said Mr. Miller, "and even if she had objected, I was going to send the Doctor out, and I know *he* would bring her to terms."

Fanny blushed, and her father said, "Do you think so? Well, I'm glad on't. I'd as soon she'd have him as any body, and she's worthy of him too, for if she can love such a hideous old clown as I am, she'll stick to such a nice man as Dr. Lacey through thick and thin. But what do *you* say to goin', Tempest?"

Julia had at first thought that nothing could induce her to become a pupil of Mr. Miller, but his allusion to Dr. Lacey decided her otherwise. It was necessary that she should go, for she did not dare trust her sister alone with the Doctor; so she swallowed her dislike to Mr. Miller, and said she should be delighted to return to school.

It was settled that they should go during the next week. This arrangement gave great pleasure to Dr. Lacey, who found it very lonely in Frankfort without Fanny, and had several times spoken of returning to New Orleans. But when he learned that Fanny was coming back, he suddenly changed his mind, and concluded that Frankfort would be a charming winter residence. This was laughingly told to Fanny by Kate, who had learned to love her very much. Julia she disliked, for she had at last drawn from Mr. Miller the whole history of her proceedings, and she could but look upon the false-hearted girl as accessory to her brother's death.

Julia knew that by the fair Northern beauty she was secretly despised, but she did not care, for she had conceived a great friendship for Mrs. Carrington, whom she often amused with her remarks about New York people. Once she said, "I do wish New York would die, or stop taking emetics, and sending the contents of her bilious stomach to Kentucky in the shape of teachers!"

Mrs. Carrington smiled and said, "I think you prefer Louisiana emetics, do you not?"

Julia blushed as she answered, "Yes, but what can I do? There's Mr. Miller ready to back up whatever Fanny does, and put down whatever I do. I'd thank him to mind his own business, and stay at his own home!"

Mrs. Carrington did not reply, for she, too, was greatly annoyed by the presence of Mr. Miller and Kate. The latter she looked upon as a rival, for she was said by every one to have the most beautiful face in Frankfort. This greatly displeased Mrs. Carrington, who, before Kate's arrival, had been considered the belle of the town, so far as beauty was concerned. She also felt great contempt for Kate's occupation as a *teacher,* and said, "she didn't see why folks should make such an ado over a *poor music teacher."*

Once, in speaking on the subject to Dr. Lacey, she said, "I am glad I was not born in New York, for then I should have been obliged to pick up chips, split wood, dig potatoes, wash dishes, and teach school!"

Dr. Lacey's reply to this remark was, "I think, Mrs. Carrington, you will admit that the young ladies who come here from the North, almost always possess superior education. Now if they spend much time in splitting wood, and digging potatoes, I am sure they could not acquire so much knowledge."

Mrs. Carrington answered, "Of course *you* feel interested in New-Yorkers, for Fanny has taken a great fancy to them, and whatever she likes, you must, of course."

"Yes, I know Fanny likes our New-York friends very much," said Dr. Lacey. "And I think you will allow that she shows good taste in the choice of her associates."

"Oh, yes, admirable," returned Mrs. Carrington, "almost as good taste as some of my acquaintance show in preferring her."

"What do you mean?" asked Dr. Lacey.

"Why, I mean," said Mrs. Carrington, "that I am puzzled to know what attraction such a simple-minded girl as Fanny can have for a person of your intelligence."

Dr. Lacey bit his lip, but forcing down his anger said, "She possesses the same attraction which every guileless, innocent person has."

"*Guileless* and *innocent*," repeated Mrs. Carrington; "rather call her artful and designing. Depend upon it, Doctor, you have only seen the bright side of her disposition. You should see her in her room, and know how much trouble her sister has with her!"

She might have said more, but Dr. Lacey stopped her by saying rather warmly, "Mrs. Carrington, you shall not talk so about Fanny; I know you do not like her, and consequently, whatever you can say of her, will have no effect upon me."

So saying he quitted the apartment, leaving Mrs. Carrington to her own reflections. They were not very pleasant, for Dr. Lacey's manner had said as plainly as words could say, that she had better mind her own business, and she began to think so herself, for she muttered, "After all, what is it to me if he does like Fanny? I am bound fast, but oh, if I were free, I'd compass heaven and earth to secure him!" Her wish to be free was realized sooner than she anticipated.

That afternoon when the Sea Gull came up from Louisville, it brought home her husband, wearied, worn out, and sick. He took his bed, and never left his room again till strong men carried him out, and laid him down to sleep in the silent graveyard. The close of his life was calm and peaceful, for he had early chosen the better part, and he looked upon the grave as but a stepping-stone from earth to heaven.

His life was a dreary pilgrimage, for though he possessed for his young, giddy wife, a strong, ardent affection, he had long known that 'twas not returned, and he felt that she would be happier if he were dead. She however paid him as much attention during his illness, as the gay life she led would allow, but she was often away, and night after night was he left alone with his Bible and his God, while she was in the midst of some fashionable amusement. Her neglect was, however, partly made up to him by the kind care of Fanny, who gave him all the time she could possibly spare from her school duties. Mrs. Carrington found it very convenient to call upon her, whenever she wished to be absent, and hour after hour the fair young girl sat by the sick man's bedside, employed either with her needle, her books, or drawing. Mr. Carrington was a fine scholar, and gave her much assistance in her studies.

When he grew too weak to read, she would read to him from the Bible, stopping occasionally, while he explained some obscure passage, or endeavored to impress on her mind some solemn truth. Thus were the seeds of righteousness sown, which afterwards sprang up and bore fruit unto everlasting life.

At last, the chilling dews came upon his forehead, his eye grew dim with the mists of death, and then he laid his cold, white hand on Fanny's head, and prayed most earnestly that Heaven's choicest blessings, both here and hereafter, might descend upon one who had so kindly smoothed his dark pathway down to the valley of death. A few words of affectionate farewell to his wife, and he was gone. His crushed, aching heart had ceased to beat, and in a few days the green sod was growing above his early grave.

Fanny begged so earnestly to have him buried by the side of Mr. Wilmot, that Mrs. Carrington finally consented, and the two, who had never seen each other on earth, now lay peacefully side by side. When the spring time came, the same fair hands planted flowers over the graves of her brothers, as she loved to call the two men, each of whom had blessed her with his dying breath. Thither would she often go with Dr. Lacey, who was each day learning to love her more and more.

Mrs. Carrington contented herself with having a few hysterical fits, shedding a few tears, dressing herself in an expensive suit of mourning, and erecting to the memory of her husband a magnificent monument. When Mr. Middleton saw the latter, he said, "Why the plague can't Dick have as good a grave stun as that young Lieutenant? He desarves it jest as much;" so out came his purse, and when Mrs. Carrington went next to visit the costly marble at her husband's grave, she was chagrined to see by its side a still more splendid one. But there was no help for it, so she had to endure in silence, consoling herself with thinking how becomingly she would dress, and how many conquests she would make, when the term of her mourning should have expired!

## Chapter VII

Our readers will not be sorry, if after a chapter of sadness and death, we turn to a more joyous one, and tell them of the bridal of Kate Wilmot and Mr. Miller. Kate wished to defer it a few months, on account of the recent death of her brother, but her lover urged his claims so strongly, that she at last yielded, and their marriage took place on Christmas Eve. Mr. W—— one of the wealthiest men in Frankfort, very kindly offered to give Kate a splendid wedding party, but she politely declined his generous offer, as she did not feel like entering into such a scene of gayety as would necessarily attend a large party.

A few of her most intimate friends assembled in Mrs. Crane's parlor, and thence proceeded to the church, which was crowded with anxious spectators, many of whom almost envied Mr. Miller his beautiful bride, while others envied her the fine looking man who stood there as the bridegroom, and all were unanimous in pronouncing it an excellent match. Kate's happiness on this occasion was not unmingled with sadness, for her thoughts went back to the time when, with a heart bursting with anguish, she had first entered that church, and passed up its broad aisle until she reached the side of her darling brother, who lay shrouded in his coffin.

Now the scene was changed; she was there as the happy bride of one to whom she had given the undivided affection of her heart, and as the solemn words were uttered which made her his forever, she felt that her brother's spirit hovered near, to bless her union with one who had ever been his true friend. She had requested that Fanny should be her bride's-maid, and the young girl now stood at the altar, with her bright face beaming with happiness, for Dr. Lacey, who was by her side, had, the night before, told her all his love, and had won from her a promise that, at some future time, she would be his. He told her that he would speak to her father the next evening.

Accordingly, after the wedding-party had returned to Mrs. Crane's, he invited Mr. Middleton to go with him for a few moments to his room. Fanny was sure of her father's consent, but she could not help feeling nervous when she saw him leave the parlor, accompanied by Dr. Lacey. A few moments after, she observed that Julia also was missing, and she trembled lest she might have suspected something, and gone to listen.

Nor was she mistaken in her fears; for Mrs. Carrington and Julia both had an inkling of what was going on, and when the latter heard Dr. Lacey say something to her father in a low tone, and then saw them leave the room together, she arose and stealthily followed them up stairs. Going out on the balcony, she stole softly up to Dr. Lacey's window, and there, unobserved, listened to a conversation which confirmed her worst fears. In a firm, decided tone, Dr. Lacey told Mr. Middleton of his love for his daughter, and said she had promised to be his if her father would consent.

Mr. Middleton replied: "And so it's my darter you want. Of course it's Sunshine?"

"Certainly, sir," answered Dr. Lacey.

"Well, I'm glad on't. I've seen it all along; but I didn't know but mebby Tempest had come it over you with her pretty face—but devil of a life you'd lead with her."

Dr. Lacey did not reply, but Julia did; and though the tones of her voice were too low to be heard, they were none the less emphatic, as she said, "And devil of a life I'll make you lead if you do not have me." At the same time she ground her glittering teeth, and shook her clenched fist at the two men, who were unconscious of the rage they were exciting.

Mr. Middleton continued, "Yes, I'll give you Sunshine, I reckon, and a hundred thousand dollars besides."

"It's Fanny I want, and not her money," said Dr. Lacey.

"Oh, yes, I know," answered Mr. Middleton; "but I reckon you won't object to a few thousand, unless you are as rich as a Jew."

Dr. Lacey replied, "I am not as rich as a Jew, but I am the only child of my father, who is said to be worth half a million."

"*Half a million!*" repeated Mr. Middleton, in astonishment. "Golly-ludy, man, what made you ever think of a poor girl like Sunshine?"

"Because I love her," answered Dr. Lacey, "and I would marry her just as soon, if she were not worth one dime."

"Maybe you would, and maybe you wouldn't," muttered Julia; "and perhaps you'll have her, and perhaps you won't. You've got *me* to deal with, and I'd like to see the person who can cross my path with impunity." So saying, she glided from her hiding-place, and went down stairs to the parlor, leaving her father and Dr. Lacey to finish their conversation.

Dr. Lacey proposed that Fanny should continue at school two years longer, and at the end of that time he would claim her as his wife.

"Why, yes," said Mr. Middleton; "I s'pose I understand; you want her to be more accomplished like, afore you take her down to New Orleans. Well, it's perfectly nateral, and old Josh'll spar no pains nor money."

And so the conference ended. When Dr. Lacey re-entered the parlor, Fanny read his success in his face. In a short time, he managed to get near her and bending down, whispered to her, "My own dear Fanny for ever." At these words, a beautiful blush suffused Fanny's usually pale cheek. It was noticed by Julia, who was watching the Doctor and her sister with a feeling of almost fiendish hatred. When she saw the bright look of joy which passed over Fanny's face as the Doctor whispered to her, she pressed her small white hands together, until her long transparent nails left their impress in her flesh!

Just then Mr. Miller, with his wife upon his arm, approached the spot where the Doctor was standing, and said, "Why, Doctor, what has happened? You look almost as happy as I feel. And little Fanny too is really looking quite rosy. I should not be surprised if my wedding should be the prelude to another."

Julia could hear no more, but sick with anger, she turned away, heartily wishing Mr. Miller was in California digging gold with the water six feet deep all around him. When the company began to disperse, Dr. Lacey whispered to Fanny that he wished her to remain a few moments, as he had something to say to her. Accordingly after the parlor was deserted, he drew her to a sofa, and placing his arm around her, told her of the plan which he had marked out for her improvement during the next two years. To all that he required Fanny promised a cheerful compliance, and he proceeded to tell her how he would in the mean time beautify his southern home and fit it up with every luxury which could please a refined, delicate female. By the time he had finished, Fanny was weeping from excess of happiness.

"It seems so strange," said she, "that you should prefer me to any one else, me who am so plain looking, so——"

"So pure minded and innocent," interrupted Dr. Lacey, "and so lovely too, for to me you are very handsome. Not as beautiful perhaps as Mrs. Miller, for there are few who are, and yet I like your looks quite as well."

Fanny did not reply, and after a few moments' silence he said, "Fanny, I shall be obliged to go to New Orleans soon."

"Go to New Orleans!" said Fanny. "Oh, don't."

"But I must," answered he. "Business of importance calls me there."

"How soon must you go?"

"In two weeks," he replied.

"And how long will you be gone?"

"Probably three months," he answered. "But I shall write to you often; twice a week, perhaps, and you will find enough to do to answer my letters and attend to your studies, besides practising your music lessons. By the way, Fanny, I wish you to pay particular attention to music, for you know I am very fond of it."

Fanny promised that she would, and they then separated for the night. While Fanny was going to her room, she determined she would tell Julia all her future prospects; but she found her sister either asleep or pretending to be (the latter was the fact); so she said nothing, but lay down without disturbing her. She could not sleep, however, and towards morning Julia called out in no very gentle tones, "Do lie still, Fan, or else get up and go down in the parlor and have another *tête-à-tête* with Dr. Lacey."

Fanny saw that her sister was awake, and she resolved to improve the opportunity even if Julia were not in a very gentle mood. So she said, "Sister, I want to tell you something, wake up, won't you?"

"Wake up!" answered Julia. "I should like to know who's been asleep, or who can sleep where you are? What is the great secret you wish to tell me?"

With many blushes and some stammering Fanny got through with her story. After she had finished, Julia was silent a few moments and then said, "Well, what of it? What if Dr. Lacey has promised to marry you? Is that any reason why you should keep me awake all night?"

Fanny did not answer, and as her mind was relieved from the weighty matter of telling her sister, she soon fell asleep, and when she awoke the sun was high in the heavens, and Mrs. Miller was bending over her, wishing her a "Merry Christmas!" That day there was sent to Mrs. Crane's a large box, which Dr. Lacey was very particular to have handled carefully. When it was opened, it was found to contain an elegant rosewood piano, and a note in which was written, "A Christmas Gift for Fanny." The delighted girl did not ask who was the giver, for she well knew; and resolved to apply herself closely to music, so as to do justice to her beautiful present.

The two weeks of Dr. Lacey's stay passed rapidly away, and at their close he bade Fanny an affectionate good-bye, promising to write regularly twice a week, and to return, if possible, at the end of three months. After he was gone it seemed to Fanny that one half of her life had left her, and she felt very unhappy. There was something in her sister's manner which she could not define, and as Julia seemed anxious to avoid her she spent much of her time with Mrs. Miller, who each day grew fonder of her little "Kentucky sister," as she often called her in imitation of her brother.

Meantime Julia spent all her leisure hours with Mrs. Carrington, to whom she confided her feelings and wishes. Mrs. Carrington was not displeased to find that Julia was determined to break the engagement between Dr. Lacey and Fanny, and secretly hoped she would succeed. Not that she wished to aid Julia in securing the Doctor, for such was not her intention. Neither did she look upon such an event as possible, for she felt sure that Dr. Lacey never would fancy Julia, even if there were no Fannys in the world; and supposing he did, she could easily remedy it by exposing Julia's wickedness.

In due course of time a letter arrived for Fanny from Dr. Lacey. It was a well-filled sheet, and so full of affection and kind suggestions for her improvement, that Fanny felt an increased pleasure in thinking that she was the object of Dr. Lacey's love. Julia watched her with an evil eye, as she read the letter, and when she saw the look of joy which lit up every feature, she thought, "Yes, read on and enjoy it,—do—, for you'll not get many more such!"

That day after school she started out for the purpose of laying the foundation for the fulfilment of a part of her plans. There was in the post-office a clerk whose name was Joseph Dunn. He was an awkward, raw-boned young man, about six feet two inches high. Until within a few months he had lived near Mr. Middleton. He had a very yellow face, yellow hair, and yellow teeth, the latter of which projected over his upper lip! He also drove a very yellow horse and rode in a yellow buggy. In his own estimation he was perfectly irresistible, and imagined he had only to say the word and all the girls in the country would eagerly accept the offer of being mistress of his fancy colored horse and person. For Fanny he had conceived a violent passion, and wondered much that she should repel all his serious advances. At last he wrote her a letter, saying that on a certain afternoon he would visit her and make a formal offer of his hand. He bade her weigh the matter seriously, so that she would have no one to blame but herself, if she should ever regret answering in the affirmative.

Fanny was very much annoyed by this letter, and when on the afternoon specified, she saw old "sorrel" coming up to the gate, she said, "Father, there is Joe coming here to offer me the honor of becoming Mrs. Dunn. He troubles me exceedingly with his attentions, and I wish you would manage to make him keep away."

Thus enlightened Mr. Middleton was ready for any emergency, and he answered Joe's confident knock in person. The young man greeted him with a very polite, "Good afternoon," to which Mr. Middleton returned a significant "Umph!"

"Is your daughter Fanny at home?" asked Mr. Dunn.

"Yes, she's at home," said Mr. Middleton. "What d'ye want of her?"

"I should like to have a few moments' private conference with her, if you've no objection, sir," replied Mr. Dunn.

"A few moments' private fiddlestick," answered Mr. Middleton. "What the devil—— whose little boy are you? Ain't you Miss Dunn's little boy? You'd better scratch gravel for home, and if I catch you here again dickerin' after Fanny, I'll pull every corn-colored har out of your head!"

This rebuff somewhat cooled the ardor of Joseph's attachment, and as he felt sure that Fanny had told her father of his coming, he from that time disliked her as much as he had before admired her. Not long after the sad finale of his *affaire du coeur,* he left his home in the country and going to Frankfort, became a clerk in the post-office. Julia well knew the old grudge which he had towards Fanny, and as he did not possess the best principles in the world, she had strong hopes of procuring his services for the accomplishment of her purpose.

Accordingly at about half-past five, she bent her steps in the direction of the post-office, hoping to see him in the street, for she knew that he usually went to his supper at that hour. She had not gone far beyond the post-office when he overtook her. She greeted him with her blandest smile, and as she seemed inclined to be very sociable, he slackened his pace for the sake of walking with her. They had not proceeded far when she said, "Mr. Dunn, if you are not in a particular hurry, I should like to have you walk on with me, as I have something to communicate to you."

Joseph was delighted, and still he knew not what to think. The haughty Julia had formerly treated him with disdain; but within a week or two her conduct towards him had changed, and she seemed to seek his society, and now she had even asked him to walk with her. What could it mean? He was not long kept in ignorance, for in a few words Julia explained her wishes.

"You know, Mr. Dunn," said she, "that I have money and I am willing to pay you almost any amount, and then it is such a rare opportunity for being revenged upon Fanny, who did abuse you shamefully, and even now makes all manner of fun of you. It will not be much trouble for you," she continued, "for you can watch our box, and whenever a letter arrives from Dr. Lacey, you can lay it aside until you have an opportunity of giving it to me, and you can do the same with Fanny's letters!"

Joseph did not hesitate long, for the love of money was strong within him, and he also had a desire for revenging his fancied insult. Julia's manner towards him too was not without its effect, for he felt greatly flattered that she should choose him for her confidant; so at last he promised to accede to her propsal on condition that he was well paid.

"It will be well enough," said Julia, "to let her have three or four letters, as it would not be natural for him to forget her immediately, you know."

"Oh, yes, ma'am," said Mr. Dunn, "I understand how to do it. Never fear but I'll fix it right."

"Well then, here is a part of your pay in advance," said Julia, as she slipped a ten dollar note into his hand. At first he seemed inclined not to take it, but finally did so, saying, "I suppose I ought to be paid, for it's mighty ticklish business."

After having arranged affairs to her satisfaction, Julia bade Mr. Dunn a very friendly good-night, and returned home, where she found Fanny employed in writing an answer to Dr. Lacey's letter. Here, for the present, we will leave them, until Julia's plot has had time to ripen.

## Chapter VIII

The reader will now accompany us to Geneva, one of the most beautiful villages in Western New York. On arriving at the depot we are beset by a host of runners, who call out lustily, "Temperance House!" "Franklyn House!" "Geneva Hotel!" "Carriage to any part of the village for a shilling!" but we prefer walking, and passing up Water street and Seneca street, we soon come to Main street, which we follow until we reach a large elegant mansion, the property of Judge Fulton, who is that evening entertaining a fashionable party. No matter if we are not invited, we can enter unperceived, and note down what is taking place.

Our attention is first directed towards the Judge and his accomplished lady, who are doing the honors of the evening. As we scan their looks closely, we are struck with the peculiarly benevolent expression which rests upon their features, and we feel sure that to them wealth was not given in vain, and that the beggar never left their door unfed, or uncared for.

Mrs. Fulton's countenance looks very familiar to us, and we wonder much where we have seen her before, or if we never have seen her, who is it that she so strongly reminds us of. Before we can solve the mystery, we observe across the room, a face which makes us start up and exclaim, "Is it possible? Can that be Dr. Lacey?" A second look at the gentleman in question, convinces us that he is two inches shorter than Dr. Lacey, and also that he wears glasses; still he bears a striking resemblance to the Doctor, and we inquire who he is. We are told that his name is Robert Stanton. He is a graduate of Yale, and a brother of Mrs. Fulton. He is intending in a few days to start for Kentucky, in company with Frederic Raymond, who was a classmate of his.

As we watch young Stanton's movements, we observe a certain restlessness in his eye, as it wanders over the crowded room, seemingly in quest of some one who is not there. At last there is a new arrival, and Miss Warner, a very prim lady, and a teacher in the Seminary, is announced, together with three of her pupils. As the young girls enter the parlor, Mr. Stanton seems suddenly animated with new life, and we feel sure that one of those young ladies has a great attraction for him. Nor are we mistaken, for he soon crosses the room, and going up to one of them, a rosy-cheeked, blue-eyed girl, he says in a low tone, "I am glad you have come, Nellie. I had almost given you up, and concluded you were doing penance for some misdemeanor, and so could not come out." Then taking her upon his arm, he kept her near him all the evening.

There was a strange history connected with Helen Ashton or Nellie, as she was more familiarly called, but of this we will speak hereafter. She was formerly a member of the young ladies' school in New Haven, where she had become acquainted with Robert Stanton, who was in college. An intimacy sprang up between them, which at last ripened into an engagement. Stanton's home was near Geneva, and when he left college, he suddenly discovered that the Geneva Seminary was superior to any other, and with but little trouble he persuaded Nellie to go there to school.

She had now been an inmate of the Seminary in that place little more than a year, during which time Robert had pursued the study of Law in Judge Fulton's office. He had always possessed a great desire to visit Kentucky, and had finally concluded to do so, determining if he liked it, to make it his permanent residence. He was to return the next autumn for Nellie, who was to remain in school until that time.

As they stood together that evening conversing about Kentucky, Nellie said, "I have an old schoolmate in Frankfort. It is Kate Wilmot. Do you not remember having seen her in New Haven?"

"Is she very beautiful?" asked Robert.

"Oh, yes, exceedingly so. She turned half the students' heads," answered Nellie.

"Yes, *I* remember her perfectly well," said Frederic Raymond, who was standing near, "and so does Bob, but he wants to pretend he does not. By the way, Miss Ashton," continued he, "are you not afraid that Kate's marvellous beauty will endanger your claim upon Robert's heart, when he shall be near her constantly, and can only think of your blue eyes as 'over the hills and far away?'"

Helen blushed, but did not answer, and Stanton said, "Never fear for me, Fred, but rather keep your own heart safely locked up, for fear some of those dark-eyed Kentucky girls will, ere you are aware, rifle you of it."

"I shall do no such thing," returned Frederic. "I am going there for the express purpose of losing my heart, and the first Kentucky girl which pleases me shall be my wife any way."

"Whether she likes you or not?" asked Nellie.

"Yes, whether she likes me or not," answered Frederic. "I shall marry her first, and make her like me afterwards."

So saying he sauntered off to another part of the room, little thinking that what he had spoken in jest would afterwards prove true. At a late hour the company began to disperse, Miss Warner keeping a watchful eye upon her pupils lest some lawless collegiate should relieve her from the trouble of seeing them safely home. This perpendicular maiden had lived forty years on this mundane sphere, without ever having had an offer, and she had come to think of gentlemen as a race of intruding bipeds, which the world would be much better without. However, if there were any of the species which she could tolerate it was Judge Fulton and Robert Stanton. The former she liked, because everybody liked him, and said he was a "nice man," and what everybody said must be true. Her partiality for the latter arose from the fact that he had several times complimented her *fine figure* and *dignified manners;* so when he that night asked the privilege of walking home with Nellie, she raised no very strong opposition, but yielded the point, by merely saying something about "child's play." She, however, kept near enough to him to hear every word of their conversation; but they consoled themselves by thinking that her wide open ears could not penetrate into the recesses of their well-filled letters which they saw in the future.

In a few days Stanton and Raymond started for Kentucky. The evening before they left was spent by Stanton in Nellie's company. Mrs. Fulton had invited her to pass the night with her, as the Judge was absent from home. About ten o'clock Mrs. Fulton very considerately grew sleepy, and retired to her own room. But long after the town clock rang out the hour of midnight, a light might have been seen gleaming from the windows of Judge Fulton's sitting-room, in which sat Robert and Nellie, repeating for the hundredth time vows of eternal constancy.

The next morning when the last rumbling sound of the eastern train died away in the streets of Geneva, Nellie Ashton sat weeping in her little room at the Seminary. She felt that now she was again alone in the wide, wide world. Eight years before she had in the short space of three weeks followed both father and mother to their last resting-place, and upon their newly made graves she had prayed the orphan's prayer, that God would protect one who was without father, mother, brother or sister in the world.

The little property of her father was sold for the payment of his debts, and Nellie, who was then but twelve years old, was obliged to labor both early and late for her daily bread. Her father had lived near the city of New-York, and not long after his death, she procured a situation in a wealthy family of that city. She was called the "girl to do *chores,*" which meant that she was kept running from garret to cellar, from parlor to kitchen, first here and then there, from earliest dawn to latest evening. It was almost always eleven o'clock before she could steal away to her low bed in the dark garret, and often, in the loneliness of the night, would the desolate child pray that the God with whom her parents dwelt, would look in pity upon the helpless orphan.

Ere long her prayer was answered, for there came to the house where she lived a gentleman and lady, who saw the "little kitchen girl." Something there was in her sad, but intelligent face, which attracted their notice, and they inquired her history of Mrs. Stanley, the lady with whom she lived.

"She is," said Mrs. Stanley, "a good enough girl, if she would only let books alone; but she seems to have a passion for study, quite unsuitable for one in her station. When she is cleaning the knives, she will have a book before her; and instead of singing the baby to sleep, she will get down and read to her, or repeat something which she has learned."

"And has she no relatives?" asked the gentleman.

"None living that I know of," said Mrs. Stanley, and then she added, "Nellie says she had a brother who was several years older than herself, and that three years ago, he was one morning missing, and they found on his table a letter, saying that he had gone to sea on a whaling voyage, and would be gone three years. Her father afterwards heard that the vessel in which his son sailed was supposed to be lost with all its crew. This is her story; but you don't know how much to believe of it."

"Did you ever detect her in a falsehood?" asked the gentleman.

"Why, no, I never did; but of course she will equivocate, for all such paupers will."

"With whom did she live before she came here?" continued the gentleman.

"With a Mr. Barnard," answered Mrs. Stanley; and she continued laughingly, "you had better inquire about her of him, as you seem so much interested in her. He lives out a few miles in the country."

The result of this conversation was, that the Mr. Barnard mentioned above, received the next day a call from a stranger, who made particular inquiry about little Helen Ashton. He seemed satisfied with the result, and as he had before learned that Mr. Barnard was a very good, honest man, he handed him five hundred dollars, telling him to take Nellie home,—as she called Mr. Barnard's house,—and to send her for two years to the district school. At the end of that time, he would furnish funds for her to be educated in New Haven.

There was a great excitement in Mrs. Stanley's family when it was known that Nellie was to go away and be sent to school in New Haven. "I wonder," said Mrs. Stanley, "who pays the expenses? It can't be Judge —— (naming the gentleman who had seemed so much interested in Nellie), for I am sure he would not be stupid enough to take a street beggar, as it were, and educate her." A second thought convinced the lady that it must be the said gentleman, and she suddenly felt an inclination to do something herself for the heretofore neglected kitchen girl.

Accordingly Nellie was summoned to the parlor and the state of her wardrobe inquired into. It was found to be lamentably deficient in even the necessary articles of clothing. Mrs. Stanley then turned her rag bag inside out, and rummaged through several boxes in the garret which had not seen the light for several years. The result of her search was three or four old cast-off garments, which the cook said "were so bad the rag man would hardly buy them." Mrs. Stanley, however, thought them quite a gift, and gave Nellie many injunctions as to when she should wear them. Nellie thought it doubtful whether she should wear them at all, but she said nothing, and in a few days she left Mrs. Stanley's house for a more pleasant home at Mr. Barnard's.

It was a great mystery to Nellie who it could be that had befriended her; but if Mr. Barnard knew, he kept the knowledge to himself, and Nellie was obliged to remain in ignorance. She was, however, satisfied that the gentleman, whoever he was, was both able and willing to carry out his plan, for money for the payment of her school-bills was regularly remitted to Mr. Barnard. At the time when she wished to leave New Haven, she had written to Mr. Barnard on the subject, and in due time had received from him a letter saying, that the gentleman who was educating her was not only willing but anxious to have her sent to Geneva.

Soon after her arrival there, she chanced to meet Judge Fulton and his wife. Something in their looks seemed familiar, and also awoke a painful reminiscence of the dark kitchen and lone garret far off in the great city. She could not remember ever having seen them, and so dismissed the subject from her mind, merely wondering if they knew that she who was to be their brother's wife, once lighted fires and cleaned potatoes as a common servant girl.

The reader will perhaps have imagined that the gentleman who befriended Nellie was none other than Judge Fulton. He was incited to this act of kindness by the same benevolent feeling which prompted all his deeds of charity. He had no daughters, and his intention was, first to see what improvement she would make of her advantages, and if he were satisfied, he would take her home as his adopted daughter. He was somewhat surprised, when two years before the time of which we are speaking, he received through Mr. Barnard a letter from Nellie addressed to, "My unknown benefactor," and desiring his consent to an engagement between herself and Robert Stanton. The same mail brought a letter from Robert, saying that he had just made an offer of his hand to a Miss Helen Ashton, who was only waiting for her guardian to sanction her choice. Judge Fulton's consent was given, and he wrote to Nellie that before she was married, he would make himself known to her, and give her a wedding at his own house.

A few weeks before Robert left for Kentucky, Judge Fulton received another letter from Nellie, saying that it was Mr. Stanton's wish to be married the ensuing autumn. To this the Judge gave his approval, and determined as soon as Robert was gone to enlighten Nellie as to who her guardian was. This, then, was the history of Nellie Ashton, whom we will leave for a time, and as our readers are probably anxious to return to the bland climate of Kentucky, we will follow young Stanton and Raymond on their journey. Having arrived at Buffalo, they took passage in the steamboat Saratoga, which landed them safely in Sandusky after a trip of about twenty-four hours. At Sandusky they took the cars for Cincinnati.

As they neared the Queen City, they noticed at one of the stations, a tall, intelligent, but rather reckless-looking young man, who entered the cars and took a seat directly opposite them. There was something peculiarly attractive to Raymond in the confident, self-possessed manner of the stranger, and ere long he had, to use a Yankee expression, "scraped acquaintance" with him, and learned that his name was Henry Ashton, and that he too was on his way to Frankfort, where he resided. As the young man told his name, Raymond turned to Stanton and said, "I should think you'd feel acquainted with this gentleman, you are so partial to his name."

Stanton did not answer and Raymond proceeded to question Mr. Ashton about Frankfort and its inhabitants. "By the way," said he, "are there any pretty girls there? substantial ones, I mean, who have a purse long enough to pay a fellow for the trouble of marrying them?"

Mr. Ashton smiled and answered, "Yes, we have a good many, and rich ones, too; but the belle of the city when I left was a Mrs. Carrington——"

"The plague it was!" interrupted Raymond, "and can't we get rid of her husband somehow? Won't he die of yellow fever, cholera, or something? Or is he a gouty old wretch, who will live forever?"

"You prevented me from telling you," said Mr. Ashton, "that Mr. Carrington has died since I left there. But you will hardly win his fair, haughty lady, unless you can plank about a million. But there are other faces, quite as pretty, I think. There is a Julia Middleton, who is attending school. She is a great beauty, but if report speaks truly, she would keep you busily employed in curbing her high temper."

"No matter about her temper—has she got the dimes?" said Raymond.

"About one hundred thousand dollars, I think," answered Ashton; "but one would need to be paid that much for having such a fury as she is, and such a queer old rat as her father."

He then proceeded to enumerate some of Mr. Middleton's oddities, at all of which his auditors laughed heartily, and expressed their determination to make the old man's acquaintance as soon as possible. When the young men reached Cincinnati, they concluded to take the stage route to Lexington and Versailles, and pay Mr. Middleton a visit before they proceeded to Frankfort. Accordingly, on Thursday afternoon, just as the sun was setting, they entered Mr. Middleton's yard, where they were received by the dogs, with just such a demonstration of anger as had greeted Mr. Wilmot more than a year before.

The master of the house was this time at home, and soon appearing at the door, he called out to the negroes who were in the yard, "Ho, thar, boys! Stuff your woolly heads down them tarnal dogs' throats, and make them stop their yellin'!" then turning to the strangers, he said, "How are you, sirs? Glad to see you—walk in. Moses and Aaron! if this ain't Ashton from Frankfort. How d'ye do? how d'ye do?"

Mr. Ashton shook hands with him, and then introduced his companions, saying they were from New-York. The word New-York seemed to thrill Mr. Middleton's nerves like an electric shock. He seized both hands of the young men, and exclaimed, "From New-York, hey? Then thrice welcome to my old cabin and hominy; old Josh's door is allus wide open to folks from New-York." Then leading the way to the sitting-room, he continued, "Yes, my own noble boy was from New York, but he died (this is my old woman, Nancy, gentlemen). I don't see why in the old Harry he couldn't of lived. But he died, and they kivered him up while I was gone, and I never seen him no more. Ho! Here, Tilda, fetch some hot water and make a little sling for these chaps. It'll do 'em good, as it's mighty cold and raw here out o' doors."

The sling was made, and Ashton and Raymond drank readily and freely; but when it was offered to Stanton, he modestly but firmly refused. "What upon airth!" said Mr. Middleton, "not drink when a frind asks you? Why, boy, take just a swaller."

Here Raymond, who was ready to adopt Mr. Middleton's language and manner, exclaimed, "I'll tell you what, old boy, Bob's left a sweetheart in New-York, and I fancy she lectured him on intemperance, for you know the women are dead set against it."

Mr. Middleton looked first at Raymond, then at Stanton, and said, "Well, he shows good sense by not touchin' on't, I reckon. Got a sweetheart, hey? That's better than to come here and marry some of our spitfires. Poor boy! Dick was engaged to one on 'em, and I've hearn that she raised a tantareen and broke his heart. But I'll fix her! I'll dock off fifty thousand and to pay for that caper."

Here Mr. Ashton asked if Mr. Middleton's daughters were still at Frankfort. "Yes," returned Mr. Middleton, "both thar, studyin' all the flat things you can think on, and thummin' away on the pianner. You'll see 'em thar: but mind me one and all, mind, I say, don't fall in love with Sunshine, for she's engaged, and I've gin my consent, and whoever meddles in that match'll find Josh arter 'em!" By way of adding emphasis to his words, he brought his fist back against a work-stand, on which stood his wife's work-basket. The stand was upset, and all the articles of the basket rolled on the floor. "Great Peter!" said Mr. Middleton, "ho! Tilda, come pick up these 'ere things!"

Tilda came at the call of her master. While she was replacing the articles in her mistress's basket, Raymond, who wished to show that he was ready to adopt all the peculiarities of the State, said, "That's a valuable looking negro girl. I suppose your property mostly consists in such as she. I don't wonder that you object to give them up just to please the North. Have you many such?"

"Yes, quite a heap on 'em. Why? Want to *steal* 'em, hey?"

Raymond reddened. His attempts at anti-abolition had not succeeded as well as he had anticipated; but he soon rallied and said, "Certainly not; I shouldn't know what to do with your slaves, if I had them; besides, I have no inclination to interfere with your Southern institutions. I am too much of a pro-slavery man myself."

"Likely enough," said Mr. Middleton, rather gruffly, for he did not much like the appearance of Raymond, "likely enough. But, young man, let old Josh give you a little advice. I've seen more'n double your years, I reckon, and I never seen a man come from the free States yit, that wasn't a leetle tached with abolitionism. It's nateral like, and it's onnateral to change their mind so mighty soon. So I advise you to keep your opinions to yourself for a spell, any way. A heap on 'em come here, and are surprised not to find a whippin' post stuck up in a corner of every yard. I don't say you are one on 'em; but we don't think no better of a body when they jine in with us so soon."

This speech somewhat disconcerted young Raymond, who was anxious to get into Mr. Middleton's good graces, but his discomfiture was soon removed by his saying, "Boy, don't take what I've said in high dudgeon. Folks allus see the roughest side on me first; I'm a frind to you, and allus will be as long as you do well." Then chancing to think his guests were hungry, he called out, "Saints and angels! Why don't you bring in supper, you lazy bones thar in the kitchen? Do you hear?"

"Yes, marster," said three or four negroes at once, "supper'll be done ready d'rectly."

In a few moments the nicely-cooked spare-rib was smoking on the table, together with hot coffee, boiled turnips, and egg bread, which Southern cooks know so well how to make. Besides this there was the golden-colored butter, white flaky honey-comb, and the Sunday pitcher overflowing with rich creamy milk. "Come, boys, set by and have some fodder!" said Mr. Middleton.

The young gentlemen took their seats at the table and Mr. Middleton continued, "Now lay into't and help yourselves. I ain't used to perlite strains, and if I should try you'd all larf at me—mebby you want to now. Tempest says I'm enough to make a dog larf."

"Who is Tempest? one of your servants?" asked Stanton.

"Christopher Columbus! one of my servants!" answered Mr. Middleton. "How Tempest would rar to hear that! Why, she's my oldest gal."

"I beg your pardon," said Stanton.

"Not a bit on't," answered Mr. Middleton. "I don't wonder you thought so, such an oddun name! Her real name is Julia, but I call her Tempest, 'cause that's jist like her. She's a regular thunderstorm of lightning, hail, and iron slugs. You'll see her in Frankfort. Goin' into the law thar, are you?"

Stanton answered that he thought he should.

"Well," said Mr. Middleton, "I'll give you all my suits, just because you wouldn't drink and tell a lie to that little gal at home. I despise liars. Let me catch a body telling me a lie, I tell you——"

Here he lifted up his huge foot which was encased in a cow-hide boot, something smaller than a canal boat. He gave the table a kick which set all the spoons, knives and forks to dancing, spilt the milk and upset the gravy pot.

"Why, Mr. Middleton!" interposed his wife.

"I am sorry, honey," said he, "but I'll be hanged if that 'ar sling ain't gettin' the better of the old man."

After supper was over and the effects of the sling had left Mr. Middleton's head, he inquired further into the intentions of his guests. On learning that Raymond would teach, if he could get a chance, Mr. Middleton said, "I reckon you can teach in Mr. Miller's school. I'll write to him about you."

It was well for Raymond that Mr. Middleton did not observe his smile of contempt at the idea of being recommended by such an "old cur," as he secretly styled him.

At a late hour Mr. Middleton conducted the young men to their room, saying as he entered it, "This was Dick's room, poor dear boy! For his sake I wish 'twas better, for it was sometimes cold like in the winter; but he's warm enough now, I reckon, poor fellow!" So saying he left the room; but Stanton noticed upon the old tin candlestick which his host had put upon the table, something which looked very much like tears, so large that he was sure no one but Mr. Middleton could have wept them.

## Chapter IX

Among Mr. Middleton's negroes was a boy twelve years of age whose name was Bob. On the morning following the incidents narrated in the last chapter, Bob was sent up to make a fire for "the young marsters." He had just coaxed the kindlings and coal into a blaze, when Raymond awoke, and spying the negro, called out, "Hallo there! Tom, Dick, Harry, what's your name?"

"My name is Bob, sar," said the negro.

"Oh, Bob, is it? Bob what? Have you no other name?"

"No, sar, 'cept it's Marster Josh. I 'longs to him."

"Belong to Marster Josh, do you? His name isn't Josh, it is Joshua."

"Yes, marster."

"Well then, Bob, if his name is Joshua, what must yours be?" said Raymond.

"Dun know, unless it's *Bobaway*," answered the negro with a broad grin.

"Bobaway! that's rich," said Raymond, laughing heartily at the rapid improvement of his pupil.

After a moment's pause, he again called out, "I say, Bobaway, did it snow last night?"

"No, sar, it didn't snew; it done frosted," said Bob.

"Done frosted, hey?" said Raymond. "You're a smart boy, Bob. What'll you sell yourself for?"

"Dun know; hain't nothin' to sell 'cept my t'other hat and a bushel of hickory nuts," answered Bob; "but I reckon how marster ax about five hundred, 'case I's right spry when I hain't got the rheumatiz."

"Got the *rheumatiz*, have you, Bob? Where?"

"In my belly, sar," answered Bob. Here all the young men burst into a loud laugh, and Raymond said, "Five hundred is cheap, Bob; I'll give more than that."

Bob opened his large white eyes to their utmost extent, and looking keenly at Raymond, slowly quitted the room. On reaching the kitchen he told Aunt Judy, who was his mother, "that ef marster ever acted like he was goin' for to sell him to that ar chap, what poked fun at him, he'd run away, sartin."

"And be cotched and git shet up," said Aunt Judy.

"I'd a heap rather be shet up 'tarnally than to 'long to any body 'sides Marster Josh," said Bob.

During breakfast Mr. Middleton suddenly exclaimed, while looking at

Stanton, "I've been tryin' ever since you've been here, to think who you look like, and I've just thought. It's Dr. Lacey."

"Who, sir?" said Stanton in some surprise.

"Dr. Lacey. D'ye know him?" asked Mr. Middleton.

"Dr. Lacey of New Orleans?" asked Stanton.

"The same," returned Mr. Middleton. "You look as much alike as two peas, only you wear goggles. Connection of your'n, I reckon?"

"Yes, sir," answered Stanton, "Dr. Lacey of New Orleans is my cousin. I have been told that we resemble each other."

"By Jupiter!" said Mr. Middleton, "that's just the checker. No wonder I like you so well. And Dr. Lacey goin' to marry Sunshine too. Your sweetheart ought to look like Fanny. Got her picter, hey?"

Stanton handed him Nellie's daguerreotype, and he pretended to discover a close resemblance between her and Fanny; but neither Mrs. Middleton, nor Mr. Ashton could trace any; for which Mr. Middleton called them both blockheads.

"I think," said Mrs. Middleton, "that she looks more like Mr. Ashton, than she does like Fanny."

"It is similarity of name which makes her resemble him," said Raymond.

"Why, is her name Ashton?" asked Middleton.

"Yes, sir," said Stanton.

"Mebby she's your sister, Ashton. But Lord knows she don't look no more like you than she does like old Josh."

"She cannot be my sister," said Ashton, "for I had but one, and she is dead."

After breakfast Mr. Middleton ordered out his carriage, and bade Ike drive the gentlemen to Frankfort.

"I'd go myself," said he, "but I've got a fetched * headache. Give my love to my gals, and tell 'em I'm comin' to see 'em shortly. You'd better go to the *Whizzakor* House, till you find out whether or no Miss Crane'll board you."

The young men thanked him for his hospitality, and bade him good morning. As they were leaving the yard, they passed Bob, who was still limping with the rheumatiz. Raymond bade Ike stop, while he threw "Bobaway" some pennies. Bob picked them up and looked at them with a rueful face.

"What's the matter, Bobaway?" said Raymond. "Don't they suit?"

"No, sar," said Bob. "I likes fopences; I don't want nothin' of these old iron rocks."

Each of the men threw Bob a sixpence, for which they were rewarded with a sight of his ivories and a loud "thank-ee, sar." After a ride of two hours they reached the Weisiger House in Frankfort. Soon after arriving there, Mr. Ashton introduced Stanton into one of the best law offices in town, and then repaired to his former lodgings.

In the course of the afternoon Raymond sought out Mr. Miller, and with a somewhat quizzical face, handed him Mr. Middleton's letter of intro-

* Pronounced in two syllables.

duction. After reading it, Mr. Miller offered his hand to Raymond, and said, "I am glad, Mr. Raymond, that you happened here just at this time, for my school is large, and I am in want of a classical teacher. You are a graduate of Yale, it seems?"

"Yes, sir," returned Raymond; "and, by the way, Mr. Middleton told me that you had won a New Haven girl—Miss Kate Wilmot. I knew her very well."

"Ah, is it possible?" said Mr. Miller, his face beaming with animation at the mention of his beautiful wife. "Come with me to Mrs. Crane's," said he; "Kate will be glad to see an old friend."

"Thank you," answered Raymond; "but I have a companion with me, a Mr. Stanton, who also knew Miss Wilmot. He is going into a law office here. We both of us intend calling at Mrs. Crane's this evening, and if possible we shall procure board there."

So they parted, and Raymond returned to the Weisiger House, while Mr. Miller hastened home to make some inquiries of Kate, concerning his new assistant, and to inform Mrs. Crane of her prospect for more boarders.

That evening Stanton and Raymond called. They found assembled in Mrs. Crane's parlor, Mr. and Mrs. Miller, Mrs. Carrington and Julia. Kate instantly recognized the young gentlemen as old acquaintances, and presented them to her friends. When Stanton entered the room, all observed the strong resemblance between him and Dr. Lacey. At last Mr. Miller spoke of it, and Stanton replied, "Yes, I've been told so before. Dr. Lacey is my cousin."

"Indeed!" said Mr. Miller. Then turning to his wife, he added, "Where is Fanny? She ought to be here. It might do her almost as much good as seeing the Doctor himself."

"I should like to see Miss Fanny," said Stanton, "as I am told she is to be my cousin."

A malicious smile curled Julia's lip, as she thought, "I think it is very doubtful whether she is ever your cousin;" but Mrs. Miller arose and said, "I think she is in her room. I will call her."

Going to Fanny's room, she knocked gently at the door; there was no response, and she knocked again more loudly. But still there was no answer; and Mrs. Miller thought she could distinguish a low stifled sob. Pushing open the door, she saw the usually gay-hearted Fanny seated on the floor, her head resting on a chair, over which her long bright hair fell like a golden gleam of sunlight. A second glance convinced Kate that Fanny was weeping.

"Why, Fanny," said she, "what is the matter? What are you crying for?"

Fanny did not reply, but as Mrs. Miller drew her up from the floor and placed her on the sofa, she laid her head in Kate's lap and wept still more passionately. At length Mrs. Miller succeeded in soothing her, and then insisted on knowing what was the cause of her distress.

"Oh," said Fanny, "do not ask me, for I can only tell you that nobody loves me long at a time—nobody but my dear old father, mother, and the blacks."

"You should not say so, Fanny, dear," said Kate. "You know we all love

you very much, and you say that within a few weeks Julia has been uni-
formly kind and affectionate to you."

"Yes, I know she is, but——"

"But what?" said Mrs. Miller. "Any thing the trouble with Dr. Lacey?"

"Yes, that's it! that's it!" said Fanny, in a low tone.

"Why, what is the matter? Is he sick?" asked Kate.

"Oh, no. If he were I would go to him. But, Mrs. Miller, for four long
weeks he has not written me one word. Now if he were sick or dead, somebody would write to me; but it isn't that,—I am afraid he's false. Julia
thinks he is, and she is sorry for me, there is some comfort in that."

"Not written in four weeks? Perhaps he has written and his letters have
been miscarried," said Kate.

"Oh, no, that cannot be," answered Fanny. "His. first four letters came in
the course of two weeks, but since then I have not had a word."

"Have you written to him since his letters ceased?" asked Kate.

"Yes, once, and I am sorry I did," answered Fanny; "but I asked Julia,
if I had better write, and she said it would do no harm."

"Perhaps," said Mrs. Miller, "he is intending to return soon and wishes
to surprise you, or it may be he is testing the strength of your attachment.
But I would not suffer myself to be so much distressed until I was sure he
was false. Come, dry your eyes and go with me to the parlor. There are some
young gentlemen there from New-York. One of them is Dr. Lacey's cousin.
He wishes to see you."

"Oh, no, no!" said Fanny quickly. "I cannot go down. You must excuse
me to him."

So Mrs. Miller returned to the parlor, and said Fanny was not feeling very
well and wished to be excused.

Stanton and Raymond passed a very pleasant evening, and ere its close
they had arranged with Mrs. Crane for rooms and board. On their way to the
Hotel, Raymond suddenly exclaimed, "I say, Bob, I'm over head and ears
in love!"

"In love with whom?" was Stanton's quiet reply.

"In love with whom?" repeated Raymond. "Why, Bob, is it possible your
head is so full of Nellie Ashton, that you do not know that we have been in
company this evening with a perfect Hebe, an angel, a divine creature?"

"Please stop," said Stanton, "and not deal in so many superlatives. Which
of the fair ladies made such havoc of your heart? Was it Mrs. Crane?"

"Mrs. Crane! Witch of Endor, just as soon," answered Raymond. "Why,
man alive, 'twas the beautiful Mrs. Carrington. I tell you what, Bob, my
destiny is upon me and she is its star. I see in her my future wife."

"Why, Fred," said Stanton, "are you crazy? Mrs. Carrington is at least
nearly thirty, and you are not yet twenty-five."

"I don't care for that," replied Raymond. "She may be thirty, and she
may be a hundred; but she looks sixteen. Such glorious eyes I never saw.
And she almost annihilated me with one of her captivating smiles. Her
name, too, is my favorite."

"Her name? Pray how did you learn her name?" asked Stanton.

"Why," answered Raymond, "you know we were talking together a part of the evening. Our conversation turned upon names and I remarked that *Ida* was my favorite. Bob, you ought to have seen her smile as she told me Ida was her own name. Perhaps I said something foolish, for I replied that Ida was a beautiful name and only fitted for such as she; but she smiled still more sweetly, and said I knew how to flatter."

"Well," observed Stanton, "I hardly think you will win her if what our friend Ashton said is true. You have no million to offer her."

"Oh, fly on your million!" said Raymond. "She's got to have me any way. If I can't get her by fair means, I'll resort to stratagem."

Thus the young man raved for nearly half an hour about Mrs. Carrington, whose handsome features, glossy curls, bright eyes, brilliant complexion and agreeable manners had nearly turned his head. Mrs. Carrington too had received an impression. There was something in Raymond's dashing manner, which she called "air," and she felt greatly pleased with his flattering compliments. She thought he would be a very pleasant companion to flirt with for an hour or two; but could she have known what his real intentions concerning her were, she would have spurned him with contempt,—as she afterwards did.

The next day at dinner Stanton and Raymond took their seats at Mrs. Crane's table. To Raymond's great delight, Mrs. Carrington sat opposite him. Stanton occupied Dr. Lacey's seat, which brought Fanny directly in front of him. Fanny had been prepared in a measure for the striking resemblance between Stanton and Dr. Lacey; but when she was introduced to him, his looks brought Dr. Lacey so forcibly before her, that she instantly grew pale, and half wished to leave the room. But a look of Mrs. Miller reassured her and she took her accustomed seat at the table.

Ere dinner was over, she had forgotten for the time her lover's neglect, and was in the midst of an animated conversation with Stanton, who was much pleased with his cousin's choice. Stanton's looks and manners were so much like Dr. Lacey's, that Fanny felt herself irresistibly drawn towards him, and her face assumed a brighter aspect than it had worn for many days. Julia watched her closely, and felt that nothing could please her better than a flirtation between Stanton and her sister.

But such was not a part of Fanny's intention. She liked Stanton because he was agreeable, intelligent, and Dr. Lacey's cousin; but she would sooner have parted with her right hand than have done anything inconsistent with her engagement with Dr. Lacey. On the other hand, Stanton's heart was too strongly fortified with Nellie's charms to admit of an entrance to the gentle Fanny. But he admired her very much, and seemed to think that she had some claim upon him in the absence of his cousin.

Thus as days wore on, his polite attentions towards Fanny increased, and Julia resolved to make this fact work for the accomplishment of her designs.

## Chapter X

Let us now go back for a few weeks, and watch Julia's plot as it progresses. We have learned from Fanny that four letters arrived from Dr. Lacey; but the fifth she was destined never to receive. She was expecting it on Tuesday, and was about going to the post-office, when Julia said, "Fanny, I feel just like walking this morning; suppose you let *me* run round to the office and get your expected letter."

"Very well," answered Fanny; "but don't be gone long."

"I won't," said Julia gaily. "You sit down by the window, and when I come round the corner on my return home I will hold up your letter, so you will know you have one at least a minute before I reach home."

So saying she departed, and Fanny sat down by the window to await her return. For several days past there had been a great change in Julia's deportment. She was very amiable and kind to the household in general and to Fanny in particular. This was a part of her plan, so that in the catastrophe which was to follow, she might not be suspected of foul play.

At first Fanny was surprised at her affectionate advances, but it was so pleasant to have a sister who would love her, that she did not ask the reason of so sudden a change, and when Julia *very humbly* asked forgiveness for all her former unkindness, the innocent-hearted Fanny burst into tears, and declared she had nothing to forgive, if her sister would only continue to love her always. Julia placed a Judas-like kiss on Fanny's pure brow, and gave a promise that she would try to be good; but she thought to herself "this seeming change will make a favorable impression on Dr. Lacey, when he hears of it."

She knew that Fanny was expecting a letter on the Tuesday morning of which we have spoken, and fearing that by some means Mr. Dunn might fail of securing it, she determined to go herself for the mail. When she reached the post-office, the sinister smile with which Mr. Dunn greeted her, assured her that he had something for her, and she readily conjectured that it was Fanny's expected letter.

"Good morning, Mr. Dunn!" said she. "Any thing for me this morning?"

"Yes, ma'am," answered Dunn with a very low bow; and casting a very furtive glance around to make sure that no one saw him, he drew from his pocket a letter, on which Julia instantly recognized Dr. Lacey's handwriting. She took it and placed it in the pocket of her dress.

On her way home, conscience clamored loudly in behalf of Fanny's rights. It said "Beware, what you do! Give Fanny her letter. It is a crime to withhold it." But again the monitress was stilled, and the crafty girl kept on her way, firm in her sinful purpose, until she reached the corner which brought her in sight of the window where Fanny was impatiently watching for her. The sight of that bright, joyous face, as it looked from the window, anxious for the expected sight of her letter, made Julia for a moment waver. She thought how gentle and loving Fanny had always been to her, and involuntarily her hand sought the letter which lay like a crushing weight in her pocket. It was half drawn from its hiding-place, when the spirit of evil which seemed ever to follow Julia's footsteps, whispered, "Let it alone. You have gone too far to retract. You have Dr. Lacey to win, and it can be done in no other way."

Julia listened to the tempter, her hand was withdrawn and Fanny looked in vain for her letter. A faint sickness stole over her for a moment, but she thought, "Perhaps Julia means to tease me. I will appear very unconcerned, and not ask for it." So when Julia entered the room, she found that her sister's attention was suddenly attracted by something in the street; but Fanny was not accustomed to dissemble, and the rosy flush on her cheek showed how anxious she was.

At last Julia said, "Why do you not ask for your letter, Fanny?"

Oh, how eager was the expression on the sweet, pale face which was instantly turned towards the speaker. Springing up, she exclaimed, "Oh, Julia, you have got me one, haven't you? please give it to me."

"I will to-morrow when it arrives," said Julia. "It has probably been delayed."

Fanny's countenance fell, and she said, "Then you haven't got me a letter? Oh, I'm so sorry!"

"Never mind, sister," said Julia. "It will come to-morrow, and will seem all the better for waiting."

To-morrow came, but with it came no letter, and days wore on, until at last it was Saturday night. Alone in her room poor Fanny was weeping bitterly. Was Dr. Lacey sick or dead? This was the question which she continually asked herself. A suspicion of his unfaithfulness had not yet entered her mind. While she was yet weeping, an arm was thrown affectionately round her, and a voice whispered in the sweetest possible tones, "Dear sister, do not weep so. If he were dead, some one would inform you. And now I think of it, why do you not write to him? There would be no harm in doing so. Come, sit down, and write him a few lines before dark, and I will take them to the office."

So Fanny sat down to her writing-desk, and the *few lines* proved to be a long letter ere she had finished. It was a most touchingly sad letter, and ought to have drawn tears from Julia, instead of forcing the malicious smile which played round her mouth while reading her sister's effusion. It is needless to say that, although Julia went to the post-office, this letter never did, but was placed in a little box by the side of two others, which had arrived from Dr. Lacey that week.

After Julia returned from her walk that evening, she said, "Fanny, if I were you I would not tell anyone that I did not hear from Dr. Lacey, for you know it's just possible that he may not be sick, and in that case your best way would be to seem quite as forgetful of him."

"Forgetful!" said Fanny, "why, Julia, what do you mean? You cannot,—oh, no, I know you do not think Dr. Lacey untrue to me?" And Fanny's large blue eyes were fixed on her sister with as much earnestness as though her answer would decide her fate for ever.

"I do not like to think so, any more than you do," said Julia, "but Dr. Lacey is now in the gay city of New Orleans, surrounded by beauty and fashion, and were I his betrothed, I should not think it strange if he did not remain true to me."

Fanny answered slowly, as if speaking were painful to her, "Oh, no, no! he cannot be false,—any thing but that."

It was a new idea to her, and that night a weight of sadness, heavier than she had ever known before, filled her heart. She thought, "I will wait and see if he answers my letter before I believe him unfaithful." The next day was the Sabbath. About church time Julia announced her intentions of remaining at home on the plea of a violent headache. Fanny immediately offered to stay with her, but Julia declined, saying that sooner than both should be absent from church she would go herself.

Accordingly Julia was left alone. She watched her sister until she disappeared down the street. Then she arose, and locking the door, drew from her pocket a small key, and unlocking a rosewood box, took from it one of Dr. Lacey's letters. Going to her writing-desk, she sat down, and commenced imitating his handwriting. She was very skilful in the art of imitation, and was delighted to find herself rapidly succeeding in her attempts at counterfeiting. So busily engaged was she, that she did not heed the lapse of time, until her sister's footsteps were heard ascending the stairs. She sprang hastily up, and thrusting her writing materials into the box, locked it, and had just time to throw herself upon the sofa, when Fanny knocked at the door. Julia allowed her to knock twice, and then getting up she unfastened the door, at the same time yawning and rubbing her eyes as if just awakened from a sound slumber.

"Why, sister, I woke you up, didn't I?" said Fanny, "I am sorry."

"No matter," answered Julia with another yawn, "I feel better. My nap has done my head good."

In the afternoon Fanny again went to church, and Julia resumed the occupation of the morning. She succeeded so well, that before church was out, she felt sure that after a few more attempts she could imitate Dr. Lacey's writing so exactly as to thoroughly deceive Fanny. "But not yet," said she to herself; "I do not wish to test my skill yet. It is hardly time."

Thus the days glided away. Nearly two weeks passed, and there had come no answer to Fanny's letter. She did not know that regularly—twice a week, letters had arrived from New Orleans, and had been handed to Julia by Mr. Dunn. In the last of these letters, Dr. Lacey complained because Fanny had neglected writing so long. We will give the following extract:

"MY PRECIOUS SUNSHINE,

"—Can it be that you are sick? I do not wish to think so; and yet what else can prevent your writing? I have not a thought that you are forgetful of me, for you are too pure, too innocent, to play me false.

And yet I am sometimes haunted by a vague fear that all is not right, for a dark shadow seems resting over me. One line from you, dearest Fanny, will fill my heart with sunshine again——"

Thus wrote the Doctor, and Julia commented on it as follows: "Yes, you are haunted, and I am glad of it. The pill is working well; I'll see whether 'Sunshine,' as you and my old fool father call her, will steal away everybody's love from me. I suppose I'm the dark shadow, for father calls me a spirit of darkness, and yet, perhaps, if he had been more gentle with me I might have been better; but now it's too late." And the letter was placed in the rosewood box by the side of its companions.

Slowly but surely the painful conviction fixed itself upon Fanny's mind that Dr. Lacey was false. It was dreadful to think so, but there seemed no other alternative, and Fanny's heart grew sadder, and her step less joyous and elastic, while her merry laugh was now seldom heard ringing out in its clear, silvery tones, making the servants stop their work to listen and exclaim, "How lonesome 'twould be without Miss Fanny; she's the life of the house, Lor' bless her."

The change was noticed and spoken of by the inmates of Mrs. Crane's dwelling. Mr. Miller attributed it to a too close application to books, and recommended her to relax somewhat in her studies. Fanny had too much of woman's pride to allow any one except Julia to know the real cause of her sadness, and was glad to have her languor ascribed to over exertion. On the night when Kate had found her weeping, she had involuntarily told her secret, but she went to Mrs. Miller the next morning, and won from her a promise not to mention what she had revealed, even to her husband.

Mr. Stanton's presence seemed to divert Fanny's mind, and the two weeks following his arrival passed away more pleasantly than she had thought two weeks could pass, uncheered by a line from Dr. Lacey. At the end of that time it pleased Julia that Fanny should have a pretended letter from New Orleans. Several days were spent in preparing it, but at last it was completed, folded, sealed, and directed. Mr. Dunn pronounced the deception perfect. He stamped it with the Frankfort postmark so slightly that one would as soon have called it "New Orleans" as any thing else.

Fanny was seated in the parlor in company with Stanton, when Julia suddenly entered the room, and said, "Oh, here you are, sister. I've looked every where for you. Here is a letter."

One glance at the superscription assured her that it was from Dr. Lacey. A bright, beautiful flush suffused Fanny's face, which became irradiated with a sudden joy. Asking Mr. Stanton to excuse her, she went to her room, so as to be alone when she perused the precious document. After she was gone, Julia spoke of Dr. Lacey, and asked Stanton if he ever heard from him. Stanton replied, "While Dr. Lacey was in college, he spent a part of his vacations at my father's; but I almost always chanced to be absent at school, and consequently we are not much acquainted. He did write to me a few times while I was in college, but our correspondence gradually ceased, and I have not heard from him in a long time. I hope he will return to Frankfort, for I should like to renew our acquaintance."

This answer gave Julia great relief; she had feared Stanton might write to Dr. Lacey, and that by some means her scheme might be ruined. But all was safe, and in a few moments she arose to go to her room and witness the result of the letter. Let us go before her, and see the effect for ourselves.

On reaching her apartment, Fanny sat down on the sofa, while a tremulous nervousness shook her frame. She dreaded to open the letter, for a strange foreboding of evil came over her. At last the seal was broken, and Fanny's heart stood still, and a dizziness crept over her as she read. For the reader's benefit, we will look over her shoulder and read with her the following:

> *"My once dear and still much admired Fanny:*
> "I hardly know how to write what I wish to tell you. If I knew exactly your opinion concerning me I might feel differently. As it is, I ardently hope that your extreme youth prevented my foolish, but then sincere attentions, from making any very lasting impression on you. But why not come to the point at once? Fanny, you must try and forget that you ever knew one so wholly unworthy of you as I am. It gives me great pain to write it, but I am about to engage myself to another.
>
> "Do not condemn me unheard. There is a young lady in this city, who is beautiful, wealthy, and accomplished. Between her father's family and mine there has long existed an intimacy, which our fathers seem anxious to strengthen by a union between myself and the young lady I have mentioned. For a time I resisted manfully. For, ever between me and the tempting bait, came the image of a pale, bright-haired girl, whose blue eyes looked mournfully into mine and whispered, 'Do not leave me.' But at last I yielded, and now, Fanny, will you forgive me? It cost me more anguish to give you up, than I hope you will ever feel. Be happy, Fanny, and sometime when I am travelling through Kentucky, let me find you the cheerful, contented wife of one more suitable for you than I am.
>
> "With many kind wishes for your happiness, I remain your true friend,
>
> "GEORGE LACEY."
>
> "P.S. It is just possible that the young lady and myself may not become engaged, but if we do not, after what has passed, it will be best for you and me to forget each other. Give my compliments to your sister Julia. By the way, do you know that I always admired her very much! What a sensation she would make in the fashionable world of New Orleans! But pshaw! what nonsense I am writing."

Alas for Fanny! she did not need to read the letter twice, for every syllable had burned into her soul, and she could have repeated each word of the cruel message. This, then, was the end of all her bright dreams of bliss! She did not weep, for she could not. The fountain of her tears seemed dried up. A heavy weight had suddenly fallen on all her faculties. The objects in the room chased each other in rapid circles, while Dr. Lacey stood in the distance mocking her anguish. A faint feeling gathered round her heart. She uttered a low cry and fell heavily forward.

When Julia entered the room, she found her sister extended on the floor, cold and white as a piece of marble, while the blood was gushing from her nostrils and moistening the long curls of her hair. Julia's first feeling was one of intense horror, for fear her sister might be dead, but a touch assured her that Fanny had only fainted. So she lifted her up and bearing her to the window, applied the usual restoratives. As Julia looked on the deathlike face of her young sister, she murmured, "Had I thought she loved him so well, never would I have done so wickedly."

But she made no promise to repair the mischief, and stifled all the better impulses of her nature, by saying, "It is too late now; it is too late." At last Fanny opened her eyes. Her first thought was for her letter, which was still tightly clenched in her hand. Passing it to Julia, she said faintly, "Read it, sister; read it."

Julia took it, and pretending to read it, burst into a violent passion, abusing Dr. Lacey for his meanness, and ending by telling Fanny that she ought to consider herself fortunate in escaping from so unprincipled a man. Fanny seemed disturbed to hear evil spoken of Dr. Lacey, so Julia changed her manner, and said, "I do not wonder you feel badly, Fanny. You and I can sympathize together now."

Fanny looked at her sister in some surprise, but at last answered, "Oh, no, you cannot know how I feel. Mr. Wilmot loved you to the last. Dr. Lacey is not dead, but——"

Here Julia interrupted her by saying, "I do not mean to refer to Mr. Wilmot. I was flattered by his attentions, but I never knew what it was to love, until I saw *Dr. Lacey!*"

"Dr. Lacey!—*You* love Dr. Lacey!" said Fanny, and again she fell back, cold and motionless. A second time Julia restored her to consciousness, but for an hour she did not speak or scarcely move. At the end of that time, calling her sister to her, in a low, subdued tone, she said, "Tell me all, Julia. I can bear it. I am calm now."

The traitoress kissed her cheek, and taking one of the little hands in hers, told her how truly she had loved Dr. Lacey, and how she had struggled against it when she saw that he loved another. "I have," said she, "lain awake many a night, and while you slept sweetly, dreaming, perhaps, of your lover, I have wept bitter tears because I must go alone through the cold world, unloved and uncared for. And forgive me, Fanny, but sometimes I have felt angered at you, because you seemed to steal everybody's love from me. Our old father never speaks to me with the same affection which marks his manner when addressing you."

"I know it, I know it," said Fanny. "I wish he would not do so, but Dr. Lacey—Dr. Lacey—I never thought you wanted him to love you; if I had——"

"What would you have done?" asked Julia eagerly.

The voice was mournfully low which replied, "I would have given him up to you. I could not have married one whom my sister loved." And then she suddenly added, "It seems doubtful whether he marries that young lady. If he should not, he may yet make you his wife."

"And you, what would you do?" asked Julia.

"Oh, it is impossible for me to marry him now," said Fanny; "but if you were happy with him, I would try to be happy too."

"God bless you, sweet sister," said Julia; "but it will never be."

Fanny did not reply, and after a moment's silence Julia said, "Sister, if I were you, I would keep all this a secret, and even if I were unhappy, I would try to assume a forced cheerfulness, for fear people would suspect the truth, and call me *lovesick*."

Fanny did not reply to this either. She was trying to still the painful throbs of her aching heart. Through all the long, weary hours of that night, she was awake. Sometimes she would watch the myriad host of stars, as they kept on their unwearied course through the clear, blue sky, and would wonder if there was room beyond them, for such as she, should she die thus early. Then she would muse on the past days of happiness now forever gone, and though a choking sensation was in her throat, not a tear moistened her cheek. "I shall never weep again," thought she, "and why should I? The world shall not know what I suffer. I will be as gay and merry as ever." And a fearful laugh rang through the room as she said, "Yes, how gayly I'll dance at the wedding. I'll hold my heart so fast that none shall ever know in how many pieces it is broken." Thus she talked on. Delirium was stealing over her, and when morning broke, the rapid moving of her bright eye, and the crimson spot which burned on either cheek, showed that brain fever was doing its work.

A physician was immediately called, and by the means of powerful remedies, the progress of the disease was checked, so that Fanny was seriously ill for only a week. She was delirious a great part of the time, but Julia was delighted to find that not one word of Dr. Lacey ever passed her lips. At the commencement of her illness, her father and mother were sent for. The old man came quickly, for Fanny was his idol, and if she should die, he would be bereaved indeed. With untiring love, he watched by her bedside until the crisis was passed. He would fan her fevered brow, moisten her parched lips, chafe her hot, burning hands, smooth her tumbled pillow, and when at last he succeeded in soothing her into a troubled slumber, he would sit by her, and gaze on her wan face with an earnestness which seemed to say that she was his all of earth, his more than all of heaven.

Julia too was all attention. Nothing tired her, and with unwearied patience she came and went at her father's bidding, doing the thousand little offices pertaining to a sick chamber. For once her father's manner softened towards her, and the tones of his voice were gentle and his words kind while speaking to his first-born. Could he have known what part she had in causing the illness of his "darling Sunshine," all Frankfort would have shaken with the heavy artillery of oaths and execrations, which would have been disgorged from his huge lungs, like the eruption of some long pent-up volcano! But he did not suspect the truth, and in speaking of Fanny's illness, he said, "It is studyin' so close, that ailded her. As ever she can bar to be moved we will carry her home, and Aunt Katy'll nuss her up quicker."

Accordingly as soon as the physician pronounced it safe to move her, she was taken home, and by her mother's assiduous care, and Aunt Katy's skilful nursing, her physical health was soon much improved. But no medicine could reach the plague-spot which preyed upon her heart, and cast a dark shadow over every feeling of pleasure. As soon as her health was fully restored, she asked permission to return to school. At first Mr. Middleton refused, but not long did he ever withstand any request which "Sunshine" made. So at last he consented, on condition that she would give up the study of the Latin, and promise not to apply herself too closely to any thing. To this Fanny readily agreed, and in a few days she was again in Frankfort, occupying her accustomed seat at Mrs. Crane's table and bending over her task in the old schoolroom, which seemed suddenly illuminated by her presence.

The school-girls welcomed back their young companion with many demonstrations of joy, for they said, "the schoolroom seemed dark and lonely when she was absent." Dear little Fanny! There was love enough left for her in the hearts of all who knew her, but it did not satisfy. There was still an aching void, which one love alone could fill, and that love she thought was lost to her for ever. She was mistaken.

During her illness she thought much of what Julia had said relative to concealing her disappointment with an assumed gayety, and she resolved to do so, partly from wounded pride, and partly from love of her dear old father, who seemed distressed whenever any thing troubled his "Sunshine." When she returned to Frankfort, none but the most acute observer would have suspected that the sparkling eye and dancing footstep were the disguise of a desolate, aching heart, and that the merry laugh and witty repartee were but the echoes of a knell of sadness, whose deepest tones were stifled ere they reached the ear of the listener. In the darkness of night, however, all was changed. The *Sunshine* was obscured, and Julia alone knew what anguish Fanny endured. Still the cruel girl never wavered in her purpose. "The worst is over," said she. "She will not die now, even if she saw him wedded to me." So she suffered her sister's cheek to grow paler, and her delicate form thinner, at the supposed desertion of her lover. Little did Fanny think that he, whose false-heartedness she deplored, dreamed each night of his distant dear one, and that each day his warm heart beat more quickly, because no tidings came from her.

A few days after Fanny's return there came cards of invitation for a large party at the residence of a Mr. C——. The evening was propitious, and at the usual hour Mrs. C——'s parlors were filled with the beauty and fashion of the city. Among all the belles, who that evening graced the brilliantly lighted drawing-rooms, none was so much admired as Julia Middleton, who appeared dressed in a rich crimson velvet robe, tastefully trimmed with ermine. Magnificent bracelets, which had cost her father almost as many oaths as dollars, glittered on her white rounded arms. Her snowy neck, which was also uncovered, was without ornament. Her glossy hair, dark as night, was arranged in the most becoming manner.

At the time Mr. Middleton had given Julia her bracelets, he had presented Fanny with a bandeau of pearls. But Julia found it an easy task to persuade her sister that pearls were not becoming to her style of beauty; so on the evening of the party they gleamed amid the heavy braids of Julia's hair. Wherever she went she was followed by a train of admirers, who little thought that that soft smile and beautiful face concealed a heart as hard as the flinty rock.

Contrary to all the rules of propriety, the heartless Mrs. Carrington was there, dealing out her fascinating smiles and bland words. She had thrown aside her mourning for the occasion and was arrayed in a dress of black velvet. An elegant lace bertha covered her white, beautiful neck, while one of her fair arms was clasped by a diamond bracelet. To this bracelet was attached a small locket, which contained the daguerreotype of him, upon whose quiet grave the suns of scarce five months had risen and set. Amid that brilliant scene she had no thought for the dead, but others wondered much that he should be so soon forgotten. She was attended by Raymond, who scarcely left her side during the whole evening, although she made several ineffectual attempts to shake him off, for she did not care to be too much noticed by a "poor Yankee schoolmaster."

Henry Ashton was also there, but his attention was wholly engrossed by the bright eyes and sunny face of Florence Woodburn, who had recently returned from Philadelphia, where she had been attending school for the last two years. Florence was the only daughter of the Mr. Woodburn, who was mentioned in the first chapter of this narrative. Her father lived several miles from the city, but she had friends in town and spent much of her time there. She was very handsome and very agreeable, and as she would probably be quite an heiress, her appearance in the fashionable world created a great sensation.

During the evening, as she was standing by Ashton and commenting upon Julia's wondrous beauty, she asked "Where is the younger Miss Middleton? Is she as handsome as her sister?"

Ashton replied, "She is not called half as beautiful, but she is much more amiable; but see, there she comes," continued he, as Fanny entered the room leaning on Stanton's arm.

She was so pale that her skin seemed almost transparent, but the excitement of the evening brought a bright glow to her cheek which greatly enhanced her loveliness. She was simply attired in a plain white muslin, low at the neck, which was veiled by the soft curls of her silken hair. Her arms were encircled by a plain band of gold, and a white, half opened rosebud, was fastened to the bosom of her dress.

As she entered the room many admiring eyes were turned towards her, and Miss Woodburn exclaimed, "Oh, how lovely she is! Her sister seems more like the flashing diamond, while Fanny's beauty is like the soft lustre of the pearl. But tell me," she continued, "is she not engaged to a Dr. Lacey of New Orleans?"

"Yes, or that is, it was so rumored," answered Ashton, "but he has gone home, and since then I have heard nothing of it. Young Stanton seems very attentive. I should not wonder if something grew out of it."

"Always making matches, Mr. Ashton," said Mrs. Carrington, who for a moment rid herself of Raymond and now came near Ashton and Florence. She had heard them speak of Dr. Lacey and Fanny, and as she knew Florence was soon going to New Orleans, she wished to give her a little Frankfort gossip to take with her.

"Oh, Mrs. Carrington," said Mr. Ashton, bowing politely, "allow me to introduce Miss Woodburn. We were just talking of the probability of Miss Fanny's being engaged to Dr. Lacey. Perhaps you can enlighten us somewhat."

"Oh," said Mrs. Carrington, "I assure you I know but little about the matter. It is rather uncertain whom Miss Fanny likes or dislikes. It is currently reported that she was in love with a Mr. Wilmot, who died, and who was known to be engaged to her sister. Since then Dr. Lacey has flirted with her, but whether seriously or not, I cannot tell; I should rather think not, however, for Mr. Stanton now seems to be the favored one."

"Oh," said Mr. Ashton, "I never supposed Fanny was so much of a coquette."

"Neither do I think she is," said Florence, whose heart warmed towards Fanny as soon as she saw her.

"Perhaps she is not," said Mrs. Carrington. "Fanny is very young yet, but when fully matured will perhaps make a noble woman, but she has not the solidity of her sister, who tries hard to keep her from assuming the appearance of a flirt." Then turning to Florence, she said, "I believe you are soon going to New Orleans?"

"Yes, madam," answered Florence.

"You will probably meet Dr. Lacey there," continued Mrs. Carrington. "Perhaps you had better say nothing to him about Fanny's flirtation with Stanton, for he would hardly believe it."

Florence merely nodded, thinking to herself that she should do as she chose about it. From the first she had been attracted towards Fanny. There was something in her face and in the expression of her eye, which interested Florence. It seemed to her that Fanny would gladly have left that scene of gayety, and going out by herself, would have poured out her soul in tears. She earnestly desired an introduction, and at last it was obtained. There seemed to be some secret magnet which attracted these two young girls towards each other, for in a few moments they were arm in arm talking familiarly upon different topics as though they had been acquainted a lifetime.

Florence was a warm-hearted, affectionate girl, and after a time she said, "Miss Middleton, I am going to New Orleans soon. I believe you have an acquaintance there. If I see him, what shall I tell him?"

Fanny's voice trembled slightly as she answered, "Tell whom?"

"Oh, Miss Middleton," said Florence, laughing gayly, "how that blush becomes you! Tell whom? Why, who should it be but Dr. Lacey, whom every body except Mrs. Carrington says is engaged to you."

The fire shot from Fanny's eyes, but one look at the open face at her side assured her, and she answered, "I am not answerable for what the world pleases to say of me."

"I am to consider the report true, then," persisted Florence.

A momentary struggle took place in Fanny's mind. Love and resentment strove for the mastery. The latter conquered, and the voice was calm and decided which replied, "I assure you, Miss Woodburn, that Dr. Lacey bears no relation to me except that of a common acquaintance."

"Indeed," said Florence. "I am sorry, for I was anticipating much pleasure in describing Dr. Lacey's intended lady to the New Orleans girls."

Fanny did not answer, and as Stanton just then approached, and asked her to go to the music-room, she took his arm readily, glad to escape from so painful a conversation.

"She is a strange girl," thought Florence, "and yet I know I should love her. I wonder what makes her so sad. Can it be that she really loved that Mr. Wilmot? At any rate I am sorry for her, and hope she will marry Mr. Stanton, who seems much pleased with her."

Thus was an impression left on Florence's mind, which was productive of much mischief. At a late hour the company dispersed. Fanny returned home, weary and sick at heart. Her conversation with Florence had awakened painful reminiscences of the past, and the gray daylight was beginning to streak the eastern horizon ere her heavy eyelids closed in slumber. In a few days Florence Woodburn departed for New Orleans, where her mother's brother resided. We will take passage with her and pay a visit to Dr. Lacey in his southern home.

## Chapter XI

The house which Dr. Lacey occupied, was situated on one of the pleasantest streets in New Orleans. It was a large, airy structure, which had formerly been owned by a wealthy French gentleman, who had spared neither money nor pains to adorn it with every elegance which could minister to the luxurious habits common to a southern clime. When it passed into the hands of Dr. Lacey's father, he gratified his northern taste, and fitted it up with every possible convenience, moulding its somewhat ancient aspect into a more modern style.

When Dr. Lacey reached the age of twenty-one, his father made him the owner of the house, he himself removing to another part of the city. At the time of which we are speaking, nothing could exceed the beauty of the house and grounds.

The yard which surrounded the building was large, and laid out with all the taste of a perfect connoisseur. In its centre was a fountain, whose limpid waters fell into a large marble basin, while the spray which constantly arose from the falling stream, seemed to render the heat of that sultry climate less oppressive. Scattered throughout the yard were the numerous trees and flowering shrubs which grow in such profusion at the "sunny South." Here the beautiful magnolia shook its white blossoms in the evening breeze, and there the dark green foliage of the orange trees formed an effectual screen from the midday sun.

The building was surrounded on all sides by a double piazza, the slender pillars of which were entwined by the flowering honey-suckle, and luxuriant passion-flower, which gave the house the appearance of a closely wreathed arbor. Within, the piazza was filled with rare tropical plants. The beautiful oleander, magnificent rose, and sweet-scented geranium, here united their fragrance, while the scarlet verbenum and brilliant heliotrope added beauty to the scene.

The interior of the building corresponded with the exterior. The rooms, large and airy, were carpeted with velvet, and adorned with costly marble and rosewood furniture. The windows, which were constructed in the French style, that is, reaching to the floor, were curtained with richly-embroidered lace. Let us ascend the winding staircase, and enter the dressing-room of the owner of all this splendor.

Half reclining on a crimson lounge sits Dr. Lacey, dressed in a fashionable brocade morning-gown. On first glancing at him, we think there is no change in his countenance, since we last saw him on Mrs. Crane's steps in Frankfort, but as we note the expression of his face, we can perceive a shade of anxiety resting there. At last he rises and rather impatiently pulls the bell-rope.

His summons is immediately answered by an exquisite dandy, who is neither African, European, French, nor Spanish, but an odd mixture of the four. He is dressed in the extreme of fashion, and on entering the room, bows most gracefully, at the same time casting an admiring glance at himself in the large mirror, and passing his hand carelessly through his perfumed locks. With the utmost deference he awaits the commands of his master.

"Well, Rondeau," said Dr. Lacey, "haven't you finished breakfast yet?"

"Yes, marster," answered Rondeau, with a very low bow. "I've got through a moment since. What can I do for you? Will you ride this morning?"

"No," answered Dr. Lacey, "I do not wish to ride, but I want you to go to the post-office and back immediately; remember now, and not stop to gossip."

"Certainly not," said the negro. "When marster's in a hurry, Rondeau is never found foolin' away time."

"And don't stop more than an hour in the kitchen to talk to Leffie. Do you understand?" continued the Doctor.

"Oh, yes, I won't," said Rondeau, extending his mouth into a broad grin, at his master's allusion to Leffie, a bright looking handsome mulatto girl, whom next to himself, Rondeau thought was the prettiest creature in the world.

At last he bowed himself out of the room, and proceeded to execute his master's commands. On passing the kitchen, he "just looked in a little," and the sight of Leffie's bright eyes and rosy lips, made him forgetful of his promise. Going up to her, he announced his intention of kissing her. A violent squabble ensued, in which the large china dish, which Leffie held in her hand, was broken, two pickle jars thrown down, chairs upset, the baby scalded, and the dog Tasso's tail nearly crushed! At last Aunt Dilsey, the head cook and the mother of Leffie, interposed, and seizing the soup ladle as the first thing near her, she laid about her right and left, dealing no very gentle blows at the well oiled hair of Rondeau, who was glad to beat a retreat from the kitchen, amidst the loud laughter of the blacks, who had witnessed the scene.

Leaving the house he was soon on his way to the post-office and having procured his master's mail he started for home. At length slackening his pace, he took from his pocket the letters and carefully scrutinized the inscription of each. He was in the habit of going to the post-office, and after his master's return from Kentucky, he had noticed two or three letters written in what he called "a mighty fineified hand," and he had whispered to Leffie as a great secret that "'twas his private opinion, marster was going to marry some Kentucky girl." Recently he had noticed the absence of those letters, and also the absence of his master's accustomed cheerfulness. Rondeau was pretty keen, and putting the two circumstances together, he again had a whispered conference with Leffie, whom he told that, "most probably the Kentucky girl had *flunked*, for marster hadn't had a letter in ever so long, and every time he didn't get one, he looked as blue as a whet-stone!"

"Glad on't, said Leffie. "Hope he won't have any your foreigners. Allus did wish he'd have Miss Mortimer. Next to old marster and young marster Lacey, her father's the toppinest man in New Orleans. And it's a pity for young marster to stoop."

After examining all the letters closely, Rondeau came to the conclusion that the right one wasn't there, and he thought, "Well, Leffie'll be glad, and marster'll be sorry, and hang me if I ain't sorry too, for marster's a plaguey fine chap, and desarves any body there is in Kentucky."

Meantime Dr. Lacey was anxiously awaiting Rondeau's return, and when he caught sight of him, coming at an unusually rapid rate towards the house, he thought, "Surely Rondeau would never hurry so, if he had not good news for me," but the next thought was, "How should *he* know what it is I am so anxious to get?" Still he waited rather impatiently for Rondeau to make his appearance. In a moment he entered the room, and commenced pulling the letters from his pocket, saying, "I've got a heap this time, marster."

He then laid them one by one on the marble dressing table, counting them as he did so; "Thar's one, thar's two, thar's three, thar's four."

"Stop counting them, can't you, and give me all you have directly," said Dr. Lacey, as his eye ran hurriedly over the superscription of each, and found not the one he sought.

"That's jist what I've done, marster," said Rondeau bowing. "The one you want wasn't thar."

Dr. Lacey glanced hastily at his servant, and felt assured that the quick-witted negro was in possession of his secret. "You may go," said he, "and mind, never let me hear of your commenting about my letters."

"No, marster, never; 'strue's I live," said Rondeau, who left the room and went in quest of Leffie. But he did not dare to repeat the scene of the morning, for Aunt Dilsey was present, bending over a large tub of boiling suds, and he felt sure that any misdemeanor on his part would call forth a more affectionate shower-bath than he cared about receiving. So he concluded to bring about his purpose by complimenting Aunt Dilsey on her fine figure (she weighed just two hundred!) .

"Aunt Dilsey," said he, " 'pears to me you have an uncommon good form, for one as plump and healthy-like as you are."

Aunt Dilsey was quite sensitive whenever her size was alluded to, and she replied rather sharply, "You git along, you bar's ile skullcap. 'Twon't be healthy for you to poke fun at me."

" 'Pon my word," said the mischievous Rondeau, "I ain't poking fun at you. I do really think so. I thought of it last Sunday, when you had on that new gown, that becomes you so well."

"Which one?" said Aunt Dilsey, a little mollified, "the blue and yaller one?"

"The same," answered Rondeau. "It fits you good. Your arms look real small in it."

Leffie was nearly convulsed with laughter, for she had tried the experiment, and found that the distance round her mother's arm, was just the distance round her own slender waist.

"Do tell!" said Aunt Dilsey, stopping from her work and wiping the drops of perspiration from her shining forehead. "Do tell! It feels drefful sleek on me, but my old man Claib says it's too tight."

"Not an atom too tight," answered Rondeau, at the same time getting nearer and nearer to Leffie, and laying his hand on her shoulder.

Before she was aware of his intention, he stole the kiss he was seeking for. Leffie rewarded him by spitting in his face, while Aunt Dilsey called out, "Ain't you 'shamed to act so, Leffie? Don't make a fool of yourself!"

Assured by this speech, Rondeau turned, and kissing Aunt Dilsey herself, was off just in time to escape a basin of hot suds, which that highly scandalized lady hurled after him.

"I'll tell marster this minute," said she, "and see if he hain't got nothin' to set the lazy lout a doin'." So saying, the old lady waddled into the house, and going up stairs, knocked at Dr. Lacey's door.

"Come in," said the Doctor, and Aunt Dilsey entered. In a very sad tone, she commenced telling how "that 'tarnal Rondeau was raisin' Cain in the kitchen. He's kissed Leffie, and me too!"

"Kissed *you*, has he?" said Dr. Lacey.

"Yes, sar, he done that ar very thing, spang on the mouth," said Dilsey.

"Well, Dilsey," said the Doctor with a roguish twinkle of the eye, "don't you think he ought to be paid?"

Aunt Dilsey tried to cry, and said, "I never thought that marster would larf at poor old Aunt Dilsey."

"Neither will I," said the Doctor. Then tossing her a picayune, he said, "Take that, Aunt Dilsey. I reckon it will pay for the kiss. I'll see that Rondeau does not repeat his offence on you at least."

Aunt Dilsey went back to the kitchen, thinking that "Marster George was the funniest and best marster on arth."

While Rondeau was carrying on this flirtation in the kitchen, Dr. Lacey was differently employed. Hope deferred had well nigh made his heart sick. "What can be the reason," thought he, "that Fanny does not write? I have written repeatedly for the last two months and have had no answer." Then as a new idea struck him, he added, "Yes, I'll write to Mr. Miller, and ask him what has happened." Suiting the action to the word, he drew up his writing desk, and in a short time a letter was written, and directed to Mr. Miller.

He arose to summon Rondeau to take it to the office, but ere he had touched the bell-rope, pride whispered. "Don't send that letter, don't let Mr. Miller into your private affairs. If Fanny were sick, some one would write to you."

So the bell was not rung, and during the next half hour, Dr. Lacey amused himself by mechanically tearing it into small fragments. Ah, Dr. Lacey, 'twas a sorry moment when you listened to the whispering of that pride! Had that letter been sent, it would have saved you many sleepless nights of sorrow. But 'twas not to be.

That night there was to be a large party at the house of Mr. Mortimer, whom Leffie had mentioned as second to the Laceys in wealth. Mr. Mortimer was the uncle at whose house Florence Woodburn was visiting, and the party was given partly in honor of her arrival, and partly to celebrate Mabel Mortimer's birthday. Mabel was an intelligent, accomplished girl, and besides being something of a beauty, was the heiress expectant of several hundred thousand. This constituted her quite a belle, and for three or four years past, she and Dr. Lacey had been given to each other by the clever gossips of New Orleans. Mr. Lacey, senior, was also rather anxious that his son should marry Mabel; so Julia was not far out of the way, when she wrote to Fanny that Dr. Lacey's parents wished to secure a match between him and a New Orleans belle. Had Dr. Lacey never seen Fanny, he possibly might have wedded Mabel. But his was a heart which could love but once, and although the object of his love should prove untrue, his affections could not easily be transferred to another; so, 'twas all in vain that Mabel Mortimer, on the evening of the party, stood before her mirror arranging and rearranging the long curls of her dark hair, and the folds of her rich white satin, wondering all the while, if Dr. Lacey would approve her style of dress.

Turning to Florence she said, "Cousin, did you see Dr. Lacey, while he was in Frankfort?"

"No, I did not," answered Florence; "but I do hope he will be here to-night, for I am all impatience to see this lion who has turned all your heads."

A slight shade of displeasure passed over Mabel's fine features, but quickly casting it off, she said, "Why are you so anxious, Florence? Have you any designs on him? If you have, they will do you no good, for I have a prior claim, and you must not interfere."

"Dear me, how charmingly you look!" said Florence. "But, fair coz, do not be too sanguine. Suppose I should tell you that far off in old Kentuck, as the negroes say, there is a golden-haired little girl, who has——"

"Stop, stop," said Mabel. "You shall not tell me; I will not hear it."

At that instant the door bell rang, and in a moment several young girls entered the dressing-room, and in the chattering and laughing and fixing which followed, Mabel forgot what her cousin had been saying. After a time the young ladies descended to the spacious drawing-rooms, which were rapidly filling with the elite of the city.

Mabel's eye took in at a glance all the gentlemen, and she felt chagrined to find Dr. Lacey absent. "What if he should not come?" thought she. "The party would be a dreadfully dull affair to me." Some time after, she missed Florence and two or three other girls, and thinking they were in the parlor above, she went in search of them. She found them on the balcony, not far from the gentlemen's dressing-room, the windows of which were open. As she approached them, they called out, "Oh, here you are, Mabel! Florence is just going to tell us about Dr. Lacey's sweetheart."

"Dr. Lacey's sweetheart!" repeated Mabel. "Who is Dr. Lacey's sweetheart, pray?"

"Do not blush so, Mabel; we do not mean you," said Lida Gibson, a bright-eyed witty girl, with a sprinkling of malice in her nature.

"Of course you do not mean me," said Mabel laughingly. "But come, cousin; what of her?" And the young girls drew nearer to each other, and waited anxiously for Florence's story.

Little did they suspect that another individual, with flushed brow, compressed lip, and beating heart, was listening to hear tidings of her whom Florence had designated as his sweetheart. Dr. Lacey had entered the gentlemen's dressing-room unobserved. He heard the sound of merry voices on the balcony, and was about to step out and surprise the girls, when he caught the sound of his own name coupled with that of Fanny Middleton. His curiosity was aroused, and he became a listener to the following conversation:

"Come, Florence," said Lida, "do not keep us in suspense any longer. Tell us whether she is black or white, fat or lean, rich or poor?"

"But first," said Mabel, "tell us how you know she is any thing to Dr. Lacey."

"That is what I don't know," said Florence. "I am only speaking of what has been."

"Well then," said Mabel, more gayly, "go on."

"This Fanny Middleton," said Florence, "looks just as you would imagine a bright angel to look."

How Dr. Lacey blessed her for these words.

"But," continued Florence, "there is a singularly sad expression on her marble face."

"I never observed it," thought Dr. Lacey.

"What makes her sad?" asked Lida.

"That is a mystery to me," answered Florence. "Report says that she loved a Mr. Wilmot, who was engaged to her sister."

"Engaged to her sister!" repeated Mabel. "How strange. But won't it make trouble?"

"It cannot," said Florence. "Mr. Wilmot is dead, and it is whispered that Fanny's heart was buried with him. I should not be surprised if it were so, for Fanny has the saddest face I ever saw. It made me want to cry when I looked at her. I should have pitied her more, however, had she not been so well cared for by a Mr. Stanton, from New-York."

Large drops of perspiration stood thickly on Dr. Lacey's forehead, and his hands, convulsively clasped, were pressed against his heart; still he did not lose a syllable, as Florence continued, "I did not blame her for liking Stanton, for he would break half your hearts and turn the rest of you crazy."

"But the sister," asked all the young ladies, "how was she affected to think Fanny loved her betrothed?"

"Oh, that sister!" said Florence. "You ought to see her. She is beautiful, beyond any thing I can describe. She eclipsed every thing and every body."

"And is she as agreeable as handsome?" asked Mabel, whose fears were aroused that Julia might be her rival, instead of Fanny.

Florence replied, "I was told that she was formerly very passionate, so much so that her father nicknamed her Tempest. Within a few months she has entirely changed, and is now very amiable; but I liked Fanny's looks the best."

"But, Dr. Lacey,—what had he to do with Fanny?" asked Lida.

"It was said they were engaged; but I do not think they are. In fact I know they are not, from what Fanny said herself; for she assured me that Dr. Lacey was nothing to her more than a common acquaintance; and the sad but sweet smile which broke over her face whenever she raised her soft blue eyes to Stanton's animated countenance, confirmed what she said."

"So, Mabel, you can have the Doctor after all," said Lida. "You know you used to say that 'twas all settled, for your parents and his had arranged it."

Dr. Lacey waited for no more. He knew of a back stairway, down which he could escape into the open air unobserved. In a moment he stood alone, in Mr. Mortimer's garden, but the evening breeze, although it cooled his brow, failed to calm his excited feelings. Suddenly it occurred to him that his absence from Mr. Mortimer's would excite attention in those who saw him enter, so he made a desperate effort to be calm, and retracing his steps, was soon in the drawing-room, with Mabel Mortimer on his arm, much to that young lady's satisfaction.

As they passed near a group of young girls, in the centre of which stood Florence Woodburn, Mabel suddenly said, "Oh, Dr. Lacey, let me introduce you to cousin Florence. She has just come from Frankfort, and knows some of your acquaintances there."

So saying she drew him towards Florence, who had all the evening been waiting for an introduction to him. Dr. Lacey rather wished to avoid making Florence's acquaintance, fearing that she might say something to him of Fanny. But there was no escape, and he greeted Florence with a smile and bow, which, to use her own words, "Nearly drove every idea from her head."

Once during the evening he found himself standing with Florence, alone, near an open window. Florence improved her opportunity, and raising her bewitching hazel eyes to the Doctor's face, said, "Why do you not ask me about your Kentucky friends, Dr. Lacey?"

Had Florence observed her companion closely, she would have noticed the pallor, which, for an instant, overspread his face. It passed away, and he replied with an assumed gayety, "How should I know that we have any acquaintances in common in Frankfort?"

Before Florence had time to reply Mabel joined them. She was unwilling to risk a tête-à-tête between the Doctor and her fascinating, graceful cousin, and as soon as she found them standing alone, she went up to them. Her example was followed by several other young ladies, among whom was Lida Gibson, who began by saying, "Doctor, do you know that Miss Florence has told us all about your love affair, and also described the Golden Fairy? Now why didn't you fall in love with her sister? Florence says she is far more beautiful."

Dr. Lacey answered calmly, "What reason has Miss Woodburn to think I am in love with either?"

"No reason," said Mabel quickly; "neither does she think you are in love with either."

"Dear me!" said Lida. "Of course you do not wish to think so, and we all know why; but never mind frowning so dreadfully, Mabel; I won't tell!" and the mischievous girl glided away, laughing to think that she had succeeded so well in teasing Mabel Mortimer.

After a moment Dr. Lacey turned to Florence, and said, "It seems you saw Julia Middleton. Do you not think her very handsome?"

"Yes, very," answered Florence; "but I liked Fanny's looks the best."

A pang shot through Dr. Lacey's heart at the mention of Fanny's name, but he continued to inquire concerning his friends in Kentucky. Before the party closed, Florence, Mabel, and Lida, had each managed to repeat to him all the conversation which he had overheard in the first part of the evening, never once thinking how desolate was the heart which beat beneath the calm manner and gay laugh of him who listened to their thoughtless raillery.

At length the party drew to a close. Dr. Lacey was among the first that left. He longed to be alone with his troubled thoughts. Mechanically bidding Mabel "Good night," he ran down the marble steps, and stepping into his carriage, ordered Claib, the coachman, to drive home as soon as possible. There was no particular necessity for this command, for Claib had been fretting for the last hour about "white folks settin' up all night and keepin' niggers awake. Darned if he didn't run the horses home like Satan, and sleep over next day, too."

With such a driver the horses sped swiftly over the smooth road, and in a very few minutes Dr. Lacey was at home, alone in his room. Then the full tide of his sorrow burst forth. He did not weep. He would scorn to do that. But could one have seen him as he hurriedly paced the apartment he would have said his was a sorrow which could not vent itself in tears. Occasionally he would whisper to himself, "My Fanny false!—she whom I believed so truthful, so loving, so innocent! And she loves another,—one, too, whom it were almost a sin to love. Fool, that I did not see it before, for what but love could have drawn such devotion to him on his death-bed? And yet she assured me that I was the first, the only one, she had ever loved; and I believed it, and gave her the entire affection of my heart."

Then came a reaction. Resentment towards Fanny for thus deceiving him mingled with his grief. But he had loved her too deeply, too truly, to cherish an unkind feeling towards her long. Throwing himself upon the sofa, and burying his face in his hands, he went back in fancy through all the many happy hours he had spent in her society. While doing this sleep descended upon him, and in his dreams he saw again his darling Fanny, not false and faithless as he had feared, but arrayed in a spotless bridal robe. She stood by his side as his own wedded wife. Was that dream ever realized? We shall see.

## Chapter XII

The next morning Rondeau waited a long time for his master's usual orders that he should go to the post-office, but no such command came, and as Dr. Lacey had not been heard moving in his room yet, Rondeau concluded to go at all events.

"I know," said he, "that'll be the first thing he'll tell me to do, and I may as well go on my own hook, as to wait and be sent."

Accordingly he again started for the post-office, thinking to himself, "I hope that marster'll git a letter this time, for he don't seem no more like the wide-awake chap he did when he first come from Kentuck, than nothin'. I don't want him to have Miss Mabel no how; for their niggers say she's awful spunky."

By the time this soliloquy was ended, he had reached the office. The clerk handed him two letters, both of which Rondeau eyed sharply. On looking at the second, the cavity between his ears widened to an enormous extent, and he gave vent to his joy by uttering aloud, "Crackee, this is jest the thing!"

"What's the matter, Rondeau. Can you read writing?" asked the clerk in some surprise.

"No, sir, not but a little," said Rondeau; "but I know this handwrite, I reckon."

In a twinkling, he was in the street. "This is a fine morning," thought he. "I've got the right letter this time, so I won't hurry home, for marster ain't goin' to find any fault if I don't get thar till noon."

So the next hour was spent in gossiping with all the blacks which could be found lounging round the streets. Suddenly one of the negroes called out, "Ho, Rondeau! thar's yer old marster Lacey comin'. You'd better cut stick for home, or he'll be in yer har."

Rondeau instantly started for home, where he was greeted by Aunt Dilsey with a torrent of abuse, that good lady rating him soundly for being gone so long. "Warn't he 'shamed to be foolin' away his time? 'Twarn't his time nuther, 'twas marster's time. Was that ar' fulfillin' of Scripter, which says 'ye must all be eye sarvents,' which means ye must all keep clus where yer marsters can see you?"

How long Aunt Dilsey might have gone on expounding Scripture is not known! for Rondeau interrupted her by saying, "Don't scold so, old lady. Marster ain't a goin' to care, for I've got him something this time better than victuals or drink."

"What is it?" said Leffie, coming forward. "Have you got him a letter from Kentuck?"

"I hain't got him nothin' else, Miss Leffie Lacey, if you please," said Rondeau, snapping his fingers in her face, and giving Aunt Dilsey's elbow a slight jostle, just enough to spill the oil, with which she was filling a lamp.

"Rondeau, I 'clar' for't," said Aunt Dilsey, setting down her oil can. "If marster don't crack your head, my old man Claib shall, if he ever gits up agin. Thar he is in his bunk, snorin' like he was a steamboat; and marster's asleep up stars, I reckon. Well, 'tain't no way to live. Things would go to rack and ruin, if I didn't sweat and work to keep 'em right eend up, sartin."

Aunt Dilsey was really a very valuable servant, and had some reason for thinking herself the main spoke in the wheel which kept her master's household together. She had lived in the family ever since Dr. Lacey's earliest recollection, and as she had nursed him when an infant, he naturally felt a great affection for her, and intrusted her with the exclusive management of the culinary department, little negroes and all. His confidence in her was not misplaced, for from morning till night she was faithful to her trust, and woe to any luckless *woolly head* who was found wasting "marster's" time or pilfering Dilsey's sweetmeats and pickles.

On the first head Aunt Dilsey was very sensitive, for being naturally active and stirring herself, "She," to use her own words, "couldn't bar to see folks lazin' round like thar was nothin' to do, but to git up and stuff themselves till they's fit to bust." She also felt annoyed whenever her young master indulged himself in a morning nap. "Ought to be up," she said, "and airin' hisself."

On the morning following the party, her patience was severely taxed in two ways. First, Claib, her husband, had adhered to his resolution of "sleeping over," and long after the clock struck eleven, he was snoring profoundly. He had resisted all Aunt Dilsey's efforts to rouse him. Her scoldings, sprinklings with both hot and cold water, punching with the carving fork, had all proved ineffectual, and as a last resort, she had put the baby on his bed, thinking, "that would surely fetch him up standin', for 'twasn't in natur to sleep with the baby wallopin' and mowin' over him." Her master, too, troubled her. Why he couldn't get up, she didn't see. "His breakfast was as cold as a grave stun, and she didn't keer if 'twas. She had enough to do, 'tendin' to other affars, without keepin' the niggers and dogs from pokin' thar noses in it."

At a late hour Dr. Lacey awoke from his uneasy slumber. The return of morning brought comparative calmness to his troubled spirit. Hope whispered that what he had heard might be a mistake. At least he would wait for further confirmation. He did not know how near that confirmation was. Rondeau had been waiting for his master's summons until his patience was exhausted. So, relying on the letter to counteract any apparent disrespect, he stalked up stairs and knocked at Dr. Lacey's door, just as that gentleman was about ringing for him.

As soon as he entered the room, he called out, "Here, marster, I've got 'em this time!" at the same time extending a letter, the superscription of which made Dr. Lacey turn pale, for he recognized, as he supposed, Fanny's delicate handwriting.

"You may leave me alone, Rondeau," said he, "and I will ring for you when I want you." So Rondeau departed with the remaining letter in his pocket. He had forgotten to deliver it, but it was not missed.

Oh, Rondeau, Rondeau! It was very unfortunate that you forgot that letter, and suffered it to remain in your pocket unheeded for many days. Its contents would have scattered the dark, desolating *tempest* which was fast gathering o'er your young master's pathway.

As soon as Dr. Lacey was alone, he sat down, anxious, yet fearing to know the contents of his letter. At last he resolutely broke the seal, thinking to himself, "It cannot contain any thing worse than I already know." One glance at the beginning and end of the letter confirmed his fears, and for a few moments he was unable to read a line; then summoning all his remaining courage, he calmly read the letter through, not omitting a single word, but comprehending the meaning of each sentence. It was as follows:

"*Frankfort, March 25th, 18—*

"DR. LACEY,

"SIR:—Have you, during some weeks past, ever wondered why I did not write to you? And in enumerating to yourself the many reasons which could prevent my writing, has it ever occurred to you that possibly I might be false? Can you forgive me, Dr. Lacey, when I tell you that the love I once fancied I bore you, has wholly subsided, and I now feel for you a friendship, which I trust will be more lasting than my transient, girlish love.

"Do you ask how I came to change so suddenly? I can only answer by another confession still more painful and humiliating to me. When I bade you adieu, I thought I loved you as well as I ever could love *again*. I say *again*, for——but how shall I tell you? How confess that my first attention was not given to you? Yes, ere I had ever seen you, I loved another, and one, too, whom some would say it were sinful to love.

"But why harrow my feelings, by awakening the past? Suffice it to say that he whom I loved is dead. We both saw him die, and I received upon my lips his last breath. Truly, if he were Julia's in life, he was mine in death. Did you never suspect how truly I loved Mr. Wilmot? You were blinded by your misplaced affection for me, if you did not. Julia, my noble-hearted sister Julia, knew it all. I confessed my love to her, and on my knees begged her not to go to him, but to let me take her place at his bedside. She complied with my request, and then bravely bore in silence the reproaches of the world for her seeming coldness.

"Dear Julia! she seems strangely changed recently, and you would hardly know her, she is so gentle, so obliging and amiable. You ought to have heard her plead your cause with me. She besought me almost with tears not to prove unfaithful to you, and when I convinced her that 'twas impossible for me to love another as I had Mr. Wilmot, she insisted upon my writing, and not keeping you in suspense any longer. Dr. Lacey, if you could transfer your affection from me—but no, why should I speak of such a thing? You will probably despise all my family. Yet do not, I beseech you, cast them off for poor Fanny's sin. They respect you highly, and Julia would be very angry if she knew that I am about to tell you how much she admires a certain Southern friend, who probably, by this time, thinks with contempt of little

"FANNY MIDDLETON."

There was no perceptible change in Dr. Lacey's manner after reading the above heartless forgery, but the iron had entered his soul, and for a time he seemed benumbed with its force. Then came a moment of reflection. His love had been trampled upon, and thrown back as a thing of naught by her who had fallen from the high pedestal on which he had enthroned the idol of his heart's deepest affection.

"I could have pitied, and admired her too," thought he, "had she candidly confessed her love for Mr. Wilmot; but to be so basely deceived by one whom I thought incapable of deception is too much."

Seizing the letter, he again read it through, and this time he felt his wounded pride somewhat soothed by thinking that the beautiful Julia admired and sympathized with him. "But, pshaw!" he exclaimed, "most likely Julia is as hollow-hearted as her sister, and yet many dark spots on her character seem to be wiped away by Fanny's confession." Throwing the letter aside, he rang the bell, and ordered his breakfast to be sent up to him.

That afternoon he called on Mabel Mortimer and her cousin. He found the young ladies in the drawing-room, and with them a dark, fine-looking, middle-aged gentleman, whom Mabel introduced as Mr. Middleton. Something in the looks as well as name of the stranger made Dr. Lacey involuntarily start with surprise, and he secretly wondered whether the gentleman was in any way connected with the Middletons of Kentucky. He was not kept long in doubt, for Florence, who was very talkative, soon said, "We were just speaking of you, Dr. Lacey, and Mr. Middleton seems inclined to claim you as an acquaintance, on the ground of your having been intimate with his brother's family in Kentucky."

"Indeed!" said Dr. Lacey; then turning to Mr. Middleton he said, "Is it possible that you are a brother of Mr. Joshua Middleton?"

"Yes, sir," returned the stranger, eyeing Dr. Lacey closely; "Joshua is my brother, but for more than twenty years, I have not seen him, or scarcely heard from him."

"Ah!" answered Dr. Lacey in some astonishment, and then, as he fancied there was something in Mr. Middleton's former life which he wished to conceal, he changed the subject, by asking if Mr. Middleton had been long in the city.

"Only two weeks," he replied, and he proceeded to speak of himself, saying, "For many years past I have been in the Indies. About the time my brother Joshua was married, my father died. When his will was opened, I thought it a very unjust one, for it gave to my brother a much larger share than was given to me. In a fit of anger I declared I would never touch a penny of my portion, and leaving college, where I was already in my senior year, I went to New-York, and getting on board a vessel bound for the East Indies, tried by amassing wealth in a distant land, to forget that I ever had a home this side of the Atlantic. During the first years of my absence my brother wrote to me frequently, and most of his letters I answered, for I really bore him no malice on account of the will. I had not heard a word from him for a long time, until I reached this city."

"Are you going to visit Kentucky?" asked Dr. Lacey.

"It is my present intention to do so," answered Mr. Middleton; "but first I wish to purchase a summer residence near the Lake, and after fitting it up tastefully, I shall invite my nieces to visit me. You are acquainted with them, I believe?"

Dr. Lacey answered in the affirmative, and Mr. Middleton continued, "I am told by Miss Woodburn that they are very beautiful, especially one of them, and quite accomplished. Is it so?"

Dr. Lacey replied very calmly, "The world, I believe, unites in calling Miss Julia very beautiful."

"But what of the other one?" asked Mr. Middleton. "I am prepossessed in her favor, for she bears the name of the only sister I ever had."

Dr. Lacey sighed, for he remembered the time when he was drawn towards Fanny, because he fancied she resembled the only sister *he* ever had. Mr. Middleton observed it, and immediately said, "Does it make you sigh just to mention Fanny? What is the matter? Has she jilted you? If she has, she does not partake of the nature of the Middletons, for they could never stoop to deceit."

Here Florence came to Dr. Lacey's relief, by saying, "Why, Dr. Lacey, Mr. Middleton wants you to repeat what I have already told him, that Julia is exceedingly beautiful, and that Fanny is as lovely as a Houri, and has the saddest, sweetest face I ever saw, and the softest, mildest blue eye."

Dr. Lacey laughingly said, "Thank you, Miss Florence; Mr. Middleton will please take what you have said as my opinion concerning his fair nieces."

Mr. Middleton bowed and then said, "How does my brother appear? He used to be very rough and abrupt in his manner."

Dr. Lacey laughed. He could not help it. His risible faculties were always excited when he thought of Joshua Middleton, and he answered, that although he highly esteemed Mr. Middleton, he feared his manners were not much improved.

"I dare say not," said the brother. "When he was at home, he was always saying things which our mother called 'impolite,' our father 'outlandish,' and the blacks, 'right down heathenish.' However, with all his roughness, I believe there never was a more truly honorable man, or a more sincere friend."

After a few moments of general conversation, Mr. Middleton said, turning to Dr. Lacey, "I feel some anxiety about this summer residence which I intend purchasing. I am told that you have fine taste both in selecting a good locality, and in laying out grounds. If you have leisure, suppose you accompany me on my exploring excursion, and I will reward you by an invitation to spend as much time with me as you like after my nieces arrive."

Dr. Lacey thanked Mr. Middleton for the compliment paid to his taste, and he politely expressed his willingness to assist his friend in the selection of a country-seat. "By the way," continued he, "you are stopping at the St. Charles, I believe. Suppose you exchange your rooms at the hotel for a home with me, and become my guest until you leave the city for Kentucky?"

Mr. Middleton accepted Dr. Lacey's invitation willingly, and the three weeks which he spent at his residence passed rapidly and pleasantly away. During that time Dr. Lacey met with a gentleman who owned a very handsome villa near the lake shore. This he wished to dispose of, and Mr. Middleton and Dr. Lacey went down to inspect it. They found it every way desirable, and Mr. Middleton finally purchased it at an enormous price, and called it the "Indian Nest." "Here," said he, speaking to Dr. Lacey, "here I shall at last find that happiness which I have sought for in vain during forty years. I shall have both my nieces with me, besides Miss Mortimer and Miss Woodburn. I suppose I shall have to invite some other young gentleman besides yourself, for the girls will hardly fancy the old Indian for a beau."

Dr. Lacey did not reply. He was thinking how much pleasure such an arrangement would have given him a few months ago; but now all was changed, and the thought of again meeting Fanny afforded him more pain than pleasure.

Mr. Middleton noticed his silence, and as he was slightly tinctured with the abruptness which characterized his brother, he said, "Why, young man, what is the matter? Have you been disappointed, or what makes you manifest so much indifference to spending the summer, or a part of it, with four agreeable girls?"

Dr. Lacey saw the necessity of rousing himself from his melancholy mood, and assuming a gayety he did not feel, he said, "I feel very much flattered, Mr. Middleton, with the honor you confer upon me, but I have, for some time past, been subject to low spirits; so you must not mind it, if I am not always gay. Come, let us go into the garden and see what improvements are needed there."

So saying, they turned together into the large terraced garden. While they were engaged in walking over the handsome grounds which surrounded "The Indian Nest," Rondeau, who had accompanied his master, was differently occupied. Strolling down to the lake shore, he amused himself for a time by watching the waves as they dashed against the pebbly beach, and by fancying that each of them reflected the image of Leffie's bright round face. Then buttoning up his coat he would strut back and forth, admiring his shadow, and thinking how much more the coat became him than it did his young master. It had been given to him by Dr. Lacey, with the order "not to wear it out in two days;" so Rondeau had not worn it before since the morning when he gave his master one letter and forgot the other. He had brought it with him to the lake, and was trying the effect of his elegant appearance.

Chancing to thrust his hand in his pocket, he felt the long-forgotten letter and drew it forth, then looking at it with wide open eyes and mouth, gave vent to his surprise as follows: "Who'd a b'leved it? Here's this letter been in my pocket two weeks! I deserve to be cracked over the head, and anybody but marster would do it. I'll run and give it to him now,—but no, I won't," said he, suddenly slackening his pace, "I've heard him say he could always trust me, and if I own up this time, he'll lose his—what's the word? conference?—yes, conference in me. I don't believe this letter's of any account, for it's a great big letter, just like a man's handwrite. Any way, I'll wait till I get home and consult Leffie."

The letter was accordingly placed in his pocket, and in a few moments he rejoined his master and Mr. Middleton. The next day they returned home. Rondeau's first act was to draw Leffie aside, and after winning from her various strong promises of secrecy, he imparted to her the astounding fact that, "He had found one of marster's letters in his trousers—no, his coat pocket. It had been there two weeks, and he didn't know what in Cain to do with it. If he gave it to marster now, 'twould make him lose faith in him, and so forth."

Leffie heard him through, and then fully agreed with him that 'twas best not to tell marster at this late hour. "But," said she, "I'd put it out of the way, so 'twouldn't be poppin' out in sight some time."

"Shall I burn it?" asked Rondeau.

"Oh, no," said Leffie; "keep it so marster can have it if he ever hears of it. There's your cigar box, take it and bury the letter in it."

"Whew—ew," said Rondeau with a prolonged whistle, "it takes you women to calculate any thing cute!"

The cigar box was brought out, and in a few moments the poor letter was lying quietly under a foot and a half of earth.

"There," said Leffie, as Rondeau laid over the spot a piece of fresh green turf, "nobody'll ever have any idea whose grave this is."

Rondeau rolled up his eyes, and assuming a most doleful expression, said, "Couldn't you manage to bust a tear or two just to make it seem more like a real buryin'?"

Leffie answered him by a sound box on his ear, at the same time threatening to expose his wickedness at the next class meeting. Aunt Dilsey's voice was now heard calling out, "Leffie, Leffie, is you stun deaf and blind now that fetched Rondeau's done got home? Come here this minute!"

Rondeau and Leffie returned to the house, leaving buried a letter, the reading of which would have changed the whole tenor of their master's feelings.

For a knowledge of its contents, as well as of its author, we must go back for a time to Frankfort, whence it came, premising that Mr. Middleton will follow us in a few days.

## Chapter XIII

In order to keep the threads of our narrative connected, it is necessary that we go back for a time, and again open the scene in Frankfort, on the 24th of March, several days after the party at which Florence Woodburn met Fanny Middleton. Seated at her work-table, in one of the upper rooms of Mrs. Crane's boarding-house, is our old friend, Kate Miller. Her dazzling beauty seems enhanced by the striking contrast between the clearness of her complexion and the sable hue of her robe.

On a low stool, at her feet, sits Fanny. Her head is resting on Mrs. Miller's lap, and she seems to be sleeping. She has been excused from school this afternoon, on account of a sick, nervous headache, to which she has recently been frequently subject. Finding the solitude of her own chamber rather irksome, she had sought Mrs. Miller's room, where she was ever a welcome visitor. To Kate she had imparted a knowledge of the letter which she supposed Dr. Lacey had written.

Mrs. Miller's sympathy for her young friend was as deep and sincere as was her resentment against the supposed author of this letter. As yet, she had kept Fanny's secret inviolate, and not even her husband had ever suspected the cause of Fanny's failing strength. But, this afternoon, as she looked on the fair girl's sad, white face, which seemed to grow whiter and thinner each day, she felt her heart swell with indignation towards one who had wrought this fearful change. "Surely," thought she, "if Dr. Lacey could know the almost fatal consequence of his faithlessness, he would relent; and he must, he shall know it. I will tell Mr. Miller, and he, I know, will write immediately." Then came the thought that she had promised not to betray Fanny's confidence; but she did not despair of gaining her consent that Mr. Miller should also know the secret.

For a time, Fanny slept on sweetly and quietly; then she moved uneasily in her slumber, and finally awoke.

"How is your head, now?" asked Mrs. Miller, at the same time smoothing the disordered ringlets which lay in such profusion over her lap.

"Oh, much better," said Fanny. "I had a nice sleep, and so pleasant dreams, too."

"Did you dream of *him?*" said Mrs. Miller, in a low tone.

Quick as thought, the crimson tide stained Fanny's cheek and forehead, but she answered, somewhat bitterly, "Oh, no, no! I never dream of him now, and I am trying hard to forget him. I do not think I love him half as well now, as I once thought I did."

Poor little Fanny! How deceived she was! After a time, Mrs. Miller said, "Fanny, Mr. Miller seems very anxious about your altered and languid appearance. May I not tell him the truth? He will sympathize with you as truly as I do; for he feels for you almost the affection of a brother."

At first Fanny objected. "I know," said she, "that Mr. Miller would only think me a weak, silly girl." Mrs. Miller, however, finally gained permission to tell every thing to her husband. "I know though," persisted Fanny, "that he will laugh at me. You say he likes me; I know he did once, but, since the time when he visited my father's, more than a year ago, he has not treated me with the same confidence he did before. I never knew the reason, unless it was that foolish, romping mistake which I made, by riding into the school-house!"

With many tears and some laughing—for the remembrance of the exploit always excited her mirth—Fanny told a part of what we already know, concerning Mr. Miller's visit at her father's, the winter previous. She related the adventure of the sled-ride, and said that the morning after she noticed a change in Mr. Miller's manner towards her. The unsuspecting girl little thought what was the true reason of that change.

While she was yet speaking, Mr. Miller entered the room. On seeing Fanny there, and weeping, he said: "What, Sunshine, in tears? That is hardly the remedy I would prescribe for headache. But come, Fanny, tell me what is the matter."

"Oh, I cannot, I cannot!" said Fanny, and again she buried her face in Kate's lap.

Mr. Miller looked inquiringly at his wife, who had not yet ceased laughing at Fanny's ludicrous description of her sled-ride; but overcoming her merriment, she at length found voice to say, "Fanny is crying because she thinks you do not like her as well as you used to."

Kate had never dreamed that her husband had once felt more than a brother's love for the weeping girl before her, and she did not know what pain her words inflicted on his noble heart. Neither did she think there was the least ground for Fanny's supposition, and she desired her husband to say so.

"I cannot say so, and tell the truth," said Mr. Miller, "but I can assure you that Bill Jeffrey's sled had nothing to do with it."

"What was it then?" asked Kate and Fanny both in the same breath.

Mr. Miller drew Fanny towards him with the freedom of an elder brother, and, in a low, earnest tone, said: "Did nothing else occur during my visit, which could have changed my opinion of you?"

Fanny lifted her large blue eyes to Mr. Miller's face with so truthful, wondering a gaze, that he was puzzled. "Can it be," thought he, "that I did not hear aright, that I was deceived? I will, at least, ask her how she spent that evening," so he said: "Fanny, do you remember where you were, or how you were occupied during the last evening of my stay at your father's?"

At first, Fanny seemed trying to recall the events of that night; then she said: "Oh, yes, I remember now perfectly well. You and Mr. Wilmot had letters to write, and went to your room early, while father and mother went to one of the neighbor's, leaving Julia and me alone in the sitting-room."

"Did you both remain in the sitting-room, during the evening?" continued Mr. Miller.

"Yes," said Fanny, "or, that is, I staid there all the time, but Julia was gone a long time, and when she returned she would not tell me where she had been."

"But were not you and Luce in your own room, at all, that evening?" continued Mr. Miller.

"Luce!" said Fanny; "I do not remember having seen her once that night; neither was I in my own room until bed-time."

There was so much frankness and apparent truth in Fanny's face and manner, that Mr. Miller never for a moment doubted her. His first feeling was one of intense happiness, at finding that Fanny was, indeed, all he had once fancied her to be. Back through the channels of his heart rolled, for an instant, the full tide of his once secretly nurtured affection for her. It was for an instant, however; for one look at the beautiful Kate convinced him that the love he once bore the gentle, timid girl at his side was naught when compared with the deep, ardent affection which he now felt for his own cherished wife. "Fanny," said he, "I have wronged you in thought, but never in word or deed, to my knowledge. I was, however, grossly deceived, although I can see no object for the deception."

"What can you mean?" asked Kate, rather anxiously. "Do explain yourself, and not deal in mysteries any longer. What dreadful thing did you imagine Fanny had done?—set the stables on fire, or abused the blacks—which?"

Mr. Miller did not immediately answer; and Fanny said: "Come, Mr. Miller, it is not fair to suspect me of something evil and not tell what it is."

"I will tell you," said Mr. Miller; and, in as few words as possible, he repeated to Fanny the conversation which he had overheard, between Luce and herself, as he supposed.

When he finished speaking, both Kate and Fanny were silent for a moment; then Kate said: "It was Julia, I know it was. Did you ever notice how much alike their voices are? And, besides, I once heard Julia lay a wager with Mr. Raymond that she could imitate her sister's voice so exactly, that one not seeing her, would be thoroughly deceived."

"Oh, Mrs. Miller," said Fanny, "it cannot be! Why should Julia wish to do so wicked a thing? And yet I now remember that when I was sick, Luce came to me one night and asked me to forgive her for everything bad she had ever done to me. I assured her I knew of nothing to forgive, and then she cried, and said I did not know all she did about her wickedness. She must have referred to that night. I can forgive her; for she is a poor ignorant girl, and much afraid of Julia. But how could my own sister do me so great a wrong, and what could have been her object?"

Here Fanny burst into tears, while Kate gave vent to her indignation by expressing her opinion pretty freely of Miss Julia.

"I can see," said she, "what Julia's object was. I fancy she was always fearful lest my brother should like Fanny the best; and she probably took this method to make you both think meanly of Fanny."

"Your idea is, probably, the correct one," said Mr. Miller, who would have added more; but Kate interrupted him by saying, "Yes, I think I understand it all now. Julia is, probably, at the foundation of Dr. Lacey's neglect. Most likely she's been writing him some base falsehood."

"Dr. Lacey's neglect!" repeated Mr. Miller. "What do you mean?"

Kate commenced an explanation, but Fanny started up, saying: "Please, Mrs. Miller, wait until I am gone."

She then quitted the apartment, and sought her own room, of which Julia had been sole occupant for more than an hour. On her return from school, this hopeful young lady was pleased to find her sister absent. Seating herself near the window, with paper and pencil, she began the composition of that letter, which, as we have seen, widened the breach between Dr. Lacey and Fanny. This unhallowed work cost her a world of pains. Many times were the lines crossed out and rewritten, before they quite suited her. The letter was but half completed, when Fanny was heard coming slowly through the upper hall. Springing up, Julia darted through the window out upon the balcony, and by the time Fanny reached the room, she was seated at the furthest end of the verandah, busily engaged with her forgery.

When she at last returned to her room, and tried to converse with her sister, she observed that Fanny shrank from her approach and that she had been weeping. In a very ironical tone Julia said, "What now is the matter? I declare, Fan., I believe you are a perfect little simpleton. I wouldn't be such a cry-baby, anyway, and make so much fuss about one good-for-nothing Doctor."

Fanny replied very calmly, and without once taking her eyes from her sister's face, "If you think I have been crying about Dr. Lacey, you are mistaken."

"Pray what did you cry for?" said Julia, laughingly. "Did somebody look sideways at you, or omit to call you by some pet baby name?"

"I cried," said Fanny, "because I feared you had been acting very wickedly towards me."

In an instant Julia's assurance left her. The bright color forsook her cheek, which became perfectly white. Fanny noticed the change, and it confirmed her fears. She did not know that the circumstances to which she alluded had long since faded from Julia's memory, and that her present agitation arose from the fear that she might have been detected in her work of deception, and that, after all, she might be foiled and entangled in her own meshes. A glance of intense anger flashed from her large black eye, as she muttered between her closed teeth: "Has the wretch dared to betray me?"

Fanny supposed she referred to Luce; and her first feeling was to save the helpless servant girl from Julia's displeasure; so she said, "Do not condemn Luce; she did not tell me. I received my information from our teacher, Mr. Miller."

"Luce! Mr. Miller! What do you mean?" asked Julia, her eyes lessening to their usual size, and the color again coming to her cheeks and lips. This sudden change in her sister's appearance puzzled Fanny; but she proceeded to relate what she had just heard from Mr. Miller. Julia was so much relieved to find her fears unfounded, and her darling secret safe, that she burst into a loud laugh, which was continued for some time. During this fit of laughter, she was determining whether it were best to confess the whole, and seem sorry for it, or to strenuously deny it. Finally she decided on the former, but resolved not to give the right reason for her conduct; so she said, with an air of great penitence: "Yes, Fanny, I am guilty, and I am glad you know it, too. I have been on the point of acknowledging it to you many times, but shame kept me silent."

"How could you do it, and what did you do it for?" asked Fanny.

Julia replied, "Truth compels me to say that I feared your influence over Mr. Wilmot. I knew how much he admired amiability in females, and I wished to make him think you were no more amiable than other people."

"And yet you say you never cared for his love," continued Fanny.

Miss Julia was getting cornered; but her evil genius did not forsake her, and she answered, "True, I did not care much for him; but I felt flattered with his attention, and I ardently desired to have one person prefer me to you. I know it was wicked in me to do what I did; but you will forgive me, will you not? and I will promise never again to act so deceitfully towards you."

Always sincere in what she said herself, Fanny could not think her sister otherwise; so her hand was extended in token of forgiveness. Julia took it, and raising it to her lips, kept it there for an instant, in order to conceal the treacherous smile of exultation which played round her mouth. "I shall yet triumph," thought she, and in the exuberance of her joy, she kissed again the soft hand which she held in her grasp. Could Fanny have looked into the heart of her sister, and beheld all its dark designs, she would have fled from her presence as from a poisonous serpent. But, though she was deceived, there was one, the All-seeing One, whose eye was ever upon the sinful girl; and though for a while she seemed to prosper; the same mighty Power so ordered it, that after a time, she who had sown the tempest reaped the whirlwind; and the clouds which hung so heavy and dark around the pathway of her innocent victim, afterwards burst with terrific violence upon her own head.

We will now return to Mrs. Miller, whom we left relating to her husband the supposed neglect of Dr. Lacey. She finished her narrative by saying, "I cannot help thinking that, by some means, Julia is at the foundation of all this mischief. You and Dr. Lacey were good friends; suppose you write to him, and then we shall at least know the truth of the matter."

"Yes, I will," said Mr. Miller; "I will write tomorrow."

"But why not write to-night?" asked Kate, who was in a hurry.

"Because," answered Mr. Miller, "I shall be engaged to-night, and to-morrow will do just as well."

Kate could not help feeling that, possibly, "to-morrow" might not do as well; but she said no more on the subject, and waited patiently for the morrow, when, true to his promise, her husband commenced the important letter. We have said that Mr. Miller had never liked Julia. In his letter, however, he spoke as favorably of her as he could; but he told how basely she had once deceived himself and Mr. Wilmot, with regard to Fanny, and also hinted his own and his wife's suspicion, that, in some way or other, Julia was connected with Dr. Lacey's long silence, as well as with the heartless letter which Fanny had received from New Orleans.

"Yes, this will do," said Kate, as she read what her husband had written. "But," she added, "I cannot help feeling sorry that it was not sent yesterday."

"Oh, Kate," said Mr. Miller, gayly, "your anxiety for Fanny has made you nervous, and now you are almost superstitious. One day can make no possible difference in the result of this letter."

Afterwards, when it was too late, he learned how much difference the delay of one day caused. By its means, that letter which would have set all aright, was sent in the same package with Julia's amiable production, and, as we have seen, was not received by its owner, but was safely stowed away in a cigar box under ground.

Soon after Mr. Miller deposited his letter in the post-office, a young girl, closely veiled, entered the same building, and looked anxiously round until her eye fell upon her accomplice, Mr. Dunn. That worthy young man instantly came forward, grinning and bowing, and almost upsetting another clerk, who was also hastening to wait upon the beautiful Miss Middleton.

"Good morning, Miss Julia!" said Mr. Dunn; "glad to see you. Fine morning."

Julia did not deign to reply, for Mr. Dunn's familiarity was exceedingly disgusting to her. She however handed him her letter, which he looked at in some surprise, and said, in a low tone, "From Fanny, or you?"

"From me; send it," answered Julia, at the same time managing to slip an eagle into the hands of the honest clerk.

Leaving the office the young lady proceeded homeward, thinking to herself, "There, that will settle *him,* I hope. I am getting on swimmingly."

When Mr. Miller entered his room, on his return from the office, Kate said, "In the course of two weeks, you or Fanny or both, will hear from Dr. Lacey."

"Do not be too sanguine, Katy," answered Mr. Miller; "you may be disappointed."

"Well," continued Kate, "if he pays no attention to your letter, I shall be satisfied that he really is undeserving of Fanny's esteem. I'll not tell her that you have written, for fear of the consequence."

So days came and went, week followed week, in rapid succession, until five weeks were numbered with the past since Mr. Miller's letter had been dispatched. Kate had waited and watched until even her sanguine nature had ceased to hope; for there had come no tidings from the far off Crescent City, and both she and her husband had unwillingly come to the conclusion that Dr. Lacey was really false. Kate manifested her disappointment by an increased tenderness of manner towards Fanny, whom she sincerely loved, and by a more gracious deportment towards Julia, whom she began to fear she had wronged by suspecting her of being accessory to Dr. Lacey's conduct.

## Chapter XIV

It was now the first day of May, and as it was also Fanny's seventeenth birthday, her school companions determined to celebrate it by a May party, of which Fanny was unanimously chosen queen. The fête took place in a handsome grove, on a hill-side, which overlooks the city of Frankfort. All of Mr. Miller's pupils were present, together with most of their parents and many of their friends. Mrs. Miller had taken great pains that Fanny should be arrayed becomingly for the occasion, and many and flattering were the compliments paid to the youthful queen, who indeed looked bewitchingly beautiful.

Her dress was a white muslin, festooned with wild flowers, some of which were fastened here and there by a pearl or brilliant. The gayety of the little party was at its height, and when Fanny, gracefully kneeling, received upon her head the crown, and was proclaimed "Queen of the May," a strange voice called out in loud musical tones, "Vive la Reine." The whole company instantly caught up the words, and "Long live the Queen," was echoed and re-echoed on all sides.

When the tumult had somewhat subsided, the eyes of those present were turned towards the spot whence the words "Vive la Reine" had proceeded. Leaning against one of the tall shade trees were two gentlemen, who had joined them unobserved. The elder of the strangers was a middle aged man, in whose piercing black eyes, and dark complexion, we recognize the Mr. Middleton whom we left with Dr. Lacey in New Orleans. His companion was many years younger, and there was something in his appearance which instantly interested and attracted the notice of strangers. There was a nobleness in the intellectual cast of his high, white forehead, round which his rich brown hair lay in thick masses, as if unwilling to part with the curl which must have been natural to it in childhood.

No sooner did Kate's eye fall upon the young man, then she darted forward with a cry of recognition and exclaimed, "Why, Frank Cameron, how came you here?"

But before he answers Kate's question, we will introduce him to our readers. Frank Cameron was a cousin of Kate Wilmot. His father, who was a lawyer by profession, had amassed a large fortune, on the interest of which he was now living in elegant style in the city of New-York. Frank, who was the eldest child, had chosen the profession of his father contrary to the wishes of his proud lady mother, who looked upon all professions as too plebeian to suit her ideas of gentility. This aristocratic lady had forgotten the time when, with blue cotton umbrella and thick india-rubbers, she had plodded through the mud and water of the streets in Albany, giving music lessons for her own and widowed mother's maintenance. One of her pupils was Kate Wilmot's mother, Lucy Cameron. While giving lessons to her, she first met Lucy's brother, Arthur Cameron, who afterwards became her husband. He was attracted by her extreme beauty, and his admiration was increased on learning her praiseworthy efforts to maintain herself and mother. They were married, and with increasing years came increasing wealth, until at length Mr. Cameron was a millionaire and retired from business.

As riches increased, so did Mrs. Cameron's proud spirit, until she came to look upon herself as somewhat above the common order of her fellow-beings. She endeavored to instil her ideas of exclusiveness into the minds of her children. With her daughter Gertrude, she succeeded admirably, and by the time that young lady had reached her eighteenth year, she fancied herself a kind of queen, to whom all must pay homage. But Frank the poor mother found perfectly incorrigible. He was too much like his father to think himself better than his neighbor on account of his wealth. Poor Mrs. Cameron had long given him up, only asking as a favor that he would not disgrace his family by marrying the washerwoman's daughter. Frank promised he would not, unless perchance he should fall in love with her, "And then," said he, with a wicked twinkle of his handsome hazel eyes, "then, my dear Mrs. Cameron, I cannot be answerable for consequences."

He had always greatly admired his cousin Kate, and often horrified his mother by declaring that if Kate were not his cousin, he would surely marry her. "Thank the Lord, then, that she is so near a relative! for now you will not stoop to marry a music teacher," said Mrs. Cameron.

The old roguish expression danced in Frank's eye, as he said, "Most noble mother Adelaide, will you tell me whether it wrenched father's back much, when he stooped to a music teacher?"

The highly indignant lady was silent, for Frank had a way of reminding her of the past, which she did not quite relish; so she let him alone, secretly praying that he would not make a fool of himself in his choice of a wife. He bade her be easy on that point, for 'twasn't likely he would ever marry, for he probably would never find a wife who would suit him.

Such was Frank Cameron. Business for his father had taken him to Louisville, and he determined to visit his cousin Kate, ere he returned home. He took passage in the Blue Wing, on board of which was Mr. Middleton, who soon made his acquaintance. As they were bound for the same place, they kept together, and on reaching Frankfort, went immediately to Mrs. Crane's, where they were entertained by Mrs. Carrington, who wondered much who the distinguished looking strangers could be. Concluding that the older one must of course be married, she turned her attention to Frank, who was much amused at her airs and coquettish manners. He had inquired for Mrs. Miller, and at length Mrs. Carrington asked if she were an acquaintance of his.

"Yes, ma'am," answered Frank with great gravity, "she is my wife's cousin."

In an instant Mrs. Carrington's coquetry vanished, and rising upon her dignity, she soon gave the gentlemen directions where to find the May party. As they were proceeding thither, Mr. Middleton said, "Why, Cameron, I understood you to say upon the boat, that you were not married?"

"Neither am I," answered Frank. "I merely wished to get a dissolving view of that lady's manoeuvres. Besides, I was actually afraid of being annihilated by her eyes and smiles. I'll manage to let her know that you are marketable, and then she'll turn her artillery towards you."

"But was it quite right," said Mr. Middleton, "to give her a wrong impression?"

"No, I suppose not," answered Frank. "But if I ever marry, Kate *will* be my wife's cousin."

By this time they had reached the entrance of the grove and caught a sight of the fair queen. "The fates protect me!" said Frank, suddenly stopping, and planting himself against a tree. "It would be suicide to advance another step. And she is your niece, you say. Pray intercede for me, or in less than a month I shall be making faces through the iron grating of some mad-house."

Mr. Middleton did not reply. His eyes were riveted on Fanny, whose face and figure recalled to his remembrance his only sister, who was the playmate of his childish years. Many long years had rolled away, since that bright summer morning, when with a sad heart he bade adieu to that sister, who, a young happy bride, was leaving her native land for a home on a foreign shore. Weeks passed, and there came intelligence that the ill-fated vessel in which she embarked was a total wreck. Among the lost were his sister and her husband, who now slept quietly beneath the billowy surf of the Atlantic.

Fanny so strongly resembled her aunt, that 'twas not strange Mr. Middleton for an instant fancied he again looked on the features of his long lost sister. But the illusion soon vanished, and when Kate bounded forward and saluted her cousin, his eye was wandering over the group of young girls in quest of his other niece. He, however, looked in vain. Julia was not there. When urged to attend the party, she had tossed her head in scorn, saying that she unfortunately had no taste for child's play. She preferred remaining at home, where she could spend her time more profitably. Oh, Julia! Julia! it is a pity you did not dare assign your true reason for absenting yourself from the party. Of this reason we will speak hereafter. We are not quite through with the May party.

We left Kate interrogating her cousin as to how he chanced to be there, and the remainder of the company looking in wonder upon the strangers, who seemed so suddenly to have dropped in their midst. After Frank had answered his cousin's questions, he introduced his companion, and said, "He has two nieces here, I believe. He has recognized one of them in your charming Queen. Will you please point out the other, and then introduce him?"

"I am sorry to say Julia is not present," answered Kate. "But come with me, Mr. Middleton," continued she, "and I will present you to Fanny." Then turning to Frank, she added, "I remember you to be a woman hater, Master Frank, so you can remain where you are."

"I'd laugh to see myself doing it," answered Frank, as he followed his gay cousin to the spot where Fanny was standing. All eyes were upon them, while Kate introduced the tall, distinguished looking gentleman to Fanny as her uncle.

"My uncle!" said Fanny, in some surprise: "my uncle!"

A slight shade of disappointment was visible on Mr. Middleton's face, as he took the offered hand of his niece, but he said, "Yes, your uncle. Did you never hear your father speak of his brother *Bill?*"

"Oh, yes, yes," said Fanny, joyfully. "I do know you now. You are my Uncle William, from the Indies. Father will be delighted to see you, for he has long feared you were dead." At the same time the affectionate girl again took her uncle's hand and raised it to her lips.

The tears started to Mr. Middleton's eyes, but hastily dashing them away, he said, "I suppose the fair Queen Fanny knows that bad *bills* always return?"

Fanny replied by again kissing the sunburned hand of her uncle. "King Ferdinand!" thought Frank, "I'd endure the rack for the sake of being in the old fellow's boots." Frank had been standing near Fanny, fixing upon her a gaze so intensely earnest, that when she at last raised her eyes to his, she blushed deeply, for there was no mistaking the look of deep admiration with which he regarded her.

Kate immediately introduced him. Fanny received him very politely, but said playfully, "I was in hopes, Mr. Cameron, that you would prove to be my cousin."

Mr. Middleton instantly answered, "No, dear Fanny, he is not your cousin, but he seems very desirous of being my nephew."

Fanny did not apply this to herself, but answered very demurely, "I don't know what he'll do, Uncle. You'll have to talk the matter over with sister Julia, who unfortunately is not here."

"You are a modest little *puss*," said Mr. Middleton. "But do you always give up every thing so quietly to Julia?"

Fanny said, somewhat sadly, "I've nothing to give."

Here Mr. Miller joined them, and said it was time to make preparations for returning home. Accordingly in a short time the company were dispersing. When our party reached Mrs. Crane's, Fanny went directly to Julia, whom she found most becomingly dressed, and apparently anxiously awaiting her return.

That excellent young lady had heard from Mrs. Carrington of the strangers' visit, and as she was impatient to know who they were, she had dispatched a negro girl to reconnoitre and report. The girl soon came back, her eyes projecting like coffee saucers, and the little braided tags of her hair seemingly standing upright.

"Oh, Miss Julia!" said she, "that 'ar tall, black man—no, I ax yer pardon, Miss—that 'ar tall, yaller man, done shook hands 'long of Miss Fanny, who kissed him, and called him Uncle William. She said how he done been with the Injuns."

"*Her Uncle William!*" repeated Julia, in amazement. "And who is the other one? His son?"

"Yes, reckon so," said the negro. "They done call him Mr. Camel, or Camlet, or suthin. I tell you he's han'some; and I reckon he's tuk with Miss Fanny. Jiminy hoecake, ain't she pooty? She looked a heap han'somer than you—no I don't mean so—I axes pardon agin." And the negro bobbed out of the door, just in time to dodge a ball of soap, which Julia hurled at her head.

"It's of no use fretting so," said Mrs. Carrington, who was present. "The young man is married, for he spoke of his wife."

Julia did not answer, and Mrs. Carrington soon after left the room. When she was gone, Julia muttered to herself, "Uncle William, from the Indies; rich as Croesus, of course. What a fool I was not to go to the party. Most likely, Fanny has won his good graces by this time. However, I'll dress myself and surprise him with my beauty, if nothing else."

Accordingly, the next hour was spent in decorating her person, and when Fanny came for her, she was ready to make an assault upon the good opinion of her rich India uncle. Not a thing was out of place, from the shining braids of her dark hair to the tiny slipper on her delicate foot.

Fanny's first exclamation on entering the room, was, "How beautifully you look, Julia! It is exceedingly fortunate that you are dressed so becomingly; for, will you believe it, Uncle William is down stairs!"

"Is it possible?" said Julia, affecting much surprise.

"Yes," answered Fanny. "You know father thinks him dead. But come, he is anxious to see you."

Julia arose to go with her sister, and said, "Isn't there a young man with him?"

"How did you know that?" asked Fanny, in some astonishment.

"I saw them from the window," was Julia's ready reply.

Fanny did not think of doubting her sister, and she answered, "It is a Mr. Cameron. He is cousin to Mrs. Miller."

By this time, they had reached the parlor, which was open. Here Julia thought proper to be seized with a fit of modest diffidence, and hesitated a moment before entering the room. Her uncle, however, immediately came forward and relieved her from all embarrassment, by saying, "And this, I suppose, is Julia. My brother is a happy man to be father of two such charming girls."

Julia received him graciously, but rather haughtily offered him her cold, white hand. "I will not kiss him," thought she; "Fanny did that. It's too childish. I'll be more dignified."

Could she have known the contrast which her uncle was drawing between

her own and Fanny's reception of him, she would not have felt much
flattered; but, before her uncle had time to say anything further, Fanny
introduced her to Frank, whose keen eye had read her character at a glance,
and read it aright, too. His ideas and words were after the following fashion:

"Pshaw! what a bundle of pride and stuck-up-ishness! She's handsome,
though, but isn't to be named the same day with Fanny."—"How do you
do, Miss Middleton?"—"What an affected little curtsy!"—"Hope to see you
well, ma'am."—"I'd laugh to see her trip and fall flat."

Such were Frank's thoughts while undergoing the ceremony of an introduction to Julia, who never for a moment doubted she was making an
impression upon the handsome young stranger, his supposed wife to the
contrary notwithstanding. The introductions being over, Julia seated herself on the sofa, while Fanny took a seat on a low ottoman near her uncle,
but partially behind him. She had chosen this place, because she fancied
it would screen her somewhat from Frank's eyes, which she felt, rather
than saw, were fixed upon her constantly.

During the conversation which followed, Julia, as if by mere accident,
mentioned New Orleans. She was anxious to know whether her uncle saw
or heard of Dr. Lacey. Her curiosity was soon gratified; for, at the mention
of New Orleans, Mr. Middleton, as if suddenly recollecting himself, said,
turning to Fanny, "I saw two of your acquaintances in New Orleans, and
one of them gave me a most glowing description of you."

"I wonder if it were a gentleman," thought Frank.

Julia's thoughts were similar, and she bit her lip, while Fanny's cheek
glowed with unwonted brilliancy, as she quietly asked, "Pray, who was it,
Uncle?"

"It was Miss Woodburn, who praised you so highly," answered Mr.
Middleton.

Julia immediately asked, "And who was the other acquaintance?"

"Dr. Lacey," answered her uncle. "I spent three weeks at his house."

Without knowing it, Fanny drew nearer to her uncle, and laid her hand
on his. He seemed dearer to her from the fact that he had spent so much
time with one whose image was ever before her, and whom she vainly fancied
she was trying to forget.

Frank noticed Fanny's manner and interpreted it according to his fears.
"There's mischief here," thought he. "I hope this doctor lives in a good
locality for yellow fever."

"Is Dr. Lacey about to be married?" asked Julia.

"Married," repeated Mr. Middleton; "I should say matrimony was very
far from his thoughts, at present. I fancied he had met with some disappointment, and I sometimes feared lest the fair deceitful one were one
of my nieces. Can any one set me right on the subject?"

Mr. Middleton had no idea how painfully his words affected her who
sat by his side, and looked up so imploringly in his face, as if begging
him to stop. There was an embarrassing silence, which Julia presently broke,
by saying, "While Dr. Lacey was here, he and Fanny got up a flirtation;
but nothing serious will result from it, I reckon."

"It's Fanny's own fault, then, I imagine," said Mr. Middleton, laying his hand on the head which had drooped lower and lower, until at last it rested heavily upon his knee.

Fanny made no reply; but, when she lifted up her head, there was something so sad in the expression of her face, that Mr. Middleton immediately surmised that there was, or had been, something between Dr. Lacey and Fanny more serious than a mere flirtation; so he very kindly changed the conversation, which now turned upon indifferent subjects, until the supper bell rang out its summons, when they all repaired to the dining-room.

At the supper table Mr. Middleton and Frank were introduced to Mrs. Carrington, Mr. Stanton and Raymond. Mrs. Carrington acknowledged her introduction to Cameron merely by a haughty, disdainful bow. She had learned from Kate that he was not married; and, feeling indignant at the deception he attempted to practise upon her, she resolved to treat him with contempt. Accordingly, although seated opposite him, she deigned him neither look nor word, but divided her time between laughing and coquetting with Raymond, and trying the power of her charms upon Mr. Middleton, who, she had been told, was a bachelor, and possessed of unbounded wealth. With the old Indian, however, she made but little headway; and Frank was right when he thought, "You'll get tired of that play, madam, the game is too old to be caught with chaff." With Raymond she succeeded better. He was delighted with her unusually flattering notice; and ere supper was over, he had, in Frank's estimation, made a perfect fool of himself.

Frank's attention was, however, soon diverted towards Mr. Middleton, who said, speaking to Stanton, "Were it not for your name and glasses, I should address you as Dr. Lacey. Are you related to him?"

Stanton replied, "Yes, sir; he is my cousin. I think I must resemble him, as I have been told so, frequently."

Mr. Middleton then spoke of Dr. Lacey in the highest terms of commendation, and concluded his remarks by saying, "I have recently purchased a residence, near Lake Pontchartrain, and am beating up recruits to spend the summer there with me. I am sure of Dr. Lacey, Miss Woodburn, and her cousin, Miss Mortimer. My nieces I shall take back with me, any way; and shall be happy to prevail on you, Mr. Stanton, to accompany me also."

Stanton thanked him for his kind invitation, but at the same time declined it, saying that business would call him to New-York in the autumn. The deep blush which accompanied these words caused Raymond to burst into a laugh. Mr. Middleton looked inquiringly at him, and he said, "Pardon me for laughing; I was thinking of the important *business* which calls Bob to New-York."

"Nothing bad, I hope?" said Mr. Middleton.

"Nothing worse than going for a wife," answered Raymond. "He is not suited with Kentucky girls, but must needs plod back to New-York."

"If appearances do not deceive, *you*, at least, seem likely to be suited by a Kentuckian," replied Mr. Middleton, at the same time turning his black eyes on Mrs. Carrington, with something of a quizzical expression.

Raymond colored. He did not know how this speech would be received by the fair lady. She soon satisfied him, however, for tossing her head proudly, she said, "As far as my experience goes, New-Yorkers are more easily suited than Kentuckians: at least, I find them generally to be exceedingly disagreeable."

"I am afraid some of them are so easily suited that they catch a *Tartar* sometimes," said Frank, whose feelings were roused at hearing this rude speech.

Mrs. Carrington gave him a look which she meant should say, "I wonder who you think you are. I'd thank you to mind your business."

But Frank thought he was minding his business; for he was looking at Fanny, who had not taken her eyes from her plate since her uncle had proposed taking herself and Julia to New Orleans. Her first feeling was one of joy. She would go, for she would then see Dr. Lacey; but the next thought was, "No, I will not. He has spurned me, and why should I put myself in his way?"

Julia's feelings were different. She could scarcely conceal her delight. Her artful mind took in the future at a glance. She felt sure that Fanny would not go; but *she* would, and could thus make Dr. Lacey believe that she, of all others, was just suited for him. Here we may as well give Julia's real reason for absenting herself from the May party. She had begun to fear that all her fine scheming might come to naught; for in all probability Dr. Lacey would not return to Kentucky in a long time. What could she do? She would write him a letter in her own name. In it she would modestly express her opinion of Fanny's conduct; sympathize with him in his disappointment, and end by inviting him to Frankfort, saying she hoped he would not absent himself from his friends on Fanny's account; for there were many who would welcome him back to Kentucky with pleasure. It was for the sake of manufacturing this letter that Julia had remained at home. But now there was no need of sending it, for she was going to New Orleans herself. Her joy was complete; and from that time she looked upon Dr. Lacey as belonging exclusively to herself. She would win him. He would yet be hers.

On returning to the parlor after supper, she seated herself close to her uncle, upon whom she lavished so many caresses that he wondered much what had come over her, and began to think that he was mistaken in supposing her to be cold-hearted and indifferent to him. As he looked at her beautiful, animated face, and the sparkling brilliancy of her eyes, he felt a moment's vanity in thinking how proud he should be to introduce her as his niece among the fashionables of New Orleans.

During the evening Mr. Ashton called. He had heard of the arrival of a Mr. Middleton from the Indies, and he had his own particular reason for wishing to see him. Soon after entering the room, he addressed Mr. Middleton, saying, "Were you in Calcutta twelve years ago?"

"Yes, sir; I was there twenty years ago," answered Mr. Middleton.

"Do you remember transacting business with the captain of the English vessel 'Delphine?' "

Mr. Middleton thought a moment, and then answered, "Yes, I remember that vessel and its captain well."

"And do you remember a poor cabin boy, who was sick and worn out with ship fever?" continued Mr. Ashton.

"Oh, yes, yes; I remember him well," said Mr. Middleton. "I had him removed to my own house, and nursed him until he was nearly well; and then, he one night ran away from me. I have never heard from him since; but there was an American vessel anchored near the shore, and I always supposed he went on board and sailed for home. I would give much to know what became of him."

"He stands before you," said Mr. Ashton, rising and grasping Mr. Middleton's hand. "He is here to thank you for your kindness, and is both able and willing to repay you for the care you took of him who was alone and friendless in a distant land."

"Can it be," said Mr. Middleton, with much emotion, "that you really are Henry Ashton? I should never have recognized you."

"I presume not," answered Ashton. "Twelve years have transformed the pale, emaciated youth into the tall, full-grown man. But I should have known you anywhere."

Here Raymond called out, "Why, Ashton, have *you* been to the Indies? Why did you never tell us?"

"Because," replied Ashton, "there was so much of homesickness and suffering attending that voyage to India, that I never like to speak of it." Then turning to Mr. Middleton, he said, "I have met your brother often, but never suspected him to be a relative of yours. Have you seen him yet?"

"I have not," answered Mr. Middleton. "I intend visiting him to-morrow, and shall be glad to take as many of you with me as are willing to go. I wish to be introduced to him as a Mr. Stafford from New Orleans."

After some further conversation, it was arranged that Mr. Miller, Ashton, Stanton, Raymond, and Cameron, should all accompany Mr. Middleton on his projected visit to his brother. Soon after Mr. Ashton departed for his boarding-place, and the remainder of the company separated for the night.

## Chapter XV

Julia's first exclamation on waking next morning was, "I am glad I'm not expected to go home with uncle to-day, and see father make a precious fool of himself, as he surely will."

"How can you say so, Julia?" answered Fanny, "I wish I was going, for I think I could smooth father down a little, if he got to using too strong language."

"Nonsense, Fan.," said Julia. "Why don't you confess that you wish to go because that handsome Cameron is going? Didn't I see how much he looked at you, and how you blushed, too? But no matter. I would get him, if I were you!"

Julia was getting very generous, now that she thought herself sure of Dr. Lacey. Further remark from her, however, was prevented by the ringing of the breakfast bell.

"What shall I tell your parents?" said Mr. Middleton to his nieces, as he stood in the hall, waiting for the driver to open the carriage door and let down the steps.

Julia made no reply, but Fanny said, "Give them my love, and tell them I am getting better every day, and shall want to come home soon," and then she added in a lower tone, "You will not laugh at father much, will you, or make fun of him either, if he does act oddly?"

"God bless you, sweet girl," said Mr. Middleton, stooping to kiss the innocent face which looked up into his with so much earnestness. "For your sake, if for no other, your father shall not be laughed at."

As the carriage drove off, Julia turned to Fanny and said, "Won't they have fun, though, with the old man? I can fancy it all. Father's beard will probably be long enough to do up in papers, and it will be a miracle if he does not have on those horrid old bagging pants of his."

Fanny was only too fearful that 'twould all be as Julia predicted, but she made no answer, and soon returned to her room.

We will now follow the carriage, which, with its load of gentlemen was proceeding rapidly towards the house of our friend, Uncle Joshua. Mr. William Middleton, or Mr. Stafford as we will call him for a time, seemed to grow excited as he approached nearer to a brother whose face he had not looked upon for more than twenty long years.

"I say, boys," said he, speaking to his companions, "you must help me, and when I begin to ask Joshua concerning his parents and brothers, you, too, must talk, or he will suspect I have some design in questioning him."

The gentlemen all promised to do their best, except Frank, who could promise nothing, because he knew nothing concerning the man they were going to visit. His curiosity, however, was roused, and forgetting the presence of Mr. William Middleton, he asked, "Do they keep the old fellow caged? And must we pay any thing for seeing him?"

These questions were greeted with a burst of laughter, and Raymond said, "No—admittance is free, but you'll be more amused to see him and hear him talk, than you would in visiting Barnum's Museum!"

By this time the carriage had entered the woods, and they soon came in sight of the house. Mr. Stafford leaned from the window, and said, "Is it possible that my brother with all his wealth, lives in such a heathenish place as this!"

"When you see him," said Raymond, "you'll think the nest just suited to the bird."

They were now in the yard, which was so filled with farming utensils, that the driver found it difficult to effect a passage up to the door. The gentlemen were about concluding to alight where they were, when Mr. Middleton was heard calling out, "Ho! thar, driver, don't run agin that ar ox-cart; turn a leetle to the right, can't ye? Now be keerful and not run afoul of the plaguey lye leech! I b'lieve the niggers would move the old hut, Josh and all, into the yard, if they could only make a raise!"

Mr. Stafford and Frank looked eagerly out at the speaker, who fully realized Frank's idea of him. His beard was as long and black as a rapid growth of three weeks could make it. As Julia had feared, he was dressed in his favorite bagging pants, which hung loosely even 'round his huge proportions, and looked as if fitted to some of his out buildings. It was very warm, and he wore neither coat nor vest, while his feet, whose dimensions we have mentioned before, were minus either shoes or stockings. He appeared in the doorway buttoning one of his suspenders. The truth was, he had spied the carriage in the distance, and as his linen was none the cleanest, he hastened to change it, and was now putting the finishing touch to his toilet. When he caught sight of the occupants of the carriage, he thought to himself, "Thar's a heap on 'em. Nancy'll have to rout the whole gang of niggers, field hands and all, to huntin' hin's neests after eggs enough for dinner."

By this time the gentlemen had alighted, and Mr. Middleton went forward to receive them. "How d'ye do, how d'ye do?" said he; "I'm mighty glad you've come. I wish you'd brought the whole city."

"We came pretty near it, I think," said Mr. Miller, at the same time presenting Mr. Stafford and Mr. Cameron.

Mr. Middleton continued talking as if replying to Mr. Miller's first remark, "No consequence, no consequence; Mr. Stafford, Mr. Cameron, how are you? The more the merrier. I s'pose they've told you all about Josh, so I needn't make b'lieve any,—but come in,—the house looks better inside than it does out. Ho! Luce," continued he, "where the old boy is your mistress? Tell her thar's heaps of folks here, and mind tell Aunt Judy to get us up a whalin' dinner."

Here he stopped to take a breath a moment, and then proceeded, "You must excuse my rig, gentlemen, or rather, you must excuse what ain't rigged; mebby if I'd known all you city buggers was comin', I'd a kivered my bar feet."

"You go barefoot for comfort, I suppose," said Mr. Miller.

"Why, yes, mainly for that, I suppose," answered Mr. Middleton, "for I've got such fetched big corns on my feet that I ain't goin' to be cramped with none of your toggery. My feet happen to be clean, for I washed 'em in the watering trough this mornin'. How d'ye leave my gals?"

"They are well," answered Mr. Miller, "or rather Julia is, and Fanny is improving every day."

"I've often wondered," said Mr. Middleton, "what 'twas ailded Sunshine when she was sick. She didn't seem to have no disease in particular, and I reckon nothin's on her mind, for all's straight between her and Dr. Lacey, as far as I know."

"Dr. Lacey," repeated Frank, without knowing what he said.

"Yes, Dr. Lacey—know him?" asked Mr. Middleton.

"No, sir," answered Frank, and Ashton rejoined, "I imagine he wishes Fanny had never known him."

Mr. Middleton turned, and for a moment regarded Frank intently. Frank stood the inspection manfully, and Mr. Middleton said, "You are from New-York, hey? I like New-Yorkers, and if Sunshine wasn't done promised to Dr. Lacey and never had seen him, and I liked you, I'd as soon you'd have her as anybody."

Mr. Stafford now said that he was acquainted with Dr. Lacey, and proceeded to speak of the pleasant time he had spent with him. This occupied the time until dinner was ready.

"Come, haul up," said Mr. Middleton, "haul up; we didn't expect so many to dinner, but the old table'll stretch, and you mus' set clus; but don't none on you step on my corns, for thunder's sake!"

Frank thought if his host kept on talking, he should not be able to eat for laughing, but the old man was but just getting into the merits of the case!

When his guests were seated, he said to Mr. Stafford, "Your white neck-cloth looks like you might belong to the clargy. If you do, you can say a short prar over the eggs and bacon, but Lord's sake be spry, for I'm blasted hungry!"

But for the remembrance of his promise to Fanny, Mr. Stafford would have screamed. It is needless to say that he declined his host's invitation, and the company began their dinner.

Suddenly Mr. Stafford asked if Mr. Middleton had any brothers.

"Yes,—no, or, that is, I had one once," answered Mr. Middleton, "but he's deader than a door nail afore this, I reckon."

"And what makes you think he is dead?" asked Stafford.

"Why, you see," returned Mr. Middleton, "when our old pap died, something in his will stuck crossways in Bill's swaller, and he left college and put out to sea, and I hain't heard from him in fifteen years."

"Did he look like you?" said Raymond.

"He was four years younger than I," answered Mr. Middleton, "but no more like me than Sunshine's pet kitten is like our old watch dog, Tige. He was soft like in his ways and took to book larnin' mightily, and I'm— but every body knows what old Josh is. Hold on thar! Save the pieces!" said he to Frank, who, unable longer to restrain his mirth, had deluged his plate with coffee.

"Pray excuse me," said Frank, mortified beyond measure at his mishap.

His discomfiture was, however, somewhat relieved by his companions, all of whom burst into a fit of laughter, in which Mr. Stafford heartily joined, forgetful of his promise to Fanny. By this time dinner was over and the company repaired to the porch, where Ashton and Raymond betook themselves to their cigars, while Mr. Middleton puffed away at his old cob pipe.

Mr. Stafford at length resumed the dinner table conversation, by saying, "If I were you, Mr. Middleton, I would not give up my brother yet; 'Hope on, hope ever,' is my motto."

"Hope on," repeated Mr. Middleton. "I have hoped on till I'm tired on't, and yet by spells, I have dreams in which it seems like my brother was alive and had come back, and then my old gourd shell of a heart gives a thunderin' thump and fetches me up wide awake. I hate dreams mightily, for it takes me an all-fired while to get to sleep all over, and when I do, I hate to be waked up by a dream."

"I hope you'll live to see your brother, though," said Frank.

"No, I shan't," answered Mr. Middleton, again filling his cob pipe. "Every thing that I loved has always died."

"Have you lost many friends?" asked Mr. Stafford.

"Considerable many," said Mr. Middleton, "considerin' how few I ever had. First, thar was mother died, when Bill and I was little boys; I remember how we cried when we stood by her grave, and I was so feared Bill would bust his jacket open, that I whispered to him not to take on so, for I'd be his mother now. And then that night, which was the longest and darkest I ever knew, we took turns rocking and singing to our little baby sister, just as we had seen mother do."

Here he stopped a moment, and Raymond, who was rather impatient, said, "Don't stop; go on."

The old man wiped his eyes, and said, "Heavens and arth! don't hurry a fellow so; can't you let him wait till the big bumps gits out of his throat, or would you have me bellerin' here like a calf?"

"Take your time, Mr. Middleton," said Mr. Stafford, who was as much affected as his brother at the remembrance of that sad night, when he first felt what it was to be motherless.

After an instant Mr. Middleton continued, "Directly that sister got big enough, she was married and started to go to England, but the vessel went to smash and the crew went to the bottom. Poor gal, she always hated salt, but she's used to it by this time, I reckon. Then thar was pap died next, but he was old and gray-headed and sick-hearted like, and wanted to go, but it made it jest as bad for me. Then thar was Bill."

Here Mr. Stafford moved his chair, so as to hide his face from the speaker, who continued, "I did think I might have one left, but 'twasn't to be. He went, too, and Josh was left alone."

Mr. Middleton cleared his throat a little, refilled his cob pipe and proceeded, "The Lord gin me two gals, and then he sent me as noble a boy as ever was, I don't care where t'other comes from. He wasn't mine, but I loved him all the same. You, Mr. Miller, knew him, but you didn't know— no, nor begin to know, how old Josh loved him, and what a tremendous wrench it gin my old heart when I come home and found he was dead. But, Lord, hain't he got a fine grave stun, though! You go to the cimetry at Frankfort, and you'll see it, right alongside of Leftenant Carrington's, whose widow's a flirtin' with everybody in creation any way, and Frankford, sartin.

"I've now told you of all that's dead," continued he, striking the ashes out of his pipe and wiping it on his bagging trousers, "but I hain't told you yit what troubles me more than all. Thar's something haunts old Josh, that makes his heart stand still with mortal fear. Thar's Sunshine, dearer to her old pap than his own life. You've all seen her, and I reckon she's made some of your hearts ache, but something's come over her. She seems delicate like and is fadin' away."

Here two big tears, that couldn't be mistaken, rolled down Mr. Middleton's cheek, as he added emphatically, "and by Jehu, if Sunshine goes, old Josh'll bust up and go too!"

The winding up of Uncle Joshua's story, was so odd and unexpected, that all the gentlemen, Mr. Stafford included, laughed loudly.

"'Tain't no laughin' matter, boys," said Mr. Middleton, "and so you'll all think if you ever have a gal as sweet and lovin'-like as Sunshine."

Here Mr. Stafford said, "Your sister's name was Fanny, I believe."

"Yes, 'twas; who told you?" asked Mr. Middleton.

"No one. I knew it myself," answered Mr. Stafford, looking his brother earnestly in the face.

Mr. Middleton seemed puzzled, and after closely scrutinizing Mr. Stafford's features, he said, "Confound it, am I in a nightmare? I thought for a minute, —but no, it can't be neither, for you've got too thunderin' black a hide to be Bill!"

Before Mr. Stafford replies to this remark we will take the reader to the kitchen, where a group of negroes are assembled round old Aunt Katy, and are listening with breathless interest to what she is saying. Aunt Katy was so infirm that she kept her bed for the greater part of the time, but on this day she was sitting up, and from her low cabin window had caught a view of the visitors as they alighted from the carriage. When Mr. Stafford appeared, she half started from her chair and said aloud, "Who upon airth can that be and whar have I seen him? Somewhar, sartin."

It then occurred to her that she would go to the kitchen, and inquire who "that tall darkish-looking gentleman was." Accordingly she hobbled out to make the inquiry. She was much disappointed when she heard the name. "No," said she, "'tain't nobody I ever knowed, and yet how like he is to somebody I've seen."

Not long after the old negress again muttered to herself, "Go way now; what makes me keep a thinkin' so of Marster William this mornin'? 'Pears like he keeps hauntin' me." Then rising she went to an old cupboard, and took from it a cracked earthen teapot. From this teapot, she drew a piece of brown paper, and opening it, gazed fondly on a little lock of soft brown hair.

"Bless the boy," said she, "I mind jest how he looked when I cut this har from his head, the very day his mother was buried. Poor Marster William," continued she, "most likely he's gone to 'tarnity 'fore this time."

As she said this, tears, which were none the less sincere because she who wept them belonged to Afric's sable race, fell upon the once bright but now faded lock of hair, which the faithful creature had for more than forty years preserved as a memento of him whom she had long since looked upon as dead, although she had never ceased to pray for him, and always ended her accustomed prayer, "Now I lay me——" with the petition that "God would take keer of Marster William and bring him home again." Who shall say that prayer was not answered?

Going back to her seat, she took up her knitting and was soon living over the past, when she was young and dwelt with "the old folks at home." Suddenly there came from the house the sound of merry laughter. High above all the rest was a voice, whose clear, ringing tones made Katy start up so quickly that, as she afterwards described it, "a sudden misery cotched her in the back, and pulled her down quicker." There was something in the sound of that laugh, which seemed to Katy like an echo of the past. "But," thought she, "I'm deaf like, and mebby didn't hear straight. I'll go to the kitchen agin and hark."

In a few minutes she was in the kitchen and dropping down on the meal chest as the first seat handy, she said, "Ho! Judy, is you noticed the strange gentleman's laugh?"

"I hain't noticed nothing," answered Judy, who chanced to be out of sorts, because, as she said, "the white folks had done et up every atom of egg; they didn't even leave her the yaller of one!"

"Well, suthin' in his laugh kerried me back to the old plantation in Carlina, and I b'lieve, between you and me, Judy, that Marster William's here," said Katy.

"Marster William, Marster William; what on airth do you mean?" asked Judy, forgetting the eggs in her surprise.

At the mention of "Marster William," who was looked upon as a great man, but a dead one, the little negroes gathered round, and one of them, our old friend Bobaway, said, "Oh, Laddy, I hope 'tis Marster William, for Marster Josh'll be so tickled that he won't keer if we don't do nothin' for a week; and I needn't milk the little red heifer nuther. Oh, good, good!"

"You go 'long you Bob," said Aunt Judy, seizing a lock of his wool between her thumb and finger, "let me catch you not milkin' the heifer, and I'll crack you."

Again there was the sound of laughter, and this time Judy dropped her dishcloth, while Katy sprang up, saying, " 'Tis, I know 'tis, anyways I'll walk round thar as if for a little airin', and I can see for myself."

Accordingly old Katy appeared round the corner of the house just as Mr. Middleton had spoken to his brother of his color. The moment Mr. Stafford's eye rested on his old nurse, he knew her. Twenty years had not changed her as much as it had him. Starting up he exclaimed, "Katy, dear old mammy Katy," while she uttered a wild, exultant cry of joy, and springing forward threw her thin, shrivelled arms round his neck, exclaiming, "My darling boy, my sweet Marster William. I knowed 'twas you. I knowed your voice. You are alive; I've seen you, and now old Katy's ready to die."

White as ashes grew the face of Uncle Joshua. The truth had flashed upon him, and almost rendered him powerless. Pale and motionless he sat, until William, freeing himself from Aunt Katy, came forward and said, "Joshua, I am William, your brother; don't you know me?"

Then the floodgates of Uncle Joshua's heart seemed unlocked, and the long, fervent embrace, which followed between the rough old man and his newly found brother, made more than one of the lookers-on turn away his face, lest his companions should detect the moisture in his eyes, which seriously threatened to assume the form of tears.

When the first joy and surprise of this unexpected meeting was over, Mr. Joshua Middleton said, as if apologizing for his emotion, "I'm dumbly afeared, Bill, that I acted mighty baby like, but hang me if I could help it. Such a day as this I never expected to see, and yet I have lain awake o' nights thinkin' mebby you'd come back. But such idees didn't last long, and I'd soon give you up as a goner."

"That's jest what I never did," said Aunt Katy, who still stood near.

In the excitement of the moment, she had forgotten that she had long thought of "Marster William" as dead; she continued, "A heap of prars I said for him, and it's chiefly owin' to them prars, I reckon, that he's done fished up out o' the sea."

"I've never been in the sea yet, Aunt Katy," said Mr. Middleton, desirous of removing from Aunt Katy's mind the fancy that any special miracle had been wrought in his behalf.

"Whar in fury have you been, and what's the reason you hain't writ these dozen years? Come, give us the history of your carryin's on," said Mr. Joshua Middleton.

"Not now," answered his brother. "Let us wait until evening, and then you shall hear my adventures; now let me pay my respects to your wife."

While he was introducing himself to Mrs. Middleton, Katy went back to the kitchen, whither the news had preceded her, causing Bob in his joy to turn several summersets. In the last of these, he was very unfortunate, for his heels, in their descent, chanced to hit and overturn a churn full of buttermilk! When Aunt Katy entered, she found Bob bemoaning the back ache, which his mother had unsparingly given him! Aunt Judy herself, having cleared away the buttermilk, by sweeping it out doors, was waiting eagerly to know, "if Marster William done axed arter her."

"Why, no, Judy," said Katy, somewhat elated because she had been first to recognize and welcome the stranger, "why, no I can't say he did, and 'tain't nateral like that he should set so much store by you, as by me. Ain't I got twenty years the start on you, and didn't I nuss him, and arter his mother died, didn't I larn him all his manners?"

Aunt Judy was on the point of crying, when who should walk in but "Marster William" himself. "I am told," said he, "that Judy is here, Judy, that I used to play with."

"Lor' bless you, Marster William," exclaimed Judy, at the same time covering his hand with tears and kisses, "I's Judy, I is, I know'd you hadn't done forgot me."

"Oh, no, Judy," said he, "I have not forgotten one of you, but I did not know whether you were living or not, so I did not bring you presents, but I'll get you something in a few days. Meantime take this," said he, slipping a silver dollar into the hands of Aunt Katy and Aunt Judy, each of whom showered upon him so many blessings and "thankies" that he was glad to leave the kitchen and return to his companions, who were talking to Uncle Joshua without getting any definite answer.

His brother's sudden return had operated strangely upon him, and for a time he seemed to be in a kind of trance. He would draw his chair up closely to William, and, after gazing intently at him for a time, would pass his large rough hand over his hair, muttering to himself, "Yes, it *is* Bill, and no mistake, but who'd a thought it?"

At last rousing himself he turned to his other guests, and said, "You mustn't think hard on me, if I ain't as peart and talkin' like for a spell; Bill's comin' home has kinder oversot the old man, and I'm thinkin' of the past when we's little boys and lived at home on pap's old plantation afore any of us was dead."

The young gentlemen readily excused the old man's silence, and when the slanting beams of the setting sun betokened the approach of night, they all, with the exception of Ashton, began to speak of returning home. Mr. Middleton urged them to stay, saying, "What's the use of goin'? Nancy's got beds enough, I reckon, and will be right glad of a chance to show her new calico kiverlids, and besides, we are goin' to have some briled hen in the morning, so stay."

But as the next day was the Sabbath, the gentlemen declined the invitation, and bidding their host "good bye," they were soon on their way homeward, each declaring that he had seldom spent a pleasanter day. As they can undoubtedly find their way to Frankfort without our assistance, we will remain at Uncle Joshua's, together with Mr. William Middleton and Ashton. The latter felt as if he had suddenly found an old friend, and as nothing of importance required his presence at home, he decided to remain where he was until Monday.

That evening, after every thing was "put to rights," and Mr. Middleton had yelled out his usual amount of orders, he returned to the porch, where his brother and Ashton were still seated. Lighting his old cob pipe, he said, "Come, Bill, Nancy'll fetch out her rockin' cheer and knittin' work, and we'll hear the story of your doin's in that heathenish land, but be kinder short, for 'pears like I'd lived a year to-day, and I feel mighty like goin' to sleep."

After a moment's silence Mr. Middleton commenced: "I shall not attempt to justify myself for running away as I did, and yet I cannot say that I have ever seriously regretted visiting those countries, which I probably shall never look upon again. I think I wrote to you, Joshua, that I took passage in the ship Santiago, which was bound for the East Indies. Never shall I forget the feeling of loneliness which crept over me, on the night when I first entered the city of Calcutta and felt that I was indeed alone in a foreign land, and that more than an ocean's breadth rolled between me and my childhood's home. But it was worse than useless to dwell upon the past. I had my fortune to make, and I began to look about for some employment. At last I chanced to fall in with an intelligent Spaniard, Signor de Castello. He was a wealthy merchant, and for several years had resided in Calcutta. As he spoke the English language fluently, I found no trouble in making his acquaintance. He seemed pleased with me, and offered me the situation of clerk in his counting-room. I accepted his offer, and also became an inmate of his dwelling, which was adorned with every conceivable luxury. His family consisted of himself and his daughter, Inez."

At the mention of Inez, Ashton half started from his chair, but immediately reseating himself, listened while Mr. Middleton proceeded: "I will not attempt to describe Inez, for I am too old now to even feel young again, by picturing to your imagination the beauty of that fair Spaniard. I will only say that I never saw one whose style of beauty would begin to compare with hers, until I beheld my niece, Julia."

"Lord knows I hope she warn't like Tempest," said Uncle Joshua, at the same time relieving his mouth of its overflowing contents.

"I do not know whether she was or not," answered Mr. Middleton, "I only know that Inez seemed too beautiful, too gentle, for one to suspect that treachery lurked beneath the soft glance of her dark eyes. I know not why it was, but Castello, from the first, seemed to entertain for me a strong friendship, and at last, I fully believe the affection he felt for me was second only to what he felt for his daughter. But he could not remain with us, and in eighteen months after I first knew him, he took one of the fevers common to that sultry climate, and in the course of a few days he was dead. I wrote to you of his death, but I did not tell you that he left a will, in which all his immense wealth was equally divided between myself and Inez. He did not express his desire that we should marry, but I understood it so, and thenceforth looked upon Inez as belonging exclusively to myself."

"You didn't marry her, though, I take it," said Joshua making a thrust at an enormous musquito, which had unceremoniously alighted upon his brawny foot.

"No," answered William, "I did not marry her, but 'twas not my fault. She played me false. Six months after her father's death we were to be married. The evening previous to our wedding arrived. I was perfectly happy, but Inez seemed low-spirited, and when I inquired the cause she answered, "Nothing, except a little nervous excitement." I readily believed her; but when the morning came the cause of her low spirits was explained. The bird had flown, with a young Englishman, Sir Arthur Effingham, who had been a frequent guest at my house."

"That was one of Tempest's capers to a dot," said Uncle Joshua, "but go on, Bill, and tell us whether the disappointment killed you or not."

So William proceeded: "Instead of my bride, I found a note from Inez, in which she asked pardon for what she had done, saying she had long loved Sir Arthur, but did not dare tell me so. They were going to England, whither she wished me to send a part of her portion, as her husband was not wealthy. I understood Inez's character perfectly, and could readily see that she preferred a titled, but poor Englishman, to a wealthy, but plain American, so I gave her up quietly."

"And was mighty lucky to get shut of her so," interrupted Joshua.

"From that time," continued William, "I gave up all thoughts of marriage, and devoted myself to increasing my wealth, and spending it for my own comfort and the good of others. Twelve years ago I chanced to go on board the English vessel Delphine, and there I found our friend Ashton."

"Look at him, for gracious' sake," said Uncle Joshua, pointing towards Ashton. "Why, man, you are as white as one of Judy's biscuits; what ails you?"

"Nothing," answered Ashton, who really was much affected by Mr. Middleton's narrative; but he said, "I am only thinking of the long, weary days I passed in the Delphine before Mr. Middleton kindly cared for me."

This seemed quite natural, and Mr. Middleton continued, "Ashton was wasted to a mere skeleton by ship fever, and my heart yearned towards him. Perhaps I felt a stronger sympathy for him when I learned that he was an American. He, like myself, had run away. The vessel, in which he had embarked, had been wrecked, and he, with two others, were saved in a small boat. For days they floated over the broad expanse of waters, until at length the Delphine picked them up, and brought them to India. I had Ashton removed to my house, but as soon as he recovered, he too took French leave of me. From that time I lived alone. I wrote to you frequently, but got no answer. My letters must have been lost, but I then concluded you were dead. At last I began to have such an ardent desire to tread my native soil once more that I disposed of my property and set out for home, so here I am and have told you my history; what do you think of it?"

There was no answer save the sound of heavy breathing. Uncle Joshua had probably got to sleep "all over." The cessation of his brother's voice awoke him, and rubbing his eyes he said, "Yes, yes, Ashton had the ship fever. I hope he can't give it now, for I am mortal feared on't."

Ashton assured him there was no danger, and then, turning to William, said, "Have you ever heard from Inez?"

"Yes," said Mr. Middleton. "About a year after her marriage, I heard of the birth of a daughter, whom she called Inez Middleton. I have heard of them once or twice since, but not recently."

After a moment's silence, Ashton, with some hesitation, said, "If I mistake not, I know Inez Effingham well."

"*You* know Inez, my Inez,—where,—how,—tell me all," said Mr. Middleton, grasping Ashton's hand as if a new link were suddenly added to the chain of friendship, which already bound them together.

"You probably remember," said Ashton, "that when I left you so suddenly, there was an American vessel in port. I was anxious to return home, but fancied you would oppose it, so I left you without a word, and went on board the ship. During the voyage, I found that one of the crew was from my own native town. I eagerly inquired after my parents and the little sister Nellie, whom you so often heard me mention; judge of my feelings when told that they were all dead. In the agony of the moment I attempted to throw myself overboard, but was prevented. From that time all desire to return was gone, and when at last we stopped at one of the ports in England, I left the vessel, determining to try my fortune in the mother country."

"But Inez," said Mr. Middleton, "what of Inez?"

"I will tell you," answered Ashton. "After remaining in England some years, I became acquainted with her father, Sir Arthur Effingham, who lived about forty miles from London. He invited me to visit his house, and there I first saw Inez and her mother. To know Inez was to love her, but I

could not hope to win the haughty Englishman's daughter, and besides, she
was so young that I did not believe I had made any impression upon her.
But encouraged by Lady Effingham, I at length ventured to ask Inez of her
father. I did not wish to marry her then, as she was only fourteen, but her
father spurned me with contempt, and bade me never again enter his house.
I obeyed, but tried many times to procure an interview with Inez. I succeeded, and told her I was about to leave England for America, but should
never forget her. I would not suffer her to bind herself to me by any
promise, but expressed my belief that at some future time she would be
mine. It is three years since we parted. I came immediately to America, but
I could not bear to return to my old home and see it occupied by others,
so I wandered this way, and at last settled in Frankfort as a merchant."

Here he stopped, and Mr. Middleton said, "You have not told me of the
mother. Does she still live?"

Ashton answered, "She was living when I left England, but Inez has
since written to me of her death."

"That will do, Ashton; that will do. I do not wish to hear any more
now," said William.

While Mr. Middleton and Ashton were relating their adventures, Aunt
Katy was busily engaged in superintending the arrangement of "Marster
William's" sleeping room. Mrs. Middleton had bidden Judy to see that
everything was put in order, but Aunt Katy seemed to think nothing would
be done right unless she had an oversight of it. So she was walking back
and forth, consulting with Judy a little and ordering her a good deal.

"Now, Judy," said she, "hain't you no more idees of ilegance than to
push the bedstead smack up agin the clarbuds; just pull it out a foot or
two, as old miss use to do."

Judy complied with her request and she continued: "Lordy sakes,—don't
Miss Nancy know no better than to put Marster William to sleep in sich
coarse sheets," at the same time casting a rueful glance at the linen which
Judy had put upon the bed. "You set down, Judy," said Aunt Katy, "and
I'll tend to the bed myself."

So saying she hobbled off to her cabin and opening her "old red chist,"
drew from it a pair of half worn, but very fine linen sheets. These she shook
most lustily in order to free them from the rose leaves, lavender sprigs, and
tobacco which she had placed between their folds. With the former she
thought to perfume them, while the latter was put there for the purpose
of keeping out moths. The old creature had heard that tobacco was good
to keep moths from woollen, and she knew of no reason why it would not
answer every purpose for linen.

"Thar," said she, on returning to the house, "these begins to look a leetle
like Marster William. They was gin to me by old marster, jest afore he died.
They 'longed to old miss, and if any one on us could read, I reckon we
should find her name on 'em somewhar writ in brawdery."

When the bed and room were adjusted to her satisfaction, she went down
to the kitchen and took a seat there. Here Aunt Judy found her about
ten o'clock that night.

"What on airth you sittin' here for?" said she.

"Oh, I's only waitin' till Marster William gets a little used to his room, afore I axes him how he likes it and does he want anything."

Accordingly not long after Aunt Katy stole up stairs and opening the door, called out, "Ho! Marster William, does you want any thing, and is you got enough kivers?"

But "Marster William's" senses were too soundly locked in sleep to heed the faithful creature, and after standing still a moment, she said to herself, "I'm mighty feared he'll cotch cold."

So back she went to her cabin and from the same "red chist" she took a many colored patchwork quilt. This she carried to the house and spread carefully over Mr. Middleton, saying, "He won't be none too comfortable, and in the mornin' he'll see it, and I'll tell him how I done pieced it and quilted it my own self."

The consequence of this extra covering was, that Mr. Middleton awoke in the night, with the impression that he was being suffocated in the hot climate of Calcutta. He did not know that she, to whom he was indebted for his warm berth, was now sleeping quietly and dreaming, "how tickled Marster William would be when he knew she had lent him her spar sheets and bed quilt!"

## Chapter XVI

The next day was the Sabbath. Contrary to their usual custom on such mornings, Mr. Middleton and his negroes were astir at an early hour. The female portion of the latter were occupied in preparing a great breakfast in honor of "Marster William's" arrival, while Mr. Middleton busied himself in removing a part of his dark, heavy beard.

When William made his appearance in the sitting-room, he was greeted by his brother with, "How are you, Bill? Hope you slept better than I did, for 'pears like I couldn't get asleep no how, till towards mornin', and then I was mighty skeary about wakin' up, for fear I should find it all moonshine, and no Bill here after all." After a moment's pause, he added, "Whar's t'other chap? If he don't come directly, the hen'll spile, for Judy's had it ready better than half an hour."

Ashton soon appeared, and the party did ample justice to Aunt Judy's well-cooked breakfast. That meal being over, Mr. Middleton said, "Now, boys, what do you say to goin' to meetin'? The Babtiss have preachin', and

I've a mind to go. How the folks'll star though to see Bill. Say, will you go?"

The gentlemen signified their assent; and at the usual hour they proceeded to the church, which was situated about two miles from Mr. Middleton's. We are sorry for it, but truth compels us to say, that on this day Uncle Joshua was not quite as devotional as usual. He was looking over the congregation to see what effect his brother's presence was producing. When he saw that no one exclaimed or turned pale, and that even the minister kept on the even tenor of his discourse, he inwardly accused them all of being "doughheads," and wondered he had never before discovered how little they knew. However, when meeting was over, the neighbors crowded around the old man, congratulating him on the unexpected return of his brother, whom they welcomed so warmly that Uncle Joshua began to think he had been too hasty in condemning them, for "after all, they knew a heap."

That night, after supper, Mr. Middleton was again seated in the little porch with his guests. They had been speaking of the sermon they had heard, when Mr. Middleton said, "That's the right kind of meetin' to my notion. A feller can sleep a bit, if he feels like it; but whar my gals go, in Frankford, they have the queerest doin's—keep a gittin' up and sittin' down; 'pears like you don't more'n git fairly sot, afore you have to hist up agin, and you can't sleep to save you. Then they have streaked yaller and black prar-books and keep a-readin' all meetin' time."

"Do your daughters prefer that church?" asked William.

"Why, yes," returned his brother; "or, that is, Dick, poor boy Dick, belonged thar; so did the young Lefftenant Carrington; so does Dr. Lacey; and that's reason enough why Sunshine should prefer it. Tempest goes thar, I reckon, because it's fashionable, and she can have a nice prar-book to show. You ought to see the one I bought for Sunshine. It's all velvety, and has gold clasps, with jest the word 'Sunshine' writ on it. Tempest has got a more common one. It didn't cost half as much."

"I notice that you make quite a distinction between your daughters," said William. "May I ask why you do it?"

Mr. Middleton stopped smoking, and said, "If you please, Bill, I'd rather say nothin' about that now. I make it a rule never to swar Sundays, and if I git to goin' it about Tempest, and the way she used poor Dick, I should have to swar and no mistake. Mebby you think I'd better not swar any time."

"Yes," answered William; "I should be glad if you would not. It is a bad habit, and I wish you would discontinue it."

"Well now, Bill," said Mr. Middleton, "Lord knows—no, I mean *I* know— I've tried a heap of times to break off, and now I'll try again. I'll not cuss a word till I forget. Dick used to want me to stop, and when he died I promised myself I would; but the pigs and horses got into the corn, and fust I knew I was swarin' wus than ever. I wish you had seen Dick; but it can't be—he's gone for ever."

"Have you no daguerreotype of him?" asked William.

"No, I hain't, but his folks have; and Mr. Miller and Kate are goin' home this summer, and they'll fetch me one. That makes me think Sunshine is so puny and sick like, that I'm goin' to let her go North with them. It'll do her good; and I'm goin' to buy her four silk gowns to go with, but for Lord's—no, for land's sake, don't tell Tempest."

"I hope you are not very anxious to have Fanny go North," said William; "for it will seriously affect a plan which I have formed."

"Well, what is it?" asked Mr. Middleton.

William then told of the house he had purchased, and of his intention to take both his nieces back with him. "I know," said he, "that it seems strange to take them there in hot weather; but down by the lake it will be pleasant and cool, and I must have them with me."

"Have you said anything to them about it?" asked Mr. Middleton.

"Yes," answered his brother. "I have mentioned it to them."

"What did they say?"

"Fanny said nothing, but Julia seemed much pleased with the idea," said William.

"I'll warrant that," returned Mr. Middleton. "She's tickled enough, and in her own mind she's run up a bill agin me for at least five hundred. Sunshine is so modest, I s'pose, because Dr. Lacey will be there, that she does not want to seem very glad; but she'll go. I'll have them come home to-morrow, and will talk the matter over. I'd as soon have her go to New Orleans as to New-York."

Here the conversation was interrupted by Mrs. Middleton, who came to tell her husband that 'twas past nine. Mr. Middleton had a great horror of being up after that hour, so he hastily bade his brother and Ashton good-night, saying to the former, "Now I've got kinder used to your being alive, Bill, I hope I shan't have such pesky work goin' to sleep."

Next morning Ashton returned to Frankfort in the carriage which Mr. Middleton had sent for the purpose of bringing his daughters home. For once in her life, Julia was delighted with the idea of visiting her parents. She had learned from a note which her mother had written, that the reason of their being sent for was to talk over the matter of going to New Orleans. Fanny felt differently. She wished, yet dreaded to go home. She too knew why they were sent for; but as she was determined not to go to New Orleans, it would be necessary at last to tell her father the true reason. She was certain he would be unsparing in his wrath against Dr. Lacey, and she almost trembled for the consequences.

When at last she was ready, she descended to the parlor and sitting down to her piano, ran her fingers lightly over the keys. At that moment Frank Cameron entered. He had learned from his cousin, Kate, enough of Fanny's history to make him fear that she never could be aught to him; and yet the knowledge that he could not, must not, hope to win her only rendered the attraction stronger. He was intending to start for home the next day, and had now come to spend a few moments alone with Fanny, ere he bade her good-bye. As he entered the room, she ceased playing, and said, "I believe you leave town to-morrow, do you not?"

"I do," replied Frank, "and am come to bid you good-bye now; for when you return, I shall probably be looking on the dust, smoke, and chimneys of the Empire City." As Fanny made no answer, Frank continued,

"Miss Middleton, we shall meet again, I trust. Kate tells me that you are to accompany them to New-York this summer. I shall expect you, and shall watch anxiously for your coming."

Fanny replied, "I have thought of going North with Mrs. Miller, but it is possible I may be disappointed."

"Disappointed!" repeated Frank; "you must not be disappointed, or disappoint me either. I would hardly be willing to leave Frankfort if I did not hope to see you again. And yet if we never do meet, I shall know that I am a better man for having once seen and known you; and I shall look back upon the few days spent in Kentucky as upon one of the bright spots in my life."

We do not know what Fanny would have replied; for ere she had time to answer, Julia appeared in the door, calling out, "Come, Fan., the carriage is ready. But, pray excuse me," continued she, as she saw Frank. "I had no idea that I was interrupting so interesting a conversation as your looks seem to indicate."

This increased Fanny's confusion, but she endeavored to appear at ease; and rising up, she offered Frank her hand, saying, "I must now bid you farewell, Mr. Cameron."

Frank took her hand, and quick as thought, raised it to his lips. Fanny's cheeks reddened as she hastily withdrew her hand, saying, rather indignantly, "Mr. Cameron, I am surprised!"

Frank expected as much, and he said, rather gaily, "Pardon me, Miss Middleton, I could not help it, and would not if I could. It is all I ever hope to receive from you; and years hence, when I am a lone, lorn old bachelor, I shall love to think of the morning when I bade good-bye to and kissed Fanny Middleton."

A moment more, and the carriage drove rapidly away. Frank watched it until it disappeared down the street; then turning away, he thought, "I have met and parted with the only person on earth who has power to awaken in me any deeper feeling than that of respect."

When Julia and Fanny reached home, they were greeted kindly both by their parents and uncle. The latter had resolved to watch them closely, in order to ascertain, if possible, the reason of his brother's evident preference for Fanny. During the day, nothing was said of the projected visit to New Orleans; and Julia was becoming very impatient, but she knew better than to broach the subject herself; so she was obliged to wait.

That evening the family, as usual, assembled on the little porch. Fanny occupied her accustomed seat and low stool by the side of her father, whose pipe she filled and refilled; for he said, "The tobacker tasted a heap better after Sunshine had handled it."

Julia could wait no longer, and she began the conversation by asking her uncle something about New Orleans.

"Thar, I knew 'twould be so," said Mr. Middleton. "Tempest is in a desput hurry to know whether I'm going to cash over and send her to market in New Orleans."

"Well, father," said Julia, coaxingly, "you are going to let Fanny and me go with Uncle William, I know."

It was lucky for Julia that she chanced to mention her sister; for however much her father might be inclined to tease *her*, the word "Fanny" mollified him at once, and he answered, "Why, yes; I may as well let you go as to keep you here doing nothing, and eating up my corn bread." Then drawing Fanny nearer to him, he said, "I've talked some of letting Sunshine go to New-York, but she'll jump at the chance of going to New Orleans, I reckon."

There was no answer, and as Julia was not particularly desirous of having her sister's silence questioned, she rattled on about her expected visit, and even went so far as to caress her father, because he had given his consent to her going. It was decided that Mr. William Middleton should return, as he had intended, in two weeks' time, so as to have every thing in readiness for the reception of his nieces, who were to come on as soon as school closed, which would be about the tenth of June.

During all this time, Fanny said not a word; and at last it occurred to her father, that she had neither expressed her desire nor willingness to go; so he said, "Come, Sunshine, why don't you hold up your head and talk about it? We all know *you* want to go mightily, and see that little Doctor."

Fanny knew it was of no use delaying longer, and she answered gently, but decidedly, "Father, I have no desire to go to New Orleans. I cannot go."

"Fudge on being so very modest," replied Mr. Middleton. "It is nateral-like that you should want to see him and nobody'll think less of you."

Fanny answered, "You know I have thought of going to New-York with Mr. and Mrs. Miller. I am still anxious to do so; but to New Orleans I cannot, shall not go, unless you command me to do so."

"Saint Peter!" said Mr. Middleton. "What's the row now? What's happened to make little Sunshine spirt up so? Don't you want to see Dr. Lacey, child?"

"No, father; I never desire to see him again."

The old cob pipe dropped from Mr. Middleton's mouth and springing up, he confronted Fanny, saying, "What in fury is the racket? You not wish to go to New Orleans, or see Dr. Lacey either! I half wish you was Tempest for a spell, so I could storm at you; but as it is Sunshine, I can't even feel mad."

"Oh, father, father!" said Fanny, weeping; "if you knew all that has occurred, you would not blame me."

"What do you mean, darling?" asked Mr. Middleton, suddenly becoming cool. "What has happened?" Then looking at Julia, whose face was crimson, a new idea struck him, and he exclaimed, more wrathfully, "How now, Tempest? What makes *you* turn as red as a hickory fire. Have you been raising a rumpus between Dr. Lacey and Sunshine? Out with it, if you have."

It was now Julia's turn to cry and appeal to her uncle if it were not unjust in her father always to suspect her of evil, if any thing were wrong. William very wisely kept silent, but Fanny said, "Do not accuse Julia, for she is not guilty. She knows it all, however, and is sorry for it."

"Knows what? Sorry for what? Why don't you tell?" said Mr. Middleton, stalking back and forth through the porch, and setting down his feet as heavily as if he would crush every thing which might chance to fall beneath his footsteps.

"I cannot tell you now," said Fanny; "but when we are alone, you shall know all."

In a few moments William thought proper to retire, and as his example was soon followed by Julia, Fanny was left alone with her parents. Drawing her stool nearer to her father, and laying her hot, feverish forehead upon his hand, she said, "Before I give any explanation I wish you to make me a promise."

"Promise of what?" asked her father and mother, simultaneously.

"It is not probable," answered Fanny, "that you will ever see Dr. Lacey again, but if you do, I wish you never to mention to him what I am about to tell you."

The promise was readily given by Mrs. Middleton, but her husband demurred, saying, "I shan't commit myself until I know what 'tis. If Dr. Lacey has been cuttin' up, why I'll cowhide him, that's all."

"Then I shall not tell you," was Fanny's firm reply.

Her father saw she was in earnest, and replied, "What's got your back up so high, Sunshine? I never knew you had so much grit. What's the reason you don't want Dr. Lacey to hear of it?"

"Because," said Fanny, hesitatingly, "because I do not wish him to know how much I care about it; and besides, it can do no possible good. Now, father, promise you will not tell him or any one else."

Mr. Middleton was finally persuaded, and his promise given. Fanny knew it would not be broken, for her father prided himself on keeping his word. So she gave an account of Dr. Lacey's conduct, and ended her narrative by producing the letter, which she supposed came from him. Up to this moment Mr. Middleton had sat perfectly still; but meantime his wrath had waxed warmer and warmer, until at last it could no longer be restrained, but burst forth in such a storm of fury as made Fanny stop her ears.

She, however, caught the words: "And I was fool enough to promise not to say a word. Well, thank the Lord, I didn't promise not to shoot the puppy. Let me catch him within pistol shot of me, and I'll pop him over as I would a woodchuck. And if he don't come back, I'll go all the way to Orleans for the sake of doin' on't. I'll larn him to fool with my gal; yes, I will!"

Fanny's fears for Dr. Lacey's safety were immediately roused; and again were her arms wound round the neck of her enraged father, while she begged of him to be quiet, and think reasonably of the matter. Not long could any one resist the arguments of Fanny; and in less than half an hour her father grew calm, and said more gently, "I shouldn't have been so rarin' mad, if it had been any body besides you, Sunshine. I s'pose I did go on high, and swar like a pirate. I didn't mean to do that, for I promised Bill I'd try and leave off."

"Leave swearing?" said Fanny; "Oh, I am so glad! I hope you will. Now promise that you will, dear father, and say again that you will not mention Dr. Lacey's conduct either to him or any one else."

"I have promised *once*," said Mr. Middleton, "and one promise is as good as forty. Old Josh'll never break his word as long as he has his senses. But that paltry Doctor owes his life to you, Sunshine. Half an hour ago, I was as fully set to knock him over as I am now determined to let the varmint go to destruction his own way."

Fanny shuddered at the idea of her father becoming the murderer of Dr. Lacey, and Mrs. Middleton rejoined, "I am glad, husband, to hear you talk more sensibly. It can do no possible good for you to shoot Dr. Lacey, and then lose your own life, as you assuredly would; besides, I think the less we say of the matter, the better it will be."

"I reckon you are right, Nancy," said Mr. Middleton, "but hang it all, what excuse shall I give Bill for not lettin' the gals go to New Orleans?"

"But, father," said Fanny, "you will let Julia go, of course. Uncle knows I do not intend to go, and consequently will think nothing of that; and there is no reason why Julia should not go to New Orleans, and I to New-York. Now say we may, that's a dear father."

"I s'pose I'll have to, honey," answered Mr. Middleton, "but if I can see ahead an inch, you're bitin' your own nose off by sending Tempest to New Orleans without you."

Afterwards Fanny remembered his speech, and understood it too; but now she was prevented from giving it a thought by her father, who continued, "Doesn't that Cameron chap live some'us in New-York?"

There was no reason for it, but Fanny blushed deeply as she replied, "Yes, sir, Mr. Cameron lives in New-York city; but I am not going to see him."

"Mebby not," answered her father; "but my name ain't Josh if he won't be on the lookout for you. And 'twixt us, darling, now the Doctor's sarved you such a scaly trick, I shouldn't pitch and dive much if I heard that you and Cameron were on good terms."

"That will never, never be," answered Fanny. "I shall always live at home with you and mother."

"You are a blessed daughter," said Mr. Middleton, "and I hope thar's better fortin in store for you than to stay hived up with us two old crones, and I can't help thinkin' that you'll have Dr. Lacey yet, or somebody a heap better. Now go to bed, child, for your eyes are gittin' red like, and heavy."

Fanny obeyed and retired to her room, where she found Julia sitting up and waiting for her. As soon as Fanny appeared she began, "Fan., you are a real good girl. I was pleased to hear you talk. Nobody but you could have done any thing with the old heathen."

"What are you talking about?" asked Fanny.

"Why," said Julia, "I had my head out of the window listening all the time, and overheard what you said. Once I trembled for fear father would take it into his head not to let me go any way; but you fixed it all right, and I thank you for it." As Fanny made no answer, Julia continued, "I heard, too, all about Frank Cameron. Now, Fan., I know he admires you, and I really hope you'll not be silly enough to discourage him. I shall expect you to write that you have promised to become Mrs. Cameron."

"Will you please, Julia, say no more on that subject?" said Fanny. "I do not suppose Frank Cameron has any particular regard for me; and if he has, it will do no good."

Thus the conversation ended for that night. The next day Mr. William Middleton was informed that Julia would spend the summer in New Orleans, but that Fanny preferred going North. He was rather disappointed. His preference, if he had any, was for Fanny. She was so quiet, so gentle, he could not help loving her; but Julia puzzled him. There was a certain bold assurance in her manner which he disliked. Besides, he could not help fearing there was some good reason why her father censured her so much. "I will watch her closely," thought he, "and if possible, discover her faults and help her correct them."

It would seem that Julia suspected her uncle's intentions, for she intended to be very correct and amiable in her deportment, whenever he was present. Thought she, "I shall thus retain his good opinion; and by so doing I shall more easily win Dr. Lacey's regard."

In the course of a few days, Fanny and Julia returned to school; the one, elated with the prospect of going to New Orleans, and the other, quietly anticipating a pleasant but rather sad journey to New-York. Two weeks after their return to Frankfort, their uncle called upon them, on his way South. He again repeated his invitation that Stanton and Ashton would spend a part of the summer with him. Ashton consented, but Stanton still pleaded his *important business* North, and his excuse was considered a sufficient one.

Mrs. Carrington, who had become rather weary of Raymond's attentions, and was longing for a change of place and scene, now tried by every possible manoeuvre to induce Mr. Middleton to invite her also. Julia readily understood her; and as she feared Mrs. Carrington's presence would frustrate her plans, she resolutely determined that she should *not* be invited. Consequently, when that lady talked to Mr. Middleton of New Orleans, and the desire she had of again visiting that city, Julia would adroitly change the conversation to some other subject; and once, when Mr. Middleton had actually opened his mouth and commenced giving the desired invitation, Julia, as if suddenly recollecting herself, started up, saying, "Excuse me, Uncle, but I have a painting in my room which I wish you to see. Pray come with me now, for I cannot bring it down, and as it is getting dark, there is no time to be lost."

Mr. Middleton arose and followed his niece, who congratulated herself on the success of her stratagem. After reaching her room, and exhibiting her painting she said to her uncle, "I do hope you will not ask Mrs. Carrington to go to New Orleans this summer."

"Why not?" said Mr. Middleton. "She seems anxious that I should do so."

"I know it," answered Julia; "but I am afraid she is not a good woman. At least, she has a bad influence over me, and I always feel wicked after being with her a while."

As Julia had supposed, this had the desired effect. Mr. Middleton would not ask one to visit him whose influence over his niece was bad. Consequently, all Mrs. Carrington's hints were unnoticed or misunderstood.

She, however, knew tolerably well to whom she was indebted for the slight; and when, after Mr. Middleton's departure, Julia said to her, "I wonder Uncle did not invite you too; I thought he was going to do so," she replied, rather sharply, "I fancy I should have been under no obligations to you, Miss Julia, if I had received an invitation." Then turning, she hastily entered her room, and throwing herself upon the sofa, she tried to devise some scheme by which she could undermine Julia, provided Dr. Lacey should show her any marked attention.

Mrs. Carrington was not in a very enviable mood. The night before Raymond had offered her his heart and hand, and of course had been rejected. He was in the parlor when Julia so abruptly took her uncle away. As there was no one present besides Mrs. Carrington, he seized upon that moment to declare his love. It is impossible to describe the loathing and contempt which she pretended to feel for him who sued so earnestly for her hand, even if her heart did not accompany it. Nothing daunted by her haughty refusal, Raymond arose, and standing proudly before the indignant lady, said, "Ida Carrington, however much dislike you may profess to feel for me, I do not believe it. I know I am not wholly disagreeable to you, and were I possessed of thousands, you would gladly seize the golden bait. I do not ask you to love me, for it is not in your nature to love any thing. You are ambitious, and even now are dreaming of one whom you will never win; for just as sure as yon sun shall set again, so sure you, proud lady, shall one day be my wife."

When Mrs. Carrington had recovered a little from the surprise and anger into which Raymond's fiery speech had thrown her, he was gone and she was alone. "Impudent puppy!" said she; "and yet he was right in saying he was not disagreeable to me. But I'll never be his wife. I'd die first!" Still, do what she would, a feeling haunted her that Raymond's prediction would prove true. Perhaps it was this which made her so determined to supplant Julia in Dr. Lacey's good opinion, should he ever presume to think favorably of her. How she succeeded we shall see hereafter.

## Chapter XVII

Three weeks after Mr. Middleton's departure for New Orleans, Mr. Miller's school closed. Uncle Joshua was present at the examination, and congratulated himself much because he did not feel at all "stuck up" at seeing both Julia and Fanny acquit themselves so creditably. After the exercises were concluded, he returned with Mr. Miller to Mrs. Crane's. Just before he started for home, he drew from his sheepskin pocket-book five hundred dollars, which he divided equally between his daughters, saying, "Here, gals, I reckon this'll be enough to pay for all the furbelows you've bought, or will want to buy. I'll leave you here the rest of the week to see to fixin' up your rig, but Saturday I shall send for you."

Fanny was surprised at her father's unlooked-for generosity, and thanked him again and again. Julia was silent, but her face told how vexed and disappointed she was. As soon as her father was gone, her rage burst forth. "Stingy old thing," said she, "and yet he thinks he's done something wonderful. Why, my bill at C.'s already amounts to two hundred, and I want as much more. What I am to do, I don't know."

She would have said more, but Fanny quieted her by saying, "Don't talk so about father, Julia. It was very liberal, and really I do not know what to do with all mine."

"I could find ways enough to dispose of it, I imagine," said Julia.

But we will not continue the conversation. Suffice it to say that when Julia retired that night, her own money was safe in her purse, and by the side of it lay the hundred dollars which she had coaxed from Fanny. As they were preparing to return home, on Saturday, Julia said to her sister, "Fan., don't let father know that you gave me a hundred dollars, for I fear all your powers of persuasion would be of no avail to stay the storm he would consider it his bounden duty to raise."

There was no need of this caution, for Fanny was not one to do a generous act and then boast of it, neither did her father ask her how she had disposed of her money. He was satisfied to know that the "four silk gowns" were purchased, as, in his estimation, they constituted the essential part of a young lady's wardrobe.

Since Fanny had disclosed the heartless desertion of Dr. Lacey, she seemed to be doubly dear to her father; for pity now mingled with the intense love he had always borne for his youngest and best loved daughter. Often, during the three days which she passed at home, prior to her departure for New-York, he would sit and gaze fondly upon her until the tears would blind his vision, then springing up, he would pace the floor, impetuously muttering, "The scamp!—the vagabond!—but he'll get his pay fast enough,—and I'd pay him, too, if I hadn't done promised not to. But 'tain't worth a while, for I reckon 'twould only make her face grow whiter and thinner if I did anything."

At length the morning came on which Julia and Fanny were to leave for the first time their native State. Side by side near the landing at Frankfort lay the two boats, Blue Wing and Diana. The one was to bear Fanny on her Northern tour, and the other would convey Julia as far as Louisville on her way South. Mr. Woodburn, who had business in New Orleans, was to take Julia under his protection.

And now but a short time remained ere the Diana would loose her moorings and be under way. These few moments were moments of sorrow to Mr. and Mrs. Middleton, who had accompanied their daughters to Frankfort. Uncle Joshua particularly was much depressed, and scarce took his eyes from his treasure, who might be leaving him for ever. In his estimation the far-off North was a barren, chilly region, and although he did not quite believe his Fanny would be frozen to death, he could not rid himself of the fear that something would befall her.

"You'll take good keer of her, won't you, Miller?" said he, "and bring her safely back to us?"

Mr. Miller gave the promise, and then observing that there was something else on Mr. Middleton's mind, he said, "What is it, Mr. Middleton? What more do you wish to say?"

Mr. Middleton struggled hard with his feelings, and his voice sank to a whisper as he answered, "I wanted to tell you that if—if she should die, bring her home,—bring her back, don't leave her there all alone."

The old man could say no more, for the bell rang out its last warning. The parting between Fanny and her parents was a sad one, and even Julia wept as she kissed her sister, and thought it might be for the last time.

Soon after the Diana, with its precious freight, disappeared from view, Mr. Middleton was called upon to bid another farewell to his eldest daughter. "Reckon the old fellow likes one girl better than the other," said a bystander, who had witnessed both partings. And yet Mr. Middleton did well, and his look and manner were very affectionate as he bade Julia good-bye, and charged her "not to be giddy and act like a fool, nor try to come it over Dr. Lacey. Though," thought he, "it'll be sarvin' the rascal right if he should have to live with Tempest all his life."

It is not our intention at present to follow Julia in her passage to New Orleans. In another chapter we will take up that subject and narrate her adventures. Now we prefer going North with the other party, which consisted of Mr. and Mrs. Miller, Fanny and Raymond. The latter had, in a fit of desperation, determined to quit Frankfort, and go no one knew whither. He accompanied his friends as far as Cincinnati, and there bade them adieu, saying that they would hear of him again in a way they little dreamed of.

Mr. Miller was sorry to part with one who had proved so valuable an assistant in his school, but all his arguments had failed and he was obliged to give him up, saying, "I hope, Raymond, that all your laudable enterprises may be successful."

"I shall succeed," were Raymond's emphatic words, "and she, the haughty woman, who tried to smile so scornfully when I bade her farewell, will yet be proud to say that she has had a smile from me, the poor school-master."

"Well, Raymond," said Mr. Miller, "you have my good wishes, and if you ever run for President, I'll vote for you. So now good-bye."

Raymond wrung his friend's hand, and then stepped from the cars, which soon rolled heavily from the dépot. Faster and faster sped the train on its pathway over streamlet and valley, meadow and woodland, until at last the Queen City with its numerous spires was left far behind. From the car windows Fanny watched the long blue line of hills, which marks the Kentucky shore, until they too disappeared from view.

For a time now we will leave her to the tender mercies of the Ohio railroad, and a Lake Erie steamer, and hurrying on in advance, we will introduce the reader to the home where once had sported Richard Wilmot and his sister Kate. It stood about a half a mile from the pleasant, rural village of C—— in the eastern part of New-York. The house was large and handsome, and had about it an air of thrift and neatness, which showed its owner to be a farmer who not only understood his business, but also attended to it himself. Between the house and road was a large, grassy lawn, in which was growing many a tall, stately maple and elm, under whose wide-spreading branches Kate and her brother had often played during the gladsome days of their childhood. A long piazza ran around two sides of the building. Upon this piazza the family sitting-room opened.

Could we have entered that sitting-room the day on which our travellers arrived, we should have seen a fine-looking, middle-aged lady, whose form and features would instantly have convinced us that we looked upon the mother of Kate. Yes, what Kate Miller is now, her mother was once; but time and sorrow have made inroads upon her dazzling beauty, and here and there the once bright locks of auburn are now silvered over, and across the high, white brow, are drawn many deep-cut lines. Since Kate last saw her mother, these lines have increased, for the bursting heart has swelled with anguish, and the dark eye has wept bitter tears for the son who died far away from his childhood's home. Even now the remembrance of the noble youth, who, scarce two years ago, left her full of life and health, makes the tear drop start as she says aloud, "How can I welcome back my darling Kate, and know that he will never come again?"

The sound of her voice aroused old Hector, the watch dog, who had been lying in the sun upon the piazza. Stretching his huge limbs and shaking his shaggy sides, he stalked into the sitting-room, and going up to his mistress laid his head caressingly in her lap. The sight of Hector made Mrs. Wilmot's tears flow afresh, for during many years he had been the faithful companion of Richard, whose long absence he seemed seriously to mourn. For days and weeks he had watched by the gate, through which he had seen his young master pass, and when at last the darkness of night forbade a longer watch, he would lay his head on the ground and give vent to his evident disappointment in a low, mournful howl.

Mrs. Wilmot was not superstitious; but when, day after day, the same sad cry was repeated, it became to her an omen of coming evil; and thus the shock of her son's death, though none the less painful, was not quite as great as it would otherwise have been. For Kate, too, old Hector had wept, but not so long nor so mournfully; still, he remembered her, and always evinced his joy whenever her name was spoken.

On the morning of the day on which she was expected home, a boy who had lived in the family when she went away, called Hector to him, and endeavored by showing him some garment which Kate had worn, and by repeating her name, to make him understand that she was coming home. We will not say that Hector understood him, but we know that during the day he never for a moment left the house or yard, but lay upon the piazza, looking eagerly towards the road which led from the village. Whenever he saw a carriage coming, he would start up and gaze wistfully at it until it had passed, then he would again lie down and resume his watch. Mrs. Wilmot noticed this, and when Hector, as we have seen, walked up to her and looked so sympathizingly in her face, she patted his head, saying, "Poor Hector; good fellow; you will see Kate at least to-day."

Nor was she mistaken, for about three that afternoon, an omnibus drew up before the gate. Kate immediately sprang out, and was followed by Mr. Miller and Fanny. Their arrival was first made known to Mrs. Wilmot by the cry of joy which Hector sent forth at sight of Kate. With lightning speed he bounded over the lawn to meet the travellers. Fanny, who was accustomed to the savage watch dogs of Kentucky, sprang back in terror and clung to Mr. Miller for protection; but Kate cried out, "Do not fear; it is only Hector, and he wouldn't harm you for the world." Then she ran forward to meet him, and embraced him as fondly as though he had really been a human being, and understood and appreciated it all. And he did seem to, for after caressing Kate, he looked about as if in quest of the missing one. Gradually he seemed to become convinced that Richard was not there, and again was heard the old wailing howl, but this time it was more prolonged, more despairing. Faithful creature! Know you not that summer's gentle gale and winter's howling storm have swept over the grave of him whom you so piteously bemoan?

Fanny stopped her ears to shut out the bitter cry, but if Kate heard it she heeded it not, and bounded on over the gravelled walk towards her mother, who was eagerly waiting for her. In an instant parent and child were weeping in each other's arms.

"My Kate, my darling Kate, are you indeed here?" said Mrs. Wilmot.

Kate's only answer was a still more passionate embrace. Then recollecting herself, she took her husband's hand and presented him to her mother, saying, "Mother, I could not bring you Richard, but I have brought you another son. Will you not give him room in your heart?"

Mrs. Wilmot had never seen Mr. Miller before, but she was prepared to like him, not only because he was her daughter's choice, but because he had been the devoted friend of her son; consequently she greeted him with a most kind and affectionate welcome.

During all this time Fanny was leaning against one of the pillars of the piazza, but her thoughts were far away. She was thinking of her distant Kentucky home, and a half feeling of home-sickness crept over her, as she thought how joyfully she would be greeted there, should she ever return. Her reverie was of short duration, for Kate approached, and leading her to her mother, simply said, "Mother, this is Fanny."

'Twas enough. The word Fanny had a power to open the fountains of that mother's heart. She had heard the story of the young girl, who had watched so unweariedly by the bedside of Richard—she had heard too of the generous old man, whose noble heart had cared for and tenderly cherished the stranger, and she knew that she, who advanced towards her so timidly, was the same young girl, the same old man's daughter; and could Mr. Middleton have witnessed her reception of his Sunshine, he would have been satisfied.

A messenger was dispatched for Mr. Wilmot, who was superintending some workmen in a field not far from the house. Mr. Wilmot was a tall, noble-looking man, whose fine figure was slightly bowed by the frosts of sixty winters. As he advanced with breathless haste towards the house, Kate ran to meet him, and the tears which the strong man wept, told how dear to him was this, his beautiful daughter, and how forcibly her presence reminded him of his first-born, only son, who went away to die among strangers.

When he was presented to Mr. Miller and Fanny, a scene similar to the one we have already described took place. As he blessed Fanny for Richard's sake, she felt that though in a strange land, she was not alone or unloved. Her home-sickness soon vanished; for how could she be lonely and sad, where all were so kind, and where each seemed to vie with the other in trying to make every thing agreeable to her. It was strange how soon even Hector learned to love the fair Kentuckian. He would follow her footsteps wherever she went, and affectionately kiss her hands. But then, as Kate said, "Hector had more common sense than half the people in the world," and he seemed to know by instinct that she, whom he so fondly caressed, had once watched over and wept for his young master, who was now sleeping in his silent grave, unmindful that in his home he was still sincerely mourned even by old Hector.

Not many days after Fanny's arrival at Mr. Wilmot's she was told that a gentleman wished to see her in the parlor. On entering the room how was she surprised at beholding Frank Cameron. He had learned by a letter from Kate that Fanny was in C—— and he immediately started for his uncle's. Since his return from Kentucky he had thoughts of little else save Fanny Middleton. Waking or sleeping, she was constantly in his mind, and still with happy thoughts of her, there ever came a sadder feeling, a fear that his love for her would be in vain. But since the morning when he bade her adieu, her name had never once passed his lips.

When his sister Gertrude questioned him concerning the Kentucky girls, he had described to her in glowing terms the extreme beauty of Julia, and the handsome eyes of "the vidder," as he called Mrs. Carrington, but of Fanny he had never spoken. He could not bear that even his own sister should mention Fanny in connection with any one else. However, when Kate's letter arrived, he passed it over to Gertrude, whose curiosity was instantly roused, and she poured forth a torrent of questions as to *who* that Fanny Middleton was.

"I suppose she must be old Mr. Middleton's daughter," was Frank's teasing reply.

"Of course I know that," said Gertrude, "but what of her? Who is she?"

"Why, I've told you once, she is Fanny Middleton," said Frank.

These and similar answers were all Gertrude could draw from him, and she fell into a fit of pouting; but Frank was accustomed to that, and consequently did not mind it. Next day he announced his intention to visit his Uncle Wilmot. Gertrude instantly exclaimed, "Now, Frank, you are too bad. Just as soon as you hear Fanny Middleton is in New-York, you start off to see her, without even telling me who she is, or what she is. In my opinion you are in love with her, and do not wish us to know it."

This started up Mrs. Cameron's ideas, and she said, "Frank, I am inclined to believe Gertrude is right; but you surely will be respectful enough to *me* to answer my questions civilly."

"Certainly," said Frank. "Ask any thing you please; only be quick, for it is almost car time."

"Well then, do you intend to make this Miss Middleton your wife?"

"I do, if she will have me," said Frank.

The distressed lady groaned audibly, but continued, "One more question, Frank. Is she *rich,* and well connected?"

Frank passed his hand through the thick curls of his brown hair, and seemed to be trying hard to think of something. Finally he answered, "Why, really, mother, I never once thought to ask that question."

"But," persisted Mrs. Cameron, "you can judge by her appearance, and that of her parents. Did you not see them?"

Frank laughed loudly as the image of Uncle Joshua, as he first saw him in the door, buttoning his suspenders, presented itself to his remembrance; but he answered, "Yes, mother, I did see her father and 'twas the richest sight I ever saw."

He then proceeded to give a description of Mr. Middleton to his astonished sister and mother, the latter of whom exhibited such distress, that Frank very compassionately asked, "if she had the toothache."

Before she had time to answer Frank was gone, leaving his mother to lament over the strange infatuation which always led Frank in pursuit of somebody beneath him.

"I know," said she to Gertrude, "that this Fanny Middleton is from a horrid low family, and is as poor as a church mouse."

So, while Frank was hurrying on towards the village of C——, his mother and sister were brooding over the disgrace which they feared threatened them. They could have spared all their painful feelings, for she of the "low family" was destined to be another's.

During Frank's ride to C—— he determined, ere his return, to know the worst. "She can but refuse me," thought he, "and even if she does, I shall feel better than I do now." When he met Fanny his manner was so calm and collected, that she never dreamed how deep was the affection she had kindled in his heart. She received him with real pleasure, for he seemed like a friend from Kentucky. He staid with her but three days, and when he left, he bore a sadder heart than he had ever felt before. Fanny had refused him; not exultingly, as if a fresh laurel had been won only to be boasted of, but so kindly, so delicately, that Frank felt almost willing to act it all over again for the sake of once more hearing Fanny's voice, as she told him how utterly impossible it was for her ever again to love as a husband should be loved.

"Then," said Frank, somewhat bitterly, "you acknowledge that you have loved another."

"Yes," answered Fanny, "but no other circumstances could have wrung the confession from me. I've loved and been deceived. I will not say my faith in man's honor is wholly gone, for I believe you, Mr. Cameron, to be perfectly sincere and honorable in your professions of regard. Had we met earlier, all might have been different, but now it is too late. If my friendship is worth having, it is yours. I have never had a brother, but will look upon and love you as one;—with that, you must be satisfied."

And he did try to be satisfied, but only because there was no other alternative. Still he felt a pleasure in being near her, in breathing the same atmosphere and gazing on the same scenes. Before he returned home he had decided upon accompanying her, together with Mr. and Mrs. Miller, on their contemplated trip to Saratoga; thence they would go on to New-York city, and visit at his father's.

"I am sorry," said he, "that it is not the season for parties, as I should love dearly to show off Fanny in opposition to our practised city belles, and now I think of it," continued he, "isn't Mr. Stanton coming North this summer after a certain Miss Ashton?"

"I believe he is," answered Kate.

"Now then," said Frank, "I have it exactly. Judge Fulton, who is Miss Ashton's guardian, has recently removed to the city. I know him well, and have been introduced to Miss Helen. Stanton has already invited us all to his wedding, and as Miss Ashton will of course repeat the invitation, Fanny will thus have an opportunity of seeing a little of the gay world in New-York."

"You seem to think any praise bestowed upon Fanny as so much credit for yourself," said Kate, mischievously.

Frank made no reply, and soon bidding good-bye to his friends, he was on his way to the city. On reaching home he found his mother and sister in a state of great anxiety concerning "the odious old scarecrow's corn-cake daughter," as Gertrude styled Fanny. Her first question after asking about Kate was, "Well, Frank, tell me, did you propose to Miss Middleton?"

"Most certainly I did. That was one object in going," was Frank's quiet reply.

The horrified Mrs. Cameron, throwing up both hands in a most theatrical manner, exclaimed, "Mon Dieu!" It was the only French phrase she knew, and she used it upon all occasions. This time, however, it was accompanied by a loud call for her vinaigrette and for *air,* at the same time declaring it was of no use trying to restore her, for her heart was broken, and she was going to faint.

"Let me wash these *red spots* off from your cheek. You can't faint gracefully with so much color," said Frank, gravely, at the same time literally deluging his mother's face with cologne, much against the blooming lady's inclination. This little scene determined Frank not to tell that he was rejected. At first he had intended to disclose all, but now he decided otherwise. "They may as well fret about that as any thing else," thought he, "and when they see Fanny, I shall have a glorious triumph." So he kept his own secret, and commenced teasing Gertrude about going to Saratoga with himself, their cousin Kate and Fanny.

"I shall do no such thing, Master Frank," said Gertrude. "I am willing enough to see Kate, and invite her here too, for she is fine looking and appears well, even if she is a music teacher; but this Fanny Middleton—Ugh! I'll never associate with *her* on terms of equality, or own her as my sister either."

"I do not think you will," said Frank, but Gertrude knew not what cause he had for so saying.

After he had quitted the apartment, Mrs. Cameron and Gertrude tried to think of some way to let Fanny know that she was not wanted in their family. "Dear me," said Gertrude, "I will *not* go to Saratoga, and be obliged to see Frank made a dolt of himself with this plebeian Kentuckian. If she were only rich and accomplished, why, it would be different, and the fact of her being from Kentucky would increase her attractions. But now it is too bad!" and Gertrude actually cried with vexation and mortified pride. Poor creature! How mistaken she was with regard to Fanny Middleton, and so she one day learned.

But as the reader is doubtless anxious to hear of Fanny's introduction to Mrs. Cameron and Gertrude, we will give a description of it in the next chapter.

## *Chapter XVIII*

Contrary to his first intention, Stanton concluded to come North in July. He had of course learned from Nellie that her mysterious guardian had proved to be Judge Fulton, his sister's husband. And more recently she had written to him of Judge Fulton's removal to New-York city. Mr. Miller was apprised of Stanton's return by a letter, in which he was also informed that the wedding would take place in Grace Church on the morning of the 22d.

Not long after there came invitations for himself, wife and Fanny, to attend the bridal party, at the residence of Judge Fulton, on the evening of July 25th. Frank, who was also invited, had his own reason for not wishing his mother or sister to see Fanny until they met her at Judge Fulton's. Consequently he was not sorry when both ladies graciously informed him that Miss Middleton would not be invited by them to visit at their house. "Of course," said Mrs. Cameron, "we shall invite Kate and her husband, and shall be glad to see them. If you choose, *you* can in your own name invite Fanny, but if she knows any thing she will not come."

Frank knew there was no possible danger of Fanny's accepting an invitation which came simply from himself, but he did not say so, and next day he started again for his uncle Wilmot's. To his cousin Kate he imparted a knowledge of his mother's and Gertrude's feelings, and also told of his own plans. Kate readily fell in with them, and when Frank returned to the city he was accompanied by Mr. Miller, Kate and Fanny, who took rooms at the Astor House. As soon as Mrs. Cameron and Gertrude learned that Kate was in the city, they called upon her. Fanny they of course did not see, neither did they mention her name. Kate expected as much, but nevertheless felt vexed, and when they urged her to spend the remainder of her time with them, she replied, "I have a young friend from Kentucky with me, and unless you invite her too, I do not feel at liberty to accept your polite invitation."

In answer to this, Gertrude muttered something about "not wishing to enlarge the circle of her acquaintance," while Mrs. Cameron said nothing, and the two ladies soon swept haughtily out of the room.

"Never mind," said Frank, to whom Kate related her adventure, "they will both sing another tune ere long," and he was right, too.

The 25th of July at last arrived. Frank had informed Gertrude that she must look to their father for a beau that evening, as he should be otherwise engaged; so she was not surprised when her brother, long before sunset, left the house all equipped for the party. She well knew where he was going and for whose society she was deserted. One hour later found her seated in a large arm-chair before the mirror in her dressing-room.

Gertrude was a tall, fine-looking girl, but in the expression of her handsome features there was something wanting. She lacked *soul,* and no one ever looked on the cold, proud face of Gertrude Cameron without being convinced that she was altogether heartless and selfish.

On this occasion, as she sat in the large arm-chair, she said to her waiting-maid, "I say, Jane, you must do your best to-night to have me splendidly dressed."

"Yes, ma'am, I understand," said Jane, and she proceeded to bedeck her young mistress with all sorts of finery. Her dress consisted of a rich, white satin, over which was thrown a skirt of handsomely embroidered lace. All the ornaments of gold and diamonds for which a place could possibly be found were heaped upon her, and when her toilet was completed she seemed one gorgeous mass of jewelry.

"There, that will do," said she, as Jane clasped the last diamond bracelet on her arm. "I presume this Fanny Middleton has never dreamed of so costly a dress as I shall appear in to-night."

Meantime in another part of the city, another toilet was being made, but of a different nature. Kate and Frank both were anxious that for once Fanny should deviate from her usually simple style of dress, and adopt something more in keeping with her father's wealth. At first Fanny hesitated, but was finally persuaded, and gave Kate permission to select for her any thing she chose. As, on the evening of the party, she glanced at the image which her mirror reflected, she was pardonable for feeling a slight thrill of pleasure. Frank was in raptures, declaring nothing had ever been seen in New-York so perfectly lovely. And truly, Fanny was beautiful as she stood there arrayed for the party.

She was dressed in a French robe of white tarletane, embroidered in bouquets of lilies of the valley in silver. A single japonica rested among the curls of her bright hair, while her neck was encircled by a necklace of pearls, and costly bracelets of the same clasped her white, slender wrists.

"Why, Fanny," said Mr. Miller, "how beautiful you look! What would your father say could he see you now?"

At the mention of her father's name the tear drops glistened for a moment in Fanny's eye, and she felt how gladly she would have foregone all the expected pleasure of that night for the sake of again seeing her distant father. She, however, dashed the tear away, and replied, "I fear he would think his Sunshine wholly covered up and spoiled by *trumpery,* as he calls fashionable dress."

Frank noticed her emotion when speaking of her father, and he thought how priceless must be the love of one who thus so truly honored her parents. A feeling of sadness was blended with his admiration of Fanny, for constantly in his heart was the knowledge that she never would be his. And here Frank showed how truly noble he was, for he could still love and cling to Fanny, although he knew that for him there was no hope.

Let us now transport our readers to the elegant residence of Judge Fulton, which was situated upon Fifth Avenue. Stanton, with his fair bride, had returned from visiting his parents near Geneva, and now in the large parlors of Judge Fulton, they were receiving the congratulations of their friends, whose numbers each moment increased, until the rooms were filled to overflowing. Frank and his party had not yet arrived. He designed to be late. For he well knew his mother and sister would not be early, and he wished to give them the full benefit of Fanny's introduction into the drawing-room.

But a part of his scheme was frustrated, for his mother, who was suffering with a violent headache, was obliged to remain above stairs for a time, and Gertrude alone witnessed her brother's triumph. She was standing near Mr. and Mrs. Stanton, carelessly twirling a costly bouquet, which one of her obsequious beaux had given her, when she overheard Nellie saying to her husband, "I do hope she will come, for I am all impatience to see one whom you have praised until I am half jealous."

Gertrude wondered much whom Mrs. Stanton could mean, but her wonder soon ceased, for there was a stir at the door. The crowd around it fell back as Frank Cameron walked proudly into the room, bearing upon his arm, Fanny Middleton. Her fame had preceded her, for many of those present had learned that a Kentucky belle and heiress was stopping at the Astor, and would be present at the party. As she advanced into the room, Gertrude felt, rather than heard, the murmur of admiration which ran round the room, and her quick ear caught the words, "Yes, that's she; that's the heiress; that's Miss Middleton from Frankfort."

Gladly would Gertrude have escaped her brother's eye, which instantly sought her out; but she felt unable to move, and stood watching the animated face and graceful manners of Fanny, who, in being presented to Mrs. Fulton and Stanton, passed near her. Every article of Fanny's dress was noted, and an estimate made as to its probable cost. "She must be wealthy," thought she, "or she could not dress so expensively." Suddenly one of Gertrude's acquaintances touched her elbow and said, "Come, Miss

Cameron, do gratify our curiosity and tell us about this Kentucky belle. Of course you know her, as she is attended by your brother."

Deeply mortified, Gertrude was obliged to confess that she had no acquaintance with her. "That's strange," said the lady. "We all supposed she stopped at your father's with your cousin."

A new idea entered Gertrude's mind, and instead of replying to this last remark, she said, "I shall know her well, though, for Frank has proposed to her."

"Did she accept him?" asked the lady eagerly.

"Of course," was Gertrude's haughty answer. "Do you think he would offer himself unless sure of success?"

Ten minutes more, and dozens of persons were gossiping about the engagement between Frank Cameron and the beautiful Kentuckian. Scores of questions were poured in upon Gertrude, relative to her future sister-in-law, but none of them could she answer. Vexed at her own ignorance, she ran up stairs to her mother whom she told to "come down immediately and see what fools they had made of themselves."

"Why, what is the matter, child?" said Mrs. Cameron alarmed at Gertrude's excited looks and manners.

"All the city are ready to fall down and worship this Fanny Middleton, whom we have treated with such neglect," said Gertrude, and then she added, what was of more consequence than all the rest, "Why, mother, she's the most elegantly dressed lady in the room!"

In a moment Mrs. Cameron was descending the broad staircase. There was the sound of the piano and some one singing. Gertrude pressed eagerly forward until she caught sight of the singer, then pulling her mother's sleeve, she whispered, "This way, mother; that is Miss Middleton playing."

Mrs. Cameron's first emotion, on beholding Fanny and the flattering attentions she every where received, was one of intense mortification, to think *she* had not been first to notice and chaperone her. "I will, however, make all possible amends now," thought she, and finding Frank she desired for herself and Gertrude an introduction to Miss Middleton; but Frank did not feel disposed to grant his mother's request immediately, and he said, "Pardon me, mother, but you see Miss Middleton is very much engaged at present with some of her friends, so you must wait awhile."

Mrs. Cameron was too proud to ask any one else to introduce her, and it seemed that she and Gertrude were not likely to make Fanny's acquaintance at all. Towards the close of the party, however, Frank thought proper to introduce them. Mrs. Cameron determined to do her best, and she overwhelmed Fanny with so much flattery, that the poor girl longed for some way of escape, thinking to herself, "Is it possible that Frank Cameron's mother is such a silly woman?" Once Mrs. Cameron went so far as to hint the probability that Miss Middleton would one day be her daughter.

"What can she possibly mean?" thought Fanny; at the same time gracefully excusing herself she ran up stairs after her shawl and veil, as Kate had signified her intention of returning home. But Mrs. Cameron was not to be thus foiled. She started in pursuit, and reaching the bonnet room as soon as Fanny, insisted that she and Kate should stop with her during the remainder of her stay in the city. As Frank soon appeared and joined his entreaties with those of his mother, Fanny said she would do just as Mrs. Miller thought proper. Kate, who had expected a similar denouement, expressed her perfect willingness to visit at her uncle's.

Accordingly the next morning they left their rooms at the Astor House and repaired to Mrs. Cameron's, where they were most *affectionately* received by Mrs. Cameron and Gertrude. And now commenced a series of *toadyism* which was vastly amusing to their acquaintances, many of whom had witnessed Mrs. Cameron's manners at the party and had since learned a part of the story. It was strange how soon Mrs. Cameron and Gertrude discovered how many fine qualities Fanny possessed. Even the "odious scarecrow of a father" was transformed into an "odd old gentleman," and in speaking of him to one of her acquaintances, Mrs. Cameron said, "he was a very generous, wealthy, but eccentric old man and was one of the first citizens in Frankfort." The good lady forgot that Uncle Joshua did not reside in Frankfort, but twelve miles from that city! Her word, however, was not questioned, for of course she would know all about the family of her son's intended wife.

Meantime the report of Frank's engagement was circulating freely, and the whole matter would undoubtedly have been arranged, marriage ceremony and all, had not Frank put an end to the matter by utterly denying the story. Some young gentlemen were one morning congratulating him on his future prospects, and declaring their intention of going to Kentucky, if there were any more Fannys there, when Frank asked upon whose authority they were repeating a story for which there was no foundation.

"Why," answered one of them, "my sister heard it from your sister Gertrude."

"From Gertrude!" said Frank in amazement, "from Gertrude! Well, I cannot answer for what Gertrude says, but I assure you I am not engaged to Miss Middleton, and never have been."

This was in the morning, and that evening when Frank entered the sitting-room where his mother and sister were, they beset him to know why he had denied his engagement with Fanny.

"Because," said he rather indignantly, "there is no engagement between us."

"Oh, Frank," said Gertrude, "you told us so."

"I never told you so," answered he rather warmly. "I told you I had proposed, and I *did* propose, and was refused."

"But why didn't you tell us?" continued Gertrude.

"Because you didn't ask me," replied Frank. "You supposed of course none could refuse me, so jumped at conclusions and have got yourself into a fine spot."

There was no need of telling this, for Mrs. Cameron readily saw it, and went off into a fit of hysterics, while Gertrude burst into tears.

"What a strange girl you are!" said Frank. "Once you cried because you thought I *was* engaged to Fanny, and now you cry because I am not." So saying he gave a low mocking whistle and left his mother and sister to console themselves as best they could.

We will not weary the reader by repeating the conversation between Gertrude and her mother. We will only say that Mrs. Cameron decided to go as soon as possible to Saratoga, "and when once there," said she, "I will use all my influence with Miss Middleton; nay, if necessary, I will even beg of her to marry Frank, for I know she likes him."

Gertrude was delighted with this idea. She had forgotten how determined she once was not to visit Saratoga with Fanny Middleton. Next morning Mrs. Cameron proposed to her guests that as the weather was getting warm, they should start directly for the Springs. The visitors of course could make no objection, and as Mr. and Mrs. Stanton, who were to accompany them, also acquiesced in the plan, two days more found our friends at Saratoga, together with crowds more of the fashionable from the north, south, east and west.

On the first day of their arrival, Fanny noticed seated opposite her at the dinner table, a dark-eyed sprightly looking girl, whose eyes so constantly met hers, that at last both blushed and the stranger girl half smiled. By her side sat a gentleman, who Fanny concluded was the young lady's brother. Something in their appearance interested Fanny, and she could not help thinking that they were from the South. That evening as she was walking alone upon the piazza, she was suddenly joined by the unknown lady, who accosted her with, "Pardon me, ma'am, but am I not speaking to Miss Middleton from Kentucky?"

Fanny was too much surprised to answer immediately but soon recovering her self-possession, she answered, "You are, but I have not the pleasure of knowing you."

"I presume not," said the lady. "We have never met before, and yet I knew *you* instantly."

"Knew me! how?" asked Fanny.

"From description," replied the lady. "You have been so accurately described to me by our mutual friend, Miss Woodburn, of New Orleans, that I could not mistake you."

"Florence Woodburn! New Orleans!" exclaimed Fanny. "And are you from New Orleans, and do you know Florence, and have you seen Julia?"

To all these questions the stranger answered "Yes," continuing, "And now let me introduce myself. I am Lida Gibson, but I might as well be *John Smith* for any idea my name will convey. However, I am from New Orleans, and know Florence and your uncle William well. Just before I left the city, I made your sister's acquaintance. When she learned I was coming this way, she said I possibly might see you, and made me the bearer of many messages of love."

Fanny had never heard of Lida Gibson, but it was sufficient that she knew her uncle and Julia, so her hand was immediately offered, and the remainder of the evening the two young girls promenaded the piazza arm in arm, talking of their distant homes and absent friends.

"Where did you see Julia?" asked Fanny.

"Your uncle's house was not quite ready, consequently he and Julia were spending a few days at the residence of Dr. Lacey," answered Lida.

"Dr. Lacey!" said Fanny in some surprise. "Julia at Dr. Lacey's?"

"Yes, why not?" said Lida, laughing merrily at Fanny's manner. "There is nothing improper about that, for Dr. Lacey's father was then absent, and his mother, for the time, staid with her son. I fancied it was not at all unpleasant either to Dr. Lacey or Julia, that they were thus thrown together, and I should not wonder if the Doctor should one day call you *sister!*"

Lida Gibson, whom our readers will recollect as having met at Mabel Mortimer's party in New Orleans, was a thoughtless, but kind-hearted girl, and never felt happier than when employed in canvassing matches. On the morning when the Cameron party arrived at the Springs, she had sent her brother to learn the names of the new comers. On his return he mentioned Fanny Middleton as being one of the new arrivals, so 'twas not surprising that Lida should so readily recognize her.

As days passed on Lida, too, heard of the supposed engagement between Fanny and Frank Cameron, and for once kept silent upon the subject, at least in Fanny's presence. Dearly as she loved to discuss such matters, she felt there was something in the character of her new friend which forbade an approach to any thing like jesting about so personal an affair as one's own engagement. She, however, fully believed the report; for everything she saw tended to confirm it, and she was anxious to return home, that she might carry the important news to Julia and Dr. Lacey. Poor Fanny! The clouds were gathering darkly about her, but she, all unconscious of the consequence, talked, laughed, rode and sang with Frank, never thinking that she was thus confirming Lida in a belief which would tend to remove Dr. Lacey farther and farther from her. Could Lida have heard a conversation, which, one evening, took place between Mrs. Cameron and Fanny, different, very different, would have been the report which she carried back.

One evening as Fanny, Lida and Gertrude were walking upon the piazza, a servant came, saying that Mrs. Cameron desired to see Miss Middleton in her room. Fanny immediately obeyed the summons, and as soon as she had gone Lida laughingly congratulated Gertrude upon the prospect of having so pleasant a sister. Gertrude smilingly received Miss Gibson's congratulations, "for," thought she, "even if Fanny does not marry Frank, Miss Gibson will probably never know it, as she is to leave in a few days."

Let us now with Fanny repair to Mrs. Cameron's room, but not like her wondering *why* she was sent for. We well know why, and consequently are prepared for the look of mingled indignation and astonishment, which appeared on Fanny's face when she learned that Mrs. Cameron was pleading the cause of her son! Fanny answered, "Madam, I have always entertained the highest respect for your son, but I must confess it is lessened if it is with his knowledge you are thus speaking to me."

Mrs. Cameron, who had at first intimated that it was Frank's request that she should thus intercede for him, now saw her mistake, and veering about, declared, what indeed was true, that Frank was wholly ignorant of the whole. Then followed a long, eloquent speech, in which Mrs. Cameron by turns tried to coax, flatter, importune, or frighten Fanny into a compliance with her wishes, but Fanny could only repeat her first answer: "I cannot, Mrs. Cameron, I cannot marry Frank. I acknowledge that I like him, but only as I would love a brother. Further remonstrance is useless, for I shall never marry him."

"And why not?" asked Mrs. Cameron. "Do you love another? Are you engaged to another?"

"I cannot answer these questions," said Fanny. "Frank knows my reason and has my permission to give it to you." Then rising, she added, "I suppose our conference is now ended, and with your leave I will retire."

Mrs. Cameron nodded her head in assent and Fanny immediately left the room. A moment after she quitted the apartment Gertrude entered, all impatience to know her mother's success.

"Baffled, baffled," was Mrs. Cameron's reply to her interrogatories. "I can do nothing with her. She is as stubborn as a mule, and we shall either have to conjure up for some reason why the engagement was broken off, or else run the risk of being well laughed at among our circle in New-York."

A few days after this, Lida Gibson started for the South, promising Fanny that she would see Julia as soon as possible after her return home. Ere long Mrs. Cameron, too, was seized with a desire to return to the city. The remainder of the party made no objections, and accordingly Mr. and Mrs. Stanton, Mrs. Cameron, Frank and Gertrude were soon in New-York.

Soon after their return, Mrs. Cameron said, in speaking of Fanny, "that 'twas quite doubtful whether Frank would marry her or not. She was so young, and had, too, so many suitors in Kentucky, that she probably would soon forget him, and for her part she was pleased enough to have it so."

## Chapter XIX

Summer was gone, and the first bright sunny days of autumn had come.

Again in Kate Wilmot's home, were tears wept and blessings breathed, as Mr. and Mrs. Wilmot bade farewell to their "children," as they affectionately called all three of the individuals who were that morning to start for their home in Kentucky.

"God bless you Kate, my darling Kate," said Mrs. Wilmot, as she fondly kissed her only child. Then turning to Fanny, she said, "And you, too, my other daughter, you have my love and earnest prayers for your happiness."

Mr. Wilmot could not speak, but his feelings were not less deep, as he embraced his child and shook the hands of Mr. Miller and Fanny. Old Hector, too, shared in the general sorrow, but for some undefinable reason he seemed to cling more closely to Fanny. He would look up in her face and howl, as if he knew that *she* was leaving him for ever. "Noble Hector!" said Fanny, "and do you indeed love me so well?" then kneeling down by him, she drew from her neck a tiny locket, in which was a daguerreotype of herself. To this she attached a blue ribbon, which she fastened around Hector's neck, saying, "I cannot stay with you, Hector, but you shall have my likeness." Afterwards when strangers visited at the house, and marvelled at Hector's unusual neck gear, they were shown the fair, sweet face, which looked forth from the golden casing, and were told the story of the young girl, whose presence had been like sunshine in Richard Wilmot's darkened home.

Mr. Miller was not willing that Fanny should leave New-York without having first visited Niagara. Accordingly, they stopped at the Falls, and were there joined by Mr. and Mrs. Stanton and Frank, the latter of whom was desirous of seeing Fanny as long as possible. He accompanied them to Buffalo, and staid upon the boat which was to bear them away until the last bell rang out its warning. As he was leaving them Kate playfully asked if they were taking any thing of his with them. "Yes, every thing, every thing," he answered.

Soon the steamer was moving proudly over the blue waters of Lake Erie. On the upper deck our Kentucky friends were waving their handkerchiefs to Frank, who stood upon the wharf as long as one bright-haired girl could be distinguished by the light of the harvest moon, whose rays fell calmly upon the placid waters.

In a few days Mr. Middleton again folded to his bosom his Sunshine, now more precious than ever, because as he said, "He'd lain awake a heap o' nights, worryin' about her. The dogs had howled, the death watches had ticked in the wall, and every thing had carried on, t'other side up, ever since she'd been gone. But look, Nancy," continued he to his wife, "she's fattin' up right smart. Her journey has done her a heap of good, and I'm glad I let her go."

The blacks now crowded round, delighted to welcome home their young mistress, who had a kind word and some little gift for each. Particularly were Aunt Katy and Aunt Judy pleased with the present of a tasty lace cap, whose value was greatly increased from the fact that they were bought in New-York city. In these simple creatures' estimation, New-York and Frankfort were the largest places in the world. "I s'pose," said Aunt Katy, "that this New-York is mighty nigh three times as large as Frankfort!"

"Three times as large!" repeated Fanny. "Why yes, Katy, *forty* times as large."

From that time Aunt Katy looked upon Fanny as one not long for this world! "'Tain't in natur," said she, "that she should stay long. Allus was peart like and forrud, and now has been ridin' in the railroad all over the airth, and hain't got lost nuther, besides a sailin' along in the steam engine over the salt water."

It was indeed marvellous how much Fanny had seen, and when she came to tell the wonder-stricken negroes of the cataract of Niagara, their amazement knew no bounds. Our friend Bobaway did not fail to ease himself by a round of sommersets, his usual manner of expressing surprise or pleasure. At the same time he whispered to Lucy, that "He's mistaken if Miss Fanny wan't tellin' 'em a stretcher this time," for which declaration, Lucy rewarded him with a smart box on the ear, saying, "Is you no better manners than to 'cuse white folks of lyin'? Miss Fanny never'd got as well as she is if she'd picked up a mess of lies to tell us."

Fanny's health was indeed much improved, and for a day or two after her return home, she bounded about the house and grounds as lightly and merrily as she had done in childhood. Mr. Middleton noticed the change and was delighted. "I b'lieve she's forgettin' that paltry Doctor," said he, but he was wrong.

The third day after her return she was sitting with her parents, relating to them an account of her journey, when Ike entered the room. He had been sent to the post-office and now came up to Fanny saying, "There, I done got this air," at the same time handing her a letter, which she instantly saw was from her sister. Eagerly taking it, she said, "A letter from Julia. I am so delighted. It is a long time since I have heard from her." Then quickly breaking the seal, she commenced reading it.

Gradually as she read there stole over her face a strange expression. It was a look of despair,—of hope utterly crushed, but she finished the letter, and then mechanically passing it to her father, she said, "Read it; it concerns us all," and then rising she went to her own room, leaving her father to read and swear over Julia's letter at his leisure. That he did so no one will doubt when they learn its contents.

The first page was filled with assurances of love; the second congratulated Fanny upon her engagement with Frank, but chided her for suffering Lida Gibson to be the bearer of the news. "Why did you not write to me yourself?" said she;—"that is the way I shall do, and now to prove my words, you will see how confiding I am." Then followed the intelligence that Dr. Lacey had, the night before, offered his *heart* and hand, and of course had been accepted. You will not wonder at it," she wrote, "for you know how much I have always loved him. I was, however, greatly surprised, when he told me he always preferred me to you, but was prevented from telling me so by my silly engagement with Mr. Wilmot and my supposed affection for him." The letter ended by saying that Dr. Lacey would accompany her home some time during the latter part of October, when their marriage would probably take place. There was also a P.S. in which Julia wrote, "Do, Fan., use your influence with the old man, and make him fix up the infernal old air castle. I'd as soon be married in the horse barn as there."

This, then, was the letter, which affected Fanny so, and called all of Uncle Joshua's biggest oaths into use. Mrs. Middleton tried to calm her husband, and reminded him of his promise not to swear. "I know it," he said, "I know I promised not to swar, and for better than two months I hain't swore, but I can't help it now. And yet I expected it. I know'd 'twould be so when I let Tempest go to Orleans. But he'll run himself into a hornet's neast, and I ain't sure but it's jest the punishment for him."

"Why, then, do you rave so?" asked Mrs. Middleton.

"Because," answered her husband, "when I let Tempest go, I'd no idee Sunshine cared so much for him. If I had I'd have slung a halter round Tempest's neck and tied her up in the hoss barn she likes so well!"

The old man was evidently piqued at Julia's thrust at his old house. "Fix up! A heap I'll fix up for her to be married," continued he.

"Then you intend to give your consent?" said Mrs. Middleton.

"Consent! Who's asked any consent?" replied he, "and 'tain't likely they will nuther; and if I should refuse, Tempest wouldn't mind clamberin' out of the chimbly to run away, and the Doctor has showed himself jest as mean. No;—he may have her and go to the old boy for all of Josh. But what's that about this Cameron. I hope 'tis so, but I'm mighty feared it ain't. Sunshine can't love two at a time."

While Mr. Middleton was thus expending his fury Fanny was alone in her room, struggling hard to subdue the bitter feelings which were rising in her heart. Until now she had not been aware how much she loved Dr. Lacey. True, she had said it was impossible she could ever marry him; and she had believed she was trying to forget him; but ever in her heart she had, perhaps unconsciously, cherished a half-formed belief that all would yet be well, and when she refused the noble, generous heart which Frank Cameron laid at her feet, it was with a vague hope that Dr. Lacey would yet be hers. But now every hope was gone. "There is nothing left for me," said Fanny, "but woe, woe!" 'Twas fearful,—the tide of sorrow which swept over the young girl, but amid the wild storm of passion came the echo of a still small voice, whispering of one who loves with a more than earthly love, who never proves faithless,—never fails. Fanny listened to the Spirit's pleadings and resolved that henceforth she would seek to place her affections where "there is no variableness, neither shadow of turning."

The whirlwind of excitement passed over, leaving no trace to mark its passage, save a fixed, calm expression of features, which troubled Mr. Middleton more than a more violent demonstration of feeling would have done.

The week following the receipt of Julia's letter Mr. Middleton had business which took him to Frankfort. Fanny accompanied him and remained several days. The morning after her arrival she and Mr. Stanton were walking upon the upper balcony at Mrs. Crane's, when they were joined by Ashton, who had returned from New Orleans a few days before. He had always been a frequent visitor there, but since his return his visits had been more frequent and of longer duration. There was to him something very fascinating about Stanton's fair bride, and yet he always felt uneasy when with her, for her manners and appearance reminded him of the past, but in what way he could not tell.

This morning, however, the mystery was explained. Soon after his appearance on the balcony, Nellie pointed to a gentleman, who was crossing the street and inquired his name. On being told, she replied, "He looks very much like a Mr. Barnard I used to know years ago in ——," mentioning the town where she was born.

"Used to know where?" asked Ashton quickly.

Nellie repeated the name and Ashton said, "Why, that's my native town, and I knew Mr. Barnard well." Then as if the light of a sudden revelation fell upon him, he added, "And your name, too, was Nellie Ashton? I once had a sister Nellie, on whose rosy cheeks I dropped a tear the night I ran away to sea. Can it be that you are that Nellie?"

A few moments more sufficed for them to discover what we have long surmised, viz., that Henry Ashton and Nellie Stanton were brother and sister. The surprise and pleasure of their recognition is better imagined than described. We will only say that when Stanton, on his return from the office, stepped out upon the balcony in quest of his wife, he was greatly shocked at beholding her in Ashton's arms, and his amazement was increased, when he saw that she not only suffered his caresses, but also returned them in a manner highly displeasing to the young husband. Fanny, however, soon explained all, and Stanton gladly received Ashton as a newly found brother.

It is unnecessary for us to repeat what Nellie and her brother had to relate concerning themselves since the night when Ashton so unceremoniously took leave of his home. With the important points in their history the reader is already acquainted, so for the present we leave them, while we take a brief glance at Mrs. Carrington. The reader will doubtless think that for once in her life that estimable lady has done a good deed, although her motive was not the best in the world. Before Julia went to New Orleans, Mrs. Carrington so far overcame her dislike as to ask her to write. Julia did not promise to do so, but probably concluded she would, for soon after her arrival in New Orleans, she wrote to her a letter, in which she hinted at the probable result of her visit. She was then a guest of Dr. Lacey, and she spoke of his attention and politeness in the most extravagant terms. This so provoked Mrs. Carrington that she determined at once to write to Dr. Lacey, and give him an insight into Julia's real character.

The letter was accordingly written. We must do Mrs. Carrington the justice to say, that though her object in writing was purely selfish, she asserted nothing in her letter but what she knew to be strictly true. She was ignorant of Julia's conduct concerning Fanny, consequently she said nothing upon that head, but she spoke of her generally deceitful character, and mentioned several instances, in which she had not hesitated to stoop to the basest falsehood for the accomplishment of her purpose.

As she was folding the letter, it occurred to her that by some accident Julia might possibly get hold of it, "and then," thought she, "she will recognize my handwriting, and curiosity will impel her to open the letter, after which she wouldn't hesitate a moment to destroy it."

The next moment Mrs. Carrington was rapping at the door of Mrs. Miller's room. Kate opened it and was greatly surprised at beholding her visitor, who seldom came there. Mrs. Carrington, however, smilingly presented her letter to Mr. Miller, saying that she had business with Dr. Lacey, which rendered it necessary for her to write to him, and as she did not care to have the post-office clerks gossip about her writing to a gentleman, she wished him to direct it for her. Mr. Miller complied with her request and the next morning the important document was on its way to New Orleans. As our readers have twice made the voyage of the Mississippi, they will not refuse, again, to run the risk of its floating snags, sandbars, and boat-races;

so stepping on board the same steamer which bears Mrs. Carrington's letter, we will once more visit Louisiana, and stopping with Dr. Lacey, will see how much of Julia's letter to her sister was true.

# Chapter XX

The first three weeks of Julia's stay in New Orleans were, as we have learned, spent at the house of Dr. Lacey. His mother was present, and although she readily acknowledged the uncommon beauty of her fair visitor, yet from the first she disliked her.

The servants, too, as if adopting the opinion of their mistress, felt and expressed among themselves an aversion to the "evil-eyed lady," as they termed Julia. Aunt Dilsey, in particular, soon had her own reason for disliking her. The second day after Julia's arrival, as she was strolling through the yard, she encountered Andrew Jackson, a bright little fellow, three years of age, and Aunt Dilsey's only son. Jack, as he was usually called, was amusing himself by seeing how far he could *spit!* Unfortunately he spit too far, and hit Miss Julia's pink muslin. In an instant her white, slender fingers were buried in his wool. His screams soon brought Aunt Dilsey to the rescue. Upon learning the dreadful crime of which Jack had been guilty, she snatched him from Julia's grasp, and hurried him into the house without a word. From that time Dilsey was Julia's sworn enemy, and Jack was taught to make up faces at her whenever he could do so without being discovered.

The servants, however, were too well trained to manifest any open disrespect, for they knew she was "marster's guest," and as such, was entitled to every possible attention.

When first she arrived Dr. Lacey felt exceedingly uncomfortable, for her presence constantly reminded him of the past, and his reminiscences of Julia were not particularly pleasant. Gradually this feeling wore away, for she appeared greatly changed. There was a softness,—a gentleness, in her manner, which seemed to Dr. Lacey like Fanny, and then her voice, too, was so like her sister's that ere long she ceased to be disagreeable to him, and instead of avoiding her society, as at first he had done, he now sought it.

Julia saw her advantage, and determined to follow it up. Nothing could exceed her extreme amiability, and apparent sweetness of disposition. Even Mrs. Lacey was partially deceived, and concluded she had been too hasty in her estimation of Miss Middleton. Still she watched her son's movements narrowly, and hoped he had no intentions of making Julia his wife.

She was in New Orleans three weeks before her uncle's house was in readiness; but at the end of that time, she, together with Dr. Lacey, Mabel Mortimer and Florence Woodburn, were about to exchange the heat and dust of the city for a cooler residence near the lake. The day before they left was hot and sultry, and in the morning Julia sought the shade of a large vine-wreathed summer-house which stood in the garden, near by the tree, under which Rondeau had buried his master's letter.

One word now about our old friend Rondeau. The buried letter had cost him a world of trouble. He was constantly fearful lest he should be detected. Particularly was he afraid that the author of the letter, failing to receive an answer, would write again, and thus he might be exposed. Twice had he dug up the epistle upon occasions when he fancied some one of his master's letters bore a similar superscription. In this way, he had become tolerably familiar with Mr. Miller's handwriting, which was rather peculiar, being a large, heavy, black hand.

On the morning when Julia was snugly ensconced in the summer-house, Rondeau returned from the post-office in great tribulation.

"What's up now?" asked Leffie, whom Rondeau drew aside, with a dolefully-grave face.

"Nothing's up," answered Rondeau, "but the letter has got to come up! I ain't going to feel like I was a whipped dog any longer. I'll confess all to Marster George, for see, here's another just like the buried one." So saying he held up Mrs. Carrington's letter, on the envelope of which was Mr. Miller's writing.

Leffie offered no remonstrance, and as Aunt Dilsey just then screamed for her, Rondeau went alone to the garden and proceeded to disinter the buried document. 'Twas but the work of a moment, and could Julia have been cooling herself in Greenland, as she ought to have been, all would have ended well. And now I suppose some indignant reader will say, "Why didn't you put her in Greenland, then, or some worse place?" but patience, patience, a little longer. You would have us tell things just as they were, I suppose, so we must not only suffer Miss Julia to be in the summer-house, but we must also allow her to be a spectator of Rondeau's proceedings.

She was greatly surprised when she saw him take from the cigar-box a much soiled, yellowish-looking letter, and she could not help feeling that in some way it concerned herself. Suddenly appearing, she startled Rondeau by saying, "What are you doing? Whose is that? Give it to me?"

Rondeau was anxious to conceal from her his long-buried treasure, and he passed her the other. She took it and recognizing Mr. Miller's writing, knew also that Rondeau had given her the wrong one, so she said in a commanding tone, "What does all this mean? Give me the other one immediately."

The submissive African, ever obedient to his superiors, handed her the other letter, and then in a few words told his story, and announced his intention of confessing all to his master, at the same time extending his hand to take the letters. But Julia did not mean he should have them, and she said coaxingly, "You have done very wrong, Rondeau, and your master will undoubtedly be very angry, but I will take them to him and intercede for you, as you are on the whole a pretty fine fellow. He'll forgive you for me. I know he will; but mind, don't *you* say any thing to him about it until you've seen me again."

So saying she returned to the house, and going to her room, bolted the door. After which, breaking the seal of the oldest letter, she deliberately read it through, occasionally uttering a malediction against Mr. Miller, thanking the good luck which brought it to her hands instead of Dr. Lacey's, and making remarks generally. Said she, "Mighty good opinion Mr. *Quilting-frames* has of me (alluding to Mr. Miller's height), glad I know his mind. A heap of good the answer to this did him, and his doll wife, too. Hadn't *I* better answer it myself? I'd write after this fashion:—'Mr. Miller,—At first I thought I would treat your letter with silent contempt, but recently I have concluded to write and thank you to mind your own business. By order of George Lacey, Esq.—Julia Middleton, Secretary,'—Yes, that would serve the meddling old Yankee Dictionary right," continued she, and then as her eye fell upon the remaining letter, she added, "Yes, I'll read this one, too, and see what new thing I'm guilty of!"

As soon as she broke it open and glanced at the handwriting, she knew it to be from Mrs. Carrington, "What now?" said she, "what has Mrs. Carrington got to say about me?"

A rapid perusal of the letter showed her what Mrs. Carrington had to say, and she continued her remarks as follows: "She has described me quite accurately. I didn't suppose she knew me so well. I wonder who'll write next! It seems every body is in league against me, but I'm enough for any body there is in Kentucky; and," she added, in a lower tone, "I wouldn't hesitate to try my strength with Satan himself;" but even then the dark girl trembled as she thought there was a God, whom none could withstand, and who, one day, would inevitably overtake her.

Quickly as possible she drove such unpleasant thoughts from her mind, and then tried to devise the best plan for managing Mrs. Carrington. "For Mr. Miller's letter," said she, "I care nothing. It was written so long ago that he has ceased expecting an answer, but I well know Mrs. Carrington's designs, and she will continue to write until she receives some reply. I have once successfully counterfeited Dr. Lacey's handwriting, and can do it again. I'll send her something that will quiet her nerves better than assafoetida!"

This settled, she went in quest of Rondeau, whom she told, that, as she had expected, his master was very much displeased, "but," said she, "after I interceded a while for you, he said he would forgive you on condition that you were never guilty of the like again, and never mention the subject to him in any way, as it makes him angry to talk about it." To both these conditions Rondeau readily agreed, and Julia left him, thinking she was safe in that quarter.

Several days after, Mrs. Carrington received a letter which she supposed came from Dr. Lacey. In it she was coolly requested not to interfere in other people's matters, and told that any efforts on her part to engraft herself into Dr. Lacey's good graces by maligning Julia, would be useless, and only serve to confirm him in his present low opinion of her, while, at the same time, it would increase the high estimation in which he held Miss Middleton!

After that Mrs. Carrington troubled Dr. Lacey with no more letters, but busied herself in anticipating the capture of a wealthy gentleman, who, Ashton told her, was, in the course of two or three months, coming on from Charleston, South Carolina.

The scene now changes from Dr. Lacey's to the "Indian Nest," on the lake shore. 'Twas a charming spot, and looked as if intended only for the habitation of the pure and innocent. Yet even there, was crafty ambition and base deceit. Julia was there, eagerly seeking to wind her coils securely around her long-watched-for prey. To all eyes but her own she seemed not likely to succeed, for though Dr. Lacey admired her, and possibly treated her with more attention than he did either Mabel or Florence, yet his heart still turned to Fanny, and for hours he would sit, talking to Julia of her sister, while she schooled herself to answer all his questions without one sign of impatience.

Occasionally she would speak to Dr. Lacey of his cousin, young Stanton, and would tell how much pleasure Fanny seemed to take in *his* society. But this produced no effect, for Dr. Lacey had learned from Stanton himself of his approaching marriage with Miss Ashton. Then Julia pulled another string and expatiated so largely upon Frank Cameron's sayings and doings, that Dr. Lacey became really uneasy, for recently he had thought seriously of again writing to Fanny, and now he determined to do so.

Without knowing it, Julia was herself the means of causing this determination to be carried into effect. One night she and Dr. Lacey had been strolling for more than an hour through the many delightful walks in the garden, which lay upon the lake shore. To her great satisfaction, they were entirely alone, for Mr. Middleton and Florence were engaged in their favorite game of chess, while Mabel was eagerly listening to Ashton, who was relating to her some of his India adventures. Mabel had good sense enough to know that her efforts to win Dr. Lacey would be useless, and rather reluctantly she had given him up. Now her eyes grew brighter and her heart beat faster whenever Ashton approached. But, fair Mabel, your hopes are all in vain.

> "For Inez, the Spaniard,
> Is o'er the blue sea,
> And the heart thou wouldst win
> Is not destined for thee."

As we have before said, Julia was delighted at having Dr. Lacey thus to herself, and she resolved to increase the favorable impression she knew she had already made upon him. Most admirably was her part played. Fanny herself could not have been more gentle and agreeable, than was Julia, as together with Dr. Lacey, she traversed the broad walks of the garden. Sweet and soothing were the words she poured into his ear, occasionally administering a little well-timed flattery, and wishing, as she had once done before to another individual in similar circumstances, that Dr. Lacey had been her brother. He did not, like Mr. Wilmot, follow up this wish by a proposition that as he was not her brother, she should accept him for a husband, but he pressed the hand, which, with seeming unconsciousness, had been placed on his, and said, "God knows how ardently I once hoped to be your brother, Julia."

"And would you then have loved me?" said Julia, "me whom few have ever loved, because they did not know me; say, would you have loved me as a sister?"

The face of her who awaited Dr. Lacey's answer was very beautiful, while tears moistened the long eyelashes, which veiled the large, bright eyes, and the tones of her voice, now more like Fanny's than ever, thrilled his every nerve. What wonder, then, that his lips for the first time touched the polished brow of the tempter, as he said, "It would be no hard task, Julia, to love you with *more* than a brother's love."

"One more well aimed blow," thought Julia, "and I shall have him at my feet;" but she was mistaken. Between herself and Dr. Lacey there rose the image of one, the remembrance of whom had a power to prevent the utterance of words, which otherwise might have been spoken.

Abruptly changing the conversation, he drew her rather reluctantly towards the house, which they reached just in time to hear Florence exclaim as she scattered the chessmen over the floor, "Why, Uncle Billy Middleton, what do you mean? Put yourself up to be played for, and then cheat me; shame, shame."

"What is all this about?" asked Dr. Lacey, having some inkling of the truth.

"Why," answered Florence, "you see, Mr. Middleton has conceived a fatherly affection for me, and as he is rather rusty in such matters, he could think of no better way of proposing, than to put himself up as a prize, and tell me if I beat him in playing chess, he would be mine, or in other words, make me Mrs. Billy Middleton."

"And who beat?" asked Julia.

"Why, Mr. Middleton was ill-mannered enough to win," said Florence, "but then, it was such fun to see how desperately he played for fear I should get him! Now, Dr. Lacey, I suppose you have been proposing to Julia in the real old orthodox way, but that is too common. You must sit down at the chess-board and let Julia play for you," and she pushed them both towards the chairs, which she and Mr. Middleton had just vacated.

Julia did not refuse, but Dr. Lacey, freeing himself from Florence, said, "Excuse me to-night, Miss Woodburn. Perhaps at some other time I will comply with your request," then bowing, he left the verandah and went to his own room.

When there he strove to recall the events of the evening, and the words he had involuntarily spoken to Julia. "Why is it," said he, "that I feel so uneasy whenever I am alone with her? Is it that I love her and am afraid I shall tell her so? No, that cannot be. I do not love her; and yet, next to Fanny, she is more agreeable to me than anyone else."

Memories of other days came thronging about him, and he then resolved again to write, and beseech Fanny at least to grant him her second love, even if her first, best affections had been given to another.

"Suppose she refuse you," seemed whispered in his ear.

It must have been some evil spirit which prompted the reply. "Then I will marry Julia, as being next and nearest to Fanny." His resolution once taken, he proceeded to carry it into effect. The letter was written, and over Dr. Lacey came a sense of relief,—a feeling that he had escaped from something, he knew not what. But she, who was upon his track, was more wily, more crafty, than any thing he had ever imagined.

This time, however, her interference was not necessary, for early next morning, a carriage drew up in front of the Indian Nest. From it sprang Lida Gibson, who had recently returned from New-York. She was full of talk, and within an hour after her arrival, the story of Fanny's engagement with Frank Cameron had been repeated in Dr. Lacey's hearing, at least three times.

"It must be true," said Lida, "for every one said so, and their actions proclaimed it, if nothing more; besides, Mr. Cameron's sister Gertrude herself told me it was so."

"I am not surprised," said Julia and her uncle both.

For Julia's opinion Dr. Lacey possibly might not have cared, but when Mr. Middleton too added his testimony, the matter was settled. *The letter was not sent.*

During the day Lida wondered much why Dr. Lacey stayed so closely in his room. "I should think he would roast in there," said she. "I do wonder what he is about."

"I fancy," answered Florence, "that he still loves Fanny, and now that she is engaged, he is staying alone until he gets his rebellious heart tied up."

When Lida afterwards learned the truth, she expressed a wish that her tongue might have been cut out, ere she had been the bearer of news which caused so much trouble.

While Dr. Lacey was securely bolted in his room, nerving himself to bear this fresh disappointment, and striving to drive each thought of Fanny from him, Julia too was alone, and busily engaged. What pains she took to rub and soil those tiny sheets of paper, until they assumed a worn and crumpled look. Then dipping her finger in the silver goblet at her side, what perfect *tear blots* she made, and how she exulted over the probable success of her morning's work. When it was finished, she placed it in her portfolio, and waited for a favorable opportunity.

It came not that day, however, for save at meal time Dr. Lacey made not his appearance. To Mr. Middleton's inquiries concerning the reason of his seclusion, he replied, "that he was busy with important matters;" but his abstracted manner led Mr. Middleton to believe what he had long suspected, viz., that Dr. Lacey's heart was wholly centered upon Fanny, and that the news of her coming marriage was the cause of his unhappiness.

Next morning's sun rose clear and bright, but it brought a day which Dr. Lacey long, long remembered, and which Julia, in the bitterness of her heart, cursed many and many a time. In the early part of the morning, Dr. Lacey wandered down to a small arbor, which stood at the foot of the garden. He had not been there long before Julia, too, came tripping down the walk, with her portfolio and drawing pencil. So *absorbed* was she in her own thoughts that she of course did not see Dr. Lacey until she had entered the arbor; then, with a most becoming blush and start, she said, "Pray pardon me for disturbing you. I had no idea you were here."

Dr. Lacey, of course, insisted upon her staying. She knew he would, and sitting down, she busied herself in looking over the contents of her portfolio. Suddenly she heaved a deep sigh, and Dr. Lacey looked up just in time to see her wipe something from her eyes, or pretend to, which *must* have been tears. At the same time she hastily thrust a paper back into her portfolio, which she immediately shut.

"What is the matter?" asked Dr. Lacey. "For whom was that sigh, and those tears?"

"For poor Fan.," answered Julia. "I have accidentally found a part of an old journal, which she kept while Mr. Wilmot was living."

"May I see it?" asked Dr. Lacey.

Julia seemed at first reluctant, but finally replied, "Perhaps it will be as well to let you do so, for you may then judge more kindly of Fanny;" and she placed in his hands the soiled sheets of paper, which we saw in her room.

Leaning back, she watched him while he read. As we have as much right to read Fanny's journal as Dr. Lacey, we will give a few brief extracts:—

*April.*—"Cease your wild beatings, my heart. Mr. Wilmot is promised to Julia. He will never be mine, but nought can prevent my loving him; aye, for ever and ever."

*August 1st.* "I do not believe I am indifferent to Mr. Wilmot, but he will be true to his vows,—he will wed Julia; and this doctor that bothers me so, what of him? Why, he is wealthy, and high, and handsome,—but I do not love him; and yet, if he offers himself I shall say yes, for, as Mrs. Carrington says, 'he is a great *catch.*'"

*Sept. 5th.* "Mr. Wilmot is dead, and with him died my poor, poor heart. Had he lived, he possibly might have turned to me, for Julia knew how much I loved him. Dear, generous Julia, how I wish Dr. Lacey would love her, for she is more worthy of him than I am."

*Jan. 1st.* Heigh ho, I'm engaged to Dr. Lacey! Who would think it? Now am I happy? Oh, no.—Out in the graveyard lies one who could have made me happy. Ought I thus to deceive Dr. Lacey? Why, yes; if he is satisfied, it is well enough. I am ambitious, and if I can't marry for love, I will for money. And then he's given me so beautiful a piano. Oh, I hope he'll send me more presents after he gets home!"

*Jan. 15th.* "Dr. Lacey has gone, and I feel relieved. But just think of it,—*Julia loves him devotedly.* I wish he knew it. She has always loved him and tries to make me do the same. She read me a sermon to-day two hours long, about my duty. Fudge on my duty! As long as I can make *Joshua* and Dr. Lacey think I'm all sunshine, it's no matter if my *love* is all moonshine."

This journal was interspersed here and there with *tears,* and was so exact an imitation of Fanny's writing that Dr. Lacey was completely duped. He, however, wondered that Julia should show it to him. She had foreseen this, and as he was reading the last few lines, she was looking over her portfolio. Suddenly springing up she snatched the paper from his hands, saying, "Oh, what have I done? I've shown you the wrong part of the journal. I did not mean you to see *this.* What *shall* I do? You'll hate Fanny and despise me."

"Why despise you?" asked Dr. Lacey.

"Because," replied Julia, "you will dislike me for the foolish thing which Fan wrote about me. I could not help her writing it."

"And is it true?" asked Dr. Lacey.

"Oh, you must not ask me that—I can't tell,—I shan't tell," and seizing her portfolio, Julia darted off towards the house, thinking possibly she should be pursued. But she was not.

During the reading of the journal, Dr. Lacey's heart seemed to go through a benumbing process, which rendered it perfectly palsied. No emotion either of love or anger did he feel towards Fanny. She was naught to him.

And how did the knowledge that Julia loved him affect him? Answer, any man, whether your wounded pride is never soothed by woman's sympathy and love, come in what garb it may. And in Dr. Lacey's case, it was a being of wondrous beauty, who knew well what she was about, and had marked each inch of ground ere she trod upon it. What marvel then that Dr. Lacey turned towards her? *You* would have done so; aye, perchance, sooner than he did.

That evening after supper, as Dr. Lacey was walking upon the verandah, Florence approached him, saying, "Come, Dr. Lacey, now fulfill your promise of playing with Julia," at the same time leading him towards the place where her companions were seated. "Now," said she, placing the chessboard in his hands, "I am mistress of ceremonies. We will have a fair understanding. If Julia beats, you shall be hers; if you beat, Mabel and Lida shall draw cuts for you. Do you agree to it?'

"Certainly," was Dr. Lacey's reply, at the same time seating himself opposite Julia, who gave him a look of searching inquiry. He understood her and in a low tone answered, "I am in earnest. Do your best."

And she did do her best. With one strong effort of the will, she concentrated all her energies upon that game, which she felt would decide her fate. Dr. Lacey, too, as if resolved to conquer, played most skilfully. The bystanders for a time looked on, and as Lida noticed the livid hue of Julia's face, she said, "Pray, Julia, don't burst a blood-vessel, for may be Dr. Lacey will have you, even if you do not beat."

But the ear she addressed was deaf save to the quiet sound of the chess-men. The contest was long and severe. Nine, ten, eleven, struck the little clock in the hall. One by one the spectators stole away. Florence's parting words were, "If Dr. Lacey beats, be sure and wake us, Julia, so Mabel and Lida can draw cuts."

And now they were alone. Once and only once Julia glanced at the face of her antagonist. It was white and colorless as her own hand, which wandered steadily over the chess-board. The final spell was upon him and he seemed striving hard to shake it off. 'Twas all in vain. The little clock struck the hour of midnight. The game was ended. Julia had won! Dr. Lacey was checkmated!

With one hand he rapidly swept the board of its occupants, while the other he extended towards Julia, saying, "Take it.—'Tis all I can offer, for you well know I have no *heart* to give. My hand and name you have won,— they are yours."

A person less intriguing or determined than Julia, would have scorned to receive a hand so coldly offered. But not so with her. She did not expect any protestations of love, for she knew he felt none. Yet she was hardly satisfied, and resolved upon one movement more ere she accepted what she felt was reluctantly given.

"You are mistaken in me," said she, "if you think I will play for a husband, and then expect him to comply with the terms, unless he chooses to do so."

Dr. Lacey replied, "When I consented to play, I knew what I was about, and I know, too, that you love me. I cannot say the same to you in return, but you are far from being indifferent to me. When I first knew you, I disliked you, for I believed you to be passionate, jealous and designing, nor do I think my opinion of you then was wrong; but you are changed, very much changed. Continue to be what you are now, and we may be happy, for I may learn to love you, but never as fondly, as madly, as I loved your sister; aye, as I could love her again; but enough of this. She was false; she deceived me, and now I will wed you."

And what said Julia to all this? Why, she sat bolt upright, listening attentively while Dr. Lacey expressed his former and present opinion of her. When he had finished, she ventured to acknowledge her love for him; said she had always loved him, and that as his wife she would try to make him happy. Perhaps she was sincere in this, for she did love Dr. Lacey as well as her selfish nature would suffer her to love any one, and she had resolved, if she ever married him, to do all in her power to atone, if possible, for the past.

A half hour longer they conversed of the future, and arranged the plan, which Julia next day wrote to her sister. At last Dr. Lacey exclaimed, "Come, Julia, you must go now; it is getting late, for see,"—pointing to the little clock—but as if astonished at what it had heard, *the clock had stopped!*

## Chapter XXI

Great was Mr. Middleton's surprise when informed by Dr. Lacey of his engagement with Julia. Something in his countenance must have betrayed it, for Dr. Lacey said, "You seem astonished, sir. Are you displeased?"

"Certainly not; I am glad," answered Mr. Middleton. "Yet I confess I was surprised, for I had never thought of such a thing. Once I hoped you would marry Fanny, but since Frank Cameron has rendered that impossible, you cannot do better than take Julia. She is intelligent, accomplished and handsome, and although she has some faults, your influence over her will lead her to correct them."

Unlike this was the reception which the intelligence met with from Dr. Lacey's negroes.

"What's that ar you sayin'?" asked Aunt Dilsey of Rondeau, who was communicating the important news to Leffie.

"You'd better ask," replied Rondeau. "Who do you suppose Marster George is goin' to fetch here to crack our heads for us?"

"Dun know,—Miss Mabel, mebby," said Aunt Dilsey.

"No, sir; Miss Mabel is bad enough, but she can't hold a candle to this one," answered Rondeau.

"You don't mean Miss July," shrieked, rather than asked Aunt Dilsey.

"I don't mean nobody else, mother Dilsey," said Rondeau.

Up flew Aunt Dilsey's hands in amazement, and up rolled her eyes in dismay. "I clar for't," said she, "if Marster George has done made such a fool of hisself, I hope she'll pull his har a heap worse than she did Jack's."

"No danger but what she will, and yours too," was Rondeau's consoling reply.

"Lord knows," said Aunt Dilsey, "fust time she sasses me, I'll run away 'long of Jack and the baby. I'll tie up my new gown and cap in a handkercher this night."

Leffie now proposed that her mother should defer her intended flight until the arrival of the dreaded Julia, while Rondeau added, "Besides, Dilsey, if you should run away, your delicate body couldn't get further than the swamp, where you'd go in up to your neck first lunge, and all marster's horses couldn't draw you out."

This allusion to her size changed the current of Aunt Dilsey's wrath, which now turned and spent itself on Rondeau. Her impression of Julia, however, never changed, although she was not called upon to run away.

Mrs. Lacey, too, received the news of her son's engagement with evident dissatisfaction; but she thought remonstrance would be useless, and she kept silent, secretly praying that Julia might prove better than her fears. In due course of time there came from Kentucky a letter of congratulation from Fanny; but she was so unaccustomed to say or write what she did not feel, that the letter, so far as congratulations were concerned, was a total failure. She, however, denied her engagement with Frank, and this, if nothing else, was sufficient reason why Julia refused to show it to Dr. Lacey. Julia knew the chain by which she held him was brittle and might at any time be broken, and 'twas not strange that she longed for the last days of October, when with Dr. Lacey she would return to Kentucky.

They came at last, and one bright cloudless morning Uncle Joshua got out his carriage and proceeded to Frankfort, where, as he had expected, he met Julia and his future son-in-law. His greeting of the former was kind and fatherly enough, but the moment he saw the latter, he felt, as he afterwards said, an almost unconquerable desire to flatten his nose, gouge his eyes, knock out his teeth, and so forth, which operations would doubtless have greatly astonished Dr. Lacey, and given him what almost every man has, viz., a most formidable idea of his wife's relations.

He, however, restrained his wrath, and when, at a convenient time, Dr. Lacey, with a few ominous "ahems" and made-up coughs, indicated his intention of asking for Julia, Uncle Joshua cut him short by saying, "Never mind, I know what you want. You may have her and welcome. I only wish she would make as good a wife as you will a husband. But mind now, when you find out what for a fury you've got, don't come whinin' round me, for I give you fa'r warnin'."

Here Dr. Lacey thought proper to say that possibly Mr. Middleton did not understand his daughter.

"Not understand her," repeated Mr. Middleton. "What's to hinder? She's my own gal, and I like her well enough; but don't I know she's as fiery as a baker's oven?"

"She is greatly changed," continued Dr. Lacey. "Don't you give her credit for that?"

"Changed!" replied Mr. Middleton. "So's lightnin' changed! It's one of her tricks. Depend on't, you'll find it so." And Mr. Middleton walked off in search of his promising daughter.

Strange as it may seem, the old man's remarks had no other effect upon Dr. Lacey than to cause him to pity Julia, who he fancied was misunderstood and misused. He believed her reformation to be sincere, and could not help feeling that Mr. Middleton was mistaken in his opinion of both his daughters.

After tramping all over the house, banging doors, and shouting at least a dozen times, "Ho! Tempest, whar for gracious' sake are you?" Mr. Middleton at length found his daughter in Mrs. Miller's room consulting with Kate about her bridal dress. Kate, too, was wholly deceived by Julia's gentleness and apparent frankness of manner, and readily complied with her request that she should be with her the two days preceding the marriage, for the purpose of assisting in the arrangement of affairs. This being settled, Mr. Middleton and his daughter started for home, which they reached about sunset.

Julia leaped gaily from the carriage, and running into the house embraced her mother, and received the blacks as affectionately as Fanny herself could have done; then missing her sister, she asked, "Where is Fan., why does she not come to meet me?"

Mrs. Middleton looked inquiringly at her husband, who replied, "No, I hain't told her, jest because she didn't ask me. Sunshine is sick,—sick in bed, and has had the potecary three times."

"Fanny sick?" said Julia. "Where is she? In her room? I will go to her immediately."

But in going to Fanny, it was necessary to pass the parlor, and Julia could not resist the temptation to look in and see, "if the old man had fixed up any."

"Oh, how neat! how pleasant!" was her first exclamation, and truly the cheerless old room had undergone a great renovation. It had been thoroughly cleaned and repainted. The walls were hung with bright, cheerful-looking paper. A handsome carpet covered the floor, while curtains of corresponding beauty shaded the windows. The furniture, tastefully arranged, was nearly all new, and in the waxen flowers, which filled the vases on the mantel-piece, Julia recognized the handiwork of her sister.

Yes, Fanny's love had wrought this change. At first her father had refused to do any thing. "No, I won't," said he. "It's good enough, and if it don't suit lady Tempest, she can go to the hoss barn; that's just fit for 'em."

"Then, father," said Fanny, "do it for my sake. It would please me to have a pleasanter parlor."

This was sufficient. A well-filled purse was placed in Fanny's hands, with liberty to do as she pleased. Then with untiring love, aching heart and throbbing temples, she worked on day after day, until all was completed; parlor, bridal chamber and all. The hangings and drapery of the latter were as white and pure as was she who so patiently worked on, while each fresh beauty added to the room pierced her heart with a deeper anguish, as she thought what and whom it was for. When her mother remonstrated against such unceasing toil, she would smile a sweet, sad smile and say, "Don't hinder me, dear mother; 'tis all I can do to show my love for Julia, and after I am gone they will perhaps think more kindly of me when they know how I worked for them."

At last all was done; the finishing stroke was given, and then came a reaction. Fanny took her bed, and her father, instantly alarmed, called the nearest physician. Dr. Gordon readily saw that Fanny's disease was in her mind, and in reply to Mrs. Middleton's inquiries he frankly told his opinion, and said that unless the cause of her melancholy could be removed the consequence might be fatal.

"Don't tell my husband," said Mrs. Middleton; "his life is bound up in Fanny, and the day that sees her dead will, I fear, also make me a widow." Accordingly Mr. Middleton was deceived into a belief that Fanny's illness was the result of over exertion, and that she would soon recover.

In a day or two she seemed better, but was not able to come down stairs. Indeed she had no desire or intention of doing so until after the wedding, for she felt she could not, would not, see Dr. Lacey for the world. Since the receipt of her sister's letter, she had been given a holier love, a firmer faith, than aught on earth can bestow, and she was now under the influence of religion; of lasting, true religion. This then was the reason why she welcomed her sister so affectionately, and felt no emotion either of resentment or anger towards those who were thus trampling upon the bleeding fibres of her heart.

As Julia kissed the almost transparent brow of her sister, and clasped her thin, white fingers, tears gathered in her eyes, and she thought, "This ruin have I wrought, and for it I must answer;" but not long did she ever suffer her conscience to trouble her, and the next hour she was chatting away to Fanny about the preparations for her wedding, which was to take place one week from that day. Fanny listened as one who heard not. She was praying for more grace, more strength to endure yet a little longer.

Slowly to Julia dragged the days of that week, while to Fanny they sped on rapid wing. And now every thing within and without the house betokened the coming event. Servants scampered hither and thither, thinking they were doing it all, while in reality they were doing nothing. Mrs. Middleton scolded the blacks, and Uncle Joshua scolded Mrs. Middleton, at the same time walking mechanically from the kitchen to the parlor, from the parlor to Fanny's sick-room, and from Fanny's sick-room back to the kitchen, occasionally kicking from his path some luckless kitten, dog, or black baby, which latter set up most lusty yells, just to vary the scene.

In the midst of all this Fanny lay calmly and quietly on her low bed, counting each succeeding sun as it rose and set, bringing nearer and nearer a day she so much dreaded. True to her promise, Kate Miller came two days before the wedding. Fanny was asleep when she entered the room to see her, but on the white, wasted face, Kate's tears fell as she said, "Poor Fanny! I did not know she was so ill."

Mr. Middleton, who was present, muttered: "Yes, cursed be the one who made her so!" He knew not that he cursed his own child.

The next day Mr. William Middleton arrived, bringing the intelligence that Florence and Mabel had accompanied him, and would next evening be present at the wedding. Slowly the last rays of a bright October sun faded in the west, giving no sign of the stormy day which was to succeed. Long after midnight a lone watcher sat by the window in Fanny's room, gazing at the stars, which looked down so quietly from their distant homes, and praying, not for herself, but for Dr. Lacey, that he might be happy with her he had chosen. At last, chilled with the night air, she crept shivering to her pillow, nor woke again until aroused by the fierce moaning of the autumn wind, which shook the casement, and by the sound of the driving rain, which beat against the pane. Yes, the morning which dawned on Julia's bridal day was wild and stormy, but before noon the clouds cleared away, and the afternoon was hot, sultry and oppressive, a precursor of the mightier and more wrathful storm which followed.

About five o'clock there was a noise in the yard, and Kate, who was in Fanny's room, arranging her young friend's hair, looked from the window and said, "It is Dr. Lacey. Julia has looked for him more than three hours."

Quickly Fanny hurried to the window. She could not meet Dr. Lacey face to face, but she wished to look at him once more. She was too late, however. He had entered the house, and soon the sound of his voice reached her ear. He had not been there long ere he asked for Fanny. On being told she was sick, he seemed rather disturbed. Possibly, however, he felt relieved to know she would not be present when he took upon him vows which should have been breathed to her. Ashton, Florence and Mabel now arrived, and soon after came Mr. and Mrs. Stanton, accompanied by Mrs. Carrington, who had been invited because it would not do to slight her, and who came because she had a mind to!

The ceremony was to take place at seven o'clock, and guests each moment arrived, until the parlor seemed nearly full. Alone in her chamber sat Fanny listening to the sounds of mirth, which grated harshly on her ear. Night, dark and stormy, was gathering over the earth, but a darker night lay round the heart of the young girl, as she watched from her window a dense, black pile of clouds, which had appeared in the west, and now increased until the whole sky was overspread, as with a pall of darkness, while distant peals of muttered thunder announced the coming storm.

And now louder roared the howling wind, and brighter the glaring lightning flashed, while fiercer grew the conflict in Fanny's bosom. Her faith was weak, and well-nigh blotted with tears of human weakness. But He, whose power could stay the storm without, could also still the agony within, and o'er the troubled waters of that aching heart, there fell a peaceful calm.

Suddenly the door opened and a creature of wondrous, dazzling beauty appeared. It was Julia, in her bridal robe. She would fain have her sister's blessing ere she descended to the parlor. The struggle was over, and the blessing which Fanny gave her sister, was sincere, but when Julia asked forgiveness for all the evil she had ever done, the reply was prevented by a crash of thunder, so terrific, that Julia trembled with terror, and hastily left the room.

In a moment there was a light step upon the stairs. Fanny knew it was Dr. Lacey, for he soon returned with Julia, and as they passed her door, she heard the merry laugh of Florence, who was bridesmaid. In an instant they were in the parlor, throughout which a general gloom seemed to reign. Perhaps it was owing to the wildness of the storm, which each moment increased in fury. The bridal party took their places, and Uncle Joshua shut his eyes, while the marriage ceremony commenced.

The reader may now accompany me to the borders of yonder wood, where stands a low-roofed building, the property of Mrs. Dunn. There, in a darkened room, lay the widow's only son, raving in the madness of delirium. The fever-flame burned in each vein, and as he tossed from side to side, he would shriek out, "Quick, I tell you, or you are too late. She must not wed him. Don't you know she's doubly, trebly, steeped in guilt? Go quick, I tell you, and stop it."

Mrs. Dunn could only weep, for she knew not, dreamed not, what her son could mean. Soon he grew calm, and fell into a deep sleep. When he awoke, Billy Jeffrey, who lived near, was sitting by him. To Mrs. Dunn's delight, Joseph was sane, and calling her to him, he said, "Isn't Julia Middleton to be married to-night?"

"She is," answered his mother.

"At what hour?"

"At seven."

"What time is it now?"

"Half-past six," replied Mrs. Dunn.

"It must not be," said Joseph, and turning to Bill he added, "Listen, William, to what I have to tell, then speed away, on the lightning's wing, and tear her from the altar; take her from his side, I say, and put there the other one, the pale, golden-haired one;" then, as he noticed the vacant look on Bill's face, he added, "Oh, no, you can't tell it. You wouldn't understand it. Mother, bring me a pen and some paper."

The paper was brought, and as soon as possible Joseph wrote a confession of his own and Julia's guilt. "Now, Bill," said he, "run for your life, and give this to Dr. Lacey. Do it for the sake of Fanny."

Bill needed no second bidding. His obtuse intellect had gathered that in some way Fanny was in danger, and away he flew over bushes, briers, rocks and ditches. But alas! the way was long and dark, and ere he was aware of it, he was precipitated into one of the sink-holes, which are so common in the limestone soil of Kentucky. The fall sprained his ankle, but gathering himself up, he continued on, slowly and painfully.

Meantime delirium had again crept over Joseph Dunn, and he forgot that he had sent Billy, but concluded he must go himself. Watching a time when his mother was from the room, he arose, and throwing on his double-gown, went forth into the storm, and was soon far on his road towards Mr. Middleton's.

The man of God had scarcely finished the second paragraph of the Episcopal marriage ceremony, beginning with, "I require and charge you both," &c., when a shriek, wild, unearthly and horrid, rent the air. It was succeeded by a thunder-crash, so deafening, that the ladies paled with terror. The large maple tree, which stood by the front door, and which Julia had called hers, was shivered by lightning, but no one heeded it, for again was heard that fearful, maniacal shriek, and this time could be distinguished the sound as of some one struggling with the blacks, who were huddled together in the hall.

"Let me go, I tell you," said the voice. "It shall not go on!"

All eyes turned towards the door, as Joseph Dunn appeared, shouting, "Stop it! stop it! *She forged those letters!* She broke her sister's heart! Stop it, I say!" Every person in the room seemed terror-stricken at the wild spectacle he presented. His face, wasted to a mere skeleton, was ghastly white, while his long, yellow hair hung in matted locks about his brow, and a look of wild frenzy was in his eye, as darting towards the paralyzed Julia, he seized her as with a lion's grasp and shook her most furiously!

Bill Jeffrey was close behind. He had lost his hat, and the rain had soaked his thick, black hair, until it clung closely to his head, giving him, too, a strange appearance. Mr. William Middleton now came forward, to ask an explanation of Joseph, who, chancing to discover Bill, said, "He has got the letter,—my confession. Read that, I am too exhausted," and he fell upon the floor.

No one noticed him, for all gazed intently at Bill, who drew from his pocket a paper and presented it to Dr. Lacey. In a calm, clear voice, Dr. Lacey read aloud the confession, in the midst of thunder, lightning, groans, cries and oaths, the latter of which were the spontaneous production of Uncle Joshua, who sat still in his chair, until the confession was read through; then with one bound he reached Julia, and raising her from the floor, said, "Speak, Satan, and tell if this be true!"

Julia was overtaken, surrounded on all sides, and there was no way of escape. Mechanically she answered, "I am guilty," while a burst of execration ran round the room. A stifled moan of agony came from Dr. Lacey's parted lips, and he asked in a voice which plainly told his suffering, "Oh, why was I suffered to go thus far? Why, why did no one write?"

"I did," answered Mrs. Miller.

"And I too," repeated Mrs. Carrington, "but you spurned my letter and treated me with contempt."

"Never, never," scarcely articulated Dr. Lacey. "I never received them, but call Rondeau; he must know something of it."

Rondeau, who had accompanied his master, was called. Explanation followed explanation, testimony crowded upon testimony, and Julia acknowledged all, until at length Dr. Lacey, frantic with the sense of wrong done him, turned to her and said, "Base woman, why have you done this? Your sin has found you out ere it was too late; for, thank God, you are not my wife, nor ever will be!"

Julia now lost all command of herself. Tearing the bridal veil from her brow, she rent it in twain; then from her arm she snatched her diamond bracelet, and trampled it under her feet, while a stream of blood issued from her mouth, and stained her white satin dress. A moment more, and she, too, was extended upon the floor by the side of her ally.

Where, during this exciting scene, was Fanny? The direful sounds had reached her ear, and now at the head of the stairs, she listened to the Babel, which reigned in the parlor. High above all other voices, she distinguished her father's, who, in his uncontrollable fury, was calling into use all the oaths he had ever heard of, besides manufacturing some expressly for the occasion! Then there was a heavy fall, accompanied with a cry from Mrs. Middleton, of, "Lift her up—carry her out. Don't you see she is dying?"

Fanny hesitated no longer, but quickly descending the stair, she forced her way through the blacks into the parlor, where she stood appalled at the scene before her. On the floor lay Julia, who a few moments before stood there resplendent in beauty. Near her sat the maniac, Joseph Dunn. He had recovered from his fainting fit, and was now crouching over the prostrate form of Julia, laughing in delirious glee, as he wiped from her lips the red drops of blood! In a corner of the room a group had gathered, near an open window, through which they were bearing an inanimate object. It was Florence, who had fainted, and as it seemed impossible to effect a passage through the hall, so filled was it with the terrified servants, they had sought the window as the best means of egress.

Suddenly over that excited assembly there came a deep silence. It was caused by the appearance of Fanny, who, with her loose white muslin wrapper, and long curls, which floated over her shoulders, seemed like some being from another world, come to stay that storm of passion. Mabel, who was occupied with her cousin, looked back as the calm hush fell upon them, and then and there she first saw Fanny Middleton. The scene was too much for Fanny, and she too would have fainted, had not Dr. Lacey caught her in his arms. Clasping her slight form passionately to his bosom, he exclaimed, "My own,—my Fanny,—my wife, for such you are, such you shall be!"

Mr. William Middleton and Mr. Miller, who were bearing Julia from the room, now passed them. Dr. Lacey glanced once at the corpse-like face over which the heavy braids of long, black hair had fallen, then with a shudder he again strained Fanny to his heart, saying, "Thank God, thank God, I escaped her in time!" Then turning to the minister, who, all this time had stood looking on in mute astonishment, he added in an authoritative manner, "Go on with the ceremony, sir, and make her my wife." But a new thought entering his mind, he released Fanny, and said: "Pardon me, dear Fanny; sorrow has well-nigh bereft me of my senses. In my first joy at finding you innocent, I forgot that you could not be mine, for you belong to another—to Mr. Cameron."

"Cameron go to thunder!" exclaimed Uncle Joshua, who was still standing near. "That's another of Tempest's lies. She never was engaged to him; never loved him, or any other mortal man, save yourself."

Here Fanny, who, it will be remembered, was all this time ignorant of the truth, asked if some one would not explain what she saw and heard. "I will," said Dr. Lacey, "it is my duty to do so;" and he led her to the window, where he hurriedly told her all,—everything which he himself knew, intermingling his words with so many passionate embraces that his sanity was much to be doubted. He had scarcely finished his story, when Kate approached him, saying, "For humanity's sake, Dr. Lacey, if you have any medical skill, exert it in behalf of Julia, who seems to be dying."

Dr. Lacey arose, and winding his arm about Fanny as if afraid he should lose sight of her, moved towards the room where Julia lay. They had borne her to the bridal chamber which Fanny had arranged with so much care, and as Dr. Lacey appeared at the door, Uncle Joshua met him and said, "I know she sarved you mean, but I would not have her die. She is my own child, and you must save her if you can." At the same time he pointed to Julia, who lay in the same death-like trance, with the blood still issuing slowly from her livid lips. All that Dr. Lacey could do, he did, but when Dr. Gordon arrived, he gladly gave up his charge to him, and turned his attention towards Fanny, who, overcome with what she had seen and heard, had fainted and been carried to her own room, where she was surrounded by Mrs. Carrington, Florence and Mabel. These ladies ran against each other, upset the camphor-bottle, dropped the lamp, and spilled half the cologne, in their zealous efforts to take care of their patient!

In the midst of their confusion Dr. Lacey entered, and they immediately gave up to him the task of restoring her. This he soon did, for it would seem that his very voice had a power to recall Fanny's suspended faculties. Slowly her eyes unclosed; then, as if wearied out, she again closed them, and for a time slept sweetly, calmly, on Dr. Lacey's bosom.

The guests now began to depart, and Bill Jeffrey, who had been sent to inform Mrs. Dunn of her son, returned with some of the neighbors, and carried Joseph away. Owing to the darkness of the night, the company from Frankfort remained until morning, but no eyelid closed in sleep. With maternal solicitude, Mrs. Middleton sat by the bed-side of her daughter Julia, whose eyes opened once, but on seeing Dr. Lacey standing near her, she closed them again with a shudder, and a faint wail of anguish. She had ruptured a small blood-vessel, but Dr. Gordon said there was no danger if she could be kept quiet for a few days.

Uncle Joshua, thus relieved from alarm concerning her, walked back and forth from her room to Fanny's, swearing that "He knew the devil was let loose that night for his special benefit, and that he had come there to see how much of a row he could get up!"

"He succeeded admirably, I think," said Florence, who, having recovered from her first fright, was now ready to extract whatever *fun* could be gathered from surrounding circumstances.

In the kitchen the blacks canvassed the matter after their fashion. Aunt Judy lamented because none of the tempting supper in the dining-room was touched, while Bob did not fail to turn his usual round of summersets, thus evincing his joy that so many good things were left for him to eat. " 'Cause," said he, "in course we allus has all that comes off the table!"

Aunt Katy took occasion to lecture the young black girls on the awful sin of "conceit," as she called it, pointing them for an example to Julia, "who," she said, "would most likely have to live an old maid all her days." She couldn't have threatened a worse punishment, for many of the negresses had already their own preferences in favor of certain mulatto boys on their master's plantation and others adjoining.

Rondeau seemed to think his sympathy was only needed by his young master, whom he looked upon as a much abused man. From the first he had felt great contempt for the old house, its master, servants and all; and had come to the conclusion that "they were of no 'count any how." This opinion would doubtless have been reserved for Leffie's ear, had not affairs taken so unexpected a turn. Now, however, Rondeau felt at liberty to express his mind so freely, that Ike considered it his duty to resent the insult.

A regular negro fight ensued, in which Aunt Katy, who was not very active, was thrown down, and as she loudly protested, "every atom of breath was knocked out of her." The big chicken pie was also turned over into Rondeau's new hat, greatly to the satisfaction of Tiger and the other dogs, who had mingled in the fracas! The riot was finally quelled by Mr. William Middleton and Dr. Lacey, Uncle Joshua declaring, *"he* wouldn't interfere that night if the niggers all fit till they killed themselves!"

## Chapter XXII

The morning which succeeded the events narrated in the last chapter, was clear and bright. Nature, beautiful as ever, looked as if laughing defiance at the fearful storm, which so lately had swept over the earth. Beautifully over hill and valley, fell the sun's red rays, but when they penetrated the dwelling of Mr. Middleton, they shone on the anxious, careworn faces of those who had been sleepless during the dark hours of that dreadful night. Even the merry-hearted Florence seemed sad and spiritless as she hurried from room to room, urging Ashton to accelerate their departure. By eight o'clock, the last guest was gone. Around the old stone house a gloomy silence settled, broken only by the heavy tramp of Uncle Joshua, whose cowhides came down with a vengeance, as up and down the yard he strode, talking to Dr. Lacey, who walked by his side.

"Now," said he, "if this isn't a leetle the allfiredest muss a feller ever got into, Josh ain't no judge. Of course the papers have nothing to do but to flout it all over the country. For myself I don't care a copper, but 'twill be mighty mortifyin' to you, though I think you desarve some mortifyin', for how in thunder a chap of your sense ever come to be made such a precious fool of, is more'n I can tell."

"If you knew all the arts she employed, you would not wonder quite so much," said Dr. Lacey; and Mr. Middleton answered, "Know all her arts! Don't I know 'em? Don't I know that she rummaged heaven and 'arth for ways and means?"

"I hardly think she went to the former place for assistance," said Dr. Lacey; and Mr. Middleton continued, "You are right, but I'll be bound Satan hadn't any tricks but what he told her of. 'Pears like she's been possessed ever since she first opened her big black eyes in the very room where the row was last night. Oh, how happy I was," he continued, "when I took her in my arms, a little soft, tender baby, and knew she was mine and Nancy's, and thought what a comfort she'd be to me; but, George, I tell you what," said he, as he placed one hand on Dr. Lacey's arm and passed the other through the grizzly locks which lay around his brow, "I tell you what, these gray hairs come a heap too soon, and all for her, for her! Oh, Julia, Julia, what trouble have you not caused me!" and in his hands Uncle Joshua buried his face, while through his large red fingers the tears trickled slowly, and fell upon the ground. For a moment he wept, and then wiping his eyes, said, "But wasn't it lucky that long-legged, salmon-colored Joe got here as he did? Another minute and you'd have been clinched, but now the tempest has blowed over, and for the rest of your life, you'll have nothin' but sunshine."

The overseer now approached to ask orders concerning a piece of work in which the negroes were employed. Mr. Middleton accompanied him to the field, while Dr. Lacey returned to the house in quest of Fanny. He was told that she was with Julia, and with an involuntary shudder, he approached the chamber which contained one who had well-nigh been his wife! His wife! the very idea filled him with loathing when associated with her, and still he pitied the suffering girl, who divested of her bridal attire, now lay moaning in her pain. With coming day, had come a burning fever, which increased so rapidly that Dr. Gordon shook his head when questioned as to the result.

The change of affairs had also wrought a change in Fanny, who seemed and really was better than she had been for many days. Gladly would she have stayed with Dr. Lacey, but she felt that duty called her to Julia's bedside. With unwearying devotion she hung over the pillow of her sister, who seemed more quiet when she knew Fanny was near. Once she looked wistfully in her face, and appeared as if anxious to speak, but Fanny gently laid her hand on her lips, saying, "No, no, Julia, you must not."

She did, however, and the word "forgive" met Fanny's ear. Had Fanny been less of a Christian, forgiveness might have been hard, but now she answered sincerely, truthfully, "As I hope for pardon in heaven, so do I forgive you for the great wrong you have done me."

At the mention of the word "heaven," Julia shuddered, and after a time repeated, "Heaven! You will find it, but I,—never,—never!"

Earnestly then did Fanny speak of a Saviour's love, which receives all, pardons all, who come to him. Julia shook her head despairingly, and as the conversation seemed to annoy her, Fanny ceased talking, while a voice behind her said, "Teach me, too, the way of life, for I fear I have never walked in it."

It was Dr. Lacey, who, unobserved by either of the girls, had entered and been a listener to what Fanny said. As Julia heard the sound of his voice, she turned towards him a look so imploring, so full of contrition and entreaty, that he was moved, and approaching the bedside, took the vacant seat near Fanny. But he did not, like her, breathe words of forgiveness, for his heart was full of bitterness towards her. As he sat there, gazing coldly, sternly at her, she again spoke, "If you *can,* if you only *will* forgive me."

Dr. Lacey's brow grew dark and his manner excited as he replied, "Forgive you! In time I may learn to do so, but to forget will take me my lifetime, and yet I blame myself not less than I do you for having been so duped."

A low sob was Julia's only answer as Dr. Lacey arose to leave, announcing to Fanny his intention of visiting Joseph Dunn, who was said to be dying. As he entered the house where Joseph lay, tossing in feverish agony, the sick man's eyes glared wildly upon him, as he shrieked, "Why have you come to taunt me with my crime? Is it not enough that the room is full of little demons who creep over my pillow, and shout in my ear as they hold to view the letters I withheld? *I* did not do it alone! *She* bribed me with gold and that infernal smile which lured you too, sir, to the verge of destruction!" For a time he was silent and then he continued, "Yes, she bribed me with gold, and now when I am dead, who will take care of my mother? She will be cold when the winter winds blow, and hungry when the summer corn ripens."

Dr. Lacey drew nearer to him and stooping down, whispered, "Is your mother very poor and you all her dependence?"

"Yes, yes," answered Joseph, whose almost only virtue was the love he bore his mother.

"Fear not, then," said Dr. Lacey, "I will care for her; for though you did me a great wrong, you saved me from being to-day the most wretched of men."

That night as the October sun went down there was heard beneath that lonely roof the piteous cry of a widowed mother, for Joseph, her first-born, her only child, was dead. Next day they buried him, as is frequently the custom in Kentucky, beneath a large shade-tree in the garden. Many words of sympathy were spoken to the bereaved mother, but none fell so soothingly on her ear as did those of Dr. Lacey, who was present at the funeral, and led the weeping mother to the grave.

After the burial was over, he whispered to her, "I will surely remember you, for, erring though your son may have been, I owe him a debt of gratitude." So saying he walked hastily away towards Mr. Middleton's, where he was met by alarmed faces, soft footsteps and subdued whispers. In reply to his inquiries, he was told by Aunt Judy, that "somehow or 'nother, Miss Julia had got wind of Mr. Dunn's death, and it had gone to her head, makin' her ravin' mad, and the Doctor said she wouldn't get well."

Aunt Judy was right; Julia had accidentally heard of Mr. Dunn's death, and it added greatly to the nervous excitement which she was already suffering, and when Dr. Gordon came, he was surprised to find the dangerous symptoms of his patient increased to an alarming extent. The fever had settled upon her brain, and for many days she lay at the very gates of death.

Incessantly she talked of Dr. Lacey, Fanny, and Mr. Wilmot, the latter of whom, in her disordered imagination, was constantly pursuing her. "Go back—go back to your grave," she would say; "there are tears enough shed for you, but none will fall for me when I am dead. *He* will laugh and be glad, and the first moon that shines on my grave, will light the marriage train to the altar." Then, as if the phantom still were near her, she would cry out, "Take him away, I tell you! What have *I* to do with coffins, and white faces, and broken hearts? I killed him, I know, and he loved me, too, as no one else ever has, but I madly loved another, and now *he* hates me, spurns me!" Then turning to Fanny she would say, "I broke your heart, too, and still pressed on when I saw it was killing you, but you forgave me, and now you must plead with him, who loves the air you breathe, to think compassionately of me. I do not ask him to *love* me, for that I know is impossible; but he can, at least, forgive and forget the past."

Sometimes she would speak of her father, saying, "He will be glad when the *tempest* is still and ceases to trouble him, for he never loved me, never spoke to me as he did to Fanny. I know I did not deserve his love, but I should have been better if he had given me a *little*, yes, just a little."

"God knows she speaks the truth," said Uncle Joshua, wiping away the tears he was not ashamed to weep. "I have been mighty hard on her, but I never s'posed she cared."

Such were the scenes which daily occurred in Julia's sick room, until at last, from utter exhaustion, she became still, and for many days she lay in a dreamy kind of sleep.

"Will she live?" asked Mr. Middleton of Dr. Gordon, as he one day left the sick room.

"With proper care, I think she may," was the answer, and then Dr. Lacey again urged the request he had once before made of Mr. Middleton.

But Uncle Joshua answered, "No, George, wait a little longer. Nothin' 'ill come betwixt you again, I reckon, and I wouldn't have you marry her while t'other one is so low."

So Dr. Lacey was obliged to wait, but though he would much rather have remained near Fanny, he deemed it expedient to change his abode and remove to Mrs. Crane's. He was partly induced to do this on Rondeau's account, who, being Ike's sworn enemy, was the cause of no little annoyance to Mr. Middleton, who, with his negroes, was much nettled by the air of superiority which that young gentleman thought proper to assume.

Greatly was Rondeau delighted to exchange the crazy old stone house, with its corn-bread and fried bacon, for Mrs. Crane's elegant place, with its oyster soups and ice creams, a part of which the head cook always reserved for the "colored gentleman from New Orleans," who assured her, that though when at home, he didn't exactly eat at the same table with his master, he still lived on the *top shelf!* Not long, however, did Rondeau enjoy his new quarters, for about that time Mr. William Middleton returned to New Orleans, and Dr. Lacey sent with him his servant Rondeau, nothing loath to return home, for Leffie's face of late had haunted him not a little.

Dr. Lacey's return to Mrs. Crane's gave great satisfaction to Mrs. Carrington, who, though she had no hopes of winning him, still, to use her own words, "took great delight in reminding him of the snare into which he had fallen, notwithstanding his profound wisdom and boasted foresight." It required all the good breeding he was master of to answer politely, when after returning from a visit to Mr. Middleton's, she would jeeringly ask him concerning "his *bride's* health!"

But Mrs. Carrington's levity was brought to an end by an unforeseen circumstance. It was now six weeks since the evening of the denouement, and Julia's health was so much improved that Dr. Lacey began to speak confidently of the day when Fanny would be his own. Uncle Joshua had given his consent, and preparations for the marriage had actually commenced, when Julia, in whose room Mrs. Middleton had been in the habit of sleeping, insisted upon being left alone. "I am well now," she said, "and do not need you."

Mrs. Middleton was finally persuaded, but charged her daughter to be sure and call her if she wished for her during the night.

Over Julia's face a meaning smile flitted as she answered, "I hope to trouble no one much longer," but it was unnoticed by Mrs. Middleton, and Julia was left alone. Early next morning Luce went as usual to make a fire for her young mistress, after which she softly drew back the bed curtains to see if Julia slept. How was she surprised to find no Julia there, neither were there signs of her having been there during the night. With a loud cry Luce summoned to the room both Mr. and Mrs. Middleton, the former of whom on seeing how matters stood, exclaimed, "So ho! up to her tricks again. I thought she couldn't hold good long,

> " 'The de'il when sick, a saint would be,
> But when he got well, the de'il a saint was he.' "

"Don't, husband," said Mrs. Middleton; "perhaps she will never come back alive, and then you will be sorry."

Uncle Joshua readily guessed his wife's meaning, and turning to Luce, said, "Rout out the whole gang and set 'em to huntin'."

In less than two hours scores of men on horseback were seen hunting in all directions, looking, as Bob expressed it, "for all the world like they was huntin' a runaway." Ere long the news reached Frankfort, causing Mrs. Carrington to sneeringly advise Dr. Lacey "by all means to join in the hunt." He deigned her no reply, but mounting his horse, took the road to Mr. Middleton's, where he was welcomed with tears by Mrs. Middleton and Fanny, whose fears he strove to allay.

Meanwhile the search went on, headed by Uncle Joshua, who, late in the afternoon, unconsciously led a part of the company to the banks of the river, not far from a point called Woodford Landing. Dismounting, he strolled along the shore for several rods, when suddenly a loud cry turned towards him the attention of the party. Near the water's edge he had discovered a shawl, which he knew belonged to Julia, and near by lay a pair of slippers, on the inside of which her name was marked. Instantly the conviction flashed upon all,—*Julia was drowned!*

Upon a large flat rock Uncle Joshua sat down, while his long gray locks were tossed by the November wind which swept mournfully by, bearing on its wing the bitter tones with which the stricken father bewailed his loss. "Every thing goes agin me," said he, "every thing—she's dead, and worse than all, died by her own hand." Then, as if void of reason, he arose, and over the craggy hillside, and down the dark rolling river echoed the loud, shrill cry, of "Julia, Julia, oh, my child! come back, come back! why was you left to break your old father's heart?" and to that wail of sorrow only the moaning wind replied, and faster the waters of the Kentucky rolled on.

They took the old man home, and long weary days went by, during which the river near the landing was dragged again and again, and still no trace of the missing girl was found. Then, as hope began to whisper that possibly she was not dead, the papers far and near contained advertise-

ments for her, and by the side of that advertisement appeared another for
a lunatic girl, who had escaped from the Asylum at Lexington.

Four weeks went by, and the waters of the Kentucky frowned angrily
"in the gray December light," making Uncle Joshua shudder whenever he
chanced to pass by, and thought perhaps his daughter lay sleeping in their
cold embrace. A gloomy, drizzly day was settling into a dark rainy night,
when two young men, who, either for business or pleasure, had rowed
across the river some miles from Woodford Landing, started to return home.
They had stepped into their boat and were about pushing off, when among
some drift wood which lay not far from the shore, they thought they
descried a female's garment floating on the water. The spot was soon
reached, and to their horror they discovered the body of a young girl, which
from its appearance must have been in the water some time. They had
heard the story of Julia and readily concluded that the bloated, disfigured
form before them must have been she. Taking her to the nearest dwelling,
they dispatched a messenger for Mr. Middleton, who, now that his worst
fears were confirmed, seemed paralyzed with the shock.

"Oh, I cannot go!" said he, "I cannot. Is there no one to do it for me?"

Dr. Lacey, who chanced to be present, said, "For your sake, sir, and for
Fanny's, I will go."

"God bless you, George!" answered Mr. Middleton. "She don't desarve it
from you, but if you only will!" and in a few moments Dr. Lacey departed.

With a thrill of horror he looked upon the swollen, discolored face,
round which the long black hair clung, matted and slimy from being so long
saturated with water, and thought that this was once the beautiful Julia,
though now so fearfully changed that no one could possibly have recognized
her. Owing to the state which the body was in, Dr. Lacey thought proper
to procure a coffin before removing her home; consequently, it was nearly
ten o'clock the following morning ere the little procession slowly entered the
yard, from which, with wonderful forethought, Mr. Middleton had ordered
to be removed some half dozen carts, corn cribs, &c. Fanny was pressing forward to look at her unfortunate sister when Dr. Lacey, gently but firmly
led her away, saying, "No, Fanny, you must not see her. The sight would
haunt you for months and years." Then as her tears fell fast, he strove
in various ways to divert her mind from Julia's untimely end.

About noon a middle-aged man came to the house, and asked permission
to see the body. His request was granted but he almost immediately turned
away from the coffin, saying, by way of explanation, "I am the father of
the maniac girl, who, some time since, escaped from Lexington, and I
thought perhaps this might be my daughter; but it is not, and even if it
were I could not recognize her."

On Mr. Middleton's farm and not far from the house, was a small yard
which had been inclosed as a burial-place for the family. On this spot Fanny
had expended much time and labor. Roses and honeysuckles there bloomed
in their season, while the dark evergreen and weeping willow waved their
branches, and beckoned the passer-by to rest beneath their shadow. In one
corner was a tall forest maple, where Julia and Fanny often had played, and
where Fanny once, when dangerously ill in childhood, had asked to be laid.

As yet no mound had rendered that spot dearer for the sake of the lost one who slept there, but now in the scarcely frozen ground, the ringing of the spade was heard; shovelfull after shovelfull of earth was thrown up, and into that cold, damp grave, at the sun setting, they lowered the remains of Julia, who once little thought that she first of all would break the turf of the family graveyard.

That night was fast merging into the hours of morning, ere the sound of Uncle Joshua's footsteps ceased, as again and again he traversed the length and breadth of his sleeping-room, occasionally stopping before the window, and peering out in the darkness towards the spot where he knew lay that newly-made grave. Memory was busily at work, and in the events which marked Julia's short life, oh! how much he saw for which to blame himself. Remorse mingled in the old man's cup of affliction, and while the hot tears rolled down his cheeks, he exclaimed, "If she could only come back, and I could do it over, I'd love her more, and maybe she'd be better. But I treated her mean. I gin her only harsh words and cross looks." Then as his wife's tears mingled with his, he took her hand, saying, "Don't take on so, Nancy, you've nothin' to cry for. You's always good to her, and kind o' took up for her when I got sot agin her."

Mrs. Middleton could only answer by her tears to this touching attempt at sympathy, but she finally succeeded in quieting her husband, and before daybreak he had forgotten in sleep the injustice done to Julia. All thoughts of Fanny's marriage for the present were of course given up, although Mr. Middleton promised that when the autumn came round again, he would surely give his treasure to the care of another.

Two weeks after Julia's burial, all of which time was passed at Mr. Middleton's, Dr. Lacey went back to New Orleans, having first placed in Mr. Middleton's care a sum of money for the benefit of Mrs. Dunn, promising Fanny that with the spring he would come again. He bade her adieu, praying that nothing might come between them again. Heavily now dragged the days at Mr. Middleton's, until Uncle Joshua hit upon a plan which would not only give pleasure to Fanny, but would also relieve the tedium of his own life. It was nothing more nor less than the erection of a new house on a grassy lawn, which Fanny had frequently pointed out as being a good location. Long he revolved in his own mind the for and against, but the remembrance of Julia's wish to have the "old shell fixed up," finally decided him. "If 'twasn't good enough for her to be married in, it surely wasn't good enough for Sunshine."

At the breakfast table he first announced his intention, causing Fanny in her surprise and joy not only to drop her knife, but also to upset her coffee. "All right," said he, "I'll do it, if it breaks me. We'll have a buster," said he, "marble manteltrys, windows that come to the floor, Brussels carpets, and if you're a mind to, you may have them four-legged split things; though Lord knows I'll never eat with them."

In a short time the necessary arrangements were completed. A large number of men were hired, and matters progressed so rapidly that there was every probability of the house being completed early in June, should the winter season prove favorable.

Here we may as well relate a little circumstance which occurred to Fanny during the winter. Bill Jeffrey, who, it will be remembered, had always felt a predilection for her, emboldened by the kindness of her manner, now determined to make his wishes known. Accordingly, he sent her numerous little cakes of maple sugar, besides giving her many knowing winks, his usual method of showing his preference.

As she was one day strolling in the woods, she suddenly encountered Bill, who thought this was as favorable an opportunity as he would probably have. He was rather awkward and unaccustomed to lovemaking, but he resolved to do his best. Planting his foot upon a log, he with one hand drew from his head his old wool cap and thrust it under his arm, while with the other he twirled a huge, brass watch-key, which hung suspended from his pocket. (He had the day before traded off an old jack-knife, two puppies, and a cracked fiddle, for a brass watch which would only go by shaking.)

Tiger, who had accompanied Fanny, eyed Bill's movements uneasily. He was, however, unnoticed by the young man, who had got his mouth open, and at last found courage to say, "I always liked you, Fanny, 'cause you never laughed at me, nor called me a fool, and now if you'll have me, you may carry my watch, and I'll work for your father two seasons in the hemp field." This last was wonderful, for Bill was notoriously lazy.

Involuntarily Fanny laughed, but Bill construed it into approval, and was about to sit down by her, when Tiger, with an angry growl, sprang forward and precipitated the wooing swain over the log into the dirt. Fanny called off the dog, and Bill gathered himself up, carefully brushing the dirt from his Sunday suit. Fearing he would repeat his offer Fanny said, "I appreciate your kindness, Billy, but you see Tiger doesn't seem to approve your proposal, and as I have great confidence in his judgment, I think I, too, must follow his example, and though I shan't knock you down, I shall have to tell you, 'No.' "

She might as well have knocked him down, for he instantly sat down, and covering his face with his hands, burst into such a fit of crying, that Fanny, half laughing at and half pitying him, said, "Poor Billy, I am sorry for you, and though I cannot marry you, I will like you just as well as you fancy I always have."

This failed to quiet Bill, who kept on crying, until Tiger made so many threatening demonstrations of anger, that Bill thought it wise to leave before he got another tumble.

He had hardly disappeared when a loud voice called out, "Bravo, Tiger! You know how to fix 'em." Looking round, Fanny saw her father, who had been a silent spectator of the scene, and now came forward laughing heartily at his would-be son-in-law. "Pretty well done, Sunshine," said he. "Let's see, how many offers does this make? Thar's Joe's one; the Doctor's two; Yankee Cameron's three; and lubberin' Bill Jeffrey's four, and you not quite eighteen. That'll do; that'll do!" Afterwards, when Mr. Middleton wished to entertain his visitors with any thing "extra," he would rehearse to them, with some exaggerations, Bill Jeffrey's proposal to Fanny.

Glancing backwards a few pages, we find we have omitted to repeat what occurred among Dr. Lacey's blacks, during the days when they were anxiously but vainly watching for the coming of their young master and his bride. For a whole week Aunt Dilsey was unusually crusty, and all her attempts at cookery invariably failed, plainly showing her mind to be in a disturbed state.

"I don't keer," she would say, "if the cakes is all dough and the 'sarves all froth. They's good enough for her, any day." Then she would call out, "Get along, you Jack, pokin' your fingers into the 'lasses cup; make yourself scarce in this kitchen, or I'll crack your head mighty nigh as hard as the new Miss will." Then she would scold Leffie, who, she said, "was of no more account than a burnt stick, now she was 'spectin' Rondeau. Pity but the boat he come on wouldn't blow up and let 'em all into perdition together."

Leffie knew her mother didn't mean more than half what she said, but she chose to keep silent, hoping each morning that the close of the day would bring the long absent Rondeau. Thus between scolding and fretting, cooking and sweating, Aunt Dilsey passed the time until the day arrived on which, as she said, "they'd come if they ever did."

Mrs. Lacey, whose husband had not yet received his son's letter announcing the catastrophe, came out to superintend affairs and receive her new daughter. In the large, handsome dining-room, the supper table was neatly spread, while Aunt Dilsey bustled about with the air of one who felt her time was short, but was determined to contest every inch of ground, ere yielding it to another. She had condescended to put on her new calico gown (the one she proposed taking with her in a "handkercher,") and had even washed the grease and molasses from Jack's and the baby's faces, telling the former that "he needn't mind about making up faces at the lady that night."

Claib had gone to the landing, and now Mrs. Lacey and the servants were gathered upon the upper piazza, waiting his return. Suddenly Dilsey, whose eyesight seemed wonderfully sharpened, exclaimed, "Thar, that's Claib. I could tell my old man, if I should meet him at a camp-meeting!"

Mrs. Lacey looked in the direction of the city and saw the carriage, which Dilsey had pointed out. It proved to be Claib; and Leffie, who was rather nearsighted, strained her eyes to see if Rondeau too was on the box.

"Thar's nobody in that ar," said Dilsey. "Reckon the boat has run into the ground, or bust her riggin'; so, Leffie, you've put on your pink gown for nothin'."

The elder Mr. Lacey was, however, in the carriage, and alighting, he advanced towards his wife and gave her the letter he had just received from his son. Mrs. Lacey read it, while the blacks crowded around Claib, asking him scores of foolish questions, such as, "Was Marster George in the boat? and why wasn't he thar? and when would he be thar?"

When Mrs. Lacey finished reading the letter she said to Leffie, who was still standing near, "Rondeau is well, and will be at home in a few days."

"When's the new Miss a comin'?" asked Aunt Dilsey.

"Not at all," was Mrs. Lacey's reply.

"Glad on't," said Dilsey, "for now Jack can spit as fur and as big spits as he wants to."

Nothing more was known by the blacks until many days after, when Rondeau returned home, and related the whole story with many embellishments. He omitted to tell of the whipping which Ike had given him, but spoke with unqualified contempt of the old house and every thing belonging to it, except Miss Fanny, who, he said, "Looked just like an angel, only a heap better."

"You ought to have seen her," said he, "that night when every thing was t'other side up; folks a yellin' like they was crazy, and one man was stark mad. Miss Julia lay on the floor, the blood pourin' out of her eyes and mouth by pails full; Miss Florence, she fainted, and they had to throw her out of the window, glass and all, because there was so many low, ill-mannered niggers crowded in the hall."

"I s'pose you's one of the niggers?" said Aunt Dilsey.

"Why, yes," returned Rondeau; "but then I was helpin' and was tryin' to push them all back so I could get to marster, who was feelin' so bad that they sent for me, because nobody else could comfort him."

Here Rondeau began to fumble in his pocket, as if in search of something. Having found it, he continued, "Marster got hold of her hand and grabbed off the wedding ring so quick that it broke her finger. Then he threw it from him and I picked it up. Here 'tis," said he, holding up a plain gold ring.*

"That's a likely story," interrupted Aunt Dilsey. "If they wasn't married, how came the ring on her finger!"

Rondeau saw he had *stretched* a *trifle* too much, but he answered, "Well, any how he throwed it away, and I'm going to keep it till,—till, you know when, Dilsey."

"Keep it till you're gray," said Aunt Dilsey. "Leffie ain't goin' to be married with no such flummery."

Here Leffie, anxious to change the conversation, asked, "What of Miss Fanny?"

"Why, yes," answered Rondeau, "that's what I'm going to tell. Right in the middle of the fuss, I heard something moving softly down the stairs, and I saw a thing all as white as snow. Her hair, which was about the color of Leffie's neck,—real handsome,—was hanging in long curls down her back. I thought it was an angel, and kinder touched her as she passed, to see if she had wings. But the niggers said, 'It's Miss Fanny,' and next I heard, 'twas all as still in the room, and marster was huggin' and kissin' her and cryin' over her. Then, when I tried to get nearer and see more, they crowded me into such a little spot that I didn't breathe again for a week."

"Why didn't you get out of the crowd then?" asked Dilsey.

"How could I?" answered Rondeau. "Lord, Dilsey, I'd like to have seen *you* there; but then there wouldn't have been room for any body else, for the hall wouldn't more than hold you."

Here the conversation ended, but for a long time Rondeau carried on his arm the marks of Aunt Dilsey's finger and thumb.

* Rondeau had bought the ring in Frankfort.

## Chapter XXIII

From the grassy hillside and bright green plains of Kentucky, the frosts of winter were gone. By the dancing brook and in the shady nooks of the quiet valleys, the warm spring sun had sought out and brought to life thousands of sweet wild blossoms, which in turn had faded away, giving place to other flowers of a brighter and gayer hue.

Each night from the upper balcony of her father's handsome dwelling, Fanny watched in vain for the coming of Dr. Lacey, whose promised return had been long delayed by the dangerous illness of his father. Over the wooded hills the breath of summer was floating, hot, arid, and laden with disease. Death was abroad in the land, and as each day exaggerated rumors of the havoc made by cholera in the sultry climate of Louisiana reached Fanny, fearful misgivings filled her mind, lest Dr. Lacey, too, should fall a victim to the plague.

For herself she had no fears, though slowly but surely through her veins the fever flame was creeping, scorching her blood, poisoning her breath and burning her cheek, until her father, alarmed at her altered and languid appearance, inquired for the cause of the change. "Nothing but a slight headache," was the reply.

Next to the cholera Mr. Middleton most feared the typhoid fever, several cases of which had recently occurred in the neighborhood, and fearing lest the disease might be stealing upon his darling, he proposed calling the physician. But this Fanny would not suffer, and persisted in saying that she was well, until at last she lay all day upon the sofa, and Aunt Katy, when her favorite herb teas failed of effecting their wonted cure, shook her head, saying, "I knew 'twould be so. I always told you we couldn't keep her long."

Dr. Gordon was finally called, and pronounced her disease to be typhoid in its worst form. Days went by, and so rapid was the progress of the fever that Mr. Middleton trembled lest of him it had been decreed, "He shall be childless." To Fanny the thought of death was familiar. For her it had no terrors, and as her outward strength decayed, her faith in the Eternal grew stronger and brighter, yet she could not die without an assurance that again in the better world she would meet the father she so much loved. For her mother she had no fears, for during many years she had been a patient, self-denying Christian. At first Mr. Middleton listened in silence to Fanny's gentle words of entreaty, but when she spoke to him of her own death and the love which alone could sustain him then, he clasped her tightly to his heart, as if his arm alone could keep her there for ever saying, "Oh, no,

you must not tell me that; you will not die. Even now you are better."
And the anxious father did try to deceive himself into the belief that Fanny
was better, but when each morning's light revealed some fresh ravage the
disease had made;—when the flush on her cheek grew deeper, and the light
of her eye wilder and more startling, an agonizing fear held the old man's
heart in thrall. Many and many a weary night found him sleepless, as he
wet his pillow with tears. Not such tears as he wept when Richard Wilmot
died, nor such as fell upon the grave of his first-born, for oh! his grief then
was naught compared with what he now felt for his Sunshine, his idol, his
precious Fanny. "I cannot, cannot let her die," was the cry which hourly
welled up from the depths of that fond father's aching heart. "Take all,
take every thing I own, but leave me Sunshine; *she* mustn't, mustn't die."

Earnestly did Fanny pray that her father might be enabled better to bear
his affliction. But he turned a deaf ear alike to her and his gentle, enduring
wife, who, bowed with sorrow, yet sought to soothe her grief-stricken husband.
Sadly he would turn away, saying, "It's of no use talking; I can't be pious,
if they take Fanny away. I can see why t'other one died. 'Twas to bring me
to my senses, and show me how bad I used her; but Fanny, my Sunshine,
what *has* Josh done that she should leave him, too? Oh, it's more than I
can bar!"

At Dr. Gordon's request a council of physicians in Frankfort was called.
As the one who came last was about to enter her room, Mr. Middleton detained him while he said: "Save her, Doctor, save her, and you shall have
all I'm worth." Impatiently he awaited the decision. It came, but alas! it
brought no hope.

Mr. William Middleton, who had recently come from New Orleans, broke
the news to his unhappy brother. Terrible was the anguish of Uncle Joshua,
when he became convinced that he *must* lose her. Nothing could induce
him to leave her room; and as if endowed with superhuman strength, he
watched by her constantly, only leaving her once each day to visit the
quiet grave, the bed of his other daughter, where now the long, green grass
was waving, and the summer flowers were blooming—flowers which Fanny's
hand had planted, and the father's tears had watered.

One night they were alone, the old man and his child. For several hours
Fanny had turned uneasily upon her pillow, but she at last fell into a deep
sleep. For a time her father sat quietly listening to the sound of her breathing, then arising, he softly drew aside the curtains, and looked long and
anxiously at her as she slept.

Suddenly lifting his hands, he exclaimed, "Oh, God! save her, or help
me to bear it if she dies." It was the first prayer which for long, long years
had passed his lips, but it had a power to bring back the olden feeling, when
a happy boy, he had knelt at his mother's side, and was not ashamed to
pray. Falling on his knees, he tried to recall the words of prayer his mother
had taught him, but one petition alone came from his heart in that dark,
midnight hour, "Oh, don't let Fanny die, don't let her die, for who will
comfort old Joshua when she is gone?"

"The Saviour: he who once wept at the grave of Lazarus, will be more
to you than *I* ever was, or ever can be," said Fanny.

In her sleep she dreamed that her father prayed. She awoke and found it true. "Come nearer to me, father," said she. He did so, and then among his thick gray locks she laid her thin white hand and prayed.

It was a beautiful sight, and methinks the angels hovered round as that young disciple, apparently so near the portals of Heaven, sought to lead her weeping father to the same glad world. Her words were soothing, and o'er his darkened mind a ray of light seemed feebly, faintly shining. Before the morning dawned, he had resolved that if there still was hope for him he would find it. Many a time during the succeeding days he prayed in secret, not that Fanny might be spared, but that he might be reconciled to God. His prayer at length was answered, and Uncle Joshua was a changed man. He showed it in every thing, in the expression of his face and in the words he uttered. For his Sunshine he still wept, but with a chastened grief, for now he knew that if she died, he should see her in Heaven.

Where now was Dr. Lacey? Knew he not of the threatened danger? At his father's bedside, where for many days his place had been, he had received from Mr. William Middleton a letter announcing Fanny's illness, which, however, was not then considered dangerous. On learning the contents of the letter, the elder Mr. Lacey said, turning to his son, "Go, George, go; I would not keep you from her a moment." The Doctor needed no second bidding, and the first steamer which left New Orleans bore him upon its deck, anxious and impatient.

Fast the days rolled on, and they who watched Fanny alternately hoped and feared, as she one day seemed better and the next worse. Of those days we will not speak. We hasten to a night three weeks from the commencement of her illness, when gathered in her room were anxious friends, who feared the next day's sun would see her dead. Florence, Kate and Mr. Miller were there, with tearful eyes and saddened faces. Frank Cameron, too, was there. Business, either real or fancied, had again taken him to Kentucky, and hearing of Fanny's illness he had hastened to her.

She had requested to be raised up, and now, leaning against her Uncle William, she lay in a deep slumber. In a corner of the room sat Uncle Joshua, his head bowed down, his face covered by his hands, while the large tears fell upon the carpeting, as he sadly whispered to himself, "It'll be lonesome at night; it'll be lonesome in the morning; it'll be lonesome every whar."

Florence stood by him, and tried by gently smoothing his tangled hair, to express the sympathy she could not speak. Suddenly there was the sound of fast-coming wheels, and Kate, thinking it must be Dr. Gordon, whom they were each moment expecting, ran out to meet him. Nearer and nearer came the carriage, and as Kate was peering through the darkness to see if it were the expected physician, Dr. Lacey sprang quickly to her side.

In Frankfort he had heard that Fanny could not live, and now he eagerly asked, "Tell me, Mrs. Miller, is she yet alive?"

Kate replied by leading him directly towards the sick chamber. As he entered the room Uncle Joshua burst into a fresh flood of tears, saying as he took the Doctor's offered hand, "Poor boy! poor George. You're losing a great deal, but not as much as I, for you can find another Fanny, but for me thar's no more Sunshine, when they carry her away."

Dr. Gordon now came, and after feeling her pulse and listening to the sound of her breathing, he said, "When she wakes from this sleep I think the matter will be decided. She will be better or worse."

And he was right, although the old clock in the hall told the hour of midnight ere she roused from the deep slumber which had seemed so much like the long last sleep of death. Her first words were for "water, water," and as she put up her hand to take the offered glass, Dr. Gordon whispered to Dr. Lacey, "She is better, but must not see you tonight."

In a twinkling Mr. Middleton's large hand was laid on Dr. Lacey's shoulder, and hurrying him into the adjoining room, he said, "Stay here till mornin', and neither breathe nor stir!"

Dr. Lacey complied with this request as far as it was possible, though never seemed a night so long, and never dawned a morning so bright as did the succeeding one, when through the house the joyful tidings ran, that the crisis was past, and Fanny would live.

In the course of the morning, Fanny asked Kate, who alone was attending her, if Dr. Lacey were not there?

"What makes you think so?" said Kate.

"Because," answered Fanny, "I either heard him, or dreamed that I did."

"And if he is here, could you bear to see him now?"

"Oh, yes, yes," was the eager answer, and the next moment Dr. Lacey was by her side.

Intuitively Kate left the room, consequently we have no means of knowing what occurred during that interview, when Dr. Lacey as it were received back from the arms of death his Fanny, whose recovery from that time was sure though slow. Mr. Middleton, in the exuberance of his joy at having his Sunshine restored, seemed hardly sane, but frequently kept muttering to himself, "Yes, yes, I remember,—I'll do it, only give me a little time"; at the same time his elbow moved impatiently, as if nudging off some unseen visitor. What it was that he remembered, and would do, was not known for several days, and then he informed his wife, that when at first he feared lest Fanny should not live, he had racked his brain to know why this fresh evil was brought upon him, and had concluded that it was partly to punish him for his ill-treatment of Julia when living, and partly because that now she was dead he had neglected to purchase for her any grave-stones; and I promised, said he "that if she was spar'd, I'd buy as nice a grave-stun as I would if 'twas Sunshine." Three weeks from that time there stood by the mound in the little graveyard a plain handsome monument, on which was simply inscribed, "Julia, aged twenty."

One after another those who had been with Fanny during her illness departed to their homes. Frank Cameron lingered several weeks in Frankfort. Florence, too, was there with some relatives. Now, reader, if you value our friendship, you will not accuse him of being fickle. He had loved Fanny long and faithfully, but he knew the time was coming when he would see her the wife of another. What wonder was it then, if he suffered his eye occasionally to rest admiringly upon Florence Woodburn's happy face, or that he frequently found himself trying to trace some resemblance between the dark *hazel* of Florence's eyes and the deep *blue* of Fanny's!

With woman's quick perception Florence divined Frank's thoughts, and although she professed herself to be "terribly afraid of his Presbyterian smile and deaconish ways," she took good care *not* to discourage him. But she teased him unmercifully, and played him many sorry tricks. He bore it all good-humoredly, and when he started next for New-York he had with him a tiny casing, from which peeped the merry face of Florence, looking as if just meditating some fresh mischief.

And what of Florence? Why, safely stowed away at the bottom of her bureau-drawer, under a promiscuous pile of gloves, ribbons, laces and handkerchiefs, was a big daguerreotype; but as Florence guarded that drawer most carefully, always keeping the key in her pocket, we are unable to say any thing certain upon the subject. Up to this day we don't know exactly whose face it was, that led Florence to the drawer so many times a day, but we are safe in saying, that it looked *frank* enough to be Frank himself!

Here for a time we leave her, and return to Mr. Middleton's, where Fanny was improving each day. Dr. Lacey watched her recovery anxiously, fearing continually lest some new calamity should happen to take his treasure from him. Owing to the protracted illness of his father it became necessary that he should go back to New Orleans; but as soon as possible he would return, and then,—Fanny could have told you what then, and so too could we, but we prefer keeping you in suspense.

## Chapter XXIV

The autumn months were gone; December had come and "Christmas was coming." The negroes, far and near, had counted the days which must pass before their expected holidays. In Uncle Joshua's kitchen there was much talking and laughing, fixing and fussing, and some crying. Had you asked the cause of the crying, you would have been told that Miss Fanny was to be married Christmas Eve, and the week following she would leave them, and start for New Orleans.

Preparations commenced on a large scale; for Uncle Joshua, a little proud, it may be, of his handsome house, had determined on a large party. The old gentleman even went so far as to order for himself a new suit of broadcloth, saying, by way of apology, that, "though the jeens coat and bagging pants did well enough for Josh, they wouldn't answer no how for the father of Mrs. Dr. George Lacey."

In every corner might be seen little negroes engaged in stoning raisins, with here and there a *seed* sticking to their shining faces. Owing to some unaccountable reason, when the raisins were finished, nearly half of the original quantity was found missing. Aunt Judy's suspicions instantly alighted upon Bob, notwithstanding his vehement denial of having even *tached* a raisin while stoning them. Alas, for poor Bob! He had taken too many, and his stomach began to show threatening signs of dislodging its contents. Vomiting was the result, during which process Aunt Judy shook him lustily, declaring, "he had done et enough raisins to give an ostrich the misspepsy!"

Bob didn't know who *she* was, but he gladly made his escape from his mother's hands, muttering to himself, "I don't care a darn how many Miss Betsy's I git; they can't none on em be worse than mother. High, she's a roarer," and with this consoling reflection he betook himself to the barn in quest of eggs, as his mother had bidden him not to come in her sight again, unless his cap were full of eggs. " 'Sposin' I can't find none," said he, "wonder if she 'spects me to lay 'em."

Bob was naturally of an inquiring mind, and for many days back he had been troubled to know exactly what *relationship* would exist between Dr. Lacey and himself when the former should be Fanny's husband. He could not settle the point satisfactorily, and when he thought his mother had forgotten the raisins he ventured to ask her opinion.

"Why, Bob," said she, " 'tain't no ways likely *you'll* be connection at all, for he won't have such a limb in his family, but *I* am Fanny's aunt, and that'll make Dr. Lacey my niece."

Bob never thought of doubting his mother's word, but he lamented his numerous misdemeanors, which would prevent him, too, from being Dr. Lacey's aunt.

A week before the wedding, Florence, who loved dearly to be in a bustle, came laden with bandboxes and carpet bags. Hourly through the house rang her merry laugh, as she flitted hither and thither, actually doing nothing in her zeal to do every thing. She had consented to be bridesmaid on condition that she should choose her own groomsman, who, she said, should be "Uncle Billy," as she always called Mr. William Middleton, "unless Providence sent her some one she liked better." Whether it were owing to Providence or to an invitation, which went from Florence to New-York, we are unable to say, but two days before the 24th, Uncle Joshua surprised Florence and Fanny by opening the door of the room where they were sitting, and saying, "Ho! my boy, here they be;—come on."

The girls started up, and in a moment Frank stood between them, with an arm thrown around each. "Why, Mr. Cameron," said Florence, "what did you come for, and who knew you were coming?"

"I came to see *you,* and *you* knew I was coming," answered Frank.

"Well then," returned Florence, "if you came to see me, do look at me, and not keep your eyes fixed so continually on Fanny. In a few days you will be breaking that part of the tenth commandment, which says, 'Thou shalt not covet thy neighbor's wife.' "

"Possibly I might, had I never seen *you*," answered Frank.

At a late hour that night Florence moved with soft footsteps about her sleeping room, fearing lest she should awaken Fanny. Her precautions were useless, for Fanny was awake; looking at Florence, she, said, "Oh, Flory, you naughty girl; what makes you blush so dreadfully?"

The next half hour was spent by Florence in telling Fanny what Frank had just asked her in four or five words and which she had answered in *one*, viz., if she would be his wife; "but then," said Florence, pretending to pout, "he was so very conscientious that he had to tell me what I already knew, which was, that he once loved you better than he should ever love another."

Frank had asked Florence to share his lot through life and she, like any other good, prompt Kentucky girl, had readily answered "Yes," although she was frightened next moment for fear she had been too easily won by the "cold Yankee," as she called him, and she proposed taking back what she had said just for the sake of being *teased*. Mr. Woodburn came next day to bring Florence some article of dress, which she would need. He was not surprised when Frank, taking him aside, modestly asked for his daughter; he said, "Yes," almost as readily as Florence had done, and then it was hard telling which seemed most happy, Frank or Dr. Lacey.

The 24th of December came at last. We, at the North, who, during six months of the year, blow our benumbed fingers, can scarcely imagine how bright and beautiful are some of the clear warm days of a Kentucky winter. On this occasion, as if nature had resolved to do her best, the day was soft and sunny as in early autumn, presenting a striking contrast to the wild, angry storm, which rent the sky, when once before 'neath Uncle Joshua's roof, a bridal party was assembled.

As night approached, carriage after carriage rolled up the long, gravelled pathway, until Ike declared, "Thar was no more room in the barns, and if any more came he'd have to drive 'em into the kitchen."

Up and down the broad stairway tripped light and joyous footsteps, until the rooms above, which Luce had put in so exact order, presented a scene of complete confusion. Bandboxes were turned bottom side up, and their contents indiscriminately scattered until it was impossible to tell what was yours and what wasn't. Merry voices were heard, talking, laughing, and asking, "How do I look?" to which question those present invariably answered, "Oh, beautifully," without ever looking up! But the answer was correct enough, for the young girls, who that night assembled at Fanny's bridal, were beautiful enough to make even Mr. William Middleton talk of trying *Twiggs' Preparation* on his slightly whitened locks!

In one room there was rather more order. 'Twas where Florence and Fanny were dressing. Once Florence stopped in the midst of her toilet, and throwing her arms about Fanny, said, "Oh, I am so glad you are the bride, for I would not live that other dreadful night over again for any thing. Why, I actually found two white hairs in my head within a week after, and I know 'twas all owing to my fright!"

Just before Fanny was ready, a servant entered, bringing to her a singularly-looking bouquet. It consisted of three large, *full blown* roses, round which were ranged in a perfect circle, some dark green leaves of rose geranium. The whole was tied with a piece of white tape. It was the gift of Bill Jeffrey, who had brought it himself with the request that Fanny would accept it, as he had nothing else to give. Mrs. Jeffrey had quite a passion for flowers, and for many days Bill had watched these roses, fearing they would not be fully blown by the time he wanted them. Some one had suggested to him that *buds* were preferable, but he resented the advice as an insult, saying, "he reckoned he knew better than to offer Miss Fanny stingy little rosebuds." Fanny accepted the bouquet, and ordered it to be placed with the remainder of her bridal presents. Then learning that Billy was still waiting, she sent an invitation that he should stay and witness the ceremony.

At length the noise up stairs subsided, and was transferred to the parlors below, but even there it ceased, as through the door came Dr. Lacey and Fanny, followed by Frank Cameron and Florence. The ceremony was not interrupted by the thunder's roar, nor the company blinded by the lightning's flash, but throughout the rooms was a solemn hush as Fanny was made Dr. Lacey's wife. Firmly Dr. Lacey held her hand until the last word was spoken; then when he felt sure that she was his, he stooped down and whispered in her ear, "Thank God, you are mine at last."

Their friends now crowded round offering their congratulations to Dr. and *Mrs. Lacey*, who looked as they felt, perfectly happy. Uncle Joshua too came forward, and taking the hand of his son-in-law, said, "George, I have now gin you my only gal, and I've got nothin' left, but I am old and before long shall go home. I needn't tell you to be good-natured and kind to Sunshine, for I know you will be, and if an old man's blessing is of any account, you both have mine." Here he entirely broke down, and drawing Fanny to him, sobbed out, "Oh, what shall I do without you? What shall I do without my Sunshine?"

Dr. Lacey tried to soothe him, and by the time supper was announced he had become calm. He led the way to the dining-room, saying, "Come on, as many as you as can squeeze in, and the rest can sit on the stars. That's plates enough to go 'round, I reckon, for Nancy borrowed all Miss Thornton and Widder Brown had."

Judy had no fears this time that the supper would not be eaten, while Bob, who was watching the proceedings through the window, expressed his fears that "they'd clear the table, smack and clean," hoping that if they did, "they'd all vomuk a heap worse than he did when he et the raisins."

But Bob was mistaken in his estimate of things, and when at a late hour that night he held the lantern until Ike had harnessed the last horse, he crept to his rude bed with a sick head and a sick stomach, the result of a very light supper of half a chicken, four tarts, five pieces of cake, three saucers of ice cream, four pickles, and two cups of strong coffee! He, however, forgot his troubles by morning and said, "he allus did like to go to Miss Fanny's wedding 'cause he had sich tall things to eat."

Three days after the wedding Mr. Middleton's carriage again stood before the door, while Ike tried to conceal his tears by fixing and refixing the travelling trunks in their proper places. Fanny had been the playmate of his childhood and the affection conceived for her then had increased as he grew older. Now she was leaving him, and the poor black boy cried as he thought how lonesome the old place would be without her. Her parents thought so too, but they tried to appear composed, for they would not add unnecessary grief to their daughter's parting. When all was ready, Uncle Joshua kneeled down, and winding his arm about Fanny, prayed in simple, touching language that God would protect his Sunshine, and at last bring them all to the same home. "All of us; don't let *one* be missing thar." There was a peculiar pathos in the tone of his voice as he said the last words, and all knew to whom he referred.

Long and wearisome at Mr. Middleton's were the days succeeding Fanny's departure, while in Dr. Lacey's home all was joy and gladness, as Aunt Dilsey "put her best foot forward to get ready for the new Miss." Tarts, or "little pies," as she called them, were her special favorites, and now Aunt Dilsey was not a little puzzled to know which kind would suit Fanny best.

"Wish I knew," said she, "which she likes most, grape sass ones, or blackb'ry ones."

"Let me fix 'em," said Rondeau. "You make a heap of both kinds, and mebby I can manage to worry down a little of what she don't eat."

Rondeau was in high spirits these days, for his master had promised to give him Leffie one week after his return home. This, of course, made Leffie good for nothing, and Rondeau a good deal worse. He was continually in the kitchen, playing off some prank on Aunt Dilsey, who declared, "She hoped marster would come pretty soon and tend to him, or she shouldn't have a spoonful of sense left."

Her wish was gratified, for one afternoon there came word that Dr. Lacey was in the city. He had arrived a day sooner than he had expected to, and in a few hours would be at home, where he hoped to find all in readiness to receive him. Every thing and every body was in a flurry. Fires had to be lighted in the parlors, supper-table spread in the dining-room, coffee put a boiling, and chickens set to broiling, while Jack was continually reminded how to "hold up his head and make a bow to the new lady, like he had some manners."

Then came the making of Aunt Dilsey's toilet, which was no small matter considering the amount of labor necessary to get her dress together, but then, of course, 'twas very loose, for "she didn't b'lieve in having tight dresses, and wouldn't neither, if she was as big agin."

About dark Dr. Lacey arrived. Happy as a bird, Fanny sprang up the steps. Every thing about her seemed homelike and cheerful. Dusky, but kind faces peered at her from every corner, while Aunt Dilsey, with a complacent smile, stood ready to receive her. Fanny was prepared to like every thing, but there was something peculiarly pleasing to her in Dilsey's broad, good-humored face. Going up to her, she took both her hands, and said, "I know we shall be good friends. I shall like you, and you will love me a little, won't you, just as the old aunties did, I left in Kentucky?"

Aunt Dilsey hadn't expected all this, and the poor creature burst into tears, saying, "Lord bless the sweet Miss, I'd die for her this minute, I would."

Rondeau, Leffie, and the other blacks belonging to the establishment now came forward, and in the crowd little Jack's bow was entirely unappreciated; but Fanny next day made amends by giving him nearly a pound of candy, which had the effect of making him sick a week, but he got well in time to be present at Leffie's wedding, which took place just a week after Dr. Lacey's return.

Leffie, who chanced to be just the size of her young mistress, was thrown into ecstasies by the gift of a thin pink and white silk, which Fanny presented to her for a bridal dress. Aunt Dilsey, in order to show her thanks, went down on her knees, a thing she never attempted again, as it took her such an unheard-of length of time to recover a standing posture. Dr. Lacey had made Leffie the present of a pair of gold ear-rings, so that she was really a pretty bride, and Rondeau was the happiest negro in all New Orleans.

As weddings seem to be the order of this chapter, we may here, as well as any where, dispose of Mrs. Carrington, whom, you will remember, Raymond said he would one day marry. When he left Frankfort, he had no definite idea as to what he should do, but after reaching Cincinnati, it occurred to him that his mother had a wealthy old bachelor-uncle living in St. Louis, and thither he determined to go. This uncle, Mr. Dunlap, received the young man cordially, for he was the first relative he had met with in years. There was something, too, in the manner with which Raymond introduced himself, that won for him a place in the crusty old man's good opinion.

"I am Fred Raymond," said he, "your niece Helen's son, and as poor a jack as there is this side of California. They say you are a stingy old customer, but I don't care for that. You have got to give me some business, and a home, too."

Had Raymond come cringingly about his uncle, he most likely would have been sent away. But Mr. Dunlap was a somewhat uncivil man, and Raymond's uncivil speech charmed him, and he answered, "Upon my word, Fred, you are well stocked with impudence, if you haven't any thing else. But I like that much better than palaver. Want some business, hey? Well, what can you do? Nothing, I'll warrant."

"I can do anything *you* can, sir," answered Raymond, unhesitatingly. "Only give me something that will bring money, for money I *must* and *will* have."

Without knowing it, he had touched the right chord, for a young man who wished to work and make money, was a novel sight to old Dunlap, who held laziness in great abhorrence. He was a wealthy merchant, and fortunately was just wanting a young man in his counting-room. This situation, with a liberal salary, he offered to Raymond, who eagerly accepted it. That day seemed to Raymond of interminable length, for in his haste to find his uncle, he had neglected to take breakfast, and when dinner hour arrived, he was greatly surprised to see Mr. Dunlap walk off without saying a word to him.

"Wonder if he means to starve me," thought Raymond. The old gentleman soon returned, and Raymond thought there was a mischievous look in his gray eye, but he kept silent until the bells of the city rang for nine. Then as he saw his uncle about to leave, he took his hat and accompanied him. When they were in the street, Mr. Dunlap said, "Are you going any where in particular, Fred?"

"I don't know whether I am or not," answered Raymond. "I am going home with you, and am going to have some supper, too."

Nothing more was said until they reached a large, remarkably handsome building, which they entered. Mr. Dunlap rang the bell and ordered supper for himself and Raymond. While waiting for it, Raymond had time to look about him. He was surprised at the costly furniture, and argued from that, that he should soon have a warm supper of corresponding goodness. Greatly was he disappointed on entering the dining-room, to find nothing but a few thin slices of bread, already buttered, and some tolerably decent coffee. (The table was covered with a fine damask cloth and adorned with silver plate.)

Mr. Dunlap sat down and passed the bread to Raymond, who instantly took two thirds of the whole. With the utmost sang froid Mr. Dunlap continued holding the plate saying, "Better take it *all.*"

Raymond did so, and ate it too, then seizing the bell, he asked the servant who appeared, if there was any cold meat in the house?

"Yes, marster."

"Well, bring me some, quick."

"Yes, marster."

And she immediately placed before him some cold roast beef, with its appendages. While he was carving and helping himself, Mr. Dunlap said, quietly, "Perhaps you mean to board with me?"

"Yes, sir, I do," answered Raymond.

"Was you going to pay?"

Raymond hesitated a moment, and then said, "No, *sir,* I'm not going to spend my salary for board!"

"Very well," answered his uncle, "when you finish that joint of beef, I'll show you your room, for I'm afraid you'll be walking into my best bed, boots and all."

Raymond did not eat quite all the beef, and in a few moments found himself in a snug, pleasant little room, which his uncle said he might call his. As Mr. Dunlap was leaving the room, Raymond called after him, saying, "Ho! old fellow, have some nice beef steak in the morning, will you?"

His uncle did not answer, but trod heavily down the winding stairway, muttering to himself, "He's some, and no mistake, but I like his grit, any way."

Mr. Dunlap was a wealthy, but miserly man. He, however, liked to show off, and to appear well in society. Accordingly, his house was furnished expensively, and he kept numerous servants. Four times a year he gave large dinner-parties, at which he spared neither money nor pains, but to make amends for such extravagance, he almost starved himself the remainder of the time.

Recently he had begun to find his life lonely, and he looked upon Raymond as a godsend to cheer his solitude. He wished, however, to know something of him before taking him into his confidence, and consequently treated him as we have seen. But the die was cast, and Raymond was soon perfectly at home in his uncle's house, where he called every thing *his*. He even succeeded in making a change in the board, saying, he could not work on such meagre fare, and what was more, he would not. Mr. Dunlap yielded the point quietly, merely saying, "he hoped Fred would let him know before he concluded to sell the house!"

When Raymond had been with his uncle about three months, the junior partner died, and Mr. Dunlap proposed that Raymond should take his place. "I haven't any money," said Raymond, "but it won't hurt you a bit to take me without any capital, and give me a fair share of the profits." In a few days the old sign board, which for thirty years had proclaimed the firm of "Dunlap & Johnson," was exchanged for a new one, on which was written in large letters, "Dunlap & Raymond."

Raymond now was on the road to wealth, but he never for a moment forgot his design of eventually marrying Mrs. Carrington. He had once accidentally mentioned her in the presence of his uncle, who immediately asked, "Who *is* Mrs. Carrington?" In a few moments Raymond told who and what she was, sparing none of her faults, but making the most of her virtues, and speaking too of his own views and feelings with regard to her.

Mr. Dunlap listened attentively, and when Raymond finished speaking, he said, "Yes,—Mrs. Carrington,—Well—I don't think she would feel *much* flattered with your description of her. And you like her, and think she would marry you, if you were rich, hey?"

"I know she would," said Raymond, warmly.

"Well, we shall see, we shall see," answered his uncle.

The spring following Julia Middleton's death, Mrs. Carrington, thinking she was not appreciated in Frankfort, determined on going to St. Louis. Several of her relatives resided there, besides a rich bachelor old enough to be her father, to whom she had once been engaged, but had jilted for Mr. Carrington. Now, however, she resolved to make another attack upon him, feeling tolerably sure of success, for she knew he had once idolized her.

Raymond was first apprised of her being in St. Louis by accidentally meeting her in the street, accompanied by her cousin, Miss Howard, who was something of a belle. The cold, frigid bow which Mrs. Carrington had prepared to greet Raymond with melted into a smile of pleased recognition, when she saw how familiarly her cousin received and chatted with him. Still, she was somewhat on her guard, but before they parted, Miss Howard had invited him to call upon them that evening, saying that she and Mrs. Carrington would be alone.

When Raymond returned home to tea, he casually mentioned to his uncle that he should be absent that evening, as he was intending to call upon some ladies.

"Singular coincidence," returned Mr. Dunlap, "for I too shall be engaged in the same business."

"*You* call upon the ladies!" said Raymond.

"Yes, why not?" returned his uncle, slightly reddening. "There's not a fashionable mother in St. Louis but weekly lectures her daughter on the importance of treating the ugly, but *rich* old Dunlap, with due respect."

At an early hour Raymond started for Mr. Howard's. Since morning Mrs.

Carrington had learned from her cousin Jane the position which Raymond occupied in society, and she received him with great cordiality of manner, although she appeared ill at ease, and started nervously each time the sound of footsteps was heard. Soon there was a sound of a loud, hasty ring at the door, and in a moment, who should enter the room but Mr. Dunlap, who walked across the room and greeted Mrs. Carrington with the freedom of an old friend, saying, "I scarcely hoped ever again to see you, Ida."

Raymond's jealousy was instantly roused. He had heard the clerks hint that eight or nine years before, his uncle had been disappointed by a young lady many years his junior, and that this disappointment had increased the natural moroseness of his nature. He had never asked the name of the lady, but he was now convinced that 'twas none other than Ida Carrington.

An awkward restraint seemed suddenly to have fallen upon the little company, and as Raymond thought *he* was the cause, he soon took his leave. What occurred that night between Mr. Dunlap and Mrs. Carrington, Raymond never exactly knew, but when next morning he met his uncle at breakfast, he fancied there was the same mischievous look in his eye which he remembered having seen once before.

After a time Mr. Dunlap said, "Fred, do you still love Mrs. Carrington well enough to marry her?"

"Yes, don't you?" answered Raymond.

Mr. Dunlap did not reply to this question, but continued, "Ten years ago, Fred, I made a fool of myself by fancying that a young girl, scarcely twenty-one, loved me and my ugly face well enough to marry me, but when a younger, handsomer, and nearly as wealthy a man, presented himself, Ida Lindsey all at once discovered that thirty-five years difference in our ages was altogether too much. She left me and married young Carrington. But now that he is dead, she is willing old Dunlap should again bend his rheumatic knees before her, for she thinks me rich; but *I* shan't do it. I have, however, spoken a word for you, and she will not tell you 'No' again."

The next time Raymond saw Mrs. Carrington, she met him with her sweetest smile, but he all at once discovered many perfections in Jane Howard, and for three weeks he flirted with *her,* utterly neglecting Mrs. Carrington, who tried in vain to win him to her side. At the end of that time his flirtation was cut short by the return of a gentleman from Europe, to whom Jane had long been engaged.

When next Raymond and Mrs. Carrington were alone, he abruptly said, "Mrs. Carrington, I will marry you, if you want me to!"

She probably did want him to, for four weeks from that time Mr. Dunlap's house was thrown open to a large party who assembled to pay their respects to Mr. and Mrs. Raymond. Mrs. Carrington soon found that the man she had to deal with this time was not so patient and all-enduring as her first husband had been. He was not unkind, but he exercised over his wife a surveillance exceedingly annoying, and she learned too late that she had not only chosen a husband but an exacting master, who, although he treated her with attention, was still determined that she should pay due deference to *him* and his wishes.

She was also disappointed in her expectations of a fortune, for within two years after her marriage Mr. Dunlap suddenly died. He had intended to make his will and make Raymond his heir, but like many other men, he put it off until it was too late, and his property, which was found to be less than was supposed, went back to his brothers and sisters, and from them to their children and grandchildren, so that Raymond got but a small share.

He, however, retained his position as a merchant, and struggled hard to keep his wife in the same circumstances to which she had been accustomed. She appreciated his kindness, and when at the end of three years she was the mother of three children, she concluded it was time to lay aside all desire for fashionable amusements, and she became a tolerably affectionate wife, and a wonderfully indulgent mother.

# Chapter XXV

It was a day of unusual rejoicing in the establishment over which Miss Dillon presided as fashionable dressmaker, milliner, &c., in Cincinnati. Faces which for many weeks had scarcely worn a smile when in the presence of their grim mistress, now broke forth in merry peals of laughter, and backs which for the same length of time had bent in a sort of half-circle over brocades, silks and satins, were now erect, while needles which should have been better employed, now stuck stiff and straight in the mammoth pin-cushion on the little workstand. The cause of all this change was this: Miss Dillon, the crabbed, cross-grained, parsimonious proprietor of the shop, had gone for two weeks to the country, leaving her affairs in the charge of her foreman, Lizzie Copeland, a chubby, good-natured girl, whom no body feared, and every body loved.

Hardly had the last tones of Miss Dillon's harsh voice subsided in the workroom, ere a dozen girls exclaimed at once, "Oh, good! now what shall we do, and what shall we have nice to eat, whilst the stingy old thing is gone?" There was, however, one drawback to their pleasure. A large quantity of work was on hand to finish which somebody must labor both early and late.

"Dear me," said Jenny Carson, as before the glass she brushed and admired her bright auburn hair, "how I wish some raw apprentice who knows how to sew would happen along! Wouldn't we make her work while we rested?" and Jenny threw herself on the faded calico lounge with the air and manner of one who had nothing to do, and no wish to do it.

The girls looked at her and then at Lizzie Copeland, who was about to reprove the notoriously lazy Jenny, when tingle, tingle, went the bell in the front shop, and out went Miss Copeland to see what was wanted. In an instant Jenny was on her feet, saying, "Who knows but it's the apprentice I was wishing for!" Then up to the little glass door she stole, and lifting one corner of the curtain, peeped cautiously out at the stranger, who was talking with Lizzie.

"Shame on you, Jenny," said one of the older girls. "Come back to your work and behave yourself."

But Jenny paid no heed to her companion, but continued her espionage, until suddenly starting back she exclaimed, "Laws of mercy! what horrible eyes, and she saw me looking at her, too."

This brought up half a dozen more girls, who crowded round the glass door, curiously eyeing the stranger, who seemed desirous of coming amongst them. One of Miss Dillon's last orders to Lizzie was, that if during her absence two or three decent-looking girls should apply for situations, she should engage them, and the girl who now stood before Lizzie was certainly decent-looking, yes, and more than that, for humble as was her dress and appearance, there was something about her that inspired Miss Copeland with a feeling slightly akin to awe. She gave her name as Lucy Brown, and said she was from the country. After a little further conversation, Lizzie concluded to receive her, and she was ushered into the workroom through the glass door, from which the half-dozen girls beat a precipitate retreat, Jenny falling down and upsetting the pile of bonnet boxes, which rolled promiscuously over the floor.

When order was somewhat restored, twenty pair of eyes were turned towards the new comer. She was a young girl apparently eighteen or twenty years of age. Her face was pale, almost startlingly so, and her glossy black hair was cut short in the neck, giving her a strange, unusual appearance. Her most remarkable feature was her large, black, glittering eyes, whose glance was so proudly defiant that Jenny at once despaired of making her presence any way subservient to her wishes.

Jenny had a great fancy for tracing back one's origin and ancestry, consequently the name of the stranger girl, Lucy Brown, was not a little displeasing. "It might as well be John Smith," thought she, "for who is ever going to be at the trouble of running through the whole race of Browns for the sake of alighting upon her great-grandfather? However, I'll make her acquaintance, and question her a little."

Accordingly she moved towards the corner where Lucy sat quietly sewing on a black skirt, which Lizzie had given her to make. She commenced the conversation with, "I suppose you have made skirts before, haven't you?"

"No," was the laconic reply.

"What! never made a skirt?"

"Never!"

"That's queer! Why, you must be as old as I, are you not?"

"I don't know."

"Well, I'm seventeen; are you older than that?"

"Yes."

Jenny was puzzled, but determining to persevere, she said, "Are you always so quiet and still as you seem to be now?"

"Very seldom," was the reply, while the fiery flash from her glittering eyes made Jenny conclude not to question her any more for the present.

Scarcely was the conclusion formed when the ringing of the door-bell was heard, and up bounced Jenny, saying, "Let me go this time, for my head aches so I can't see any way." Away she ran, but soon returned bringing the Daily Cincinnati Commercial in her hand, and saying, "Won't I have a nice time now, reading the rest of that story?"

The girls well knew it was impossible to make Jenny work when Miss Dillon was absent, therefore they listened, nothing loth, to the conclusion of a story, which had been in progress for several days. That being finished, Jenny looked the paper over and suddenly exclaimed, "Oh, girls, don't you remember the advertisement which appeared two weeks ago concerning Julia Middleton, of whom cousin Mary told us so much?"

"Yes, what of it?" asked a dozen voices, while Lucy Brown accidentally dropped her thimble, occupying quite a little time in finding it.

Jenny answered, "She's dead,—drowned! But let me read it," and in a few moments she read the first notice, headed, "Supposed Suicide."

Jenny was a kind-hearted girl, and as she finished reading, two large tears dropped from her eyes and fell upon the paper.

"Oh, Jenny Carson," said one of the girls, "I do believe you're crying for that bag of deceit! If what your cousin Mary told us about her were true, she deserves drowning a dozen times."

"Perhaps she does," answered Jenny; "but then she was so young, so handsome, and then you know her father was not so kind to her as he was to the other one—the one he called Sunshine. Now if he had been better to Julia, she might have been better to him. Don't you think so?"

"I don't think anything about it," said her companion. "I only know I'm glad she's getting her pay for all her badness."

"Oh, awful!" said Jenny. "Not even willing that she should live until she had time to repent."

Here the conversation ceased. Lucy Brown certainly couldn't have liked her seat; for while the girls were talking, she moved uneasily, and at last turned entirely around, sitting with her back to them. Upon what had been said she made no comment; but most wonderfully she unbent towards Jenny, who, when next she made advances, was pleased to find herself met more than half-way.

It was strange how strong a friendship soon sprang up between the cold, silent Lucy, and the merry, romping Jenny. It was not unlike the friendship which might be supposed to exist between a playful, though somewhat in-dolent kitten and a fierce mastiff, or between a dove and an eagle, or better yet, between a sunbeam and a lowering cloud laden with gleams of lightning.

Jenny looked up to Lucy with feelings of love and fear, while Lucy looked down upon Jenny with a mixture of love, censure and contempt; —love for her affectionate nature, censure for her notorious laziness, and contempt for suffering herself to be so easily led and influenced by others; but in no way was this last fault so clearly manifested as in the power which she herself soon possessed over her. She, better than any one else, could coax Jenny to work, although she did it not so much by words as by the glance from her black eyes, which Jenny greatly feared.

Once, when both words and eyes had failed, the little dark hand was for an instant buried in the soft, plump flesh of Jenny's round, plump shoulder, who, sinking into a chair thought, "I do believe Lucy is the old one himself."

Jenny would have sworn that these thoughts were not expressed in words, but they were, and Lucy stooping down whispered, "Others have thought so, too."

Jenny was confounded, and Lucy's power over her greatly increased. To do Lucy justice, we must say that during her stay at Miss Dillon's, the influence she exerted over Jenny was seldom used to her injury, but many times after Jenny was asleep, would Lucy stitch away on a piece of work which had been assigned to her friend, and which otherwise would have been unfinished at the appointed time.

Two weeks had passed since Lucy had been in the shop, when one morning Jenny exclaimed, "To-day the Madam comes home, and oh, my—won't Jenny Carson have to work for the next three months!" She was right in one conjecture at least; for about noon Miss Dillon came, bringing a little girl ten or twelve years of age. Her first inquiry was for Lizzie Copeland, whom she took aside and questioned concerning what had been done during her absence. Lizzie told her of Lucy, whom she described as quite a treasure, saying, "that she already did as much work as a girl and a half." This put Miss Dillon in fine spirits; and as it was her custom to appear amiable in the eyes of each new girl, she entered the workroom, where she not only shook hands with, but kissed each girl until she came to Lucy, who haughtily drew back from the offered familiarity, merely extending her white slender fingers. Miss Dillon reddened, and turning away went in quest of the little girl, whom she introduced as "My niece Lottie." She was an ugly-looking, sour-faced child; and ere she had been in the house twenty-four hours every girl was her enemy. For several weeks she continued to be a perfect pest, hiding the girls' spools and scissors, nudging their elbows, pulling their hair, repeating to Miss Dillon every word they said, and annoying them in various ways.

One day her pranks seemed to have reached their crisis. For three hours she had been in the workroom playing off all manner of tricks upon the girls. As yet she had never dared molest Lucy, but now sidling up to her she jogged her elbow just in time to send the sharp-pointed needle far under the thumb nail! Up sprang Lucy, and seizing the little wretch, she shook her furiously, at the same time dealing her a few sound cuffs, and finishing up by sending her through a window which chanced to be open! Lottie's outcries brought in Miss Dillon, whom, with flashing eyes and fiercely set teeth, Lucy confronted, and explained the cause of the disturbance.

Miss Dillon's face was livid with rage, but Lucy was too valuable to be discharged, as many another girl would have been; so she partly suppressed her wrath, and said, "It is your first offence, Lucy, so I overlook it; but if it is repeated, you will leave my employ. Do you understand?"

"I shall probably not repeat it," answered Lucy, and, Miss Dillon, somewhat cooled, and wishing to conciliate Lucy, said, "I am sure you will not. You have too much good sense."

"You mistake me, Madam," interrupted Lucy. "I probably shall not repeat it, because there will be no occasion; but if that piece of impudence is not kept out of here, or if she does not behave when in here, I'll——"

"What will you do, Miss?" asked Miss Dillon, again towering high with indignation.

"I'll shake her twice as hard, and if the *top* window chances to be open instead of the lower one, I'll hurl her through that!"

Nothing but Lucy's tact at turning off work readily saved her from being discharged; but from that time Miss Lottie kept out of the way, or managed to behave when she was in the way.

On a few more occasions did Lucy's temper boil over. Once she made an assertion to which one of her companions replied, "That's a lie." Quick as thought the big shears were thrown at the offender's head, which they missed, and passing on stuck in the wall.

Always after these ebullitions, Lucy would relapse for weeks into a silent, moody fit, answering in monosyllables to every one save Jenny. And yet she was a favorite, although the girls united in saying that she was a strange, inexplicable girl.

The story of Julia Middleton had several times been brought up and discussed; and once, several months after Lucy's arrival, Jenny said, "Ever since Lucy has been here, I've been trying to think who she resembles, and now I've thought."

"Who is it?" asked Lucy, and Jenny answered, "To be sure *I* never saw her, but from what my cousin Mary said, you must look like Julia Middleton, only not quite so well."

Two crimson spots burned on Lucy's cheeks, and Jenny, clapping her hands, said, "That's it,—now I am sure you look exactly like her."

"And do I act like her?" asked Lucy.

"No, not exactly," returned Jenny; "and yet when you threw Lottie through the window, and the shears at Sarah's head, I thought of her." Then, as a new idea entered her brain, she said, "Oh, girls, won't it be nice when Miss Dillon goes away, to have some more tableaux, and take that wedding for the scene. You know a lady who was present told cousin Mary all about it, and she has described it accurately enough for us to imitate."

Tableaux was the favorite amusement of these over-worked, half-fed girls, and the place which they were in offered many inducements to such pastime, as every needful article of dress could generally be procured. Accordingly, Jenny's suggestion was readily received, and ere bed-time the girls of two or three other shops were notified of the coming event. In a few weeks Miss Dillon went away, and the third night of her absence was fixed for the play. Jenny Carson, never idle when fun was afoot, was chosen mistress of ceremonies.

"Now," said she, "let us choose characters. I will be Fanny, because I've got curly hair. Lizzie Copeland shall be the minister,—she's just good enough for that. Sarah Burnett shall be Dr. Lacey, because Bill Dillon's clothes fit her so well; and now," said she, looking over the girls, "who'll be the bride?"

"Why, Lucy, of course," said three or four voices. "You say she looks like her."

"So she does," answered Jenny, "but somebody has got to be the old man. He, you know, will rave, and shake Julia, and Lucy can do that so well."

"Yes, I can personate him to perfection," said Lucy, somewhat bitterly.

But Jenny was overruled, and Lottie, who was large of her age, was appointed to personate Mr. Middleton, whose six feet and a half would have felt insulted at being represented by a girl of twelve.

"Yes, that will do," said Jenny, "for next to Lucy Lottie is most of a spitfire."

After some more talk it was decided that Lucy should be the bride, to which she consented rather unwillingly. Wednesday evening came, and Jenny was appointed to dress the bride, which she did with a great deal of care, continually lamenting Lucy's obstinacy in wearing her hair short in her neck.

"Now if 'twere only long," said she, "I could arrange it beautifully."

"Never mind, Jenny," said Lucy. "I am Julia Middleton enough without the hair."

At last all was ready. To be sure, Lottie's clothes did not fit exactly, but the wrinkles and cavities were filled out with aprons, towels, &c.; so that when her toilet was completed, she was a tolerably good picture of a short, red-faced, portly old man. Near the door stood Lizzie Copeland, with black dressing-gown and prayer book. Two or three times Jenny had nearly spoiled the scene by running down stairs to see the fun go on. At last through the door came Sarah Burnett and Lucy, and as the latter swept into the room, all marvelled at the whiteness of her face. Greatly, too, did their wonder and admiration increase at the facility with which she acted her part. Julia herself could not have done better; and when at the final winding up Joseph Dunn appeared, she fainted and fell to the floor "so naturally."

Meantime Jenny came tripping in, and Sarah Burnett instantly caught her in her arms. Either by mistake or design, Jenny called out, "Come, Sally, that will do. Put me down. You've squeezed me most to death now," and the whole party burst into a loud laugh.

Lucy still lay upon the floor, and Jenny, who bent down to speak to her, screamed out, "Oh, girls, mercy,—she's cold,—she's dead,—or fainted, one or the other."

Half out of their senses with fright, the girls lifted her up, and carrying her to her room, placed her upon her bed. She soon opened her eyes, and glancing at the bridal dress in which she was still attired, shuddered as she said, "Come, girls, help me off with this foolery."

They did so, and in a short time she was able to sit up, talking and laughing about the tableaux and her fainting fit, saying she was accustomed to them, and had felt sick and dizzy all day.

In two weeks' time Miss Dillon returned, bringing with her, as Jenny said, the cholera,—not that she actually brought it in any one of her numerous trunks or bandboxes, but on the same day that she returned, the first case of cholera was reported in the city. Rapidly the disease spread, and one by one Miss Dillon's girls went home, until none were left save Lucy and Jenny;—the former stayed because she had no home to go to, she said;— Jenny's mother was a widow and lived with a married son in Sandusky, where the disease was making fearful ravages. Consequently it was safe for Jenny to stay in Cincinnati as it was to venture home.

Nearer and nearer came the pestilence, and more and more terrified grew Miss Dillon, until at last she, too, was smitten. If she had valued Lucy Brown as a workwoman, how much more did she now prize her as a nurse. Utterly fearless of the disease she stood with untiring patience by Miss Dillon's bedside, while in the farthest attic of the house Jenny held camphor to her nose, or entirely suspended her respiration, if by chance she was obliged to pass Miss Dillon's door. Alas, poor Jenny! Up in that little attic the destroyer found her. With an agonizing shriek of terror she threw herself into Lucy's arms, exclaiming, "I've got it! I've got it! I shall die! Oh, my poor mother! If I could see her again!" Terrible were her sufferings. For three long hours Lucy stood by her, and when at last the little parched hand fell heavily at her side, and o'er the laughing eyes the heavy eyelids closed, when the last spasm came and went, she lay in Lucy's arms, and as falls the rain in the dark November days, so fell Lucy's tears on the face of the pale, dead Jenny!

More than a year had passed since the curtain fell upon Jenny, cold and still, and Lucy weeping passionately over her. In Miss Dillon's workroom are assembled nearly all our old friends, though one seat,—the little stool by Lucy's side is vacant, and in the common grave-yard is a grassy mound, on whose plain marble slab is the single word, "Jenny." The girls do not play at tableaux now, for the moving spirit of fun is gone, and the motto at Miss Dillon's seems to be, "Work, work, till the eyes grow dim."

On this afternoon several of the girls are engaged upon an elegant party dress, which must be finished by sunset. Among them is Lucy, who, since Jenny's death has grown more grave and taciturn, seldom asking a favor, though often doing one. At last the dress was completed, neatly folded and placed in a bandbox, while Lucy asked permission to carry it home. Her request was granted, and with the dress and Miss Dillon's bill, she started for Mr. Graham's, which was distant nearly a mile. It was dark when she reached the house, where she was seated in the hall while the servant took the dress and bill to Miss Woodburn, who was in the adjoining parlor with her friend, Alice Graham.

"Here, ma'am, is your dress and a note," said the girl.

"My dress," exclaimed Florence, for she it was. "Oh, Allie, isn't it beautiful! But where is the girl? Is she waiting to be paid?"

"Yes, ma'am,—in the hall."

"Well, she wants to rest, and I want to finish reading my letter, so ask her to wait a moment."

Lucy merely bowed to the message which the girl delivered, and then listened eagerly while Florence read aloud a letter which she had just received from Nellie Stanton. In the letter Nellie said that Mrs. Middleton, whose health had long been failing, was not expected to live; Dr. Lacey and Fanny had come from New Orleans and were now with her; that Mr. William Middleton and Ashton had gone to England, ostensibly to attend the World's Fair, but in reality on a wild goose chase after a little Spaniard. When Florence appeared in the hall, Lucy's green veil was drawn closely over her face, and after receiving the money she immediately departed.

That night Miss Dillon was surprised when Lucy requested the payment of a part or all of her wages then due, saying she was intending to take the morning stage for Lexington. At first Miss Dillon was angry, but Lucy persisted, saying by way of explanation that she had that night heard something which made it necessary for her to go, that she was not what she seemed, neither was her name Lucy Brown. "But do not question me," said she. " 'Twill do no good, and some time I will tell you all."

The stars were still shining in the sky of a September morning, when the stage-coach stopped before Miss Dillon's gate. A group of pale, sickly-looking girls assembled in the hall, and with many tears bade their companion good-bye. Miss Dillon warmly pressed Lucy's hand, and in a low voice said, "Will you not tell me who you are?"

Lucy whispered in her ear a name which made her reel and fall backwards upon the stairs. When she recovered, the stage was far down the stony street and Lucy was gone.

> "Now far away, far away, over valley and plain,
> To the land of Kentucky we'll speed us again."

In Uncle Joshua's home there were sad, troubled faces and anxious hearts, as the husband and daughter watched by the wife and mother, whose life on earth was well-nigh ended. From her mother's family Mrs. Middleton had inherited the seeds of consumption, which had fastened upon her.

Day by day they watched her, and when at last she left them, it seemed so much like falling away to sleep that Mr. Middleton, who sat by her, knew not the exact moment which made him a lonely widower. The next afternoon sympathizing friends and neighbors assembled to pay the last tribute of respect to Mrs. Middleton, and many an eye overflowed, and more than one heart ached as the gray-haired old man bent sadly above the coffin, which contained the wife of his early love. But he mourned not as one without hope, for her end had been peace, and when upon her face his tears fell, he felt assured that again beyond the dark river of death he should meet her.

The night succeeding the burial, Mr. Middleton's family, overcome with fatigue and grief, retired early to their rooms, but Fanny could not sleep, and between ten and eleven she arose and throwing on her dressing-gown nervously walked up and down her sleeping-room. Through the closed shutters the rays of a bright September moon were stealing, and attracted by the beauty of the night, Fanny opened the blinds and the room was filled with a flood of soft, pale light. From the window where she stood she could distinguish the little grave-yard, with its cypress and willow trees, and its white monument gleaming through the silvery moonlight, and near that monument was a darker spot, the grave of her beloved mother. "If all nights were as lovely as this," thought she, "it would not seem half so dreary to sleep in the cold dark grave," and then Fanny fell into a fit of musing of the night that would surely come when she would first be left alone in the shadowy grave-yard.

In the midst of her reverie her attention was attracted by a slight female figure, which from some quarter had approached unperceived, and now upon the newly made grave was bowing itself and apparently weeping. The size and form of the girl were so much like Luce, that Fanny concluded it must be she, at the same time wondering how, with her superstitious ideas, she dared venture alone near a grave in the night-time. In a moment, however, she saw that Tiger, the watch-dog, was with her, and the same instant the sound of a suppressed sob fell on her ear. "Poor Luce," said she, "I did not think she loved my mother so well. I will go to her, and mingle my tears with hers."

In a short time Fanny was in the open air, and on her way to the grave-yard. As she approached her mother's grave, she said, gently, "Luce, Luce, why are you out so late?"

The person addressed partially raised her head and answered hurriedly, "Oh, Fanny, Fanny, do not be frightened and leave me; I am not dead, and never was buried in that grave as you suppose, but am here to-night, a living, repentant woman," and throwing back her bonnet, the thin, white face of Julia Middleton was in the bright moonlight perfectly distinguishable to Fanny, who at first recoiled in fear and leaned for support against the marble pillar near which she was standing.

She, however, soon recovered her self-command and, glancing at the object on the grave, saw that she was caressing Tiger, who seemed trying various ways to evince his joy at finding one whom he had long missed, for he had ever been Julia's favorite. Their fiery natures accorded well. Again Julia spoke, "Fanny, dear Fanny; in an adjoining State I heard of mother's illness and hastened to see her, but I am too late. Now do not think me a phantom, for see, Tiger recognizes me and welcomes me home, and will not you?"

An instant Fanny wavered, then with a half-fearful, half-joyful cry she went forward, and by the grave of the mother that day lowered to the dust, the sisters met in a long, fervent embrace.

Into the best chamber of their father's house Fanny led the weeping, repentant girl, and gently removing her bonnet and shawl, bade her lie down upon the nicely-cushioned lounge, while she went for their father. As she was leaving the room Julia arose and laid her small, bony hand on Fanny's shoulder. It had rested there before, for in the grave-yard, with their buried mother between them, Julia's arms had encircled her sister's neck; but the first excitement was over, and now involuntarily Fanny shrank from that touch, for spite of all her courage, she could not help associating Julia with the grass-grown grave, and the large white monument.

"What is it, Julia?" she said calmly. "Do you not wish to see father?"

"Oh, yes, yes," answered Julia, "but not *him,* the other one;—at least not to-night. You understand."

"I do," said Fanny, and she glided down the stairs towards her father's room. He was awake, for ere her hand touched the door knob, his sonorous, "Who's thar?" fell on her ear. This somewhat disconcerted her, for she had intended stopping near his door, to devise the best means by which to break the intelligence. But "Who's thar?" was again repeated, and entering the room she said softly, "It's I, father."

"Why, sure enough," said he, and then as the light from her lamp fell on her features, he exclaimed, "Why, how white you be! What's the matter? Who's up stairs? Is George sick?"

"No, George is not sick," said Fanny, "but—," and then as well as she could she told him all she knew.

Uncle Joshua's nervous system was unstrung, and his physical health impaired by long nights of watching with his wife, and now when this fresh shock came upon him he fell back half fainting upon his pillow. Then rousing himself, he said, "Alive, and come back! I didn't desarve this. But where is she? I will go to her."

Fanny directed him where to find her and then returned to Julia, whither her father soon followed. Uncle Joshua was not prepared for the change in his daughter. He did not even think of her as he saw her last, wasted by sickness, but in imagination he beheld her as she was in her days of health and dazzling beauty, when with diabolical cunning she had brought Dr. Lacey to her feet. Now, however, her face was thin, white and haggard, for a life at Miss Dillon's had never conduced to the beauty and health of any one, except the merry Jenny, who was too indolent to grow poor. Her eyes, sunken in their sockets, and swollen with recent weeping, looked frightfully large and wild, and to complete the metamorphosis, her beautiful, glossy hair was now cut short in her neck, and pushed far back from a brow, across which lay more than one premature wrinkle.

The sight of her for a time unsettled the old man's reason. Taking her in his arms, he alternately cried and laughed over her, saying, "I knew you'd come, I expected it. I've waited for you," and then in a whisper he added, "Why didn't you bring your poor mother? Didn't she tell you how lonesome I was, and didn't she say that I *did* love you more'n you thought I did?" Then laying her down, he turned to Fanny, who was alarmed at his manner, and said, "Come, Sunshine, darling, go to the grave-yard agin, and mebby you'll fetch Nancy this time. Oh, I wish you would. I'm so sorry and sick without her." Seeing that Fanny did not move, he continued more imploringly, "Oh, Sunshine, do go. You can bring her back, if any body can. Tell her how dark 'tis here at home, and how long I've lived since she went away."

"Poor dear father!" said Julia, while Fanny, winding her arms about his neck, said, "Oh, father, father, don't talk so, mother's in heaven. You wouldn't have her back, would you?"

His daughters' sympathy made him weep, but tears relieved him, and his mind again became calm and clear. Still Julia's altered appearance troubled him, and drawing her head down upon his bosom, and laying his hand on her thin, white face, he said, "Poor child, what has changed you so, and whar have you been; and who did I buy that big stun for if 'twasn't for you?"

"Not to-night, dear father," answered Julia. "Let me rest to-night, and to-morrow I will tell you all."

Uncle Joshua arose to leave the room, but at the door he turned back and said, "Are you sure you won't clamber out o' the window, and be gone in the mornin'?"

"Perfectly sure," was the reply, and then Julia was alone.

## Chapter XXVI

In the breakfast room the table was neatly spread, Aunt Judy wondering much, "what had got into marster that he would have the best cheeny dishes and the damson table-cloth." Doubts of his sanity had entered her mind, and when he ordered her to arrange the table for four, she muttered to herself, "Wonder if he 'spects any of the dead to come back to breakfast."

"Yes, I do," said he.

"Which one?" asked Judy, wishing to humor his whim.

Uncle Joshua waited until the pile of china coffee cups was set upon the table, and out of all danger of being broken, and then he answered, "Your young Miss Julia."

Judy's worst fears were now confirmed, and she said pityingly, "Poor dear marster! Trouble's done driv him clearn mad."

"I am not mad," answered Uncle Joshua, "I am in earnest. Julia never was dead, never was drownded. She has come back, and is up stars in the best room."

"Gone clearn mad!" was Judy's only answer, and Uncle Joshua's stock of patience, which even now was not remarkably large, was fast oozing out, when Fanny appeared in the room, and at her father's request, corroborated what he had said.

Had a powder mill exploded near Judy's feet, she could not have been more startled. Retreating to the kitchen she repeated what she had heard, with many little embellishments of her own. Surprise and alarm were depicted on every face as Aunt Judy told her story, which she ended with, "I wonder what possessed her to come back. 'Pears like marster and I have as much trouble now as we can bar without her. Why couldn't she lie still like other folks when she was dead, and not be a gittin' up and comin' back where she ain't wanted?"

Aunt Katy tried to reason the case, saying, "It was perfectly nateral, for she never did do nothin' like no body else, and if she took a notion not to be dead 'twarn't in natur that she should be."

Here the conversation was interrupted by Mr. Middleton, who screamed out, "Ho! Judy, gals, fetch in your vittles." He had first asked Fanny to go for her sister, and she arose to obey him. Overcome with fatigue and excitement, Julia, immediately after her father left her on the preceding night, had fallen into a deep sleep, which was unbroken till long after day dawn. Then she was aroused by her father calling up the negroes. Her first impression was that it was Miss Dillon's harsh, unwelcome voice, and, hastily starting up, she looked around her. That pleasant room, with its handsome furniture, and those downy pillows, with their fine white linen, belonged not to Miss Dillon, and for a moment Julia strove to recall what had happened. Soon she remembered all, and burying her face in the pillows, she sobbed out, "Father, I thank thee; the prodigal is at last at home." It was not Julia's first prayer, for since Jenny's death, Lucy Brown had learned to pray.

Hastily arising she proceeded with her toilet, which was nearly completed when Fanny tapped gently at the door, and immediately entered the room, saying, "Good morning, dear Julia. I am so glad you really are here, and that it is not a dream. But come, breakfast is waiting and so is father, and so is,—so is,—George."

"Oh, I can't see him, I can't," said Julia, and Fanny answered, "Oh, never mind him. I have told him all about it, and he is ready to receive you as a sister."

Julia's eyes were fixed upon Fanny's face, and for the first time she seemed to discover how greatly she had improved in looks. The exceeding paleness of her cheek was gone, and the bright, healthful bloom which had taken its place, though differing in shade, was equally as beautiful as the roses of which Julia once had boasted. Her hair, too, which after her illness had nearly all fallen off, had grown out greatly improved in beauty, being now a rich golden brown and Uncle Joshua had frequently lamented that he had lost his little yellow-haired girl. They were standing together before a long mirror, and involuntarily Julia glanced at the faces which it revealed. The contrast affected her painfully, and instead of replying to what Fanny had said, she asked, "Am I indeed so greatly changed, or is it you who have grown so beautiful?"

Fanny, too, looked in the glass, and guessing the cause of her sister's thoughts, placed her arm around her neck and said, "Never mind that either. You have had a hard time, somewhere. Now that you are at home, you will grow strong and handsome again. But come, father does not like waiting for breakfast any better than he used to."

So saying she led the reluctant girl down the long staircase, through the wide hall to the door of the breakfast room, where Mr. Middleton stood waiting for them. His tones and manner were very, very affectionate, as he kissed the wanderer and said, "I am so glad you're here."

Julia could have wept, but she would not. There was yet another to meet, and choking down her tears she nerved herself to the trial. Of what occurred next she knew nothing until her cold hand was clasped by another so warm, so life-giving in its touch, that she raised her eyes and met the calm, quiet gaze of Dr. Lacey. Neither of them spoke until Julia, averting her eyes, said, "Am I forgiven?"

"You are," was the answer, and then Uncle Joshua exclaimed, "Thar, that'll do. Now come to your breakfast, children, for I'm mighty hungry, and shan't wait another minute."

After breakfast Julia was greatly surprised at seeing her father take from the book-case the old family bible, on whose dark dusky cover she remembered having many a time written her name. All was now explained. Her father's gentleness of look and manner was accounted for; and as, for the first time in her life, she knelt by his side and heard him as he prayed, her heart swelled with emotion, and she longed to tell him, though she dared not hope she was a Christian, she was still trying to lead a different, a better life.

That afternoon in her chamber were seated Mr. Middleton and Fanny, while Julia recounted the story of her wanderings. "The idea of leaving my home," said she, "was not a sudden impulse, else had I returned sooner, but it was the result of long, bitter reflection. In the first days of my humiliation I wished that I might die, for though the thought of death and the dread hereafter made me tremble, it was preferable to the scorn and contempt I should necessarily meet if I survived. Then came a reaction and when our angel mother glided so noiselessly around my sick room when you, darling Fanny, nursed me with so much care, and even father's voice grew low and kind as he addressed me, my better nature, if I have any, was touched, and I thought I would like to live for the sake of retrieving the past. But the evil spirit which has haunted me from infancy, whispered, that as soon as I was well all would be changed. You, Fanny, would hate me, and father would treat me as he always had, only worse."

"Poor dear child! I didn't ort to do so, I know," said Uncle Joshua, and Julia continued: "Then I thought how the world would loathe, and despise, and point at me, until I was almost maddened, and when Dr. Gordon said I would live, the tempter whispered *suicide;* but I dared not do that. About that time I heard rumors of a marriage which would take place as soon as I was well; and, Fanny, will you forgive me? I tried to be sick as long as possible for the sake of delaying your happiness."

A pressure of the hand was Fanny's only answer, and Julia proceeded: "I could not see you married to him. I could not meet the world and its censure, so I determined to go away. I had thirty dollars in my purse, of which no one knew, and taking that I started, I knew not where. On reaching the schoolhouse something impelled me to enter it, and I found there a young girl about my own size. Under other circumstances I might have been frightened, but now utterly fearless, I addressed her, and found from her answers that she was crazy. A sudden idea entered my brain. I would change clothes with her, and thus avoid discovery. She willingly acceded to my proposition, and in my new attire I again started towards Lexington, which I reached about four in the morning. I had no definite ideas as to where I wanted to go, but the sight of the Cincinnati stage drawn up before the

Phoenix, determined me. I had purposely kept my own bonnet and veil, as the maniac girl wore neither. Drawing the latter over my face, I kept it there while securing my seat in the coach, and until we were many miles from the city. Passengers entered and left, and some looked inquisitively at me and my slightly fantastic dress.

"We reached Cincinnati about ten in the evening, and with a long, glad breath I stepped from the coach, and felt that Kentucky and my notorious character were behind. I stopped at the —— Hotel, and the next two days were spent in procuring myself a decent outfit. Each night I went to a different house, for the sake of avoiding suspicion, and as my bills were promptly paid, no questions were ever asked. At the D—— House I saw in a paper an advertisement for a teacher in a school in one of the interior towns. I had formed some such plan for the future, and instantly determined personally to apply for the situation. I did so, but credentials were required, and I had none to give. Somewhat weary of my adventure I returned to Cincinnati, and in passing through one of the streets, my eye caught the sign 'Fashionable Dressmaking and Millinery.' I knew I had a taste for that, and I concluded to offer myself as an apprentice."

Then she told them how in the unwholesome atmosphere of Miss Dillon's crowded shop, she had toiled on day after day with dim eye and aching head, while thoughts of home and remorse for the past preyed on her heart.

"But why did you not come back?" asked Fanny. "We would have received you most gladly."

"I felt that I could not do that," said Julia. "I knew that you thought me dead, and I fancied that father at least would feel relieved."

"Oh, child," groaned Uncle Joshua, "don't say so I was mighty mean, I know, but I never got to that."

After a moment Julia continued: "In those close, heated rooms, there was a ray of sunlight, which in its gentle love for me, reminded me of Fanny." And then she told them of poor Jenny, of her sufferings, and early death. "After Jenny's death," said she, "I was desolate indeed. She seemed constantly before me, and I was haunted by the thought, 'What if it had been I, with all my load of guilt!' Among Jenny's books was a Bible, which I had frequently seen her read. When her clothes were sent to her mother, I kept the Bible, reading it at first for Jenny's sake, and afterwards for the precious truths it contained, and now though I may not hope I am a Christian, I am changed in more points than one."

Then she told them of the letter she had heard Florence read, and which had determined her to return home. "We reached Lexington," said she, "about nine o'clock in the evening, and as I thought my baggage might incommode me, I purposely left it there, but hired a boy to bring me home. When we reached the gate at the entrance of the woods, I told him he could return, as I preferred going the remainder of the way alone. He seemed surprised, but complied with my request. I had never heard of the new house, and as I drew near I was puzzled, and fancied I was wrong; but Tiger bounded forward, at first angrily, then joyfully, and I knew I was right. All about the house was so dark, so still, that a dreadful foreboding filled my heart,—a fear that mother might be dead. I remembered the little grave-yard, and instantly bent my steps thither. I saw the costly marble and the carefully kept grave, and a thrill of joy ran through my veins, for they told me I was kindly remembered in the home I had so darkened. But another object riveted my attention. It was a fresh mound, and I knew full well who rested there. Never had I shed such tears of anguish as fell upon the sod which covers my sainted mother. In the intensity of my grief I was not conscious of Fanny's approach until she stood near me. The rest you know; and now, father, will you receive to your home and affection one who has so widely strayed?"

"Willin'ly, most willin'ly," said Uncle Joshua, as he folded her to his bosom, "and if I'd done as I ort to, a heap of this wouldn't have happened. Oh, I didn't ort to do so, I didn't and I ain't goin' to, any more. You shall live with me when Sunshine's gone; and we would be so happy, if your poor mother could only see us and know it all."

From that time, nothing could exceed Uncle Joshua's kindness to his daughter. He seemed indeed trying to make up for the past, and frequently would he whisper to himself, "No, I didn't ort to do so. I see more and more that I didn't." Still his fondness for Fanny was undiminished, and occasionally, after looking earnestly at both his children, he would exclaim, "Hang me, if I don't b'lieve Sunshine is a heap the handsomest"; but if these words caused Julia any emotion, 'twas never betrayed.

From Julia's story, there could be no doubt that the maniac girl was laid in the grave, which Uncle Joshua had thought belonged to his daughter. No tidings of her had been heard, although one gentleman *thought* that he once had met with a girl answering to her description in the stage-coach between Lexington and Cincinnati. All search in that quarter was unavailing, and over her fate a dark mystery lay, until Julia suddenly appeared and threw light upon the matter. The afflicted father (for she had no mother) was sent for, and when told where his child was laid, asked permission to have her disinterred and taken to his family burial place. His request was granted, the grave was opened, and then refilled and levelled with the earth. The monument Julia took care to have carefully preserved as a memento of the olden time.

As will be supposed, Julia's return furnished the neighborhood and surrounding country with a topic of conversation for many weeks. At first nearly all treated her with cool neglect; but as she kept entirely at home, curiosity to see one who had, as it were, come back from the dead, triumphed over all other feelings; and at last, all who came to see Fanny asked also for her sister.

Among the few who at once hastened to give the penitent girl the hand of friendship, was Kate Miller; and as she marked her gentle manners and the subdued glance of her still somewhat haughty eyes, she wound her arm about her neck and whispered, "I shall in time learn to love you dearly for the sake of more than one."

Julia comprehended her, or thought she did, and answered, "Oh, Mrs. Miller, that one dreadful crime has troubled me more than all the rest. I killed him, your noble brother, and from the moment I deliberately determined to do so, I became leagued with the tempter, who lured me madly on.

But I outdid myself, and was entangled in the snare my own hands had laid."

"It is ever so," answered Kate. "Our most secret sins will in the end surely find us out."

Lest the reader should think us guilty of exaggeration and so credit nothing we have written, we must tell them that Julia was not wholly and entirely changed. But that good influences were at work, no one would doubt who had seen her once and who saw her now. Even Judy, who had predicted all manner of evil for her colored brethren, when Julia should be sole mistress of the house, now changed her mind, and admitted that "though Miss Julia wasn't to be named the same day 'long of Sunshine, she done pretty well, considerin'." Occasionally flashes of her hasty temper appeared; but, like "heat lightning," they did no harm, and were followed by no thunder, Uncle Joshua having ceased to act in that capacity!

Before Dr. Lacey and Fanny returned to New Orleans they saw Florence Woodburn, with a happy, loving heart, give her hand to Frank Cameron, who ever cherished for his young wife a tenderness as deep as he ever could have felt for Fanny Middleton. When he took his bride to New-York, she was received by his mother and sister with a profusion of love, so perfectly overwhelming, that poor Florence was guilty of several misdemeanors. We cannot do better than to give a part of a letter which she wrote to Fanny two weeks after her arrival in the city:

"DEAR FAN.:—

"Why, in the name of all the Woodburns and Camerons that ever were or ever will be, didn't you tell me what kind of mussy, fussy, twisted up things both Mrs. Cameron Senior, and Mrs. Cameron Senior's daughter, are. Why, the very first evening of our arrival, Mrs. Senior met me on the steps, and hugged me so hard that I really thought she was opposed to the match, and meant to kill me at once. In her zeal she actually kissed off both veil and bonnet, and as the latter disappeared, and she got a view of my face, on which the dust and cinders were an inch thick, she exclaimed, 'Oh, bootiful, bootiful! Why, Frank, half hasn't been told me.'

"By this time what little sense of propriety I ever had entirely left me, and I burst into a long, loud laugh. Frank put on his very longest Sunday face, and said softly, 'Don't, Florence.'

"But Mrs. Cameron apologized for me herself, saying, 'Hysterical, perhaps.'

"I have since asked her forgiveness, and she pretended to forgive me, but I don't more than half think she has, for between you and me, Fanny, I actually think she intends to roast me alive, and all on the plea of my having come from Kentucky, where she imagines the thermometer is always at the boiling point. She keeps the hottest fires I ever felt, and if by accident I open the window for a breath of air, she shuts it down, with a bang that would make me start, were I not so perfectly weakened by heat. I don't know what will be the end of all this, but I think by the time this letter reaches you, you may safely think of me as being *done brown!* If I am not roasted, stewed, fried and baked by New Years, Frank and I are going to keeping house. Oh, won't that be nice? I shan't have a fire again in a month, and the first thing I do will be to open all the doors and windows in the house!

"Gertrude pleases me well enough, but I shall like her better when she marries a certain Timothy Towzer, or some other awful name. Mr. Cameron I like very, very much, and call him father, too; he is exactly like Frank, and the only silly thing he ever did was when he married his wife. Do you suppose any body will ever say so of Frank? *Mais n'importe:* he says he's suited, and thinks he loves me quite as well as he ever did you——"

The next letter which came from Florence brought the intelligence that Gertrude was married to a Mr. *Somebody* and gone *Somewhere,* Halifax perhaps; that Florence and Frank were keeping house, and that Mrs. *Senior* came around every day to see who had called, and if Mrs. *Junior* had a cold.

Two years after Florence again wrote that Mrs. *Grandma* now came twice a day and petted little Frank until he actually began to look and act just like her!

The reader is perhaps anxious to know whether back across the Atlantic, Ashton brought his Spanish bride. Yes, he did. Mr. William Middleton accompanied him to the house of Sir Arthur Effingham, whom they found to be dying; his property was gone, and he feared that he must leave the youthful Inez to the cold charities of the world and a miserly brother. When Mr. Middleton made himself known, the dying man pointed to Inez and said, "You once loved the mother; care for the daughter when I am gone, will you?"

"I will," answered Mr. Middleton, "on condition that you consent to having a young friend of mine share the care with me." At the same time he presented Ashton.

Sir Arthur recognized him immediately and answered, "Willingly, most willingly; I was a fool to spurn you once as I did."

In a few hours Sir Arthur was dead, and Inez was an orphan. But her grief was soothed by the presence of Ashton, who, a few days before sailing for America, made her his wife. During the voyage Mr. Middleton informed Ashton, that as soon as he reached home he intended making his will, by which he should bequeath his property to Inez. Said he, "I have spent so many years of my life in India, that I find the climate of New Orleans more congenial to my feelings than a colder one would be, consequently I shall purchase a house in that city, and as I look upon you and Inez as my children, I shall insist upon you living with me, if you have no objections."

Ashton had never looked for such good fortune. Years before, he had been of rather reckless, dissipated habits, and his appearance still showed marks of having lived too fast. But recently he was very much changed, and with Nellie for a sister and Inez for a wife, he became a substantial and highly respectable man. Mr. Middleton purchased for a winter residence, a house near Dr. Lacey's, and between Fanny and Inez there sprang up a strong, ardent affection. Inez had never had a sister and she readily turned to Fanny, who reciprocated her love.

The spring following Dr. Lacey's return to New Orleans, Uncle Joshua was thrown into a great ferment by a letter from Fanny, in which she said it would be impossible for them to visit Kentucky that summer, and that they would spend the season near the Lake, where she urged her father and Julia to join them. This last proposal was out of the question, as Mr. Middleton was sure he could not exist in a climate where the thermometer stood a degree higher than it did in Kentucky, and Julia felt a decided aversion to New Orleans. So for two weeks Uncle Joshua fretted because Fanny could not come, wondering what was in the wind and making himself and every body else generally uncomfortable.

At last Julia, whom her father now honored with the appellation of his "Gale," suggested that as they could not see Fanny and would not go to New Orleans, they might take a trip through the Northern States, saying that she knew her Uncle William could be pleased to accompany them. "Well, we'll see," said her father, who seemed rather pleased with the idea.

The result of his *seeing* was that about the middle of June a party of three stepped from the Diana at Cincinnati, and took the morning train for Cleveland. In the features and dress of one of the individuals we readily recognize Uncle Joshua, who, with a little pardonable pride managed to let more than one fellow-traveller know that "he was a heap richer than he looked to be;" that "he owned fifty niggers and as many horses;" that "the handsome young lady with the dark blue travelling dress, buttoned with real gold buttons, was his daughter;" that "she had a sister married to Dr. Lacey, of New Orleans;" and lastly, that "the gentlemanly looking man, who accompanied them and seemed to know so much more about marners and travellin' than he did, was his brother Bill, who made his fortin' in the Indies and was now livin' on the interest on't."

They were an interesting group and attracted the attention of many, who wondered why Julia should seem so sad and her father so frequently called her his "Gale." They went through the Northern States, visiting the principal cities and watering-places, where it required all of Julia's watchfulness and forebearance to keep the father straight. Twice the old gentleman lost his temper, because she insisted upon his having a clean collar every day. "No use on't," said he, the morning after their arrival at Saratoga, as on the piazza they were reasoning the matter. "No use on't. I never wore none at home, and they make me feel so starched up and stiff like."

This was said in the hearing of two ladies, both of whom were coolly inspecting our friend through an opera glass. With a suppressed giggle they turned to enter the house, the eldest of them saying, "Do, Gertrude, try and find your father and ask him who that old savage is?"

"Ho! my fine madam," said the "old savage," "I can tell you and save you the trouble. I'm Josh Middleton, from Kentucky, and this is my daughter Julia."

"Fanny Middleton's father," said Mrs. Cameron, immediately changing her manner and offering her hand, while Gertrude flew to Julia's side, overwhelming her with a thousand questions concerning "Cousin Kate," and Fanny, the latter of whom, "we were so delighted with."

But neither Mr. Middleton nor his daughter could be talked over, and before they left the Springs Mrs. Cameron decided that the father was "not half civilized," and the daughter "quite ordinary looking."

About the middle of September our friends started to return home. At Cincinnati they called upon Miss Dillon, who was delighted at again seeing "Lucy Brown." Several of the old girls were there, but they seemed somewhat awed by the elegant appearance of their former companion. Before leaving the city Julia and her father visited Jenny's grave. On it there bloomed a fair white rose, which Julia gathered and still preserves as a memorial of her young friend.

The last week in September they reached home, greatly to Uncle Joshua's satisfaction, as he said, "he'd been so cramped up and purlite, that he hadn't more'n half enjoyed himself, and it had cost him a heap of money too." For a long time after his return he tried hard to introduce upon his plantation the same conveniences, order and thrift, which had pleased him so much at the North, but like all other slaveholders he was obliged to give it up, saying, that "if he would have niggers, he s'posed he must put up with nigger fixin'."

During the winter, Fanny wrote frequently to her father urging him to visit her; but this he declined doing, and early the following May, he stood one evening impatiently awaiting the arrival of Ike, who had gone to Frankfort with the expectation of meeting Fanny and her husband. Every thing had been put in readiness. The parlors and best chamber were opened and aired. The carriage and carriage horses had been brushed up, a new saddle had been bought for Fanny's pony, and a new dress for each of the black women, and every thing and every body seemed expecting a joyful time. With praiseworthy perseverance Julia had at length coaxed her father into one of the offending collars, and for the twentieth time he had in the same breath declared, that "he wouldn't war it, and that he'd gin up looking for Sunshine, for she wasn't coming," when from the group of woolly heads perched on the fence in the rear of the house, there came the glad cry, "Thar, that's Ike. Some body's with him. They're comin'."

In an instant the collar was forgotten, and as the carriage approached the house, Uncle Joshua looked wistfully towards it, trying to catch a glimpse of "Sunshine," whom he had not seen for nearly a year and a half. But only the face of a little negro girl was seen looking from the window, and Uncle Joshua exclaimed, "Now, what's possessed them to fetch that yaller gal! I've got niggers enough to wait on 'em."

But the "yaller gal" knew very well why she was there, and so ere long did Uncle Joshua. The steps were let down and there, blithesome and gay as ever, Fanny sprang from the carriage and ran into the arms of her father, who kissed her again and again, holding her off to look at her and then again drawing her to him and saying, "You're handsomer than ever."

During this process the yellow girl, Rose, had brought from the carriage a mysterious looking bundle of flannel and white cambric, which now in

Dr. Lacey's arms, was crowing with delight as its little nurse bobbed up and down, making at it all sorts of grimaces.

"What the—, no I forgot, I didn't mean so. But *what—is—that!!*" said Uncle Joshua, releasing Fanny and advancing towards Dr. Lacey, who proudly placed in his arms a beautiful nine months old baby saying, "We have brought you a second Sunshine."

Then through the house there echoed a laugh so long and loud that all the blacks who were not on the spot hastened thither, and on learning the cause of the disturbance, they, too, joined in the general joy with noisy demonstrations. "Oh, a baby, a little live baby, and Miss Fanny's baby too! How funny!" said Bob, as his heels flew into the air, and he went through with a set of gymnastic exercises, which would have done credit to the most practised circus performer.

Meantime little Anna Lacey, on whose account all this rejoicing was made, was amusing herself by burying her little chubby hands in her grand-father's hair. Fanny remonstrated, but her father said, "Let her alone;—let her work. She may pull every hair out of my head if she wants to. But what made you keep it so still? Why didn't you write about it?"

"Because," answered Fanny, "we at first thought you would surely visit us in the winter, and we wished to surprise you; but you did not come, and then I took a fancy to keep it from you until we came home; so I did not write, and I made Inez and Uncle William promise not to. Perhaps it was wrong, but I shan't do it again, for I did so want to tell you."

"All right, all right," said Uncle Joshua, "and tomorrow I'll go after Kate and her boy, and have 'em all here together."

But when the morrow came he found it impossible to leave his new Sunshine, and Ike was sent for Mrs. Miller, who came gladly to see her old friend. All that afternoon Uncle Joshua sat with his grand-daughter on one knee and little Dick Wilmot on the other, dancing them up and down in a manner highly alarming to their mothers and highly pleasing to the babies. The next day Kate returned home. As she was stepping into the carriage Uncle Joshua placed in her hands a sealed package, saying, "Wait till you get home before you open it." She did so, and then found it to be a deed to little Richard of a house and lot which Mr. Middleton owned in Frankfort. Accompanying the deed was a note, in which was written, "Don't hurt yourselves a thankin' me, for it's Julia's doin's. She first thought on't and put me up to it, though she don't want you to know it. I reckon she did it because the boy is named after poor Dick."

When next Mr. Middleton went to Frankfort, both Mr. Miller and Kate remonstrated at receiving so much at his hands, but he replied, "You may as well take it, for if poor boy Dick had lived I should have gin him a heap more, and a house won't come amiss to you and Katy. I s'pose you're too good abolitionists to own niggers, so I'll lend you Luce, who'll be mighty tickled to come and live with you, for she thinks there's only two ladies in the world; one's Sunshine and t'other's Kate."

In a few days Mr. William Middleton, Inez and her husband, came from New Orleans. The greater part of the summer they spent at the house of

Uncle Joshua, where, together with Dr. Lacey and Fanny, they formed as happy a party as one will often find.

Julia alone seemed not to share the general happiness. She could not forget the past, and whenever Dr. Lacey was present, seemed under a painful restraint. Frequently she would steal away, taking with her Anna, and if he were present little Richard, whom she seemed to love even better than she did her niece. For hours she would amuse them in her own room, much to the satisfaction of the little negro girls who had the charge of them, and who spent the time in a manner far more congenial to their tastes.

During the summer Lida Gibson wrote to Fanny, saying that Mabel Mortimer, having lost both the Doctor and Mr. Ashton, had at last taken up with her brother John, who had danced attendance upon her for several years. "As for me," said Lida, "I have reached the advanced age of twenty-two without ever having had an offer, so I have given up in despair and am looking forward to a long life of single-blessedness."

"Fetch her up with you next summer," said Uncle Joshua," and if Bill Jeffrey is alive she'll have a chance to brag of at least one offer."

In November Dr. Lacey again went South. Uncle Joshua accompanied them as far as Frankfort, clinging till the last to little Anna, whom he had petted till she was nearly spoiled. Dreary and desolate indeed seemed the house when the old man returned to it. Every thing reminded him of the absent ones, and when he accidentally came upon a bauble with which Anna had played, he was entirely overcome, and laying his head upon the table, cried like a child.

Softly a dark-eyed girl approached him, and throwing her arm across his neck and wiping away his tears, said, "Father, don't do so. They'll come again, and besides that, you are not all alone, for I am left, and you love me a little, don't you?"

"Yes, yes!" said he, and drying his eyes, he drew her near to him, and added, "thank God, who restored you to me, my Tempest, my Gale, my Julia."

# THE LAMPLIGHTER

BY MARIA SUSANNA CUMMINS

❀❀❀❀❀❀❀❀❀❀❀❀❀❀❀❀❀❀❀❀❀❀❀❀

# Chapter I

*Good God! to think upon a child*
*That has no childish days,*
*No careless play, no frolics wild,*
*No words of prayer and praise!*
LANDON

It was growing dark in the city. Out in the open country it would be light for half an hour or more; but within the close streets where my story leads me it was already dusk. Upon the wooden door-step of a low-roofed, dark, and unwholesome-looking house, sat a little girl, who was gazing up the street with much earnestness. The house-door, which was open behind her, was close to the side-walk; and the step on which she sat was so low that her little unshod feet rested on the cold bricks. It was a chilly evening in November, and a light fall of snow, which had made everything look bright and clean in the pleasant open squares, near which the fine houses of the city were built, had only served to render the narrow streets and dark lanes dirtier and more cheerless than ever; for, mixed with the mud and filth which abound in those neighborhoods where the poor are crowded together, the beautiful snow had lost all its purity.

A great many people were passing to and fro, bent on their various errands of duty or of pleasure; but no one noticed the little girl, for there was no one in the world who cared for her. She was scantily clad, in garments of the poorest description. Her hair was long and very thick; uncombed and unbecoming, if anything could be said to be unbecoming to a set of features which, to a casual observer, had not a single attraction,—being thin and sharp, while her complexion was sallow, and her whole appearance unhealthy.

She had, to be sure, fine, dark eyes; but so unnaturally large did they seem, in contrast to her thin, puny face, that they only increased the peculiarity of it, without enhancing its beauty. Had any one felt any interest in her (which nobody did), had she had a mother (which, alas! she had not), those friendly and partial eyes would perhaps have found something in her to praise. As it was, however, the poor little thing was told, a dozen times a day, that she was the worst-looking child in the world; and, what was more, the worst-behaved. No one loved her, and she loved no one; no one treated her kindly; no one tried to make her happy, or cared whether she were so. She was but eight years old, and all alone in the world.

There was one thing, and one only, which she found pleasure in. She loved to watch for the coming of the old man who lit the street-lamp in front of the house where she lived; to see the bright torch he carried flicker in the wind; and then, when he ran up his ladder, lit the lamp so quickly and easily, and made the whole place seem cheerful, one gleam of joy was shed on a little desolate heart, to which gladness was a stranger; and, though he had never seemed to see, and certainly had never spoken to her, she almost felt, as she watched for the old lamplighter, as if he were a friend.

"Gerty," exclaimed a harsh voice within, "have you been for the milk?"

The child made no answer, but, gliding off the door-step, ran quickly round the corner of the house, and hid a little out of sight.

"What's become of that child?" said the woman from whom the voice proceeded, and who now showed herself at the door.

A boy who was passing, and had seen Gerty run,—a boy who had caught the tone of the whole neighborhood, and looked upon her as a sort of imp, or spirit of evil,—laughed aloud, pointed to the corner which concealed her, and, walking off with his head over his shoulder, to see what would happen next, exclaimed to himself, as he went, "She'll catch it! Nan Grant 'll fix her!"

In a moment more, Gerty was dragged from her hiding-place, and, with one blow for her ugliness and another for her impudence (for she was making up faces at Nan Grant with all her might), she was despatched down a neighboring alley with a kettle for the milk.

She ran fast, for she feared the lamplighter would come and go in her absence, and was rejoiced, on her return, to catch sight of him, as she drew near the house, just going up his ladder. She stationed herself at the foot of it, and was so engaged in watching the bright flame, that she did not observe when the man began to descend; and, as she was directly in his way, he hit against her, as he sprang to the ground, and she fell upon the pavement. "Hollo, my little one!" exclaimed he, "how's this?" as he stooped to lift her up.

She was upon her feet in an instant; for she was used to hard knocks, and did not much mind a few bruises. But the milk!—it was all spilt.

"Well! now, I declare!" said the man, "that's too bad!—what'll mammy say?" and, for the first time looking full in Gerty's face, he here interrupted himself with, "My! what an odd-faced child!—looks like a witch!" Then, seeing that she looked apprehensively at the spilt milk, and gave a sudden glance up at the house, he added, kindly, "She won't be hard on such a mite of a thing as you are, will she? Cheer up, my ducky! never mind if she does scold you a little. I'll bring you something, tomorrow, that I think you'll like, may be; you're such a lonesome sort of a looking thing. And, mind, if the old woman makes a row, tell her I did it.—But didn't I hurt you? What was you doing with my ladder?"

"I was seeing you light the lamp," said Gerty, "and I an't hurt a bit; but I wish I hadn't spilt the milk."

At this moment Nan Grant came to the door, saw what had happened, and commenced pulling the child into the house, amidst blows, threats, and profane and brutal language. The lamplighter tried to appease her; but she shut the door in his face. Gerty was scolded, beaten, deprived of the crust which she usually got for her supper, and shut up in her dark attic for the night. Poor little child! Her mother had died in Nan Grant's house, five years before; and she had been tolerated there since, not so much because when Ben Grant went to sea he bade his wife be sure and keep the child until his return (for he had been gone so long that no one thought he would ever come back), but because Nan had reasons of her own for doing so; and, though she considered Gerty a dead weight upon her hands, she did not care to excite inquiries by trying to dispose of her elsewhere.

When Gerty first found herself locked up for the night in the dark garret (Gerty hated and feared the dark), she stood for a minute perfectly still; then suddenly began to stamp and scream, tried to beat open the door, and shouted, "I hate you, Nan Grant! Old Nan Grant, I hate you!" But nobody came near her; and, after a while, she grew more quiet, went and threw herself down on her miserable bed, covered her face with her little thin hands, and sobbed and cried as if her heart would break. She wept until she was utterly exhausted; and then gradually, with only now and then a low sob and catching of the breath, she grew quite still. By and by she took away her hands from her face, clasped them together in a convulsive manner, and looked up at a little glazed window by the side of the bed. It was but three panes of glass unevenly stuck together, and was the only chance of light the room had. There was no moon; but, as Gerty looked up, she saw through the window shining down upon her *one* bright star. She thought she had never seen anything half so beautiful. She had often been out of doors when the sky was full of stars, and had not noticed them much; but this one, all alone, so large, so bright, and yet so soft and pleasant-looking, seemed to speak to her; it seemed to say, "Gerty! Gerty! *poor* little Gerty!" She thought it seemed like a kind face, such as she had a long time ago seen or dreamt about. Suddenly it flashed through her mind, "Who lit it? Somebody lit it! Some good person, I know! O! how could he get up so high!" And Gerty fell asleep, wondering who lit the star.

Poor little, untaught, benighted soul! Who shall enlighten thee? Thou art God's child, little one! Christ died for thee. Will he not send man or angel to light up the darkness within, to kindle a light that shall never go out, the light that shall shine through all eternity!

## Chapter II

*Who shall assuage thy griefs, "thou tempest-toss'd!"*
*And speak of comfort, "comfortless!" to thee?*
                                        EMILY TAYLOR

Gerty awoke the next morning, not as children wake who are roused by each other's merry voices, or by a parent's kiss, who have kind hands to help them dress, and know that a nice breakfast awaits them. But she heard harsh voices below; knew, from the sound, that the men who lived at Nan Grant's (her son and two or three boarders) had come in to breakfast, and that her only chance of obtaining any share of the meal was to be on the spot when they had finished, to take that portion of what remained which Nan might chance to throw or shove towards her. So she crept down stairs, waited a little out of sight until she smelt the smoke of the men's pipes as they passed through the passage, and, when they had all gone noisily out, she slid into the room, looking about her with a glance made up of fear and defiance. She met but a rough greeting from Nan, who told her she had better drop that ugly, sour look; eat some breakfast, if she wanted it, but take care and keep out of her way, and not come near the fire, plaguing round where she was at work, or she'd get another dressing, worse than she had last night.

Gerty had not looked for any other treatment, so there was no disappointment to bear; but, glad enough of the miserable food left for her on the table, swallowed it eagerly, and, waiting no second bidding to keep herself out of the way, took her little old hood, threw on a ragged shawl, which had belonged to her mother, and which had long been the child's best protection from the cold, and, though her hands and feet were chilled by the sharp air of the morning, ran out of the house.

Back of the building where Nan Grant lived, was a large wood and coal yard; and beyond that a wharf, and the thick muddy water of a dock. Gerty might have found playmates enough in the neighborhood of this place. She sometimes did mingle with the troops of boys and girls, equally ragged with herself, who played about in the yard; but not often,—there was a league against her among the children of the place. Poor, ragged and miserably cared for, as most of them were, they all knew that Gerty was still more neglected and abused. They had often seen her beaten, and daily heard her called an ugly, wicked child, told that she belonged to nobody, and had no business in any one's house. Children as they were, they felt their advantage, and scorned the little outcast. Perhaps this would not have been the case if Gerty had ever mingled freely with them, and tried to be on friendly terms. But, while her mother lived there with her, though it was but a short time, she did her best to keep her little girl away from the rude herd. Perhaps that habit of avoidance, but still more a something in the child's nature, kept her from joining in their rough sports, after her mother's death had left her to do as she liked. As it was, she seldom had any intercourse with them. Nor did they venture to abuse her, otherwise than in words; for, singly, they dared not cope with her;—spirited, sudden and violent, she had made herself feared, as well as disliked. Once a band of them had united in a plan to tease and vex her; but, Nan Grant coming up at the moment when one of the girls was throwing the shoes, which she had pulled from Gerty's feet, into the dock, had given the girl a sound whipping, and put them all to flight. Gerty had not had a pair of shoes since; but Nan Grant, for once, had done her good service, and the children now left her in peace.

It was a sunshiny, though a cold day, when Gerty ran away from the house, to seek shelter in the wood-yard. There was an immense pile of timber in one corner of the yard, almost out of sight of any of the houses.

Of different lengths and unevenly placed, the planks formed, on one side, a series of irregular steps, by means of which it was easy to climb up. Near the top was a little sheltered recess, overhung by some long planks, and forming a miniature shed, protected by the wood on all sides but one, and from that looking out upon the water.

This was Gerty's haven of rest, her sanctum, and the only place from which she never was driven away. Here, through the long summer days, the little, lonesome child sat, brooding over her griefs, her wrongs and her ugliness; sometimes weeping for hours. Now and then, when the course of her life had been smooth for a few days (that is, when she had been so fortunate as to offend no one, and had escaped whipping, or being shut up in the dark), she would get a little more cheerful, and enjoy watching the sailors belonging to a schooner hard by, as they labored on board their vessel, or occasionally rowed to and fro in a little boat. The warm sunshine was so pleasant, and the men's voices at their work so lively, that the poor little thing would for a time forget her woes.

But summer had gone; the schooner, and the sailors, who had been such pleasant company, had gone too. The weather was now cold, and for a few days it had been so stormy, that Gerty had been obliged to stay in the house. Now, however, she made the best of her way to her little hiding-place; and, to her joy, the sunshine had reached the spot before her, dried up the boards, so that they felt warm to her bare feet, and was still shining so bright and pleasant, that Gerty forgot Nan Grant, forgot how cold she had been, and how much she dreaded the long winter. Her thoughts rambled about some time; but, at last, settled down upon the kind look and voice of the old lamplighter; and then, for the first time since the promise was made, it came into her mind, that he had engaged to bring her something the next time he came. She could not believe he would remember it; but still, he might, he seemed to be so good-natured, and sorry for her fall.

What could he mean to bring? Would it be something to eat? O, if it were only some shoes! But he wouldn't think of *that*. Perhaps he did not notice but she had some.

At any rate, Gerty resolved to go for her milk in season to be back before it was time to light the lamp, so that nothing should prevent her seeing him.

The day seemed unusually long, but darkness came at last; and with it came True—or rather Trueman—Flint, for that was the lamplighter's name.

Gerty was on the spot, though she took good care to elude Nan Grant's observation.

True was late about his work that night, and in a great hurry. He had only time to speak a few words in his rough way to Gerty; but they were words coming straight from as good and honest a heart as ever throbbed. He put his great, smutty hand on her head in the kindest way, told her how sorry he was she got hurt, and said "It was a plaguy shame she should have been whipped too, and all for a spill o' milk, that was a misfortin', and no crime."

"But here," added he, diving into one of his huge pockets, "here's the critter I promised you. Take good care on't; don't 'buse it; and, I'm guessin', if it's like the mother that I've got at home, 't won't be a little ye'll be likin' it, 'fore you're done. Good-by, my little gal;" and he shouldered his ladder and went off, leaving in Gerty's hands a little gray-and-white kitten.

Gerty was so taken by surprise, on finding in her arms a live kitten, something so different from what she had anticipated, that she stood for a minute irresolute what to do with it. There were a great many cats, of all sizes and colors, inhabitants of the neighboring houses and yard; frightened-looking creatures, which, like Gerty herself, crept or scampered about, and often hid themselves among the wood and coal, seeming to feel, as she did, great doubts about their having a right to be anywhere. Gerty had often felt a sympathy for them, but never thought of trying to catch one, carry it home and tame it; for she knew that food and shelter were most grudgingly accorded to herself, and would not certainly be extended to her pets. Her first thought, therefore, was to throw the kitten down and let it run away.

But, while she was hesitating, the little animal pleaded for itself in a way she could not resist. Frightened by its long imprisonment and journey in True Flint's pocket, it crept from Gerty's arms up to her neck, clung there tight, and, with its low, feeble cries, seemed to ask her to take care of it. Its eloquence prevailed over all fear of Nan Grant's anger. She hugged pussy to her bosom, and made a childish resolve to love it, feed it, and, above all, keep it out of Nan's sight.

How much she came in time to love that kitten, no words can tell. Her little, fierce, untamed, impetuous nature had hitherto only expressed itself in angry passion, sullen obstinacy, and even hatred. But there were in her soul fountains of warm affection yet unstirred, a depth of tenderness never yet called out, and a warmth and devotion of nature that wanted only an object to expend themselves upon.

So she poured out such wealth of love on the little creature that clung to her for its support as only such a desolate little heart has to spare. She loved the kitten all the more for the care she was obliged to take of it, and the trouble and anxiety it gave her. She kept it, as much as possible, out among the boards, in her own favorite haunt. She found an old hat, in which she placed her own hood, to make a bed for pussy. She carried it a part of her own scanty meals; she braved for it what she would not have done for herself; for she almost every day abstracted from the kettle, when she was returning with the milk for Nan Grant, enough for pussy's supper; running the risk of being discovered and punished, the only risk or harm the poor ignorant child knew or thought of, in connection with the theft and deception; for her ideas of abstract right and wrong were utterly undeveloped. So she would play with her kitten for hours among the boards, talk to it, and tell it how much she loved it. But, when the days were very cold, she was often puzzled to know how to keep herself warm out of doors, and the risk of bringing the kitten into the house was great. She would then hide it in her bosom, and run with it into the little garret-room where she slept; and, taking care to keep the door shut, usually eluded Nan's eyes and ears. Once or twice, when she had been off her guard, her little playful pet had escaped from her, and scampered through the lower room and passage. Once Nan drove it out with a broom; but in that thickly-peopled region, as we have said, cats and kittens were not so uncommon as to excite inquiry.

It may seem strange that Gerty had leisure to spend all her time at play. Most children living among the poorer class of people learn to be useful even while they are very young. Numbers of little creatures, only a few years old, may be seen in our streets, about the yards and doors of houses, bending under the weight of a large bundle of sticks, a basket of shavings, or, more frequently yet, a stout baby, nearly all the care of which devolves upon them. We have often pitied such little drudges, and thought their lot a hard one. But, after all, it was not the worst thing in the world; they were far better off than Gerty, who had nothing to do at all, and had never known the satisfaction of *helping* anybody. Nan Grant had no babies; and, being a very active woman, with but a poor opinion of children's services, at the best, she never tried to find employment for Gerty, much better satisfied if she would only keep out of her sight; so that, except her daily errand for the milk, Gerty was always idle,—a fruitful source of unhappiness and discontent, if she had suffered from no other.

Nan was a Scotchwoman, no longer young, and with a temper which, never good, became worse and worse as she grew older. She had seen life's roughest side, had always been a hard-working woman, and had the reputation of being very smart and a driver. Her husband was a carpenter by trade; but she made his home so uncomfortable, that for years he had followed the sea. She took in washing, and had a few boarders; by means of which she earned what might have been an ample support for herself, had it not been for her son, an unruly, disorderly young man, spoilt in early life by his mother's uneven temper and management, and who, though a skilful workman when he chose to be industrious, always squandered his own and a large part of his mother's earnings. Nan, as we have said, had reasons of her own for keeping Gerty, though they were not so strong as to prevent her often having half a mind to rid herself of the encumbrance.

❀❀❀❀❀❀❀❀❀❀❀❀❀❀❀❀❀❀❀❀❀❀❀❀❀❀❀

## *Chapter III*

*Mercy and Love have met thee on thy road,*
*Thou wretched outcast!*

WORDSWORTH

When Gerty had had her kitten about a month, she took a violent cold from being out in the damp and rain; and Nan, fearing she should have trouble with her if she became seriously ill, bade her stay in the house, and keep in the warm room where she was at work. Gerty's cough was fearful; and it would have been a great comfort to sit by the stove all day and keep warm, had it not been for her anxiety about the kitten, lest it should get lost, or starve, before she was well enough to be out taking care of it; or, worst of all, come running into the house in search of her. The whole day passed away, however, and nothing was seen of pussy. Towards night, the men were heard coming in to supper. Just as they entered the door of the room where Nan and Gerty were, and where the coarse meal was prepared, one of them stumbled over the kitten, which had come in with them, unperceived.

"Cracky! what's this 'ere?" said the man, whom they all were accustomed to call Jemmy; "a cat, I vow! Why, Nan, I though you kind o' hated cats!"

"Well, 't an't none o' mine; drive it out," said Nan.

Jemmy started to do so; but puss, suddenly drawing back, and making a circuit round his legs, sprang forward into the arms of Gerty, who was anxiously watching its fate.

"Whose kitten's that, Gerty?" said Nan.

"Mine!" said Gerty, bravely.

"Well, how long have you kept cats? I should like to know," said Nan. "Speak! how came you by this?"

The men were all looking on. Gerty was afraid of the men. They sometimes teased, and were always a source of alarm to her. She could not think of acknowledging to whom she was indebted for the gift of the kitten; she knew it would only make matters worse, for Nan had never forgiven True Flint's rough expostulation against her cruelty in beating the child for spilling the milk; and Gerty could not summon presence of mind to think of any other source to which she could ascribe the kitten's presence, or she would not have hesitated to tell a falsehood; for her very limited education had not taught her a love or habit of truth where a lie would better serve her turn, and save her from punishment. She was silent, and burst into tears.

"Come," said Jemmy, "give us some supper, Nan, and let the gal alone till arterwards."

Nan complied, ominously muttering, however.

The supper was just finished, when an organ-grinder struck up a tune outside the door. The men stepped out to join the crowd, consisting chiefly of the inmates of the house, who were watching the motions of a monkey that danced in time to the music. Gerty ran to the window to look out. Delighted with the gambols of the creature, she gazed intently, until the man and monkey moved off; so intently, that she did not miss the kitten, which, in the mean time, crept down from her arms, and, springing upon the table, began to devour the remnants of the repast. The organ-grinder was not out of sight when Gerty's eyes fell upon the figure of the old lamplighter coming up the street. She thought she would stay and watch him light his lamp, when she was startled by a sharp and angy exclamation from Nan, and turned just in time to see her snatch her darling kitten from the table. Gerty sprang forward to the rescue, jumped into a chair, and caught Nan by the arm; but she firmly pushed her back with one hand, while with the other she threw the kitten half across the room. Gerty heard a sudden splash and a piercing cry. Nan had flung the poor creature into a large vessel of steaming-hot water, which stood ready for some household purpose. The little animal struggled and writhed an instant, then died in torture.

All the fury of Gerty's nature was roused. Without hesitation, she lifted a stick of wood which lay near her, and flung it at Nan with all her strength. It was well aimed, and struck the woman on the head. The blood started from the wound the blow had given; but Nan hardly felt the blow, so greatly was she excited against the child. She sprang upon her, caught her by the shoulder, and, opening the house-door, thrust her out upon the side-walk. "Ye'll never darken my doors again, yer imp of wickedness!" said she, as she rushed into the house, leaving the child alone in the cold, dark night.

When Gerty was angry or grieved, she always cried aloud,—not sobbing, as many children do, but uttering a succession of piercing shrieks, until she sometimes quite exhausted her strength. When she found herself in the street, she commenced screaming;—not from fear at being turned away from her only home, and left all alone at nightfall to wander about the city, and perhaps freeze before morning (for it was very cold),—she did not think of herself for a moment. Horror and grief at the dreadful fate of the only thing she loved in the world entirely filled her little soul. So she crouched down against the side of the house, her face hid in her hands, unconscious of the noise she was making, and unaware of the triumph of the girl who had once thrown away her shoes, and who was watching her from the house-door opposite. Suddenly she found herself lifted up and placed on one of the rounds of Trueman Flint's ladder, which still leaned against the lamp-post. True held her firmly, just high enough on the ladder to bring her face opposite his, recognized her as his old acquaintance, and asked her, in the same kind way he had used on the former occasion, what was the matter.

But Gerty could only gasp and say, "O, my kitten! my kitten!"

"What! the kitten I gave you? Well, have you lost it? Don't cry! there—don't cry!"

"O, no! not lost! O, poor kitty!" and Gerty began to cry louder than ever, and coughed at the same time so dreadfully, that True was quite frightened for the child. Making every effort to soothe her, and having partially succeeded, he told her she would catch her death o' cold, and she must go into the house.

"O, she won't let me in!" said Gerty, "and I wouldn't go, if she would!"

"Who won't let you in?—your mother?"

"No! Nan Grant."

"Who's Nan Grant?"

"She's a horrid, wicked woman, that drowned my kitten in bilin water!"

"But where's your mother?"

"I han't got none."

"Who do you belong to, you poor little thing!"

"Nobody; and I've no business anywhere!"

"But who do you live with, and who takes care of you?"

"O, I lived with Nan Grant; but I hate her. I threw a stick of wood at her head, and I wish I'd killed her!"

"Hush! hush! you mustn't say that! I'll go and speak to her."

True moved towards the door, trying to draw Gerty in with him; but she resisted so forcibly that he left her outside, and, walking directly into the room, where Nan was binding up her head with an old handkerchief, told her she had better call her little girl in, for she would freeze to death out there.

"She's no child of mine," said Nan; "she's been here long enough; she's the worst little creature that ever lived; it's a wonder I've kept her so long; and now I hope I'll never lay eyes on her agin,—and, what's more, I don't mean to. She ought to be hung for breaking my head! I believe she's got an ill-spirit in her, if ever anybody did have in this world!"

"But what'll become of her?" said True. "It's a fearful cold night. How'd you feel, marm, if she were found to-morrow morning all *friz* up just on your door-step?"

"How'd I feel?—That's your business, is it? S'posen you take care on her yourself! Yer make a mighty deal o' fuss about the brat. Carry her home, and try how yer like her. Yer've been here a talkin' to me about her once afore; and I tell you I won't hear a word more. Let other folks see to her, I say; I've had more'n my share; and, as to her freezin', or dyin' any-how, I'll risk her. Them children that comes into the world nobody knows how, don't go out of it in a hurry. She's the city's property—let 'em look out for her; and you'd better go long, and not meddle with what don't consarn you."

True did not wait to hear more. He was not used to women; and an angry woman was the most formidable thing to him in the world. Nan's flashing eyes and menacing attitude were sufficient warning of the coming tempest, and he wisely hastened away before it should burst upon his head.

Gerty had ceased crying when he came out, and looked up into his face with the greatest interest.

"Well," said he, "she says you shan't come back."

"O, I'm so glad!" said Gerty.

"But where'll you go to?"

"I don't know; p'raps I'll go with you, and see you light the lamps."

"But where'll you sleep to-night?"

"I don't know where; I haven't got any house. I guess I'll sleep out, where I can see the stars. I don't like dark places. But it'll be cold, won't it?"

"My goodness! You'll freeze to death, child."

"Well, what'll become of me, then?"

"The Lord only knows!"

True looked at Gerty in perfect wonder and distress. He knew nothing about children, and was astonished at her simplicity. He could not leave her there, such a cold night; but he hardly knew what he could do with her if he took her home, for he lived alone, and was poor. But another violent coughing spell decided him at once to share with her his shelter, fire and food, for one night, at least. So he took her by the hand, saying, "Come with me;" and Gerty ran along confidently by his side, never asking whither.

True had about a dozen more lamps to light before they reached the end of the street, when his round of duty was finished. Gerty watched him light each one with as keen an interest as if that were the only object for which she was in his company; and it was only after they had reached the corner of the street, and walked on for some distance without stopping, that she inquired where they were going.

"Going home," said True.

"Am I going to your home?" said Gerty.

"Yes," said True, "and here it is."

He opened a little gate close to the side-walk. It led into a small and very narrow yard, which stretched along the whole length of a decent two-storied house. True lived in the back part of the house; so they went through the yard, passed by several windows and the main entrance, and, keeping on to a small door in the rear, opened it and went in. Gerty was by this time trembling with the cold; her little bare feet were quite blue with walking so far on the pavements. There was a stove in the room into which they had entered, but no fire in it. It was a large room, and looked as if it might be pretty comfortable, though it was very untidy. True made as much haste as he could to dispose of his ladder, torch, &c., in an adjoining shed; and then, bringing in a handful of wood, he lit a fire in the stove. In a few minutes there was a bright blaze, and the chilly atmosphere grew warm. Drawing an old wooden settle up to the fire, he threw his shaggy great-coat over it, and lifting little Gerty up, he placed her gently upon the comfortable seat. He then went to work to get supper; for True was an old bachelor, and accustomed to do everything for himself. He made tea; then, mixing a great mug full for Gerty, with plenty of sugar, and all his cent's worth of milk, he produced from a little cupboard a loaf of bread, cut her a huge slice, and pressed her to eat and drink as much as she could; for he judged well when he concluded, from her looks, that she had not always been well fed; and so much satisfaction did he feel in her evident enjoyment of the best meal she had ever had, that he forgot to partake of it himself, but sat watching her with a tenderness which proved that the unerring instinct of childhood had not been wanting in Gerty, when she felt, as she watched True about his work, so long before he ever spoke to her, that he was a friend to everybody, even to the most forlorn little girl in the world.

Trueman Flint was born and brought up in New Hampshire; but, when fifteen years old, being left an orphan, he had made his way to Boston, where he supported himself for many years by whatever employment he could obtain; having been, at different times, a newspaper carrier, a cab-driver, a porter, a wood-cutter, indeed, a jack-at-all-trades; and so honest, capable and good-tempered, had he always shown himself, that he everywhere won a good name, and had sometimes continued for years in the same employ. Previous to his entering upon the service in which we find him, he had been for some time a porter in a large store, owned by a wealthy and generous merchant. Being one day engaged in removing some heavy casks, he had the misfortune to be severely injured by one of them falling upon his chest. For a long time no hope was entertained of his recovering from the effects of the accident; and when he at last began to mend, his health returned so gradually that it was a year before he was able to be at work again. This sickness swallowed up the savings of years; but his late employer never allowed him to want for any comforts, provided an excellent physician, and saw that he was well taken care of.

True, however, had never been the same man since. He rose up from

his sick bed ten years older in constitution, and his strength so much enfeebled that he was only fit for some comparatively light employment. It
was then that his kind friend and former master obtained for him the
situation he now held as lamplighter; in addition to which, he frequently
earned considerable sums by sawing wood, shovelling snow, &c.

He was now between fifty and sixty years old, a stoutly-built man, with
features cut in one of nature's rough moulds, but expressive of much
good-nature. He was naturally silent and reserved, lived much by himself,
was known to but few people in the city, and had only one crony, the
sexton of a neighboring church, a very old man, and one usually considered
very cross-grained and uncompanionable.

But we left Gerty finishing her supper; and now, when we return to her,
she is stretched upon the wide settle, sound asleep, covered up with a
warm blanket, and her head resting upon a pillow. True sits beside her; her
little thin hand lies in his great palm,—occasionally he draws the blanket
closer round her. She breathes hard; suddenly she gives a nervous start,
then speaks quickly; her dreams are evidently troubled. True listens intently to her words, as she exclaims, eagerly, "O, don't! don't drown my
kitty!" and then again, in a voice of fear, "O, she'll catch me! she'll catch
me!" once more; and now her tones are touchingly plaintive and earnest,—
"Dear, dear, good old man! let me stay with you, *do* let me stay!"

Great tears are in Trueman Flint's eyes, and rolling down the furrows of
his rough cheeks; he lays his great head on the pillow and draws Gerty's
little face close to his; at the same time smoothing her long, uncombed
hair with his hand. He too is thinking aloud;—what does *he* say?

"Catch you!—no, she *shan't!* Stay with *me!*—so you shall, I promise you,
poor little birdie! All alone in this big world, and so am I. Please God,
we'll bide together."

## Chapter IV

*That Nature's first, last lesson to mankind.*
*In age, in infancy, from others' aid*
*Is all our hope; to teach us to be kind:*
YOUNG

Little Gerty had found a friend and a protector; and it was well she had,
for suffering and neglect had well-nigh cut short her sad existence, and
ended all her sorrows. The morning after True took her home, she woke
in a high fever, her head and limbs aching, and with every symptom of

severe illness. She looked around, and found she was alone in the room; but there was a good fire, and preparation for some breakfast. For a moment or two she was puzzled to know where she was, and what had happened to her; for the room seemed quite strange, now that she first saw it by daylight. A look of happiness passed over her little sick face when she recalled the events of the previous night, and thought of kind old True, and the new home she had found with him. She got up and went to the window to look out, though her head was strangely giddy, and she tottered so that she could hardly walk. The ground was covered with snow, and it was still stormy without. It seemed as if the snow dazzled Gerty's eyes; for she suddenly found herself quite blinded, her head grew dizzy, she staggered and fell.

Trueman came in, a moment after, and was very much frightened at seeing Gerty stretched upon the floor; but soon found out the real state of the case, for he had made up his mind during the night that she was a very sick child, and was not surprised that she had fainted in endeavoring to walk. He placed her in bed, and soon succeeded in restoring her to consciousness; but, for three weeks from that time, she never sat up, except when True held her in his arms. True was a rough and clumsy man about most things; but not so in the care of his little charge. He knew a good deal about sickness; was something of a doctor and nurse in his simple way; and, though he had never had much to do with children, his warm heart was a trusty guide, and taught him all that was necessary for Gerty's comfort, and far, far more kindness than she had ever experienced before.

Gerty was very patient. She would sometimes lie awake whole nights, suffering from pain and extreme weariness at her long confinement to a sick bed, without uttering a groan, or making any noise, lest she might waken True, who slept on the floor beside her, when he could so far forget his anxiety about her as to sleep at all. Sometimes, when she was in great pain, True had carried her in his arms for hours; but even then Gerty would try to appear relieved before she really was so, and even feign sleep, that he might put her back to bed again, and take some rest himself. Her little heart was full of love and gratitude to her kind protector, and she spent much of her time in thinking what she could ever do for him when she got well, and wondering whether she were capable of ever learning to do any good thing at all. True was often obliged to leave her, to attend to his work; and, during the first week of her sickness, she was much alone, though everything she could possibly want was put within her reach, and many a caution given to her to keep still in bed until his return. At last, however, she grew delirious, and for some days had no knowledge how she was taken care of. One day, after a long and quiet sleep, she woke quite restored to sense and consciousness, and saw a woman sitting by her bedside sewing.

She sprang up in bed to look at the stranger, who had not observed her open her eyes, but who started the moment she heard her move, and exclaimed, "O, lie down, my child! lie down!" at the same time laying her hand gently upon her, to enforce the injunction.

"I don't know you," said Gerty; "where's my Uncle True?" for that was the name by which True had told her to call him.

"He's gone out, dear; he'll be home soon. How do you feel,—better?"

"O, yes! much better. Have I been asleep long?"

"Some time; lie down now, and I'll bring you some gruel; it will be good for you."

"Does Uncle True know you are here?"

"Yes. I came in to sit with you while he was away."

"Came in?—From where?"

"From my room. I live in the other part of the house."

"I think you're very good," said Gerty. "I like you. I wonder why I did not see you when you came in."

"You were too sick, dear, to notice; but I think you'll soon be better now."

The woman prepared the gruel, and after Gerty had taken it reseated herself at her work. Gerty laid down in bed, with her face towards her new friend, and, fixing her large eyes upon her, watched her some time while she sat sewing. At last the woman looked up, and said, "Well, what do you think I'm making?"

"I don't know," said Gerty; "what are you?"

The woman held up her work, so that Gerty could see that it was a dark calico frock for a child.

"O! what a nice gown!" said Gerty. "Who is it for?—Your little girl?"

"No," said the woman, "I haven't got any little girl; I've only got one child, my boy, Willie."

"Willie; that's a pretty name," said Gerty. "Is he a good boy?"

"Good?—He's the best boy in the world, and the handsomest!" answered the woman, her pale, care-worn face lit up with all a mother's pride.

Gerty turned away, and a look so unnaturally sad for a child came over her countenance, that the woman, looking up, thought she was getting tired, and ought to be kept very quiet. She told her so, and bade her shut up her eyes and go to sleep again. Gerty obeyed the first injunction, and lay so still that the latter seemed in a fair way to be fulfilled, when the door opened gently, and True came in.

"O! Miss Sullivan," said he, "you're here still! I'm very much obleeged to you for stayin'; I hadn't calkerlated to be gone so long. And how does the child seem to be, marm?"

"Much better, Mr. Flint. She's come to her reason, and I think, with care, will do very well now.—O! she's awake," she added, seeing Gerty open her eyes.

True came up to the bedside, stroked back her hair, now cut short and neatly arranged, felt of her pulse, and nodded his head satisfactorily. Gerty caught his great hand between both of hers, and held it tight. He sat down on the side of the bed, and, glancing at Mrs. Sullivan's work, said, "I shouldn't be surprised if she needed her new clothes sooner than we thought for, marm. It's my 'pinion we'll have her up and about afore many days."

"So I was thinking," said Mrs. Sullivan; "but don't be in too great a hurry. She's had a very severe sickness, and her recovery must be gradual. Did you see Miss Graham to-day?"

"Yes, I did see her, poor thing! The Lord bless her sweet face! She axed a sight o' questions about little Gerty here, and gave me this parcel of *arrer*root, I think she called it. She says it's excellent in sickness. Did you ever fix any, Miss Sullivan, so that you can jist show me how, if you'll be so good; for I declare I don't remember, though she took a deal o' pains to tell me."

"O, yes; it's very easy. I'll come in and prepare some, by and by. I don't think Gerty'll want any at present; she's just had some gruel. But father has come home, and I must be seeing about our tea. I'll come in again, this evening, Mr. Flint."

"Thank you, marm, thank you; you're very kind."

During the few following days Mrs. Sullivan came in and sat with Gerty several times. She was a gentle, subdued sort of woman, with a placid face, that was very refreshing to a child that had long lived in fear, and suffered a great deal of abuse. She always brought her work with her, which was usually some child's garment that she was making.

One evening, when Gerty had nearly recovered from her tedious fever, she was sitting in True's lap by the stove fire, carefully wrapped up in a blanket. She had been talking to him about her new acquaintance and friend; suddenly looking up in his face, she said, "Uncle True, do you know what little girl she's making a gown for?"

"For a little girl," said True, "that needs a gown, and a good many other things; for she hasn't got any clothes, as I know on, except a few old rags. Do you know any such little girl, Gerty?"

"I guess I do," said Gerty, with her head a little on one side, and a very knowing look.

"Well, where is she?"

"Ain't she in your lap?"

"What, you!—Why, do you think Mrs. Sullivan would spend her time making clothes for you?"

"Well," said Gerty, hanging her head, "I shouldn't *think* she would; but then you *said*—"

"Well, what did I say?"

"Something about new clothes for me."

"So I did," said True, giving her a rough hug; "and they *are* for you;—two whole suits, and shoes and stockings into the bargain."

Gerty opened her large eyes in amazement, laughed and clapped her hands. True laughed too; they both seemed very happy.

"Did she buy them, Uncle True? Is she rich?" said Gerty.

"Miss Sullivan?—no, indeed!" said True. "Miss Graham bought 'em, and is going to pay Miss Sullivan for making them."

"Who is Miss Graham?"

"She's a lady too good for this world—that's sartin. I'll tell you about her, some time; but I better not now, I guess; it's time you were abed and asleep."

One Sabbath, after Gerty was nearly well, she was so much fatigued with sitting up all day, that she went to bed before dark, and for two or three hours slept very soundly. On awaking, she saw that True had company.

An old man, much older, she thought, than True, was sitting on the opposite side of the stove, smoking a pipe. His dress, though of ancient fashion, and homely in its materials, was very neat; and his hair, of which he had but little, and that perfectly white, growing in two long locks just behind his ears, was nicely combed up, and tied on the top of his head, which was elsewhere bald and shiny. He had sharp features, and Gerty thought, from his looks, it must be easy for him to say sharp things; indeed, rather hard for him to say anything pleasant. There was a sarcastic expression about the corners of his mouth, and a disappointed look in his whole face, which Gerty observed, though she could not have defined, and from which she drew her conclusions with regard to his temper. She rightly conjectured that he was Mrs. Sullivan's father, Mr. Cooper; and in the opinion she formed of him from her first observation she did not widely differ from most other people who knew the old church-sexton. But both his own face and public opinion somewhat wronged him. It was true his was not a genial nature. Domestic trials, and the unkindness and fickleness of fortune, had caused him to look upon the dark side of life,—to dwell upon its sorrows, and frown upon the bright hopes of the young and the gay, who, as he was wont to say, with a mysterious shake of his head, knew but little of the world. The occupation, too, which had of late years been his, was not calculated to counteract a disposition to melancholy; his duties in the church were mostly solitary, and, as he was much withdrawn in his old age from intercourse with the world at large, he had become severe towards its follies, and unforgiving towards its crimes. There was much that was good and benevolent in him, however; and True Flint knew it, and loved to draw it out. True liked the old man's sincerity and honesty; and many a Sabbath evening had they sat by that same fireside, and discussed all those questions of public policy, national institutions, and individual rights, which every American feels called upon to take under his especial consideration, besides many matters of private feeling and interest, without their friendly relations being once disturbed or endangered; and this was the more remarkable, inasmuch as Trueman Flint was the very reverse of old Paul Cooper in disposition and temper, being hopeful and sanguine, always disposed to look upon the bright side of things, and, however discouraging they might seem, ever averring that it was his opinion 't would all come out right at last. On the evening of which we are speaking, they had been talking on several of their usual topics; but when Gerty awoke she found herself the subject of conversation. Of course she soon became deeply interested.

"Where," said Mr. Cooper, "did you say you picked her up?"

"At Nan Grant's," said True. "Don't you remember her? she's the same woman whose son you were called up to witness against, at the time the church-windows were broken, the night afore the 4th of July. You can't have forgotten her at the trial, Cooper; for she blew you up with a vengeance, and didn't spare his honor the Judge, either. Well, 't was just such a rage she was in with this 'ere child, the first time I see her; and the *second* time she'd just turned her out o' doors."

"Ah, yes, I remember the she-bear. I shouldn't suppose she'd be any too gentle to her own child, much less a stranger's; but what are you going to do with the foundling, Flint?"

"Do with her?—Keep her, to be sure, and take care on her."

Cooper laughed rather sarcastically.

"Well, now, I s'pose, neighbor, you think its rather freakish in me to be adoptin' a child at my time o' life; and p'raps it is; but I'll explain to you just how 't was. She'd a died that night I tell yer on, if I hadn't brought her home with me; and a good many times since, what's more, if I, with the help o' your darter, hadn't took mighty good care on her. Well, she took on so in her sleep, the first night ever she came, and cried out to me all as if she never had a friend afore (and I doubt me she never had), that I made up my mind then she should stay, at any rate, and I'd take care on her, and share my last crust with the wee thing, come what might. The Lord's been very marciful to me, Mr. Cooper, very marciful. He's raised me up friends in my deep distress. I knew, when I was a little shaver, what a lonesome thing it was to be fatherless and motherless; and when I see this little sufferin' human bein', I felt as if, all friendless as she seemed, she was more par- tickerlerly the Lord's, and as if I could not sarve him more, and ought not to sarve him less, than to share with her the blessins he has bestowed on me. You look round, neighbor, as if you thought 't wan't much to share with any one; and 't ain't much there is here, to be sure; but it's a *home*,—yes, a *home;* and that's a great thing to her that never had one. I've got my hands yet, and a stout heart, and a willin' mind. With God's help, I'll be a father to that child; and the time may come when she'll be God's embodied blessin' to me."

Mr. Cooper shook his head doubtfully, and muttered something about children, even one's own, not being apt to prove blessings.

But he had not power to shake Trueman's high faith in the wisdom, as well as righteousness, of his own proceedings. He had risen in the earnest- ness with which he had spoken, and, after pacing the room hastily and with excitement, he returned to his seat, and said: "Besides, neighbor Cooper, if I had not made up my mind the night Gerty came here, I wouldn't have sent her away after the next day; for the Lord, I think, spoke to me by the mouth of one of his holy angels, and bade me persevere in my resolution. You've seen Miss Graham. She goes to your church regular, with the fine old gentleman, her father. I was at their house shovelling snow, after the great storm three weeks since, and she sent for me to come into the kitchen. Well may I bless her angel face, poor thing!—if the world is dark to her, she makes it light to other folks. She cannot see Heaven's sunshine outside; but she's better off than most people, for she's got it in her, I do believe, and when she smiles it lets the glory out, and looks like God's rainbow in the clouds. She's done me many a kindness, since I got hurt so bad in her father's store, now some five years gone; and she sent for me that day, to ask how I did, and if there was anything I wanted that she could speak to the master about. So I told her all about little Gerty; and, I tell you, she and I both cried 'fore I'd done. She put some money into my hand, and told me to get Miss Sullivan to make some clothes for Gerty; more than that, she promised to help me if I got into trouble with the care of her; and when

I was going away, she said, 'I'm sure you've done quite right, True; the Lord will bless and reward your kindness to that poor child.' "

True was so excited and animated by his subject, that he did not notice what the sexton had observed, but did not choose to interrupt. Gerty had risen from her bed and was standing beside True, her eyes fixed upon his face, breathless with the interest she felt in his words. She touched his shoulder; he looked round, saw her, and stretched out his arms. She sprang into them, buried her face in his bosom, and, bursting into a paroxysm of joyful tears, gasped out the words, "Shall I stay with you always?"

"Yes, just as long as I live," said True, "you shall be my child."

◎◉◎◉◎◉◎◉◎◉◎◉◎◉◎◉◎◉◎◉◎◉◎◉◎◉◎◉◎

## Chapter V

*A light, busy foot astir*
*In her small housewifery; the blithest bee*
*That ever wrought in hive.*

MITFORD

It was a stormy evening. Gerty was standing at the window, watching for True's return from his lamplighting. She was neatly and comfortably dressed, her hair smooth, her face and hands clean. She was now quite well—better than for years before her sickness. Care and kindness had done wonders for her, and, though still a pale and rather slender-looking child, with eyes and mouth disproportionately large to her other features, the painful look of suffering she had been wont to wear had given place to a happy though rather grave expression. On the wide window-sill in front of her sat a plump and venerable cat, parent to Gerty's lost darling, and for that reason very dear to her; she was quietly stroking its back, while the constant purring that the old veteran kept up proved her satisfaction at the arrangement.

Suddenly a rumbling, tumbling sound was heard in the wall. The house was old, and furnished with ample accommodations for rats, who seemed, from the noise, to have availed themselves of this fact to give a ball, such an excitement were they manifesting. One would almost have thought a chimney was falling down, brick by brick. It did not alarm Gerty, however; she was used to old, rat-inhabited walls, and too much accustomed to hearing such sounds all around her, when she slept in the garret at Nan Grant's, to be disturbed by them. Not so, however, with the ancient grimalkin, who pricked up her ears, and gave every sign of a disposition to rush into battle. No war-horse could have been more excited by the sound of the trumpet, than was puss at the rushing of her foes through the ceiling.

"Lie still, pussy," said Gerty, "lie still, I say; don't you be running off after rats. You must sit up straight, and be good, till you see Uncle True coming, so's to hear what he'll say when he sees the room and *me*."

Here Gerty turned and glanced around the room with an air of infinite satisfaction; then, clambering upon the wide, old-fashioned window-sill, where she could see up the yard, and have a full view of the lamplighter the moment he entered the gate, she took the cat in her arms, smoothed down her dress, gave a look of interest and pride at her shoes and stockings, and then composed herself, with a determined effort to be patient. It would not do, however; she could not be patient; it seemed to her that he never came so late before, and she was just beginning to think he never would come at all, when he turned into the gate. It was nearly dark, but Gerty could see that there was some person with him. He did not look tall enough to be Mr. Cooper, and did not step like him; but she concluded it must be he, for whoever it was stopped at his door further up the yard, and went in. Impatient as Gerty had been for True's arrival, she did not run to meet him as usual, but waited in a listening attitude, until she heard him come in through the shed, where he was in the habit of stopping to hang up his ladder and lantern, and remove the soiled frock and overalls which he wore outside his clothes when about his work. She then ran and hid behind the door by which he must enter the room. She evidently had some great surprise in store for him, and meant to enjoy it to the utmost. The cat, not being so full of the matter, whatever it was, was more mindful of her manners, and went to meet him, rubbing her head against his legs, which was her customary welcome.

"Hollo, whiskers!" said True; "where's my little gal?"

He shut the door behind him as he spoke, thus disclosing Gerty to view. She sprang forward with a bound, laughed, and looked first at her own clothes, and then in True's face, to see what he would think of her appearance.

"Well, I declare!" said he, lifting her up in his arms and carrying her nearer to the light; "little folks do look famous! New gown, apron, shoes! —got 'em all on! And who fixed your hair? My! you an't none too handsome, sartain, but you do look famous nice!"

"Mrs. Sullivan dressed me all up, and brushed my hair; and *more too*— don't you see what *else* she has done?"

True followed Gerty's eyes as they wandered around the room. He looked amazed enough to satisfy her anticipations, great as they had been; and no wonder. He had been gone since morning, and things had indeed undergone a transformation. Woman's hands had evidently been at work, clearing up and setting to rights.

Until Gerty came to live with True, his home had never been subjected to female intrusion. Living wholly by himself, and entertaining scarcely any visitors, it had been his habit to make himself comfortable in his own way, utterly regardless of appearances. In his humble apartment sweeping-day came but seldom, and spring cleaning was unknown. Two large windows, facing the yard, were treated with great injustice, the cheerful light they were capable of affording being half obscured by dirt and smoke. The corners of the ceiling were festooned with cobwebs; the high, broad mantel-piece had accumulated a curious medley of things useful and useless; while there was no end to the rubbish that had collected under the stove. Then the furniture, some of which was very good, was adjusted in the most inconvenient manner, and in a way to turn the size of the room to the least possible advantage. During Gerty's illness, a bed made up on the floor for True's use, and the various articles which had been required in her sick-room, had increased the clutter to such an extent that one almost needed a pilot to conduct him in safety through the apartment.

Now, Mrs. Sullivan was the soul of neatness. Her rooms were like wax-work. Her own dress was almost quaker-like in its extreme simplicity, and freedom from the least speck or stain. No one could meet her old father, or her young son, even in their working dress, without perceiving at once the evidence of a careful daughter and mother's handiwork. It was to nurse Gerty, and take care of her in True's absence, that she first entered a room so much the reverse of her own; and it is not easy to appreciate the degree in which the virtue and charity of her so doing was enhanced, unless one can realize how painful the contrast was to her, and how excessively annoying she found it, to spend sometimes a whole afternoon in a room, which, as she expressed herself afterwards at home, it would have been a real pleasure to her to clear up and put to rights, if it were only to see how it would look, and whether anybody would recognize it. Mrs. Sullivan was a little bit of a woman, but had more capability and energy than could have been found in any one among twenty others twice her size. She really pitied those whose home was such a mass of confusion; felt sure that they could not be happy; and inwardly determined, as soon as Gerty got well, to exert herself in the cause of cleanliness and order, which was in her eyes the cause of virtue and happiness, so completely did she identify outward neatness and purity with inward peace. She pondered in her own mind how she could broach the subject of a renovation in his affairs to True himself, without wounding his feelings; for she was herself so sensitive on a point of neatness, that she imagined he must be somewhat the same,—and the little woman, being as tender-hearted as she was tidy, would not have mortified him for the world,—when a mode of action was suggested to her by Gerty herself.

On the day previous to that on which the great cleaning operations took place, Gerty was observed by Mrs. Sullivan standing in the passage near her door, and looking shyly but wistfully in.

"Come in, Gerty," said the kind little woman; "come in and see me.— Here," added she, seeing how timid the child felt about intruding herself into a strange room; "you may sit up here by the table, and see me iron. This is your own little dress. I am smoothing it out, and then your things will all be done. You'll be glad of some new clothes, shan't you?"

"Very glad, marm," said Gerty. "Am I to take them away, and keep them all myself?"

"Yes, indeed," said Mrs. Sullivan.

"I don't know where I'll put 'em all; there an't no place in our room,—at least, no very nice place," said Gerty, glancing with admiration at the open drawer, in which Mrs. Sullivan was now placing the little dress, adding it to a pile of neatly-folded garments.

"Why, part of them, you know, you'll be wearing," said Mrs. Sullivan; "and we must find some good place for the rest."

"You've got good places for things," said Gerty, looking round the room; "this is a beautiful room, isn't it?"

"Why, it isn't very different from Mr. Flint's. It's just about the same size, and two front-windows like his. My cupboard is the best; yours is only a three-cornered one; but that's about all the difference."

"O, but then yours don't look one bit like ours. You haven't got any bed here, and all the chairs stand in a row, and the table shines, and the floor is so clean, and the stove is new, and the sun comes is so bright! O! I wish our room was like this! I shouldn't think ours was more than half as big, either. Why, Uncle True stumbled over the tongs, this morning, and he said there wasn't room there to swing a cat."

"Where were the tongs?" said Mrs. Sullivan.

"About in the middle of the floor, marm."

"Well, you see I don't keep things in the middle of the floor. I think, if your room were all cleaned up, and places found for everything, it would look almost as well as mine."

"I wish it could be fixed up nice," said Gerty; "but what could be done with those beds?"

"I've been thinking about that. There's that little pantry,—or bathing-room, I think it must have been once, when this house was new, and rich people lived in it; that's large enough to hold a small bedstead and a chair or two; 't would be quite a comfortable little chamber for you. There's nothing in it but rubbish, that might just as well be thrown away, or, if it *were* good for anything, put in the shed."

"O, that'll be nice!" said Gerty; "then Uncle True can have his bed back again, and I'll sleep on the floor in there."

"No," said Mrs. Sullivan; "it won't be necessary for you to sleep on the floor. I've got a very good little cross-legged bedstead, that my Willie slept on when he lived at home; and I will lend it to you, if you'll try to take good care of it, and of everything else that is put into your room."

"O, I will," said Gerty.—"But can I?" added she, hesitating; "do you think I can? I don't know how to do anything."

"You never have been taught to do anything, my child; but a girl eight years old can do a great many things, if she is patient and tries hard to learn. I could teach you to do a great deal that would be useful, and that would help your Uncle True very much."

"What could I do?"

"You could sweep the room up every day; you could make the beds, after a fashion, with a little help in turning them; you could set the table, toast the bread, and wash the dishes. Perhaps you would not do these things in the best manner at first; but you would keep improving, and by and by get to be quite a nice little house-keeper."

"O, I wish I could do something for Uncle True!" said Gerty; "but how could I ever begin?"

"In the first place, you must have things cleaned up for you. If I thought Mr. Flint would like it, I'd get Kate McCarty to come in some day and help us; and I think we could make a great improvement in his home."

"O, I know he'd like it," said Gerty; " 'twould be grand! May I help?"

"Yes, you may do what you can; but Kate'll be the best hand; she's strong, and knows how to do cleaning very well."

"Who's she?" said Gerty.

"Kate?—She's Mrs. McCarty's daughter, in the next house. Mr. Flint does them many a good turn,—saws wood, and so on. They do most of his washing; but they can't half pay him all the kindness he's done that family. Kate's a clever girl; she'll be glad to come and work for him, any day. I'll ask her."

"Will she come to-morrow?"

"Perhaps she will."

"Uncle True's going to be gone all day to-morrow," said Gerty; "he's going to get in Mr. Eustace's coal. Wouldn't it be a good time?"

"Very," said Mrs. Sullivan. "I'll try and get Kate to come to-morrow."

Kate came. The room was thoroughly cleaned, and put in complete order. Gerty's new clothes were delivered over to her own keeping; she was neatly dressed in one suit, the other placed in a little chest which was found in the pantry, and which accommodated her small wardrobe very well.

It was the result of all Mrs. Sullivan's, Kate's and Gerty's combined labor which called forth True's atonishment on his return from his work; and the pleasure he manifested made the day a memorable one in Gerty's life, one to be marked in her memory as long as she lived, as being the first in which she had known *that* happiness—perhaps the highest earth affords—of feeling that she had been instrumental in giving joy to another. Not that Gerty's assistance had been of any great value; or that all could not have been done as well, or even better, if she had been where Nan Grant always put her,—out of the way. But the child did not realize that: she had been one of the laborers; she had entered heart and soul into every part of the work; wherever she had been allowed to lend a helping hand, she had exerted her whole strength. She could say, with truth, "*We* did it,—Mrs. Sullivan, Kate and *I*."

None but a loving heart, like Mrs. Sullivan's, would have understood and sympathized in the feeling which made Gerty so eager to help. But *she* did, and allotted to her many little services, which the child felt herself more blessed in being permitted to perform than she would have done at almost any gift or favor that could have been bestowed upon her.

She led True about to show him how judiciously and ingeniously Mrs. Sullivan had contrived to make the most of the room and the furniture; how, by moving the bed into a deep recess, which was just wide enough for it, she had reserved the whole square area, and made, as True declared, a parlor of it. It was some time before he could be made to believe that half his property had not been spirited away, so incomprehensible was it to him that so much additional space and comfort could be acquired by a little system and order.

But his astonishment and Gerty's delight reached their climax, when she introduced him into the former lumber-closet, now transformed into a really snug and comfortable bed-room.

"Well, I declare! Well, I declare!" was all the old man could seem to say. He sat down beside the stove, now polished, and made, as Gerty declared, new, just like Mrs. Sullivan's; rubbed his hands together, for they were cold with being out in the frosty evening, and then, spreading them in front of the fire, took a general view of his reformed domicile, and of Gerty, who, according to Mrs. Sullivan's careful instructions, was preparing to set the table and toast the bread for supper. She was standing on a chair, taking down the cups and saucers from among the regular rows of dishes shining in the three-cornered cupboard, having already deposited on the lower shelf, where she could reach it from the floor, a plate containing some smoothly-cut slices of bread, which the thoughtful Mrs. Sullivan had prepared for her. True watched her motions for a minute or two, and then indulged in a short soliloquy. "Mrs. Sullivan's a clever woman, sartain, and they've made my old house here complete, and Gerty's gettin' to be like the apple of my eye, and I'm as happy a man as—"

## Chapter VI

*Some dream that they can silence, when they will,*
*The storm of passion, and say peace, be still!*

COWPER.

Here True was interrupted. Quick, noisy footsteps in the passage were followed by a sudden and unceremonious opening of the door.

"Here, Uncle True," said the new comer; "here's your package. You forgot all about it, I guess; and I forgot it, too, till mother saw it on the table, where I'd laid it down. I was so taken up with just coming home, you know."

"Of course,—of course!" said True. "Much obleeged to you, Willie, for fetchin' it for me. It's pretty brittle stuff it's made of, and most like I should a smashed it, 'fore I got it home."

"What is it?—I've been wondering."

"Why, it's a little knick-knack I've brought home for Gerty, here, that—"

"Willie! Willie!" called Mrs. Sullivan from the opposite room, "have you been to tea, dear?"

"No, indeed, mother;—have you?"

"Why, yes; but I'll get you some."

"No, no!" said True; "stay and take tea with us, Willie; take tea here, my boy. My little Gerty is makin' some famous toast, and I'll put the tea a steepin' presently."

"So I will," said Willie; "I should like to, first-rate. No matter about any supper for me, mother; I'm going to have my tea here, with Uncle True. Come, now, let's see what's in the bundle; but first I want to see little Gerty; mother's been telling me about her. Where is she?—has she got well? She's been very sick, hasn't she?"

"O, yes, she's nicely now," said True. "Here, Gerty, look here! Why, where is she?"

"There she is, hiding up behind the settle," said Willie, laughing. "She an't afraid of me, is she?"

"Well, I didn't know as she was shy," said True. "You silly little girl," added he, going towards her, "come out here, and see Willie. This is Willie Sullivan."

"I don't want to see him," said Gerty.

"Don't want to see Willie!" said True; "why, you don't know what you're sayin'. Willie's the best boy that ever was; I 'spect you and he'll be great friends, by and by."

"He won't like me," said Gerty; "I know he won't!"

"Why shan't I like you?" said Willie, approaching the corner where Gerty had hid herself. Her face was covered with her hands, according to her usual fashion when anything distressed her. "I guess I shall like you first-rate, when I see you."

He stooped down as he spoke, for he was much taller than Gerty, and, taking her hands directly down from her face and holding them tight in his own, he fixed his eyes full upon her, and, nodding pleasantly, said,

"How do do, Cousin Gerty,—how do do?"

"I an't your cousin!" said Gerty.

"Yes you are," said Willie, decidedly; "Uncle True's your uncle, and mine too;—so we're cousins—don't you see?—and I want to get acquainted."

Gerty could not resist Willie's good-natured words and manner. She suffered him to draw her out of the corner, and towards the lighter end of the room. As she came near the lamp, she tried to free her hands, in order to cover her face up again; but Willie would not let her, and, attracting her attention to the unopened package, and exciting her curiosity as to what it might contain, he succeeded in diverting her thoughts from herself, so that in a few minutes she seemed quite at her ease.

"There, Uncle True says it's for you," said Willie; "and I can't think what 't is, can you? Feel—it's hard as can be."

Gerty felt, and looked up wonderingly in True's face.

"Undo it, Willie," said True.

Willie produced a knife, cut the string, took off the paper, and disclosed one of those white plaster images, so familiar to every one, representing the little Samuel in an attitude of devotion.

"O, how pretty!" exclaimed Gerty, full of delight.

"Why didn't I think?" said Willie; "I might have known what 't was, by the feeling."

"Why! did you ever see it before—" said Gerty.

"Not this same one; but I've seen lots just like it."

"Have you?" said Gerty. "I never did. I think it's the beautifullest thing that ever was. Uncle True, did you say it was for me? Where did you get it?"

"It was by an accident I got it. A few minutes before I met you, Willie, I was stoppin' at the corner to light my lamp, when I saw one of those *furren* boys with a sight o' these sort of things, and some black ones too, all set up on a board, and he was walkin' with 'em a-top of his head. I was just a wonderin' how he kept 'em there, when he hit the board agin my lamp-post, and, the first thing I knew, whack they all went! He'd spilt 'em every one. Lucky enough for him, there was a great bank of soft snow close to the side-walk, and the most of 'em fell into that, and wasn't hurt. Some few went on to the bricks, and were smashed. Well, I kind o' pitied the feller; for it was late, and I thought like enough he hadn't had much luck sellin' of 'em, to have so many left on his hands—"

"On his head, you mean," said Willie.

"Yes, Master Willie, or on the snow," said True; "any way you're a mind to have it."

"And I know what you did, Uncle True, just as well as if I'd seen you," said Willie; "you set your ladder and lantern right down, and went to work helping him pick 'em all up,—that's just what you'd be sure to do for anybody. I hope, if ever you get into trouble, some of the folks you've helped will be by to make return."

"This feller, Willie, didn't wait for me to get into trouble, he made return right off. When they were all set right, he bowed, and scraped, and touched his hat to me, as if I'd been the biggest gentleman in the land; talkin', too, he was, all the time, though I couldn't make out a word of his lingo; and then he insisted on my takin' one o' the figurs. I wasn't agoin to, for I didn't want it; but I happened to think little Gerty might like it."

"O, I shall like it!" said Gerty. "I shall like it better than—no, not better, but almost *as well* as my kitten; not *quite* as well, because that was alive, and this isn't; but *almost*. O, an't he a cunning little boy?"

True, finding that Gerty was wholly taken up with the image, walked away and began to get the tea, leaving the two children to entertain each other.

"You must take care and not break it, Gerty," said Willie. "We had a Samuel once, just like it, in the shop; and I dropped it out of my hand on to the counter, and broke it into a million pieces."

"What did you call it?" said Gerty.

"A Samuel; they're all Samuels."

"What are *Sammles?*" said Gerty.

"Why, that's the name of the child they're taken for."

"What do you s'pose he's sittin' on his knee for?"

Willie laughed. "Why, don't you know?" said he.

"No," said Gerty; "what is he?"

"He's praying," said Willie.

"Is that what he's got his eyes turned up for, too?"

"Yes, of course; he looks up to heaven when he prays."

"Up to where?"

"To heaven."

Gerty looked up at the ceiling in the direction in which the eyes were turned, then at the figure. She seemed very much dissatisfied and puzzled.

"Why, Gerty," said Willie, "I shouldn't think you knew what praying was."

"I don't," said Gerty; "tell me."

"Don't you ever pray,—pray to God?"

"No, I don't.—Who is God? Where is God?"

Willie looked inexpressibly shocked at Gerty's ignorance, and answered, reverently, "God is in heaven, Gerty."

"I don't know where that is," said Gerty. "I believe I don't know nothin' about it."

"I shouldn't think you did," said Willie. "I *believe* heaven is up in the sky; but my Sunday-school teacher says, 'heaven is anywhere where goodness is,' or some such thing," he said.

"Are the stars in heaven?" said Gerty.

"They look so, don't they?" said Willie. "They're in the sky, where I always used to think heaven was."

"I should like to go to heaven," said Gerty.

"Perhaps, if you're good, you will go, some time."

"Can't any but good folks go?"

"No."

"Then I can't ever go," said Gerty, mournfully.

"Why not?" said Willie; "an't you good?"

"O, no! I'm very bad."

"What a queer child!" said Willie. "What makes you think yourself so very bad?"

"O! I *am*," said Gerty, in a very sad tone; "I'm the worst of all. I'm the worst child in the world."

"Who told you so?"

"Everybody. Nan Grant says so, and she says everybody thinks so; I know it, too, myself."

"Is Nan Grant the cross old woman you used to live with?"

"Yes. How did you know she was cross?"

"O, my mother's been telling me about her. Well, I want to know if she didn't send you to school, or teach you anything?"

Gerty shook her head.

"Why, what lots you've got to learn! What did you used to do, when you lived there?"

"Nothing."

"Never did anything, and don't know anything; my gracious!"

"Yes, I do know one thing," said Gerty. "I know how to toast bread;—your mother taught me;—she let me toast some by her fire."

As she spoke, she thought of her own neglected toast, and turned towards the stove; but she was too late,—the toast was made, the supper ready, and True was just putting it on the table.

"O, Uncle True," said she, "I meant to get the tea."

"I know it," said True, "but it's no matter; you can get it to-morrow." The tears came into Gerty's eyes;—she looked very much disappointed, but said nothing. They all sat down to supper. Willie put the Samuel in the middle of the table for a centre ornament, and told so many funny stories, and said so many pleasant things, that Gerty laughed heartily, forgot that she did not make the toast herself, forgot her sadness, her shyness, even her ugliness and wickedness, and showed herself, for once, a merry child. After tea, she sat beside Willie on the great settle, and, in her peculiar way, and with many odd expressions and remarks, gave him a description of her life at Nan Grant's, winding up with a touching account of the death of her kitten.

The two children seemed in a fair way to become as good friends as True could possibly wish. True himself sat on the opposite side of the stove, smoking his pipe; his elbows on his knees, his eyes bent on the children, and his ears drinking in all their conversation. He was no restraint upon them. So simple-hearted and sympathizing a being, so ready to be amused and pleased, so slow to blame or disapprove, could never be any check upon the gayety or freedom of the youngest, most careless spirit. He laughed when they laughed; seemed soberly satisfied, and took long whiffs at his pipe, when they talked quietly and sedately; ceased smoking entirely, letting his pipe rest on his knee, and secretly wiping away a tear, when Gerty recounted her childish griefs. He had heard the story before, and he cried then. He often heard it afterwards, but never *without crying*.

After Gerty had closed her tale of sorrows, which was frequently interrupted by Willie's ejaculations of condolence or pity, she sat for a moment without speaking; then, becoming excited, as her ungoverned and easily roused nature dwelt upon its wrongs, she burst forth in a very different tone from that in which she had been speaking, and commenced uttering the most bitter invectives against Nan Grant; making use of many a rough and coarse term, such as she had been accustomed to hear used by the ill-bred people with whom she had lived. The child's language expressed unmitigated hatred, and even a hope of future revenge. True looked worried and troubled at hearing her talk so angrily. Since he brought her home he had never witnessed such a display of temper, and had fondly believed that she would always be as quiet and gentle as during her illness and the few weeks subsequent to it. True's own disposition was so placid, amiable and forgiving, that he could not imagine that any one, and especially a little child, should long retain feelings of anger and bitterness. Gerty had shown herself so mild and patient since she had been with him, so submissive to his wishes, so anxious even to forestall them, that it had never occurred to him to dread any difficulty in the management of the child. Now, however, as he observed her flashing eyes, and noticed the doubling of her little fist, as she menaced Nan with her future wrath, he had an undefined, half-formed presentiment of coming trouble in the control of his little charge; a feeling almost of alarm, lest he had undertaken what he could never perform. For the moment, she ceased, in his eyes, to be the pet and plaything he had hitherto considered her. He saw in her something which needed a check, and felt himself unfit to apply it.

And no wonder. He *was* totally unfit to cope with a spirit like Gerty's. It was true he possessed over her one mighty influence,—her strong affection for him, which he could not doubt. It was that which made her so submissive and patient in her sickness, so grateful for his care and kindness, so anxious to do something in return. It was that deep love for her first friend, which, never wavering, and growing stronger to the last, proved, in after years, a noble motive for exertion, a worthy incentive to virtue. It was that love, fortified and illumined by a higher light, which came in time to sanctify it, that gave her, while yet a mere girl, a woman's courage, a woman's strength of heart and self-denial. It was that which cheered the old man's latter years, and shed joy on his dying bed.

But for the present it was not enough. The kindness she had received for the few weeks past had completely softened Gerty's heart towards her benefactors; but the effect of eight years' mismanagement, ill treatment, and want of all judicious discipline, could not be done away in that short time. Her unruly nature could not be so suddenly quelled, her better capabilities called into action.

The plant that for years has been growing distorted, and dwelling in a barren spot, deprived of light and nourishment, withered in its leaves and blighted in its fruit, cannot at once recover from so cruel a blast. Transplanted to another soil, it must be directed in the right course, nourished with care and warmed with Heaven's light, ere it can recover from the shock occasioned by its early neglect, and find strength to expand its flowers and ripen its fruit.

So with little Gerty;—a new direction must be given to her ideas, new nourishment to her mind, new light to her soul, ere the higher purposes for which she was created could be accomplished in her.

Something of this True felt, and it troubled him. He did not, however, attempt to check the child. He did not know what to do, and so did nothing.

Willie tried once or twice to stop the current of her abusive language; but soon desisted, for she did not pay the least attention to him. He could not help smiling at her childish wrath; nor could he resist sympathizing with her in a degree, and almost wishing he could have a brush with Nan himself, and express his opinion of her character in one or two hard knocks. But he had been well brought up by his gentle mother, was conscious that Gerty was exhibiting a very hot temper, and began to understand what made everybody think her so bad.

After Gerty had railed about Nan a little while, she stopped of her own accord; though an unpleasant look remained on her countenance, one of her old looks, that it was a pity should return, but which always did when she got into a passion. It soon passed away, however, and when, a little later in the evening, Mrs. Sullivan appeared at the door, Gerty looked bright and happy, listened with evident delight while True uttered warm expressions of thanks for the labor which had been undertaken in his behalf, and, when Willie went away with his mother, said her good-night and asked him

to come again so pleasantly, and her eyes looked so bright as she stood
holding on to True's hand in the doorway, that Willie said, as soon as they
were out of hearing, "She's a queer little thing, an't she, mother? But I kind
o' like her."

## Chapter VII

*Prayer is the burden of a sigh,*
*The falling of a tear,*
*The upward glancing of an eye,*
*When none but God is near.*
MONTGOMERY

It would have been hard to find two children, both belonging to the
poorer class, whose situations in life had, thus far, presented a more complete contrast than those of Gerty and Willie. With Gerty's experiences the
reader is somewhat acquainted. A neglected orphan, she had received little
of that care, and still less of that love, which Willie had always enjoyed.
Mrs. Sullivan's husband was an intelligent country clergyman; but, as he
died when Willie was a baby, leaving very little property for the support
of his family, the widow went home to her father, taking her child with her.
The old man needed his daughter; for death had made sad inroads in his
household since she left it, and he was alone.

From that time the three had lived together in humble comfort; for,
though poor, industry and frugality secured them from want. Willie was
his mother's pride, her hope, her constant thought. She spared herself no
toil or care to provide for his physical comfort, his happiness, and his growth
in knowledge and virtue.

It would have been strange enough if she had not been proud of a boy
whose uncommon beauty, winning disposition, and early evidences of a
manly and noble nature, won him friends even among strangers. He had
been a handsome child; but there was that observable in him, now that he
had nearly reached his thirteenth year, far excelling the common boyish
beauty, which consists merely in curly hair, dark eyes and rosy cheeks. It was
his broad, open forehead, the clearness and calmness of his full gray eye,
the expressive mouth, so determined and yet so mild, the well-developed
figure and ruddy complexion, proclaiming high health, which gave promise
of power to the future man. No one could have been in the boy's company
half an hour, without loving and admiring him. He had naturally a warm-
hearted, affectionate disposition, which his mother's love and the world's

smiles had fostered; an unusual flow of animal spirits, tempered by a natural politeness towards his elders and superiors; a quick apprehension; a ready command of language; a sincere sympathy in others' pleasures and pains; in fine, one of those genial natures, that wins hearts one knows not how. He was fond of study, and until his twelfth year his mother kept him constantly at school. The sons of poor parents have, in our large cities, almost every educational advantage that can be obtained by wealth; and Willie, having an excellent capacity, and being constantly encouraged and exhorted by his mother to improve his opportunities to the utmost, had attained a degree of proficiency quite unusual at his age.

When he was twelve years old he had an excellent opportunity to enter into the service of an apothecary, who did an extensive business in the city, and wanted a boy to assist in his store. The wages that Mr. Bray offered were not great, but there was the hope of an increased salary; and, at any rate, situated as Willie was, it was not a chance to be overlooked. Fond as he was of his books, he had long been eager to be at work, helping to bear the burden of labor in the family. His mother and grandfather assented to the plan, and he gladly accepted Mr. Bray's proposals.

He was sadly missed at home; for, as he slept at the store during the week, he rarely had much leisure to make even a passing visit to his mother, except on Saturday, when he came home at night and passed Sunday. So Saturday night was Mrs. Sullivan's happy night, and the Sabbath became a more blessed day than ever.

When Willie reached his mother's room on the evening of which we have been speaking, he sat down with her and Mr. Cooper, and for an hour conversation was brisk with them. Willie never came home that he had not a great deal to relate concerning the occurrences of the week; many a little anecdote to tell; many a circumstance connected with the shop, the customers, his master the apothecary, and his master's family, with whom he took his meals. Mrs. Sullivan was interested in everything that interested Willie, and it was easy to see that the old grandfather was more entertained by the boy than he was willing to appear; for, though he sat with his eyes upon the floor, and did not seem to listen, he usually heard all that was said, as was often proved afterwards by some accidental reference he would make to the subject. He seldom asked questions, and indeed it was not necessary, for Mrs. Sullivan asked enough for them both. He seldom made comments, but would occasionally utter an impatient or contemptuous expression regarding individuals or the world in general; thereby evidencing that distrust of human nature, that want of confidence in men's honesty and virtue, which formed, as we have said, a marked trait in the old man's character. Willie's spirits would then receive a momentary check; for *he* loved and trusted *everybody*, and his grandfather's words, and the tone in which they were spoken, were a damper to his young soul; but, with the elasticity of youth and a gay heart, they would soon rebound, and he would go on as before. Willie did not fear his grandfather, who had never been severe to him, never having, indeed, interfered at all with Mrs. Sullivan's management; but he sometimes felt chilled, though he hardly knew why, by his want of sympathy with his own warm-heartedness. On the present occasion, the conversation having turned at last upon True Flint and his adopted child, Mr. Cooper had been unusually bitter and satirical, and, as he took his lamp to go to bed, wound up with remarking that he knew very well Gerty would never be anything but a trouble to Flint, who was a fool not to send her to the alms-house at once.

There was a pause after the old man left the room; then Willie exclaimed, "Mother, what makes grandfather hate folks?"

"Why, he don't, Willie."

"I don't mean exactly *hate,*—I don't suppose he does *that, quite;* but he don't seem to *think* a great deal of anybody—do you think he does?"

"O, yes; he don't show it much," said Mrs. Sullivan; "but he thinks a great deal of you, Willie, and he wouldn't have anything happen to me for the world; and he likes Mr. Flint, and—"

"O, yes, I know that, of course; I don't mean that; but he doesn't think there's much goodness in folks, and he don't seem to think anybody's going to turn out well, and—"

"You're thinking of what he said about little Gerty."

"Well, she an't the only one. That's what made me speak of it now, but I've often noticed it before, particularly since I went away from home, and am only here once a week. Now, you know I think everything of Mr. Bray; and when I was telling to-night how much good he did, and how kind he was to old Mrs. Morris and her sick daughter, grandfather looked just as if he didn't believe it, or didn't *think* much of it, somehow."

"O, well, Willie," said Mrs. Sullivan, "you mustn't wonder much at that. Grandpa's had a good many disappointments. You know he thought everything of Uncle Richard, and there was no end to the trouble he had with him; and there was Aunt Sarah's husband—he seemed to be such a fine fellow when Sally married him, but he cheated father dreadfully at last, so that he had to mortgage his house in High-street, and finally give it up entirely. He's dead now, and I don't want to say anything against him; but he didn't prove what we expected, and it broke Sally's heart, I think. That was a dreadful trial to father, for she was the youngest, and had always been his pet. And, just after that, mother was taken down with her death-stroke, and there was a quack doctor prescribed for her, that father always thought did her more hurt than good. O, take it altogether, he's had a great deal to make him look on the dark side now; but you mustn't mind it, Willie; you must take care and turn out well yourself, my son, and then he'll be proud enough; he's as pleased as he can be when he hears you praised, and expects great things of you, one of these days."

Here the conversation ended; but not until the boy had added another to the many resolves already made, that, if his health and strength were spared, he would prove to his grandfather that hopes were not always deceitful, and that fears were sometimes groundless.

O! what a glorious thing it is for a youth when he has ever present with him a high, a noble, an unselfish motive! What an incentive is it to exertion, perseverance and self-denial! What a force to urge him on to ever-increasing efforts! Fears that would otherwise appall, discouragements that would dishearten, labors that would weary, obstacles that would dismay, opposition that would crush, temptation that would overcome, all, all lie disarmed and powerless, when, with a single-hearted and worthy aim, he struggles for the victory!

And so it is, that those born in honor, wealth and luxury, seldom achieve greatness. They were not *born* for labor; and, without labor, nothing that is worth having can be won. Why will they not make it their great and absorbing motive (a worthy one it certainly would be), to overcome the disadvantages of their position, and make themselves great, learned, wise and good, in spite of those riches, that honorable birth, that opportunity for luxurious sloth, which are, in reality, to the clear-judging eye of wise men and angels, their deadliest snare? A motive Willie had long had. His grandfather was old, his mother weak, and both poor. He must be the staff of their old age; he must labor for their support and comfort; he must do *more;*—they hoped great things of him; they *must* not be disappointed. He did not, however, while arming himself for future conflict with the world, forget the present, but sat down and learned his Sunday-school lessons. After which, according to custom, he read aloud in the Bible; and then Mrs. Sullivan, laying her hand on the head of her son, offered up a simple, heartfelt prayer for the boy,—one of those mother's prayers, which the child listens to with reverence and love, and remembers in the far-off years; one of those prayers which keep men from temptation, and deliver them from evil.

After Willie went home that evening, and Gerty was left alone with True, she sat on a low stool beside him for some time, without speaking. Her eyes were intently fixed upon the white image which lay in her lap; that her little mind was very busy, there could be no doubt, for thought was plainly written on her face. True was not often the first to speak; but, finding Gerty unusually quiet, he lifted up her chin, looked inquiringly in her face, and then said:

"Well, Willie's a pretty clever sort of a boy, isn't he?"

Gerty answered, "Yes;" without, however, seeming to know what she was saying.

"You like him, don't you?" said True.

"Very much," said Gerty, in the same absent way. It was not Willie she was thinking of. True waited for Gerty to begin talking about her new acquaintance; but she did not speak for a minute or two. Then looking up suddenly, she said:

"Uncle True?"

"What say?"

"What does Samuel pray to God for?"

True stared. "Samuel!—pray!—I guess I don't know exactly what you're saying."

"Why," said Gerty, holding up the image, "Willie says this little boy's name is Samuel; and that he sits on his knee, and puts his hands together *so,* and looks up, because he's praying to God, that lives up in the sky. I don't know what he means,—*way* up in the sky,—do you?"

True took the image and looked at it attentively; he moved uneasily upon his chair, scratched his head, and finally said:

"Well, I s'pose he's about right. This 'ere child is prayin', sartain, though I didn't think on it afore. But I don't jist know what he calls it a Samuel for. We'll ask him, some time."

"Well, what does he pray for, Uncle True?"

"O! he prays to make him good; it makes folks good to pray to God."

"Can God make folks good?"

"Yes. God is very great; he can do anything."

"How can he *hear?*"

"He hears everything and sees everything in the world."

"And does he live in the sky?"

"Yes," said True, "in heaven."

Many more questions Gerty asked; many strange questions, that True could not answer; many questions that he wondered he had not oftener asked himself. True had a humble, loving heart, and a child-like faith; he had enjoyed but little religious instruction, but he earnestly endeavored to live up to the light he had. Perhaps, in his faithful practice of the Christian virtues, and especially in his obedience to the great law of Christian charity, he more nearly approached to the spirit of his Divine Master than many who, by daily reading and study, are far more familiar with Christian doctrines. But he had never inquired deeply into the sources of that belief which it had never occurred to him to doubt; and he was not at all prepared for the questions suggested by the inquisitive, keen and newly-excited mind of little Gerty. He answered her as well as he could, however; and, where he was at fault, hesitated not to refer her to Willie, who, he told her, went to Sunday-school, and knew a wonderful sight about such things. All the information that Gerty could gain amounted to the knowledge of these facts: that God was in heaven; that his power was great; and that people were made better by prayer. Her little eager brain was so intent upon the subject, however, that, as it grew late, the thought even of sleeping in her new room could not efface it from her mind. After she had gone to bed, with the white image hugged close to her bosom, and True had taken away the lamp, she lay for a long time with her eyes wide open. Just at the foot of the bed was the window. Gerty could see out, as she had done before in her garret at Nan Grant's; but, the window being larger, she had a much more extended view. The sky was bright with stars; and the sight of them revived her old wonder and curiosity as to the author of such distant and brilliant lights. Now, however, as she gazed, there darted through her mind the thought, "God lit them! O, how great he must be! But a *child* might pray to him!" She rose from her little bed, approached the window, and, falling on her knees and clasping her hands precisely in the attitude of the little Samuel, she looked up to heaven. She spoke no word, but her eyes glistened with the dew of a tear that stood in each. Was not each tear a prayer? She breathed no petition, but she longed for God and virtue. Was not that very wish a prayer? Her little uplifted heart throbbed vehemently. Was not each throb a prayer? And did not God in heaven, without whom not a sparrow falls to the ground, hear and accept that first homage of a little, untaught child; and did it not call a blessing down?

Many a petition did Gerty offer up in after years. In many a time of trouble did she come to God for help; in many an hour of bitter sorrow did she from the same source seek comfort; and, when her strength and heart failed her, God became the strength of her heart. But never did she approach his throne with a purer offering, a more acceptable sacrifice, than when, in her first deep penitence, her first earnest faith, her first enkindled hope, she took the attitude, and her heart uttered, though her lips pronounced them not, the words of the prophet-child, "Here am I, Lord!"

❂❂❂❂❂❂❂❂❂❂❂❂❂❂❂❂❂❂❂❂❂❂❂❂❂❂❂❂❂❂

# *Chapter VIII*

> "——*Revenge, at first though sweet,*
> *Bitter ere long back on itself recoils.*"
> MILTON

The next day was Sunday. True was in the habit of going to church half the day at least, with the sexton's family; but Gerty, having no bonnet, could not go, and True would not leave her. So they spent the morning together, wandering round among the wharves and looking at the ships, Gerty wearing her old shawl pinned over her head. In the afternoon, True fell asleep by the fireside, and Gerty played with the cat.

Willie came in the evening; but it was only to say good-by, before going back to Mr. Bray's. He was in a hurry, and could not stop at all; for his master had a sober household, and liked to have his doors closed early, especially Sunday night. Old Mr. Cooper, however, made his usual visit; and, when he had gone, True, finding Gerty sound asleep on the settle, thought it a pity to wake her, and laid her in bed with her clothes on.

She did not wake until morning; and then, much surprised and amused at finding herself dressed, sprung up and ran out to ask True how it happened. True was busy making the fire; and Gerty, having received satisfactory answers to her numerous inquiries,—when and where she fell asleep, and how she came in bed,—applied herself earnestly to help in every possible way about getting the breakfast and putting the room in order. She followed Mrs. Sullivan's instructions, all of which she remembered, and showed a wonderful degree of capability in everything she undertook. In the course of the few following weeks, during which her perseverance held out surprisingly, she learned how to make herself useful in many ways, and, as Mrs. Sullivan had prophesied, gave promise of becoming, one day, quite a clever little housekeeper. Of course, the services she performed were trifling; but her active and willing feet saved True a great many steps, and she was of essential aid in keeping the rooms neat, that being her especial ambition.

She felt that Mrs. Sullivan expected her, now that the dust and cobwebs were all cleared away, to take care that they should not accumulate again; and it was quite an amusing sight, every day, when True had gone out as usual to fill and clean the street-lamps, to see the little girl diligently laboring with an old broom, the handle of which was cut short to make it more suitable for her use. Mrs. Sullivan looked in occasionally, to praise and assist her; and nothing made Gerty happier than learning how to do some new thing. She met with a few trials and discouragements, to be sure. In two or three instances the toast got burned to a cinder; and, worse still, she one day broke a painted teacup, over which she shed many a tear; but, as True never thought of blaming her for anything, she forgot her misfortunes, and experience made her careful.

Kate McCarty thought her the smartest child in the world, and would sometimes come in and wash up the floor, or do some other work, which required more strength or skill than Gerty possessed.

Prompted by her ambition to equal Mrs. Sullivan's expectations, and still more by her desire to be useful to True, and in some degree manifest her love to him by her labors, Gerty was usually patient, good-natured and obliging. So very indulgent was True, that he rarely indeed laid a command upon the child, leaving her to take her own course, and have her own way; but, undisciplined as she was, she willingly yielded obedience to one who never thwarted her, and the old man seldom saw her exhibit in his presence that violent temper, which, when roused, knew no restraint. She had little to irritate her in the quiet home she now enjoyed; but instances sometimes occurred which proved that the fire of her little spirit was not quenched, or its evil propensities extinguished.

One Sunday, Gerty, who had now a nice little hood which True had bought for her, was returning with Mr. Cooper, Mr. Flint and Willie, from the afternoon service at church. The two old men were engaged in one of their lengthy discussions, and the children, having fallen into the rear, had been talking earnestly about the church, the minister, the people and the music, all of which were new to Gerty, and greatly excited her wonder and astonishment.

As they drew near home, Willie remarked how dark it was growing in the streets; and then, looking down at Gerty, whom he held by the hand, he said, "Gerty, do you ever go out with Uncle True, and see him light the lamps?"

"No, I never did," said Gerty, "since the first night I came. I've wanted to, but it's been so cold Uncle True would not let me; he said I'd just catch the fever again."

"It won't be cold this evening," said Willie; "it'll be a beautiful night; and, if Uncle True's willing, let's you and I go with him. I've often been, and it's first rate; you can look into the windows and see folks drinking tea, and sitting all round the fire in the parlors."

"And I like to see him light those great lamps," interrupted Gerty; "they make it look so bright and beautiful all round. I hope he'll let us go; I'll ask him; come," said she, pulling him by the hand; "let's catch up with them and ask him now."

"No,—wait;" said Willie; "he's busy talking with grandpa; and we're almost home,—we can ask him then."

He could hardly restrain her impatience, however; and, as soon as they reached the gate, she suddenly broke away from him, and, rushing up to True, made known her request. The plan was willingly acceded to, and the three soon started on the rounds.

For some time Gerty's attention was so wholly engrossed by the lamplighting that she could see and enjoy nothing else. But, when they reached the corner of the street, and came in sight of a large apothecary's shop, her delight knew no bounds. The brilliant colors displayed in the windows, now for the first time seen by the evening light, completely captivated her fancy; and when Willie told her that his master's shop was very similar, she thought it must be a fine place to spend one's life in. Then she wondered why this was open on Sunday, when all the other stores were closed; and Willie, stopping to explain the matter to her, and to gratify her curiosity on many other points, found, when they again started on their way, that True was some distance in advance of them. He hurried Gerty along, telling her that they were now in the finest street they should pass through, and that they must make haste, for they had nearly reached the house he most wanted her to see. When they came up with True, he was just placing his ladder against a post opposite a fine block of buildings. Many of the front windows were shaded, so that the children could not see in; some, however, either had no curtains, or they had not yet been drawn. In one parlor there was a pleasant wood-fire, around which a group were gathered; and here Gerty would fain have lingered. Again, in another, a brilliant chandelier was lit, and though the room was vacant, the furniture was so showy, and the whole so brilliant, that the child clapped her hands in delight, and Willie could not prevail upon her to leave the spot, until he told her that further down the street was another house, equally attractive, where she would perhaps see some beautiful children.

"How do you know there'll be children there?" said she, as they walked along.

"I don't know, certainly," said Willie; "but I think there will. They used always to be up at the window, when I came with Uncle True, last winter."

"How many?" asked Gerty.

"Three, I believe; there was one little girl with such beautiful curls, and such a sweet, cunning little face. She looked like a wax doll, only a great deal prettier."

"O, I hope we shall see her!" said Gerty, dancing along on the tops of her toes, so full was she of excitement and pleasure.

"There they are!" exclaimed Willie; "all three, I declare, just as they used to be!"

"Where?" said Gerty; "where?"

"Over opposite, in the great stone house. Here, let's cross over. It's muddy; I'll carry you."

Willie lifted Gerty carefully over the mud, and they stood in front of the house. True had not yet come up. It was he that the children were watching for. Gerty was not the only child that loved to see the lamps lit.

It was now quite dark, so that persons in a light room could not see any one out of doors; but Willie and Gerty had so much the better chance to look in. It was indeed a fine mansion, evidently the home of wealth. A clear coal-fire, and a bright lamp in the centre of the room, shed abroad their cheerful blaze. Rich carpets, deeply-tinted curtains, pictures in gilded frames, and huge mirrors, reflecting the whole on every side, gave Gerty her first impressions of luxurious life. There was an air of comfort combined with all this elegance, which made it still more fascinating to the child of poverty and want. A table was bountifully spread for tea; the cloth of snow-white damask, the shining plate, above all, the home-like hissing tea-kettle, had a most inviting look. A gentleman in gay slippers was in an easy-chair by the fire; a lady in a gay cap was superintending a servant-girl's arrangements at the tea-table, and the children of the household, smiling and happy, were crowded together on a window-seat, looking out, as we have said.

They were, as Willie had described them, sweet, lovely-looking little creatures; especially a girl, about the same age as Gerty, the eldest of the three. Her fair hair fell in long ringlets over a neck as white as snow; she had blue eyes, a cherub face, and a little round, plump figure. Gerty's admiration and rapture were such that she could find no expression for them, except in jumping up and down, shouting, laughing, and directing Willie's notice first to one thing and then another.

"O, Willie! isn't she a darling? and see what a beautiful fire,—what a splendid lady! And look! look at the father's shoes! What is that on the table? I guess it's good! There's a big looking-glass; and O, Willie! an't they dear little handsome children?"

In all her exclamations, she began and ended with her praises of the children. Willie was quite satisfied; Gerty was as much pleased as he had expected or wished.

True now came up, and, as his torch-light swept along the sidewalk, Gerty and Willie became, in their turn, the subjects of notice and conversation. The little curly-haired girl saw them, and pointed them out to the notice of the other two. Though Gerty could not know what they were saying, she did not like the idea of being stared at and talked about; and, hiding behind the post, she would not move or look up, though Willie laughed at her, and told her it was now her *turn* to be looked at. When True took up his ladder, however, and started to move off, she commenced following him at a run, so as to escape observation; but Willie calling to her, and saying that the children were gone from the window, she ran back as quickly to have one more look, and was just in time to see them taking their places at the tea-table. The next instant the servant-girl came and drew down the window-shades. Gerty then took Willie's hand again, and they hastened on once more to overtake True.

"Shouldn't you like to live in such a house as that, Gerty?" said Willie.

"Yes, indeed," said Gerty; "an't it splendid?"

"I wish I had just such a house," said Willie. "I mean to, one of these days."

"Where will you get it?" exclaimed Gerty, much amazed at so bold a declaration.

"O, I shall work, and grow rich, and buy it."

"You can't; it would take a lot o' money."

"I know it; but I can earn a lot, and I mean to. The gentleman that lives in that grand house was a poor boy when he first came to Boston; and why can't one poor boy get rich, as well as another?"

"How do you suppose he got so much money?"

"I don't know how *he* did; there are a good many ways. Some people think it's all luck, but I guess it's as much smartness as anything."

"Are you smart?"

Willie laughed. "An't I?" said he. "If I don't turn out a rich man, one of these days, you may say I an't."

"I know what I'd do, if I was rich," said Gerty.

"What?" asked Willie.

"First, I'd buy a great, nice chair, for Uncle True, with cushions all in the inside, and bright flowers on it,—just exactly like that one the gentleman was sitting in; and next, I'd have great big lamps, ever so many all in a bunch, so's to make the room as *light*—as *light* as it could be!"

"Seems to me you're mighty fond of lights, Gerty," said Willie.

"I be," said the child. "I hate old, dark, black places; I like stars, and sunshine, and fires, and Uncle True's torch—"

"And I like bright eyes!" interrupted Willie; "yours look just like stars, they shine so to-night. An't we having a good time?"

"Yes, real."

And so they went on. Gerty jumping and dancing along the side-walk, Willie sharing in her gayety and joy, and glorying in the responsibility of entertaining and at the same time protecting the wild little creature. They talked much of how they would spend that future wealth which, in their buoyant hopefulness, they both fully calculated upon one day possessing; for Gerty had caught Willie's spirit, and she, too, meant to work and grow rich. Willie told Gerty of the many plans he had for surrounding his mother and grandfather, and even herself and Uncle True, with every comfort and luxury he had ever heard or dreamt of. Among other things, his mother was to wear a gay cap, like that of the lady they had seen through the window; and at this Gerty had a great laugh. She had an innate perception of the fact that the quiet, demure little widow would be ridiculous in a flowered head-gear. Good taste is inborn, and Gerty had it in her. She felt that Mrs. Sullivan, attired in anything that was not simple, neat and sober-looking, would altogether lose her identity. Willie had no selfish schemes; the generous boy suggested nothing for his own gratification; it was for the rest he meant to labor, and in and through them that he looked for his reward. Happy children! happy as children only can be! What do they want of wealth? What of anything, material and tangible, more than they now possess? They have what is worth more than riches or fame. They are full of childhood's faith and hope. With a fancy and imagination unchecked by disappointment, they are building those same castles that so many thousand children have built before,—that children always will be building, to the end of time. Far off in the distance, they see bright things, and know not what myths they are. High up they rise, and shine, and glitter; and the little ones fix their eyes on them, overlook the rough, dark places that lie between, see not the perils of the way, suspect not the gulfs and snares into which many are destined to fall; but, confident of gaining the glorious goal, they set forth on the way rejoicing. Blessings on that childhood's delusion, if such it be. Undeceive not the little believers, ye wise ones! Check not that God-given hopefulness, which will, perhaps, in its airy flight, lift them in safety over many a rough spot in life's road. It lasts not long, at the best; then check it not, for as it dies out the way grows hard.

One source of the light-heartedness that Willie and Gerty experienced undoubtedly lay in the disinterestedness and generosity of the emotion which occupied them; for, in the plans they formed, neither seemed actuated by selfish motives. They were both filled with the desire to contribute to the comfort of their more aged friends. It was a beautiful spirit of grateful love which each manifested,—a spirit in a great degree natural to both. In Willie, however, it had been so fostered by pious training that it partook of the nature of a principle; while in Gerty it was a mere impulse; and, alas for poor human nature, when swayed by its own passions alone! The poor little girl had—as who has not?—other less pleasing impulses; and, if the former needed encouraging and strengthening, so did the latter require to be uprooted and destroyed.

They had reached the last lamp-post in the street, and now turned another corner; but scarcely had they gone a dozen steps, before Gerty stopped short, and, positively refusing to proceed any further, pulled hard at Willie's hand, and tried to induce him to retrace his steps.

"What's the matter, Gerty?" said he; "are you tired?"

"No, O no! but I can't go any further."

"Why not?"

"O, because—because—" and here Gerty lowered her voice, and, putting her mouth close to Willie's ear, whispered,—"there is Nan Grant's; I see the house! I had forgot Uncle True went there; and I can't go,—I'm afraid!"

"Oho!" said Willie, drawing himself up with dignity, "I should like to know what you're afraid of, when I'm with you! Let her touch you, if she dares! And Uncle True, too!—I *should* laugh." Very kindly and pleasantly did Willie plead with the child, telling her that Nan would not be likely to see *them*, but that perhaps they should see *her;* and that was just what he wanted,—nothing he should like better. Gerty's fears were easily allayed. She was not naturally timid; it was only the suddenness of the shock she received, on recognizing her old home, that had revived, with full force, her dread and horror of Nan. It needed but little reasoning to assure her of the perfect safety of her present position; and her fears soon gave place to the desire to point out to Willie her former persecutor. So, by the time they stood in front of the house, she was rather hoping, than otherwise, to catch sight of Nan. And never had any one a fairer chance to be looked at than Nan at that moment. She was standing opposite the window, engaged in an animated dispute with one of her neighbors. Her countenance expressed angry excitement; and, an ill-looking woman at best, her face now was so sufficient an index to her character, that no one could see her thus and afterwards question her right to the title of vixen, virago, scold, or anything else that conveys the same idea.

"Which is she?" said Willie; "the tall one, swinging the coffee-pot in her hand? I guess she'll break the handle off, if she don't look out."

"Yes," said Gerty, "that's Nan."

"What's she doing?"

"O, she's fighting with Miss Birch; she does most always with some-body. She don't see us, does she?"

"No, she's too busy. Come, don't let's stop; she's an ugly-looking woman, just as I knew she was. I've seen enough of her, and I'm sure you have,— come."

But Gerty lingered. Courageous in the knowledge that she was safe and unseen, she was attentively gazing at Nan, and her eyes glistened, not, as a few minutes before, with the healthy and innocent excitement of a cheerful heart, but with the fire of kindled passion,—a fire that Nan had kindled long ago, which had not yet gone out, and which the sight of Nan had now revived in full force. Willie, thinking it was time to be hurrying home, and perceiving once more that Mr. Flint and his torch were far down the street, now left Gerty, and started himself, as an expedient to draw her on, saying, at the same time, "Come, Gerty, I can't wait."

Gerty turned, saw that he was going, then, quick as lightning, stooped, and, picking up a stone from the side-walk, flung it at the window. There was a crash of broken glass, and an exclamation in Nan's well-known voice; but Gerty was not there to see the result of her work. The instant the stone had left her hand, and she heard the crash, her fears all returned, and, flying past Willie, she paused not until she was safe by the side of True. Willie did not overtake them until they were nearly home, and then came running up, exclaiming, breathlessly, "Why, Gerty, do you know what you did?—You broke the window!"

Gerty jerked her shoulders from side to side to avoid Willie, pouted, and declared that was what she meant to do.

True now inquired what window; and Gerty unhesitatingly acknowledged what she had done, and avowed that she did it on purpose. True and Willie were shocked and silent. Gerty was silent, too, for the rest of the walk; there were clouds on her face, and she felt unhappy in her little heart. She did not understand herself, or her own sensations: we may not say how far she was responsible for them, but this much is certain, her face alone betrayed that, as evil took violent possession of her soul, peace and pleasantness fled away. Poor child! how much she needs to learn the truth! God grant that the inward may one day become as dear to her as now the outward light!

Willie bade them good-night at the house-door, and, as usual, they saw no more of him for a week.

## Chapter IX

*But peace! I must not quarrel with the will*
*Of highest dispensation, which herein*
*Haply had ends above my reach to know.*
                                                    MILTON

"Father," said Mrs. Sullivan, one afternoon, as he was preparing to go out and to take with him a number of articles which he wanted for his Saturday's work in the church, "why don't you get little Gerty to go with you, and carry some of your things? You can't take them all at once; and she'd like to go, I know."

"She'd only be in the way," said Mr. Cooper; "I can take them myself."

But when he had swung a lantern and an empty coal-hod on one arm, taken a little hatchet and a basket of kindlings in his hand, and hoisted a small ladder over his shoulder, he was fain to acknowledge that there was no accommodation for his hammer and a large paper of nails.

So Mrs. Sullivan called Gerty, and asked her to go to the church with Mr. Cooper, and help him carry his tools.

Gerty was very much pleased with the proposal, and, taking the hammer and nails, started off with great alacrity.

When they reached the church, the old sexton took them from her hands, and, telling her she could play about until he went home, but to be sure and do no mischief, left her and went down into the vestry-room to commence there his operation of sweeping, dusting, and building fires. Gerty was thus left to her own amusement; and ample amusement she found it, for some time, to wander round among the empty aisles and pews, and examine closely what, hitherto, she had only viewed from a corner of the gallery. Then she ascended the pulpit, and in imagination addressed a large audience. She was just beginning to grow weary and restless, however, when the organist, who had entered unperceived, commenced playing some low, sweet music; and Gerty, seating herself on the pulpit-stairs, listened with the greatest attention and pleasure. He had not played long before the door at the foot of the broad aisle opened, and a couple of visitors entered, in observing whom Gerty was soon wholly engrossed. One was an elderly man, dressed like a clergyman, short and spare, with hair thin and gray, forehead high, and features rather sharp; but, though a plain man, remarkable for his calm and benignant expression of countenance. A young lady, apparently about twenty-five years of age, was leaning on his arm. She was attired with great simplicity, wearing a dark-brown cloak, and a bonnet of the same color, relieved by some light-blue ribbon about the face. The only article of her dress which was either rich or elegant was some beautiful dark fur, fastened at her throat with a costly enamelled slide. She was somewhat below the middle size, but had a pleasing and well-rounded figure. Her features were small and regular; her complexion clear, though rather pale; and her light-brown hair was most neatly and carefully arranged. She never lifted her eyes as she walked slowly up the aisle, and the long lashes nearly swept her cheek.

The two approached the spot where Gerty sat, but without perceiving her. "I am glad you like the organ," said the gentleman; "I'm not much of a judge of music, myself, but they say it is a superior instrument, and that Hermann plays it remarkably well."

"Nor is my opinion of any value," said the lady; "for I have very little knowledge of music, much as I love it. But that symphony sounds very delightful to me; it is a long time since I have heard such touching strains; or, it may be, it is partly owing to their striking so sweetly on the solemn quiet of the church, this afternoon. I love to go into a large church on a week-day. It was very kind in you to call for me this afternoon. How came you to think of it?"

"I thought you would enjoy it, my dear. I knew Hermann would be playing about this time; and, besides, when I saw how pale you were looking, it seemed to me the walk would do you good."

"It has done me good. I was not feeling well, and the clear cold air was just what I needed; I knew it would refresh me; but Mrs. Ellis was busy, and I could not, you know, go out alone."

"I thought I should find Mr. Cooper, the sexton, here," said the gentleman. "I want to speak to him about the light; the afternoons are so short now, and it grows dark so early, I must ask him to open more of the blinds, or I cannot see to read my sermon to-morrow. Perhaps he is in the vestry-room; he is always somewhere about here on Saturday; I think I had better go and look for him."

Just then Mr. Cooper entered the church, and, seeing the clergyman, came up, and, after receiving his directions about the light, seemed to request him to accompany him somewhere; for the gentleman hesitated, glanced at the young lady, and then said, "I suppose I ought to go to-day; and, as you say you are at leisure, it is a pity I should not; but I don't know—"

Then, turning to the lady, he said, "Emily, Mr. Cooper wants me to go to Mrs. Glass' with him; and I suppose I should have to be absent some time. Do you think you should mind waiting here until I return? She lives in the next street; but I may be detained, for it's about that matter of the library-books being so mischievously defaced, and I am very much afraid that oldest boy of hers had something to do with it. It ought to be inquired into before to-morrow, and I can hardly walk so far as this again to-night, or I would not think of leaving you."

"O! go, by all means," said Emily; "don't mind me; it will be a pleasure to sit here and listen to the music. Mr. Hermann's playing is a great treat to me, and I don't care how long I wait; so I beg you won't hurry on my account, Mr. Arnold."

Thus assured, Mr. Arnold concluded to go; and, having first led the lady to a chair beneath the pulpit, went away with Mr. Cooper.

All this time Gerty had been quite unnoticed, and had remained very quiet on the upper stair, a little secured from sight by the pulpit. Hardly had the doors closed, however, with a loud bang, when the child got up, and began to descend the stairs. The moment she moved, the lady, whose seat was very near, started, and exclaimed, rather suddenly, "Who's that?"

Gerty stood quite still, and made no reply. Strangely enough, the lady did not look up, though she must have perceived that the movement was above her head. There was a moment's pause, and then Gerty began again to run down the stairs. This time the lady sprung up, and, stretching out her hand, said, as quickly as before, "Who is it?"

"Me," said Gerty, looking up in the lady's face; "it's only me."

"Will you stop and speak to me?" said the lady.

Gerty not only stopped, but came close up to Emily's chair, irresistibly attracted by the music of the sweetest voice she had ever heard. The lady placed her hand on Gerty's head, drew her towards her, and said, "Who are you?"

"Gerty."

"Gerty who?"

"Nothing else but Gerty."

"Have you forgotten your other name?"

"I haven't got any other name."

"How came you here?"

"I came with Mr. Cooper, to help him bring his things."

"And he's left you here to wait for him, and I'm left too; so we must take care of each other, mustn't we?"

Gerty laughed at this.

"Where were you?—On the stairs?"

"Yes."

"Suppose you sit down on this step by my chair, and talk with me a little while; I want to see if we can't find out what your other name is. Where do you say you live?"

"With Uncle True."

"True?"

"Yes. Mr. True Flint, I live with now. He took me home to his house, one night, when Nan Grant put me out on the sidewalk."

"Why! are you that little girl? Then I've heard of you before. Mr. Flint told me all about you."

"Do you know my Uncle True?"

"Yes, very well."

"What's your name?"

"My name is Emily Graham."

"O! I know," said Gerty, springing suddenly up, and clapping her hands together; "I know. You asked him to keep me; he said so,—I *heard* him say so; and you gave me my clothes; and you're beautiful; and you're good; and I love you! O! I love you ever so much!"

As Gerty spoke with a voice full of excitement, a strange look passed over Miss Graham's face, a most inquiring and restless look, as if the tones of the voice had vibrated on a chord of her memory. She did not speak, but, passing her arm round the child's waist, drew her closer to her. As the peculiar expression passed away from her face, and her features assumed their usual calm composure, Gerty, as she gazed at her with a look of wonder (a look which the child had worn during the whole of the conversation), exclaimed, at last, "Are you going to sleep?"

"No.—Why?"

"Because your eyes are shut."

"They are always shut, my child."

"Always shut!—What for?"

"I am blind, Gerty; I can see nothing."

"Not see!" said Gerty; "can't you see anything? Can't you see me now?"

"No," said Miss Graham.

"O!" exclaimed Gerty, drawing a long breath, *"I'm so glad."*

*"Glad!"* said Miss Graham, in the saddest voice that ever was heard.

"O, yes!" said Gerty, "so glad you can't see me!—because now, perhaps, you'll love me."

"And shouldn't I love you if I saw you?" said Emily, passing her hand softly and slowly over the child's features.

"O, no!" answered Gerty; "I'm so ugly! I'm glad you can't see how ugly I am."

"But just think, Gerty," said Emily, in the same sad voice, "how would you feel if you could not see the light, could not see anything in the world?"

"Can't you see the sun, and the stars, and the sky, and the church we're in? Are you in the dark?"

"In the dark, all the time, day and night in the dark."

Gerty burst into a paroxysm of tears. "O!" exclaimed she, as soon as she could find voice amid her sobs, "it's too bad! it's too bad!"

The child's grief was contagious; and, for the first time for years, Emily wept bitterly for her blindness.

It was for but a few moments, however. Quickly recovering herself, she tried to compose the child also, saying, "Hush! hush! don't cry; and don't say it's too bad! It's not too bad; I can bear it very well. I'm used to it, and am quite happy."

*"I* shouldn't be happy in the dark; I should *hate* to be!" said Gerty. "I *an't* glad you're blind; I'm real *sorry.* I wish you could see me and everything. Can't your eyes be opened, anyway?"

"No," said Emily, "never; but we won't talk about that any more; we'll talk about you. I want to know what makes you think yourself so very ugly."

"Because folks say that I'm an ugly child, and that nobody loves ugly children."

"Yes, people do," said Emily, "love ugly children, if they are good."

"But I an't good," said Gerty; "I'm real bad!"

"But you *can be good,"* said Emily, "and then everybody will love you."

"Do you think I can be good?"

"Yes, if you try."

"I will try."

"I *hope* you will," said Emily. "Mr. Flint thinks a great deal of his little girl, and she must do all she can to please him."

She then went on to make inquiries concerning Gerty's former way of life, and became so much interested in the recital of the little girl's early sorrows and trials, that she was unconscious of the flight of time, and quite unobservant of the departure of the organist, who had ceased playing, closed his instrument, and gone away.

Gerty was very communicative. Always a little shy of strangers at first, she was nevertheless easily won by kind words; and, in the present case, the sweet voice and sympathetic tones of Emily went straight to her heart. Singularly enough, though her whole life had been passed among the poorer, and almost the whole of it among the lowest class of people, she seemed to feel none of that awe and constraint which might be supposed natural, on her encountering, for the first time, one who, born and bred amid affluence and luxury, showed herself, in every word and motion, a lady of polished mind and manners. On the contrary, Gerty clung to Emily as affectionately, and stroked her soft boa with as much freedom, as if she had herself been born in a palace, and cradled in sable fur. Once or twice she took Emily's nicely-gloved hand between both her own, and held it tight; her favorite mode of expressing her enthusiastic warmth of gratitude and admiration. The excitable but interesting child took no less strong a hold upon Miss Graham's feelings. The latter saw at once how totally neglected the little one had been, and the importance of her being educated and trained with care, lest early abuse, acting upon an impetuous disposition, should prove destructive to a nature capable of the best attainments. The two were still entertaining each other, and, as we have said, unconscious of the lateness of the hour, when Mr. Arnold entered the church hastily, and somewhat out of breath. As he came up the aisle, when he was yet some way off he called to Emily, saying, "Emily, dear, I'm afraid you thought I had forgotten you, I have been gone so much longer than I intended. Were you not quite tired and discouraged?"

"Have you been gone long?" replied Emily. "I thought it was but a very little while; I have had company, you see."

"What, little folks!" said Mr. Arnold, good-naturedly. "Where did this little body come from?"

"She came to the church this afternoon, with Mr. Cooper. Isn't he here for her?"

"Cooper?—No: he went straight home, after he left me; he's probably forgotten all about the child. What's to be done?"

"Can't we take her home? Is it far?"

"It is two or three streets from here, and directly out of our way; altogether too far for you to walk."

"O no, it won't tire me; I'm quite strong now, and I wouldn't but know she was safe home, on any account. I'd rather get a little fatigued."

If Emily could but have seen Gerty's grateful face that moment, she would indeed have felt repaid for almost any amount of weariness.

So they went home with Gerty, and Emily kissed Gerty at the gate; and Gerty was a happy child that night.

# Chapter X

*By the strong spirit's discipline,*
*By the fierce wrong forgiven,*
*By all that wrings the heart of sin,*
*Is woman won to Heaven.*
                                        N. P. WILLIS

As may be supposed, the blind girl did not forget our little Gerty. Emily Graham never forgot the sufferings, the wants, the necessities, of others. She could not see the world without, but there was a world of love and sympathy within her, which manifested itself in abundant benevolence and charity, both of heart and deed. She lived a life of love. She loved God with her whole heart, and her neighbor as herself. Her own great misfortunes and trials could not be helped, and were borne without repining; but the misfortunes and trials of others became her care, the alleviation of them her greatest delight. Emily was never weary of doing good. Many a blessing was called down upon her head, by young and old, for kindness past; many a call was made upon her for further aid; and to the call of none was she ever deaf. But never had she been so touched as now by any tale of sorrow. Ready listener, as she was, to the story of grief and trouble, she knew how many children were born into the world amid poverty and privation; how many were abused, neglected and forsaken; so that Gerty's experience was not new to her. But it was something in the child herself that excited and interested Emily in an unwonted degree. The tones of her voice, the earnestness and pathos with which she spoke, the confiding and affectionate manner in which she had clung to her, the sudden clasping of her hand, and, finally, her vehement outbreak of grief when she became conscious of Emily's great misfortune,—all these things so haunted Miss Graham's recollection, that she dreamt of the child at night, and thought much of her by day. She could not account to herself for the interest she felt in the little stranger; but the impulse to see and know more of her was irresistible, and, sending for True, she talked a long time with him about the child.

True was highly gratified by Miss Graham's account of the meeting in the church, and of the interest the little girl had inspired in one for whom he felt the greatest admiration and respect. Gerty had previously told him how she had seen Miss Graham, and had spoken in the most glowing terms of the dear lady, who was so kind to her, and brought her home when Mr. Cooper had forgotten her, but it had not occurred to the old man that the fancy was mutual.

Emily asked him if he didn't intend to send her to school.

"Well, I don't know," said he; "she's a little thing, and an't much used to being with other children. Besides, I don't exactly like to spare her; I like to see her round."

Emily suggested that it was time she was learning to read and write; and that the sooner she went among other children, the easier it would be to her.

"Very true, Miss Emily, very true," said Mr. Flint. "I dare say you're right; and, if you think she'd better go, I'll ask her, and see what she says."

"I would," said Emily. "I think she might enjoy it, besides improving very much; and, about her clothes, if there's any deficiency, I'll—"

"O, no, no, Miss Emily!" interrupted True; "there's no necessity; she's very well on 't now, thanks to your kindness."

"Well," said Emily, "if she should have any wants, you must apply to me. You know we adopted her jointly, and I agreed to do anything I could for her; so you must never hesitate,—it will be a pleasure to serve either of you. Father always feels under obligations to you, Mr. Flint, for faithful service, that cost you dear in the end."

"O, Miss Emily," said True, "Mr. Graham has always been my best friend; and as to that 'ere accident that happened when I was in his employ, it was nobody's fault but my own; it was my own carelessness, and nobody's else."

"I know you say so," said Emily, "but we regretted it very much; and you mustn't forget what I tell you, that I shall delight in doing anything for Gerty. I should like to have her come and see me, some day, if she would like to, and you'll let her."

"Sartain, sartain," said True, "and thank you kindly; she'd admire to come."

A few days after, Gerty went with True to see Miss Graham; but the housekeeper, whom they met in the hall, told them that she was ill and could see no one. So they went away full of disappointment and regret.

It proved afterwards that Emily took a severe cold the day she sat so long in the church, and was suffering with it when they called; but, though confined to her room, she would have been glad to have a visit from Gerty, and was sorry and grieved that Mrs. Ellis should have sent them away so abruptly.

One Saturday evening, when Willie was present, True broached the subject of Gerty's going to school. Gerty herself was very much disgusted with the idea; but it met with Willie's warm approbation, and when Gerty learned that Miss Graham also wished it, she consented, though rather reluctantly, to begin the next week, and try how she liked it. So, on the following Monday, Gerty accompanied True to one of the primary schools, was admitted, and her education commenced. When Willie came home the next Saturday, he rushed into True's room, full of eagerness to hear how Gerty liked going to school. He found her seated at the table, with her spelling-book; and, as soon as he entered, she exclaimed, "O, Willie! Willie! come and hear me read!"

Her performance could not properly be called reading. She had not got beyond the alphabet, and a few syllables which she had learned to spell; but Willie bestowed upon her much well-merited praise, for she had really been very diligent. He was astonished to hear that Gerty liked going to school, liked the teacher and the scholars, and had a fine time at recess. He had fully expected that she would dislike the whole business, and very probably go into tantrums about it,—which was the expression he used to denote her fits of ill-temper. On the contrary, everything, thus far, had gone well, and Gerty had never looked so animated and happy as she did this evening. Willie promised to assist her in her studies; and the two children's literary plans soon became as high-flown as if one had been a poet-laureate and the other a philosopher.

For two or three weeks all appeared to go on smoothly. Gerty went regularly to school, and continued to make rapid progress. Every Saturday Willie heard her read and spell, assisted, praised and encouraged her. He had, however, a shrewd suspicion that, on one or two occasions, she had come near having a brush with some large girls, for whom she began to show symptoms of dislike. Whatever the difficulty originated in, it soon reached a crisis.

One day, when the children were assembled in the school-yard, during recess, Gerty caught sight of True in his working-dress, just passing down the street, with his ladder and lamp-filler. Shouting and laughing, she bounded out of the yard, pursued and overtook him. She came back in a few minutes, seeming much delighted at the unexpected rencounter, and ran into the yard out of breath, and full of happy excitement. The troop of large girls, whom Gerty had already had some reason to distrust, had been observing her, and, as soon as she returned, one of them called out, saying,

"Who's that man?"

"That's my Uncle True," said Gerty.

"Your what?"

"My uncle, Mr. Flint, that I live with."

"So you belong to him, do you?" said the girl, in an insolent tone of voice. "Ha! ha! ha!"

"What are you laughing at?" said Gerty, fiercely.

"Ugh! Before I'd live with him!" said the girl, "old Smutty!"

The others caught it up, and the laugh and epithet Old Smutty circulated freely in the corner of the yard where Gerty was standing.

Gerty was furious. Her eyes glistened, she doubled her little fist, and, without hesitation, came down in battle upon the crowd. But they were too many for her, and, helpless as she was with passion, they drove her out of the yard. She started for home on a full run, screaming with all her might.

As she flew along the side-walk, she brushed roughly against a tall and rather stiff-looking lady, who was walking slowly in the same direction, with another and much smaller person leaning on her arm.

"Bless me!" said the tall lady, who had almost lost her equilibrium from her fright and the suddenness of the shock. "Why, you horrid little creature!" As she spoke, she grasped Gerty by the shoulder, and, before the child could break away, succeeded in giving her a slight shake. This served to increase Gerty's anger, and, her speed gaining in proportion, it was but a few minutes before she was at home, crouched in a corner of True's room behind the bed, her face to the wall, and, as usual, on such occasions, covered with both her hands. Here she was free to cry as loud as she pleased; for Mrs. Sullivan was gone out, and there was no one in the house to hear her,—a privilege, indeed, of which she fully availed herself.

But she had not had time to indulge long in her tantrum, when the gate at the end of the yard closed with a bang, and footsteps were heard coming towards Mr. Flint's door. Gerty's attention was arrested, for she knew by the sound that it was the step of a stranger who was approaching. With a strong effort, she succeeded, after one or two convulsive sobs, in so far controlling herself as to keep quiet. There was a knock at the door, but Gerty did not reply to it, remaining in her position concealed behind the bed. The knock was not repeated, but the stranger lifted the latch and walked in.

"There doesn't seem to be any one at home," said a female voice; "what a pity!"

"Isn't there? I'm sorry," replied another, in the sweet, musical tones of Miss Graham.

Gerty knew the voice, at once.

"I thought you'd better not come here yourself," rejoined the first speaker, who was no other than Mrs. Ellis, the identical lady whom Gerty had so frightened and disconcerted.

"O, I don't regret coming," said Emily. "You can leave me here while you go to your sister's, and very likely Mr. Flint or the little girl will come home in the mean time."

"It don't become you, Miss Emily, to be carried round everywhere, and left, like an expressman's parcel, till called for. You caught a horrid cold, that you're hardly well of now, waiting there in the church for the minister; and Mr. Graham will be finding fault next."

"O, no, Mrs. Ellis; it's very comfortable here; the church must have been damp, I think. Come, put me in Mr. Flint's arm-chair, and I can make myself quite contented."

"Well, at any rate," said Mrs. Ellis, "I'll make up a good fire in this stove before I go."

As she spoke, the energetic housekeeper seized the poker, and, after stirring up the coals, and making free with all True's kindling-wood, waited long enough to hear the roaring and see the blaze; and then, having laid aside Emily's cloak and boa, went away with the same firm, steady step with which she had come, and which had so overpowered Emily's noiseless tread, that Gerty had only anticipated the arrival of a single guest. As soon as Gerty knew, by the swinging of the gate, that Mrs. Ellis had really departed, she suspended her effort at self-control, and, with a deep-drawn sigh, gasped out, "O, dear! O, dear!"

"Why, Gerty!" exclaimed Emily, "is that you?"

"Yes," sobbed Gerty.

"Come here."

The child waited no second bidding, but, starting up, ran, threw herself on the floor by the side of Emily, buried her face in the blind girl's lap, and once more commenced crying aloud. By this time her whole frame was trembling with agitation.

"Why, Gerty!" said Emily; "what is the matter?"

But Gerty could not reply; and Emily, finding this to be the case, desisted from her inquiries until the little one should be somewhat composed. She lifted Gerty up into her lap, laid her head upon her shoulder, and with her own handkerchief wiped the tears from her face.

Her soothing words and caresses soon quieted the child; and when she was calm, Emily, instead of recurring at once to the cause of her grief, very judiciously questioned her upon other topics. At last, however, she asked her if she went to school.

"I *have been*," said Gerty, raising her head suddenly from Emily's shoulder; "but I won't ever go again!"

"What!—Why not?"

"Because," said Gerty, angrily, "I hate those girls; yes, I hate 'em! ugly things!"

"Gerty," said Emily, "don't say that; you shouldn't hate anybody."

"Why shouldn't I?" said Gerty.

"Because it's wrong."

"No, it's not *wrong; I* say it *isn't!*" said Gerty; "and I do hate 'em; and I hate Nan Grant, and I always shall! Don't *you* hate anybody?"

"No," answered Emily; "*I don't.*"

"Did anybody ever drown your kitten? Did anybody ever call your father Old Smutty?" said Gerty. "If they had, I know you'd hate 'em, just as I do."

"Gerty," said Emily, solemnly, "didn't you tell me, the other day, that you were a naughty child, but that you wished to be good, and would try?"

"Yes," said Gerty.

"If you wish to become good and be forgiven, you must forgive others."

Gerty said nothing.

"Do you not wish God to forgive and love you?"

"God, that lives in heaven,—that made the stars?" said Gerty.

"Yes."

"Will he love me, and let me some time go to heaven?"

"Yes, if you try to be good, and love everybody."

"Miss Emily," said Gerty, after a moment's pause, "I can't do it,—so I s'pose I can't go."

Just at this moment a tear fell upon Gerty's forehead. She looked thoughtfully up in Emily's face, then said,

"Dear Miss Emily, are you going?"

"I am trying to."

"I should like to go with you," said Gerty, shaking her head, meditatively.

Still Emily did not speak. She left the child to the working of her own thoughts.

"Miss Emily," said Gerty, at last, in the lowest whisper, "I mean to *try,* but I don't think I *can.*"

"God bless you, and help you, my child!" said Emily, laying her hand upon Gerty's head.

For fifteen minutes, or more, not a word was spoken by either. Gerty lay perfectly still in Emily's lap. By and by the latter perceived, by the child's breathing, that, worn out with the fever and excitement of all she had gone through, she had dropped into a quiet sleep. When Mrs. Ellis returned, Emily pointed to the sleeping child, and asked her to place her on the bed. She did so, wonderingly; and then, turning to Emily, exclaimed, "Upon my word, Miss Emily, that's the same rude, bawling little creature, that came so near being the death of us!" Emily smiled at the idea of a child eight years old overthrowing and annihilating a woman of Mrs. Ellis' inches, but said nothing.

Why did Emily weep long that night, as she recalled the scene of the morning? Why did she, on bended knee, wrestle so vehemently with a mighty sorrow? Why did she pray so earnestly for new strength and heavenly aid? Why did she so beseechingly ask of God his blessing on the little child? Because she had felt, in many a year of darkness and bereavement, in many an hour of fearful struggle, in many a pang of despair, how a temper like that which Gerty had this day shown might, in one moment of its fearful reign, cast a blight upon a lifetime, and write in fearful lines the mournful requiem of earthly joy. And so she prayed to Heaven that night for strength to keep her firm resolve, and aid in fulfilling her undying purpose, to cure that child of her dark infirmity.

## Chapter XI

*Her influence breathes, and bids the blighted heart
To life and hope from desolation start.*

HEMANS

The next Sabbath afternoon found Gerty seated on a cricket, in front of a pleasant little wood-fire in Emily's own room. Her large eyes were fixed upon Emily's face, which always seemed, in some unaccountable way, to fascinate the little girl; so attentively did she watch the play of the features in a countenance the charm of which many an older person than Gerty had felt, but tried in vain to describe. It was not beauty,—at least, not brilliant beauty,—for that Emily had not possessed, even when her face was illumined, as it had once been, by beautiful hazel eyes; nor was it the effect of what is usually termed fascination of manner, for Emily's manner and voice were both so soft and unassuming that they never took the fancy by storm. It was not compassion for her blindness, though so great a misfortune might well, and always did, excite the warmest sympathy. But it was hard to realize that Emily *was* blind. It was a fact never forced upon her friends' recollection by any repining or selfish indulgence on the part of the sufferer; and, as there was nothing painful in the appearance of her closed lids, shaded and fringed as they were by her long and heavy eyelashes, it was not unusual for those immediately about her to converse upon things which could only be evident to the sense of sight, and even direct her attention to one object and another, quite forgetting, for the moment, her sad deprivation; and Emily never sighed, never seemed hurt at their want of consideration, or showed any lack of interest in objects thus shut from her gaze; but, apparently quite satisfied with the descriptions she heard, or the pictures which she formed in her imagination, would talk pleasantly and playfully upon whatever was uppermost in the minds of her companions. Some said that Emily had the sweetest mouth in the world, and they loved to watch its ever-varying expression. Some said her chief attraction lay in a small dimple in her right cheek; others (and these were young girls who wanted to be charming themselves) remarked that if they thought they could make their hair wave like Emily's, they'd braid it up every night: it was *so* becoming! But the chosen few, who were capable, through their own spirituality, of understanding and appreciating Emily's character,—the few, the very few, who had known her struggles, and had witnessed her triumphs,—had *they* undertaken to express their belief concerning the source whence she derived that power by which her face and voice stole into the hearts of young and old, and won their love and admiration, *they* would have said, as Gerty did, when she sat gazing so earnestly at Emily on the very Sunday afternoon of which we speak, "Miss Emily, I know you've been with God."

Gerty was certainly a strange child. All untaught as she was, she had felt Emily's entire superiority to any being she had ever seen before; and, yielding to that belief in her belonging to an order above humanity, she reposed implicit confidence in what she told her, allowed herself to be guided and influenced by one whom she felt loved her and sought only her good; and, as she sat at her feet and listened to her gentle voice while she gave her her first lesson upon the distinction between right and wrong, Emily, though she could not see the little thoughtful face that was looking up at her, knew, by the earnest attention she had gained, by the child's perfect stillness, and, still more, by the little hand which had sought hers, and now held it tight, that one great point was won.

Gerty had not been to school since the day of her battle with the great girls. All True's persuasions had failed, and she would not go. But Emily understood the child's nature so much better than True did, and urged upon her so much more forcible motives than the old man had thought of employing, that *she* succeeded where *he* had failed. Gerty considered that her old friend had been insulted, and that was the chief cause of indignation with her; but Emily placed the matter in a different light, and, convincing her at last that, if she loved Uncle True, she would show it much better by obeying his wishes than by retaining her foolish anger, she finally obtained Gerty's promise that she would go to school the next morning. She also advised her how to conduct herself towards the scholars whom she so much disliked, and gave her some simple directions with regard to her behavior the next day; telling her that perhaps Mr. Flint would go with her, make suitable apologies to the teacher for her absence, and that, in such case, she would have no further trouble.

The next morning True, much pleased that Gerty's repugnance to the school was at last overcome, went with her, and, inquiring for the teacher at the door, stated the case to her in his blunt, honest way, and then left Gerty in her special charge.

Miss Browne, who was a young woman of good sense and good feelings, saw the matter in the right light; and, taking an opportunity to speak privately to the girls who had excited Gerty's temper by their rudeness, made them feel so ashamed of their conduct, that they no longer molested the child; and, as Gerty soon after made friends with one or two quiet children of her own age, with whom she played in recess, she got into no more such difficulties.

The winter passed away. The pleasant, sunny spring days came, days when Gerty could sit at open windows, or on the door-step, when birds sang in the morning among the branches of an old locust-tree that grew in the narrow yard, and the sun at evening threw bright rays across True's great room, and Gerty could see to read almost until bed-time. She had been to school steadily all winter, and had improved as rapidly as most intelligent children do, who are first given the opportunity to learn at an age when, full of ambition, the mind is most fertile and capable of progress. She was looking healthy and well; her clothes were clean and neat, for her wardrobe was well stocked by Emily, and the care of it superintended by Mrs. Sullivan. She was bright and happy too, and tripped round the house so joyously and lightly, that True declared his birdie knew not what it was to touch her heel to the ground, but flew about on the tips of her toes.

The old man could not have loved the little adopted one better had she been his own child; and, as he sat by her side on the wide settle, which, when the warm weather came, was moved outside the door, and listened patiently and attentively while she read aloud to him story after story, of little girls who never told lies, boys who always obeyed their parents, or, more frequently still, of the child who knew how to keep her temper, they seemed, as indeed they were, most suitable companions for each other. The old man's interest in the story-books, which were provided by Emily, and read and re-read by Gerty, was as keen and unflagging as if he had been a child himself; and he would sit with his elbows on his knees, hearing the simple stories, laughing when Gerty laughed, sympathizing as fully and heartily as she did in the sorrows of her little heroines, and rejoicing with her in the final triumph of truth, obedience and patience.

Emily knew the weight that such tales often carried with them to the hearts of children, and most carefully and judiciously did she select books for Gerty. Gerty's life was now as happy and prosperous as it had once been wretched and miserable. Six months before, she had felt herself all alone, unloved, uncared-for. Now she had many friends, and knew what it was to be thought of, provided for, and caressed. All the days in the week were joyous; but Saturday and Sunday were marked days with her, as well as with Mrs. Sullivan; for Saturday brought Willie home to hear her recite her lessons, walk, laugh and play, with her. He had so many pleasant things to tell, he was so full of life and animation, so ready to enter into all her plans, and in every way promote her amusement, that on Monday morning she began to count the days until Saturday would come again. Then, if anything went wrong or got out of order,—if the old clock stopped, or her toys got broken, or, worse still, if her lessons troubled, or any little childish grief oppressed her,—Willie knew how to put everything right, to help her out of every difficulty. So Willie's mother looked not more anxiously for his coming than Gerty did.

Sunday afternoon Gerty always spent with Emily, in Emily's own room, listening to her sweet voice, and, half-unconsciously, imbibing a portion of her sweet spirit. Emily preached no sermons, nor did she weary the child with exhortations and precepts. Indeed, it did not occur to Gerty that she went there to be *taught* anything; but simply and gradually the blind girl imparted light to the child's dark soul, and the truths that make for virtue, the lessons that are divine, were implanted in her so naturally, and yet so forcibly, that she realized not the work that was going on; but long after,— when goodness had grown strong within her, and her first feeble resistance of evil, her first attempts to keep her childish resolves, had matured into deeply-rooted principles, and confirmed habits of right,—she felt, as she looked back into the past, that on those blessed Sabbaths, sitting on her cricket at Emily's knee, she had received into her heart the first beams of that immortal light that never could be quenched.

Thus her silent prayer was answered. God had chosen an earthly messenger to lead his child into everlasting peace; a messenger from whose closed eyes the world's paths were all shut out, but who had been so long treading the heavenly road, that it was now familiar ground. Who so fit to guide the little one as she, who with patience had learned the way? Who so well able to cast light upon the darkness of another soul as she, to whose own darkened life God had lent a torch divine?

It was a grievous trial to Gerty, about this time, to learn that the Grahams were soon going into the country for the summer. Mr. Graham owned a pleasant residence about six miles from Boston, to which he invariably resorted as soon as the planting-season commenced; for, though devoted to business during the winter, he had of late years allowed himself much relaxation from his counting-room in the summer; and legers and day-books were now soon to be supplanted, in his estimation, by the labors and delights of gardening. Emily promised Gerty, however, that she should come and pass a day with her when the weather was fine; a visit which Gerty enjoyed three months in anticipation, and more than three in retrospection.

It was some compensation for Emily's absence that, as the days became long, Willie was frequently able to leave the shop and come home for an hour or two in the evening; and Willie, as we have said, always knew how to comfort Gerty, whatever the trouble might be.

# Chapter XII

"Let every minute, as it springs,
Convey fresh knowledge on its wings;
Let every minute, as it flies,
Record thee good, as well as wise."

COTTON

It was one pleasant evening in the latter part of April, that Gerty, who had been to see Miss Graham and bid her good-by, before her departure for the country, stood at the back part of the yard weeping bitterly. She held in her hand a book and a new slate, Emily's parting gifts; but she had not removed the wrapper from the one, and the other was quite besmeared with tears. She was so full of grief at the parting (with her, the first of those many sad partings life is so full of), that she did not hear any one approach, and was unconscious of any one's presence, until a hand was placed upon each of her shoulders; and, as she turned round, she found herself encircled by Willie's arms, and face to face with Willie's sunny countenance.

"Why, Gerty!" said he, "this is no kind of a welcome, when I've come home on a week-night, to stay with you all the evening. Mother and grandfather are both gone out somewhere, and then, when I come to look for you, you're crying so I can't see your face through such oceans of tears. Come, come! *do* leave off; you don't know how shockingly you look!"

"Willie!" sobbed she, "do you know Miss Emily's gone?"

"Gone where?"

"Way off, six miles, to stay all summer!"

But Willie only laughed. "Six miles!" said he; "that's a terrible way, certainly!"

"But I can't see her any more!" said Gerty.

"You can see her next winter," rejoined Willie.

"O, but that's so long!" said the child.

"What makes you think so much of her?" asked Willie.

"She thinks much of me; she can't see me, and she likes me better than anybody but Uncle True."

"I don't believe it; I don't believe she likes you half as well as I do. I *know* she don't! How can she, when she's blind, and never saw you in her life, and I see you all the time, and love you better than I do anybody in the world, except my mother?"

"Do you *really*, Willie?"

"Yes, I do. I always think, when I come home, Now I'm going to see Gerty; and everything that happens all the week, I think to myself—I shall tell Gerty that."

"I shouldn't think you'd like me so well."

"Why not?"

"O, because you're so handsome, and I an't handsome a bit. I heard Ellen Chase tell Lucretia Davis, the other day, that she thought Gerty Flint was the worst-looking girl in school."

"Then she ought to be ashamed of herself," said Willie. "I guess she an't very good-looking. I should hate the looks of *her,* or any *other* girl that said that."

"O, Willie!" exclaimed Gerty, earnestly, "it's true; as true as can be."

"No, it an't *true,*" said Willie. "To be sure, you haven't got long curls, and a round face, and blue eyes, like Belle Clinton's, and nobody'd think of setting you up for a beauty; but when you've been running, and have rosy cheeks, and your great black eyes shine, and you laugh so heartily as you do sometimes at anything funny, I often think you're the brightest-looking girl I ever saw in my life; and I don't care what other folks think, as long as I like your looks. I feel just as bad when you cry, or anything's the matter with you, as if it were myself, and worse. George Bray struck his little sister Mary yesterday, because she tore his kite; I should have liked to give him a flogging. I wouldn't strike you, Gerty, if you tore all my playthings to pieces."

Such professions of affection on Willie's part were frequent, and always responded to by a like declaration from Gerty. Nor were they mere professions. The two children loved each other dearly. They were very differently constituted, for Willie was earnest, persevering and patient, calm in his temperament, and equal in his spirits. Gerty, on the other hand, excitable and impetuous, was constantly thrown off her guard; her temper was easily roused, her spirits variable, her whole nature sensitive to the last degree. Willie was accustomed to be loved, expected to be loved, and *was* loved by everybody. Gerty had been an outcast from all affection, looked not for it, and, except under favorable circumstances and by those who knew her well, did not readily inspire it. But that they loved *each other* there could be no doubt; and, if in the spring the bond between them was already strong, autumn found it cemented by still firmer ties; for, during Emily's absence, Willie filled her place and his own too, and though Gerty did not forget her blind friend, she passed a most happy summer, and continued to make such progress in her studies at school, that, when Emily returned to the city in October, she could hardly understand how so much had been accomplished in what had seemed to her so short a time.

The following winter, too, was passed most profitably by Gerty. Miss Graham's kindly feeling towards her little protegée, far from having diminished, seemed to have been increased by time and absence, and Gerty's visits to Emily became more frequent than ever. The profit derived from these visits was not all on Gerty's part. Emily had been in the habit, the previous winter, of hearing her read occasionally, that she might judge of her proficiency; now, however, she discovered, on the first trial, that the little girl had attained to a greater degree of excellence in this accomplishment than is common among grown people. She read understandingly, and her accent and intonations were so admirable, that Emily found rare pleasure in listening to her.

Partly with a view to the child's benefit, and partly for her own gratification, she proposed that Gery should come every day and read to her for an hour. Gerty was only too happy to oblige her dear Miss Emily, who, in making the proposal, represented it as a personal favor to herself, and a plan by which Gerty's eyes could serve for them both. It was agreed that when True started on his lamp-lighting expeditions he should take Gerty to Mr. Graham's, and call for her on his return. Owing to this arrangement, Gerty was constant and punctual in her attendance at the appointed time; and none but those who have tried it are aware what a large amount of reading may be accomplished in six months, if only an hour is devoted to it regularly each day. Emily, in her choice of books, did not confine herself to such as come strictly within a child's comprehension. She judged, rightly, that a girl of such keen intelligence as Gerty was naturally endowed with would suffer nothing by occasionally encountering what was beyond her comprehension; but that, on the contrary, the very effort she would be called upon to make would enlarge her capacity, and be an incentive to her genius. So history, biography, and books of travels, were perused by Gerty at an age when most children's literary pursuits are confined to stories and pictures. The child seemed, indeed, to give the preference to this comparatively solid reading; and, aided by Emily's kind explanations and encouragement, she stored up in her little brain many an important fact and much useful information. At Gerty's age the memory is strong and retentive, and things impressed on the mind then are usually better remembered than what is learned in after years, when the thoughts are more disturbed and divided.

Her especial favorite was a little work on astronomy, which puzzled her more than all the rest put together, but which delighted her in the same proportion; for it made some things clear, and all the rest, though a mystery still, was to her a beautiful mystery, and one which she fully meant some time to explore to the uttermost. And this ambition to learn more, and understand better, by and by, was, after all, the greatest good she derived. Awaken a child's ambition, and implant in her a taste for literature, and more is gained than by years of school-room drudgery, where the heart works not in unison with the head.

From the time Gerty was first admitted, until she was twelve years old, she continued to attend the public schools, and was rapidly advanced and promoted; but what she learned with Miss Graham, and acquired by study with Willie at home, formed nearly as important a part of her education. Willie, as we have said, was very fond of study, and was delighted at Gerty's warm participation in his favorite pursuit. They were a great advantage to each other, for each found encouragement in the other's sympathy and coöperation. After the first year or two of their acquaintance, Willie could not be properly called a child, for he was in his fifteenth year, and beginning to look quite manly. But Gerty's eagerness for knowledge had all the more influence upon him; for, if the little girl ten years of age was patient and willing to labor at her books until after nine o'clock, the youth of fifteen must not rub his eyes and plead weariness. It was when they had reached these respective years that they commenced studying French together. Willie's former teacher continued to feel a kindly interest in the boy, who had long been his best scholar, and who would certainly have borne away from his class the first prizes, had not a higher duty called him to inferior labors previous to the public exhibition. Whenever he met him in the street, or elsewhere, he inquired concerning his mode of life, and whether he continued his studies. Finding that Willie had considerable spare time, he earnestly advised him to learn the French language,—that being a branch of knowledge which would undoubtedly prove useful to him, whatever business he might chance to pursue in life,—and offered to lend him such books as he would need at the commencement.

Willie availed himself of his teacher's advice, and his kind offer, and began to study in good earnest. When he was at home in the evening, he was in the habit of coming into True's room, partly for the sake of quiet (for True was a quiet man, and had too great a veneration for learning to interrupt the students with his questions), and partly for the sake of being with Gerty, who was usually, at that time, occupied with her books. Gerty, as may be supposed, conceived a strong desire to learn French, too. Willie was willing she should try, but had no confidence that she would long persevere. To his surprise, however, she was not only discovered a wonderful determination, but a decided talent for language; and, as Emily furnished her with books similar to Willie's, she kept pace with him, oftentimes translating more during the week than he could find time to do. On Saturday evening, when they always had a fine study time together, True would sit on his old settle by the fire, watching Willie and Gerty, side by side, at the table, with their eyes bent on the page, which to him seemed the greatest of earthly labyrinths. Gerty always looked out the words, in which employment she had great skill, her bright eyes diving, as if by magic, into the very heart of the dictionary, and transfixing the right word at a glance, while Willie's province was to make sense. Almost the only occasion when True was known to disturb them, by a word even, was when he first heard Willie talk about making sense. "Making sense, Willie?" said the old man; "is that what ye 're after? Well, you couldn't do a better business. I'll warrant you a market for it; there's want enough on 't in the world!"

It was but natural that, under such favorable influences as Gerty enjoyed, with Emily to advise and direct, and Willie to aid and encourage, her intellect should rapidly expand and strengthen. But how is it with that little heart of hers, that, at once warm and affectionate, impulsive, sensitive and passionate, now throbs with love and gratitude, and now again burns as vehemently with the consuming fire that a sense of wrong, a consciousness of injury, to herself or her friends, would at any moment enkindle? Has she, in two years of happy childhood, learned self-control? Has she also attained to an enlightened sense of the distinction between right and wrong, truth and falsehood? In short, has Emily been true to her self-imposed trust, her high resolve, to soften the heart and instruct the soul of the little ignorant one? Has Gerty learned religion? Has she found out God, and begun to walk patiently in that path which is lit by a holy light, and leads to rest?

She has *begun;* and though her footsteps often falter, though she sometimes quite turns aside, and, impatient of the narrow way, gives the rein to her old irritability and ill-temper, she is yet but a child, and there is the strongest foundation for hopefulness in the sincerity of her good intentions, and the depth of her contrition when wrong has had the mastery. Emily has spared no pains in teaching her where to place her strong reliance, and Gerty has already learned to look to higher aid than Emily's, and to lean on a mightier arm.

Miss Graham had appointed for herself no easy task, when she undertook to inform the mind and heart of a child utterly untaught in the ways of virtue. In some important points, however, she experienced far less diffi- culty than she had anticipated. For instance, after her first explanation to Gerty of the difference between honesty and dishonesty, the truth and a lie, she never had any cause to complain of the child, whose whole nature was the very reverse of deceptive, and whom nothing but extreme fear had ever driven to the meanness of falsehood. If Gerty's greatest fault lay in a proud and easily-roused temper, that very fault carried with it its usual accompaniment of frankness and sincerity. Under almost any cir- cumstances, Gerty would have been too proud to keep back the truth, even before she became too virtuous. Emily was convinced, before she had known Gerty six months, that she could always depend upon her word; and noth- ing could have been a greater encouragement to Miss Graham's unselfish efforts than the knowledge that truth, the root of every holy thing, had thus easily and early been made to take up its abode in the child. But this sensitive, proud temper of Gerty's seemed an inborn thing; abuse and tyranny had not been able to crush it; on the contrary, it had flourished in the midst of the unfavorable influences amid which she had been nur- tured. Kindness could accomplish almost anything with her, could con- vince and restrain; but restraint from any other source was unbearable, and, however proper and necessary a check it might be, she was always dis- posed to resent it. Emily knew that to such a spirit even parental control is seldom sufficient. She knew of but one influence that is strong enough, one power that never fails to quell and subdue earthly pride and passion; the power of Christian humility, engrafted into the heart,—the humility of *principle,* of *conscience,*—the only power to which native pride ever will pay homage.

She knew that a command, of almost any kind, laid upon Gerty by her- self or Uncle True, would be promptly obeyed; for, in either case, the little girl would know that the order was given in love, and she would fulfill it in the same spirit; but, to provide for all contingencies, and to make the heart right as well as the life, it was necessary to inspire her with a higher motive than merely pleasing either of these friends; and, in teaching her the spirit of her Divine Master, Emily was making her powerful to do and to suffer, to bear and to forbear, when, depending on herself, she should be left to her own guidance alone. How much Gerty had improved in the two years that had passed since she first began to be so carefully instructed and provided for, the course of our story must develop. We cannot pause to dwell upon the trials and struggles, the failures and victories, that she experienced. It is sufficient to say that Miss Graham was satisfied and hopeful, True proud and overjoyed, while Mrs. Sullivan, and even old Mr. Cooper, declared she had improved wonderfully in her behavior and her looks, and was remarkably mannerly for such a child.

## Chapter XIII

*No caprice of mind,*
*No passing influence of idle time,*
*No popular show, no clamor from the crowd,*
*Can move him, erring, from the path of right.*
W. G. SIMMS

One Saturday evening in December, the third winter of Gerty's residence with True, Willie came in with his French books under his arm, and, after the first salutations were over, exclaimed, as he threw the grammar and dictionary upon the table, "O, Gerty! before we begin to study, I *must* tell you and Uncle True the funniest thing, that happened to-day; I have been laughing so at home, as I was telling mother about it!"

"I heard you laugh," said Gerty. "If I had not been so busy, I should have gone into your mother's room, to hear what it was so very droll. But, come, do tell us!"

"Why, you will not think it's anything like a joke when I begin; and I should not be so much amused, if she hadn't been the very queerest old woman that ever I saw in my life."

"Old woman!—You haven't told us about any old woman!"

"But I'm going to," said Willie. "You noticed how everything was covered with ice, this morning. How splendidly it looked, didn't it? I declare, when the sun shone on that great elm-tree in front of our shop, I thought I never saw anything so handsome in my life. But, there, that's nothing to do with my old woman,—only that the side-walks were just like everything else, a perfect glare."

"I know it," interrupted Gerty; "I fell down, going to school."

"Did you?" said Willie; "didn't you get hurt?"

"No, indeed. But go on; I want to hear about your old woman."

"I was standing at the shop-door, about eleven o'clock, looking out, when I saw the strangest-looking figure that you ever imagined, coming down the street. I must tell you how she was dressed. She did look so ridiculous! She had on some kind of a black silk or satin gown, made very scant, and trimmed all round with some brownish-looking lace (black, I suppose it had been once, but it isn't now); then she had a gray cloak, of some sort of silk material, that you certainly would have said came out of the ark, if it hadn't been for a little cape, of a different color, that she wore outside of it, and which must have dated a generation further back. I would not undertake to describe her bonnet; only I know it was twice as big as anybody's else, and she had a figured lace veil thrown over one side, that reached nearly to her feet. But her goggles were the crowner; such immense, horrid-looking things, I never saw! She had a work-bag, made of black silk, with pieces of cloth of all the colors in the rainbow sewed on to it, zigzag; then her pocket-handkerchief was pinned to her bag, and a great feather fan (only think, at this season of the year!), that was pinned on somewhere (by a string, I suppose), and a bundle-handkerchief and a news-paper! O, gracious! I can't think of half the things; but they were all pinned together with great brass pins, and hung in a body on her left arm, all depending on the strength of the bag-string. Her dress, though, wasn't the strangest thing about her. What made it too funny was to see her way of walking; she looked quite old and infirm, and it was evident she could hardly keep her footing on the ice; and yet she walked with such a smirk, such a consequential little air! O, Gerty, it's lucky you didn't see her; you'd have laughed from then till this time."

"Some poor crazy crittur', wasn't she?" asked True.

"O, no!" said Willie, "I don't think she was; queer enough, to be sure, but not crazy. Just as she got opposite the shop-door her feet slipped, and, the first thing I knew, she fell flat on the side-walk. I rushed out, for I thought the fall might have killed the poor little thing; and Mr. Bray, and a gentle-man he was waiting upon, followed me. She did appear stunned, at first; but we carried her into the shop, and she came to her senses in a minute or two. Crazy, you asked if she were, Uncle True! No, not she! She's as bright as a dollar. As soon as she opened her eyes, and seemed to know what she was about, she felt for her work-bag and all its appendages; counted them up, to see if the number were right, and then nodded her head very satisfactorily. Mr. Bray poured out a glass of cordial, and offered it to her. By this time she had got her airs and graces back again; so, when he rec-ommended to her to swallow the cordial, she retreated, with a little old-fashioned curtsey, and put up both hands to express her horror at the idea of such a thing. The gentleman that was standing by smiled, and advised her to take it, telling her it would do her no harm. Upon that, she turned round, made another curtsey to him, and answered, in a little, cracked voice, 'Can you assure me, sir, as a gentleman of candor and gallantry, that it is not an exhilarating potion?' The gentleman could hardly keep from laughing; but he told her it was nothing that would hurt her. 'Then,' said she, 'I will venture to sip the beverage; it has a most aromatic frag-rance.' She seemed to like the taste, as well as the smell, for she drank every drop of it; and, when she had set the glass down on the counter, she turned to me and said, 'Except upon this gentleman's assurance of the harmlessness of the liquid, I would not have swallowed it in your presence, my young master, if it were only for the *example*. I have set my seal to no temperance-pledge, but I am abstemious because it becomes a lady;—it is with me a matter of choice—a matter of *taste.'* She now seemed quite restored, and talked of starting again on her walk; but it really was not safe for her to go alone on the ice, and I rather think Mr. Bray thought so, for he asked her where she was going. She told him, in her roundabout way, that she was proceeding to pass the day with Mistress somebody, that lived in the neighborhood of the Common. I touched Mr. Bray's arm, and said, in a low voice, that, if he could spare me, I'd go with her. He said he shouldn't want me for an hour; so I offered her my arm, and told her I should be happy to wait upon her. You ought to have seen her then! If I had been a grown-up man, and she a young lady, she couldn't have tossed her head or giggled more. But she took my arm, and we started off. I knew Mr. Bray and the gentleman were laughing to see us, but I didn't care; I pitied the old lady, and I did not mean she should get another tumble.

"Every person we met stared at us; and it's no wonder they did, for we must have been a most absurd-looking couple. She not only accepted my offered crook, but clasped her hands together round it, making a complete handle of her two arms; and so she hung on with all her might.—But, there, I ought not to laugh at the poor thing; for she needed somebody to help her along, and I'm sure she wasn't heavy enough to tire me out, if she did make the most of herself. I wonder who she belongs to. I shouldn't think her friends would let her go about the streets so, especially such walking as it is to-day."

"What's her name?" inquired Gerty. "Didn't you find out?"

"No," answered Willie; "she wouldn't tell me. I asked her; but she only said, in her little, cracked voice (and here Willie began to laugh immoderately), that she was the *incognito,* and that it was the part of a true and gallant knight to discover the name of his fair lady. O, I promise you, she was a case! Why, you never heard any one talk so ridiculously as she did! I asked her how old she was.—Mother says that was very impolite, but it's the only uncivil thing I did, or said, as the old lady would testify herself, if she were here."

"How old is she?" said Gerty.

"Sixteen."

"Why, Willie, what do you mean?"

"That's what she told me," returned Willie; "and a true and gallant knight is bound to believe his fair lady."

"Poor body!" said True; "she's childish!"

"No, she isn't, Uncle True," said Willie; "you'd think so, part of the time, to hear her run on with her nonsense; and then, the next minute, she'd speak as sensibly as anybody, and say how much obliged she was to me for showing such a spirit of conformity as to be willing to put myself to so much trouble for the sake of an old woman like her. Just as we turned into Beacon-street, we met a whole school of girls, blooming beauties, handsome enough to kill, my old lady called them; and, from the instant they came in sight, she seemed to take it for granted I should try to get away from her, and run after some of them. But she held on with a vengeance! It's lucky I had no idea of forsaking her, for it would have been impossible. Some of them stopped and stared at us,—of course, I didn't care how much they stared; but she seemed to think I should be terribly mortified; and when we had passed them all, she complimented me again and again on my spirit of conformity,—her favorite expression."

Here Willie paused, quite out of breath. True clapped him upon the shoulder. "Good boy, Willie!" said he; "clever boy! You always look out for the old folks; and that's right. Respect for the aged is a good thing; though your grandfather says it's very much out of fashion."

"I don't know much about fashion, Uncle True; but I should think it was a pretty mean sort of a boy that would see an old lady get one fall on the ice, and not save her from another by seeing her safe home."

"Willie's always kind to everybody," said Gerty.

"Willie's either a hero," said the boy, "or else he has got two pretty good friends,—I rather think it's the latter. But, come, Gerty; Charles the XII. is waiting for us, and we must study as much as we can to-night. We may not have another chance very soon; for Mr. Bray isn't well this evening; he seems threatened with a fever, and I promised to go back to the shop after dinner to-morrow. If he should be sick, I shall have plenty to do, without coming home at all."

"O, I hope Mr. Bray is not going to have a fever," said True and Gerty, in the same breath.

"He's such a clever man!" said True.

"He's so good to you, Willie!" added Gerty.

Willie hoped not, too; but his hopes gave place to his fears, when he found, on the following day, that his kind master was not able to leave his bed, and the doctor pronounced his symptoms alarming.

A typhoid fever set in, which in a few days terminated the life of the excellent apothecary.

The death of Mr. Bray was so sudden and dreadful a blow to Willie, that he did not at first realize the important bearing the event had upon his own fortunes. The shop was closed, the widow having determined to dispose of the stock and remove into the country as soon as possible.

Willie was thus left without employment, and deprived of Mr. Bray's valuable recommendation and assistance. His earnings during the past year had been very considerable, and had added essentially to the comfort of his mother and grandfather, who had thus been enabled to relax the severity of their own labors. The thought of being a burden to them, even for a day, was intolerable to the independent and energetic spirit of the boy; and he earnestly set himself to work to obtain another place. He commenced by applying to the different apothecaries in the city. But none of them wanted a youth of his age, and one day was spent in fruitless inquiries.

He returned home at night, disappointed, but not by any means discouraged. If he could not obtain employment with an apothecary, he would do something else.

But what should he do? That was the question. He had long talks with his mother about it. She felt that his talents and education entitled him to fill a position equal, certainly, to that he had already occupied; and could not endure the thought of his descending to more menial service. Willie, without too much self-esteem, thought so too. He knew, indeed, that he was capable of giving satisfaction in a station which required more business talent than his situation at Mr. Bray's had ever given scope to. But, if he could not obtain such a place as he desired, he would take what he could get. So he made every possible inquiry; but he had no one to speak a good word for him, and he could not expect people to feel confidence in a boy concerning whom they knew nothing.

So he met with no success, and day after day returned home silent and depressed. He dreaded to meet his mother and grandfather, after every fresh failure. The care-worn, patient face of the former turned towards him so hopefully, that he could not bear to sadden it by the recital of any new disappointment; and his grandfather's incredulity in the possibility of his ever having anything to do again was equally tantalizing, so long as he saw no hope of convincing him to the contrary. After a week or two, Mrs. Sullivan avoided asking him any questions concerning the occurrences of the day; for her watchful eye saw how much such inquiries pained him, and therefore she waited for him to make his communications, if he had any.

Sometimes nothing was said, on either side, of the manner in which Willie had passed his day. And many an application did he make for employment, many a mortifying rebuff did he receive, of which his mother never knew.

❁❁❁❁❁❁❁❁❁❁❁❁❁❁❁❁❁❁❁❁❁❁❁❁❁

## Chapter XIV

*Yet where an equal poise of hope and fear*
*Does arbitrate the event, my nature is*
*That I incline to hope, rather than fear.*
COMUS

This was altogether a new experience to Willie, and one of the most trying he could have been called upon to bear. But he bore it, and bore it bravely; kept all his worst struggles from his anxious mother and desponding grandfather, and resolved manfully to hope against hope. Gerty was now his chief comforter. He told her all his troubles, and, young as she was, she was a wonderful consoler. Always looking on the bright side, always prophesying better luck to-morrow, she did much towards keeping up his hopes, and strengthening his resolutions. Gerty was so quick, sagacious and observing, that she knew more than most children of the various ways in which things are often brought about; and she sometimes made valuable suggestions to Willie, of which he gladly availed himself. Among others, she one day asked him if he had applied at the intelligence-offices. He had never thought of it,—wondered he had not, but would try the plan the very next day. He did so, and for a time was buoyed up with the hopes held out to him; but they proved fleeting, and he was now almost in despair, when his eye fell upon an advertisement in a newspaper, which seemed to afford still another chance. He showed the notice to Gerty. It was just the thing. He had only to apply; he was the very boy that man wanted;—just fifteen, smart, capable and trustworthy; and would like, when he had learned the business, to go into partnership. That was what was required; and Willie was the very person, she was sure.

Gerty was so sanguine, that Willie presented himself the next day at the place specified, with a more eager countenance than he had ever yet worn. The gentleman, a sharp-looking man, with very keen eyes, talked with him some time; asked a great many questions, made the boy very uncomfortable by hinting his doubts about his capability and honesty, and, finally, wound up by declaring that, under the most favorable circumstances, and with the very best recommendations, he could not think of engaging with any young man, unless his friends were willing to take some interest in the concern, and invest a small amount on his account.

This, of course, made the place out of the question for Willie, even if he had liked the man; which he did not, for he felt in his heart that he was a knave, or not many degrees removed from one.

Until now, he had never thought of despairing; but when he went home after this last interview, it was with such a heavy heart, that it seemed to him utterly impossible to meet his mother, and so he went directly to True's room. It was the night before Christmas. True had gone out, and Gerty was alone. There was a bright fire in the stove, and the room was dimly lighted by the last rays of the winter sunset, and by the glare of the coals, seen through one of the open doors of the stove.

Gerty was engaged in stirring up an Indian cake for tea,—one of the few branches of the cooking department in which she had acquired some little skill. She was just coming from the pantry, with a scoop full of meal in her hand, when Willie entered at the opposite door. The manner in which he tossed his cap upon the settle, and, seating himself at the table, leaned his head upon both his hands, betrayed at once to Gerty the defeat the poor boy had met with in this last encounter with ill-fate. It was so unlike Willie to come in without even speaking,—it was such a strange thing to see his bright young head bowed down with care, and his elastic figure looking tired and old,—that Gerty knew at once his brave heart had given way. She laid down the scoop, and, walking softly and slowly up to him, touched his arm with her hand, and looked up anxiously into his face. Her sympathetic touch and look were more than he could bear. He laid his head on the table, and in a minute more Gerty heard great heavy sobs, each one of which sank deep into her soul. She often cried herself,—it seemed only natural, but Willie,—the laughing, happy, light-hearted Willie,—she had never seen *him* cry; she didn't know he *could*. She crept up on the rounds of his chair, and, putting her arm round his neck, whispered, "I shouldn't mind, Willie, if I didn't get the place; I don't believe it's a *good* place."

"I don't believe it is, either," said Willie, lifting up his head; "but what shall I do? I can't get *any* place, and I can't stay here, doing nothing."

"We like to have you at home," said Gerty.

"It's pleasant enough to be at home. I was always glad enough to come when I lived at Mr. Bray's, and was earning something, and could feel as if anybody was glad to see me."

"*Everybody* is glad to see you *now.*"

"But not as they were *then,*" said Willie, rather impatiently. "Mother always looks as if she expected to hear I'd got something to do; and grand- father, I believe, never thought I should be good for much; and now, just as I was beginning to earn something, and be a help to them, I've lost my chance!"

"But that an't your fault, Willie; you couldn't help Mr. Bray's dying. I shouldn't think Mr. Cooper would blame you for not having anything to do *now.*"

"He don't *blame* me; but, if you were in my place, you'd feel just as I do, to see him sit in his arm-chair, evenings, and groan and look up at me, as much as to say, 'it's *you* I'm groaning about.' He thinks this is a dreadful world, and that he's never seen any good luck in it himself; so I suppose he thinks I never shall."

"*I* think you will," said Gerty. "I think you'll be rich, some time,—and *then* won't he be astonished?"

"O, Gerty! you're a nice child, and think I can do anything. If ever I am rich, I promise to go shares with you; but," added he, despondingly, "'t an't so easy. I used to think I could make money when I grew up; but it's pretty slow business."

Here he was on the point of leaning down upon the table again, and giv- ing himself up to melancholy; but Gerty caught hold of his hands. "Come," said she, "Willie. Don't think any more about it. People have troubles al- ways, but they get over 'em; perhaps next week you'll be in a better shop than Mr. Bray's, and we shall be as happy as ever. Do you know," said she, by way of changing the subject (a species of tact which children understand as well as grown people), "it's just two years to-night since I came here?"

"Is it?" said Willie. "Did Uncle True bring you home with him the night before Christmas?"

"Yes."

"Why, that was Santa Claus carrying you to good things, instead of bringing good things to you, wasn't it?"

Gerty did not know anything about Santa Claus, that special friend of children; and Willie, who had only lately read about him in some book, undertook to tell her what he knew of the veteran toy-dealer.

Finding the interest of the subject had engaged his thoughts in spite of himself, Gerty returned to her cooking, listening attentively, however, to his story, while she stirred up the corn-cake. When he had finished, she was just putting her cake in the oven; and, as she sat on her knee by the stove, swinging the handle of the oven-door in her hand, her eyes twinkled with such a merry look that Willie exclaimed, "What are you thinking of, Gerty, that makes you look so sly?"

"I was thinking that perhaps Santa Claus would come for you to-night. If he comes for folks that need something, I expect he'll come for you, and carry you to some place where you'll have a chance to grow rich."

"Very likely," said Willie, "he'll clap me into his bag, and trudge off with me as a present to somebody,—some old Croesus, that will give me a fortune for the asking. I do hope he will; for, if I don't get something to do before New Year, I shall give up in despair."

True now came in, and interrupted the children's conversation by the display of a fine turkey, a Christmas present from Mr. Graham. He had also a book for Gerty, a gift from Emily.

"Isn't that queer?" exclaimed Gerty. "Willie was just saying you were my Santa Claus, Uncle True; and I do believe you are." As she spoke, she opened the book, and in the frontis-piece was a portrait of that individual. "It looks like him, Willie! I declare it does!" shouted she; "a fur cap, a pipe, and just such a pleasant face! O! Uncle True, if you only had a sack full of toys over your shoulder, instead of your lantern and that great turkey, you would be a complete Santa Claus. Haven't you got anything for Willie, Uncle True?"

"Yes, I've got a little something; but I'm afeared he won't think much on 't. It's only a bit of a note."

"A note for me?" inquired Willie. "Who can it be from?"

"Can't say," said True, fumbling in his great pockets; "only, just round the corner, I met a man who stopped me to inquire where Miss Sullivan lived. I told her she lived jist here, and I'd show him the house. When he saw I belonged here too, he give me this little scrap o' paper, and asked me to hand it over, as it was directed to Master William Sullivan. I s'pose that's you, an't it?"

He now handed Willie the slip of paper; and the boy, taking True's lantern in his hand, and holding the note up to the light, read aloud:

"R. H. Clinton would like to see William Sullivan on Thursday morning, between ten and eleven o'clock, at No. 13 —— Wharf."

Willie looked up in amazement. "What does it mean?" said he; "I don't know any such person."

"I know who he is," said True; "why, it's he as lives in the great stone house in —— street. He's a rich man, and that's the number of his store— his counting-room, rather,—on —— Wharf."

"What! father to those pretty children we used to see in the window?"

"The very same."

"What can he want of me?"

"Very like he wants your sarvices," suggested True.

"Then it's a place!" cried Gerty, "a real good one, and Santa Claus came and brought it! I said he would! O, Willie, I'm so glad!"

Willie did not know whether to be glad or not. It was such a strange message, coming too from an utter stranger. He could not but hope, as Gerty and True did, that it might prove the dawning of some good fortune;

but he had reasons, of which they were not aware, for believing that no offer from this quarter could be available to him, and therefore made them both promise to give no hint of the matter to his mother or Mr. Cooper.

On Thursday, which was the next day but one, being the day after Christmas, Willie presented himself at the appointed time and place. Mr. Clinton, a gentlemanly man, with a friendly countenance, received him very kindly, asked him but few questions, and did not even mention such a thing as a recommendation from his former employer; but, telling him that he was in want of a young man to fill the place of junior clerk in his counting-room, offered him the situation. Willie hesitated; for, though the offer was most encouraging to his future prospects, Mr. Clinton made no mention of any salary; and that was a thing the youth could not dispense with. Seeing that he was undecided, Mr. Clinton said, "Perhaps you do not like my proposal, or have already made some other engagement."

"No, indeed," answered Willie, quickly. "You are very kind to feel so much confidence in a stranger as to be willing to receive me, and your offer is a most unexpected and welcome one; but I have been in a retail store, where I obtained regular earnings, which were very important to my mother and grandfather. I had far rather be in a counting-room, like yours, sir, and I think I might learn to be of use; but I know there are numbers of boys, sons of rich men, who would be glad to be employed by you, and would ask no compensation for their services; so that I could not expect any salary, at least for some years. I should, indeed, be well repaid, at the end of that time, by the knowledge I might gain of mercantile affairs; but unfortunately, sir, I can no more afford it than I could afford to go to college."

The gentleman smiled. "How did you know so much of these matters, my young friend?"

"I have heard, sir, from boys who were at school with me, and are now clerks in mercantile houses, that they received no pay, and I always considered it a perfectly fair arrangement; but it was the reason why I felt bound to content myself with the position I held in an apothecary's shop, which, though it was not suited to my taste, enabled me to support myself, and to relieve my mother, who is a widow, and my grandfather, who is old and poor."

"Your grandfather is—"

"Mr. Cooper, sexton of Mr. Arnold's church."

"Aha!" said Mr. Clinton; "I know him."

"What you say, William," added he, after a moment's pause, "is perfectly true. We are not in the habit of paying any salary to our young clerks, and are overrun with applications at that rate; but I have heard good accounts of you, my boy (I shan't tell you where I had my information, though I see you look very curious), and, moreover, I like your countenance, and believe you will serve me faithfully. So, if you will tell me what you received from Mr. Bray, I will pay you the same next year, and, after that, increase your salary, if I find you deserve it; and, if you please, you shall commence with me the first of January."

Willie thanked Mr. Clinton in the fewest possible words, and hastened away.

The senior clerk, who, as he leaned over his accounts, listened to the conversation, thought the boy did not express much gratitude, considering the unusual generosity of the merchant's offer. But the merchant himself, who was watching the boy's countenance, while despondency gave place to surprise, and surprise again was superseded by hope, joy, and a most sincere thankfulness, saw there a gratitude too deep to express itself in words, and remembered the time when he too, the only son of his mother, and she a widow, had come alone to the city, sought long for employment, and, finding it at last, had sat down to write and tell her how he hoped soon to earn enough for himself and her.

The grass had been growing on that parent's grave, far back in the country, more than twenty years, and the merchant's face was furrowed with the lines of care; but, as he returned slowly to his desk, and unconsciously traced, on a blank sheet of paper, and with a dry pen, the words "Dear mother," she for the time became a living image; he, a boy again; and those invisible words were the commencement of the very letter that carried her the news of his good fortune.

No. The boy was not ungrateful, or the merchant would not thus have been reminded of the time when his own heart had been so deeply stirred.

And the spirits of those mothers who have wept, prayed, and thanked God over similar communications from much-loved sons, may know how to rejoice and sympathize with good little Mrs. Sullivan, when she heard from Willie the joyful tidings. Mr. Cooper and Gerty also have their prototypes in many an old man, whose dim and world-worn eye lights up occasionally with the hope that, disappointed as he has been himself, he cannot help cherishing for his grandson; and in many a proud little sister, who now sees her noble brother appreciated by others, as he has always been by her. Nor, on such an occasion, is the band of rejoicing ones complete, without some such hearty friend as True to come in unexpectedly, tap the boy on the shoulder, and exclaim, "Ah! Master Willie, they needn't have worried about you, need they? I've told your grandfather, more than once, that I was of the 'pinion 't would all come out right, at last."

The great mystery of the whole matter was Mr. Clinton's ever having heard of Willie at all. Mrs. Sullivan thought over all her small circle of acquaintances, and suggested a great many impossible ways. But as, with much conjecturing, they came no nearer to the truth, they finally concluded to do as Gerty did, set it all down to the agency of Santa Claus.

✿✿✿✿✿✿✿✿✿✿✿✿✿✿✿✿✿✿✿✿✿✿✿✿✿✿✿✿✿✿

## Chapter XV

*Whether the day its wonted course renewed,*
*Or midnight vigils wrapt the world in shade,*
*Her tender task assiduous she pursued,*
*To soothe his anguish, or his wants to aid.*

BLACKLOCK

"I wonder," said Miss Peekout, as she leaned both her hands on the sill of the front-window, and looked up and down the street,—a habit in which she indulged herself for about ten minutes, after she had washed up the breakfast things, and before she trimmed the solar-lamp,—"I wonder who that slender girl is that walks by here every morning, with that feeble-looking old man leaning on her arm! I always see them at just about this time, when the weather and walking are good. She's a nice child, I know, and seems to be very fond of the old man,—probably her grandfather. I notice she's careful to leave the best side of the walk for him, and she watches every step he takes; she needs to, indeed, for he totters sadly. Poor little thing! she looks pale and anxious; I wonder if she takes all the care of the old man!" But they are quite out of sight, and Miss Peekout turns round to *wonder* whether the solar-lamp doesn't need a new wick.

"I *wonder*," said old Mrs. Grumble, as she sat at her window, a little further down the street, "if I should live to be old and infirm (Mrs. Grumble was over seventy, but as yet suffered from no infirmity but that of a very irritable temper),—I *wonder* if anybody would wait upon me, and take care of me, as that little girl does of her grandfather! No, I'll warrant not! Who can the patient little creature be?"

"There, look Belle!" said one young girl to another, as they walked up the shady side of the street, on their way to school; "there's the girl that we meet every day with the old man. How can you say you don't think she's pretty? I admire her looks!"

"You always do manage, Kitty, to *admire* people that everybody else thinks are horrid-looking."

"Horrid-looking!" replied Kitty, in a provoked tone; "she's anything but *horrid-looking!* Do notice, now, Belle, when we meet them, she has the *sweetest* way of looking up in the old man's face, and talking to him. I *wonder* what is the matter with him! Do see how his arm shakes,—the one that's passed through hers."

The two couples are now close to each other, and they pass in silence.

"*Don't you* think she has an interesting face?" said Kitty, eagerly, as soon as they were out of hearing.

"She's got handsome eyes," answered Belle. "I don't see anything else that looks interesting about her. I *wonder* if she don't hate to have to walk in the street with that old grandfather; trudging along so slow, with the sun shining right in her face, and he leaning on her arm, and shaking so he can hardly stand on his feet! I wouldn't do it for anything."

"Why, Belle!" exclaimed Kitty, "how can you talk so? I'm sure I pity that old man dreadfully."

"Lor!" said Belle, "what's the use of pitying? If you are going to begin to pity, you'll have to do it all the time. Look,"—and here Belle touched her companion's elbow,—"there's Willie Sullivan, father's clerk; an't he a beauty? I want to stop and speak to him."

But, before she could address a word to him, Willie, who was walking very fast, passed her with a bow, and a pleasant "Good-morning, Miss Isabel;" and, ere she had recovered from the surprise and disappointment, was some rods down the street.

"Polite!" muttered the pretty Isabel.

"Why, Belle! do see," said Kitty, who was looking back over her shoulder, "he's overtaken the old man and my interesting little girl. Look,—look! He's put the old man's other arm through his, and they are all three walking off together. Isn't that quite a coincidence?"

"Nothing very remarkable," replied Belle, who seemed a little annoyed. "I suppose they are persons he's acquainted with. Come, make haste; we shall be late at school."

Reader! Do *you wonder* who they are, the girl and the old man? or, have you already conjectured that they are no other than Gerty and Trueman Flint? True is no longer the brave, strong, sturdy protector of the feeble, lonely little child. The cases are quite reversed. True has had a paralytic stroke. His strength is gone, his power even to walk alone. He sits all day in his arm-chair, or on the old settle, when he is not out walking with Gerty. The blow came suddenly; struck down the robust man, and left him feeble as a child. And the little stranger, the orphan girl, who, in her weakness, her loneliness and her poverty, found in him a father and a mother, she now is all the world to him; his staff, his stay, his comfort and his hope. During four or five years that he has cherished the frail blossom, she has been gaining strength for the time when *he* should be the leaning, *she* the sustaining power; and when the time came,—and it came full soon,—she was ready to respond to the call. With the simplicity of a child, but a woman's firmness; with the stature of a child, but a woman's capacity; the earnestness of a child, but a woman's perseverance,—from morning till night, the faithful little nurse and housekeeper labors untiringly in the service of her first, her best friend. Ever at his side, ever attending to his wants, and yet most wonderfully accomplishing many things which he never sees her do, she seems, indeed, to the fond old man, what he once prophesied she would become,—God's embodied blessing to his latter years, making light his closing days, and cheering even the pathway to the grave.

Though disease had robbed True's limbs of all their power, the blast had happily spared his mind, which was clear and tranquil as ever; while his pious heart was fixed in humble trust on that God whose presence and love he had ever acknowledged, and on whom he so fully relied, that even in this bitter trial he was able to say, in perfect submission, "Thy will, not mine, be done!" Little did those who *wondered*, as day after day they watched the invalid and his childish guardian, at the patience and self-sacrifice of the devoted girl, little did they understand the emotions of Gerty's loving, grateful heart. Little did they realize the joy it was to her to sustain and support her beloved friend. Little did *she,* who would have been too proud to walk with the old paralytic, know what Gerty's pride was made of. She would have wondered, had she been told that the heart of the girl, whom she would have pitied, could she have spared time to pity *any one,* had never swelled with so fervent and noble a satisfaction as when, with the trembling old man leaning on her arm, she gloried in the burden.

The outward world was nothing at all to her. She cared not for the conjectures of the idle, the curious or the vain. She lived for True now; she might almost be said to live *in* him, so wholly were her thoughts bent on promoting his happiness, prolonging and blessing his days.

It had not long been thus. Only about two months previous to the morning of which we have been speaking had True been stricken down with this weighty affliction. He had been in failing health, but had still been able to attend to all his duties and labors, until one day in the month of June, when Gerty went into his room, and found, to her surprise, that he had not risen, although it was much later than his usual hour. On going to the bed-side and speaking to him, she perceived that he looked strangely, and had lost the power of replying to her questions. Bewildered and frightened, she ran to call Mrs. Sullivan. A physician was summoned, the case pronounced one of paralysis, and for a time there seemed reason to fear that it would prove fatal. He soon, however, began to amend, recovered his speech, and in a week or two was well enough to walk about, with Gerty's assistance.

The doctor had recommended as much gentle exercise as possible; and every pleasant morning, before the day grew warm, Gerty presented herself bonneted and equipped for those walks, which, unknown to her, excited so much observation. She usually took advantage of this opportunity to make such little household purchases as were necessary, that she might not be compelled to go out again and leave True alone; that being a thing she as much as possible avoided doing.

On the occasion already alluded to, Willie accompanied them as far as the provision-shop, which was their destination; and, having seen True comfortably seated, proceeded to —— Wharf, while Gerty stepped up to the counter to bargain for the dinner. She purchased a bit of veal suitable for broth, gazed wishfully at some tempting summer vegetables, turned away and sighed. She held in her hand the wallet which contained all their money; it had now been in her keeping for some weeks, and was growing light, so she knew it was no use to think about the vegetables; and she sighed, because she remembered how much Uncle True enjoyed the green peas last year.

"How much is the meat?" asked she of the rosy-cheeked butcher, who was wrapping it up in a paper.

He named the sum. It was very little; *so little* that it almost seemed to Gerty as if he had seen into her purse, and her thoughts too, and knew how glad she would be that it did not cost any more. As he handed her the change, he leaned over the counter, and asked, in an under tone, what kind of nourishment Mr. Flint was able to take.

"The doctor said any wholesome food," replied Gerty.

"Don't you think he'd relish some green peas? I've got some first-rate ones, fresh from the country; and, if you think he'd eat 'em, I should like to send you some. My boy shall take round half a peck or so, and I'll put the meat right in the same basket."

"Thank you," said Gerty; "he likes green peas."

"Very well, very well! Then I'll send him some beauties;" and he turned away to wait upon another customer, so quick that Gerty thought he did not see how the color came into her face and the tears into her eyes. But he *did* see, and that was the *reason* he turned away so quickly. He was a clever fellow, that rosy-cheeked butcher!

True had an excellent appetite, enjoyed and praised the dinner exceedingly, and, after eating heartily of it, fell asleep in his chair.

The moment he awoke, Gerty sprung to his side, exclaiming, "Uncle True, here's Miss Emily!—here's dear Miss Emily come to see you!"

"The Lord bless you, my dear, dear young lady!" said True, trying to rise from his chair and go towards her.

"Don't rise, Mr. Flint, I beg you will not," exclaimed Emily, whose quick ear perceived the motion. "From what Gerty tells me, I fear you are not able. Please give me a chair, Gerty, nearer to Mr. Flint."

She drew near, took True's hand, but looked inexpressibly shocked as she observed how tremulous it had become.

"Ah, Miss Emily!" said he; "I'm not the same man as when I saw you last; the Lord has given me a warnin', and I shan't be here long!"

"I'm so sorry I did not know of this!" said Emily. "I should have come to see you before, but I never heard of your illness until to-day. George, my father's man, saw you and Gertrude at a shop this morning, and mentioned it to me as soon as he came out of town. I have been telling this little girl that she should have sent me word."

Gerty was standing by True's chair, smoothing his gray locks with her slender fingers. As Emily mentioned her name, he turned and looked at her. O, what a look of love he gave her! Gerty never forgot it.

"Miss Emily," said he, " 't was no need for anybody to be troubled. The Lord provided for me, his own self. All the doctors and nurses in the land couldn't have done half as much for me as this little gal o' mine. It wan't at all in my mind, some four or five years gone,—when I brought the little barefoot mite of a thing to my home, and when she was sick and e'en-a-'most dyin' in this very room, and I carried her in my arms night and day,—that her turn would come so soon. Ah! I little thought then, Miss Emily, how the Lord would lay me low,—how those very same feet would run about in my service, how her bit of a hand would come in the dark nights to smooth my pillow, and I'd go about daytimes leaning on her little arm. Truly God's ways are not like our ways, nor his thoughts like our thoughts."

"O, Uncle True!" said Gerty, "I don't do much for you; I wish I could do a great deal more. I wish I could make you strong again."

"I daresay you do, my darlin', but that can't be in this world; you've given me what's far better than strength o' body. Yes, Miss Emily," added he, turning again towards the blind girl, "it's you we have to thank for all the comfort we enjoy. I loved my little birdie; but I was a foolish man, and I should ha' spiled her. You knew better what was for her good, and mine too. You made her what she is now, one of the lambs of Christ, a handmaiden of the Lord. If anybody'd told me, six months ago, that I should become a poor cripple, and sit in my chair all day, and not know who was going to furnish a livin' for me or birdie either, I should ha' said I never could bear my lot with patience, or keep up any heart at all. But I've learned a lesson from this little one. When I first got so I could speak, after the shock, and tell what was in my mind, I was so mightily troubled a' thinkin' of my sad case, and Gerty with nobody to work or do anything for her, that I took on bad enough, and said, 'What shall we do now?—what shall we do now?' And then she whispered in my ear, 'God will take care of us, Uncle True!' And when I forgot the sayin', and asked, 'Who will feed and clothe us now?' she said again, 'The Lord will provide.' And, in my deepest distress of all, when one night I was full of anxious thoughts about my child, I said aloud, 'If I die, who will take care of Gerty?' the little thing, that I supposed was sound asleep in her bed, laid her head down beside me and said, 'Uncle True, when I was turned out into the dark street all alone, and had no friends nor any home, my Heavenly Father sent you to me; and now, if he wants you to come to him, and is not ready to take me too, he will send somebody else to take care of me the rest of the time I stay.' After that, Miss Emily, I gave up worryin' any more. Her words, and the blessed teachin's of the Holy Book that she reads me every day, have sunk deep into my heart, and I'm at peace.

"I used to think that, if I lived and had my strength spared me, Gerty would be able to go to school and get a sight o' larnin', for she has a nateral lurch for it, and it comes easy to her. She's but a slender child, and I never could bear the thought of her bein' driv to hard work for a livin'; she don't seem made for it, somehow. I hoped, when she grew up, to see her a schoolmistress, like Miss Browne, or somethin' in that line; but I've done bein' vexed about it now. I know, as she says, it's all for the best, or it wouldn't be."

When he finished speaking, Gerty, whose face had been hid against his shoulder, looked up and said, bravely, "O, Uncle True, I'm sure I can do almost any kind of work. Mrs. Sullivan says I sew very well, and I can learn to be a milliner or a dressmaker; that isn't hard work."

"Mr. Flint," said Emily, "would you be willing to trust your child with me? If you should be taken from her, would you feel as if she were safe in my charge?"

"Miss Emily," said True, "would I think her safe in angel-keepin'? I should believe her in little short o' that, if she could have you to watch over her."

"O, do not say that," said Miss Emily, "or I shall be afraid to undertake so solemn a trust. I know too well that my want of sight, my ill-health and my inexperience, almost unfit me for the care of a child like Gerty. But, since you approve of the teaching I have already given her, and are so kind as to think a great deal better of me than I deserve, I know you will at least believe in the sincerity of my wish to be of use to her; and, if it will be any comfort to you to know that in case of your death I will gladly take Gerty to my home, see that she is well educated, and, as long as I live, provide for and take care of her, you have my solemn assurance (and here she laid her hand on his), that it shall be done, and that to the best of my ability I will try to make her happy."

Gerty's first impulse was to rush towards Emily, and fling her arms around her neck; but she was arrested in the act, for she observed that True was weeping like an infant. In an instant his feeble head was resting upon her bosom; her hand was wiping away the great tears that had rushed to his eyes. It was an easy task, for they were tears of joy,—of a joy that had quite unnerved him in his present state of prostration and weakness.

The proposal was so utterly foreign to his thoughts or expectations, that it seemed to him a hope too bright to be relied upon; and, after a moment's pause, an idea occurring to him which seemed to increase his doubts, he gave utterance to it in the words, "But your father, Miss Emily!—Mr. Graham! —he's partickler, and not over-young now. I'm afeared he wouldn't like a little gal in the house."

"My father is indulgent to *me*," replied Emily; "he would not object to any plan I had at heart, and I have become so much attached to Gertrude that she would be of great use and comfort to me. I trust, Mr. Flint, that you will recover a portion at least of your health and strength, and be spared to her for many a year yet; but, in order that you may in no case feel any anxiety on her account, I take this opportunity to tell you that, if I should outlive you, she will be sure of a home with me."

"Ah, Miss Emily!" said the old man, "my time's about out, I feel right sure o' that; and, since you're willin', you'll soon be called to take charge on her. I haven't forgot how tossed I was in my mind, the day after I brought her home with me, with thinkin' that p'raps I wasn't fit to undertake the care of such a little thing, and hadn't ways to make her comfortable; and then, Miss Emily, do you remember you said to me, 'You've done quite right; the Lord will bless and reward you'? I've thought many a time since that you was a true prophet, and that your words were, what I thought 'em then, a whisper right from heaven! And now you talk o' doin' the same thing yourself; and I, that am just goin' home to God, and feel as if I read his ways clearer than ever afore, *I tell you*, Miss Emily, that you're doin' right, too; and, if the Lord rewards you as he has done me, there'll come a time when this child will pay you back in love and care all you ever do for her.—Gerty?"

"She's not here," said Emily; "I heard her run into her own room."

"Poor birdie!" said True, "she doesn't like to hear o' my leavin' her; I'm sad to think how some day soon she'll almost sob her heart away over her old uncle. Never mind now! I was goin' to bid her be a good child to you; but I think she will, without biddin'; and I can say my say to her another time. Good-by, my dear young lady;"—for Emily had risen to go, and George, the man-servant, was waiting at the door for her,—"if I never see you again, remember that you've made an old man so happy that he's nothing in this world left to wish for; and that you carry with you a dyin' man's best blessin', and his prayer that God may grant such perfect peace to your last days as now He does to mine."

That evening, when True had already retired to rest, and Gerty had finished reading aloud in her little Bible, as she always did at bed-time, True called her to him, and asked her, as he had often done of late, to repeat his favorite prayer for the sick. She knelt at his bed-side, and with a solemn and touching earnestness fulfilled his request.

"Now, darlin,' the prayer for the dyin';—isn't there such a one in your little book?"

Gerty trembled. There *was* such a prayer, a beautiful one; and the thoughtful child, to whom the idea of death was familiar, knew it by heart,—but could she repeat the words? Could she command her voice? Her whole frame shook with agitation; but Uncle True wished to hear it, it would be a comfort to him, and she would try. Concentrating all her energy and self-command, she began, and, gaining strength as she proceeded, went on to the end. Once or twice her voice faltered, but with new effort she succeeded, in spite of the great bunches in her throat; and her voice sounded so clear and calm that Uncle True's devotional spirit was not once disturbed by the thought of the girl's sufferings; for, fortunately, he could not hear how her heart beat and throbbed, and threatened to burst.

She did not rise at the conclusion of the prayer,—she could not,—but remained kneeling, her head buried in the bed-clothes. For a few moments there was a solemn stillness in the room; then the old man laid his hand upon her head.

She looked up.

"You love Miss Emily, don't you, birdie?"

"Yes, indeed."

"You'll be a good child to her, when I'm gone?"

"O, Uncle True!" sobbed Gerty, "you mustn't leave me! I can't live without you, *dear* Uncle True!"

"It is God's will to take me, Gerty; he has always been good to us, and we mustn't doubt him now. Miss Emily can do more for you than I could, and you'll be very happy with her."

"No, I shan't!—I shan't ever be happy again in this world! I never was happy until I came to you; and now, if you die, I wish I could die too!"

"You mustn't wish that, darlin'; you are young, and must try to do good in the world, and bide your time. I'm an old man, and only a trouble now."

"No, no, Uncle True!" said Gerty, earnestly; "you are not a trouble, you never could be a trouble! I wish *I'd* never been so much trouble to *you.*"

"So far from that, birdie, God knows you've long been my heart's delight! It only pains me now to think that you're a spendin' all your time, and slavin' here at home, instead of goin' to school, as you used to; but, O! we all depend on each other so!—first on God, and then on each other! And that 'minds me, Gerty, of what I was goin' to say. I feel as if the Lord would call me soon, sooner than you think for now; and, at first, you'll cry, and be sore vexed, no doubt; but Miss Emily will take you with her, and she'll tell you blessed things to comfort you;—how we shall all meet again and be happy in that world where there's no partin's; and Willie'll do everything he can to help you in your sorrer; and in time you'll be able to smile again. At first, and p'raps for a long time, Gerty, you'll be a care to Miss Emily, and she'll have to do a deal for you in the way o' schoolin', clothin', and so on; and what I want to tell you is, that Uncle True expects you'll be as good as can be, and do just what Miss Emily says; and, by and by, may be, when you're bigger and older, you'll be able to do somethin' for her. She's blind, you know, and you must be eyes for her; and she's not over strong, and you must lend a helpin' hand to her weakness, just as you do to mine; and, if you're good and patient, God will make your heart light at last, while you're only tryin' to make other folks happy; and when you're sad and troubled (for everybody is, sometimes), then think of old Uncle True, and how he used to say, 'Cheer up, birdie, for I'm of the 'pinion 't will all come out right, at last.' There, don't feel bad about it; go to bed, darlin', and to-morrow we'll have a nice walk,—and Willie's goin' with us, you know."

Gerty tried to cheer up, for True's sake, and went to bed. She did not sleep for some hours; but when, at last, she did fall into a quiet slumber, it continued unbroken until morning.

She dreamed that morning was already come; that she and Uncle True and Willie were taking a pleasant walk; that Uncle True was strong and well again,—his eye bright, his step firm, and Willie and herself laughing and happy.

And, while she dreamed the beautiful dream, little thinking that her first friend and she should no longer tread life's paths together, the messenger came,—a gentle, noiseless messenger,—and, in the still night, while the world was asleep, took the soul of good old True, and carried it home to God!

❀❀❀❀❀❀❀❀❀❀❀❀❀❀❀❀❀❀❀❀❀❀❀❀

## Chapter XVI

*The stars are mansions built by Nature's hand;*
*And, haply, there the spirits of the blest*
*Dwell, clothed in radiance, their immortal vest.*
                                    WORDSWORTH

Two months have passed since Trueman Flint's death, and Gertrude has for a week been domesticated in Mr. Graham's family. It was through the newspaper that Emily first heard of the little girl's sudden loss, and, immediately acquainting her father with her wishes and plans concerning the child, she found she had no opposition to fear from him. He reminded her, however, of the inconvenience that would attend Gertrude's coming to them at once, as they were soon to start on a visit to some distant relatives, from which they would not return until it was nearly time to remove to the city for the winter. Emily felt the force of this objection; for, although Mrs. Ellis would be at home during their absence, she knew that, even were she willing to undertake the charge of Gertrude, she would be a very unfit person to console her in her time of sorrow and affliction.

This thought troubled Emily, who now considered herself the orphan girl's sole protector; and she regretted much that this unusual journey should take place so inopportunely. There was no help for it, however, for Mr. Graham's plans were arranged, and must not be interfered with, unless she would make Gertrude's coming, at the very outset, unwelcome and disagreeable. She started for town, therefore, the next morning, quite undecided what course to pursue, under the circumstances.

The day was Sunday, but Emily's errand was one of charity and love, and would not admit of delay; and, an hour before the time for morning service, Mrs. Sullivan, who stood at her open window, which looked out upon the street, saw Mr. Graham's carryall stop at the door. She ran to meet Emily, and, with the politeness and kindness always observable in her, waited upon her into her neat parlor, guided her to a comfortable seat, placed in her hand a fan (for the weather was excessively warm), and then proceeded to tell how thankful she was to see her, and how sorry she felt that Gertrude was not at home. Emily wonderingly asked where Gertrude was, and learned that she was out walking with Willie. A succession of inquiries followed, and a long and touching story was told by Mrs. Sullivan of Gertrude's agony of grief, the impossibility of comforting her, and the fears the kind little woman had entertained lest the girl would die of sorrow.

"I couldn't do anything with her myself," said she. "There she sat, day after day, last week, on her little cricket, by Uncle True's easy-chair, with her head on the cushion, and I couldn't get her to move or eat a thing. She didn't appear to hear me when I spoke to her; and, if I tried to move her, she didn't struggle (for she was very quiet), but she seemed just like a dead weight in my hands; and I couldn't bear to make her come away into my room, though I knew it would change the scene, and be better for her. If it hadn't been for Willie, I don't know what I should have done, I was getting so worried about the poor child; but he knows how to manage her a great deal better than I do. When he is at home, we get along very well; for he takes her right up in his arms (he's very strong, and she's as light as a feather, you know), and either carries her into some other room or out into the yard; and somehow he contrives to cheer her up wonderfully. Her persuades her to eat, and in the evenings, when he comes home from the store, takes long walks with her. Now, last evening they went way over Chelsea Bridge, where it was cool and pleasant, you know; and I suppose he diverted her attention and amused her, for she came home brighter than I've seen her at all, and quite tired. I got her to go to bed in my room, and she slept soundly all night, so that she really looks quite like herself to-day. They've gone out again this morning, and, being Sunday, and Willie at home all day, I've no doubt he'll keep her spirits up, if anybody can."

"Willie shows very good judgment," said Emily, "in trying to change the scene for her, and divert her thoughts. I'm thankful she has had such kind friends. I promised Mr. Flint she should have a home with me when he was taken away, and, not knowing of his death until now, I consider it a great favor to myself, as well as her, that you have taken such excellent care of her. I felt sure you had been all goodness, or it would have given me great regret that I had not heard of True's death before."

"O, Miss Emily!" said Mrs. Sullivan, "Gertrude is so dear to us, and we have suffered so much in seeing her suffer, that it was a kindness to ourselves to do all we could to comfort her. Why, I think she and Willie could not love each other better, if they were own brother and sister; and Willie and Uncle True were great friends; indeed, we shall all miss him very much. My old father doesn't say much about it, but I can see he's very down-hearted."

More conversation followed, in the course of which Mrs. Sullivan informed Emily that a cousin of hers, a farmer's wife, living in the country, about twenty miles from Boston, had invited them all to come and pass a week or two with her at the farm, and, as Willie was now to enjoy his usual summer vacation, they proposed accepting the invitation.

She spoke of Gertrude's accompanying them as a matter of course, and enlarged upon the advantage it would be to her to breathe the country air, and ramble about the fields and woods, after all the fatigue and confinement she had endured.

Emily, finding from her inquiries that Gertrude would be a welcome and expected guest, cordially approved of the visit, and also arranged with Mrs. Sullivan that she should remain under her care until Mr. Graham removed to Boston for the winter. She was then obliged to leave, without waiting for Gertrude's return, though she left many a kind message for her, and placed in Mrs. Sullivan's hands a sufficient sum of money to provide for all her wants and expenses.

Gertrude went into the country, and abundance of novelty, of country fare, healthful exercise, and heartfelt kindness and sympathy, brought the color into her cheek, and calmness and composure, if not happiness, into her heart.

Soon after the Sullivans' return from their excursion, the Grahams removed to the city, and, as we have said before, Gertrude had now been with them about a week.

"Are you still standing at the window, Gertrude? What are you doing, dear?"

"I'm watching to see the lamps lit, Miss Emily."

"But they will not be lit at all. The moon will rise at eight o'clock, and light the streets sufficiently for the rest of the night."

"I don't mean the street-lamps."

"What do you mean, my child?" said Emily, coming towards the window, and lightly resting a hand on each of Gertrude's shoulders.

"I mean the stars, dear Miss Emily. O, how I wish you could see them too!"

"Are they very bright?"

"O, they are beautiful! and there are so many! The sky is as full as it can be."

"How well I remember when I used to stand at this very window, and look at them as you are doing now! It seems to me as if I saw them this moment, I know so well how they look."

"I love the stars,—all of them," said Gertrude; "but my own star I love the best."

"Which do you call yours?"

"That splendid one, there, over the church-steeple; it shines into my room every night, and looks me in the face. Miss Emily (and here Gertrude low-ered her voice to a whisper), it seems to me as if that star were lit on purpose for me. I think Uncle True lights it every night. I always feel as if he were smiling up there, and saying, 'See, Gerty, I'm lighting the lamp for you.' Dear Uncle True! Miss Emily, do you think he loves me now?"

"I do, indeed, Gertrude; and I think, if you make him an example, and try to live as good and patient a life as he did, that he will really be a lamp to your feet, and as bright a light to your path as if his face were shining down upon you through the star."

"I was patient and good when I lived with him; at least, I almost always was; and I'm good when I'm with you; but I don't like Mrs. Ellis. She tries to plague me, and she makes me cross, and then I get angry, and don't know what I do or say. I did not mean to be impertinent to her to-day, and I wish I hadn't slammed the door; but how could I help it, Miss Emily, when she told me, right before Mr. Graham, that I tore up the last night's *Journal,* and I *know* that I did not? It was an old paper that she saw me tying your slippers up in, and I am almost sure that she lit the library fire with that very *Journal,* herself; but Mr. Graham will always think *I* did it."

"I have no doubt, Gertrude, that you had some reason to feel provoked, and I believe you when you say that you were not the person to blame for the loss of the newspaper. But you must remember, my dear, that there is no merit in being patient and good-tempered, when there is nothing to ir-ritate you. I want you to learn to bear even injustice, without losing your self-control. You know Mrs. Ellis has been here a number of years; she has had everything her own way, and is not used to young people. She felt, when you came, that it was bringing new care and trouble upon her, and it is not strange that when things go wrong she should sometimes think you in fault. She is a very faithful woman, very kind and attentive to me, and very important to my father. It will make me unhappy if I have any reason to fear that you and she will not live pleasantly together."

"I do not want to make you unhappy; I do not want to be a trouble to anybody," said Gertrude, with some excitement; "I'll go away! I'll go off somewhere, where you will never see me again!"

"Gertrude!" said Emily, seriously and sadly. Her hands were still upon the young girl's shoulders, and, as she spoke, she turned her round, and brought her face to face with herself. "Gertrude, do you wish to leave your blind friend? Do you not love me?"

So touchingly grieved was the expression of the countenance that met her gaze, that Gertrude's proud, hasty spirit was subdued. She threw her arms round Emily's neck, and exclaimed, "No! dear Miss Emily, I would not leave you for all the world! I will do just as you wish. I will never be angry with Mrs. Ellis again, for your sake."

"Not for *my* sake, Gertrude," replied Emily,—"for your own sake; for the sake of duty and of God. A few years ago I should not have expected you to be pleasant and amiable towards any one whom you felt ill-treated you; but, now that you know so well what is right; now that you are familiar with the life of that blessed Master, who, when he was reviled, reviled not again; now that you have learned faithfully to fulfil so many important duties; I had hoped that you had learned, also, to be forbearing, under the most trying circumstances. But do not think, Gertrude, because I remind you when you have done wrong, I despair of your becoming one day all I wish to see you. What you are experiencing now being a new trial, you must bring new strength to bear upon it; and I have such confidence in you as to believe that, knowing my wishes, you will try to behave properly to Mrs. Ellis on all occasions."

"I will, Miss Emily, I will. I'll not answer her back when she's ugly to me, if I have to bite my lips to keep them together."

"O, I do not believe it will be so bad as that," said Emily, smiling. "Mrs. Ellis' manner is rather rough, but you will get used to her."

Just then a voice was heard in the entry,—"To see *Miss Flint!* Really! Well, *Miss Flint* is in Miss Emily's room. She's going to entertain company, is she?"

Gertrude colored to her temples, for it was Mrs. Ellis' voice, and the tone in which she spoke was very derisive.

Emily stepped to the door, and opened it.—"Mrs. Ellis!"

"What say, Emily?"

"Is there any one below?"

"Yes; a young man wants to see Gertrude; it's that young Sullivan, I believe."

"Willie!" exclaimed Gertrude, starting forward.

"You can go down and see him, Gertrude," said Emily. "Come back here when he's gone,—and, Mrs. Ellis, I wish you would step in and put my room a little in order. I think you will find plenty of pieces for your rag-bag about the carpet,—Miss Randolph always scatters so many when she is engaged with her dress-making."

Mrs. Ellis made her collection, and then, seating herself on a couch at the side of the fireplace, with her colored rags in one hand and the white in the other, commenced speaking of Gertrude.

"What are you going to do with her, Emily?" said she; "send her to school?"

"Yes. She will go to Mr. W.'s, this winter."

"Why! Isn't that a very expensive school for a child like her?"

"It is expensive, certainly; but I wish her to be with the best teacher I know of, and father makes no objection to the terms. He thinks, as I do, that if we undertake to fit her to instruct others, she must be thoroughly taught herself. I talked with him about it the first night after we came into town for the season, and he agreed with me that we had better put her out to learn a trade at once, than half-educate, make a fine lady of her, and so unfit her for anything. He was willing I should manage the matter as I pleased, and I resolved to send her to Mr. W.'s. So she will remain with us for the present. I wish to keep her with me as long as I can, not only because I am fond of the child, but she is delicate and sensitive, and now that she is so sad about old Mr. Flint's death, I think we ought to do all we can to make her happy; don't you, Mrs. Ellis?"

"I always calculate to do my duty," said Mrs. Ellis, rather stiffly. "Where is she going to sleep when we get settled?"

"In the little room at the end of the passage."

"Then where shall I keep the linen press?"

"Can't it stand in the back entry? I should think the space between the windows would accommodate it."

"I suppose it's *got* to," said Mrs. Ellis, flouncing out of the room, and muttering to herself,—"everything turned topsy-turvy for the sake of that little upstart!"

Mrs. Ellis was vexed on more accounts than one. She had long had her own way in the management of all household matters at Mr. Graham's, and had consequently become rather tyrannical. She was capable, methodical and neat; accustomed to a small family, and now for many years quite *unaccustomed* to children; Gertrude was in her eyes an unwarrantable intruder—one who must of necessity be continually in mischief, continually deranging her most cherished plans. Then, too, Gertrude had been reared, as Mrs. Ellis expressed it, among the lower classes; and the housekeeper, who was not in reality very hard-hearted, and quite approved of all public and private charities, had a slight prejudice in favor of high birth. Indeed, though now depressed in her circumstances, she prided herself on being of a good family, and considered it an insult to her dignity to expect that she should feel an interest in providing for the wants of one so inferior to her in point of station.

More than all this, she saw in the new inmate a formidable rival to herself in Miss Graham's affections; and Mrs. Ellis could not brook the idea of being second in the regard of Emily, who, owing to her peculiar misfortune and to her delicate health, had long been her especial charge, and for whom she felt as much tenderness as it was in her nature to feel for any one.

Owing to all these circumstances, Mrs. Ellis was far from being favorably disposed towards Gertrude; and Gertrude, in her turn, was not yet prepared to love Mrs. Ellis very cordially.

# Chapter XVII

*And thou must sail upon this sea, a long,*
*Eventful voyage. The wise may suffer wreck,*
*The foolish must. O, then, be early wise.*

WARE

Emily sat alone in her room. Mr. Graham had gone to a meeting of bank-directors. Mrs. Ellis was stoning raisins in the dining-room. Willie still detained Gertrude in the little library below stairs, and Emily, with the moonlight now streaming across the chamber, which was none the less dark to her on that account, was indulging in a long train of meditation. Her head rested on her hand; her face, usually so placid, was sad and melancholy in its expression; and her whole appearance and attitude denoted despondency and grief. As thought pressed upon thought, and past sorrows arose in quick succession, her head gradually sunk upon the cushions of the couch where she sat, and tears slowly trickled through her fingers.

Suddenly, a hand was laid softly upon hers. She gave a quick start, as she always did when surprised, for her unusual preöccupation of mind had made Gertrude's approaching step unheard.

"Is anything the matter, Miss Emily?" said Gertrude. "Do you like best to be alone, or may I stay?"

The sympathetic tone, the delicacy of the child's question, touched Emily. She drew her towards her, saying, as she did so, "O, yes, stay with me;" then observing, as she passed an arm round the little girl, that she trembled, and seemed violently agitated, she added, "but what is the matter with you, Gerty? What makes you tremble and sob so?"

At this, Gertrude broke forth with, "O, Miss Emily! I thought you were crying when I came in, and I hoped you would let me come and cry with you; for I am so miserable I can't do anything else."

Calmed herself by the more vehement agitation of the child, Emily endeavored to discover the cause of this evidently new and severe affliction. It proved to be this: Willie had been to tell her that he was going away, going out of the country; as Gertrude expressed it, to the very other end of the world—to India. Mr. Clinton was interested in a mercantile house at Calcutta, and had offered William the most favorable terms to go abroad as clerk to the establishment. The prospect thus afforded was far better than he could hope for by remaining at home; the salary was, at the very first, sufficient to defray all his own expenses, and provide for the wants of those who were now becoming every year more and more dependent upon him. The chance, too, of future advancement was great; and, though the young man's affectionate heart clung fondly to home and friends, there was no hesitation in his mind as to the course which both duty and interest prompted. He agreed to the proposal, and, whatever his own struggles were at the thought of five, or perhaps ten years' banishment, he kept them manfully to himself, and talked cheerfully about it to his mother and grandfather.

"Miss Emily," said Gertrude, when she had acquainted her with the news, and become again somewhat calm, "how can I bear to have Willie go away? How can I live without Willie? He is so kind, and loves me so much! He was always better than any brother, and, since Uncle True died, he has done everything in the world for me. I believe I could not have borne Uncle True's death if it had not been for Willie; and now how can I let him go away?"

"It is hard, Gertrude," said Emily, kindly, "but it is no doubt for his advantage; you must try and think of that."

"I know it," replied Gertrude,—"I suppose it is; but, Miss Emily, you do not know how I love Willie. We were so much together; and there were only us two, and we thought everything of each other; he was so much older than I, and always took such good care of me! O, I don't think you have any idea what friends we are!"

Gertrude had unconsciously touched a chord that vibrated through Emily's whole frame. Her voice trembled as she answered, "*I*, Gertrude! *not know*, my child! I know better than you imagine how dear he must be to you. *I*, too, had"——then checking herself, she paused abruptly, and there was a few moments' silence, during which Emily got up, walked hastily to the window, pressed her aching head against the frosty glass, and then, returning to Gertrude, said, in a voice which had recovered its usual calmness, "O, Gertrude! in the grief that oppresses you now, you little realize how much you have to be thankful for. Think, my dear, what a blessing it is that Willie will be where you can often hear from him, and where he can have constant news of his friends."

"Yes," replied Gerty; "he says he shall write to his mother and me very often."

"Then, too," said Emily, "you ought to rejoice at the good opinion Mr. Clinton must have of Willie; the perfect confidence he must feel in his uprightness, to place in him so much trust. I think that is very flattering."

"So it is," said Gertrude; "I did not think of that."

"And you have lived so happily together," continued Emily, "and will part in such perfect peace. O, Gertrude! Gertrude! such a parting as that should not make you sad; there are so much worse things in the world. Be patient, my dear child, do your duty, and perhaps there will some day be a happy meeting, that will quite repay you for all you suffer in the separation."

Emily's voice trembled as she uttered the last few words. Gertrude's eyes were fixed upon her friend with a very puzzled expression. "Miss Emily," said she, "I begin to think everybody has trouble."

"Certainly, Gertrude; can you doubt it?"

"I did not use to think so. I knew *I* had, but I thought other folks were more fortunate. I fancied that rich people were all happy; and, though you are blind, and that is a dreadful thing, I supposed you were used to it; and you always looked so pleasant and quiet, I took it for granted nothing ever vexed you now. And then, Willie!—I believed once that nothing could make him look sad, he was always so gay; but when he hadn't any place, I saw him really cry; and then, when Uncle True died, and now again to-night, when he was telling me about going away, he could hardly speak, he felt so badly. And so, Miss Emily, since I see that you and Willie have troubles, and that tears will come, though you try to keep them back, I think the world is full of trials, and that everybody gets a share."

"It *is* the lot of humanity, Gertrude, and we must not expect it to be otherwise."

"Then who can be happy, Miss Emily?"

"Those only, my child, who have learned submission; those who, in the severest afflictions, see the hand of a loving Father, and, obedient to his will, kiss the chastening rod."

"It is very hard, Miss Emily."

"It is hard, my child, and therefore few in this world can rightly be called happy; but, if, even in the midst of our distress, we can look to God in faith and love, we may, when the world is dark around, experience a peace that is a foretaste of heaven."

And Emily was right. Who that is striving after the Christian life has not experienced moments when, amid unusual discouragements and disappointments, the heart, turning in love and trust to its great Source, experiences emotions of ecstatic joy and hope, that never come to the prosperous and the world-called happy? He who has had such dreams of eternal peace can form some conception of the rest which remaineth for the people of God, when, with an undivided affection, and a faith undimmed by a single doubt, the soul reposes in the bosom of its Creator.

Gertrude had often found in time and the soothing influences of religious faith some alleviation to her trials; but never, until this night, did she feel a spirit not of earth, coming forth from the very chaos of sorrow into which she was plunged, and enkindling within her the flame of a higher and nobler sensation than she ever yet had cherished.

When she left Emily that night, it was with a serenity which is strength; and, if the spirit of Uncle True, looking down upon her through the bright star which she so loved, sighed to see the tears which glittered in her eyes, it was reässured by the smile of a heaven-lit light that played over her features, and when she sunk to slumber stamped them with the seal of peace.

Willie's departure was sudden, and Mrs. Sullivan had only a week in which to make those arrangements which a mother's thoughtfulness deems necessary. Her hands were therefore full of work, and Gerty, whom Emily at once relinquished for the short time previous to the vessel's sailing, was of great assistance to her. Willie was very busy daytimes, but was always with them in the evening.

On one occasion, he returned home about dusk, and, his mother and grandfather both being out, and Gertrude having just put aside her sewing, he said to her, "Come, Gerty, if you are not afraid of taking cold, come and sit on the door-step with me, as we used to in old times; there will be no more such warm days as this, and we may never have another chance to sit there, and watch the moon rise above the old house at the corner."

"O, Willie," said Gertrude, "do not speak of our never being together in this old place again! I cannot bear the thought; there is not a house in Boston I could ever love as I do this."

"Nor I," replied Willie; "but there is not one chance in a hundred, if I should be gone five years, that there would not be a block of brick stores in this spot, when I come to look for it. I wish I did not think so, for I shall have many a longing after the old home."

"But what will become of your mother and grandfather, if this house is torn down?"

"It is not easy to tell, Gerty, what will become of any of us by that time; but, if there is any necessity for their moving, I hope I shall be able to provide a better house than this for them."

"You won't be here, Willie."

"I know it, but I shall be always hearing from you, and we can talk about it by letters, and arrange everything. The idea of any such changes, after all," added he, "is what troubles me most in going away; I think they would miss me and need me so much. Gertrude, you will take care of them, won't you?"

"I!" said Gertrude, in amazement; "such a child as I!—what can I do?"

"If I am gone five or ten years, Gerty, you will not be a child all that time, and a woman is often a better dependence than a man; especially such a good, brave woman as you will be. I have not forgotten the beautiful care you took of Uncle True; and, whenever I imagine grandfather or mother old and helpless, I always think of you, and hope you will be near them; for I know, if you are, you will be a greater help than I could be. So I leave them in your care, Gerty, though you *are* only a child yet."

"Thank you, Willie," said Gertrude, "for believing I shall do everything I can for them. I certainly will, as long as I live. But, Willie, *they* may be strong and well all the time you are gone; and *I*, although I am so young, may be sick and die,—nobody knows."

"That is true enough," said Willie, sadly; "and I may die myself; but it will not do to think of that. It seems to me I never should have courage to go, if I didn't hope to find you all well and happy when I come home. You must write to me every month, for it will be a much greater task to mother, and I am sure she will want you to do nearly all the writing; and, whether my letters come directed to her or you, it will be all the same, you know. And, Gerty, you must not forget me, darling; you must love me just as much when I am gone,—won't you?"

"Forget you, Willie! I shall be always thinking of you, and loving you the same as ever. What else shall I have to do? But you will be off in a strange country, where everything will be different, and you will not think half as much of me, I know."

"If you believe that, Gertrude, it is because you do *not* know. You will have friends all around you, and I shall be alone in a foreign land; but every day of my life my heart will be with you and my mother, and I shall live here a great deal more than there."

They were now interrupted by Mr. Cooper's return, nor did they afterwards renew the conversation on the above topics; but the morning Willie left them, when Mrs. Sullivan was leaning over a neatly-packed trunk in the next room, trying to hide her tears, and Mr. Cooper's head was bowed lower than usual, while the light had gone out in the neglected pipe, which he still held in his hand, Willie whispered to Gerty, who was standing on a small chest of books, in order to force down the lid for him to lock it, "Gerty, dear, for my sake take good care of *our* mother and grandfather, —they are *yours* almost as much as mine."

On Willie's thus leaving home, for the first time, to struggle and strive among men, Mr. Cooper, who could not yet believe that the boy would be successful in the war with fortune, gave him many a caution against indulging hopes which never would be realized, and reminded him again and again that he knew nothing of the world.

Mrs. Sullivan bestowed on her son but little parting counsel. Trusting to the lessons he had been learning from his childhood, she compressed her parental advice into few words, saying, "Love and fear God, Willie, and do not disappoint your mother."

We pause not to dwell upon the last night the youth spent at home, his mother's last evening prayer, her last morning benediction, the last breakfast they all took together (Gertrude among the rest), or the final farewell embrace.

And Willie went to sea. And the pious, loving, hopeful woman, who for eighteen years had cherished her boy with tenderness and pride, maintained now her wonted spirit of self-sacrifice, and gave him up without a murmur. None knew how she struggled with her aching heart, or whence came the power that sustained her. No one had given the little widow credit for such strength of mind, and the neighbors wondered much to see how quietly she went about her duties the day before her son sailed; and how, when he had gone, she still kept on with her work, and wore the same look of patient humility that ever characterized her.

At the present moment, when emigration offers rare hopes and inducements, there is scarcely to be found in New England a village so insignificant, or so secluded, that there is not there some mother's heart bleeding at the perhaps life-long separation from a darling son. Among the wanderers, we hope,—ay, we *believe* that there is many a one who is actuated, not by the love of gold, the love of change, the love of adventure, but by the love he bears his *mother*,—the earnest longing of his heart to save her from a life of toil and poverty. Blessings and prosperity to him who goes forth with such a motive! And, if he fail, he has not lived in vain; for, though stricken by disease or violence at the very threshold of his labors, he dies in attestation of the truth that there are sons worthy of a mother's love, a love which is the highest, the holiest, the purest type of God on earth.

And now, in truth, commenced Gertrude's residence at Mr. Graham's, hitherto in various ways interrupted. She at once commenced attending school, and until the spring labored diligently at her studies. Her life was varied by few incidents, for Emily never entertained much company, and in the winter scarcely any at all, and Gertrude formed no intimate acquaintances among her companions. With Emily she passed many happy hours; they took walks, read books and talked much with each other, and Miss Graham found that in Gertrude's observing eyes, and her feeling and glowing descriptions of everything that came within their gaze, she was herself renewing her acquaintance with the outside world. In errands of charity and mercy Gertrude was either her attendant or her messenger; and all the dependants of the family, from the cook to the little boy who called at the door for the fragments of broken bread, agreed in loving and praising the child, who, though neither beautiful nor elegantly dressed, had a fairy lightness of step, a grace of movement and a dignity of bearing, which impressed them all with the conviction that she was no beggar in spirit, whatever might be her birth or fortune,—and all were in the invariable habit of addressing her as *Miss* Gertrude.

Mrs. Ellis' prejudices against her were still strong; but, as Gertrude was always civil, and Emily prudently kept them much apart, no unhappy result had yet ensued.

Mr. Graham, seeing her sad and pensive, did not at first take much notice of her; but, having on several occasions found his newspaper carefully dried, and his spectacles miraculously restored, after a vain search on his part, he began to think her a smart girl; and when, a few weeks after, he took up the last number of the *Working Farmer,* and saw, to his surprise, that the leaves were cut and carefully stitched together, he, supposing she had done it for her own benefit, pronounced her decidedly an *intelligent* girl.

She went often to see Mrs. Sullivan, and, as the spring advanced, they began to look for news of Willie. No tidings had come, however, when the season arrived for the Grahams to remove into the country for the summer. A letter, written by Gertrude to Willie, soon after they were established there, will give some idea of her situation and mode of life.

After dwelling at some length upon the disappointment of not having yet heard from him, and giving an account of the last visit she had made his mother before leaving the city, she went on to say: "But you made me promise, Willie, to write about myself, and said you should wish to hear everything that occurred at Mr. Graham's which concerned me in any way; so, if my letter is more tedious than usual, it is your own fault, for I have much to tell of our removal to D——, and of the way in which we live here, so different from our life in Boston. I think I hear you say, when you have read so far, 'O dear! now Gerty is going to give me a description of Mr. Graham's country-house!'—but you need not be afraid; I have not forgotten how, the last time I undertook to do so, you placed your hand over my mouth to stop me, and assured me you knew the place as well as if you had lived there all your life, for I had described it to you as often as once a week ever since I was eight years old. I made you beg my pardon for being so uncivil; but I believe I talked enough about my first visit here to excuse you for being quite tired of the subject. Now, however, quite to my disappointment, everything looks smaller and less beautiful than it seemed to me then; and, though I do not mean to describe it to you again, I must just tell you that the entry and piazzas are much narrower than I expected, the rooms lower, and the garden and summer-houses not nearly so large. Miss Emily asked, me, a day or two ago, how I liked the place, and if it looked as it used to. I told her the truth; and she was not at all displeased, but laughed at my old recollections of the house and grounds, and said it was always so with things we had seen when we were little children.

"I need not tell you that Miss Emily is kind and good to me as ever; for nobody who knows her as you do would suppose she could ever be anything but the best and loveliest person in the world. I can never do half enough, Willie, to repay her for all her goodness to me; and yet, she is so pleased with little gifts, and so grateful for trifling attentions, that it seems as if everybody might do something to make her happy. I found a few violets in the grass yesterday, and when I brought them to her she kissed and thanked me as if they had been so many diamonds; and little Ben Gately, who picked a hatful of dandelion-blossoms, without a single stem, and then rang at the front-door bell and asked for Miss Ga'am, so as to give them to her himself, got a sweet smile for his trouble, and a 'thank you, Bennie,' that he will not soon forget. Wasn't it pleasant in Miss Emily, Willie?

"Mr. Graham has given me a garden, and I mean to have plenty of flowers for her, by and by,—that is, if Mrs. Ellis doesn't interfere; but I expect she will, for she does in almost everything. Willie, Mrs. Ellis is my trial, my *great* trial. She is just the kind of person I cannot endure. I believe there are some people that other people *can't* like,—and she is just the sort I can't. I would not tell anybody else so, because it would not be right, and I do not know as it is right to mention it at all; but I always tell you everything. Miss Emily talks to me about her, and says I must learn to love her; and *when I do* I shall be an angel.

"There, I know you will think that is some of Gerty's old temper; and perhaps it is, but you don't know how she tries me: it is in little things that I cannot tell very easily, and I would not plague you with them if I could, so I won't write about her any more,—I will try to be perfect, and love her dearly.

"You will think that now, while I am not going to school, I shall hardly know what to do with my time; but I have plenty to do. The first week after we came here, however, I found the mornings very dull. You know I am always an early riser; but, as it does not agree with Miss Emily to keep early hours, I never see her until eight o'clock, full two hours after I am up and dressed. When we were in Boston, I always spent that time studying; but this spring, Miss Emily, who noticed that I was growing fast, and heard Mr. Arnold observe how pale I looked, fancied it would not do for me to spend so much time at my books; and so, when we came to D——, she planned my study-hours, which are very few, and arranged that they should take place after breakfast and in her own room. She also advised me, if I could, to sleep later in the morning; but I could not, and was up at my usual time, wandering around the garden. One day I was quite surprised to find Mr. Graham at work, for it was not like his winter habits; but he is a queer man. He asked me to come and help him plant onion-seeds, and I rather think I did it pretty well; for after that he let me help him plant a number of things, and label little sticks to put down by the side of them. At last, to my joy, he offered to give me a piece of ground for a garden, where I might raise flowers. He does not care for flowers, which seems *so* strange; he only raises vegetables and trees.

"And so I am to have a garden. But I am making a very long story, Willie, and have not time to say a thousand other things that I want to. O! if I could see you, I could tell you in an hour more than I can write in a week. In five minutes I expect to hear Miss Emily's bell, and then she will send for me to come and read to her.

"I long to hear from you, dear Willie, and pray to God, morning and evening, to keep you in safety, and soon send tidings of you to your loving

GERTY."

## Chapter XVIII

*Is it not lovely? Tell me, where doth dwell*
*The fay that wrought so beautiful a spell?—*
*In thine own bosom, brother, didst thou say?*
*Then cherish as thine own so good a fay.*

DANA

A few weeks after the date of this letter, Gerty learned through George, who went daily to the city to attend to the marketing, that Mrs. Sullivan had left word at the shop of our old acquaintance, the rosy-cheeked butcher, that she had received a letter from Willie, and wanted Gerty to come into town and see it. Emily was willing to let her go, but afraid it would be impossible to arrange it, as Charlie, the only horse Mr. Graham kept, was in use, and she saw no way of sending her.

"Why don't you let her go in the omnibus?" asked Mrs. Ellis.

Gerty looked gratefully at Mrs. Ellis; it was the first time that lady had ever seemed anxious to promote her views.

"I don't think it's safe for her to go alone in the coach," said Emily.

"Safe!—What, for that great girl!" exclaimed Mrs. Ellis, whose position in the family was such that there were no forms of restraint in her intercourse with Miss Graham.

"Do you think it is?" inquired Emily. "She seems a child to me, to be sure; but, as you say, she is almost grown up, and I daresay is capable of taking care of herself. Gertrude, are you sure you know the way from the omnibus-office in Boston to Mrs. Sullivan's?"

"Perfectly well, Miss Emily."

Without further hesitation, two tickets for the coach were put into Gertrude's hand, and she set forth on her expedition with beaming eyes and a full heart. She found Mrs. Sullivan and Mr. Cooper well, and rejoicing over the happiest tidings from Willie, who, after a long but agreeable voyage, had reached Calcutta in health and safety. A description of his new home, his new duties and employers, filled all the rest of the letter, excepting what was devoted to affectionate messages and inquiries, a large share of which were for Gerty. Gertrude stayed and dined with Mrs. Sullivan, and then hastened to the omnibus. She took her seat, and, as she waited for the coach to start, amused herself with watching the passers-by. It was nearly three o'clock, and she was beginning to think she should be the only passenger, when she heard a strange voice proceeding from a person whose approach she had not perceived. She moved towards the door, and saw, standing at the back of the coach, the most singular-looking being she had ever beheld. It was an old lady, small, and considerably bent with years. Gertrude knew, at a glance, that the same original mind must have conceived and executed every article of the most remarkable toilet she had ever witnessed. But, before she could observe the details of that which was as a whole so wonderfully grotesque, her whole attention was arrested by the peculiar behavior of the old lady.

She had been vainly endeavoring to mount the inconvenient vehicle, and now, with one foot upon the lower step, was calling to the driver to come to her assistance.

"Sir," said she, in measured tones, "is this travelling equipage under your honorable charge?"

"What say marm?—Yes, I'm the driver;" saying which, he came up to the door, opened it, and, without waiting for the polite request which was on the old lady's lips, placed his hand beneath her elbow, and before she was aware of his intention lifted her into the coach and shut the door.

"Bless me!" ejaculated she, as she seated herself opposite Gertrude, and began to arrange her veil and other draperies, "that individual is not versed in the art of assisting a lady without detriment to her habiliments. O dear, O dear!" added she, in the same breath, "I've lost my parasol!"

She rose as she spoke; but the sudden starting of the coach threw her off her balance, and she would have fallen, had it not been for Gertrude, who caught her by the arm and reseated her, saying, as she did so, "Do not be alarmed madam; here is the parasol."

As she spoke she drew into view the missing article, which, though nearly the size of an umbrella, was fastened to the old lady's wrist by a green ribbon, and, having slipped out of place, was supposed lost. And not a parasol only did she thus bring to light; numerous other articles, arranged in the same manner, and connected with the same green string, now met Gertrude's astonished eyes;—a reticule of unusual dimensions and a great variety of colors, a black lace cap, a large feather fan, a roll of fancy paper, and several other articles. They were partly hidden under a thin black silk shawl, and Gertrude began to think her companion had been on a pilfering expedition. If so, however, the culprit seemed remarkably at her ease, for before the coach had gone many steps she deliberately placed her feet on the opposite seat, and proceeded to make herself comfortable. In the first place, much to Gertrude's horror, she took out all her teeth and put them in her work-bag; then drew off a pair of black silk gloves, and replaced them by cotton ones; removed her lace veil, folded and pinned it to the green string. She next untied her bonnet, threw over it, as a protection from the dust, a large cotton handkerchief, and, with some difficulty, unloosing her fan, applied herself diligently to the use of it, closing her eyes as she did so, and evidently intending to go to sleep. She probably did fall into a doze, for she was very quiet, and Gertrude, occupied with her own thoughts, and with observing some heavy clouds that were arising from the west, forgot to observe her fellow-traveller, until she was startled by a hand suddenly laid upon her own, and an abrupt exclamation of "My dear young damsel, do not those dark shadows betoken adverse weather?"

"I think it will rain very soon," replied Gertrude.

"This morn, when I ventured forth," soliloquized the old lady, "the sun was bright, the sky serene; even the winged songsters, as they piped their hymns, proclaimed their part in the universal joy; and now, before I can regain my retirement, my delicate lace flounces (and she glanced at the skirt of her dress) will prove a sacrifice to the pitiless storm."

"Doesn't the coach pass your door?" inquired Gertrude, her compassion excited by the old lady's evident distress.

"No! O, no! not within half a mile. Does it better accommodate you, my young miss?"

"No. I have a mile to walk beyond the omnibus-office."

The old lady, moved by a deep sympathy, drew nearer to Gertrude, saying, in the most doleful accents, "Alas for the delicate whiteness of your bonnet-ribbon!"

The coach had by this time reached its destination, and the two passengers alighted. Gertrude placed her ticket in the driver's hand, and would have started at once on her walk, but was prevented by the old lady, who grasped her dress, and begged her to wait for her, as she was going the same way. And now great difficulty and delay ensued. The old lady refused to pay the amount of fare demanded by the driver; declared it was not the regular fare, and accused the man of an intention to put the surplus of two cents in his own pocket. Gertrude was impatient, for she was every moment expecting to see the rain pour in torrents; but at last, the matter being compromised between the driver and his closely-calculating passenger, she was permitted to proceed. They had walked about a quarter of a mile, and that at a very slow rate, when the rain commenced falling; and now Gertrude was called upon to unloose the huge parasol, and carry it over her companion and herself. In this way they had accomplished nearly as much more of the distance, when the water began to descend as if all the reservoirs of heaven were at once thrown open. At this moment Gertrude heard a step behind them, and, turning, she saw George, Mr. Graham's man, running in the direction of the house. He recognized her at once, and exclaimed,

"Miss Gertrude, you'll be wet through; and Miss Pace too," added he, seeing Gerty's companion. "Sure and ye'd better baith hasten to her house, where ye'll be secure."

So saying, he caught Miss Pace in his arms, and signing to Gertrude to follow, rushed across the street, and hurrying on to a cottage near by, did not stop until he had placed the old lady in safety beneath her own porch; and Gerty at the same instant gained its shelter. Miss Pace—for such was the old lady's name—was so bewildered that it took her some minutes to recover her consciousness; and, in the mean time, it was arranged that Gertrude should stop where she was for an hour or two, and that George should call for her when he passed that way with the carriage, on his return from the dépôt, where he went regularly on three afternoons in the week for Mr. Graham.

Miss Patty Pace was not generally considered a person of much hospitality. She owned the cottage which she occupied, and lived there quite alone, keeping no servants and entertaining no visitors. She was herself a famous visitor; and, as but a small part of her life had been passed in D——, and all her friends and connections lived either in Boston or at a much greater distance, she was a constant frequenter of omnibuses and other public vehicles. But though, through her travelling propensities and her regular attendance at church, she was well known, Gertrude was, perhaps, the first visitor that had ever entered her house; and she, as we have seen, could scarcely be said to have come by invitation.

Even when she was at the very door, she found herself obliged to take the old lady's key, unlock and open it herself, and finally lead her hostess into the parlor, and help her off with her innumerable capes, shawls and veils. Once come to a distinct consciousness of her situation, however, and Miss Patty Pace conducted herself with all the elegant politeness for which she was remarkable. Suffering though she evidently was with a thousand regrets at the trying experience her own clothes had sustained, she commanded herself sufficiently to express nearly as many fears lest Gertrude had ruined every article of her dress. It was only after many assurances from the latter that her boots were scarcely wet at all, her gingham dress and cape not likely to be hurt by rain, and her nice straw bonnet safe under the scarf she had thrown over it, that Miss Patty could be prevailed upon to so far forget the duties of a hostess as to retire and change her lace flounces for something more suitable for home-wear.

As soon as she left the room, Gertrude, whose curiosity was wonderfully excited, hastened to take a nearer view of numbers of articles, both of ornament and use, which had already attracted her attention from their odd and singular appearance.

Miss Pace's parlor was as remarkable as its owner. Its furniture, like her apparel, was made up of the gleanings of every age and fashion, from chairs that undoubtedly came over in the Mayflower, to feeble attempts at modern pincushions, and imitations of crystallized glass, that were a complete failure. Gertrude's quick and observing eye was revelling amid the few relics of ancient elegance, and the numerous specimens of folly and bad taste, with which the room was filled, when the old lady returned.

A neat though quaint black dress having taken the place of the much-valued flounces, she now looked far more ladylike. She held in her hand a tumbler of pepper and water, and begged her visitor to drink, assuring her it would warm her stomach and prevent her taking cold; and when Gertrude, who could only with great difficulty keep from laughing in her face, declined the beverage, Miss Patty seated herself, and, while enjoying the refreshment, carried on a conversation which at one moment satisfied her visitor she was a woman of sense, and the next persuaded her that she was either foolish or insane.

The impression which Gertrude made upon Miss Patty, however, was more decided. Miss Patty was delighted with the young miss, who, she declared, possessed an intellect that would do honor to a queen, a figure that was airy as a gazelle, and motions more graceful than those of a swan.

When George came for Gertrude, Miss Pace, who seemed really sorry to part with her, cordially invited her to come again, and Gertrude promised to do so.

The satisfactory news from Willie, and the amusing adventures of the afternoon, had given to Gertrude such a feeling of buoyancy and light-heartedness, that she bounded into the house, and up the stairs, with that fairy quickness Uncle True had so loved to see in her, and which, since his death, her subdued spirits had rarely permitted her to exercise. She hastened to her own room to remove her bonnet and change her dress before seeking Emily, to whom she longed to communicate the events of the day.

At the door of her room she met Bridget, the house-maid, with a dust-pan, hand-broom, etc. On inquiring what was going on there at this unusual hour, she learned that during her absence her room, which had since their removal been in some confusion, owing to Mrs. Ellis' not having decided what furniture should be placed there, had been subjected to a thorough and comprehensive system of spring cleaning. Alarmed, though she scarcely knew why, at the idea of Mrs. Ellis having invaded her premises, she surveyed the apartment with a slight feeling of agitation, which, as she continued her observations, swelled into a storm of angry excitement.

When Gertrude went from Mrs. Sullivan's to Mr. Graham's house in the city, she carried with her, beside a trunk containing her wardrobe, an old handbox, which she stored away on the shelf of a closet in her chamber.

There it remained, during the winter, unpacked and unobserved by any one. When the family went into the country, however, the box went also, carefully watched and protected by its owner. As there was no closet or other hiding-place in Gertrude's new room, she placed it in a corner behind the bed, and the evening before her expedition to the city had been engaged in removing and inspecting a part of its contents. Each article was endeared to her by the charm of old association, and many a tear had the little maiden shed over her stock of valuables. There was the figure of the Samuel, Uncle True's first gift, now defaced by time and accident. As she surveyed a severe contusion on the back of the head, the effect of an inadvertent knock given it by True himself, and remembered how patiently the dear old man labored to repair the injury, she felt that she would not part with the much-valued memento for the world. There, too, were his pipes, of common clay, and dark with smoke and age; but, as she thought how much comfort they had been to him, she felt that the possession of them was a consolation to her. She had brought away too his lantern, for she had not forgotten its pleasant light, the first that ever fell upon the darkness of her life; nor could she leave behind an old fur cap, beneath which she had often sought a kindly smile, and, never having sought in vain, could hardly realize that there was not one for her still hidden beneath its crown. There were some toys too, and picture-books, gifts from Willie, a little basket he had carved for her from a nut, and a few other trifles.

All these things, excepting the lantern and cap, Gertrude had left upon the mantel-piece; and now, upon entering the room, her eye at once sought her treasures. They were gone. The mantel-piece was nicely dusted, and quite empty. She ran towards the corner, where she had left the old box. That too was gone. To rush after the retreating house-maid, call her back, and pour forth a succession of eager inquiries, was but the work of an instant.

Bridget was a new comer, a remarkably stupid specimen, but Gertrude contrived to obtain from her all the information she needed. The image, the pipes and the lantern, were thrown among a heap of broken glass and crockery, and, as Bridget declared, smashed all to nothing. The cap, pronounced moth-eaten, had been condemned to the flames; and the other articles, Bridget could not be sure, but "troth, she belaved she was just after laving them in the fireplace." And all this in strict accordance with Mrs. Ellis' orders. Gertrude allowed Bridget to depart unaware of the greatness of her loss; then, shutting the door, she threw herself upon the bed, and gave way to a violent fit of weeping.

So this, thought she, was the reason why Mrs. Ellis was so willing to forward my plans,—and I was foolish enough to believe it was for my own sake! She wanted to come here and rob me, the thief!

She rose from the bed as suddenly as she had thrown herself down, and started for the door; then, some new thought seeming to check her, she returned again to the bed-side, and, with a loud sob, fell upon her knees, and buried her face in her hands. Once or twice she lifted her head, and seemed on the point of rising and going to face her enemy. But each time something came across her mind and detained her. It was not fear;—O, no! Gertrude was not afraid of anybody. It must have been some stronger motive than that. Whatever it might be, it was something that had, on the whole, a soothing influence; for, after every fresh struggle, she grew calmer, and presently, rising, seated herself in a chair by the window, leaned her head on her hand, and looked out. The window was open; the shower was over, and the smiles of the refreshed and beautiful earth were reflected in a glowing rainbow, that spanned the eastern horizon. A little bird came, and perched on a branch of a tree close to the window, and shouted forth a *Te Deum*. A Persian lilac-bush in full bloom sent up a delicious fragrance. A wonderful composure stole into Gertrude's heart, and, ere she had sat there many minutes, she felt "the grace that brings peace succeed to the passions that produce trouble." She had conquered; she had achieved the greatest of earth's victories, a victory over herself. The brilliant rainbow, the carol of the bird, the fragrance of the blossoms, all the bright things that gladdened the earth after the storm, were not half so beautiful as the light that overspread the face of the young girl when, the storm within her laid at rest, she looked up to heaven, and her heart sent forth its silent offering of praise.

The sound of the tea-bell startled her. She hastened to bathe her face and brush her hair, and then went down stairs. There was no one in the dining-room but Mrs. Ellis; Mr. Graham had been detained in town, and Emily was suffering with a severe headache. Consequently, Gertrude took tea alone with Mrs. Ellis. The latter, though unaware of the great value Gertrude attached to her old relics, was conscious she had done an unkind thing; and as the injured party gave no evidence of anger or ill will, not even mentioning the subject, the aggressor felt more uncomfortable and mortified than she would have been willing to allow. The matter was never recurred to, but Mrs. Ellis experienced a stinging consciousness of the fact that Gertrude had shown a superiority to herself in point of forbearance.

The next day, Mrs. Prime, the cook, came to the door of Emily's room, and obtaining a ready admittance, produced the little basket, made of a nut, saying, "I wonder now, Miss Emily, where Miss Gertrude is; for I've found her little basket in the coal-hod, and I guess she'll be right glad on 't—'t an't hurt a mite." Emily inquired "What basket?" and the cook, placing it in her hands, proceeded with eagerness to give an account of the destruction of Gertrude's property, which she had herself witnessed with great indignation. She also gave a piteous description of the distress the young girl manifested in her questioning of Bridget, which the sympathizing cook had overheard from her own not very distant chamber.

As Emily listened to the story, she well remembered having thought, the previous afternoon, that she heard Gertrude sobbing in her room, which on one side adjoined her own, but that she afterwards concluded herself to have been mistaken. "Go," said she, "and carry the basket to Gertrude; she is in the little library; but please, Mrs. Prime, don't tell her that you have mentioned the matter to me." Emily expected, for several days, to hear from Gertrude the story of her injuries; but Gertrude kept her trouble to herself, and bore it in silence.

This was the first instance of complete self-control in Gerty, and the last we shall have occasion to dwell upon. From this time she continued to experience more and more the power of governing herself; and, with each new effort gaining new strength, became at last a wonder to those who knew the temperament she had had to contend with. She was now nearly fourteen years old, and so rapid had been her recent growth that, instead of being below the usual stature, she was taller than most girls of her age. Freedom from study, and plenty of air and exercise, prevented her, however, from suffering from this circumstance.

Her garden was a source of great pleasure to her, and, flowers seeming to prosper under her careful training, she had always a bouquet ready to place by Emily's plate at breakfast-time.

Occasionally she went to see her friend Miss Patty Pace, and always met with a cordial reception. Miss Patty's attention was very much engrossed by the manufacture of paper flowers, and, as Gertrude's garden furnished the models, she seldom went empty-handed; but, the old lady's success being very ill proportioned to her efforts, it would have been a libel upon nature to pronounce even the most favorable specimens of this sort of fancy-work true copies of the original. Miss Patty was satisfied, however; and it is to be hoped that her various friends, for whom the large bunches were intended that travelled about tied to her waist by the green string, were satisfied also.

Miss Patty seemed to have a *great many* friends. Judging from the numbers of people that she talked about to Gertrude, the latter concluded she must be acquainted with everybody in Boston. And it would have been hard to find any one whose intercourse extended to a wider circle. She had, in her youth, learned an upholsterer's trade, which she had practised for many years in the employment (as she said) of the first families in the city; and so observing was she, and so acute in her judgment, that a report at one time prevailed that Miss Pace had eyes in the back of her head, and two pair of ears. Notwithstanding her wonderful visionary and comprehending powers, she had never been known to make mischief in families. She was prudent and conscientious, and, though always peculiar in her habits and modes of expression, and so wild in some of her fancies as to be often thought by strangers a little *out,* she had secured and continued to retain the good will of a great many kindly-disposed ladies and gentlemen, at whose houses she was always well received and politely treated. She calculated, in the course of every year, to go the rounds among all these friends, and thus kept up her intimacy with households in every member of which she felt a warm personal interest.

Miss Patty labored under one great and absorbing regret, and frequently expatiated to Gertrude on the subject; it was, that she was without a companion. "Ah, Miss Gertrude," she would sometimes exclaim, seeming for the time quite forgetful of her age and infirmities, "I should do vastly well in this world, if I only had a companion;" and here, with a slight toss of the head, and a little smirking air, she would add, in a whisper, "and you must know, my dear, I somewhat meditate matrimony." Then, seeing Gertrude's look of surprise and amusement, she would apologize for having so long delayed fulfilling what had always been her intention; and, at the same time that she admitted not being as young as she had once been, would usually close with the remark, "It is true, time is inexorable; but I cling to life, Miss Gertrude, I cling to life, and may marry yet."

On the subject of fashion, too, she would declaim at great length, avowing, for her own part, a rigid determination to be modern, whatever the cost might be. Gertrude could not fail to observe that she had failed in this intention as signally as in that of securing a youthful swain; and she was also gradually led to conclude that Miss Pace, whatever might be her means, was a terrible miser. Emily, who knew the old lady very well, and had often employed her, did not oppose Gertrude's visits to the cottage, and sometimes accompanied her; for Emily loved to be amused, and Miss Patty's quaint conversation was as great a treat to her as to Gertrude. These calls were so promptly returned, that it was made very evident that Miss Patty preferred doing the greater part of the visiting herself; observing which, Emily gave her a general invitation to the house, of which she was not slow to avail herself.

## Chapter XIX

*More health, dear maid, thy soothing presence brings,*
*Than purest skies, or salutary springs.*

MRS. BARBAULD

Persons who own residences within six miles of a large city cannot be properly said to enjoy country life. They have large gardens, oftentimes extensive grounds, and raise their own fruit and vegetables; they usually keep horses, drive about and take the air. Some maintain quite a barn-yard establishment, and pride themselves upon their fat cattle and Shanghae fowls. But, after all, these suburban residents do not taste the charms of true country life. There are no pathless woods, no roaring brooks, no waving fields of grain, no wide stretches of pasture-land. Every eminence commands a view of the near metropolis, the hum of which is almost audible; and every hourly-omnibus, or train of cars, carries one's self, or one's neighbor, to or from the busy mart.

Those who seek retirement and seclusion, however, can nowhere be more sure to find it than in one of these half-country, half-city homes; and many a family will, summer after summer, resort to the same quiet corner, and, undisturbed by visitors or gossip, maintain an independence of life which would be quite impossible either in the crowded streets of the town, where one's acquaintances are forever dropping in, or in the strictly country villages, where every new comer is observed, called upon and talked about.

Mr. Graham's establishment was of the medium order, and little calculated to attract notice. The garden was certainly very beautiful, abounding in rich shrubbery, summer-houses, and arbors covered with grape-vines; but a high board-fence hid it from public view, and the house, standing back from the road, was rather old-fashioned and very unobtrusive in its appearance.

Excepting his horticultural propensities, Mr. Graham's associations were all connected with the city; and Emily, being unfitted for much general intercourse with society, entertained little company, save that of the neighbors who made formal calls, and some particular friends, such as Mr. Arnold, the clergyman, and a few intimates, who often towards evening drove out of town to see Emily and eat fruit.

The summer was passing away most happily, and Gertrude, in the constant enjoyment of Emily's society, and in the consciousness that she was, in various ways, rendering herself useful and important to this excellent friend, was finding in every day new causes of contentment and rejoicing, when a seal was suddenly set to all her pleasure.

Emily was taken ill with a fever, and Gertrude, on occasion of her first undertaking to enter the sick room, and share in its duties, was rudely repulsed by Mrs. Ellis, who had constituted herself sole nurse, and who declared, when the poor girl pleaded hard to be admitted, that the fever was catching, and Miss Emily did not want her there,—that when she was sick she never wanted any one about her but herself.

For three or four days Gertrude wandered about the house, inconsolable. On the fifth morning after her banishment from the room, she saw Mrs. Prime, the cook, going up stairs with some gruel; and, thrusting into her hand some beautiful rose-buds, which she had just gathered, she begged her to give them to Emily, and ask if she might not come in and see her.

She lingered about the kitchen awaiting Mrs. Prime's return, in hopes of some message, at least, from the sufferer. But when the cook came down the flowers were still in her hands, and, as she threw them on the table, the kind-hearted woman gave vent to her feelings.

"Well! folks do say that first-rate cooks and nurses are allers as cross as bears! 'T an't for me to say whether it's so 'bout cooks, but 'bout nurses there an't no sort o' doubt! I would not want to go there, Miss Gertrude; I wouldn't insure you but what she'd bite your head off."

"Wouldn't Miss Emily take the flowers?" asked Gertrude, looking quite grieved.

"Well, she hadn't no word in the matter. You know she couldn't see what they were, and Miss Ellis flung 'em outside the door, vowin' I might as well bring pison into the room with a fever, as them roses. I tried to speak to Miss Emily, but Miss Ellis set up such a hush-sh-sh I s'posed she was goin' to sleep, and jest made the best o' my way out. Ugh! don't she scold when there's anybody sick?"

Gertrude sauntered out into the garden. She had nothing to do but think anxiously about Emily, who, she feared, was very ill. Her work and her books were all in Emily's room, where they were usually kept; the library might have furnished amusement, but it was locked up. So the garden was the only thing left for her, and there she spent the rest of the morning; and not that morning only, but many others; for Emily continued to grow worse, and a fortnight passed away without Gertrude's seeing her, or having any other intimation regarding her health than Mrs. Ellis' occasional report to Mr. Graham, who, however, as he saw the physician every day, and made frequent visits to his daughter himself, did not require that particular information which Gertrude was eager to obtain. Once or twice she had ventured to question Mrs. Ellis, whose only reply was, "Don't bother me with questions! what do you know about sickness?"

One afternoon, Gertrude was sitting in a large summer-house at the lower end of the garden; her own piece of ground, fragrant with mignonette and verbena, was close by, and she was busily engaged in tying up and marking some little papers of seeds, the gleanings from various seed-vessels, when she was startled by hearing a step close beside her, and, looking up, saw Dr. Jeremy, the family physician, just entering the building.

"Ah! what are you doing?" exclaimed the doctor, in a quick, abrupt manner, peculiar to him. "Sorting seeds, eh?"

"Yes, sir," replied Gerty, looking up and blushing, as she saw the doctor's keen black eyes scrutinizing her face.

"Where have I seen you before?" asked he, in the same blunt way.

"At Mr. Flint's."

"Ah! True Flint's! I remember all about it. You're his girl! Nice girl, too! And poor True, he's dead! Well, he's a loss to the community! So this is the little nurse I used to see there. Bless me! how children do grow!"

"Doctor Jeremy," asked Gertrude, in an earnest voice, "will you please to tell me how Miss Emily is?"

"Emily! she an't very well, just now."

"Do you think she'll die?"

"Die! No! What should she die for? I won't let her die, if you'll help me keep her alive. Why an't you in the house, taking care of her?"

"I wish I might!" exclaimed Gertrude, starting up; "I wish I might!"

"What's to hinder?"

"Mrs. Ellis, sir; she won't let me in; she says Miss Emily doesn't want anybody but her."

"She's nothing to say about it, or Emily either; it's my business, and I want you. I'd rather have you to take care of my patients than all the Mrs. Ellises in the world. She doesn't know anything about nursing; let her stick to her cranberry-sauce and squash-pies. So, mind, to-morrow you're to begin."

"O, thank you, doctor!"

"Don't thank me yet; wait till you've tried it,—it's hard work taking care of sick folks. Whose orchard is that?"

"Mrs. Bruce's."

"Is that her pear-tree?"

"Yes, sir."

"By George, Mrs. Bruce, I'll try your pears for you!"

As he spoke, the doctor, a man some sixty-five years of age, stout and active, sprung over a stone wall, which separated them from the orchard, and, carried along by the impetus the leap had given him, reached the foot of the tree almost at a bound.

As Gertrude, full of mirth, watched the proceeding, she observed the doctor stumble over some obstacle, and only save himself from falling by stretching forth both hands, and sustaining himself against the huge trunk of the fine old tree. At the same instant a head, adorned with a velvet smoking-cap, was slowly lifted from the long grass, and a youth, about sixteen or seventeen years of age, raised himself upon his elbow, and stared at the unlooked-for intruder.

Nothing daunted, the doctor at once took offensive ground towards the occupant of the place, saying, "Get up, lazy bones! What do you lie there for, tripping up honest folks?"

"Who do you call honest folks, sir?" inquired the youth, apparently quite undisturbed by the doctor's epithet and inquiry.

"I call myself and my little friend here remarkably honest people," replied the doctor, winking at Gertrude, who, standing behind the wall and looking over, was laughing heartily at the way in which the doctor had got caught.

The young man, observing the direction of the latter's eyes, turned and gave a broad stare at Gertrude's merry face.

"Can I do anything for you, sir?" asked he.

"Yes, certainly," replied the doctor. "I came here to help myself to pears; but you are taller than I,—perhaps, with the help of that crooked-handled cane of yours, you can reach that best branch."

"A remarkably honorable and honest errand!" muttered the young man. "I shall be happy to be engaged in so good a cause."

As he spoke, he lifted his cane, which lay by his side, and, drawing down the end of the branch, so that he could reach it with his hand, shook it vigorously. The ripe fruit fell on every side, and the doctor, having filled his pockets, and both his hands, started for the other side of the wall.

"Have you got enough?" asked the youth, in a very lazy tone of voice.

"Plenty, plenty," said the doctor.

"Glad of it," said the boy, indolently throwing himself on the grass, and still staring at Gertrude.

"You must be very tired," said the doctor, stepping back a pace or two; "I'm a physician, and should advise a nap."

"Are you, indeed!" replied the youth, in the same half-drawling, half-ironical tone of voice in which he had previously spoken; "then I think I'll take your advice;" saying which, he threw himself back upon the grass and closed his eyes.

Having emptied his pockets upon the seat of the summer-house, and invited Gertrude to partake, the doctor, still laughing so immoderately at his boyish feat that he could scarcely eat the fruit, happened to bethink himself of the lateness of the hour. He looked at his watch. "Half-past four! The cars go in ten minutes. Who's going to drive me down to the dépôt?"

"I don't know, sir," replied Gertrude, to whom the question seemed to be addressed.

"Where's George?"

"He's gone to the meadow to get in some hay, but he left white Charlie harnessed in the yard; I saw him fasten him to the chain, after he drove you up from the cars."

"Ah! then you can drive me down to the dépôt."

"I can't, sir; I don't know how."

"But you must; I'll show you how. You're not afraid!"

"O, no, sir; but Mr. Graham"—

"Never you mind Mr. Graham—do you mind me. I'll answer for your coming back safe enough."

Gertrude was naturally courageous; she had never driven before, but, having no fears, she succeeded admirably, and, being often afterwards called upon by Dr. Jeremy to perform the same service, she soon became skilful in the use of the reins,—an accomplishment not always particularly desirable in a lady, but which, in her case, proved very useful.

Dr. Jeremy was true to his promise of installing Gertrude in Emily's sick room. The very next visit he made to his patient, he spoke in terms of the highest praise of Gertrude's devotion to her old uncle, and her capability as a nurse, and asked why she had been expelled from the chamber.

"She is timid," said Emily, "and is afraid of catching the fever."

"Don't believe it," said Dr. Jeremy; " 't an't like her."

"Do you think not?" inquired Emily, earnestly. "Mrs. Ellis—"

"Told a lie," interrupted the doctor. "Gerty wants to come and take care of you, and she knows how as well as Mrs. Ellis, any day; it isn't much you need done. You want quiet, and that's what you can't have, with that great talking woman about. So I'll send her to Jericho to-day, and bring my little Gertrude up here. She's a quiet little mouse, and has got a head on her shoulders."

It is not to be supposed that Gertrude could provide for Emily's wants any better, or even as well, as Mrs. Ellis; and Emily, knowing this, took care that the housekeeper should not be sent to Jericho; for, though Dr. Jeremy, a man of strong prejudices, did not like her, she was excellent in her department, and could not be dispensed with. Had it been otherwise, Emily would not have hurt her feelings by letting her see that she was in any degree superseded.

So, though Emily, Dr. Jeremy and Gertrude, were all made happy by the free admission of the latter to the sick room, the housekeeper, unhandsomely as she had behaved, was never conscious that any one knew the wrong she had done to Gertrude, in keeping her out of sight and giving a false reason for her continued absence.

There was a watchfulness, a care, a tenderness, in Gertrude, which only the warmest love could have dictated.

When Emily awoke at night from a troubled sleep, found a cooling draught ready at her lips, and knew from Mrs. Ellis' deep snoring that it was not her hand that held it,—when she observed that all day long no troublesome fly was ever permitted to approach her pillow, her aching head was relieved by hours of patient bathing, and the little feet that were never weary were always noiseless,—she realized the truth, that Dr. Jeremy had brought her a most excellent medicine.

A week or two passed away, and she was well enough to sit up nearly all the time, though not yet able to leave her room. A few weeks more, and the doctor began to insist upon air and exercise. "Drive out two or three times every day," said he.

"How can I?" said Emily. "George has so much to do, it will be very inconvenient."

"Let Gertrude drive you; she is a capital hand."

"Gertrude," said Emily, smiling, "I believe you are a great favorite of the doctor's; he thinks you can do anything. You never drove in your life, did you?"

"Hasn't she driven me to the dépôt, every day, for these six weeks?" inquired the doctor.

"Is it possible?" asked Emily, who was unaccustomed to the idea of a lady's attempting the management of a horse.

Upon her being assured this was the case, and the doctor insisting that there was no danger, Charlie was harnessed into the carryall, and Emily and Mrs. Ellis went out to drive with Gertrude; an experiment which, being often repeated, was a source of health to the invalid, and pleasure to them all. In the early autumn, when Emily's health was quite restored, old Charlie was daily called into requisition; sometimes Mrs. Ellis accompanied them, but, as she was often engaged about household duties, they usually went by themselves, in a large, old-fashioned buggy, and Emily declared that Gertrude's learning to drive had proved one of the greatest sources of happiness she had known for years.

Once or twice, in the course of the summer and autumn, Gertrude saw again the lazy youth whom Dr. Jeremy had stumbled over when he went to steal pears.

Once he came and sat on the wall while she was at work in her garden, professed himself astonished at her activity, talked a little with her about her flowers, asked some questions concerning her friend Dr. Jeremy, and ended by requesting to know her name.

Gertrude blushed; she was a little sensitive about her name, and, though she always went by that of Flint, and did not, on ordinary occasions, think much about it, she could not fail to remember, when the question was put to her point blank, that she had, in reality, no surname of her own.

Emily had endeavored to find Nan Grant, in order to learn from her something of Gertrude's early history; but Nan had left her old habitation, and, for years, nothing had been heard of her.

Gertrude, as we have said, blushed on being asked her name, but replied, with dignity, that she would tell hers, provided her new acquaintance would return the compliment.

"Shan't do it!" said the youth, impudently, "and don't care about knowing yours, either;" saying which, he kicked an apple with his foot, and walked off, still kicking it before him, leaving Gertrude to the conclusion that he was the most ill-bred person she had ever seen.

❁❁❁❁❁❁❁❁❁❁❁❁❁❁❁❁❁❁❁❁❁❁❁❁❁❁❁

## Chapter XX

*A perfect woman, nobly planned,*
*To warn, to comfort, and command,*
*And yet a spirit still, and bright,*
*With something of an angel light.*

WORDSWORTH

It was the twilight of a sultry September day, and, wearied with many hours' endurance of an excessive heat, unlooked for so late in the season, Emily Graham sat on the front piazza of her father's house, inhaling a delicious and refreshing breeze, which had just sprung up. The western sky was still streaked with brilliant lines of red, the lingering effects of a gorgeous sunset, while the moon, now nearly at the full, and triumphing in the close of day and the commencement of her nightly reign, cast her full beams upon Emily's white dress, and gave to the beautiful hand and arm, which, escaping from the draperied sleeve, rested on the side of her rustic arm-chair, the semblance of polished marble.

Ten years had passed since Emily was first introduced to the reader; and yet, so slight were the changes wrought by time upon her face and figure, that she looked scarcely any older than on the occasion of her first meeting Gertrude in Mr. Arnold's church.

She had even then experienced much of the sorrow of life, and learned how to distil from the bitter dregs of suffering a balm for every pain. Even then, that experience, and the blessed knowledge she had gained from it, had both stamped themselves upon her countenance: the one in a sobered and subdued expression, which usually belongs to more mature years; the other, in that sweet, calm smile of trust and hope, which proclaims the votary of Heaven.

Therefore time had little power upon her, and as she was then so was she now; lovely in her outward appearance, and still more lovely in heart and life. A close observer might, however, perceive in her a greater degree of buoyancy of spirit, keenness of interest in what was going on about her, and evident enjoyment of life, than she had formerly evinced; and this was due, as Emily felt and acknowledged, to her recent close companionship with one to whom she was bound by the warmest affection, and who, by her lively sympathy, her constant devotion, her natural appreciation of the entertaining and the ludicrous, as well as the beautiful and the true, and her earnest and unsparing efforts to bring her much-loved friend into communion with everything she herself enjoyed, had called into play faculties which blindness had rendered almost dormant, and become what Uncle True bade her be, eyes to her benefactor.

On the present occasion, however, as Emily sat alone, shut out from the beautiful sunset, and unconscious of the shadows that played over her in the moonlight, her thoughts seemed to be sad. She held her head a little on one side, in a listening attitude, and, as often as she heard the sound of the gate swinging in the breeze, she would start, while a look of anxiety, and even pain, would cross her features.

At length, some one emerges from behind the high fence which screens the garden from public gaze, and approaches the gate. None but Emily's quick ear could have distinguished the light step; but she hears it at once, and, rising, goes to meet the new comer, whom we must pause to introduce, for, though an old acquaintance, time has not left *her* unchanged, and it would be hard to recognize in her our little quondam Gertrude.

The present Gertrude—for she it is—has now become a young lady. She is some inches taller than Emily, and her figure is slight and delicate. Her complexion is dark, but clear, and rendered brilliant by the rosy hue that flushes her cheeks; but that may be the effect of her rapid walk from the railroad station. She has taken off her bonnet, and is swinging it by the string,—a habit she always had as a child; so we will acquit her of any coquettish desire to display an unusually fine head of hair.

Gertrude's eyes have retained their old lustre, and do not now look too large for her face; and, if her mouth be less classically formed than the strict rule of beauty would commend, one can easily forgive that, in consideration of two rows of small pearly teeth, which are as regular and even as a string of beads. Her neat dress of spotted muslin fits close to her throat, and her simple black mantle does not conceal the roundness of her taper waist.

What then? Is Gertrude a beauty?

By no means. Hers is a face and form about which there would be a thousand different opinions, and out of the whole number few would pronounce her beautiful. But there are faces whose ever-varying expression one loves to watch,—tell-tale faces, that speak the truth and proclaim the sentiment within; faces that now light up with intelligence, now beam with mirth, now sadden at the tale of sorrow, now burn with a holy indignation for that which the soul abhors, and now, again, are sanctified by the divine presence, when the heart turns away from the world and itself, and looks upward in the spirit of devotion. Such a face was Gertrude's.

There are forms, too, which, though neither dignified, queenly or fairy-like, possess a grace, an ease, a self-possession, a power of moving lightly and airily in their sphere, and never being in any one's way,—and such a form was Gertrude's.

Whatever charm these attractions might give her,—and there were those who estimated it highly,—it was undoubtedly greatly enhanced by an utter unconsciousness, on her part, of possessing any attractions at all. The early-engrafted belief in her own personal plainness had not yet deserted her; but she no longer felt the mortification she had formerly labored under on that account.

As she perceived Miss Graham coming to meet her, she quickened her pace, and, joining her near the door-step, where a path turning to the right led into the garden, passed her arm affectionately over Emily's shoulder, in a manner which the latter's blindness, and Gertrude's superior height and ability to act as guide, had of late rendered usual, and, turning into the walk which led from the house, said, while she drew the shawl closer around her blind friend,

"Here I am again, Emily! Have you been alone ever since I went away?"

"Yes, dear, most of the time, and have been quite worried to think you were travelling about in Boston this excessively warm day."

"It has not hurt me in the least; I only enjoy this cool breeze all the more; it is such a contrast to the heat and dust of the city!"

"But, Gerty," said Emily, stopping short in their walk, "what are you coming away from the house for? You have not been to tea, my child."

"I know it, Emily, but I don't want any supper."

They walked on for some time, slowly and in perfect silence. At last Emily said,

"Well, Gertrude, have you nothing to tell me?"

"O, yes, a great deal, but—"

"But you know it will be sad news to me, and so you don't like to speak it; is it not so?"

"I ought not to have the vanity, dear Emily, to think it would trouble you very much; but, ever since last evening, when I told you what Mr. W. said, and what I had in my mind, and you seemed to feel so badly at the thought of our being separated, I have felt almost doubtful what it was right for me to do."

"And I, on the other hand, Gertrude, have been reproaching myself for allowing you to have any knowledge of my feeling in the matter, lest I should be influencing you against your duty, or, at least, making it harder for you to fulfil. I feel that you are right, Gertrude, and that, instead of opposing, I ought to do everything I can to forward your plans."

"Dear Emily!" exclaimed Gertrude, vehemently, "if you thought so from what I told you yesterday, you would be convinced, had you seen and heard all that I have to-day."

"Why? are matters any worse than they were at Mrs. Sullivan's?"

"Much worse than I described to you. I did not then know myself all that Mrs. Sullivan had to contend with; but I have been at their house nearly all the time since I left home this morning (for Mr. W. did not detain me five minutes), and it really does not seem to me safe for such a timid, delicate woman as Mrs. Sullivan to be alone with Mr. Cooper, now that his mind is in such a dreadful state."

"But, do you think you can do any good, Gertrude?"

"I know I can, dear Emily; I can manage him much better than she can, and at the same time do more for his comfort and happiness. He is like a child now, and full of whims. When he can possibly be indulged, Mrs. Sullivan will please him at any amount of inconvenience, and even danger, to herself; not only because he is her father, and she feels it her duty, but I actually think she is afraid of him, he is so irritable and violent. She tells me he often takes it into his head to do the strangest things, such as going out late at night, when it would be perfectly unsafe; and sleeping with his window wide open, though his room is on the lower floor."

"Poor woman!" exclaimed Emily; "what does she do in such cases?"

"I can tell you, Emily, for I saw an instance of it to-day. When I first went in this morning, he was preparing to make a coal-fire in the grate, notwithstanding the heat, which was becoming intense in the city."

"And Mrs. Sullivan?" said Emily.

"Was sitting on the lower stair, in the front entry, crying."

"Poor thing!" murmured Emily.

"She could do nothing with him," continued Gertrude, "and had given up in despair."

"She ought to have a strong woman, or a man, to take care of him."

"That is what she dreads, more than anything. She says it would kill her to see him unkindly treated, as he would be sure to be by a stranger; and, besides, I can see that she shrinks from the idea of having any one in the house to whom she is unaccustomed. She is exceedingly neat and particular in all her arrangements, has always done her work herself, and declares she would sooner admit a wild beast into her family than an Irish girl."

"Her new house has not been a source of much pleasure to her yet, has it?"

"O, no. She was saying, to-day, how strange it seemed, when she had been looking forward so long to the comfort of a new and well-built tenement, that, just as she had moved in and got everything furnished to her mind, she should have this great trial come upon her."

"It seems strange to me," said Emily, "that she did not sooner perceive its approach. I noticed, when I went with you to the house in E—— street, the failure in the old man's intellect."

"I had observed it for a long time," remarked Gertrude, "but never spoke of it to her; and I do not think she was in the least aware of it, until about the time of their removal, when the breaking up of old associations had a sad effect upon poor Mr. Cooper."

"Don't you think, Gertrude, that the pulling down of the church, and his consequent loss of employment, were a great injury to his mind?"

"Yes, indeed, I am sure of it; he altered very much after that, and never seemed so happy, even while they were in the house in E—— street; and when the owners of that land concluded to take it for stores and warehouses, and gave Mrs. Sullivan notice that she would be obliged to leave, the old sexton's mind gave way entirely."

"Sad thing!" said Emily. "How old is he, Gertrude?"

"I don't know exactly, but I believe he is very old; I remember Mrs. Sullivan's telling me, some time ago, that he was near eighty."

"Is he so old as that? Then I am not surprised that these changes have made him childish."

"O, no. Melancholy as it is, it is no more than we may any of us come to, if we live to his age; and, as he seems for the most part full as contented and happy as I have ever seen him appear, I do not lament it so much on his own account as on Mrs. Sullivan's. But I do, Emily, feel dreadfully anxious about *her*."

"Does it seem to be so very hard for her to bear up under it?"

"I think it would not be, if she were well; but there is something the matter with her, and I fear it is more serious than she allows, for she looks very pale, and has, I know, had several alarming ill turns lately."

"Has she consulted a physician?"

"No; she doesn't wish for one, and insists upon it she shall soon be better; but I do not feel sure that she will, especially as she takes no care of herself; and that is one great reason for my wishing to be in town as soon as possible. I am anxious to have Dr. Jeremy see her, and I think I can bring it about without her knowing that he comes on her account. I'll have a severe cold myself, if I can't manage it in any other way."

"You speak confidently of being in town, Gertrude; so I suppose it is all arranged."

"O, I have not told you, have I, about my visit to Mr. W.? Dear, good man, how grateful I ought to be to him! He has promised me the situation."

"I had no doubt he would, from what you told me he said to you at Mrs. Bruce's."

"You hadn't, really! Why, Emily, I was almost afraid to mention it to him. I couldn't believe he would have sufficient confidence in me; but he was so kind! I hardly dare tell you what he said about my capacity to teach, you will think me so vain."

"You need not tell me, my darling; I know, from his own lips, how highly he appreciates your ability; you could not tell me anything so flattering as what he told me himself."

"Dear Uncle True always wanted me to be a teacher; it was the height of his ambition. He would be pleased, wouldn't he, dear Emily?"

"He would no doubt have been proud enough to see you assistant in a school like Mr. W.'s. I am not sure, however, but he would think, as I do, that you are undertaking too much. You expect to be occupied in the school the greater part of every morning, and yet you propose to establish yourself as nurse to Mrs. Sullivan, and guardian to her poor old father. My dear child, you are not used to so much care, and I shall be constantly troubled for you, lest your own health and strength give way."

"O, dear Emily, there is no occasion for any anxiety on my account; I am well and strong, and fully capable of all that I have planned for myself. My only dread is in the thought of leaving you; and the only fear I have is, that you will miss me, and perhaps feel as if—"

"I know what you would say, Gertrude. You need not fear that; I am sure of your affection. I am confident you love me next to your duty, and I would not for the world that you should give me the preference. So dismiss that thought from your mind, and do not carry with you the belief that I would be selfish enough to desire to retain you a moment. I only wish, my dear, that for the present you had not thought of entering the school. You might then have gone to Mrs. Sullivan's, staid as long as you were needed, and perhaps found, by the time we are ready to start on our southern tour, that your services could be quite dispensed with; in which case, you could accompany us on a journey which I am sure your health will by that time require."

"But, dear Emily, how could I do that? I could not propose myself as a visitor to Mrs. Sullivan, however useful I might intend to be to her; nor could I speak of nursing to a woman who will not acknowledge that she is ill. I thought of all that, and it seemed to me impossible, with all the delicacy and tact in the world, to bring it about; for I have been with you so long that Mrs. Sullivan, I have no doubt, thinks me entirely unfitted for her primitive way of life. It was only when Mr. W. spoke of his wanting an assistant, and, as I imagined, hinted that he should like to employ me in that capacity, that the present plan occurred to me. I knew, if I told Mrs. Sullivan that I was engaged to teach there, and that you were not coming to town at all, but were soon going south, and represented to her that I wanted a boarding-place for the winter, she would not only be loth to refuse me a home with her, but would insist that I should go nowhere else."

"And it proved as you expected?"

"Exactly; and she showed so much pleasure at the thought of my being with her, that I realized still more how much she needed some one."

"She will have a treasure in you, Gertrude; I know that, very well."

"No, indeed! I do not hope to be of much use. The feeling I have is, that, however little I may be able to accomplish, it will be more than any one else could do for Mrs. Sullivan. She has lived so retired that she has not an intimate friend in the city, and I do not really know of any one, except myself, whom she would willingly admit under her roof. She is used to me and loves me; I am no restraint upon her, and she allows me to assist in whatever she is doing, although she often says that I live a lady's life now, and am not used to work. She knows, too, that I have an influence over her father; and I *have*,—strange as it may seem to you,—I *have* more than I know how to account for myself. I think it is partly because I am not at all afraid of him, and am firm in opposing his unreasonable fancies, and partly because I am more of a stranger than Mrs. Sullivan. But there is still another thing which gives me a great control over him. He naturally associates me in his mind with Willie; for we were for some years constantly together, both left the house at the same time, and he knows, too, that it is through me that the correspondence with him is chiefly carried on. Since his mind has been so weak, he seems to think continually of Willie, and I can at any moment, however irritable or wilful he may be, make him calm and quiet by proposing to tell him the latest news from his grandson. It does not matter how often I repeat the contents of the last letter, it is always new to him; and you have no idea, Emily, what power this little circumstance gives me. Mrs. Sullivan sees how easily I can guide his thoughts, and I noticed what a load of care seemed to be taken from her mind by merely having me there to-day. She looked so happy when I came away to-night, and spoke so hopefully of the comfort it would be during the winter to have me with her, that I felt repaid for any sacrifice it has been to me. But when I came home, and saw you, and thought of your going so far away, and of the length of time it might be before I should live with you again, I felt as if—" Gertrude could say no more. She laid her head on Emily's shoulder, and wept.

Emily soothed her with the greatest tenderness. "We have been very happy together, Gerty," said she, "and I shall miss you sadly; half the enjoyment of my life has of late years been borrowed from you. But I never loved you half so well as I do now, at the very time that we must part; for I see in the sacrifice you are making of yourself one of the noblest and most important traits of character a woman can possess. I know how much you love the Sullivans, and you have certainly every reason for being attached to them, and desiring to repay your old obligations; but your leaving us at this time, and renouncing, without a murmur, the southern tour from which you expected so much pleasure, proves that my Gerty is the brave, good girl I always hoped and prayed she might become. You are in the path of duty, Gertrude, and will be rewarded by the approbation of your own conscience, if in no other way."

As Emily finished speaking, they reached a corner of the garden, and were here met by a servant-girl, who had been looking for them to announce that Mrs. Bruce and her son were in the parlor, and had asked for them both.

"Did you get her buttons in town, Gertrude?" inquired Emily.

"Yes, I found some that were an excellent match for the dress; she probably wants to know what success I had; but how can I go in?"

"I will return to the house with Katy, and you can go in at the side-door, and reach your own room without being seen. I will excuse you to Mrs. Bruce for the present; and, when you have bathed your eyes, and feel composed, you can come in and report concerning the errand she intrusted to you."

## Chapter XXI

*But had we best retire? I see a storm.*
MILTON

Accordingly, when Gertrude entered the room half an hour afterwards, there was no evidence in her appearance of any unusual distress of mind. Mrs. Bruce nodded to her good-naturedly from a corner of the sofa. Mr. Bruce rose and offered his chair, at the same time that Mr. Graham pointed to a vacant window-seat near him, and said, kindly, "Here is a place for you, Gertrude."

Declining, however, the civilities of both gentlemen, she withdrew to an ottoman which stood near an open glass door, where she was almost immediately joined by Mr. Bruce, who, seating himself in an indolent attitude upon the upper row of a flight of steps which led from the window to the garden, commenced conversation with her.

Mr. Bruce—the same gentleman who some years before wore a velvet smoking-cap, and took afternoon naps in the grass—had recently returned from Europe, and, glorying in the renown acquired from a moustache, a French tailor, and the possession of a handsome property in his own right, now viewed himself with more complacency than ever.

"So you've been in Boston all day, Miss Flint?"

"Yes, nearly all day."

"Didn't you find it distressingly warm?"

"Somewhat so."

"I tried to go in to attend to some business that mother was anxious about, and even went down to the dépôt; but I had to give it up."

"Were you overpowered by the heat?"

"I was."

"How unfortunate!" remarked Gertrude, in a half-compassionate, half-ironical tone of voice.

Mr. Bruce looked up, to judge, if possible, from her countenance, whether she were serious or not; but, there being little light in the room, on account of the warmth of the evening, he could not decide the question in his mind, and therefore replied, "I dislike the heat, Miss Gertrude, and why should I expose myself to it unnecessarily?"

"O, I beg your pardon; I thought you spoke of important business."

"Only some affair of my mother's. Nothing I felt any interest in, and she took the state of the weather for an excuse. If I had known that you were in the cars, as I have since heard, I should certainly have persevered, in order to have had the pleasure of walking down Washington-street with you."

"I did not go down Washington-street."

"But you would have done so with a suitable escort," suggested the young man.

"If I had gone out of my way for the sake of accompanying my escort, the escort would have been a very doubtful advantage," said Gertrude, laughing.

"How very practical you are, Miss Gertrude! Do you mean to say that, when you go to the city, you always have a settled plan of operations, and never swerve from your course?"

"By no means. I trust I am not difficult to influence when there is a sufficient motive."

The young man bit his lip. "Then you never act without a motive; pray, what is your motive in wearing that broad-brimmed hat when you are at work in the garden?"

"It is an old habit, adopted some years ago from motives of convenience, and still adhered to, in spite of later inventions, which would certainly be a better protection from the sun. I must plead guilty, I fear, to a little obstinacy in my partiality for that old hat."

"Why not acknowledge the truth, Miss Gertrude, and confess that you wear it in order to look so very fanciful and picturesque that the neighbors' slumbers are disturbed by the very thoughts of it? My own morning dreams, for instance, as you are well aware, are so haunted by that hat, as seen in company with its owner, that I am daily drawn, as if by magnetic attraction, in the direction of the garden. You will have a heavy account to settle with Morpheus, one of these days, for defrauding him of his rights; and your conscience too will suffer for injuries to my health, sustained by continued exposure to early dews."

"It is hard to condemn me for such innocent and unintentional mischief; but, since I am to experience so much future remorse on account of your morning visits, I shall take upon myself the responsibility of forbidding them."

"O! you wouldn't be so unkind!—especially after all the pains I have taken to impart to you the little I know of horticulture."

"Very little I think it must have been; or I have but a little memory," said Gertrude, laughing.

"Now, how can you be so ungrateful? Have you forgotten the pains I took yesterday to acquaint you with the different varieties of roses? Don't you remember how much I had to say at first of damask roses and damask bloom; and how, before I had finished, I could not find words enough in praise of blushes, especially such sweet and natural ones as met my eyes while I was speaking?"

"I know you talked a great deal of nonsense. I hope you don't think I listened to it all."

"O, Miss Gertrude! It is of no use to say flattering things to you; you always look upon my compliments as so many jokes."

"I have told you, several times, that it was the most useless thing in the world to waste so much flattery upon me. I am glad you are beginning to realize it."

"Well, then, to ask a serious question, where were you this morning?"

"At what hour?"

"Half-past seven."

"On my way to Boston, in the cars."

"Is it possible?—so early! Why, I thought you went at ten. Then, all the time I was watching by the garden wall to get a chance to say good-morning, you were half a dozen miles away. I wish I had not wasted that hour so; I might have spent it in sleeping."

"Very true, it is a great pity."

"And then half an hour more here this evening! How came you to keep me waiting so long?"

"I?—When?"

"Why, now, to-night."

"I was not aware of doing so. I certainly did not take your visit to myself."

"My visit certainly was not meant for any one else."

"Ben," said Mr. Graham, approaching rather abruptly, and taking part in the conversation, "are you fond of gardening? I thought I heard you just now speaking of roses."

"Yes, sir; Miss Flint and I were having quite a discussion upon flowers,— roses especially."

Gertrude, availing herself of Mr. Graham's approach, tried to make her escape and join the ladies at the sofa; but Mr. Bruce, who had risen on Mr. Graham's addressing him, saw her intention, and frustrated it by placing himself in the way, so that she could not pass him without positive rudeness. Mr. Graham continued, "I propose placing a small fountain in the vicinity of Miss Flint's flower-garden; won't you walk down with me, and give your opinion of my plan?"

"Isn't it too dark, sir, to—"

"No, no, not at all; there is ample light for our purpose; this way, if you please;" and Mr. Bruce was compelled to follow where Mr. Graham led, though, in spite of his acquaintance with Paris manners, he made a wry face, and shook his head menacingly.

Gertrude was now permitted to relate to Mrs. Bruce the results of the shopping which she had undertaken on her account, and display the buttons, which proved very satisfactory. The gentlemen, soon after returning to the parlor, took seats near the sofa, and, the company forming one group, the conversation became general.

"Mr. Graham," said Mrs. Bruce, "I have been questioning Emily about your visit to the south; and, from the route which she tells me you propose taking, I think it will be a charming trip."

"I hope so, madam,—we have been talking of it for some time; it will be an excellent thing for Emily, and, as Gertrude has never travelled at all, I anticipate a great deal of pleasure for her."

"Ah! then you are to be of the party, Miss Flint?"

"Of course, of course," answered Mr. Graham, without giving Gertrude a chance to speak for herself; "we depend upon Gertrude,—couldn't get along at all without her."

"It will be delightful for you," continued Mrs. Bruce, her eyes still fixed on Gertrude.

"I did expect to go with Mr. and Miss Graham," answered Gertrude, "and looked forward to the journey with the greatest eagerness; but I have just decided that I must remain in Boston this winter."

"What are you talking about, Gertrude?" asked Mr. Graham. "What do you mean? This is all news to me."

"And to me, too, sir, or I should have informed you of it before. I supposed you expected me to accompany you, and there is nothing I should like so much. I should have told you before of the circumstances that now make it impossible; but they are of quite recent occurrence."

"But we can't give you up, Gertrude; I won't hear of such a thing; you must go with us, in spite of circumstances."

"I fear I shall not be able to," said Gertrude, smiling pleasantly, but still retaining her firmness of expression; "you are very kind, sir, to wish it."

"Wish it!—I tell you I insist upon it. You are under my care, child, and I have a right to say what you shall do."

Mr. Graham was beginning to get excited. Gertrude and Emily both looked troubled, but neither of them spoke.

"Give me your reasons, if you have any," added Mr. Graham, vehemently, "and let me know what has put this strange notion into your head."

"I will explain it to you to-morrow, sir."

"To-morrow! I want to know now."

Mrs. Bruce, plainly perceiving that a family storm was brewing, wisely rose to go. Mr. Graham suspended his wrath until she and her son had taken leave; but, as soon as the door was closed upon them, burst forth with real anger.

"Now tell me what all this means! Here I plan my business, and make all my arrangements, on purpose to be able to give up this winter to travelling,—and that, not so much on my own account as to give pleasure to both of you,—and, just as everything is settled, and we are almost on the point of starting, Gertrude announces that she has concluded not to go. Now, I should like to know her reasons."

Emily undertook to explain Gertrude's motives, and ended by expressing her own approbation of her course. As soon as she had finished, Mr. Graham, who had listened very impatiently, and interrupted her with many a "pish!" and "pshaw!" burst forth with redoubled indignation.

"So Gerty prefers the Sullivans to us, and you seem to encourage her in it! I should like to know what they've ever done for her, compared with what I have done!"

"They have been friends of hers for years, and, now that they are in great distress, she does not feel as if she could leave them; and I confess I do not wonder at her decision."

"I must say I do. She prefers to make a slave of herself in Mr. W.'s school, and a still greater slave in Mrs. Sullivan's family, instead of staying with us, where she has always been treated like a lady, and, more than that, like one of my own family!"

"O, Mr. Graham!" said Gertrude, earnestly, "it is not a matter of preference or choice, except as I feel it to be a duty."

"And what makes it a duty? Just because you used to live in the same house with them, and that boy out in Calcutta has sent you home a camel's-hair scarf, and a cage-full of miserable little birds, and written you a great package of letters, you think you must forfeit your own interests to take care of his sick relations! I can't say that I see how their claim compares with mine. Haven't I given you the best of educations, and spared no expense either for your improvement or your happiness?"

"I did not think, sir," answered Gertrude, humbly, and yet with quiet dignity, "of counting up the favors I had received, and measuring my conduct accordingly. In that case, my obligations to you are immense, and you would certainly have the greatest claim upon my services."

"Services! I don't want your *services,* child. Mrs. Ellis can do quite as well as you can for Emily, or me either; but I like your *company,* and think it is very ungrateful in you to leave us, as you talk of doing."

"Father," said Emily, "I thought the object, in giving Gertrude a good education, was to make her independent of all the world, and not simply dependent upon us."

"Emily," said Mr. Graham, "I tell you it is a matter of feeling,—you don't seem to look upon the thing in the light I do; but you are both against me, and I won't talk any more about it."

So saying, Mr. Graham took a lamp, went to his study, shut the door hard, —not to say slammed it,—and was seen no more that night.

Poor Gertrude! Mr. Graham, who had been so kind and generous, who had seldom before spoken harshly to her, and had always treated her with great indulgence, was now deeply offended. He had called her ungrateful; he evidently felt that she had abused his kindness, and believed that he and Emily stood in her estimation secondary to other, and, as he considered them, far less warm-hearted friends. Deeply wounded and grieved, she hastened to say good-night to the no less afflicted Emily, and, seeking her own room, gave way to feelings that exhausted her spirit, and caused her a sleepless night.

❀❀❀❀❀❀❀❀❀❀❀❀❀❀❀❀❀❀❀❀❀❀❀❀❀

## Chapter XXII

*Virtue is bold, and goodness never fearful.*
SHAKSPEARE

Left at three years of age dependent upon the mercy and charity of a world in which she was friendless and alone, Gertrude had, during the period of her residence at Nan Grant's, found little of that mercy, and still less of that charity. But, although her turbulent spirit rebelled at the treatment she received, she was then too young to reason upon the subject, or come to any philosophical conclusions upon the general hardness and cruelty of humanity; and, had she done so, such impressions could not but have been effaced amid the atmosphere of love and kindness which surrounded her during the succeeding period, when, cherished and protected in the home of her kind foster-father, she enjoyed a degree of parental tenderness which rarely falls to the lot of an orphan.

And having, through a similar providence, found in Emily additional proof of the fact that the tie of kindred blood is not always needed to bind heart to heart in the closest bonds of sympathy and affection, she had hitherto, in her unusually happy experience, felt none of the evils that spring from dependence upon the bounty of strangers. The unfriendly conduct of Mrs. Ellis had, at times, been a source of irritation to her; but the housekeeper's power and influence in the family were limited by her own dependence upon the good opinion of those she served, and Gertrude's patience and forbearance had at last nearly disarmed her enmity.

From Mr. Graham she had until now experienced only kindness. On her first coming to live with them, he had, to be sure, taken very little notice of her, and, so long as she was quiet, well-mannered, and no trouble to anybody, had been quite indifferent concerning her. He observed that Emily was fond of the girl and liked to have her with her; and, though he wondered at her taste, was glad that she should be indulged. It was not long, however, before he was led to notice in his daughter's favorite a quickness of mind and propriety of deportment which had the effect of creating an interest in her that soon increased to positive partiality, especially when he discovered her taste for gardening, and her perseverance in laboring among her flowers. He not only set off a portion of his grounds for her use, but, charmed with her success during the first summer after the appropriation was made, added to the original flower-garden, and himself assisted in laying out and ornamenting it. Emily formed no plan with regard to Gertrude's education to which she did not obtain a ready assent from her father; and Gertrude, deeply grateful for so much bounty, spared no pains to evidence her sense of obligation and regard, by treating Mr. Graham with the greatest respect and attention.

But, unfortunately for the continuance of these amicable relations, Mr. Graham possessed neither the disinterested, forbearing spirit of Uncle True, or the saintly patience and self-sacrifice of Emily. Mr. Graham was a liberal and highly respectable man; he had the reputation, as the world goes, of being a remarkably high-minded and honorable man; and not without reason, for his conduct had oftentimes justified this current report of him. But, alas! he was a *selfish* man, and often took very one-sided views. He had supported and educated Gertrude,—he liked her,—she was the person whom he preferred for a travelling companion for himself and Emily,—nobody else had any claim upon her to compare with his,—and he either *could* not or *would* not see that her duty lay in any other direction.

And yet, while he was ready to act the tyrant, he deceived himself with the idea that he was the best friend she had in the world. He was not capable of understanding that kind of regard which causes one to find gratification in whatever tends to the present or future welfare of another, without reference to himself or his own interests. Acting, therefore, under the influence of his own prejudiced and narrow sentiments, Mr. Graham gave way to his ill-temper, and distressed Gertrude by the first really harsh and severe language he had ever used towards her.

During the long hours of a wakeful and restless night, Gertrude had ample time to review and consider her own situation and circumstances. At first, her only emotion was one of grief and distress, such as a child might feel on being reproved; but that gradually subsided, as other and bitter thoughts rose up in her mind. "What right," thought she, "has Mr. Graham to treat me thus,—to tell me I *shall* go with them on this southern journey, and speak as if my other friends were ciphers in his estimation, and ought to be in my own? Does he consider that my freedom is to be the price of my education, and am I no longer to be able to say yes or no? Emily does not think so; Emily, who loves and needs me a thousand times more than Mr. Graham, thinks I have acted rightly, and assured me, only a few hours ago, that it was my duty to carry out the plans I had formed. And my solemn promise to Willie! is that to be held for nothing? No," thought she, "it would be tyranny in Mr. Graham to insist upon my remaining with them, and I am glad I have resolved to break away from such thraldom. Besides, I was educated to teach, and Mr. W. says it is important to commence at once, while my studies are fresh in my mind. Perhaps, if I yielded now, and staid here living in luxury, I should continue to do so until I lost the power of regaining my independence. It is cruel in Mr. Graham to try to deprive me of my free-will."

So much said pride; and Gertrude's heart, naturally proud, and only kept in check by strict and conscientious self-control, listened a while to such suggestions. But not long. She had accustomed herself to view the conduct of others in that spirit of charity which she desired should be exercised towards her own, and milder thoughts soon took the place of these excited and angry feelings.

"Perhaps," said she to herself, as she reviewed in her mind the conversation of the evening, "it is, after all, pure kindness to me that prompted Mr. Graham's interference. He may think, as Emily does, that I am undertaking too much. It is impossible for him to know how strong my motives are, how deep I consider my obligations to the Sullivans, and how much I am needed by them at this time. I had no idea, either, that it was such an understood thing that I was to be of the party to the south; for, though Emily talked as if she took it for granted, Mr. Graham never spoke of it, or asked me to go, and I could not suppose it would be any great disappointment to him to have me refuse; but, after his planning the journey, as he says he has done, with reference to the enjoyment of us both, I do not wonder at his being somewhat annoyed. He probably feels, too, as if I had been under his guardianship so long that he has almost a right to decide upon my conduct. And he *has* been very indulgent to me,—and I a stranger, with no claims! O! I hate to have him think me so ungrateful!

"Shall I then decide to give up my teaching, go to the south, and leave dear Mrs. Sullivan to suffer, perhaps die, while I am away? No, that is impossible. I will never be such a traitor to my own heart, and my sense of right; sorry as I shall be to offend Mr. Graham, I must not allow fear of his anger to turn me from my duty."

Having thus resolved to brave the tempest that she well knew she must encounter, and committed her cause to Him who judgeth righteously, Gertrude tried to compose herself to sleep; but found it impossible to obtain any untroubled rest. Scarcely had slumber eased her mind of the weight that pressed upon it, before dreams of an equally painful nature seized upon her, and startled her back to consciousness. In some of these visions she beheld Mr. Graham, angry and excited as on the previous evening, and threatening her with the severest marks of his displeasure if she dared to thwart his plans; and then, again, she seemed to see Willie, the same boyish youth from whom she had parted nearly five years before, beckoning her with a sad countenance to the room where his pale mother lay in a swoon, as Gertrude had a few weeks before discovered her. Exhausted by a succession of such harassing images, she at length gave up the attempt to obtain any rest through sleep, and, rising, seated herself at the window, where, watching the now descending moon, and the first approach of dawn, she found, in quiet self-communing, the strength and courage which, she felt, would be requisite to carry her calmly and firmly through the following day; a day destined to witness her sad separation from Emily, and her farewell to Mr. Graham, which would probably be of a still more distressing character. It may seem strange that anything more than ordinary mental courage and decision should be needful to sustain Gertrude under the present emergency. But, in truth, it required no small amount of both these qualities for a young girl of eighteen years, long dependent upon the liberality of an elderly man, well known as a stern dictator in his household, to suddenly break the bonds of custom and habit, and mark out a course for herself in opposition to his wishes and intentions; and nothing but an urgent motive could have led the grateful and peace-loving Gertrude to such a step. The tyrannical disposition of Mr. Graham was well understood in his family, each member of which was accustomed to respect all his wishes and whims; and though he was always indulgent, and usually kind, none ever ventured to brave a temper, which, when excited, was violent in the extreme. It cannot then be surprising that Gertrude's heart should have almost failed her, when she stood, half an hour before breakfast-time, with the handle of the dining-room door in her hand, summoning all her energies for another meeting with the formidable opposer of her plans. She paused but a moment, however, then opened the door and went in. Mr. Graham was where she expected to see him, sitting in his arm-chair, and on the breakfast-table by his side lay the morning paper. It had been Gertrude's habit, for a year or two, to read that paper aloud to the old gentleman at this same hour, and it was for that very purpose she had now come.

She advanced towards him with her usual "good-morning."

The salutation was returned in a purposely constrained voice. She seated herself, and leaned forward to take the newspaper; but he placed his hand upon it and prevented her.

"I was going to read the news to you, sir."

"And I do not wish to have you read, or do anything else for me, until I know whether you have concluded to treat me with the respect I have a right to demand from you."

"I certainly never intended to treat you otherwise than with respect, Mr. Graham."

"When girls or boys set themselves up in opposition to those older and wiser than themselves, they manifest the greatest disrespect they are capable of; but I am willing to forgive the past, if you assure me, as I think you will after a night's reflection, that you have returned to a right sense of your duty."

"I cannot say, sir, that I have changed my views with regard to what that duty is."

"Do you mean to tell me," asked Mr. Graham, rising from his chair and speaking in a tone which made Gerty's heart quake, in spite of her brave resolutions, "do you mean to tell me that you have any idea of persisting in your folly?"

"Is it folly, sir, to do right?"

"Right!—There is a great difference of opinion between you and me as to what right is in this case."

"But, Mr. Graham, I think, if you knew all the circumstances, you would not blame my conduct. I have told Emily the reasons that influenced me, and she—"

"Don't quote Emily to me!" interrupted Mr. Graham, as he walked the floor rapidly. "I don't doubt she'd give her head to anybody that asked for it; but I hope I know a little better what is due to myself; and I tell you plainly, Miss Gertrude Flint, without any more words in the matter, that if you leave my house, as you propose doing, you leave it with my displeasure; and *that,* you may find one of these days, it is no light thing to have incurred,— unnecessarily, too," he muttered,—"as you are doing."

"I am very sorry to displease you, Mr. Graham, but—"

"No, you're not *sorry;* if you were, you would not walk straight in the face of my wishes," said Mr. Graham, who began to observe the expression of Gertrude's face, which, though grieved and troubled, had in the last few minutes acquired additional firmness, instead of quailing beneath his severe and cutting words;—"but, I have said enough about a matter which is not worthy of so much notice. You can go or stay, as you please. I wish you to understand, however, that, in the former case, I utterly withdraw my protection and assistance from you. You must take care of yourself, or trust to strangers. I suppose you expect your Calcutta friend will support you, perhaps come home and take you under his especial care; but, if you think so, you know little of the world. I daresay he is married to an Indian by this time, and, if not, has pretty much forgotten you."

"Mr. Graham," said Gertrude, proudly, "Mr. Sullivan will not probably return to this country for many years, and I assure you I neither look to him or any one else for support; I intend to earn a maintenance for myself."

"A heroic resolve!" said Mr. Graham, contemptuously, "and pronounced with a dignity I hope you will be able to maintain. Am I to consider, then, that your mind is made up?"

"It is, sir," said Gertrude, not a little strengthened for the dreaded necessity of pronouncing her final resolution by Mr. Graham's sarcastic speeches.

"And you go?"

"I must. I believe it to be my duty, and am therefore willing to sacrifice my own comfort, and, what I assure you I value far more, your friendship."

Mr. Graham did not seem to take the least notice of the latter part of her remark, and before she had finished speaking so far forgot his usual politeness as to drown her voice in the violent ringing of the table-bell.

It was answered by Katy with the breakfast; and Emily and Mrs. Ellis coming in at the same moment, all seated themselves at table, and the meal was commenced in unusual silence and constraint,—for Emily had heard the loud tones of her father's voice, and was filled with anxiety and alarm, while Mrs. Ellis plainly saw, from the countenances of all present, that something unpleasant had occurred.

When Mr. Graham, whose appetite appeared undiminished, had finished eating a hearty breakfast, he turned to Mrs. Ellis, and deliberately and formally invited her to accompany himself and Emily on their journey to the south, mentioning the probability that they should pass some weeks in Havana.

Mrs. Ellis, who had never before heard any intimation that such a tour was contemplated, accepted the invitation with pleasure and alacrity, and proceeded to ask a number of questions concerning the proposed route and length of absence; while Emily hid her agitated face behind her tea-cup; and Gertrude, who had lately been reading "Letters from Cuba," and was aware that Mr. Graham knew the strong interest she consequently felt in the place, pondered in her mind whether it were possible that he could be guilty of the small and mean desire to vex and mortify her.

Breakfast over, Emily hastily sought her room, where she was immediately joined by Gertrude.

In answering Emily's earnest inquiries as to the scene which had taken place, Gertrude forebore to repeat Mr. Graham's most bitter and wounding remarks; for she saw, from her kind friend's pained and anxious countenance, how deeply she participated in her own sense of wrong and misapprehension. She told her, however, that it was now well understood by Mr. Graham that she was to leave, and, as his sentiments towards her were far from kindly, she thought it best to go at once, especially as she could never be more needed by Mrs. Sullivan than at present. Emily saw the reasonableness of the proposal, assented to it, and agreed to accompany her to town that very afternoon; for, deeply sensitive at any unkindness manifested towards Gertrude, she preferred to have her depart thus abruptly, rather than encounter her father's contemptuous neglect.

The remainder of the day, therefore, was spent by Gertrude in packing, and other preparations; while Emily sat by, counselling and advising the future conduct of her adopted darling, lamenting the necessity of their separation, and exchanging with her reiterated assurances of continued and undiminished affection.

"O! if you could only write to me, dear Emily, during your long absence, what a comfort it would be!" exclaimed Gertrude.

"With Mrs. Ellis' assistance, my dear," replied Emily, "I will send you such news as I can of our movements; but, though you may not be able to hear much from me, you will be ever in my thoughts, and I shall never forget to commend my beloved child to the protection and care of One who will be to her a better counsellor and friend than I can be."

In the course of the day Gertrude sought Mrs. Ellis, and astonished that lady by announcing that she had come to have a few farewell words with her. Surprise and curiosity, however, were soon superseded by the housekeeper's eagerness to expatiate upon the kindness and generosity of Mr. Graham, and the delights of the excursion in prospect. After wishing her a great deal of pleasure, Gertrude begged to hear from her by letter during her absence; to which apparently unheard request Mrs. Ellis only replied by asking if Gertrude thought a thibet dress would be uncomfortable on the journey; and, when it was repeated with still greater earnestness, she, with equal unsatisfactoriness to the suppliant for epistolary favors, begged to know how many pairs of under-sleeves she should probably require. Having responded to her questions, and at last gained her ear and attention, Gertrude obtained from her a promise to write *one* letter, which would, she declared, be more than she had done for years.

Before leaving the house, Gertrude sought Mr. Graham's study, in hopes that he would take a friendly leave of her; but, on her telling him that she had come to bid him "good-by," he indistinctly muttered the simple words of that universal formula, so deep in its meaning when coming from the heart; so chilling when uttered, as on the present occasion, by stern and nearly closed lips; and, turning his back upon her, took up the tongs to mend his fire.

So she went away, with a tear in her eye and sadness in her heart, for until now Mr. Graham had been a good friend to her.

A far different scene awaited her in the upper kitchen, where she went to seek Mrs. Prime and Katy.

"Bless yer soul, dear Miss Gertrude!" said the former, stumbling up the staircase which led from the lower room, and wiping her hands on her apron,—"how we shall miss yer! Why, the house won't be worth livin' in when you're out of it. My gracious! If you don't come back, we shall all die out in a fortnight. Why, you're the life and soul of the place! But there, I guess you know what's right; so, if you must go, we must bear it,— though Katy and I'll cry our eyes out, for aught I know."

"Sure, Miss Gairthrude," said Irish Katy, "and it's right gude in you to be afther comin' to bid us good-by. I don't see how you gets memory to think of us all, and I'm shure yer'll never be betther off than what I wish yer. I can't but think, miss, it'll go to help yer along, that everybody's gude wishes and blessin' goes with yer."

"Thank you, Katy, thank you," said Gertrude, much touched by the simple earnestness of these good friends. "You must come and see me some time in Boston; and you too, Mrs. Prime, I shall depend upon it. Good-by;" and the good-by that *now* fell upon Gertrude's ear was a hearty and a true one; it followed her through the hall, and as the carryall drove away she heard it mingling with the rattling of the vehicle.

## Chapter XXIII

*One of that stubborn sort he is,*
*Who, if they once grow fond of an opinion,*
*They call it honor, honesty and faith,*
*And sooner part with life than let it go.*

ROWE

Passing over Gertrude's parting with Emily, her cordial reception by Mrs. Sullivan, and her commencement of school duties, we will look in upon her and record the events of a day in November, about two months after she left Mr. Graham's.

Rising with the sun, she made her neat toilet in a room so cold that before it was completed her hands were half-benumbed; nor did she, in spite of the chilling atmosphere, omit, ere she commenced the labors of the day, to supplicate Heaven's blessing upon them. Then, noiselessly entering the adjoining apartment, where Mrs. Sullivan was still sleeping, she lit a fire, the materials for which had been carefully prepared the night before, in a small grate, and, descending the stairs with the same light foot-step, performed a similar service at the cooking-stove, which stood in a comfortable room, where, now that the weather was cold, the family took their meals. The table was set, and the preparations for breakfast nearly completed, when Mrs. Sullivan entered, pale, thin and feeble in her appearance, and wrapped in a large shawl.

"Gertrude," said she, "why will you let me sleep so, mornings, while you are up and at work? I believe it has happened so every day this week."

"For the very best reason in the world, auntie; because I sleep all the early part of the night, and am wide awake at daybreak, and with you it is just the reverse. Besides, I like to get the breakfast, I make such beautiful coffee. Look!" said she, pouring some into a cup, and then lifting the lid of the coffee-pot and pouring it back again; "see how clear it is! Don't you long for some of it, this cold morning?"

Mrs. Sullivan smiled, for, Uncle True having always preferred tea, Gertrude did not at first know how to make coffee, and had been obliged to come to her for instructions.

"Now," said Gertrude, playfully, as she drew a comfortable chair close to the fire, "I want you to sit down here and watch the tea-kettle boil, while I run and see if Mr. Cooper is ready to let me tie up his cue."

She went, leaving Mrs. Sullivan to think what a good girl she was; and presently returning with the old man, who was dressed with perfect neat-ness, she placed a chair for him, and having waited, as for a child, while he seated himself, and then pinned a napkin about his throat, she proceeded to place the breakfast on the table.

While Mrs. Sullivan poured out the coffee, Gertrude, with a quiet tact which rendered the action almost unobserved, removed the skin from a baked potato and the shell from a boiled egg, and, placing both on the plate destined for Mr. Cooper, handed him his breakfast in a state of preparation which obviated the difficulty the old man experienced in performing these tasks for himself, and spared Mrs. Sullivan the anxiety she always felt at wit-nessing his clumsiness and sadly-increasing carelessness on those points of neatness so sacred in her eyes. Poor Mrs. Sullivan had no appetite, and it was with difficulty Gertrude persuaded her to eat anything; a few fried oysters, however, unexpectedly placed before her, proved such a tempta-tion that she was induced to taste and finally to eat several, with a degree of relish she rarely felt, lately, for any article of food. As Gertrude gazed at her languid face, she realized, more than ever before, the change which had come over the active, energetic little woman; and, confident that nothing but positive disease could have effected such a transformation, she resolved that not another day should pass without her seeing a physician.

Breakfast over, there were dishes to wash, rooms to be put in order, dinner to be decided on and partially prepared; and all this Gertrude exerted herself and saw accomplished, chiefly through her own labor, before she went to reärrange her dress, previous to her departure for the school, where she had now been some weeks installed as assistant teacher. A quarter before nine she looked in at the kitchen door, and said, in a cheering tone, to the old man, who was cowering gloomily over the fire,

"Come, Mr. Cooper, won't you go over and superintend the new church a little while, this morning? Mr. Miller will be expecting you; he said yesterday that he depended on your company when he was at work."

The old man rose, and taking his great-coat from Gertrude, put it on with her assistance, and accompanied her in a mechanical sort of way, that seemed to imply a great degree of indifference whether he went or stayed. As they walked in silence down the street, Gertrude could not but revolve in her mind the singular coincidence which had thus made her the almost daily companion of another infirm old man; nor could she fail to draw a comparison between the genial, warm-hearted Uncle True, and the gloomy, discontented Paul Cooper, who, never, as we have said, possessing a genial temperament, now retained, in his state of mental imbecility, his old characteristics in an exaggerated form. Unfavorable as the comparison necessarily was to the latter, it did not diminish the kindness and thoughtfulness of Gertrude towards her present charge, who was in her eyes an object of sincere compassion. They soon reached the new church of which Gertrude had spoken,—a handsome edifice, built on the site of the old building in which Mr. Cooper had long officiated as sexton. It was not yet finished, and a number of workmen were at this time engaged in the completion of the interior.

A man with a hod-full of mortar preceded Gertrude and her companion up the steps which led to the main entrance, but stopped inside the porch, on hearing himself addressed by name, and, laying down his burden, turned to respond to the well-known voice.

"Good-morning, Miss Flint," said he. "I hope you're very well, this fine day. Ah! Mr. Cooper, you've come to help me a little, I see;—that's right! We can't go on very well without you—you're so used to the place. Here, sir, if you'll come with me, I'll show you what has been done since you were here last; I want to know how you think we get along."

So saying, he was walking away with the old sexton; but Gertrude followed, and detained him a moment, to ask if he would do her the favor to see Mr. Cooper safe home when he passed Mrs. Sullivan's house on his way to dinner.

"Certainly, Miss Flint," replied the man, "with all the pleasure in the world; he has usually gone with me pretty readily, when you have left him in my care."

Having obtained this promise, Gertrude hastened towards the school, rejoicing in the certainty that Mr. Cooper would be safe and well amused during the morning, and that Mrs. Sullivan, freed from all responsibility concerning him, would be left to the rest and quiet she so much needed.

This cordial coadjutor in Gertrude's plan of diverting and occupying the old man's mind was a respectable mason, who had often been in Mr. Graham's employ, and whose good-will and gratitude Gertrude had won by the kindness and attention she had shown his family during the previous winter, when they were sick and afflicted. In her daily walk past the church, she had frequently seen Mr. Miller at his work, and it occurred to her that, if she could awaken in Mr. Cooper's mind an interest in the new structure, he might find amusement in coming there and watching the workmen. She had some difficulty in persuading him to visit a building to the erection of which he had been vehemently opposed, not only because it was inimical to his interests, but on account of the strong attachment he had for the old place of worship. Once there, however, he became interested in the work, and, as Mr. Miller took pains to make him comfortable, and even awakened in him the belief that he was useful, he gradually acquired a habit of passing the greater part of every morning in watching the men engaged in their various branches of industry. Sometimes Gertrude called for him on her return from school; and sometimes, as on the present occasion, Mr. Miller undertook to accompany him home.

Since Gertrude had been at Mrs. Sullivan's there was a very perceptible alteration in Mr. Cooper. He was much more manageable, looked better contented, and manifested far less irritability than he had previously done; and this favorable change, together with the cheering influence of Gertrude's society, had for a time produced a proportionately beneficial effect upon Mrs. Sullivan; but, within the last few days, her increased debility, and one or two sudden attacks of faintness, had awakened all, and more than all, of Gertrude's former fears. She had left home with the determination, as soon as she should be released from her school duties, to seek Dr. Jeremy and request his attendance; and it was in order to secure leisure for that purpose that she had solicited Mr. Miller's superintending care for Mr. Cooper.

Of Gertrude's school-duties we shall say nothing, save that she was found by Mr. W. fully competent to the performance of them, and that she met with those trials and discouragements only to which all teachers are more or less subjected, from the idleness, obstinacy, or stupidity of their pupils. On this day, however, she was, from various causes, detained to a later hour than usual, and the clock struck two at the very moment that she was ringing Dr. Jeremy's door-bell. The girl who opened the door knew Gertrude by sight, having often seen her at her master's house; and, telling her that, though the doctor was just going to dinner, she thought he would see her, asked her into the office, where he stood, with his back to the fire, eating an apple, as it was his invariable custom to do before dinner. He laid it down, however, and advanced to meet Gertrude, holding out both his hands. "Gertrude Flint, I declare!" exclaimed he. "Why, I'm glad to see you, my girl. Why haven't you been here before, I should like to know?"

Gertrude explained that she was living with friends, one of whom was very old, the other an invalid; and that so much of her time was occupied in school that she had no opportunity for visiting.

"Poor excuse!" said the doctor; "poor excuse! But, now we've got you here, we shan't let you go very soon;" and, going to the foot of the staircase, he called, in the loudest possible tone of voice, "Mrs. Jerry! Mrs. Jerry! come!—come down to dinner as quick as you can, and put on your best cap,—we've got company.—Poor soul!" added he, in a lower tone, addressing himself to Gertrude, and smiling good-naturedly, "she can't hurry, can she, Gerty?—she's fat."

Gertrude now protested against staying to dinner, declaring she must hasten home, and announcing Mrs. Sullivan's illness and the object of her visit.

"An hour can't make much difference in such a case," insisted the doctor. "You must stay and dine with me, and then I'll go wherever you wish, and take you with me in the buggy."

Gertrude hesitated; the sky had clouded over, and a few flakes of snow were falling; she should have an uncomfortable walk; and, moreover, it would be better for her to accompany the doctor, as the street in which she lived was principally composed of new houses, not yet numbered, and he might, if he were alone, have some difficulty in finding the right tenement.

At this stage of her reflections, Mrs. Jeremy entered. Fat she certainly was, very uncommonly fat, and flushed too with her unwonted haste, and the excitement of anticipating the company of a stranger. She kissed Gertrude in the kindest manner, and then, looking round and seeing that there was no one else present, exclaimed, glancing reproachfully at the doctor,

"Why, Dr. Jerry!—an't you ashamed of yourself? I never will believe you again; you made me think there was some great stranger here."

"And, pray, Mrs. Jerry, who's a greater stranger in this house than Gerty Flint?"

"Sure enough!" said Mrs. Jeremy. "Gertrude *is* a stranger, and I've got a scolding in store for her on that very account; but, you know, Dr. Jerry, I shouldn't have put on my lilac-and-pink for Gertrude to see; she likes me just as well in my old yellow, if she did tell me, when I bought it, the saucy girl, that I'd selected the ugliest cap in Boston. Do you remember that, Gerty?"

Gerty laughed heartily at the recollection of a very amusing scene that took place at the milliner's when she went shopping with Mrs. Jeremy. "But, come, Gerty," continued that lady, "dinner's ready; take off your cloak and bonnet, and come into the dining-room; the doctor has got a great deal to say, and has been wanting dreadfully to see you."

They had been sitting some minutes without a word's having been spoken, beyond the usual civilities of the table, when the doctor, suddenly laying down his knife and fork, commenced laughing, and laughed till the tears came into his eyes. Gertrude looked at him inquiringly, and Mrs. Jeremy said, "There, Gertrude!—for one whole week he had just such a laughing-fit, two or three times a day. I was as much astonished at first as you are; and, I confess, I don't quite understand now what could have happened between him and Mr. Graham that was so very funny."

"Come, wife," said the doctor, checking himself in his merriment; "don't you forestall my communication. I want to tell the story myself. I don't suppose," continued he, turning towards Gertrude, "you've lived five years at Mr. Graham's, without finding out what a cantankerous, opinionative, obstinate old hulk he is?"

"Doctor!" said Mrs. Jeremy, reprovingly, and shaking her head at him.

"I don't care for winking or head-shaking, wife; I speak my mind, and that's the conclusion I've come to with regard to Mr. Graham; and Gertrude, here, has done the same, I haven't a particle of doubt, only she's a good girl, and won't say so."

"I never saw anything that looked like it," said Mrs. Jeremy, "and I've seen as much of him as most folks. I meet him in the street almost every day, and he looks as smiling as a basket of chips, and makes a beautiful bow."

"I daresay," said the doctor; "Gertrude and I know what gentlemanly manners he has when one does not walk in the very teeth of his opinions,— eh, Gertrude?—but when one does—"

"In talking politics, for instance," suggested Mrs. Jeremy. "It's your differences with him on politics that have set you against him so."

"No, it isn't," replied the doctor. "A man may get angry talking politics, and be a pretty good-natured man too, in the main. I get angry *myself* on *politics*, but that isn't the sort of thing I have reference to at all. It's Graham's wanting to lay down the law to everybody that comes within ten miles of him that I can't endure; his dictatorial way of acting, as if he were the Grand Mogul of Cochin China. I thought he'd improved of late years; he had a serious lesson enough in that sad affair of poor Philip Amory's; but, fact, I believe he's been trying the old game again. Ha! ha! ha!" shouted the good doctor, leaning forward, and giving Gertrude a light tap on the shoulder,— "wasn't I glad when I found he'd met at last with a reasonable opposition?— and that, too, where he least expected it!"

Gertrude looked her astonishment at his evident knowledge of the misunderstanding between herself and Mr. Graham; and in answer to that look he continued, "You wonder where I picked up my information, and I'll tell you. It was partly from Graham himself; and what diverts me is to think how hard the old chap tried to hide his defeat, and persuade me that he'd had his own way after all, when I saw through him, and knew as well as he did that he'd found his match in you."

"Dr. Jeremy," interposed Gertrude, "I hope you don't think—"

"No, my dear, I *don't* think you a *professed pugilist;* but I consider you a girl of sense—one who knows what's right—and will do what's right, in spite of Mr. Graham, or anybody else; and when you hear my story you will know the grounds on which I formed my opinion with regard to the course things had taken, and the reasons I have for understanding the state of the case rather better than Graham meant I should. One day,—perhaps it was about two months ago—you may remember the exact time better than I do,—I was summoned to go and see one of Mr. W.'s children, who had an attack of croup. Mr. W. was talking with me, when he was called away to see a visitor; and, on his return, he mentioned that he had just secured your services in his school. I was not surprised, for I knew Emily intended you for a teacher, and I was thankful you had got so good a situation. I had hardly left Mr. W.'s door, however, before I encountered Mr. Graham, and he entertained me, as we went down the street, with an account of his plans for the winter. 'But Gertrude Flint is not going with you,' said I.—'Gertrude!' said he; 'certainly she is.'—'Are you sure of that?' I asked, 'Have you invited her?'—'Invited her!—No,' was his answer; 'but, of course, I know she will go, and be glad enough of the opportunity; it isn't every girl in her situation that is so fortunate.' Now, Gerty, I felt a little provoked at his way of speaking, and I answered, in nearly as confident a tone as his own, 'I doubt, myself, whether she will accept the invitation.' Upon that, Mr. Dignity straightened up, and such a speech as he made! I never can recall it without being amused, especially when I think of the come-down that followed so soon after. I can't repeat it; but, goodness, Gertrude! one would have thought, to hear him, that it was not only impossible you should oppose his wishes, but actual treason in me to suggest such a thing. Of course, I knew better than to tell what I had just heard from Mr. W., but I never felt a greater curiosity about anything than I did to know how the matter would end. Two or three times I planned to drive out with my wife, see Emily, and hear the result; but a doctor never can call a day his own, and I got prevented. At last, one Sunday, I heard Mrs. Prime's voice in the kitchen (her niece lives here), and down I went to make my inquiries. That woman is a friend of yours, Gertrude, and pretty sharp where you are concerned. She told me the truth, I rather think; though not, perhaps, all the particulars. It was not more than a day or two after that before I saw Graham. 'Ah!' said I; 'when do you start?'—'To-morrow,' replied he.— 'Really,' I exclaimed 'then I shan't see your ladies again. Will you take a little package from me to Gertrude?'—'I know nothing about Gertrude!' said he, stiffly.—'What' rejoined I, affecting the greatest surprise, 'has Gertrude left you?'—'She has,' answered he.—'And dared,' continued I, quoting his own words, 'to treat you with such disrespect,—to trifle so with your dignity?'—'Dr. Jeremy!' exclaimed he, 'I don't wish to hear that young person mentioned; she has behaved as ungratefully as she has unwisely.' —'Why, about the gratitude, Graham,' said I, 'I believe you said it would only be an additional favor on your part if you took her with you, and I can't say but what I think it is wisdom in her to make herself independent at home. But I really am sorry for you and Emily; you will miss her so much.'—'We can dispense with your sympathy, sir,' answered he, 'for that which is no loss.'—'Ah! really!' I replied; 'now, I was thinking Gertrude's society would be quite a loss.'—'Mrs. Ellis goes with us,' said he, with a marked emphasis, that seemed to say *she* was a person whose company compensated for all deficiencies.—'Ah!' said I, 'charming woman, Mrs. Ellis!' Graham looked annoyed, for he is aware that Mrs. Ellis is my antipathy."

"Well, you ought to have known better, Dr. Jerry," said his kind-hearted wife, "than to have attacked a man so on his weak point; it was only exciting his temper for nothing."

"I was taking up the cudgels for Gertrude, wife."

"And I don't believe Gertrude wants you to take up the cudgels for her. I have no manner of doubt that she has the kindest of feelings towards Mr. Graham, this blessed minute."

"I have, indeed, Mrs. Jeremy," said Gertrude; "he has been a most generous and indulgent friend to me."

"Except when you wanted to have your own way," suggested the doctor.

"Which I seldom did, when it was in opposition to his wishes."

"And what if it were?"

"I always considered it my duty to submit to him, until, at last, a higher duty compelled me to do otherwise."

"And then, my dear," said Mrs. Jeremy, "I daresay it pained you to displease him; and that is a right woman's feeling, and one that Dr. Jerry in his own heart, can't but approve of, though one would think, to hear him talk, that he considered it pretty in a young girl to take satisfaction in browbeating an old gentleman. But, don't let us talk any more about it; he has had his say, and now it's my turn. I want to hear how you are situated, Gerty, where you live, and how you like teaching."

Gertrude answered all these questions; and the doctor, who had heard Mrs. Sullivan spoken of as a friend of True's and Gerty's, at the time when he attended the former, made many inquiries concerning the state of her health. It was by this time beginning to snow fast, and Gertrude's anxiety to return home in good season being very manifest to her kind host and hostesss, they urged no further delay, and, after she had given many a promise to repeat her visit on the earliest opportunity, she drove away with the doctor.

## Chapter XXIV

*No simplest duty is forgot;*
*Life hath no dim and lowly spot*
*That doth not in her sunshine share.*
                                        LOWELL

"I have been thinking," said Gertrude, as she drew near home, "how we shall manage, doctor, so as not to alarm Mrs. Sullivan."

"What's going to alarm her?" asked the doctor.

"You, if she knows at once that you are a physician. I think I had better introduce you as a friend, who brought me home in the storm."

"O! so we are going to act a little farce, are we? Stage-manager, Gertrude Flint—unknown stranger, Dr. Jeremy. I'm ready. What shall I say first?"

"I leave that to a wiser head than mine, doctor, and trust entirely to your own discretion to obtain some knowledge of her symptoms, and only gradually disclose to her that you are a physician."

"Ah, yes! pretend, at first, to be only a private individual of a very inquiring mind. I think I can manage it."

They went in. As they opened the door, Mrs. Sullivan rose from her chair with a troubled countenance, and hardly waited for the introduction to Gertrude's friend before she turned to her and asked, with some anxiety, if Mr. Cooper were not with them.

"No, indeed," replied Gertrude. "Hasn't he come home?"

Upon Mrs. Sullivan's saying that she had not seen him since morning, Gertrude informed her, with a composure she was far from feeling, that Mr. Miller had undertaken the care of him, and could, undoubtedly, account for his absence. She would seek him at once.

"O, I'm so sorry," said Mrs. Sullivan, "that you should have to go out again in such a storm! but I feel very anxious about grandpa—don't you, Gerty?"

"Not very; I think he is safe in the church. But I'll go for him at once; you know, auntie, I never mind the weather."

"Then take my great shawl, dear." And Mrs. Sullivan went to the entry-closet for her shawl, giving Gertrude an opportunity to beg of Dr. Jeremy that he would await her return; for she knew that any unusual agitation of mind would often occasion an attack of faintness in Mrs. Sullivan, and was afraid to have her left alone, to dwell with anxiety and alarm upon Mr. Cooper's prolonged absence.

It was a very disagreeable afternoon, and already growing dark. Gertrude hastened along the wet side-walks, exposed to the blinding storm (for the wind would not permit her to carry an umbrella), and, after passing through several streets, gained the church. She went into the building, now nearly deserted by the workmen, saw, at once, that Mr. Cooper was not there, and was beginning to fear that she should gain no information concerning him, when she met Mr. Miller coming from the gallery. He looked surprised at seeing her, and asked if Mr. Cooper had not returned home. She answered in the negative, and he then informed her that his utmost efforts were insufficient to persuade the old man to go home at dinner-time, and that he had therefore taken him to his own house; he had supposed, however, that long before this hour he would have been induced to allow one of the children to accompany him to Mrs. Sullivan's.

As it now seemed probable that he was still at Mr. Miller's, Gertrude took the direction (for the family had moved within a year, and she did not know where to seek them), and, declining the company of the friendly mason, whom she was unwilling to take from his work, proceeded thither at once. After another uncomfortable walk, and some difficulty in finding the right street and house, she reached her destination. She knocked at the outside door; but there was no response, and, after waiting a moment, she opened it and went in. Through another door, at the right, there was the sound of children's voices, and so much noise that she believed it impossible to make herself heard, and, therefore, without further ceremony, entered the room. A band of startled children dispersed at the sight of a stranger, and ensconced themselves in corners; and Mrs. Miller, in dismay at the untidy appearance of her kitchen, hastily pushed back a clothes-horse against the wall, thereby disclosing to view the very person Gertrude had come to seek, who, in his usual desponding attitude, sat cowering over the fire. But, before she could advance to speak to him, her whole attention was arrested by another and most unexpected sight. Placed against the side of the room, directly opposite the door, was a narrow bed, in which some person seemed to be sleeping. Hardly, however, had Gertrude presented herself in the doorway, before the figure suddenly raised itself, gazed fixedly at her, lifted a hand as if to ward off her approach, and uttered a piercing shriek.

The voice and countenance were not to be mistaken, and Gertrude, pale and trembling, felt something like a revival of her old dread, as she beheld the well-known features of Nan Grant.

"Go away! go *away!*" cried Nan, as Gertrude, after a moment's hesitation, advanced into the room. Again Gertrude paused, for the wildness of Nan's eyes and the excitement of her countenance were such that she feared to excite her further.

Mrs. Miller now came forward, and interfered. "Why, Aunt Nancy!" said she, "what is the matter? This is Miss Flint, one of the best young ladies in the land."

"No, 't an't!" said Nan, fiercely. "I know better!"

Mrs. Miller now drew Gertrude aside, into the shadow of the clothes-horse, and conversed with her in an under tone, while Nan, leaning on her elbow, and peering after them into the dim corner to which they had retreated, maintained a watchful, listening attitude. Gertrude was informed that Mrs. Miller was a niece of Ben Grant's, but had seen nothing of him or his wife for years, until a few days previous, Nan had come there in a state of the greatest destitution, and threatened with the fever under which she was now laboring. "I could not refuse her a shelter," said Mrs. Miller; "but, as you see, I have no accommodation for her, and it's not only bad for me to have her sick right here in the kitchen, but, what with the noise of the children and all the other discomforts, I'm afraid the poor old thing will die."

"Have you a room that you could spare above stairs?" asked Gertrude.

"Why, there's our Jane," answered Mrs. Miller; "she's a good-hearted girl as ever lived; she said, right off, she'd give up her room to poor Aunt Nancy, and she'd sleep in with the other children; I didn't feel, though, as if we could afford to keep another fire a-going, and so I thought we'd put up a bed here for a day or two, and just see how she got along. But she's looked pretty bad to-day, and now I'm thinking, from her actions, that she's considerable out of her head."

"She ought to be kept quiet," said Gertrude; "and, if you will have a fire in Jane's room at my expense, and do what you can to make her comfortable, I'll try and send a physician here to see her." Mrs. Miller was beginning to express the warmest gratitude, but Gertrude interrupted her with saying, "Don't thank me, Mrs. Miller; Nancy is not a stranger to me; I have known her before, and, perhaps, feel more interest in her than you do yourself."

Mrs. Miller looked surprised; but Gertrude, whose time was limited, could not stop to enter into a further explanation. Anxious, however, if possible, to speak to Nan, and assure her of her friendly intentions, she went boldly up to the side of the bed, in spite of the wild and glaring eyes which were fixed steadily upon her.

"Nan," said she, "do you know me?"

"Yes! yes!" replied Nan, in a half-whisper, speaking quickly and catching her breath; "what have you come for?"

"To do you good, I hope."

But Nan still looked incredulous, and in the same undertone, and with the same nervous accent, inquired, "Have you seen Gerty? Where is she?"

"She is well," answered Gertrude, astonished, however, at the question; for she had supposed herself recognized.

"What did she say about me?"

"She says that she forgives and pities you, and is in hopes to do something to help you and make you well."

"Did she?" said the sick woman; "then you won't kill me?"

"Kill you?—No, indeed. We are in hopes to make you comfortable, and cure you."

Mrs. Miller, who had been preparing a cup of tea, now drew near, with it in her hand. Gertrude took it and offered it to Nan, who drank eagerly of it, staring at her, however, in the mean time, over the edge of the cup. When she had finished, she threw herself heavily upon the pillow, and began muttering some indistinct sentences, the only distinguishable word being the name of her son Stephen. Finding the current of her thoughts thus apparently diverted, Gertrude, now feeling in haste to return and relieve Dr. Jeremy, who had so kindly agreed to stay with Mrs. Sullivan, moved a little from the bed-side, saying, as she did so, "Good-by, I will come and see you again."

"You won't hurt me?" exclaimed Nan, starting up once more.

"O no. I will try to bring you something you will like."

"Don't bring Gerty here with you! I don't want to see her."

"I will come alone," replied Gertrude.

Nan now laid down, and did not speak again while Gertrude remained in the house, though she watched her steadily until she was outside the door. Mr. Cooper made no objection to accompanying his young guide, and, though the severity of the storm was such that they did not escape a thorough wetting, they reached home in safety, in little more than an hour from the time she started on her expedition.

Dr. Jeremy, seated at the side of the grate, with his feet upon the fender, had the contented appearance of one who is quite at home; he seemed, indeed, unconscious that he was waiting for Gertrude's return, or anything else but his own pleasure. He had been talking with Mrs. Sullivan about the people of a country town where they had both passed some time in their childhood, and the timid, retiring woman had, in the course of conversation, come to feel so much at her ease in the society of the social and entertaining physician, that, although he had, in his unguarded discourse, accidentally disclosed his profession, she allowed him to question her upon the state of her health, without any of the alarm she had nervously fancied she should feel at the very sight of a doctor. By the time Gertrude returned, he had made himself well acquainted with the case, and was prepared, on Mrs. Sullivan's leaving the room to provide dry clothes for her father, to report to Gertrude his opinion.

"Gertrude," said he, as soon as the door was shut, "that's a very sick woman."

"Do you think so, Dr. Jeremy?" said Gertrude, much alarmed, and sinking into the nearest chair.

"I do," replied he, thoughtfully. "I wish to mercy I had seen her six months ago!"

"Why, doctor! Do you date her illness so far back as that?"

"Yes, and much further. She has borne up under the gradual progress of a disease which is now, I fear, beyond the aid of medical treatment."

"Dr. Jeremy," said Gertrude, in tones of great distress, "you do not mean to tell me that auntie is going to die, and leave me and her poor old father, and without ever seeing Willie again, too! O, I had hoped it was not nearly so bad as that!"

"Do not be alarmed, Gertrude," said the doctor, kindly. "I did not mean to frighten you;—she may live some time, yet. I can judge better of her case in a day or two. But it is absolutely *unsafe* for you to be here alone with these two friends of yours,—to say nothing of its overtasking your strength. Has not Mrs. Sullivan the means to keep a nurse, or even a domestic? She tells me she has no one."

"Yes, indeed," answered Gerty; "her son supplies her wants most generously. I know that she never draws nearly the whole of the amount he is anxious she should expend."

"Then you must speak to her about getting some one to assist you at once; for, if you do not, *I* shall."

"I intend to," said Gertrude. "I have seen the necessity for some time past; but she has such a dread of strangers that I hated to propose it."

"Nonsense," said the doctor; "that's only imagination in her; she would soon get used to being waited upon."

Mrs. Sullivan now returned, and Gertrude, giving an account of her unexpected rencounter with Nan Grant, begged Dr. Jeremy, who knew the particulars of her own early life, and had frequently heard of Nan, to go the next day and see her. "It will be a visit of charity," said she, "for she is probably penniless, and, though staying with your old patients the Millers, she is but distantly connected, and has no claim upon them. That never makes any difference with you, however, I know very well."

"Not a bit, not a bit," answered the doctor. "I'll go and see her to-night, if the case require it, and to-morrow I shall look in to report how she is, and hear the rest of what Mrs. Sullivan was telling me about her wakeful nights. But, Gertrude, do you go, child, and change your wet shoes and stockings. I shall have you on my hands, next."

Mrs. Sullivan was delighted with Dr. Jeremy, and when he was gone eagerly sounded his praise. "So different," said she, "from common doctors (a portion of humanity for which she seemed to have an unaccountable aversion); so sociable and friendly! Why, I felt, Gertrude, as if I could talk to him about my sickness as freely as I could to you."

Gertrude readily joined in the praises bestowed upon her much-valued friend, and it was tea-time before Mrs. Sullivan was weary of the subject. After the evening meal was over, and Mr. Cooper, much wearied with the fatigues of the day, had been persuaded to retire to rest, while Mrs. Sullivan, comfortably reclining on the sofa, was enjoying what she always termed her happiest hour, Gertrude broached the subject recommended by Dr. Jeremy. Contrary to her expectations, Mrs. Sullivan no longer objected to the proposal of introducing a domestic into the family. She was convinced of her own incompetency to perform any active labor, and was equally opposed to the exertion on Gertrude's part which had, during the last week, been requisite. Gertrude suggested Jane Miller as a girl remarkably well suited to their wants, and it was agreed that she should be applied for on the following morning.

One more glance at Gertrude, and we shall have followed her to the conclusion of the day. She is alone. It is ten o'clock, and the house is still. Mr. Cooper is sound asleep, Gertrude has just listened at his door, and heard his loud breathing. Mrs. Sullivan, under the influence of a soothing draught recommended by Dr. Jeremy, has fallen into an unusually quiet slumber. The little Calcutta birds, ten in number, that occupy a large cage in the window, are nestled, side by side, on their slender perch, in a close, unbroken row, and Gertrude has thrown a warm covering over them, that they may not suffer from the cold night-air. She has locked the doors, made all things safe, fast and comfortable, and now sits down to read, to meditate, and pray. Her trials and cares are multiplying. A great grief stares her in the face, and a great responsibility; but she shrinks not from either. No! on the contrary, she thanks God that she is here; that she had the resolution to forsake pleasure and ease, and, in spite of her own weakness and man's wrath, to place herself in the front of life's battle, and bravely wait its issues. She thanks God that she knows where to look for help; that the bitter sorrows of her childhood and early youth left her not without a witness of His love who can turn darkness into light, and that no weight can now overshadow her whose gloom is not illumined by rays from the throne of God. But, though her heart is brave and her faith firm, she has a woman's tender nature; and, as she sits alone, she weeps—weeps for herself, and for him who, far away in a foreign land, is counting the days, the months and years, which shall restore him to a mother he is destined never to see again. With the recollection, however, that she is to stand in the place of a child to that parent, and that hers is the hand that must soothe the pillow of the invalid, a minister to all her wants, comes the stern necessity of self-control,—a necessity to which Gertrude has long since learned to submit,—and, rallying all her calmness and fortitude, she wipes away the blinding tears, commends herself to Him who is strength to the weak and comfort to the sorrowing, and, soothed by the communion of her spirit with the Father of spirits, she seeks her couch, and, worn out by the varied mental and bodily fatigues of her day's experience, follows the rest of the household to the land of dreams.

## Chapter XXV

*Some say that gleams of a remoter world
Visit the soul in sleep.*

SHELLEY

It was a fortunate thing for Gertrude that Thanksgiving week was approaching, as that was a vacation time at Mr. W.'s school, and she would thus be more at leisure to attend to her multiplied cares. She considered herself favored, too, in obtaining the services of Jane, who willingly consented to come and help Miss Gertrude. She did not, she said, exactly like the idea of living out, but couldn't refuse a young lady who had been so good to them in times past. Gertrude had feared that, with Nan Grant sick in the house, Mrs. Miller would not be able to give up her eldest daughter; but Mary, a second girl, having returned home unexpectedly, one of them could be very conveniently spared. Under Gertude's tuition, Jane, who was neat and capable, was able, after a few days, to relieve Mrs. Sullivan of nearly all her household duties, and so far provide for many of her personal wants as to leave Gertrude at liberty to pay frequent visits to the sick room of Nan, whose fever, having reached its height, rendered her claim for aid at present the most imperative.

We need hardly say that, in Gertrude's still vivid recollection of her former sufferings under the rule of Nan, there remained nothing of bitterness or a spirit of revenge. If she remembered the past, it was only to pity and forgive her persecutor; if she meditated upon the course she should herself pursue towards her once hated tyrant, it was only to revolve in her mind how she could best serve and comfort her.

Therefore, night after night found her watching by the bed-side of the sick woman, who, though still delirious, had entirely lost the fear and dread she had at first seemed to feel at her presence. Nan talked much of little Gerty,—sometimes in a way that led Gertrude to believe herself recognized, but more frequently as if the child were supposed to be absent; and it was not until a long time after that Gertrude was led to adopt the correct supposition, which was, that she had been mistaken for her mother, whom she much resembled, and whom, though tended in her last sickness by Nan herself, the fevered, diseased, and conscience-stricken sufferer believed had come back to claim her child at her hands. It was only the continued assurances of good-will on Gertrude's part, and her unwearied efforts to soothe and comfort her, that finally led Nan to the belief that the injured mother had found her child in health and safety, and was ignorant of the wrongs and unkindness she had endured.

One night—it was the last of Nan's life—Gertrude, who had scarcely left her during the previous day, and was still maintaining her watch, heard her own name mingled with those of others in a few rapid sentences. She approached the bed and listened intently, for she was always in hopes, during these partly incoherent ravings, to gain some information concerning her own early life. Her name was not repeated, however, and for some time the muttering of Nan's voice was indistinct. Then, suddenly starting up and addressing herself to some imaginary person, she shouted aloud, "Stephie! Stephie! give me back the watch, and tell me what you did with the rings!—They will ask—those folks!—and what shall I tell them?" Then, after a pause, during which her eyes were fixed steadily upon the wall, she said, in a more feeble but equally earnest voice, "No, no, Stephie, I never'll tell.—I *never, never* will!" The moment the words had left her lips, she started, turned, saw Gertrude standing by the bed-side, and, with a frightened look, shrieked, rather than asked, "Did you hear? Did you hear?—You did," continued she, "and you'll tell! O, if you *do!*" She was here preparing to spring from the bed, but, overcome with exhaustion, sunk back on the pillow. Summoning both Mr. and Mrs. Miller, who, half expecting to be called up during the night, had lain down in the next room, the agitated Gertrude, believing that her own presence was too exciting, left the now dying woman to their care, and sought in another part of the house to calm her disturbed mind and disordered nerves. Learning, about an hour afterwards, from Mrs. Miller, that Nan had become comparatively calm, but was utterly prostrated in strength, and seemed near her end, Gertrude thought it best not to enter the room again; and, sitting down by the kitchen-stove, pondered in her mind the strange scene she had witnessed. Day was just dawning when Mrs. Miller came to tell her that Nan had breathed her last.

Gerty's work of mercy, forgiveness and Christian love, being thus finished, she hastened home to recruit her wasted strength, and fortify herself, as she best might, for the labor and suffering yet in store for her.

And it was no ordinary strength and fortitude that she needed to sustain her through a period such as persons in this world are often called upon to meet, when scenes of suffering, sickness and death, follow each other in such quick succession, that, ere one shock can be recovered from, and composure of mind restored, another blow comes to add its force to the already overwhelming torrent. In less than three weeks from the time of Nan Grant's death, Paul Cooper was smitten by the destroyer's hand, and, after a brief illness, he, too, was laid to his last rest; and though the deepest feelings of Gertrude's heart were not in either case fully awakened, it was no slight call upon the mental and physical endurance of a girl of eighteen to bear up under the self-imposed duties occasioned by each event, and that, too, at a time when her mind was racked by the apprehension of a new and far more intense grief. Emily's absence was also a sore trial to her, for she was accustomed to rely upon her for advice and counsel, and, in seasons of peculiar distress, to learn patience and submission from one who was herself a living exemplification of both virtues. Only one letter had been received from the travelers, and that, written by Mrs. Ellis, contained little that was satisfactory. It was written from Havana, where they were boarding in a house kept by an American lady, and crowded with visitors from Boston, New York, and other northern cities.

"It an't so very pleasant, after all, Gertrude," wrote Mrs. Ellis, "and I only wish we were safe home again; and not on my own account, either, so much as Emily's. She feels kind of strange here; and no wonder, for it's a dreadful uncomfortable sort of a place. The windows have no glass about them, but are grated just like a prison; and there is not a carpet in the house, nor a fireplace, though sometimes the mornings are quite cold. There's a *widder* here, with a brother and some nieces. The widder is a flaunting kind of a woman, that I begin to think, if you'll believe it, is either setting her cap for Mr. Graham, or means to make an old fool of him. She is one of your loud-talking women, that dress up a good deal, and like to take the lead; and Mr. Graham is just silly enough to follow after her party, and go to all sorts of rides and excursions;—it's so *ridiculous,*— and he over sixty-five years old! Emily and I have pretty much done going into the parlor, for these gay folks don't take any sort of notice of us. Emily doesn't say a word, or complain a bit, but I know she is not happy here, and would be glad to be back in Boston; and so should I, if it wasn't for that horrid steamboat. I liked to have died with sea-sickness, Gertrude, coming out; and I dread going home so, that I don't know what to do."

Gertrude wrote frequently to Emily; but, as Miss Graham was dependent upon Mrs. Ellis' eye-sight, and the letters must, therefore, be subject to her scrutiny, she could not express her innermost thoughts and feelings as she was wont to do in conversation with her sympathizing and indulgent friend.

Every India mail brought news from William Sullivan, who, prosperous in business, and rendered happy, even in his exile, by the belief that the friends he loved best were in the enjoyment of the fruits of his exertions, wrote always in his accustomed strain of cheerfulness.

One Sabbath afternoon, a few weeks after Mr. Cooper's death, found Gertrude with an open letter in her hand, the numerous postmarks upon the outside of which proclaimed from whence it came. It had that day been received, and Mrs. Sullivan, as she lay stretched upon her couch, had been listening for the third time to the reading of its contents. The bright hopes expressed by her son, and the gay tone in which he wrote, all unconscious, as he yet was, of the cloud of sorrow that was gathering for him, formed so striking a contrast to her own reflections, that she lay with her eyes closed, and oppressed with an unwonted degree of sadness; while Gertrude, as she glanced at the passage in which Willie dilated upon the "joy of once more clasping in his arms the dear little mother whom he so longed to see again," and then turned her gaze upon the wasted form and faded cheek of that mother, felt an indescribable chill at her heart. Dr. Jeremy's first fears were all confirmed, and, her disease still further aggravated by the anxiety and agitation which attended her father's sickness and death, Mrs. Sullivan was rapidly passing away.

Whether she were herself aware that this was the case, Gertrude had not yet been able to determine. She had never spoken upon the subject, or intimated in any manner a conviction of her approaching end; and Gertrude, as she surveyed her placid countenance, was almost inclined to believe that she was yet deceiving herself with the expectation of recovery.

All doubt on this point was soon removed; for, after remaining a short time engaged in deep thought, or perhaps in prayer, Mrs. Sullivan opened her eyes, fixed them upon her young attendant, and said, in a calm, distinct voice,

"Gertrude, I shall never see Willie again!"

Gertrude made no reply.

"I wish to write and tell him so myself," she continued; "or, rather, if you will write for me, as you have done so many times already, I should like to tell you what to say; and I feel that no time is to be lost, for I am failing fast, and may not long have strength enough left to do it. It will devolve upon you, my child, to let him know when all is over; but you have had too many sad duties already, and it will spare you somewhat to have me prepare him to hear bad news. Will you commence a letter to-day?"

"Certainly, auntie, if you think it best."

"I do, Gerty. What you wrote by the last mail was chiefly concerning grandpa's sickness and death; and there was nothing mentioned which would be likely to alarm him on my account, was there?"

"Nothing at all."

"Then it is quite time he should be forewarned, poor boy! I do not need Dr. Jeremy to tell me that I am dying."

"Did he tell you so?" asked Gertrude, as she went to her desk, and began to arrange her writing-materials.

"No, Gerty! he was too prudent for that; but I told him, and he did not contradict me. You have known it some time, have you not?" inquired she, gazing earnestly in the face of Gertrude, who had returned to the couch, and, seated upon the edge of it, was bending over the invalid, and smoothing the hair from her forehead.

"Some weeks," replied Gertrude, as she spoke imprinting a kiss upon the pale brow of the sufferer.

"Why did you not tell me?"

"Why should I, dear auntie?" said Gertrude, her voice trembling with emotion. "I knew the Lord could never call you at a time when your lamp would not be trimmed and burning."

"Feebly, it burns feebly!" said the humble Christian.

"Whose, then, is bright," responded Gertrude, "if yours be dim? Have you not, for years past, been a living lesson of piety and patience? Unless it be Emily, auntie, I know of no one who seems so fit for heaven."

"O, no, Gerty! I am a sinful creature, full of weakness; much as I long to meet my Saviour, my earthly heart pines with the vain desire for one more sight of my boy, and all my dreams of heaven are mingled with the aching regret that the one blessing I most craved on earth has been denied me."

"O, auntie!" exclaimed Gertrude, "we are all human! Until the mortal puts on immortality, how *can* you cease to think of Willie, and long for his presence in this trying hour? It cannot be a sin,—that which is so natural!"

"I do not know, Gerty; perhaps it is not; and, if it be, I trust, before I go hence, I shall be blessed with a spirit of perfect submission, that will atone for the occasional murmuring of a mother's heart! Read to me, my dear, some holy words of comfort; you always seem to open the good book at the passage I most need. It is sinful, indeed, in me, Gertrude, to indulge the least repining, blessed as I am in the love and care of one who is dear to me as a daughter!"

Gertrude took her Bible, and, opening it at the Gospel of St. Mark, her eye fell at once upon the account of our Saviour's agony in the garden of Gethsemane. She rightly believed that nothing could be more appropriate to Mrs. Sullivan's state of mind than the touching description of the struggle of our Lord's humanity; nothing more likely to soothe her spirit, and reconcile her to the occasional rebellion of her own mortal nature, than the evident contest of the human with the divine so thrillingly narrated by the disciple; and that nothing could be more inspiring than the example of that holy Son of God, who ever to His thrice-repeated prayer that, if possible, the cup might pass from him, added the pious ejaculation, "Thy will, not mine, be done." Without hesitation, therefore, she read what first met her glance, and had the satisfaction of seeing that the words were not without effect; for, when she had finished, she observed that as Mrs. Sullivan lay still and calm upon her couch, her lips seemed to be repeating the Saviour's prayer. Not wishing to disturb her meditations, Gertrude made no reference to the proposed letter to Willie, but sat in perfect silence, and about half an hour afterward Mrs. Sullivan fell asleep. It was a gentle, quiet slumber, and Gertrude sat and watched with pleasure the peaceful, happy expression of her features. Darkness had come on before she awoke, and so shrouded the room that Gertrude, who still sat there, was invisible in the gloom. She started, on hearing her name, and, hastily lighting a candle, approached the couch.

"O, Gertrude!" said Mrs. Sullivan, "I have had such a beautiful dream! Sit down by me, my dear, and let me tell it to you; it could not have been more vivid, if it had all been reality. I thought I was sailing rapidly through the air, and, for some time, I seemed to float on and on, over clouds and among bright stars. The motion was so gentle that I did not grow weary, though in my journey I travelled over land and sea. At last I saw beneath me a beautiful city, with churches, towers, monuments, and throngs of gay people moving in every direction. As I drew nearer, I could distinguish the faces of these numerous men and women, and among them, in a crowded street, there was one who looked like Willie. I followed him, and soon felt sure it was he. He looked older than when we saw him last, and much as I have always imagined him, since the descriptions he has given in his letters of the change that has taken place in his appearance. I followed him through several streets, and at last he turned into a fine, large building, which stood near the centre of the city. I went in also. We passed through large halls and beautifully-furnished rooms, and at last stood in a dining-saloon, in the middle of which was a table covered with bottles, glasses, and the remains of a rich dessert, such as I never saw before. There was a group of young men round the table, all well dressed, and some of them fine-looking, so that at first I was quite charmed with their appearance. I seemed, however, to have a strange power of looking into their hearts, and detecting all the evil there was there. One had a very bright, intelligent face, and might have been thought a man of talent.—and so he was; but I could see better than people usually can, and I perceived, by a sort of instinct, that all his mind and genius were converted into a means of duping and deceiving those who were so foolish or so ignorant as to be ensnared; and, in a corner of his pocket, I knew he had a pair of loaded dice.

"Another seemed by his wit and drollery to be the charm of the company; but I could detect marks of intoxication, and felt a certainty that in less than an hour he would cease to be the master of his own actions.

"A third was making a vain attempt to look happy; but his very soul was bared to my searching gaze, and I was aware of the fact that he had the day before lost at the gaming-table all his own and a part of his employer's money, and was tortured with anxiety lest he might not this evening be fortunate enough to win it back.

"There were many others present, and all, more or less sunk in dissipation, had reached various stages on the road to ruin. Their faces, however, looked animated and gay, and, as Willie glanced from one to another, he seemed pleased and attracted.

"One of them offered him a seat at the table, and all urged him to take it. He did so, and the young man at his right filled a glass with bright wine and handed it to him. He hesitated, then took it and raised it to his lips. Just then I touched him on the shoulder. He turned, saw me, and instantly the glass fell from his hand and was broken into a thousand pieces. I beckoned, and he immediately rose and followed me. The gay circle he had left called loudly upon him to return; one of them even laid a hand upon his arm, and tried to detain him; but he would not listen or stay—he shook off the hand that would have held him, and we went on. Before we had got outside the building, the man whom I had first noticed, and whom I knew to be the most artful of the company, came out from a room near the door, which he had reached by some other direction, and, approaching Willie, whispered in his ear. Willie faltered, turned, and would perhaps have gone back; but I placed myself in front of him, held up my finger menacingly, and shook my head. He hesitated no longer, but, flinging aside the tempter, rushed out of the door, and was down the long flight of steps before I could overtake him. I seemed, however, to move with great rapidity, and soon found myself taking the lead, and guiding my son through the intricate, crowded streets of the city. Many were the adventures we encountered, many the snares we found laid for the unwary in every direction. More than once my watchful eye saved the thoughtless boy by my side from some pitfall or danger, into which, without me, he would have surely fallen. Occasionally I lost sight of him, and was obliged to turn back; now he had been separated from me by the crowd, and consequently missed his way, and now he had purposely lingered to witness or join in the amusements of the gay populace. Each time, however, he listened to my warning voice, and we went on in safety.

"At last, however, in passing through a brilliantly-lighted street,—for it was now evening,—I suddenly observed that he was absent from my side. I went backwards and forwards, but he was nowhere to be seen. For an hour I hunted the streets, and called him by name; but there was no answer. I then unfolded my wings, and, soaring high above the crowded town, surveyed the whole, hoping that in that one glance I might, as I had at first done, detect my boy.

"I was not disappointed. In a gorgeous hall, dazzlingly lit, and filled with gayety and fashion, I beheld Willie. A brilliant young creature was leaning on his arm, and I saw into her heart, and knew that she was not blind to his beauty or insensible to his attractions. But, O! I trembled for him now! She was lovely and rich, and it was evident to me, from the elegance of her dress and the attention she attracted, that she was also fashionable and admired. I saw into her soul, however, and she was vain, proud, cold-hearted and worldly; and, if she loved Willie, it was his beauty, his winning manners, and his smile that pleased her—not his noble nature, which she knew not how to prize. As they promenaded through the hall, and she, whom crowds were praising, gave all her time and thoughts to him, I, descending in an invisible shape, and standing by his side, touched his shoulder, as I had done before. He looked around, but, before he could see his mother's face, the siren's voice attracted all his attention. Again and again I endeavored to win him away; but he heard me not. At length she spoke some word that betrayed to my high-minded boy the folly and selfishness of her worldly soul. I seized the moment when she had thus weakened her hold upon him, and, clasping him in my arms, spread my wings and soared far, far away, bearing with me the prize I had toiled after and won. As we rose into the air, my manly son became in my encircling arms a child again, and there rested on my bosom the same little head, with its soft, silken curls, that had nestled there in infancy. Back we flew, over sea and land, and paused not until on a soft, grassy slope, under the shade of green trees, I thought I saw my darling Gerty, and was flying to lay my precious boy at her feet, when I awoke, pronouncing your name.

"And now, Gertrude, the bitterness of the cup I am called upon to drink is passed away. A blessed angel has indeed ministered unto me. I no longer wish to see my son again on earth, for I am persuaded that my departure is in perfect accordance with the schemes of a merciful Providence. I now believe that Willie's living mother might be powerless to turn him from temptation and evil; but the spirit of that mother will be mighty still, and in the thought that she, in her home beyond the skies, is ever watching around his path, and striving to lead him in the straight and narrow way, he may find a truer shield from danger, a firmer rest to his tempted soul, than she could have been while yet on earth. Now, O my Father, I can say, from the depths of my heart, 'Thy will, not mine, be done!' "

From this time until her death, which took place about a month afterward, Mrs. Sullivan's mind remained in a state of perfect resignation and tranquillity. As she said, the last pang had lost its bitterness. In the letter which she dictated to Willie, she expressed her perfect trust in the goodness and wisdom of Providence, and exhorted him to cherish the same submissive love for the All-wise. She reminded him of the early lessons she had taught him, the piety and self-command which she had inculcated, and made it her dying prayer that her influence might be increased, rather than diminished, and her presence felt to be a continual reality. She gave the important caution to one who had faithfully struggled with adversity, to beware of the dangers and snares which attend prosperity, and besought him never to discredit or disgrace his childhood's training.

After Gertrude had folded the letter, which she supposed completed, and left the house to attend to those duties in school which she still continued regularly to perform, Mrs. Sullivan reöpened the nearly-covered sheet, and, with her own feeble and trembling hand, recounted the disinterested, patient, loving devotion of Gertrude. "So long," said she, "my son, as you cherish in your heart the memory of your grandfather and mother, cease not to bestow all the gratitude of which that heart is capable upon one whose praises my hand is too feeble to portray."

So slow and gradual was the decline of Mrs. Sullivan, that her death at last came as an unexpected blow to Gertrude, who, though she saw the ravages of disease, could not realize that a termination must come to their work.

In the dead hours of the night, with no one to sustain and encourage her but the frightened and trembling Jane, did she watch the departing spirit of her much-loved friend. "Are you afraid to see me die, Gertrude?" asked Mrs. Sullivan, about an hour before her death. On Gertrude's answering that she was not,—"Then turn me a little towards you," said she, "that your face, my darling, may be the last to me of earth."

It was done, and, with her hand locked fast in Gertrude's, and a look that spoke of the deepest affection, she expired.

⁂⁂⁂⁂⁂⁂⁂⁂⁂⁂⁂⁂⁂⁂⁂⁂⁂⁂⁂⁂⁂⁂⁂⁂

## Chapter XXVI

*But, whatsoe'er the weal or woe*
*That Heaven across her lot might throw,*
*Full well her Christian spirit knew*
*Its path of virtue, straight and true.*
                    JOANNA BAILLIE

Not until her work of love was thus ended did Gertrude become conscious that the long continuance of her labors by night and day had worn upon her frame and utterly exhausted her strength. For a week after Mrs. Sullivan was laid in her grave, Dr. Jeremy was seriously apprehensive of a severe illness for Gertrude. But, after struggling with her dangerous symptoms for several days, she rallied, and, though still pale and worn by care and anxiety, was able to resume her classes at school, and make arrangements for providing herself with another home.

Several homes had been already offered to her, several urgent invitations given, with a warmth and cordiality which made it difficult to decline their acceptance; but Gertrude, though deeply touched by the kindness thus manifested towards her in her loneliness and desolation, preferred to abide by her previously formed resolution to seek for herself a permanent boarding-place, and, when the grounds on which she based her decision were understood by her friends, they approved her course, ceased to importune her, and manifested a sincere wish to be of service, by lending their aid to the furtherance of her plans.

Mrs. Jeremy was at first disposed to feel hurt and wounded by Gertrude's refusal to come to them without delay, and consider herself established for any length of time that she chose to remain; and the doctor himself was so peremptory with his, "Come, Gertrude, come right home with us—don't say a word!" that she was afraid lest, in her weak state of health, she should be actually carried off, without a *chance* to remonstrate. But, after he had taken upon himself to give Jane orders about packing her clothes and sending them after her, and then locking up the house and going home herself, he gave Gertrude an opportunity to expostulate, and present her reasons for wishing to decline the generous proposal.

All her reasoning upon general principles, however, proved insufficient to convince the warm-hearted couple. "It was all nonsense about independent position. She would be perfectly independent with them, and her company would be such a pleasure that she need feel no hesitation in accepting their offer, and might be sure she would herself be conferring a favor, instead of being the party obliged." At last she was compelled to make use of an argument which had greatly influenced her own mind, and would, she felt sure, carry no little weight with it in the doctor's estimation.

"Dr. Jeremy," said she, "I hope you will not condemn in me a motive which has, I confess, strengthened my firmness in this matter. I should be unwilling to mention it, if I did not know that you are so far acquainted with the state of affairs between Mr. Graham and myself as to understand, and perhaps in some degree sympathize with, my feelings. You know that he was opposed to my leaving them and remaining here this winter; and must suspect that, when we parted, there was not a perfectly good understanding between us. He hinted that I should never be able to support myself, and should be driven to a life of dependence; and, since the salary which I receive from Mr. W. is sufficient for all my wants, I am anxious to be so situated, on Mr. Graham's return, that he will perceive that my assurance, or boast (if I must call it so), that I could earn my own living, was not without foundation."

"So Graham thought that, without his sustaining power, you would soon come to beggary—did he? With your talents, too!—that's just like him!"

"O, no, no!" replied Gertrude, "I did not say that; but I seemed to him a mere child, and he did not realize that, in giving me an education, he had, as it were, paid my expenses in advance. It was very natural he should distrust my capacity—he had never seen me compelled to exert myself."

"I understand—I understand," said the doctor. "He thought you would be glad enough to come back to them;—yes, yes, just like him!"

"Well, now," said Mrs. Jeremy, "I don't believe he thought any such thing. He was provoked, and didn't mind what he said. Ten to one he will never think of it again, and it seems to me it is only a kind of pride in Gertrude to care anything about it."

"I don't know that, wife," said the doctor. "If it *is* pride, it's an honorable pride, that I like; and I am not sure but, if I were in Gertrude's place, I should feel just as she does; so I shan't urge her to do any other ways than she proposes. She can have a boarding-place, and yet spend a good share of her time with us, what with running in and out, coming to spend days, and so on; and she doesn't need to be told that, in case of any sickness or trouble, our doors are always open to her."

"No, indeed," said Mrs. Jeremy; "and, if you feel set about it, Gerty dear, I am sure I shall want you to do whatever pleases you best; but one thing I do insist on, and that is, that you leave this house, which must look dreary enough to you now, this very day, go home with me, and stay until you get recruited."

Gertrude, gladly consenting to a short visit, compromised the matter by accompanying them without delay; and it was chiefly owing to the doctor's persevering skill and care bestowed upon his young guest, and the kind and motherly nursing of Mrs. Jeremy, that she escaped the illness which had so severely threatened her.

Mr. and Mrs. W., who had felt great sympathy for Gertrude, in consequence of the acquaintance they had had with the trying nature of her winter's experience, pressed her to come to their house, and remain until the return of Mr. Graham and Emily; but, on being assured by her that she was quite unaware of the period of their absence, and should not probably reside with them for the future, they were satisfied that she acted with wisdom and judgment in at once providing herself with an independent situation.

Mr. and Mrs. Arnold, who had been constant in their attentions both to Mrs. Sullivan and Gertrude, and were the only persons, except the physician, who had been admitted to the sick room of the invalid, felt that they had a peculiar claim to the guardianship and care of the doubly-orphaned girl, and were not slow to urge upon her to become a member of their household, and accept of their protection, limiting their invitation, as the W.'s had done, to the time when Emily should be back from the south. Mr. Arnold's family, however, being large, and his house and salary small in proportion, true benevolence alone prompted this proposal; and, on Gertrude's acquainting his economical and prudent wife with the ample means she enjoyed from her own exertions, and the decision she had formed of procuring an independent home, she received the warm approbation of both, and found in the latter an excellent adviser and assistant.

Mrs. Arnold had a widowed sister, who was in the habit of adding to her moderate income by receiving into her family, as boarders, a few young ladies, who came to the city for purposes of education. Gertrude did not know this lady personally, but had heard her warmly praised; and she indulged the hope that, through her friend, the clergyman's wife, she might obtain with her an agreeable and not too expensive residence. In this she was not disappointed. Mrs. Warren had fortunately vacant, at this time, a large and cheerful front chamber; and, Mrs. Arnold having recommended Gertrude in the warmest manner, suitable terms were agreed upon, and the room immediately placed at her disposal. Mrs. Sullivan had bequeathed to her all her furniture, a part of which had lately been purchased, and was, in accordance with Willie's injunctions, most excellent, both in material and workmanship; and Mrs. Arnold and her two eldest daughters insisted that, in consideration of her recent fatigue and bereavement, she should consent to attend only to her school duties, and leave to them the task of furnishing her room with such articles as she preferred to have placed there, and superintending the packing away of all other movables; for Gertrude was unwilling that anything should be sold. It was a great relief to be thus spared the cruel trial of seeing the house her lost friend had taken so much pleasure and pride in stripped and left desolate; and though, on first entering her apartment at Mrs. Warren's, a deep sadness crept into her heart at the sight of the familiar furniture, she could not but think, as she observed the neatness, care and taste, with which everything had been arranged for her reception, that it would be a sin to repine and call one's self wretched and alone in a world which contained hearts so quick to feel, and hands so ready to labor, as those that had interested themselves for her.

On entering the dining-room the first evening after she took up her residence at Mrs. Warren's, she expected to meet only strangers at the tea-table, but was agreeably disappointed at the sight of Fanny Bruce, who, left in Boston while her mother and brother were spending the winter travelling, had now been several weeks an inmate of Mrs. Warren's house. Fanny was a school-girl, twelve or thirteen years of age; and having, for some summers past, been a near neighbor to Gertrude, had been in the habit of seeing her frequently at Mr. Graham's, had sometimes begged flowers from her, borrowed books, and obtained assistance in her fancy-work. She admired Gertrude exceedingly; had hailed with great delight the prospect of knowing her better, as she hoped to do at Mrs. Warren's; and when she met the gaze of her large, dark eyes, and saw a smile of pleasure overspread her countenance at the sight of a familiar face, she felt emboldened to come forward, shake hands, and beg that Miss Flint would sit next her at the table.

Fanny Bruce was a girl of good disposition and warm heart, but she had been much neglected by her mother, whose chief pride was in her son, the same Ben of whom we have previously spoken. She had often been left behind in some boarding-house, while her pleasure-loving mother and indolent brother passed their time in journeying; and had not always been so fortunately situated as at present. A sense of loneliness, a want of sympathy in any of her pursuits, had been a source of great unhappiness to the poor child, who labored under the painful consciousness that but little interest was felt by any one in her improvement or happiness.

Gertrude had not been long at Mrs. Warren's before she observed that Fanny occupied an isolated position in the family. She was a few years younger than her companions, three dressy misses, who could not condescend to admit her into their clique; and Mrs. Warren's time was so much engrossed by household duties that she took but little notice of her. Her apparent loneliness could not fail to excite the compassion of one who was herself suffering from recent sorrow and bereavement; and, although the quiet and privacy of her own room were, at this time, grateful to Gertrude's feelings, pity for poor Fanny induced her to invite her frequently to come and sit with her, and she often so far forgot her own griefs as to exert herself in providing entertainment for her young visitor, who, on her part, considered it privilege enough to share Gertrude's retirement, read her books, and feel confident of her friendship. During the month of March, which was unusually stormy, Fanny spent almost every evening with Gertrude; and she, who at first felt that she was making a sacrifice of her own comfort and ease by giving another such constant access to her apartment, came, at last, to realize the force of Uncle True's prophecy, that, in her efforts for the happiness of others, she would at last find her own; for Fanny's lively and often amusing conversation drew Gertrude from the contemplation of her trials, and the interest and affection she awakened saved her from the painful consciousness of her solitary situation.

April arrived, and still no further news from Emily. Gertrude's heart ached with a vain longing to once more pour out her griefs on the bosom of that dear friend, and find in her consolation, encouragement, and support. She longed to tell her how many times during the winter she had sighed for the gentle touch of the soft hand which was wont to rest so lovingly on her head, the sound of that sweet voice whose very tones were comforting. For some time Gertrude wrote regularly, but of late she had not known where to direct her letters; and since Mrs. Sullivan's death there had been no communication between her and the travellers. She was sitting at her window, one evening, thinking of that group of friends whom she had loved with a daughter's and a sister's love, and who were now separated from her by distance, or that greater barrier, death, when she was summoned below stairs to see Mr. Arnold and his daughter Anne.

After the usual civilities and inquiries, Miss Arnold turned to Gertrude and said, "Of course you have heard the news, Gertrude?"

"No," replied Gertrude, "I have heard nothing special."

"What!" exclaimed Mr. Arnold, "have you not heard of Mr. Graham's marriage?"

Gertrude started up in surprise. "Do you really mean so, Mr. Arnold? Mr. Graham married! When? To whom?"

"To the widow Holbrook, a sister-in-law of Mr. Clinton's; she has been staying at Havana with a party from the north, and the Grahams met her there."

"But, Gertrude," asked Miss Arnold, "how does it happen you had not heard of it? It is in all the newspapers—'Married in New Orleans, J. H. Graham, Esq., of Boston, to Mrs. Somebody or other Holbrook.' "

"I have not seen a newspaper for a day or two," replied Gertrude.

"And Miss Graham's blindness, I suppose, prevents her writing," said

Anne; "but I should have thought Mr. Graham would have sent wedding compliments."

Gertrude made no reply, and Miss Arnold continued, laughingly, "I suppose his bride engrosses all his attention."

"Do you know anything of this Mrs. Holbrook?" asked Gertrude.

"Not much," answered Mr. Arnold. "I have seen her occasionally at Mr. Clinton's. She is a handsome, showy woman, fond of society, I should think."

"I have seen her very often," said Anne. "She is a coarse, noisy, dashing person,—just the one to make Miss Emily miserable."

Gertrude looked distressed, and Mr. Arnold glanced reprovingly at his daughter.

"Anne," said he, "are you sure you speak advisedly?"

"Belle Clinton is my authority, father. I only judge from what I used to hear her say at school about her Aunt *Bella,* as she always used to call her."

"Did Isabel represent her aunt so unfavorably?"

"Not intentionally," replied Anne; "she meant the greatest praise, but I never liked anything she told us about her."

"We will not condemn her until we can decide upon acquaintance," said Mr. Arnold, mildly; "perhaps she will prove the very reverse of what you suppose her."

"Can you tell me anything concerning Emily?" asked Gertrude, "and whether Mr. Graham is soon to return?"

"Nothing," said Miss Arnold. "I have seen only the notice in the papers. When did you hear from them yourself?"

Gertrude mentioned the date of her letter from Mrs. Ellis, the account she had given of a gay party from the north, and suggested the probability that the present Mrs. Graham was the widow she had described.

"The same, undoubtedly," said Mr. Arnold.

Their knowledge of facts was so slight, however, that little remained to be said concerning the marriage, and other topics of conversation were introduced. But Gertrude found it impossible to give her thoughts to any other subject; the matter was one of such vital importance to Emily, that her mind constantly recurred to it, and she found it difficult to keep pace with Anne Arnold's rapidly-flowing words and ideas. The necessity which at last arose of replying to a question which she had not at all understood was fortunately obviated by the sudden entrance of Dr. and Mrs. Jeremy. The former held in his hand a sealed letter, directed to Gertrude, in the handwriting of Mr. Graham; and, as he handed it to her, he rubbed his hands, and, looking at Anne Arnold, exclaimed, "Now, Miss Anne, we shall hear all about these famous nuptials!"

Finding her visitors thus eager to learn the contents of her letter, Gertrude dispensed with ceremony, broke the seal, and hastily perused its contents.

The envelope contained two or three pages closely written by Mrs. Ellis, and also a somewhat lengthy note from Mr. Graham. Surprised as Gertrude was at any communication from one who had parted from her in anger, her strongest desire was to hear particularly from Emily, and she therefore gave the preference to the housekeeper's document, that being most likely to contain the desired information. It ran as follows:

*"New York, March 31, 1852*

"DEAR GERTRUDE: As there were plenty of Boston folks at the wedding, I daresay you have heard before this of Mr. Graham's marriage. He married the widder Holbrook, the same I wrote you about. She was determined to have him, and she's got him. I don't hesitate to say he's got the worst of the bargain. He likes a quiet life, and he's lost his chance of that,—poor man!—for she's the greatest hand for company that ever I saw. She followed Mr. Graham up pretty well at Havana, but I guess he thought better of it, and didn't really mean to have her. When we got to New Orleans, however, she was there; and the long and short of it is, she carried her point, and married him. Emily behaved beautifully; she never said a word against it, and always treated the widder as pleasantly as could be; but, dear me! how will our Emily get along with so many young folks as there are about all the time now, and so much noise and confusion? For my part, I an't used to it, and don't pretend that I think it's agreeable. The new lady is civil enough to me, now she's married. I daresay she thinks it stands her in hand, as long as she's one of the family, and I've been in it so long. But I suppose you've been wondering what had become of us, Gertrude, and will be surprised to find we've got so far as New York, on our way home,—*my* way home, I should say, for I'm the only one that talks of coming at present. The truth is, I kept meaning to write while we were in New Orleans, but there was so much going on I didn't get a chance; and, after that horrid steamboat from Charleston here, I wasn't good for anything for a week. But Emily was so anxious to have you written to that I couldn't put it off any longer than until to-day. Poor Emily isn't very well; I don't mean that she's downright sick,—it's low spirits and nervousness, I suppose, more than anything. She gets tired and worried very quick, and is easily startled and disturbed, which didn't use to be the case. I think likely it's the new wife, and all the nieces, and other disagreeable things. She never complains, and nobody would know but what she was pleased to have her father married again; but she hasn't seemed quite happy all winter, and now it troubles me to see how sad she looks sometimes. She talks a sight about you, and felt dreadfully not to get any more letters. To come to the principal thing, however, they are all going to Europe,—Emily and all. I take it it's the new wife's idea; but, whoever proposed the thing, it's all settled now. Mr. Graham wanted me to go, but I would not hear of such a thing; I would as soon be hung as venture on the sea again, and I told him so, up and down. So now he has written for you to go with Emily; and, if you are not afraid of sea-sickness, I hope you won't refuse, for it would be dreadful for her to have a stranger, and you know she always needs somebody, on account of her blindness. I do not think she has the least wish to go; but she would not ask to be left behind, for fear her father should think she did not like the new wife.

"As soon as they sail,—which will be the last of April,—I shall come back to the house in D——, and see to things there while they are away. I am going to write a postscript to you from Emily, and I believe I will add nothing more myself, except that we shall be very impatient to hear your answer; and I must say once more that I hope you will not refuse to go with Emily.

"Yours, very truly,

"SARAH H. ELLIS."

The postscript contained the following:

"I need not tell my darling Gertrude how much I have missed her, and longed to have her with me again; how I have thought of her by night and day, and prayed God to strengthen and fit her for her many trials and labors. The letter written soon after Mr. Cooper's death, is the last that has reached me, and I do not know whether Mrs. Sullivan is still living. Write to me at once, my dear child, if you cannot come to us. Father will tell you of our plans, and ask you to accompany us to Europe; my heart will be light if I can take my dear Gerty with me, but not if she leave any other duty behind. I trust to you, my love, to decide aright. You have heard of father's marriage. It is a great change for us all, but will, I trust, result in happiness. Mrs. Graham has two nieces who are with us at the hotel. They are to be of our party to go abroad, and are, I understand, very beautiful girls, especially Belle Clinton, whom you have seen in Boston some years ago. Mrs. Ellis is very tired of writing, and I must close with assuring my dearest Gertrude of the devoted affection of

EMILY GRAHAM."

It was with great curiosity that Gertrude unfolded Mr. Graham's epistle: she thought it would be awkward for him to address her, and wondered much whether he would maintain his severe and authoritative tone, or condescend to explain and apologize. Had she known him better, she would have been assured that nothing would ever induce him to do the latter, for he was one of those persons who never believe themselves in the wrong. The letter ran thus:

"MISS GERTRUDE FLINT: I am married, and intend to go abroad on the 28th of April; my daughter will accompany us, and, as Mrs. Ellis dreads the sea, I am induced to propose that you join us in New York, and attend the party, as a companion to Emily. I have not forgotten the ingratitude with which you once slighted a similar offer on my part, and nothing would compel me to give you another opportunity to manifest such a spirit, but a desire to promote the happiness of Emily, and a sincere wish to be of service to a young person who has been in my family so long that I feel a friendly interest in providing for her. I thus put it in your power, by complying with our wishes, to do away from my mind the recollection of your past behavior; and, if you choose to return to us, I shall enable you to maintain the place and appearance of a lady. As we sail the last of the month, it is important you should be here in the course of a fortnight; and, if you will write and name the day, I will myself meet you at the boat. Mrs. Ellis being anxious to return to Boston, I hope you will come as soon as possible. As you will be obliged to incur expenses, I enclose a sum of money sufficient to cover them. If you have contracted debts, let me know to what amount, and I will see that all is made right before you leave. Trusting to your being now come to a sense of your duty, I am ready to subscribe myself your friend, J. H. GRAHAM."

Gertrude was sitting near a lamp whose light fell directly upon her face, which, as she glanced over Mr. Graham's note, flushed crimson with wounded pride. Dr. Jeremy, who was watching her countenance, observed that she changed color; and during the few minutes that Mr. and Miss Arnold staid to hear the news he gave an occasional glance of defiance at the letter, and as soon as they were gone begged to be made acquainted with its contents, assuring Gertrude that if she did not let him know what Graham said, he should believe it a thousand times more insulting than it really was.

"He writes," said Gertrude, "to invite me to accompany them to Europe."

"Indeed!" said Dr. Jeremy, with a low whistle, "and he thinks you'll be silly enough to pack up and start off at a minute's notice!"

"Why, Gerty," said Mrs. Jeremy, "you'll like to go, shan't you, dear? It will be delightful."

"Delightful nonsense! Mrs. Jerry," exclaimed the doctor. "What is there delightful, I want to know, in travelling about with an arrogant old tyrant, his blind daughter, upstart, dashy wife, and her two fine-lady nieces? A pretty position Gertrude would be in, a slave to the whims of all that company!"

"Why, Dr. Jerry," interrupted his wife, "you forget Emily."

"Emily,—to be sure, she's an angel, and never would impose upon anybody, least of all her own pet; but she'll have to play second fiddle herself, and I'm mistaken if she doesn't find it pretty hard to defend her rights and maintain a comfortable position in her father's enlarged family circle."

"So much the more need, then," said Gertrude, "that some one should be enlisted in her interests, to ward off the approach of every annoyance."

"Do you mean, then, to put yourself in the breach?" asked the doctor.

"I mean to accept Mr. Graham's invitation," replied Gertrude, "and join Emily at once; but I trust the harmony that seems to subsist between her and her new connections will continue undisturbed, so that I shall have no occasion to take up arms on *her* account, and on *my own* I do not entertain a single fear."

"Then you really think you shall go," said Mrs. Jeremy.

"I do," said Gertrude; "nothing but my duty to Mrs. Sullivan and her father led me to think of leaving Emily. That duty is at an end, and now that I can be of use to her, and she wishes me back, I cannot hesitate a moment. I see very plainly, from Mrs. Ellis' letter, that Emily is not happy, and nothing which I can do to make her so must be neglected. Only think, Mrs. Jeremy, what a friend she has been to me!"

"I know it," said Mrs. Jeremy, "and I dare say you will enjoy the journey, in spite of all the scare-crows the doctor sets up to frighten you; but still, I declare, it does seem a sacrifice for you to leave your beautiful room, and all your comforts, for such an uncertain sort of life as one has travelling with a large party."

"Sacrifice!" interrupted the doctor, "it's the greatest sacrifice that ever I heard of! It is not merely giving up three hundred and fifty dollars a year of her own earning, and as pleasant a home as there is in Boston; it is relinquishing all the independence that she has been striving after, and which she was so anxious to maintain that she would not accept of anybody's hospitality for more than a week or two."

"No, doctor," said Gertrude, warmly, "nothing that I do for *Emily's* sake can be called a sacrifice; it is my greatest pleasure."

"Gerty always finds her pleasure in doing what is right," remarked Mrs. Jeremy.

"O, no," said Gertrude, "my wishes would often lead me astray; but not in this case. The thought that our dear Emily was dependent upon a stranger for all those little attentions that are only acceptable from those she loves would make me miserable; our happiness has for years been almost wholly in each other, and when one has suffered the other has suffered also. I *must* go to her; I cannot think of doing otherwise."

"I wish I thought," muttered Dr. Jeremy, "that the sacrifice you make would be half appreciated. But there's Graham, I'll venture to say, thinking it will be the greatest favor in the world to take you back again. Perhaps he addresses you as a beggar; it wouldn't be the first time he's done such a thing. I wonder what would have induced poor Philip Amory to go back." Then, in a louder tone, he inquired, "Has he made any apology in his letter for past unkindness?"

"I do not think he considered any to be needed," replied Gertrude.

"Then he didn't make any sort of excuse for his ungentlemanly behavior! I might have known he wouldn't. I declare, it's a shame you should be exposed to any more such treatment; but I always *did* hear that women were self-forgetful in their friendship, and I believe it. Gertrude makes an excellent friend. Mrs. Jerry, we must cultivate her regard, and some time or other perhaps make a loud call upon her services."

"And if ever you do, sir, I shall be ready to respond to it; if there is a person in the world who owes a debt to society, it is myself. I hear the world called cold, selfish and unfeeling; but it has not been so to me. I should be ungrateful if I did not cherish a spirit of universal love; how much more so, if I did not feel bound heart and hand to those dear friends who have bestowed upon me such affection as no orphan ever found before!"

"Gertrude," said Mrs. Jeremy, "I believe that you were right in leaving Emily when you did, and that you are right in returning to her now; and, if your being such a good girl as you are is at all due to her, she certainly has a great claim upon you."

"She has a claim indeed, Mrs. Jeremy! It was Emily who first taught me the difference between right and wrong—"

"And she is going to reap the benefit of that knowledge in you," said the doctor, in continuation of her remark. "That's fair! But, if you are resolved to take this European tour, you will be busy enough with your preparations. Do you think Mr. W. will be willing to give you up?"

"I hope so," said Gertrude; "I am sorry to be obliged to ask it of him, for he has been very indulgent to me, and I have been absent from school two weeks out of the winter already; but, as there want only a few months to the summer vacation, he will, perhaps, be able to supply my place. I shall speak to him about it to-morrow."

Mrs. Jeremy now interested herself in the details of Gertrude's arrangements, offered an attic-room for the storage of her furniture, gave up to her a dress-maker whom she had engaged for herself, and, before she left, a plan was laid out, by following which Gertrude would be enabled to start for New York in less than a week.

Mr. W., on being applied to, relinquished Gertrude, though deeply regretting, as he told her, to lose so valuable an assistant; and, after a few days busily occupied in preparation, she bade farewell to the tearful Fanny Bruce, the bustling doctor and his kind-hearted wife, all of whom accompanied her to the railroad-station. She promised to write to the Jeremys, and they, on their part, agreed to forward to her any letters that might arrive from Willie.

In less than a fortnight from the time of her departure, Mrs. Ellis returned to Boston, and brought news of the safe conclusion of Gertrude's journey. A letter, received a week after, by Mrs. Jeremy, announced that they should sail in a few days. She was, therefore, surprised, when a second epistle was put into her hands, dated the day succeeding that on which she supposed Mr. Graham's party to have left the country. It was as follows:

*"New York, April 29th.*

"My dear Mrs. Jeremy: As yesterday was the day on which we expected to sail for Europe, you will be somewhat astonished to hear that we are yet in New York, and still more so to learn that the foreign tour is now indefinitely postponed. Only two days since, Mr. Graham was seized with his old complaint, the gout, and the attack proved so violent as seriously to threaten his life. Although to-day somewhat relieved, and considered by his physician out of immediate danger, he remains a great sufferer, and a sea-voyage is pronounced impracticable for months to come. His great anxiety is to be at home; and, as soon as it is possible for him to bear the journey, we shall all hasten to the house in D——. I enclose a note for Mrs. Ellis. It contains various directions which Emily is desirous she should receive; and, as we did not know how to address her, I have sent it to you, trusting to your kindness to see it forwarded. Mrs. Graham and her nieces, who had been anticipating much pleasure from going abroad, are, of course, greatly disappointed at the entire change in their plans for the summer. It is particularly trying to Miss Clinton, as her father has been absent more than a year, and she was hoping to meet him in Paris.

"It is impossible that either Emily or myself should personally regret a journey of which we felt only dread, and, were it not for Mr. Graham's illness being the cause of its postponement, we should both, I think, find it hard not to realise a degree of selfish satisfaction in the prospect of returning to the dear old place in D——, where we hope to be established in the course of the next month. I say *we,* for neither Mr. Graham nor Emily will hear of my leaving them again.

"With the kindest regards to yourself, and my friend the doctor,
I am yours, very sincerely,
"Gertrude Flint."

# Chapter XXVII

*I see her;*
*Her hair in ringlets fluttering free,*
*And her lips that move with melody.*

*Not she.—There's a beauty that lovelier glows,*
*Though her coral lip with melody flows.*
*I see her; 't is she of the ivory brow*
*And heaven-tinged orbs: I know her now.*

*Not she.—There's another more lovely still,*
*With a chastened mind, and a tempered will.*
CAROLINE GILMAN

Mr. Graham's country-house boasted a fine, old-fashioned entry, with a door at either end, both of which usually stood open during the warm weather, admitting a cool current of air, and rendering the neighborhood of the front entrance a favorite resort for the family, especially during the early hours of the day, when the warm sun had no access to the spot; and the shady yard, which sloped gradually down to the road, was refreshing and grateful to the sight. Here, on a pleasant June morning, Isabel Clinton, and her cousin Kitty Ray, had made themselves comfortable, each according to her own idea of what constituted comfort.

Isabel had drawn a large arm-chair close to the door-sill, ensconced herself in it, and, although she held in her hand a piece of worsted-work, was gazing idly down the road. She was a beautiful girl, tall and finely formed, with a delicate complexion, clear blue eyes, and rich, light, flowing curls. The same lovely child, whom Gertrude had gazed upon with rapture, as, leaning against the window of her father's house, she watched old True while he lit his lamp, had ripened into an equally lovely woman. Her uncommon beauty aided and enhanced by all the advantages of dress which skill could suggest or money provide, she was universally admired, flattered and caressed.

At an early age deprived of her mother, and left for some years almost wholly to the care of servants, she soon learned to appreciate at more than their true value the outward attractions she possessed; and her aunt, under whose tutelage she had been since she left school, was little calculated to counteract in her this undue self-admiration. An appearance of conscious superiority which distinguished her, and the independent air with which she tapped against the door-step with her little foot, might safely be attributed, then, to her conviction that Belle Clinton, the beauty and the heiress, was looking vastly well, as she sat there, attired in a blue cashmere morning-dress, richly embroidered, and flowing open in front, for the purpose of displaying an equally rich flounced cambric petticoat. It can scarcely be wondered at that she was herself pleased and satisfied with an outward appearance that could not fail to please and satisfy the most severe critic.

On a low step at her feet sat Kitty Ray, a complete contrast to her cousin in looks, manners, and many points of character. Kitty was one of those whom the world usually calls a sweet little creature, lively, playful, and affectionate. She was so small that her childish manners became her; so full of spirits that her occasional rudeness claimed pardon on that score; too thoughtless to be always amiable or always wise; and for all other faults her warm-heartedness and generous enthusiasm must plead an excuse to one who wished, or even endeavored, to love her as she wished and expected to be loved by everybody. She was a pretty girl, always bright and animated, mirthful and happy; fond of her cousin Belle, and sometimes influenced by her, though often, on the other hand, enlisting with all her force on the opposite side of some contested question. Unlike Belle, she was seldom well dressed, for, though possessed of ample means, she was very careless. On the present occasion, her dark silk wrapper was half concealed by a crimson flannel sack, which she held tightly around her, declaring it was a dreadful chilly morning, and she was half-frozen to death— she certainly would go and warm herself at the kitchen fire, if she were not afraid of encountering that *she-dragon* Mrs. Ellis; she was sure she did not see, if they must sit in the door-way, why Belle couldn't come to the side-door, where the sun shone beautifully. "O, I forgot, though," added she; "complexion!"

"Complexion!" said Belle; "I'm no more afraid of hurting my complexion than you are; I'm sure I never freckle, or tan either."

"I know that; but you burn all up, and look like a fright."

"Well, if I didn't, I shouldn't go there to sit; I like to be at the front of the house, where I can see the passing. I wonder who those people are, coming up the road; I've been watching them for some time."

Kitty stood up, and looked in the direction to which Belle pointed. After observing the couple who were approaching for a minute or two, she exclaimed, "Why, that's Gertrude Flint! I wonder where she's been! and who can that be with her? I didn't know there was a beau to be had about here."

"Beau!" said Belle, sneeringly.

"And why not a beau, Cousin Belle! I'm sure he looks like one."

"I wouldn't give much for any of her beaux!" said Belle.

"Wouldn't you?" said Kitty. "You'd better wait until you see who they are; you near-sighted people shouldn't decide in such a hurry. I can tell you that he is a gentleman you wouldn't object to walking with, yourself; it's Mr. Bruce, the one we met in New Orleans."

"I don't believe it!" exclaimed Belle, starting up.

"You will soon have a chance to see for yourself; for he is coming home with her."

"*He is?*—What can he be walking with her for?"

"To show his taste, perhaps. I am sure he could not find more agreeable company."

"You and I don't agree about that," replied Belle. "I don't see anything very agreeable about her."

"Because you are determined not to, Belle. Everybody else thinks her charming, and Mr. Bruce is opening the gate for her as politely as if she were a queen; I like him for that."

"Do see," said Belle; "she's got on that white cape-bonnet of hers! and that checked gingham dress! I wonder what Mr. Bruce thinks of her, and he such a critic in regard to ladies' dress."

Gertrude and her companion now drew near the house; the former looked up, saw the young ladies in the door-way, and smiled pleasantly at Kitty, who was making strange grimaces, and giving significant glances, over Belle's shoulder; but Mr. Bruce, who seemed much engaged by the society he was already enjoying, did not observe either of them; and they distinctly heard him say, as he handed Gertrude a small parcel he had been carrying for her, "I believe I won't come in; it's such a bore to have to talk to strangers.—Do you work in the garden, mornings, this summer?"

"No," replied Gertrude, "there is nothing left of my garden but the memory of it."

"Why, Miss Gertrude!" said the young man, "I hope these new comers haven't interfered with—" Here, observing the direction of Gertrude's eyes, he raised his own, saw Belle and Kitty standing opposite to him, and, compelled now to recognize and speak with them, went forward to shake hands, trusting to his remarks about strangers in general, and these new comers in particular, not having been overheard.

Although overheard, the young ladies chose to take no notice of that which they supposed intended for unknown individuals.

They were mistaken, however; Mr. Bruce knew, perfectly well, that the nieces of the present Mrs. Graham were the same girls whom he had met at the south, and was, nevertheless, indifferent about renewing his acquaintance. His vanity, however, was not proof against the evident pleasure they both manifested at seeing him again, and he was in a few minutes engaged in an animated conversation with them, while Gertrude quietly entered the house, and went up stairs unnoticed. She sought Emily's room, to which she had always free access, and was giving an account of her morning's expedition to the village, and the successful manner in which she had accomplished various commissions and errands, when Mrs. Ellis put her head in at the door, and said, with a most distressed voice and countenance, "Hasn't Gertrude?—O, there you are! Do tell me what Mrs. Wilkins said about the strawberries."

"I engaged three quarts; hasn't she sent them?"

"No, but I'm thankful to hear they're coming; I have been so plagued about the dinner."

She now came in, shut the door, and, seating herself, exclaimed, with something like a groan, "I declare, Emily, such an ironing as our girls have got to do to-day! you never saw anything like it! There's no end to the fine clothes Mrs. Graham and those nieces of hers put into our wash. I declare, it's a shame! Rich as they are, they might put out their washing. I've been helping, *myself*, as much as I could; but, as Mrs. Prime says, one can't do everything at once; and I've had to see the butcher, make puddings and blanc-mange, and been worried to death, all the time, because I had forgotten to engage those strawberries. So Mrs. Wilkins hadn't sent her fruit to market when you got there?"

"No, but she was in a great hurry, getting it ready; it would have been gone in a very short time."

"Well, that was lucky. I don't know what I should have done without the berries, for I've no time to hunt up anything else for dessert. I've got just as much as I can do till dinner-time. Mrs. Graham never kept house before, and don't know how to make allowance for anything. She comes home from Boston, expects to find everything in apple-pie order, and never asks or cares who does the work."

Mrs. Prime's voice was now heard, calling at the back-staircase,—"Mrs. Ellis, Miss Wilkins' boy has fetched your strawberries, and the hulls an't off o' one on 'em; he said they hadn't no time."

"That's too bad!" exclaimed the tired, worried housekeeper. "Who's going to take the hulls off, I should like to know? Katy is busy enough, and I'm sure I can't do it."

"I will, Mrs. Ellis,—let *me* do it," said Gertrude, following Mrs. Ellis, who was now half-way down stairs.

"No, no! don't you touch to, Miss Gertrude," said Mrs. Prime; "they'll only stain your fingers all up."

"No matter if they do; my hands are not made of white kid. They'll bear washing."

Mrs. Ellis was only too thankful for Gertrude's help, and, seating herself in the dining-room, she commenced the task. In the mean while, Belle and Kitty were doing their best to entertain Mr. Bruce, who, sitting on the door-steps, and leaning back against a pillar of the piazza, from time to time cast his eyes down the entry, and up the staircase, in hopes of Gertrude's reäppearance; and, despairing of it at last, he was on the point of taking his departure, when his sister Fanny came in at the gate, and, running up the yard, was rushing past the assembled trio and into the house.

Her brother, however, stretched out his arm, caught her, and, before he let her go, whispered something in her ear.

"Who is that wild Indian?" asked Kitty Ray, as Fanny ran acoss the entry and disappeared.

"A sister of mine," answered Ben, in a nonchalant manner.

"Why! is she?" inquired Kitty, with interest; "I have seen her here several times, and never took any notice of her. I didn't know she was *your* sister. What a pretty girl she is!"

"Do you think so?" said Ben; "sorry I can't agree with you. I think she's a fright."

Fanny now reappeared, and, stopping a moment on her way up stairs, called out, without any ceremony, "She says she can't come; she's busy."

"Who?" asked Kitty, in her turn catching Fanny and detaining her.

"Miss Flint."

Mr. Bruce colored slightly, and Belle Clinton observed it.

"What is she doing?" inquired Kitty.

"Hulling strawberries."

"Where are you going, Fanny?" asked her brother.

"Up stairs."

"Do they let you go all over the house?"

"Miss Flint said I might go up and bring down the birds."

"What birds?"

"Her birds, I am going to hang them in the sun, and then they'll sing beautifully."

She ran off, and soon came back again with a cage in her hand, containing the little monias, sent by Willie from Calcutta.

"There, Kitty," cried Belle; "I think those are the birds that wake us up so early every morning with their noise."

"Very likely," said Kitty; "bring them here, will you, Fanny? I want to see them.—Goodness!" continued she, "what little creatures they are!—do look at them, Mr. Bruce,—they are sweet pretty."

"Put them down on the door-step, Fanny," said Ben, "so that we can see them better."

"I'm afraid you'll frighten them," replied Fanny; "Miss Gertrude doesn't like to have them frightened."

"No, we won't," said Ben; "we are disposed to be very friendly to Miss Gertrude's birds. Where did she get them,—do you know, Fanny?"

"Why, they are India birds; Mr. Sullivan sent them to her."

"Who is he?"

"O, he is a very particular friend; she has letters from him every little while."

"What Mr. Sullivan?" asked Belle. "Do you know his Christian name?"

"I suppose it's William," said Fanny. "Miss Emily always calls the birds little Willies."

"Belle!" exclaimed Kitty, "that's your William Sullivan!"

"What a favored man he seems to be!" said Mr. Bruce, in a tone of sarcasm; "the property of one beautiful lady, and the particular friend of another."

"I don't know what you mean, Kitty," said Belle, tartly. "Mr. Sullivan is a junior partner of my father's, but I have not seen him for years."

"Except in your dreams, Belle," suggested Kitty. "You forget."

Belle now looked angry.

"Do you dream about Mr. Sullivan?" asked Fanny, fixing her eyes on Belle as she spoke. "I mean to go and ask Miss Gertrude if she does."

"Do," said Kitty; "I'll go with you."

They ran across the entry, opened the door into the dining-room, and both put the question to her at the same moment.

Taken thus by surprise, Gertrude neither blushed nor looked confused, but answered, quietly, "Yes, sometimes; but what do you, either of you, know of Mr. Sullivan;—why do you ask?"

"O, nothing," answered Kitty; "only *some others do,* and we are inquiring round to see how many there are;" and she shut the door and ran back in triumph, to tell Belle she might as well be frank, like Gertrude, and plead guilty to the weakness; it looked so much better than blushing and denying it.

But it would not do to joke with Belle any longer; she was seriously offended, and took no pains to conceal the fact. Mr. Bruce felt awkward and annoyed, and soon went away, leaving the two cousins to settle their difficulty as they best could. As soon as he had gone, Belle folded up her work, and walked up stairs to her room with great dignity, while Kitty staid behind to laugh over the matter, and improve her opportunity to make friends with Fanny Bruce; for Kitty was not a little interested in the brother, and labored under the common, but often mistaken idea, that in cultivating the acquaintance of the sister she should advance her cause. Perhaps she was somewhat induced to this step by her having observed that Gertrude appeared to be an equal favorite with both.

She therefore called Fanny to sit beside her, put her arm round her waist, and commenced talking about Gertrude, and the origin and extent of the intimacy which seemed to exist between her and the Bruce family.

Fanny, who was always communicative, willingly informed her of the circumstances which had attached her so strongly to a friend who was some years her senior.

"And your brother," said Kitty; "he has known her some time, hasn't he?"

"Yes, indeed, I suppose so," answered Fanny, carelessly.

"Does he like her?"

"I don't know; I should think he would; I don't see how he can help it."

"What did he whisper to you, when you came up the steps?"

Fanny could not remember at once; but, on being reminded of the answer she had given, she replied, promptly,

"O, he bade me ask Miss Gertrude if she wasn't coming back to see him again, and tell her he was tired to death waiting for her."

Kitty pouted and looked vexed. "I want to know," said she, "if Miss Flint has been in the habit of receiving company here, and being treated like an equal?"

"Of course she has," answered Fanny, with spirit; "why shouldn't she? She's the most perfect lady I ever saw, and mother says she has beautiful manners, and I must take pattern by her."

"O! Miss Gertrude," called she, as Gertrude, who had been to place the strawberries in the refrigerator, crossed the back part of the long entry, "are you ready now?"

"Yes, Fanny, I shall be in a moment," answered Gertrude.

"Ready for what?" inquired Kitty.

"To read," said Fanny. "She is going to read the rest of Hamlet to Miss Emily; she read the first three acts yesterday, and Miss Emily let me sit in her room and hear it. I can't understand it, when I read it myself; but when I listen to Miss Gertrude it seems quite plain. She's a splendid reader, and I came in to-day on purpose to hear the play finished."

Kitty's last companion having deserted her, she stretched herself on the entry sofa and fell asleep. She was wakened by her aunt, who returned from the city a short time before dinner, and, finding her asleep in her morning wrapper, shook her by the arm, and said, in a voice which the best intentions could never render otherwise than loud and coarse, "Kitty Ray, wake up and go dress for dinner! I saw Belle at the chamber-window, looking like a beauty. I wish you'd take half the pains she does to improve your appearance."

Kitty yawned, and, after delaying as long as she chose, finally followed Mrs. Graham's directions. It was Kitty's policy, after giving offence to her cousin Belle, to appear utterly unconscious of the existence of any unkind feelings; and, though Belle often manifested some degree of sulkiness, she was too dependent upon Kitty's society to retain that disposition long. They were soon, therefore, chatting together as usual.

"Belle," said Kitty, as she stood arranging her hair at the glass, "do you remember a girl we used to meet every morning, on our way to school, walking with a paralytic old man?"

"Yes."

"Do you know, I think it was Gertrude Flint. She has altered very much, to be sure; but the features are still the same, and there certainly never was but one such pair of eyes."

"I have no doubt she is the same person," said Belle, composedly.

"Did you think of it before?"

"Yes, as soon as Fanny spoke of her knowing Willie Sullivan."

"Why, Belle, why didn't you speak of it?"

"Lor', Kitty, I don't feel so much interest in her as you and some others do."

"What others?"

It was now Belle's turn to be provoking.

"Why, Mr. Bruce; don't you see he is half in love with her?"

"No, I don't see any such thing; he has known her for a long time (Fanny says so), and, of course, he feels a regard and respect for a girl that the Grahams make so much account of. But I don't believe he'd think of such a thing as being in love with a poor girl like her, with no family connections to boast of."

"Perhaps he didn't *think* of being."

"Well, he *wouldn't* be. She isn't the sort of person that would suit him. He has been in society a great deal, not only at home, but in Paris; and he would want a wife that was very lively and fond of company, and knew how to make a show with money."

"A girl, for instance, like Kitty Ray."

"How ridiculous, Belle! just as if people couldn't talk without thinking of themselves all the time! What do I care about Ben Bruce?"

"I don't know that you care anything about him; but I wouldn't pull all the hair out of my head about it, as you seem to be doing. There's the dinner-bell, and you'll be late, as usual."

## *Chapter XXVIII*

*She hath a natural, wise sincerity,*
*A simple truthfulness, and these have lent her*
*A dignity as moveless as the centre.*

LOWELL

Twilight of this same day found Gertrude and Emily seated at a window which commanded a delightful western view. Gertrude had been describing to her blind friend the gorgeous picture presented to her vision by the masses of rich and brilliantly-painted cloud; and Emily, as she listened to the glowing description of nature, as she unfolded herself at an hour which they both preferred to all others, experienced a participation in Gertrude's enjoyment. The glory had now faded away, save a long strip of gold which skirted the horizon; and the stars, as they came out, one by one, seemed to look in at the chamber-window with a smile of recognition.

In the parlor below there was company from the city, and the sound of mirth and laughter came up on the evening breeze; so mellowed, however, by distance, that it contrasted with the peace of the quiet room, without disturbing it.

"You had better go down, Gertrude," said Emily; "they appear to be enjoying themselves, and I love to hear your laugh mingling with the rest."

"O, no, dear Emily!" said Gertrude; "I prefer to stay with you; they are nearly all strangers to me."

"As you please, my dear; but don't let me keep you from the young people."

"You can never keep me with you, dear Emily, longer than I wish to stay; there is no society I love so well." And so she staid, and they resumed their pleasant conversation, which, though harmonious and calm, was not without its playfulness and occasional gleams of wit.

They were interrupted by Katy, whom Mrs. Graham sent to announce a new visitor,—Mrs. Bruce,—who had inquired for Emily.

"I suppose I must go down," said Emily; "you'll come too, Gertrude?"

"No, I believe not, unless she asked for me. Did she, Katy?"

"Mrs. Graham was only afther mintioning Miss Emily," said Katy.

"Then I will stay here," said Gertrude; and Emily, finding it to be her wish, went without her.

There was soon another loud ring at the door-bell. It seemed to be a reception evening, and this time Gertrude's presence was particularly requested, to see Dr. and Mrs. Jeremy.

When she entered the parlor, she found a great number of guests assembled, and every seat in the room occupied. As she came in alone, and unexpected by the greater part of the company, all eyes were turned upon her. Contrary to the expectation of Belle and Kitty, who were watching her with curiosity, she manifested neither embarrassment nor awkwardness; but, glancing leisurely at the various groups, until she recognized Mrs. Jeremy, crossed the large saloon with characteristic grace, and as much ease and self-possession as if she were the only person present. After greeting that lady with her usual warmth and cordiality, she turned to speak to the doctor; but he was sitting next Fanny Bruce in the window-seat, and was half concealed by the curtain. Before he could rise and come forward, Mrs. Bruce nodded pleasantly from the opposite corner, and Gertrude went to shake hands with her; Mr. Bruce, who formed one in a gay circle of young ladies and gentlemen collected in that part of the room, and who had been observing Gertrude's motions so attentively as to make no reply to a question put to him by Kitty Ray, now rose and offered his chair, saying, "Miss Gertrude, do take this seat."

"Thank you," said Gertrude, "but I see my friend the doctor, on the other side of the room; he expects me to come and speak to him,—so don't let me disturb you."

Dr. Jeremy now came half-way across the room to meet her, and, taking her by both hands, led her into the recess formed by the window, and placed her in his own seat, next to Fanny Bruce. To the astonishment of all who knew him, Ben Bruce brought his own chair and placed it for the doctor opposite to Gertrude. So much respect for age had not been anticipated from the modern-bred man of fashion.

"Is that a daughter of Mr. Graham?" asked a young lady of Belle Clinton, who sat next her.

"No, indeed," replied Belle; "she is a person to whom Miss Graham gave an education, and now she lives here to read to her, and be a sort of companion; her name is Flint."

"What did you say that young lady's name was?" asked a dashing lieutenant, leaning forward and addressing Isabel.

"Miss Flint."

"Flint, ah! she's a genteel-looking girl. How peculiarly she dresses her hair!"

"Very becoming, however, to that style of face," remarked the young lady who had first spoken. "Don't you think so?"

"I don't know," replied the lieutenant; "something becomes her; she makes a fine appearance. Bruce," said he, as Mr. Bruce returned, after his unusual effort at politeness, "who is that Miss Flint?—I have been here two or three times, and I never saw her before."

"Very likely," said Mr. Bruce; "she won't always show herself. Isn't she a fine-looking girl?"

"I haven't made up my mind yet; she's got a splendid figure, but who is she?"

"She's a sort of adopted daughter of Mr. Graham's, I believe; a protegée of Miss Emily's?"

"Ah! poor thing! An orphan?"

"Yes, I suppose so," said Ben, biting his lip.

"Pity!" said the young man; "poor thing! but, as you say, Ben, she's good-looking, particularly when she smiles; there is something very attractive about her face."

There certainly was to Ben, for, a moment after, Kitty Ray missed him from the room, and immediately espied him standing on the piazza, and leaning through the open window to talk with Gertrude, Dr. Jeremy and Fanny. The conversation soon became very lively; there seemed to be a war of wits going on; the doctor, especially, laughed very loud, and Gertrude and Fanny often joined in the merry peal. Kitty endured it as long as she could, and then ran boldly across to join the party, and hear what they were having so much fun about.

But it was all an enigma to Kitty. Dr. Jeremy was talking with Mr. Bruce concerning something which had happened many years ago; there was a great deal about a fool's cap, with a long tassel, and taking afternoon naps in the grass; the doctor was making queer allusions to some old pear-tree, and traps set for thieves, and kept reminding Gertrude of circumstances which attended their first acquaintance with each other and with Mr. Bruce.

Kitty was beginning to feel that, as she was uninitiated in all they were talking about, she had placed herself in the position of an intruder, and was thereupon looking a little embarrassed and ill at ease, when Gertrude touched her arm, and, kindly making room for her next herself, motioned to her to sit down, saying, as she did so, "Dr. Jeremy is speaking of the time when he (or he and *I*, as he chooses to have it) went fruit-stealing in Mrs. Bruce's orchard, and were unexpectedly discovered by Mr. Bruce."

"You mean, my dear," interrupted the doctor, "that Mr. Bruce was discovered by us. Why, it's my opinion he would have slept until this time if I hadn't given him such a thorough waking up!"

"My first acquaintance with you was certainly the greatest awakening of my life," said Ben, speaking as if to the doctor, but looking meaningly at Gertrude; "that was not the only nap it cost me. How sorry I am, Miss Gertrude, that you've given up working in the garden, as you used to! Pray, how does it happen?"

"Mrs. Graham has had it remodelled," replied Gertrude, "and the new gardener neither needs nor desires my services. He has his own plans, and it is not well to interfere with the professor of an art; I should be sure to do mischief."

"I doubt whether his success compares with yours," said Ben. "I do not see anything like the same quantity of flowers in the room that *you* used to have."

"I don't think," said Gertrude, "that he is as fond of cutting them as I was. I did not care so much for the appearance of the garden as for having plenty of flowers in the house; but with him it is the reverse."

Kitty now addressed some remark to Mr. Bruce on the subject of gardening, and Gertrude, turning to Dr. Jeremy, continued in earnest conversation with him, until Mrs. Jeremy rose to go, when, approaching the window, she said, "Dr. Jerry, have you given Gertrude her letter?"

"Goodness me!" exclaimed the doctor, "I came near forgetting it." Then, feeling in his pocket, he drew forth an evidently foreign document, the envelope literally covered with various-colored post-office stamps. "See here, Gerty, genuine Calcutta; no mistake!"

Gertrude took the letter, and, as she thanked the doctor, her countenance expressed pleasure at receiving it; a pleasure, however, somewhat tempered by sadness, for she had heard from Willie but once since he learned the news of his mother's death, and that letter had been such an outpouring of his vehement grief that the sight of his hand-writing almost pained her, as she anticipated something like a repetition of the outburst.

Mr. Bruce, who kept his eyes upon her, and half expected to see her change color, and look disconcerted, on the letter being handed to her in the presence of so many witnesses, was reässured by the composure with which she took it, and held it openly in her hand while she bade the doctor and his wife good-evening. She followed them to the door, and was then retreating to her own apartment, when she was met at the foot of the stairs by Mr. Bruce, who had noticed the movement, and now entered from the piazza in time to arrest her steps, and ask if her letter was of such importance that she must deny the company the pleasure of her society in order to study its contents.

"It is from a friend of whose welfare I am anxious to hear," said Gertrude, gravely. "Please excuse me to your mother, if she inquires for me; and, as the rest of the guests are strangers, I shall not be missed by them."

"O, Miss Gertrude," said Mr. Bruce, "it's no use coming here to see you, you are so frequently invisible. What part of the day is one most likely to find you disengaged?"

"Hardly any part," said Gertrude. "I am always a very busy character; but good-night, Mr. Bruce,—don't let me detain you from the other young ladies;" and Gertrude ran up stairs, leaving Mr. Bruce uncertain whether to be vexed with himself or her.

Contrary to Gerty's expectations, her letter from William Sullivan proved very soothing to the grief she had felt on his account. His spirit had been so weighed down and crushed by the intelligence of the death of his grandfather, and finally of his second and still greater loss, that his first communication to Gertrude had alarmed her, from the discouraged, disheartened tone in which it was written; she had feared lest his Christian fortitude would give way to the force of this double affliction.

She was, therefore, much relieved to find that he now wrote in a calmer strain; that he had taken to heart his mother's last entreaty and prayer for a submissive disposition on his part; and that, although deeply afflicted, he was schooling himself to patience and resignation. But he did not, in this letter, dwell long upon his own sufferings under bereavement.

The three closely-written pages were almost wholly devoted to fervent and earnest expressions of gratitude to Gertrude for the active kindness and love which had cheered and comforted the last days of his much-regretted friends. He prayed that Heaven would bless her, and reward her disinterested and self-denying efforts, and closed with saying, "You are all there is left to me, Gertrude. If I loved you before, my heart is now bound to you by ties stronger than those of earth; my hopes, my labors, my prayers are all for you. God grant we may some day meet again!"

For an hour after she had finished reading, Gertrude sat lost in meditation; her thoughts went back to her home at Uncle True's, and the days when she and Willie passed so many happy hours in close companionship, little dreaming of the long separation so soon to ensue. She rehearsed, in her mind, all the succeeding events which had brought her into her present position, and was only startled at last from the revery she was indulging in by the voices of Mrs. Graham's visitors, who were now taking leave.

Mrs. Bruce and her son lingered a little, until the carriages had driven off with those of the guests who were to return to the city, and, as they were making their farewells on the door-step, directly beneath Gertrude's window, she heard Mrs. Graham say, "Remember, Mr. Bruce, we dine at two; and, Miss Fanny, we shall hope to see you also. I presume you will join the walking party."

This, then, was an arrangement which was to bring Mr. Bruce there to dinner, at no very distant period; and Gertrude's reflections, forsaking the past, began to centre upon the present.

Mr. Bruce's attentions to her had that day been marked; and the professions of admiration he had contrived to whisper in her ear had been still more so. Both these attentions and this admiration were unsought and undesired; neither were they in any degree flattering to the high-minded girl, who was superior to coquetry, and whose self-respect was even wounded by the confident and assured manner in which Mr. Bruce made his advances. As a youth of seventeen, she had marked him as indolent and ill-bred. Her sense of justice, however, would have obliterated this recollection, had his character and manners appeared changed on the renewal of their acquaintance, some years after. This was not the case, however, for the outward polish, bestowed by fashion and familiarity with society, could not cloud Gertrude's discernment; and she quickly perceived that his old characteristics still remained, heightened and rendered more glaring by an ill-concealed vanity. As a boy, he had stared at Gertrude from impudence, and inquired her name out of idle curiosity; as a youthful coxcomb, he had resolved to flirt with her, because his time hung heavy on his hands, and he could think of nothing better to do. But, to his surprise, he found the country girl (for such he considered her, never having seen her elsewhere) was quite insensible to the flattery and notice which many a city belle had coveted; appeared wholly indifferent to his admiration; and that when he tried raillery he usually proved the disconcerted party. If he sought her, as he was frequently in the habit of doing, when she was at work among the flowers, he found it impossible to distract her attention from her labors, or detain her after they were completed; if he joined her in her walks, and, with his wonted self-conceit, made her aware of the honor he supposed himself conferring, she either maintained a dignity which warded off his fulsome adulation, or, if he ventured to make her the object of direct compliment, received it as a jest, and retorted with a playfulness and wit which often left the opaque wits of poor Ben in some doubt whether he had not been making himself ridiculous; and this, not because Gertrude was willing to wound the feelings of one who was disposed to admire her, but because she perceived that he was far from being sincere, and she had an honorable pride which would not endure to be trifled with.

It was something new to Mr. Bruce to find any lady thus indifferent to his merits; and proved such an awakening to his ambition, that he resolved, if possible, to recommend himself to Gertrude, and consequently improved every opportunity of gaining admittance to her society.

While laboring, however, to inspire her with a due appreciation of himself, he fell into his own snare; for, though he failed in awakening Gertrude's interest, he could not be equally insensible to her attractions. Even the comparatively dull intellect of Ben Bruce was capable of measuring her vast superiority to most girls of her age; and her vivacious originality was a contrast to the insipidity of fashionable life, which at length completely charmed him.

His earnestness and perseverance began to annoy the object of his admiration before she left Mr. Graham's in the autumn, and she was glad soon after to hear that he had accompanied his mother to Washington, as it insured her against meeting him again for months to come.

Mr. Bruce regretted losing sight of Gertrude, but amid the gayety and dissipation of southern cities contrived to waste his time with tolerable satisfaction. He was reminded of her again on meeting the Graham party at New Orleans, and it is some credit to his understanding to say, that in the comparison which he constantly drew between her and the vain daughters of fashion she stood higher than ever in his estimation. He did not hesitate to tell her so on the morning already mentioned, when, with evident satisfaction, he had recognized and joined her; and the increased devotion of his words and manner, which now took a tone of truth in which they had before been wanting, alarmed Gertrude, and led to a serious resolve on her part to avoid him on all possible occasions. It will soon be seen how difficult she found it to carry out this resolution.

On the day succeeding the one of which we have been speaking, Mr. Graham returned from the city about noon, and, joining the young ladies in the entry, unfolded his newspaper, and, handing it to Kitty, asked her to read the news.

"What shall I read?" said Kitty, taking the paper rather unwillingly.

"The leading article, if you please."

Kitty turned the paper inside and out, looked hastily up and down its pages, and then declared her inability to find it. Mr. Graham stared at her in astonishment, then pointed in silence to the wished-for paragraph. She began, but had scarcely read a sentence before Mr. Graham stopped her, saying, impatiently, "Don't read so fast,—I can't hear a single word!" She now fell into the other extreme, and drawled so intolerably that her auditor interrupted her again, and bade her give the paper to her cousin.

Belle took it from the pouting Kitty, and finished the article,—not, however, without being once or twice compelled to go back and read more intelligibly.

"Do you wish to hear anything more, sir?" asked she.

"Yes; won't you turn to the ship-news, and read me the list by the steamer."

Belle, more fortunate than Kitty, found the place, and commenced. " 'At Canton, April 30th, ship Ann Maria, Ray, d-i-s-c-g.'—What does that mean?"

"Discharging, of course; go on."

" 'S-l-d—a-b-t 13th,' " spelt Belle, looking dreadfully puzzled all the while.

"Stupid!" muttered Mr. Graham, almost snatching the paper out of her hands; "not know how to read ship-news! Where's Gertrude? Where's Gertrude Flint? She's the only girl I ever saw that did know anything. Won't you speak to her, Kitty?"

Kitty went, though rather reluctantly, to call Gertrude, and told her for what she was wanted. Gertrude was astonished; since the day when she had persisted in leaving his house, Mr. Graham had never asked her to read to him; but, obedient to the summons, she presented herself, and, taking the seat which Belle had vacated near the door, commenced with the ship-news, and, without asking any questions, turned to various items of intelligence, taking them in the order which she knew Mr. Graham preferred.

The old gentleman, leaning back in his easy-chair, and resting his gouty foot upon an ottoman opposite to him, looked amazingly contented and satisfied; and when Belle and Kitty had gone off to their room, he remarked, "This seems like old times, doesn't it, Gertrude?" He now closed his eyes, and Gertrude was soon made aware, by his deep breathing, that he had fallen asleep.

Seeing that, as he sat, it would be impossible for her to pass without waking him, she laid down the paper, and was preparing to draw some work from her pocket (for Gertrude seldom spent her time in idleness), when she observed a shadow in the doorway, and, looking up, saw the very person whom she had yesterday resolved to avoid.

Mr. Bruce was staring in her face, with an indolent air of ease and confidence, which she always found very offensive. He had in one hand a bunch of roses, which he held up to her admiring gaze.

"Very beautiful!" said Gertrude, as she glanced at the little branches, covered with a luxurious growth of moss-rose buds, both pink and white.

She spoke in a low voice, fearing to awaken Mr. Graham. Mr. Bruce, therefore, softening his to a whisper, remarked, as he dangled them above her head, "I thought they were pretty when I gathered them, but they suffer from the comparison, Miss Gertrude;" and he gave a meaning look at the roses in her cheeks.

Gertrude, to whom this was a stale compliment, coming from Mr. Bruce, took no notice of it, but, rising, advanced to make her exit by the front-door, saying, "I will go across the piazza, Mr. Bruce, and send the ladies word that you are here."

"O, pray don't!" said he, putting himself in her way. "It would be cruel; I haven't the slightest wish to see them."

He so effectually prevented her, that she was unwillingly compelled to retreat from the door and resume her seat. As she did so, she took her work from her pocket, her countenance in the mean time expressing vexation.

Mr. Bruce looked his triumph, and took advantage of it.

"Miss Gertrude," said he, "will you oblige me by wearing these flowers in your hair to-day?"

"I do not wear gay flowers," replied Gertrude, without lifting her eyes from the piece of muslin on which she was employed.

Supposing this to be on account of her mourning (for she wore a plain black dress), he selected the white buds from the rest, and, presenting them to her, begged that, for his sake, she would display them in contrast with her dark silken braids.

"I am much obliged to you," said Gertrude; "I never saw more beautiful roses, but I am not accustomed to be so much dressed, and believe you must excuse me."

"Then you won't take my flowers?"

"Certainly I will, with pleasure," said she, rising, "if you will let me get a glass of water, and place them in the parlor, where we can all enjoy them."

"I did not cut my flowers, and bring them here, for the benefit of the whole household," said Ben, in a half-offended tone. "If you won't wear them, Miss Gertrude, I will offer them to somebody that will."

This, he thought, would alarm her, for his vanity was such that he attributed her behavior wholly to coquetry, and, as instances of this sort had always served to enhance his admiration, he believed that they were intended to produce that effect. "I will punish her," thought he, as he tied the roses together again, and arranged them for presentation to Kitty, whom he knew would be flattered to receive them.

"Where's Fanny to-day?" asked Gertrude, anxious to divert the conversation.

"I don't know," answered Ben, with a manner which implied that he had no idea of talking about Fanny.

A short silence ensued, during which he gazed idly at Gertrude's fingers, as she sat sewing.

"How attentive you are to your work!" said he, at last; "your eyes seem nailed to it. I wish I were as attractive as that piece of muslin!"

"I wish you were as inoffensive," thought Gertrude.

"I do not think you take much pains to entertain me," added he, "when I've come here on purpose to see you."

"I thought you came by Mrs. Graham's invitation," said Gertrude.

"And didn't I have to court Kitty for an hour in order to get it?"

"If you obtained it by artifice," said Gertrude, smiling, "you do not deserve to be entertained."

"It is much easier to please Kitty than you," remarked Ben.

"Kitty is very amiable and pleasant," said Gertrude.

"Yes, but I'd give more for one smile from you than—"

Gertrude now interrupted him with, "Ah! here is an old friend coming to see us; please let me pass, Mr. Bruce."

The gate at the end of the yard swung to as she spoke, and Ben, looking in that direction, beheld approaching the person whom Gertrude seemed desirous to go and meet.

"Don't be in such a hurry to leave me!" said Ben; "that little crone, whose coming seems to give you so much satisfaction, can't get here this half-hour, at the rate she is travelling."

"She is an old friend," replied Gertrude; "I must go and welcome her." Her countenance expressed so much earnestness that Mr. Bruce was ashamed to persist in his incivility, and, rising, permitted her to pass. Miss Patty Pace —for she it was who was toiling up the yard—seemed overjoyed at seeing Gertrude, and, the moment she recognized her, commenced waving, in a theatrical manner, a huge feather fan, her favorite mode of salutation. As she drew near, Miss Patty took her by both hands, and stood talking with her some minutes before they proceeded together up the yard. They entered the house at the side-door, and Ben, being thus disappointed of Gertrude's return, sallied out into the garden, in hopes to attract the notice of Kitty.

Ben Bruce had such confidence in the power of wealth and a high station in fashionable life, that it never occurred to him to doubt that Gertrude would gladly accept his hand and fortune, if it were placed at her disposal. No degree of coldness, or even neglect, on her part, would have induced him to believe that an orphan girl, without a cent in the world, would forego such an opportunity to establish herself.

Many a prudent and worldly-wise mother had sought his acquaintance; many a young lady, even among those who possessed property and rank of their own, had received his attention with favor; and believing, as he did, that he had money enough to purchase a wife any woman whom he chose to select, he would have laughed at the idea that Gertrude would presume to hold herself higher than the rest.

He had not made his mind up to such an important step, however, as the deliberate surrender of the many advantages of which he was the fortunate possessor. He had merely determined to win Gertrude's good opinion and affection; and, although more interested in her than he was aware of himself, he at present made that his ultimate object. He felt conscious that as yet she had given no evidence of his success; and, having resolved to resort to some new means of winning her, he, with a too common selfishness and baseness, fixed upon a method which was calculated, if successful, to end in the mortification, if not the unhappiness, of a third party. He intended, by marked devotion to Kitty Ray, to excite the jealousy of Gertrude; and it was with the view to furthering his intentions that he walked in the garden, hoping to attract her observation.

O! it was a shameful scheme! for Kitty liked him already. She was a warm-hearted girl,—a credulous one too, and likely to become a ready victim to his duplicity.

❀❀❀❀❀❀❀❀❀❀❀❀❀❀❀❀❀❀❀❀❀❀❀❀❀❀❀❀❀❀

# Chapter XXIX

*Is this the world of which we want a sight?*
*Are these the beings who are called polite?*
                    HANNAH MORE

A half-hour before dinner, Mrs. Graham and her nieces, Mr. Bruce, his sister Fanny, and Lieutenant Osborne, as they sat in the large parlor, had their curiosity much excited by the merriment which seemed to exist in Emily's room, directly above. It was not noisy or rude, but strikingly genuine. Gertrude's clear laugh was very distinguishable, and even Emily joined frequently in the outburst which would every now and then occur; while still another person appeared to be of the party, as a strange and most singular voice occasionally mingled with the rest.

Kitty ran to the entry two or three times, to listen, and hear, if possible, the subject of their mirth, and at last returned with the announcement that Gertrude was coming down stairs with the very queen of witches.

Presently Gertrude opened the door, which Kitty had slammed behind her, and ushered in Miss Patty Pace, who advanced with measured, mincing steps to Mrs. Graham, and, stopping in front of her, made a low curtsey.

"How do you do, ma'am?" said Mrs. Graham, half inclined to believe that Gertrude was playing off a joke upon her.

"This, I presume, is the mistress," said Miss Patty.

Mrs. Graham acknowledged her claim to that title.

"A lady of presence!" said Miss Patty to Gertrude, in an audible whisper, pronouncing each syllable with a manner and emphasis peculiar to herself. Then, turning towards Belle, who was shrinking into the shadow of a curtain, she approached her, held up both hands in astonishment, and exclaimed, "Miss Isabella, as I still enjoy existence! and radiant, too, as the morning! Bless my heart! how your youthful charms have expanded!"

Belle had recognized Miss Pace the moment she entered the room, but, with foolish pride, was ashamed to acknowledge the acquaintance of so eccentric an individual, and would have still feigned ignorance, but Kitty now came forward, exclaiming, "Why, Miss Pace, where did you come from?"

"Miss Catharina," said Miss Pace, taking her hands in an ecstasy of astonishment, *"then you knew me!* Blessings on your memory of an old friend!"

"Certainly, I knew you in a minute; you're not so easily forgotten, I assure you. Belle, don't you remember Miss Pace? It's at your house I've always seen her."

"O, is it she?" said Belle, with a poor attempt to conceal the fact that she had any previous knowledge of a person who had been a frequent visitor at her father's house, and was held in esteem by both her parents.

"I apprehend," said Miss Patty to Kitty, in the same loud whisper, "that she carries a proud heart."—Then, without having appeared to notice the gentlemen, who were directly behind her, she added, "Sparks, I see, Miss Catharina, young sparks! Whose?—yours, or hers?"

Kitty laughed, for she saw that the young men heard her and were much amused, and replied, without hesitation, "O, mine, Miss Patty, mine, both of 'em!" Miss Patty now looked round the room, and, missing Mr. Graham, advanced to his wife, saying, "And where, madam, is the bridegroom?"

Mrs. Graham, a little confused, replied that her husband would be in presently, and invited Miss Pace to be seated.

"No, mistress, I am obliged to you; I have an inquiring mind, and, with your leave, will take a survey of the apartment. I love to see everything that is modern." She then proceeded to examine the pictures upon the walls, but had not proceeded far before she turned to Gertrude and asked, still loud enough to be distinctly heard, "Gertrude, my dear, what have they done with the second wife?" Gertrude looked surprised, and Miss Pace corrected her remark, saying, "O, it is the counterfeit that I have reference to; the original, I am aware, departed long since; but where is the counterfeit of the second Mistress Graham? It always hung here, if my memory serves me."

Gertrude whispered a reply to this question, and Miss Pace then uttered the following soliloquy: "The garret! well, 't is the course of nature; what is new obliterates *the recollection, even,* of the old."

She now linked her arm in Gertrude's, and made her the companion of her survey. When they had completed the circuit of the room, she stopped in front of the group of young people, all of whom were eying her with great amusement, claimed acquaintance with Mr. Bruce, and asked to be introduced to the member of the war department, as she styled Lieutenant Osborne. Kitty introduced her with great formality, and at the same time presented the lieutenant to Gertrude, a ceremony which she felt indignant that her aunt had not thought proper to perform. A chair was now brought, Miss Patty joined their circle, and entertained them until dinner-time. Gertrude again sought Emily's room.

At the table, Gertrude, seated next to Emily, whose wants she always made her care, and with Miss Patty on the other side, had no time or attention to bestow on any one else; much to the chagrin of Mr. Bruce, who was anxious she should observe his assiduous devotion to Kitty, whose hair was adorned with moss-rose buds and her face with smiles.

Belle was also made happy by the marked admiration of her young officer, and no one felt any disposition to interfere with either of the well-satisfied girls. Occasionally, however, some remark made by Miss Pace irresistibly attracted the attention of every one at the table, and extorted either the laughter it was intended to excite, or a mirth which, though perhaps ill-timed, it was impossible to repress.

Mr. Graham treated Miss Patty with the most marked politeness and attention, and Mrs. Graham, who was possessed of great suavity of manners when she chose to exercise it, and who loved dearly to be amused, spared no pains to bring out the old lady's conversational powers. She found, too, that Miss Patty was acquainted with everybody, and made most appropriate and amusing comments upon almost every person who became the topic of conversation. Mr. Graham at last led her to speak of herself and her lonely mode of life; and Fanny Bruce, who sat next, asked her, bluntly, why she never got married.

"Ah, my young miss," said she, "we all wait our time, and I may take a companion yet."

"You should," said Mr. Graham. "Now you have property, Miss Pace, and ought to share it with some nice, thrifty man." Mr. Graham knew her weak point.

"I have but an insignificant trifle of worldly wealth," said Miss Pace, "and am not as youthful as I have been; but I may suit myself with a companion, notwithstanding. I approve of matrimony, and have my eye upon a young man."

"A *young man!*" exclaimed Fanny Bruce, laughing.

"O, yes, Miss Frances," said Miss Patty; "I am an admirer of youth, and of everything that is modern. Yes, I cling to life—I cling to life."

"Certainly," remarked Mrs. Graham, "Miss Pace must marry somebody younger than herself; some one to whom she can leave all her property, if he should happen to outlive her."

"Yes," said Mr. Graham; "at present you would not know how to make a will, unless you left all your money to Gertrude, here; I rather think *she* would make a good use of it."

"That would certainly be a consideration to me," said Miss Pace; "I should dread the thought of having my little savings squandered. Now, I know there's more than a sufficiency of pauper population, and plenty that would be glad of legacies; but I have no intention of bestowing on such. Why, sir, nine-tenths of them will *always* be poor. No, no! I shouldn't give to such! No, no! I have other intentions."

"Miss Pace," asked Mr. Graham, "what has become of Gen. Pace's family?"

"*All dead!*" replied Miss Patty, promptly, "*all dead!* I made a pilgrimage to the grave of that branch of the family. It was a melancholy and touching scene," continued she, in a pathetic tone of voice. "There was a piece of grassy ground, belted about with an iron railing, and in the centre a beautiful white-marble monument, *in which* they were all buried; it was pure as alabaster, and on it was inscribed these lines:

'PACE.' "

"What were the lines?" inquired Mrs. Graham, who believed her ears had deceived her.

"Pace, ma'am, Pace; nothing else."

Solemn as was the subject, a universal titter pervaded the circle; and Mrs. Graham, perceiving that Kitty and Fanny would soon burst into uncontrollable fits of laughter, made the move for the company to quit the table.

The gentlemen did not care to linger, and followed the ladies into the wide entry, the refreshing coolness of which invited every one to loiter there during the heat of the day. Miss Patty and Fanny Bruce compelled the unwilling Gertrude to join the group there assembled; and Mrs. Graham, who was never disposed to forego her afternoon nap, was the only member of the family who absented herself.

So universal was the interest Miss Patty excited, that all private dialogue was suspended, and close attention given to whatever topic the old lady was discussing.

Belle maintained a slightly scornful expression of countenance, and tried, with partial success, to divert Lieutenant Osborne's thoughts into another channel; but Kitty was so delighted with Miss Pace's originality, that she made no attempt at any exclusive conversation, and, with Mr. Bruce sitting beside her and joining in her amusement, looked more than contented.

Dress and fashion, two favorite themes with Miss Patty, were now introduced, and, after discoursing at some length upon her love of the beautiful, as witnessed in the mantua-making and millinery arts, she deliberately left her seat, and going towards Belle (the only one of the company who seemed desirous to avoid her), began to examine the material of her dress, and finally requested her to rise and permit her to further inspect the mode in which it was made, declaring the description of so modern and finished a master-piece of art would be a feast to the ears of some of her junior acquaintances.

Belle indignantly refused to comply, and shook off the hand of the old lady as if there had been contamination in her touch.

"Do stand up, Belle," said Kitty, in an undertone; "don't be so cross."

"Why don't you stand up yourself," said Belle, "and show off your own dress, for the benefit of her low associates?"

"She didn't ask me to," replied Kitty, "but I will, with the greatest pleasure, if she will condescend to look at it. Miss Pace," continued she, gayly, placing herself in front of the inquisitive Miss Patty, "do admire my gown at your leisure, and take a pattern of it, if you like; I should be proud of the honor."

For a wonder, Kitty's dress was pretty and well worthy of observation. Miss Patty made many comments, especially on the train, as she denominated its unnecessary and inconvenient length; and then, her curiosity being satisfied, commenced retreating towards the place she had left, first glancing behind her to see if it was still vacant, and then moving towards it with a backward motion, consisting of a series of curtseys.

Fanny Bruce, who stood near, observing that she had made an exact calculation how many steps would be required to reach her seat, placed her hand on the back of the chair, as if to draw it away; and, encouraged by a look and smile from Isabel, moved it, slightly, but still enough to endanger the old lady's safety.

On attempting to regain it, Miss Pace stumbled, and would have fallen, but Gertrude—who had been watching Fanny's proceedings—sprung forward in time to fling an arm around her, and place her safely in the chair, casting at the same time a reproachful look at Fanny; who, much confused, turned to avoid Gertrude's gaze, and in doing so accidentally trod on Mr. Graham's gouty toes, which drew from him an exclamation of pain.

"Fan," said Mr. Bruce, who had observed the latter accident only, "I wish you could learn politeness."

"Who am I to learn it from?" asked Fanny, pertly,—"you?"

Ben looked provoked, but forbore to reply; while Miss Pace, who had now recovered her composure, took up the word and said,

"Politeness! Ah, a lovely, but rare virtue; perceptibly developed, however, in the manners of my friend Gertrude, which I hesitate not to affirm would well become a princess."

Belle curled her lip, and smiled disdainfully. "Lieutenant Osborne," said she, "don't you think Miss Devereux has beautiful manners?"

"Very fine," replied the lieutenant; "the style in which she receives company, on her reception-day, is elegance itself."

"Who are you speaking of?" inquired Kitty; "Mrs. Harry Noble?"

"Miss Devereux, we were remarking upon," said Belle, "but Mrs. Noble is also very stylish."

"I think she is," said Mr. Bruce; "do you hear, Fanny?—we have found a model for you,—you must imitate Mrs. Noble."

"I don't know anything about Mrs. Noble," retorted Fanny; "I'd rather imitate Miss Flint. Miss Gertrude," said she, with a seriousness which Gertrude rightly believed was intended to express regret for her late rudeness, "how *shall I* learn politeness?"

"Do you remember," asked Gertrude, speaking low, and giving Fanny a look full of meaning, "what your music-master told you about learning to *play* with expression? I should give you the same rule for improvement in politeness."

Fanny blushed deeply.

"What is that?" said Mr. Graham; "let us know, Fanny, what is *Gertrude's* rule for politeness."

"She only said," answered Fanny, "that it was the same my music-master gave me last winter."

"And what did *he* say?" inquired her brother, with a tone of interest.

"I asked Mr. Hermann," said Fanny, "how I should learn to play with expression, and he said, 'You must cultivate your *heart*, Miss Bruce; you must cultivate your *heart.*'"

This new direction for the attainment of a great accomplishment was received with countenances that indicated as great a variety of sentiment as there was difference of character among Fanny's audience. Mr. Graham bit his lip, and walked away; for *his* politeness was founded on no such rule, and he knew that Gertrude's *was*. Belle looked glorious disdain; Mr. Bruce and Kitty, puzzled and half amused; while Lieutenant Osborne proved himself not quite callous to a noble truth, by turning upon Gertrude a glance of admiration and interest. Emily's face evidenced how fully she coincided in the opinion thus unintentionally made public, and Miss Patty unhesitatingly expressed her approbation.

"Miss Gertrude's remark is undeniably a verity," said she. "The only politeness which is trustworthy is the spontaneous offering of the heart. Perhaps this goodly company of masters and misses would condescend to give ear to an old woman's tale of a rare instance of true politeness, and the fitting reward it met."

All professed a strong desire to hear Miss Patty's story, and she began:

"On a winter's day, some years ago, an old woman of many foibles and besetting weaknesses, but with a keen eye and her share of worldly wisdom,—Miss Patty Pace by name,—started by special invitation for the house of one worshipful Squire Clinton, the honored parent of Miss Isabella, the fair damsel yonder. Every tall tree in our good city was spangled with frost-work, more glittering far than gems that sparkle in Golconda's mine, and the side-walks were a snare to the feet of the old and the unwary.

"I lost my equilibrium, and fell. Two gallant gentlemen lifted and carried me to a neighboring apothecary's emporium, restored my scattered wits, and revived me with a fragrant cordial. I went on my way with many a misgiving, however, and scarcely should I have reached my destination with bones unbroken, had it not been for a knight with a rosy countenance, who overtook me, placed my old arm within his own more strong and youthful one, and protected my steps to the very end of my journey. No slight courage either, my young misses, did my noble escort need, to carry him through what he had undertaken. Paint to your imaginations a youth fresh and beautiful as a sunbeam, straight as an arrow,—a perfect Apollo, indeed,—linked to the little bent body of poor Miss Patty Pace. I will not spare myself, young ladies; for, had you seen me then, you would consider me now vastly ameliorated in outward presentment. My double row of teeth were stowed away in my pocket, my frisette was pushed back from my head by my recent fall, and my gogs—the same my father wore before me—covered my face, and they alone attracted attention, and created some excitement. But he went on unmoved; and, in spite of many a captivating glance and smile from long rows of beautiful young maidens whom we met, and many a sneer from the youths of his own age, he sustained my feeble form with as much care as if I had been an empress, and accommodated his buoyant step to the slow movement which my infirmities compelled. Ah! what a spirit of conformity he manifested!—my knight of the rosy countenance!—Could you have seen him, Miss Catharina, or you, Miss Frances, your palpitating hearts would have taken flight forever. He was a paragon, indeed.

"Whither his own way tended I cannot say, for he moved in conformity to mine, and left me not until I was safe at the abode of Mistress Clinton. I hardly think he coveted my old heart, but I sometimes believe it followed him; for truly he is still a frequent subject of my meditations."

"Ah! then *that* was his reward!" exclaimed Kitty.

"Not so, Miss Kitty; guess again."

"I can think of *nothing so desirable,* Miss Patty."

"His *fortune in life,* Miss Catharina,—that was his reward; it may be that he cannot yet estimate the full amount of his recompense."

"How so?" exclaimed Fanny.

"I will briefly narrate the rest. Mistress Clinton encouraged me always to converse much in her presence. She knew my taste, was disposed to humor me, and I was pleased to be indulged. I told my story, and enlarged upon the merits of my noble youth, and his wonderful spirit of conformity. The squire, a gentleman who estimates good breeding, was present, with his ears open; and when I recommended my knight with all the eloquence I could command, he was amused, interested, pleased. He promised to see the boy, and did so; the noble features spake for themselves, and gained him a situation as clerk, from which he has since advanced in the ranks, until now he occupies the position of partner and confidential agent in a creditable and wealthy house. Miss Isabella, it would rejoice my heart to hear the latest tidings from Mr. William Sullivan."

"He is well, I believe," said Isabella, sulkily. "I know nothing to the contrary."

"O, Gertrude knows," said Fanny. "Gertrude knows all about Mr. Sullivan; she will tell you."

All turned, and looked at Gertrude, who, with face flushed, and eyes glistening with the interest she felt in Miss Patty's narrative, stood leaning upon Emily's chair. Miss Patty now appealed to her, much surprised, however, at her having any knowledge of her much-admired and well-remembered young escort. Gertrude drew near, and answered all her questions without the least hesitation or embarrassment, but in a tone of voice so low that the others, most of whom felt no interest in Willie, entered into conversation, and left her and Miss Patty to discourse freely concerning a mutual friend.

Gertrude gave Miss Pace a brief account of the wonder and curiosity which Willie and his friends had felt concerning the original author of his good fortune; and the old lady was so entertained and delighted at hearing of the various conjectures and doubts which arose on the reception of Mr. Clinton's unexpected summons, and of the matter being finally attributed to the agency of Santa Claus, that her laugh was nearly as loud, and quite as heart-felt, as that of the gay party near the doorstep, whom Kitty and Fanny had excited to unusual merriment. Miss Pace was just taxing Gertrude with interminable compliments and messages of remembrance to be despatched in her next letter to Willie, when Mrs. Graham presented herself, refreshed both in dress and countenance since her nap, and arrested the attention of the whole company, by exclaiming, in her abrupt manner and loud tones,

"What! are you all here still? I thought you were bound for a walk in the woods. Kitty, what has become of your cherished scheme of climbing Sunset Hill?"

"I proposed it, aunt, an hour ago, but Belle insisted it was too warm. *I* think the weather is just right for a walk."

"It will soon be growing cool," said Mrs. Graham, "and I think you had better start; it is some distance if you go round through the woods."

"Who knows the way?" asked Kitty.

No one responded to the question, and, on being individually appealed to, all professed total ignorance; much to the astonishment of Gertrude, who believed that every part of the woody ground and hill beyond were familiar to Mr. Bruce. She did not stay, however, to hear any further discussion of their plans; for Emily was beginning to suffer from headache and weariness, and Gertrude, perceiving it, insisted that she should seek the quiet of her own room, to which she herself accompanied her. She was just closing the chamber-door, when Fanny called from the staircase, "Miss Gertrude, an't you going to walk with us?"

"No," replied Gertrude, "not to-day."

"Then I won't go," said Fanny, "if you don't. Why don't you go, Miss Gertrude?"

"I shall walk with Miss Emily, by and by, if she is well enough; you can accompany us, if you like, but I think you would enjoy going to Sunset Hill much more."

Meantime a whispered consultation took place below, in which some one suggested that Gertrude was well acquainted with the path which the party wished to follow through the woods. Belle opposed her being invited to join them; Kitty hesitated between her liking for Gertrude and her fears regarding Mr. Bruce's allegiance; Lieutenant Osborne forbore to urge what Belle disapproved; and Mr. Bruce remained silent, trusting to the final necessity of her being invited to act as guide, in which capacity he had purposely concealed his own ability to serve. This necessity was so obvious, that, as he had foreseen, Kitty was at last despatched to find Gertrude and make known their request.

❀❀❀❀❀❀❀❀❀❀❀❀❀❀❀❀❀❀❀❀❀❀❀❀❀❀❀

# Chapter XXX

*There are haughty steps that would walk the globe
O'er necks of humbler ones.*

MISS L. P. SMITH

Gertrude would have declined, and made her attendance upon Emily an excuse for non-compliance; but Emily herself, believing that the exercise would be beneficial to Gertrude, interfered, and begged her to agree to Kitty's apparently very cordial proposal; and, on the latter's declaring that the expedition must otherwise be given up, she consented to join it. To change her slippers for thick walking-boots occupied a few minutes only; a few more were spent in a vain search for her flat hat, which was missing from the closet where it usually hung.

"What are you looking for?" said Emily, hearing Gertrude once or twice open and shut the door of the large closet at the end of the upper entry.

"My hat; but I don't see it. I believe I shall have to borrow your sun-bonnet again," and she took up a white sun-bonnet, the same she had worn in the morning, and which now lay on the bed.

"Certainly, my dear," said Emily.

"I shall begin to think it's mine, before long," said Gertrude, gayly, as she ran off; "I wear it so much more than you do." She found Fanny waiting for her; the rest of the party had started, and were some distance down the road, nearly out of sight. Emily now called from the staircase, "Gertrude, my child, have you thick shoes? It is always very wet in the meadow beyond the Thornton place." Gertrude assured her that she had; but, fearing that the others were less carefully equipped, inquired of Mrs. Graham whether Belle and Kitty were insured against the dampness, possibly the mud, they might encounter.

Mrs. Graham declared they were not, and was at a loss what to do, as they were now quite out of sight, and it would be so much trouble for them to return.

"I have some very light India-rubbers," said Gertrude; "I will take them with me, and Fanny and I shall be in time to warn them before they come to the place."

It was an easy matter to overtake Belle and the lieutenant, for they walked very slowly, and seemed not unwilling to be left in the rear. The reverse, however, was the case with Mr. Bruce and Kitty, who appeared purposely to keep in advance; Kitty hastening her steps from her reluctance to allow an agreeable tête-à-tête to be interfered with, and Ben from a desire to occupy such a position as would give Gertrude a fair opportunity to observe his devotion to Kitty, which increased the moment *she* came in sight whose jealousy he was desirous to arouse.

They had now passed the Thornton farm, and only one field separated them from the meadow, which, covered with grass, and fair to the eye, was nevertheless in the centre a complete quagmire, and only passable, even for the thickly shod, by keeping close to the wall, and thus skirting the field. Gertrude and Fanny were some distance behind, and already nearly out of breath with a pursuit in which the others had gained so great an advantage. As they were passing the farm-house, Mrs. Thornton appeared at the door and addressed Gertrude, who, foreseeing that she should be detained some minutes, bade Fanny run on, acquaint her brother and Kitty with the nature of the soil in advance, and beg them to wait at the bars until the rest of the party came up. Fanny was too late, notwithstanding the haste she made; they were half across the meadow when she reached the bars, proceeding, however, in perfect safety, for Mr. Bruce was conducting Kitty by the only practicable path, close under the wall, proving to Gertrude, who in a few moments joined Fanny, that he was no stranger to the place. When they were about half-way across, they seemed to encounter some obstacle, for Kitty stood poised on one foot and clinging to the wall, while Mr. Bruce placed a few stepping-stones across the path. He then helped her over, and they went on, their figures soon disappearing in the grove beyond.

Isabel and the lieutenant were so long making their appearance that Fanny became very impatient, and urged Gertrude to leave them to their fate. They at last turned the corner near the farm-house, and came on, Belle maintaining her leisurely pace, although it was easy to be seen that the others were waiting for her.

"Are you lame, Miss Clinton?" called out Fanny, as soon as they were within hearing.

"Lame!" said Belle; "what do you mean?"

"Why, you walk to slow," said Fanny, "I thought something must be the matter with your feet."

Belle disdained any reply to this, and, tossing her head, entered the damp meadow, in close conversation with her devoted young officer, not deigning even to look at Gertrude, who, without appearing to notice her haughtiness, took Fanny's hand, and, turning away from the direct path, to make the circuit of the field, said to Belle, with an unruffled ease and courtesy of manner, "This way, if you please, Miss Clinton; we have been waiting to guide you through this wet meadow."

"Is it wet?" asked Belle, in alarm, glancing down at her delicate slipper; she then added, in a provoked tone, "I should have thought you would have known better than to bring us this way. I shan't go across."

"Then you can go back," said the pert Fanny; "nobody cares."

"It was not my proposition," remarked Gertrude, mildly, though with a heightened color, "but I think I can help you through the difficulty. Mrs. Graham was afraid you had worn thin shoes, and I brought you a pair of India-rubbers."

Belle took them, and, without the grace to express any thanks, said, as she unfolded the paper in which they were wrapped, "Whose are they?"

"Mine," replied Gertrude.

"I don't believe I can keep them on," muttered Belle; "they'll be immense, I suppose."

"Allow me," said the lieutenant; and, taking one of the shoes, he stooped to place it on her foot, but found it difficult to do so, as it proved quite too small. Belle, perceiving this to be the case, bent down to perform the office for herself, and treated Gertrude's property with such angry violence that she snapped the slender strap which passed across the instep, and even then only succeeded in partially forcing her foot into the shoe.

Meantime, as she bent forward, Fanny's attention was attracted by a very tasteful broad-brimmed hat, which she wore jauntily set on one side of her head, and which Fanny at once recognized as Gertrude's. It was a somewhat fanciful article of dress, that Gertrude would hardly have thought of purchasing for herself, but which Mr. Graham had selected and brought home to her the previous summer, to replace a common garden hat which he had accidentally crushed and ruined. As the style of it was simple and in good taste, she had been in the habit of wearing it often in her country walks, and usually kept it hung in the entry closet, where it had been found and appropriated by Belle. It had been seen by Fanny in Gertrude's room at Mrs. Warren's; she had also been permitted to wear it on one occasion, when she took part in a charade, and could not be mistaken as to its identity. Having heard Gertrude remark to Emily upon its being missing, she was astonished to see it adorning Belle; and, as she stood behind her, deliberately pointed, made signs to Gertrude, opened her eyes, distorted her countenance, and performed a series of pantomimic gestures expressive of an intention to snatch it from Miss Clinton's head, and place it on that of its rightful owner.

Gertrude's gravity nearly gave way; she shook her head at Fanny, held up her finger, made signs for her to forbear, and, with a face whose laughter was only concealed by the deep white bonnet which she wore, took her hand, and hastened with her along the path, leaving Belle and beau to follow.

"Fanny," said she, "you must not make me laugh so; if Miss Clinton had seen us, she would have been very much hurt."

"She has no business to wear your hat," said Fanny, "and she shan't!"

"Yes, she shall," replied Gertrude; "she looks beautifully in it. I am delighted to have her wear it, and you must not intimate to her that it is mine."

Fanny would not promise, and there was a sly look in her eye which prophesied mischief.

The walk through the woods was delightful, and Gertrude and her young companion, in the quiet enjoyment of it, had almost forgotten that they were members of a gay party, when they suddenly came in sight of Kitty and Mr. Bruce. They were sitting at the foot of an old oak, Kitty earnestly engaged in the manufacture of an oak-wreath, which she was just fitting to her attendant's hat; while he himself, when Gertrude first caught sight of him, was leaning against the tree in a careless, listless attitude. As soon, however, as he perceived their approach, he bent forward, inspected Kitty's work, and, when they came within hearing, was uttering a profusion of thanks and compliments, which he took care should reach Gertrude's ears, and which the blushing, smiling Kitty received with manifest pleasure,—a pleasure which was still further enhanced by her perceiving that Gertrude had apparently no power to withdraw his attention from her, but that, on the contrary, he permitted her rival to seat herself at a distance, and continued to pour into her own ear little confidential nothings. Poor, simple Kitty! she believed him honest, while he bought her heart with counterfeits.

"Miss Gertrude," said Fanny, "I wish we could go into some pine woods, so that I could get some cones to make baskets and frames of."

"There are plenty of pines in that direction," said Gertrude, pointing with her finger.

"Why can't we go and look for cones?" asked Fanny; "we could get back by the time Belle Clinton reaches this place."

Gertrude professed her willingness to do so, and she and Fanny started off, having first tied their bonnets to the branch of a tree. They were gone some time, for Fanny found plenty of cones, and made a large collection of them, but was then at a loss how to carry them home. "I have thought," said she, at last; "I will run back and borrow brother Ben's handkerchief; or, if he won't let me have it, I'll take my own bonnet and fill it full." Gertrude promised to await her return, and she ran off. When she came near the spot where she had left Kitty and Mr. Bruce, she heard several voices and loud laughter. Belle and the lieutenant had arrived, and they were having great sport about something. Belle was standing with the white cape-bonnet in her hand. She had bent it completely out of shape, so as to give it the appearance of an old woman's cap, had adorned the front with white-weed and dandelions, and finally pinned on a handkerchief to serve as a veil. It certainly looked very ridiculous;—she was holding it up on the end of the lieutenant's cane, and endeavoring to obtain a bid for Miss Flint's bridal bonnet.

Fanny listened a moment with an indignant countenance, then advanced with a bound, as if just running from the woods. Kitty caught her frock as she passed, and exclaimed, "Why, Fanny, are you here? Where's Gertrude?"

"O, she's in the pine woods!" replied Fanny, "and I'm going right back; she only sent me to get her hat, the sun's so warm where we are."

"Ah, yes!" said Belle, "her Paris hat. Please give it to her, with our compliments."

"No, that isn't hers," said Fanny; "*that* is Miss Emily's. *This* is hers;" and she laid her hand upon the straw head-dress which the gentlemen had but a moment before been assuring Belle was vastly becoming, and, without ceremony, snatched it from her head.

Belle's eyes flashed angrily. "What do you mean?" said she, "you saucy little creature! Give me that hat!" and she stretched out her hand to take it.

"I shan't do any such thing," said Fanny; "it's Gertrude's hat. She looked for it this afternoon, but concluded it was either lost or stolen, and so borrowed Miss Emily's cape-bonnet; but she'll be very glad to find it, and I'll carry it to her. I rather think," said she, looking over her shoulder, as she ran off, "I rather think Miss Emily would be willing you should wear her bonnet home, if you'll be careful and not bend it!"

A few moments of embarrassment and anger to Belle, laughter from Kitty and Mr. Bruce, and concealed amusement on Lieutenant Osborne's part, and Gertrude came hastily from the woods, with the hat in her hand, Fanny following her, and taking advantage of Belle's position, with her back towards her, to resume her pantomimic threats and insinuations. "Miss Clinton," said Gertrude, as she placed the hat in her lap, "I am afraid Fanny has been very rude in my name. I did not send her for either hat or bonnet, and shall be pleased to have you wear this as often as you like."

"I don't want it," said Belle, scornfully; "I'd no idea it belonged to you."

"Certainly not; I am aware of it," said Gertrude. "But I trust that will not prevent your making use of it for to-day, at least." Without urging the matter further, she proposed that they should hasten on to the top of the hill, which they could not otherwise reach before sundown; and set the example by moving forward in that direction, Fanny accompanying her, and busying herself as she went with stripping the decorations from Emily's despised bonnet; Belle tying an embroidered handkerchief under her chin, and Mr. Bruce swinging on his arm the otherwise neglected hat.

Belle did not recover her temper for the evening; the rest found their excursion agreeable, and it was nearly dark when they reached the Thornton farm on their return. Here Gertrude left them, telling Fanny that she had promised to stop and see Jemmy Thornton, one of her Sunday-school class, who was sick with a fever, and refusing to let her remain, as her mother might not wish her to enter the house where several of the family were sick.

About an hour after, as Gertrude was walking home in some haste, she was joined near Mr. Graham's house by Mr. Bruce, who, with her hat still hanging on his arm, seemed to have been awaiting her return. She started on his abruptly joining her, for it was so dark that she did not at once recognize him, and supposed it might be a stranger.

"Miss Gertrude," said he, "I hope I don't alarm you."

"O, no," said she, reässured by the sound of his voice, "I did not know who it was."

He offered his arm, and she took it; for his recent devotion to Kitty had served in some degree to relieve her of any fear she had felt lest his attentions carried meaning with them; and, concluding that he liked to play beau-general, she had no objection to his escorting her home.

"We had a very pleasant walk, this evening," said he; "at least, *I* had. Miss Kitty is a very entertaining companion."

"I think she is," replied Gertrude; "I like her frank, lively manners much."

"I am afraid you found Fanny rather poor company. I should have joined you occasionally, but I could hardly find an opportunity to quit Miss Kitty, we were so much interested in what we were saying."

"Fanny and I are accustomed to each other, and very happy together," said Gertrude.

"Do you know we have planned a delightful drive for to-morrow?"

"No, I was not aware of it."

"I suppose Miss Ray expects I shall ask her to go with me; but supposing, Miss Gertrude, I should give you the preference, and ask you,—what should you say?"

"That I was much obliged to you, but had an engagement to take a drive with Miss Emily," replied Gertrude, promptly.

"Indeed!" said he, in a surprised and provoked tone, "I thought you would like it; but Miss Kitty, I doubt not, will accept. I will go in and ask her (for they had now reached the house). Here is your hat."

"Thank you," said Gertrude, and would have taken it; but Ben still held it by one string, and said,

"Then you won't go, Miss Gertrude?"

"My engagement with Miss Emily cannot be postponed on any account," answered Gertrude, thankful that she had so excellent a reason for declining.

"Nonsense!" said Mr. Bruce; "you could go with me if you chose; and, if you don't, I shall certainly invite Miss Kitty."

The weight he seemed to attach to this threat astonished Gertrude. "Can it be possible," thought she, "that he expects thus to pique and annoy me?" and she replied to it by saying, "I shall be happy if my declining prove the means of Kitty's enjoying a pleasant drive; she is fond of variety, and has few opportunities here to indulge her taste."

They now entered the parlor. Mr. Bruce sought Kitty in the recess of the window, and Gertrude, not finding Emily present, staid but a short time in the room; long enough, however, to observe Mr. Bruce's exaggerated devotion to Kitty, which was marked by others beside herself. Kitty promised to accompany him the next day, and did so. Mrs. Graham, Mrs. Bruce, Belle and the lieutenant, went also in another vehicle; and Emily and Gertrude, according to their original intention, took a different direction, and, driving white Charlie in the old-fashioned buggy, rejoiced in their quiet independence.

❁❁❁❁❁❁❁❁❁❁❁❁❁❁❁❁❁❁❁❁❁❁❁❁❁❁❁

# Chapter XXXI

*Sporting at will, and moulding sport to art,*
*With that sad holiness—the human heart.*

NEW TIMON

And now days and even weeks passed on, and no marked event took place in Mr. Graham's household. The weather became intensely warm, and no more walks and drives were planned. The lieutenant left the neighboring city, which was at this season nearly deserted by the friends of Mrs. Graham and her nieces; and Isabel, who could neither endure with patience excessive heat or want of society, grew more irritable and fretful than ever.

To Kitty, however, these summer-days were fraught with interest. Mr. Bruce remained in the neighborhood, visited constantly at the house, and exercised a marked influence upon her outward demeanor and her inward happiness, which were changeable and fluctuating as his attentions were freely bestowed or altogether suspended. No wonder the poor girl was puzzled to understand one whose conduct was certainly inexplicable to any but those initiated into his motives. Believing, as he did, that Gertrude would in time show a disposition to win him back, he was anxious only to carry his addresses to Kitty to such a point as would excite a serious alarm in the mind of the poor protegée of the Grahams, who dared to slight his proffered advances. Acting then as he did almost wholly with reference to Gertrude, it was only in her presence, or under such circumstances that he was sure it would reach her ears, that he manifested a marked interest in Kitty; and his behavior was, therefore, in the highest degree unequal, leading the warm-hearted Kitty to believe one moment that he felt for her almost the tenderness of a lover, and the next to suffer under the apprehension of having unconsciously wounded or offended him by her careless gayety or conversation. Unfortunately, too, Mrs. Graham took every opportunity to tease and congratulate her upon her conquest, thereby increasing the simple girl's confidence in the sincerity of Mr. Bruce's admiration.

Nor were Mr. Bruce and Kitty the only persons who found occasion for vexation and anxiety in this matter. Gertrude, whose eyes were soon opened to the existing state of things, was filled with regret and apprehension on account of Kitty, for whose peace and welfare she felt a tender and affectionate concern. The suspicions to which Mr. Bruce's conduct gave rise, during the scenes which have been detailed, were soon strengthened into convictions; for, on several occasions, after he had been offering Kitty ostentatious proofs of devotion, he thought proper to test their effect upon Gertrude by the tender of some attention to herself; more than intimating, at the same time, that she had it in her power to rob Kitty of all claim upon his favor.

Gertrude availed herself of every opportunity to acquaint him with the truth, that he could not possibly render himself more odious in her eyes than by the use of such mean attempts to mortify her; but, attributing her warmth to the very feeling of jealousy which he desired to excite, the selfish young man persevered in his course of folly and wickedness. As he only proffered his attentions, and made no offer of his heart and hand, Gertrude did not in the least trust his professions towards *herself*, considering them merely as intended, if possible, to move her from her firm and consistent course of behavior, in order to gratify his self-love. But she saw plainly that, however light and vain his motives might be in her own case, they were still more so with reference to Kitty; and she was deeply grieved at the evident unconsciousness of this fact which the simple girl constantly exhibited.

For, strangely enough, Kitty having quite forgotten that she had a few weeks back looked upon Gertrude as a rival, now chose her for her bosom friend and confidant. Her aunt was too coarse and rough, Belle too selfish and vain, to be intrusted with little matters of the heart; and, though Kitty had no idea of confessing her partiality for Mr. Bruce, the transparency of her character was such, that she betrayed her secret to Gertrude without being in the least aware that she had done so. Though no one but Gertrude appeared to observe it, Kitty was wonderfully changed;—the gay, laughing, careless Kitty had now her fits of musing,—her sunny face was subject to clouds, that flitted across it, and robbed it of all its brightness. Now, her spirits were unnaturally free and lively; and now, she wore a pensive expression, and, stealthily lifting her eyes, fixed them anxiously on the face of Mr. Bruce, as if studying his temper or his sentiments. If she saw Gertrude walking in the garden, or sitting alone in her room, she would approach, throw her arm around her, lean against her shoulder, and talk on her favorite topic. She would relate, with a mixture of simplicity and folly, the complimentary speeches and polite attentions of Mr. Bruce; talk about him for an hour, and question Gertrude as to her opinion of his merits, and the sincerity of his avowed admiration for herself. She would intimate her perception of some fault possessed by him, who was in her eyes almost perfection; and when Gertrude coïncided with her, and expressed regret at the evident failing, she would exhaust a great amount of strength and ingenuity in her efforts to prove that they were both mistaken in attributing it to him, and that, if he had a fault, it was in reality quite the reverse. She would ask if Gertrude really supposed he meant all he said, and add that of course *she* didn't believe he did,—it was all nonsense. And if Gertrude embraced the opportunity to avow the same opinion, and declare that it was not best to trust all his high-flown flatteries, poor Kitty's face would fall, and she would proceed to give her reasons for *sometimes* thinking he was sincere, he had such a *truthful, earnest* way of speaking.

It was no use to throw out hints, or try to establish safeguards. Kitty was completely infatuated. At last Mr. Bruce thought proper to try Gertrude's firmness by offering to her acceptance a rich ring. Not a little surprised at his presumption, she declined it without hesitation or ceremony, and the next day saw it on the finger of Kitty, who was eager to give an account of its presentation.

"And did you *accept* it?" asked Gertrude, with such a look of astonishment, that Kitty observed it, and evaded an acknowledgment of having done so, by saying, with a blushing countenance, that she agreed to wear it a little while.

"I wouldn't," said Gertrude.

"Why not?"

"Because, in the first place, I do not think it is in good taste to receive rich gifts from gentlemen; and then, again, if strangers notice it, you may be subjected to unpleasant, significant remarks."

"What would you do with it?" asked Kitty.

"I should give it back."

Kitty looked very undecided; but, on reflection, concluded to offer it to Mr. Bruce, and tell him what Gertrude said. She did so, and that gentleman, little appreciating Gertrude's motives, and believing her only desirous of making difficulty between him and Kitty, jumped at the conclusion that her heart was won at last, and that his triumph would now be complete. He was disappointed, therefore, when, on his next meeting with her, she treated him, as she had invariably done of late, with cool civility; indeed, it seemed to him that she was more insensible than ever to his attractions; and, hastily quitting the house, much to the distress of Kitty (who spent the rest of the day in thinking over everything she had done and said which could by any possibility have given offence), he sought his old haunt under the pear-tree, and gave himself up to the consideration of a weighty question.

Seldom did Ben Bruce feel called upon to take serious views of any subject; seldom was he accustomed to rally and marshal the powers of his mind, and deliberately weigh the two sides of an argument. Living, as he did, with no higher aim than the promoting of his own selfish gratification, he had been wont to avail himself of every opportunity for amusement and indulgence, and even to bring mean and petty artifice to the furtherance of his plans. Possessed, as he was, notwithstanding his narrow mind, with what is often called "a good look-out," he was rarely cheated or defrauded of his rights. He knew the value of his money and position in life, and never suffered himself to be sacrificed to the designs of those who hoped to reap a benefit from his companionship. *Self-sacrifice,* too, was a thing of which he had no experience, and with which, as seen in others, he felt no sympathy. Now, however, a crisis had arrived when his own interests and wishes clashed; when necessity demanded that one should be immolated at the shrine of the other, and a choice must be made between the two. It was certainly a matter which claimed deep deliberation; and if Ben Bruce, for the first time in his life, devoted a whole afternoon to careful thought, and an accurate measurement of opposing forces, the occurrence must be attributed to the fact that he was making up his mind on the most important question that ever yet had agitated it.

"Shall I," thought he, "conclude to marry this poor girl? Shall I, who am master of a handsome fortune, and have additional expectations, forego the prospect they afford me of making a brilliant alliance, and condescend to share my wealth and station in society with this adopted child of the Grahams; who, in spite of her poverty, will not grant me a smile even, except at the price of all my possessions? If she were one atom less charming, I would disappoint her, after all! I wonder how she'd feel if I should marry Kitty! I daresay I never should have the satisfaction of knowing; for she's so proud that she would come to my wedding, for aught I know, bend her slender neck as gracefully as ever, and say, 'Good-evening, Mr. Bruce,' as politely and calmly as she does now, every time I go to the house! It provokes me to see how a poor girl like that carries herself. But, as *Mrs. Bruce,* I should be proud of that manner, certainly. I wonder how I ever got in love with her;—I'm sure I don't know. She isn't handsome; at least, mother thinks she isn't, and so does Belle Clinton. But, then again, Lieutenant Osborne noticed her the minute she came into the room; and there's Fan raves about her beauty. I don't know what I think myself; I believe she's bewitched me, so that I'm not capable of judging; but, if it isn't beauty, it is because it's something more than mere good looks."

Thus he soliloquized; and as, every time he revolved the subject, he commenced by dwelling upon the immense sacrifice he was making, and ended with reflections upon Gertrude's charms, it may well be supposed that he ultimately came to the conclusion that he should suffer less by laying his fortune at her feet than by the endeavor to enjoy that fortune without her. For a few days after he arrived at a resolve on this point, he had no opportunity to address a word to Gertrude, who was now doubly anxious to avoid him, and spent nearly the whole day above stairs, except when, at Emily's request, she accompanied her for a short time into the parlor; and even then she took pains, under some pretext or other, to remain close by the side of her blind friend.

About this time, Mrs. Graham and Mrs. Bruce, with their families, received cards for a levee to be held at the house of an acquaintance nearly five miles distant. It was on the occasion of the marriage of a schoolmate of Isabel's, and both she and Kitty were desirous to be present. Mrs. Bruce, who had a close carriage, invited both the cousins to accompany her; and, as Mr. Graham's carryall, when closed, would only accommodate himself and lady, the proposal was gladly acceded to.

The prospect of a gay assembly and an opportunity for display revived Isabel's drooping spirits and energy. Her rich evening dresses were brought out, for the selection of the most suitable and becoming; and as she stood before her mirror, and tried on first one wreath and then another, and looked so beautiful in each that it was difficult to make a choice, Kitty, who stood by, eagerly endeavoring to win her attention, and obtain her advice concerning the style and color most desirable for herself, gave up in despair, and ran off to consult Gertrude.

She found her reading in her own room; but, on Kitty's abrupt entrance, she laid down her book, and gave her undivided attention to the subject which was under discussion.

"Gertrude," said Kitty, "what shall I wear this evening? I've been trying to get Belle to tell me, but she never will speak a word, or hear what I ask her, when she's thinking about her own dress!—I declare, she's dreadfully selfish!"

"Who advises *her*?" asked Gertrude.

"O, nobody; she always decides for herself; but then she has so much taste, and I haven't the least in the world!—So, do tell me, Gertrude, what had I better wear to-night?"

"I'm the last person you should ask, Kitty; I never went to a fashionable party in my life."

"That doesn't make any difference. I'm sure, if you did go, you'd look better than any of us; and I'm not afraid to trust to your opinion, for I never in my life saw you wear anything that didn't look genteel;—even your gingham morning-gown has a sort of stylish air."

"Stop, stop, Kitty! you are going too far; you must keep within bounds, if you want me to believe you."

"Well, then," said Kitty, "to say nothing of yourself (for I know you're superior to flattery, Gertrude,—*somebody* told me so), who furnishes Miss Emily's wardrobe? Who selects her dresses?"

"I have done so, lately, but—"

"I thought so! I thought so!" interrupted Kitty. "I knew poor Miss Emily was indebted to you for always looking so nice and so beautiful."

"No, indeed, Kitty, you are mistaken; I have never seen Emily better dressed than she was the first time I met her; and her beauty is not borrowed from art—it is all her own."

"O, I know she is lovely, and everybody admires her; but no one can suppose she would take pains to wear such pretty things, and put them on so gracefully, just to please herself."

"It is not done merely to please herself; it was to please her father that Emily first made the exertion to dress with taste as well as neatness. I have heard that, for some time after she lost her eye-sight, she was disposed to be very careless; but, having accidentally discovered that it was an additional cause of sorrow to him, she roused herself at once, and, with Mrs. Ellis' assistance, contrived always afterwards to please him in that particular. But you observe, Kitty, she never wears anything showy or conspicuous."

"No, indeed,—that is what I like; but, Gertrude, hasn't she always been blind?"

"No; until she was sixteen she had beautiful eyes, and could see as well as you can."

"What happened to her? How did she lose them?"

"I don't know."

"Didn't you ever ask?"

"No."

"Why not?—how queer!"

"I heard that she didn't like to speak of it."

"But she would have told you; she half worships you."

"If she had wished me to know, she would have told without my asking."

Kitty stared at Gertrude, wondering much at such unusual delicacy and consideration, and instinctively admiring a forbearance of which she was conscious she should herself have been incapable.

"But, your dress!" said Gertrude, smiling at Kitty's abstraction.

"O, yes! I had almost forgotten what I came here for," said Kitty. "What shall it be, then,—thick or thin; pink, blue, or white?"

"What has Isabel decided upon?"

"Blue,—a rich blue silk; that is her favorite color, always; but it doesn't become me."

"No, I should think not," said Gertrude; "but come, Kitty, we will go to your room and see the dresses, and I will give my opinion."

Kitty's wardrobe having been inspected, and Gertrude having expressed her preference for a thin and flowing material, especially in the summer season, a delicate white crape was fixed upon. And now there was a new difficulty; among all her head-dresses, none proved satisfactory,—all were more or less defaced, and none of them to be compared with a new and exquisite wreath which Isabel was arranging among her curls.

"I cannot wear any of them," said Kitty, "they look so mean by the side of Isabel's; but, O!" exclaimed she, glancing at a box which lay on the dressing-table, "these are just what I should like! O, Isabel, where did you get these beautiful carnations?" and she took up some flowers, which were, indeed, a rare imitation of nature, and, displaying them to Gertrude, added that they were just what she wanted.

"O, Kitty," said Isabel, angrily, turning away from the glass, and observing what her cousin had in her hand, "don't touch my flowers! you will spoil them!" and, snatching them from her, she replaced them in the box, opened a drawer in her bureau, and, having deposited them there, took the precaution to lock them up and put the key in her pocket,—an action which Gertrude witnessed with astonishment, not unmingled with indignation.

"Kitty," said she, "I will arrange a wreath of natural flowers for you, if you wish."

"Will you, Gertrude?" said the disappointed and provoked Kitty. "O, that will be delightful! I should like it, of all things! And, Isabel, you cross old miser, you can keep all your wreaths to yourself! It is a pity you can't wear two at a time!"

True to her promise, Gertrude prepared a head-dress for Kitty; and so tastefully did she mingle the choicest productions of the garden, that, when Isabel saw her cousin arrayed under a more careful and affectionate superintendence than she often enjoyed, she felt, notwithstanding her own proud consciousness of superior beauty, a sharp pang of jealousy of Kitty, and dislike to Gertrude.

It had been no small source of annoyance to Isabel, who could not endure to be outshone, that Kitty had of late been the object of marked attention to Mr. Bruce, while she herself had been entirely overlooked. Not that she felt any partiality for the gentleman whom Kitty was so anxious to please; but the dignity conferred on her cousin by his admiration, the interest the affair awakened in her aunt, and the meaning looks of Mrs. Bruce, all made her feel herself of second-rate importance, and rendered her more eager than ever to supplant, in general society, the comparatively unpretending Kitty. Therefore, when Mrs. Graham complimented the latter on her unusually attractive appearance, and declared that *somebody* would this night be more charmed than ever, Isabel curled her lip with mingled disdain and defiance, while the blushing Kitty turned to Gertrude and whispered in her ear, "Mr. Bruce likes white; he said so, the other day, when you passed through the room dressed in your mulled muslin."

❀❀❀❀❀❀❀❀❀❀❀❀❀❀❀❀❀❀❀❀❀❀❀❀❀❀

# Chapter XXXII

*Know, then, that I have supported my pretensions to your hand in the way that best suited my character.*—IVANHOE

Emily was not well this evening. It was often the case, lately, that headache, unwonted weariness, or a nervous shrinking from noise and excitement, sent her to her own room, and sometimes led her to seek her couch at an early hour. After Mrs. Graham and her nieces had gone down stairs to await Mr. Graham's pleasure and Mrs. Bruce's arrival, Gertrude returned to Emily, whom she had left only a short time before, and found her suffering more than usual from what she termed her troublesome head. She was easily induced to seek the only infallible cure—sleep; and Gertrude, seating herself on the bed-side, as she was frequently in the habit of doing, bathed her temples until she fell into a quiet slumber. The noise of Mrs. Bruce's carriage, coming and going, seemed to disturb her a little; but in a few moments more she was so sound asleep that, when Mr. and Mrs. Graham departed, the loud voice of the latter, giving her orders to one of the servants, did not startle her in the least. Gertrude sat some time longer without changing her position; then, quietly rising and arranging everything for the night, according to Emily's well-known wishes, she closed the door gently behind her, sought a book in her own room, and, entering the cool and vacant parlor, seated herself at a table, to enjoy the now rare opportunity for perfect stillness and repose.

Either her own thoughts, however, proved more interesting than the volume she held, or, it may be, the insects, attracted by the bright lamp, annoyed her; or, the beauty of the evening won her observation; for she soon forsook her seat at the table, and, going towards the open glass-doors, placed herself near them, and, leaning her head upon her hand, became absorbed in meditation.

She had not long sat thus when she heard a foot-step in the room, and, turning, saw Mr. Bruce beside her. She started, and exclaimed, "Mr. Bruce! is it possible? I thought you had gone to the wedding."

"No, there were greater attractions for me at home. Could you believe. Miss Gertrude, I should find any pleasure in a party which did not include yourself?"

"I certainly should not have the vanity to suppose the reverse," replied Gertrude.

"I wish you had a little more vanity, Miss Gertrude. Perhaps then you would sometimes believe what I say."

"I am glad you have the candor to acknowledge, Mr. Bruce, that, without that requisite, one would find it impossible to put faith in your fair speeches."

"I acknowledge no such thing. I only say to you what any other girl but yourself would be willing enough to believe; but how shall I convince you that I am serious, and wish to be so understood? How shall I persuade you to converse freely with me, and no longer shun my society?"

"By addressing me with simple truthfulness, and sparing me those words and attentions which I have endeavored to convince you are unacceptable to me and unworthy of yourself."

"But I have a meaning, Gertrude, a *deep* meaning. I have been trying for several days to find an opportunity to tell you of my resolve, and you *must* listen to me now;" for he saw her change color and look anxious and uneasy. "You must give me an answer at once, and one that will, I trust, be favorable to my wishes. You like plain speaking; and I will be plain enough, now that my mind is made up. My relatives and friends may talk and wonder as much as they please at my choosing a wife who has neither money nor family to boast of; but I have determined to defy them all, and offer, without hesitation, to share my prospects with you. After all, what is money good for, if it doesn't make a man independent to do as he pleases? And, as to the world, I don't see but you can hold your head as high as anybody, Gertrude; so, if you've no objection to make, we'll play at cross purposes no longer, and consider the thing settled;" and he endeavored to take her hand.

But Gertrude drew back; the color flushed her cheeks, and her eyes glistened as she fixed them upon his face with an expression of astonishment and pride that could not be mistaken.

The calm, penetrating look of those dark eyes spoke volumes, and Mr. Bruce replied to their inquiring gaze in these words: "I hope you are not displeased at my frankness."

"With your frankness," said Gertrude, calmly; "no, that is a thing that never displeases me. But what have I unconsciously done to inspire you with so much confidence that, while you defend yourself for defying the wishes of your friends, you hardly give me a voice in the matter?"

"Nothing," said Bruce, in an apologizing tone; "but I thought you had labored under the impression that I was disposed to trifle with your affections, and had therefore kept aloof and maintained a distance towards me which you would not have done had you known how much I was in earnest; but, believe me, I only admired you the more for behaving with so much dignity, and if I have presumed upon your favor, you must forgive me. I shall be only too happy to receive a favorable answer from you."

The expression of wounded pride vanished from Gertrude's face. "He knows no better," thought she; "I should pity his vanity and ignorance, and sympathize in his disappointment;" and, in disclaiming, with a positive-ness which left no room for further self-deception, any interest in Mr. Bruce beyond that of an old acquaintance and sincere well-wisher, she neverthe-less softened her refusal by the choice of the mildest language, and terms the least likely to grieve or mortify him. She felt, as every true woman must under similar circumstances, that her gratitude and consideration were due to the man who, however little she might esteem *him*, had paid *her* the highest honor; and, though her regret in the matter was somewhat tempered by the thought of Kitty, and the strangeness of Mr. Bruce's conduct towards her, now rendered doubly inexplicable, she did not permit *that* reflection, even, to prevent her from maintaining the demeanor, not only of a perfect lady, but of one who, in giving pain to another, laments the necessity of so doing.

She almost felt, however, as if her thoughtfulness for his feelings had been thrown away, when she perceived the spirit in which he received her refusal.

"Gertrude," said he, "you are either trifling with me or yourself. If you are still disposed to coquet with me, I desire to have it understood that I shall not humble myself to urge you further; but if, on the other hand, you are so far forgetful of your own interests as deliberately to refuse such a fortune as mine, I think it's a pity you haven't got some friend to advise you. Such a chance doesn't occur every day, especially to poor school-mistresses; and if you are so foolish as to overlook it, I'll venture to say you'll never have another."

Gertrude's *old temper* rose at this insulting language, beat and throbbed in her chafed spirit, and even betrayed itself in the tips of her fingers, which trembled as they rested on the table near which she stood (having risen as Mr. Bruce spoke); but, though this was an unlooked-for and unwonted rebellion of an old enemy, her feelings had too long been under strict regula-tion to yield to the blast, however sudden, and she replied in a tone which, though slightly agitated, was far from being angry, "Allowing I could so far forget *myself*, Mr. Bruce, I would not do *you* such an injustice as to marry you for your fortune. I do not despise wealth, for I know the blessing it may often be; but my affections cannot be bought with gold;" and as she spoke she moved towards the door.

"Stay!" said Mr. Bruce, catching her hand; "listen to me one moment; let me ask you one question. Are you jealous of my late attentions to an-other?"

"No," answered Gertrude; "but I confess I have not understood your motives."

"Did you think," asked he, eagerly, "that I cared for that silly Kitty? Did you believe, for a moment, that I had any other desire than to show you that my devotion was acceptable elsewhere? No, upon my word, I never had the least particle of regard for her; my heart has been yours all the time, and I only danced attendance upon *her* in hopes to win a glance from *you,*—an *anxious* glance, if might be. O, how often I have wished that you would show one quarter of the pleasure that she did in my society; would blush and smile as she did; would look sad when I was dull, and laugh when I was merry; so that I might flatter myself, as I could in her case, that your heart was won! But, as to *loving* her,—pooh! Mrs. Graham's poodle-dog might as well try to rival you as that soft—"

"Stop! stop!" exclaimed Gertrude; "for *my* sake, if not for your *own!* O, how—" She could say no more, but, sinking into the nearest seat, burst into tears, and hiding her face in her hands, as had been her habit in childhood, wept without restraint.

Mr. Bruce stood by in utter amazement; at last he approached her, and asked, in a low voice, "What is the matter? what have I done?"

It was some minutes before she could reply to the question; then, lifting her head, and tossing the hair from her forehead, she displayed features expressive only of the deepest grief, and said, in broken accents, "What have you done? O, how can you ask? She is gentle, and amiable, and affectionate. She loves everybody, and trusts everybody. You have *deceived* her, and *I* was the cause of it! O, how, how could you do it!"

A most disconcerted appearance did Ben present at her words, and hesitating was the tone in which he muttered, "She will get over it."

"Get over *what?*" said Gertrude; "her love for you? Perhaps so; I know not how deep it is. But, think of her happy, trusting nature, and how it has been betrayed! Think how she believed your flattering words, and how hollow they were, all the while! Think how her confidence has been abused! how that fatherless and motherless girl, who had a claim to the sympathy of all the world, has been taught a lesson of distrust!"

"I didn't think you would take it so," said Ben.

"How else could I view it?" asked Gertrude. "Could you expect that such a course would win my respect?"

"You take it very seriously, Gertrude; such flirtations are common."

"I am sorry to hear it," said Gertrude. "To my mind, unversed in the ways of society, it is a dreadful thing to trifle thus with a human heart. Whether Kitty loves you, is not for me to say; but what opinion—alas!—will she have of your sincerity?"

"I think you're rather hard, Miss Gertrude, when it was my love for you that prompted my conduct."

"Perhaps I am," said Gertrude. "It is not my place to censure; I speak only from the impulse of my heart. One orphan girl's warm defence of another is but natural. Perhaps she views the thing lightly, and does not *need* an advocate; but, O, Mr. Bruce, do not think so meanly of my sex as to believe that one woman's heart can be won to love and reverence by the author of another's betrayal! She were less than woman who could be so false to her sense of right and honor."

"Betrayal!—Nonsense! you are very high-flown."

"So much so, Mr. Bruce, that half an hour ago I could have wept that you should have bestowed your affection where it met with no requital; and if now I weep for the sake of her whose ears have listened to false professions, and whose peace has, to say the least, been *threatened* on my account, you should attribute it to the fact that my sympathies have not been exhausted by contact with the world."

A short silence ensued. Ben went a step or two towards the door, then stopped, came back, and said, "After all, Gertrude Flint, I believe the time will come when your notions will grow less romantic, and you will look back to this night and wish you had acted differently. You will find out, in time, that this is a world where people must look out for themselves."

Immediately upon this remark he left the room, and Gertrude heard him shut the hall-door with a loud bang as he went out.

A moment after, the silence that ensued was disturbed by a slight sound, which seemed to proceed from the deep recess in the window. Gertrude started, and, as she went towards the spot, heard distinctly a smothered sob. She lifted a draperied curtain, and there, upon the wide window-seat, her head bent over and buried in the cushions, and her little slender form distorted into a strange and forlorn attitude,—such as might be seen in a grieved child,—sat, or rather crouched, poor Kitty Ray. The crumpled folds of her white crape dress, her withered wreath,—which had half fallen from her head, and hung drooping on her shoulders,—her disordered hair, and her little hand clinging to a thick cord connected with the window-curtain, all added to the appearance of extreme distress.

"Kitty!" cried Gertrude, at once recognizing her, although her face was hid.

At the sound of her voice, Kitty sprung suddenly from her recumbent posture, threw herself into Gertrude's arms, laid her head upon her shoulder, and, though she did not, *could* not weep, shook and trembled with an agitation which was perfectly uncontrollable. Her hand, which grasped Gertrude's, was fearfully cold; her eyes seemed fixed; and occasionally, at intervals, the same hysterical sound which had at first betrayed her in her hiding-place alarmed her young protector, to whom she clung as if seized with sudden fear. Gertrude supported her to a seat, and then, folding the slight form to her bosom, chafed the cold hands, and again and again kissing the rigid lips, succeeded at last in restoring her to something like composure. For an hour she lay thus, receiving Gertrude's caresses with evident pleasure, and now and then returning them convulsively, but speaking no word, and making no noise. Gertrude, with the truest judgment and delicacy, refrained from asking questions, or recurring to a conversation the whole of which had been thus overheard and comprehended; but, patiently waiting until Kitty grew more quiet and calm, prepared for her a soothing draught; and then, finding her completely prostrated, both in mind and body, passed her arm around her waist, guided her up stairs, and, without the ceremony of an invitation, took her into her own room, where, if she proved wakeful, she would be spared the wonder and scrutiny of Isabel. Still clinging to Gertrude, the poor girl, to whose relief tears came at last, sobbed herself to sleep; and all her sufferings were for a time forgotten in that oblivion in which childhood and youth find a temporary rest, and often a healing balm to pain.

It was otherwise, however, with Gertrude, who, though of nearly the same age as Kitty, had seen too much trouble, experienced too much care, to enjoy, in times of disquiet, the privilege of sinking easily to repose. She felt under the necessity, too, of remaining awake until Isabel's return, that she might inform her what had become of Kitty, whom she would be sure to miss from the room which they occupied in common. She seated herself, therefore, at the window, to watch for her return; and was pained to observe that Kitty tossed restlessly on her pillows, and occasionally muttered in her sleep, as if distressed by uneasy dreams. It was past midnight when Mrs. Graham and her niece returned home, and Gertrude went immediately to inform the latter that her cousin was asleep in her room. The noise of the carriages, however, had awakened the sleeper, and when Gertrude returned she was rubbing her eyes, and trying to collect her thoughts.

Suddenly the recollection of the scene of the evening flashed upon her, and, with a deep sigh, she exclaimed, "O, Gertrude! I have been dreaming of Mr. Bruce! Should you have thought he would have treated me so?"

"No, I should not," said Gertrude; "but I wouldn't dream about him, Kitty, nor think of him any more; we will both go to sleep and forget him."

"It is different with you," said Kitty, with simplicity. "He loves you, and you do not care for him; but I—I—" Here her feelings overpowered her, and she buried her face in the pillow.

Gertrude approached, laid her hand kindly upon the head of the poor girl, and finished the sentence for her. "You have such a large heart, Kitty, that he found some place there, perhaps; but it is too good a heart to be shared by the mean and base. You must think no more of him—he is not worthy of your regard."

"I can't help it," said Kitty; "I am silly, just as he said."

"No, you are not," said Gertrude, encouragingly; "and you must prove it to him."

"How?"

"Let him see that, with all her softness, Kitty Ray is strong and brave; that she has ceased to believe his flattery, and values his professions at just what they are worth."

"Will you help me, Gertrude? You are my best friend; you took my part, and told him how wicked he had been to me. May I come to you for comfort when I can't make believe happy any longer to him, and my aunt, and Isabel?"

Gertrude's fervent embrace was assurance enough of her coöperation and sympathy.

"You will be as bright and happy as ever in a few weeks," said she; "you will soon cease to care for a person whom you no longer respect."

Kitty disclaimed the possibility of ever being happy again; but Gertrude, though herself a novice in the ways of the human heart, was much more sanguine and hopeful. She saw that Kitty's violent outburst of sobs and tears was like a child's impetuous grief, and suspected that the deepest recesses of her nature were safe, and unendangered by the storm.

She felt a deep compassion for her, however, and many fears lest she would be wanting in sufficient strength of mind to behave with dignity and womanly pride in her future intercourse with Mr. Bruce, and would also expose herself to the ridicule of Isabel, and the contempt of her aunt, by betraying in her looks and behavior her recent trying and mortifying experience.

Fortunately, the first-mentioned trial was spared her, by Mr. Bruce's immediately absenting himself from the house, and in the course of a few days leaving home for the remainder of the summer; and, as this circumstance involved both his own and Mrs. Graham's family in doubt and wonder as to the cause of his sudden departure, Kitty's outward trials consisted chiefly in the continued and repeated questionings from her aunt and cousin, to which she was incessantly exposed, as to her share in this sudden and unlooked-for occurrence. Had she refused him? Had she quarrelled with him?—and why?

Kitty denied that she had done either; but she was not believed, and the affair remained a strange and interesting mystery.

Both Mrs. Graham and Isabel were aware that Kitty's refusing at the last moment to attend the wedding levee was owing to her having accidentally learned, just before the carriage drove to the door, that Mr. Bruce was not to be of the party; and, as they wrung from her the confession that he had passed a part of the evening at the house, they came to the very natural conclusion that some misunderstanding had arisen between the supposed lovers.

Isabel was too well acquainted with Kitty's sentiments to believe she had voluntarily relinquished an admirer who had evidently been highly prized; and she also saw that the sensitive girl winced under every allusion to the deserter. One would have thought, then, that common affection and delicacy would have taught her to forbear any reference to the painful subject. But this was not the case. She made Mr. Bruce and his strange disappearance her almost constant topic; and, on occasion of the slightest difference or disagreement arising between herself and Kitty, she silenced and distressed the latter by some pointed and cutting sarcasm relative to her late love affair. Kitty would then seek refuge with Gertrude, relate her trials, and claim her sympathy; and she not only found in her a friendly listener to her woes, but invariably acquired in her society greater strength and cheerfulness than she could elsewhere rally to her aid, so that she became gradually dependent upon her for the only peace she enjoyed; and Gertrude, who felt a sincere interest in the girl who had been on her account subjected to such cruel deception, and whose drooping spirits and pensive countenance spoke touchingly of her inner sorrow, spared no pains to enliven her sadness, divert her thoughts, and win her to those occupations and amusements in which she herself had often found a relief from preying care and vexation.

A large proportion of her time was necessarily devoted to her dearest and best friend, Emily; but there was nothing exclusive in Emily's nature; when not suffering from those bodily afflictions to which she was subject, she was ever ready to extend a cordial welcome to all visitors who could find pleasure or benefit from her society; and even the wild and thoughtless Fanny never felt herself an intruder in Emily's premises, so sweet was the smile with which she was greeted, so forbearing the indulgence which was awarded to her waywardness. It can hardly be supposed, then, that Kitty would be excluded from her hospitality, especially after Emily, with a truly wonderful perception, became aware that she was less gay and happy than formerly, and had therefore an additional claim upon her kindness.

Many a time, when Isabel had been tantalizing and wounding Kitty beyond what her patience could endure, and Gertrude had been vainly sought elsewhere, a little figure would present itself at the half-open door of Miss Graham's room, and was sure to hear the sweetest of voices saying from within, "I hear you, Kitty; come in, my dear; we shall be glad of your pleasant company;" and once there, seated by the side of Gertrude, learning from her some little art in needle-work, listening to an agreeable book, or Emily's more agreeable conversation, Kitty passed hours which were never forgotten, so peaceful were they, so serene, so totally unlike any she had ever spent before. Nor did they fail to leave a lasting impression upon her, for the benefit of her mind and heart.

None could live in familiar intercourse with Emily, listen to her words, observe the radiance of her heavenly smile, and breathe in the pure atmosphere that environed her very being, and not carry away with them the *love* of virtue and holiness, if not something of their *essence*. She was so unselfish, so patient, notwithstanding her privations, that Kitty would have been ashamed to repine in her presence; and there was a contagious cheerfulness ever pervading her apartment, which, in spite of Kitty's recent cause of unhappiness, often led her to forget herself, and break into her natural tone of buoyancy and glee. As week after week passed away, and her sufferings and regrets, which at first were so vehement and severe, began to wear off as rapidly as such hurricane sorrows are apt to do, and the process of cure went on silently and unconsciously, another work at the same time progressed, to her equally salutary and important. In her constant intercourse with the pure heart and superior mind of Emily, and her still more familiar intimacy with one who had sat at her feet and learned of her, Kitty imbibed an elevation of thought and a worthiness of aim quite foreign to her quondam character.

The foolish child, whose heart was ensnared by the flatteries of Mr. Bruce, learned—partly through the example and precepts of her new counsellors and friends, and partly through her own bitter experience—the vanity and emptiness of the food thus administered to her mind; and resolving, for the first time in her life, to cultivate and cherish her immortal powers, she now developed the first germs of her better nature; which, expanding in later years, and through other influences, transformed the gay, fluttering, vain child of fashion, into the useful, estimable and lovely woman.

# Chapter XXXIII

*Small slights, neglect, unmixed perhaps with hate,*
*Make up in number what they want in weight.*
*These, and a thousand griefs minute as these,*
*Corrode our comfort and destroy our ease.*

HANNAH MOORE

Little did Gertrude imagine, while she was striving most disinterestedly to promote the welfare and happiness of Kitty, who had thrown herself upon her love and care, the jealousy and ill-will she was exciting in others. Isabel, who had never liked one whose whole tone of action and life was a continual reproach to her own vanity and selfishness, and who saw in her the additional crime of being the favored friend of a youth of whose interesting boyhood she herself retained a sentimental recollection, was ready and eager to seize the earliest opportunity of rendering her odious in the eyes of Mrs. Graham. She was not slow to observe the remarkable degree of confidence that seemed to exist between Kitty and Gertrude; she remembered that her cousin had forsaken her own room for that of the latter the very night after her probable quarrel and parting with Bruce; and, her resentment and anger excited still further by the growing friendship which her own coldness and unkindness to Kitty served only to strengthen and confirm, she hastened to communicate to Mrs. Graham her suspicion that Gertrude had, for purposes of her own, made a difficulty between Bruce and Kitty, fostered and widened the breach, and succeeded at last in breaking off the match.

Mrs. Graham readily adopted Belle's opinion. "Kitty," said she, "is weak-minded, and evidently very much under Miss Flint's influence. I shouldn't be surprised if you were right, Belle!"

Thus leagued together, they endeavored to surprise or entrap Kitty into a confession of the means which had been taken by Gertrude to drive away her lover, and out-wit herself. But Kitty, while she indignantly denied Gertrude's having thus injured her, persisted obstinately in refusing to reveal the occurrences of the eventful evening of the wedding levee. It was the first secret Kitty ever did keep; but her woman's pride was involved in the affair, and she preserved it with a care which both honor and wisdom prompted.

Mrs. Graham and Belle were now truly angry, and many were the private discussions held by them on the subject, many the vain conjectures which they conjured up; and as, day after day, they became more and more incensed against Gertrude, so they gradually began to manifest it in their demeanor.

Gertrude soon perceived the incivility to which she was constantly subjected; for, though in a great degree independent of their friendship, she could not live under the same roof without their having frequent opportunities to wound her by their rudeness, which soon became marked, and would have been unendurable to one whose disposition was less thoroughly schooled than Gertrude's.

With wonderful patience, however, did she preserve her equanimity. She had never looked for kindness and attention from Mrs. Graham and Isabel. She had seen from the first that between herself and them there could be little sympathy, and now that they manifested open dislike she struggled hard to maintain, on her part, not only self-command and composure, but a constant spirit of charity. It was well that she did not yield to this comparatively light trial of her forbearance, for a new, unexpected, and far more intense provocation was in store for her. Her malicious persecutors, incensed and irritated by an unlooked-for calmness and patience, which gave them no advantage in their one-sided warfare, now made their attack in another quarter; and Emily, the sweet, lovely, unoffending Emily, became the object against whom they aimed many of their shafts of unkindness and ill-will.

Gertrude could bear injury, injustice, and even hard and cruel language, when exercised towards herself only; but her blood boiled in her veins when she began to perceive that her cherished Emily was becoming the victim of mean and petty neglect and ill usage. To address the gentle Emily in other words than those of courtesy was next to impossible; it was equally hard to find fault with the actions of one whose life was so good and beautiful; and the somewhat isolated position which she occupied on account of her blindness seemed to render her secure from interference; but Mrs. Graham was coarse and blunt, Isabel selfish and unfeeling, and long before the blind girl was herself aware of any unkind intention on their part, Gertrude's spirit had chafed and rebelled at the sight and knowledge of many a word and act, well calculated, if perceived, to annoy and distress a sensitive and delicate spirit. Many a stroke was warded off by Gertrude; many a neglect atoned for, before it could be felt; many a nearly defeated plan, which Emily was known to have had at heart, carried through and accomplished by Gertrude's perseverance and energy; and for some weeks Emily was kept ignorant of the fact that many a little office formerly performed for her by a servant was now fulfilled by Gertrude, who would not let her know that Bridget had received from her mistress orders which were quite inconsistent with her usual attendance upon Miss Graham's wants.

Mr. Graham was, at this time, absent from home; some difficulty and anxiety in business matters having called him to New York, at a season when he usually enjoyed his leisure, free from all such cares. His presence would have been a great restraint upon his wife, who was well aware of his devoted affection for his daughter, and his wish that her comfort and ease should always be considered of first-rate importance. Indeed, his love and thoughtfulness for Emily, and the enthusiastic devotion manifested towards her by every member of the household, had early rendered her an object of jealousy to Mrs. Graham, who was therefore very willing to find ground of offence against her; and, in her case, as in Isabel's, Kitty's desertion to what her aunt and cousin considered the unfriendly party was only a secondary cause of distrust and dislike.

The misunderstanding with Mr. Bruce, and their unworthy suspicions of its having been fostered by Gertrude, aided and abetted by Emily, furnished, however, an ostensible motive for the indulgence of their animosity, and one of which they resolved to avail themselves to the utmost.

Shortly before Mr. Graham's return home, Mrs. Graham and Isabel were sitting together, endeavoring to while away the tedious hours of a sultry August afternoon by indulging themselves in an unlimited abuse of the rest of the household, when a letter was brought to Mrs. Graham, which proved to be from her husband. After glancing over its contents, she remarked, with an air of satisfaction, "Here is good news for us, Isabel, and a prospect of some pleasure in the world;" and she read aloud the following passage: "The troublesome affair which called me here is nearly settled, and the result is exceedingly favorable to my wishes and plans. I now see nothing to prevent our starting for Europe the latter part of next month, and the girls must make their arrangements accordingly. Tell Emily to spare nothing towards a full and complete equipment for herself and Gertrude."

"He speaks of Gertrude," said Isabel, sneeringly, "as if she were one of the family. I'm sure I don't see any very great prospect of pleasure in travelling all through Europe with a blind woman and her disagreeable appendages; I can't think what Mr. Graham wants to take them for."

"I wish he would leave them at home," said Mrs. Graham; "it would be a good punishment for Gertrude. But, mercy! he would as soon think of going without his right hand as without Emily."

"I hope, if ever I am married," exclaimed Isabel, "it won't be to a man that's got a blind daughter!—Such a dreadful good person, too, whom everybody has got to worship, and admire, and wait upon!"

"*I* don't have to wait upon her," said Mrs. Graham; "that's Gertrude's business—it's what she's going for."

"That's the worst of it; blind girl has to have a waiting-maid, and waiting-maid is a great lady, who doesn't mind cheating your nieces out of their lovers, and even robbing them of each other's affection."

"Well, what can I do, Belle? I'm sure I don't want Gertrude's company any more than you do; but I don't see how I can get rid of her."

"I should think you'd tell Mr. Graham some of the harm she's done already. If you have any influence over him, you might prevent her going."

"It would be no more than she deserves," said Mrs. Graham, thoughtfully, "and I am not sure but I shall give him a hint of her behavior; he'll be surprised enough when he hears of Bruce's sudden flight. I know he thought it would be a match between him and Kitty."

At this point in the conversation, Isabel was summoned to see visitors, and left her aunt in a mood pregnant with consequences.

As Isabel descended the front staircase, to meet with smiles and compliments the guests whom in her heart she wished a thousand miles away on this intensely hot afternoon, Gertrude came up by the back way from the kitchen, and passed along a passage leading to her own room. She carried, over one arm, a dress of delicate white muslin, and a number of embroidered collars, sleeves and ruffles, together with other articles evidently fresh from the ironing-board. Her face was flushed and heated; she looked tired, and, as she reached her room, and carefully deposited her burden upon the bed, she drew a long breath, as if much fatigued, seated herself by a window, brushed the hair back from her face, and threw open a blind, to feel, if possible, a breath of cool air. Just at this moment, Mrs. Prime put her head in at the half-open door, and, seeing Gertrude alone, entered the room, but stood fixed with astonishment on observing the evidences of her recent laborious employment; then, glancing directly opposite at the fruits of her diligence, she burst forth, indignantly, "My sakes alive! Miss Gertrude, I do believe you've been doin' up them muslins yourself, after all!"

Gertrude smiled, but did not reply.

"Now, if that an't too bad!" said the friendly and kind-hearted woman, "to think you should ha' been at work down in that 'ere hot kitchen, and all the rest on us takin' a spell o' rest in the heat of the day! I'll warrant, if Miss Emily knew it, she'd never put on that white gown in this 'ere world!"

"It hardly looks *fit* for her to wear," said Gertrude. "I'm not much used to ironing, and have had a great deal of trouble with it; one side got dry before I could smooth out the other."

"It looks elegant, Miss Gertrude; but what should you be doin' Bridget's work for, I want to know?"

"Bridget always has enough to do," said Gertrude, evading a direct answer, "and it's very well for me to have some practice; knowledge never comes amiss, you know, Mrs. Prime."

" 'T an't no kind of an afternoon for 'speriments o' that sort; and you wouldn't ha' done it, I'll venture to say, if you hadn't been afeard Miss Emily would want her things, and find out they wan't done. Times is changed in this house, when Mr. Graham's own daughter, that was once to the head of everything, has to have her clothes laid by to make room for other folks. Bridget ought to know better than to mind these upstarters, when they tell her, as I heard Miss Graham yesterday, to let alone that heap o' muslins, and attend to something that was o' more consequence. Our Katy would h' known better; but Bridget's a new comer, like all the rest. Thinks I to myself then, what would Miss Gertrude say, if she suspected as how Miss Emily was bein' neglected! But I'll *tell* Miss Emily, as sure as my name's Prime, just how things go;—you shan't get so red in the face with ironing agin, Miss Gertrude. If the kind o' frocks she likes to wear can't be done up at home,—and yourn too, what's more,—the washin' ought to be put out. There's money enough, and some of it ought to be spent for the use o' the ladies as is ladies! I wish to heart *that* Isabella could have to start round a little lively; 't would do her good; but, Lor', Miss Gertrude, it goes right to my heart to see all the vexatious things as is happenin' now-a-days! I'll go right to Miss Emily, this minute, and blow my blast!"

"No, you won't, Mrs. Prime," said Gertrude, persuasively, "when I ask you not to. You forget how unhappy it would make her if she knew that Mrs. Graham was so wanting in consideration. I would rather iron dresses every day, or do anything else for our dear Miss Emily, than to let her *suspect* even that anybody could willingly be unkind to her."

Mrs. Prime hesitated. "Miss Gertrude," said she, "I thought I loved our dear young lady as well as anybody could, but I believe you love her better still, to be so thoughtful and wise-like all for her sake; and I wouldn't say nothin' about it, only I think a sight o' *you*, too; you've been here ever since you was a little gal, and we all set lots by you, and I can't see them folks ride over your head, as I know they mean to."

"I know you love me, Mrs. Prime, and Emily too; so, for the sake of us both, you mustn't say a word to anybody about the change in the family arrangements. We'll all do what we can to keep Emily from pain, and, as to the rest, we won't care for ourselves; if they don't pet and indulge me as much as I've been accustomed to, the easiest way is not to notice it; and you mustn't put on your spectacles to see trouble."

"Lord bless yer heart, Miss Gertrude, them folks is lucky to have you to deal with; it isn't everybody as would put up with 'em. They don't come much in my way, thank fortin'! I let Miss Graham see, right off, that I wouldn't put up with interference; cooks is privileged to set up for their rights, and I scared her out o' my premises pretty quick, I tell yer! It's mighty hard for me to see our own ladies imposed upon; but since you say 'mum,' Miss Gertrude, I'll try and hold my tongue as long as I can. It's a shame though, I do declare!"—and Mrs. Prime walked off, muttering to herself.

An hour after, Gertrude was at the glass, braiding up the bands of her long hair, when Mrs. Ellis, after a slight knock at the door, entered.

"Well, Gertrude," said she, "I didn't think it would come to this!"

"Why, what is the matter?" inquired Gertrude, anxiously.

"It seems we are going to be turned out of our rooms!"

"Who?"

"You, and I next, for aught I know."

Gertrude colored, but did not speak, and Mrs. Ellis went on to relate that she had just received orders to fit up Gertrude's room for some visitors who were expected the next day. She was astonished to hear that Gertrude had not been consulted on the subject. Mrs. Graham had spoken so carelessly of her removal, and seemed to think it so mutually agreeable for Emily to share her apartment with her young friend, that Mrs. Ellis concluded the matter had been preärranged.

Deeply wounded and vexed, both on her own and Emily's account, Gertrude stood for a moment silent and irresolute. She then asked if Mrs. Ellis had spoken to Emily on the subject. She had not. Gertrude begged her to say nothing about it.

"I cannot bear," said she, "to let her know that the little sanctum she fitted up so carefully has been unceremoniously taken from me. I sleep in her room more than half the time, as you know; but she always likes to have me call this chamber mine, that I may be sure of a place where I can read and study by myself. If you will let me remove my bureau into your room, Mrs. Ellis, and sleep on a couch there occasionally, we need not say anything about it to Emily."

Mrs. Ellis assented. She had grown strangely humble and compliant within a few months, and Gertrude had completely won her good-will; first by forbearance, and latterly by the frequent favors and assistance she had found it in her power to render the overburdened housekeeper. So she made no objection to receive her into her room as an inmate, and even offered to assist in the removal of her wardrobe, work-table and books.

But, though yielding and considerate towards Gertrude, whom, with Emily and Mrs. Prime, she now considered members of the oppressed and injured party to which she herself belonged, no words could express her indignation with regard to the late behavior of Mrs. Graham and Isabel. "It is all of a piece," said she, "with the rest of their conduct! Sometimes I almost feel thankful that Emily is blind, it would grieve her so to see the goings on. I should have liked to box Isabella's ears for taking your seat at the table so impudently as she did yesterday, and then neglecting to help Emily to anything at all; and there sat dear Emily, angel as she is, all unconscious of her shameful behavior, and asking her for butter as sweetly as if it were by mere accident that you had been driven from the table, and she left to provide for herself. And all those strangers there, too! I saw it all from the china-closet! And then Emily's dresses and muslins!—there they laid in the press-drawer, till I thought they would mildew. I'm glad to see Bridget has been allowed to do them at last, for I began to think Emily would one of these warm days be without a clean gown in the world. But, there, it's no use talking about it; all I wish is, that they'd all go off to Europe, and leave us here to ourselves. You don't want to go, do you, Gertrude?"

"Yes, if Emily goes."

"Well, you're better than I am; I couldn't make such a martyr of myself, even for her sake."

It is needless to detail the many petty annoyances to which Gertrude was daily subjected; especially after the arrival of the expected visitors, a gay and thoughtless party of fashionables, who were taught to look upon her as an unwarrantable intruder, and upon Emily as a troublesome incumbrance. Nor, with all the pains taken to prevent it, could Emily be long kept in ignorance of the light estimation in which both herself and Gertrude were regarded. Kitty, incensed at the incivility of her aunt and Isabel, and indifferent towards the visitors, to whose folly and levity of character her eyes were now partially opened, hesitated not to express both to Emily and Gertrude her sense of the injuries they sustained, and her own desire to act in their defense. But Kitty was no formidable antagonist to Mrs. Graham and Belle, for, her spirits greatly subdued, and her fears constantly excited by her cousin's sarcastic looks and speeches, she had become a sad coward, and no longer dared, as she would once have done, to thwart their schemes, and stand between her friends and the indignities to which they were exposed.

But Mrs. Graham, thoughtless woman, went too far, and became at last entangled in difficulties of her own weaving. Her husband returned, and it now became necessary to set bounds to her own insolence, and, what was far more difficult, to that of Isabel. Mrs. Graham was a woman of tact; she knew just how far her husband's forbearance would extend,—just the point to which his perceptions might be blinded; and had also sufficient self-control to check herself in any course which would be likely to prove obnoxious to his imperious will. In his absence, however, she acted without restraint, permitted Belle to fill the house with her lively young acquaintances, and winked at the many open and flagrant violations of the law of politeness, manifested by the young people towards the daughter of their absent host, and her youthful friend and attendant. Now, however, a check must be put to all indecorous proceedings; and, unfortunately for the execution of the wife's wise precautions, the head of the family returned unexpectedly, and under circumstances which forestalled any preparation or warning. He arrived just at dusk, having come from town in an omnibus, which was quite contrary to his usual custom.

It was a cool evening; the windows and doors of the house were closed, and the parlor was so brilliantly lighted that he at once suspected the truth that a large company was being entertained there. He felt vexed, for it was Saturday night, and, in accordance with old New England customs, Mr. Graham loved to see his household quiet on that evening. He was, moreover, suffering from a violent headache, and, avoiding the parlor, he passed on to the library, and then to the dining-room; both were chilly and deserted. He then made his way up stairs, walked through several rooms, glanced indignantly at their disordered and slovenly appearance,—for he was excessively neat,—and finally gained Emily's chamber. He opened the door noiselessly, and looked in.

A bright wood-fire burned upon the hearth; a couch was drawn up beside it, on which Emily was sitting; and Gertrude's little rocking-chair occupied the opposite corner. The fire-light reflected upon the white curtains, the fragrant perfume which proceeded from a basket of flowers upon the table, the perfect neatness and order of the apartment, the placid, peaceful face of Emily, and the radiant expression of Gertrude's countenance, as she looked up and saw the father and protector of her blind friend looking pleasantly in upon them, proved such a charming contrast to the scenes presented in other parts of the house, that the old gentleman, warmed to more than usual satisfaction with both of the inmates, greeted his surprised daughter with a hearty paternal embrace, and, bestowing upon Gertrude an equally affectionate greeting, exclaimed, as he took the arm-chair which the latter wheeled in front of the fire for his accommodation, "Now, girls, this looks pleasant and homelike! What in the world is going on down stairs? What is everything up in arms about?"

Emily explained that there was company staying in the house.

"Ugh! company!" grunted Mr. Graham, in a dissatisfied tone. "I should think so! Been emptying rag-bags about the chambers, I should say, from the looks!"

Gertrude asked if he had been to tea.

He had not, and should be thankful for some;—he was tired. So she went down stairs to see about it.

"Don't tell anybody that I've got home, Gerty," called he, as she left the room; "I want to be left in peace *to-night,* at least."

While Gertrude was gone, Mr. Graham questioned Emily as to her preparations for the European tour; to his surprise, he learned that she had never received his message communicated in the letter to Mrs. Graham, and knew nothing of his plans. Equally astonished and angry, he nevertheless restrained his temper for the present;—he did not like to acknowledge to himself, far less to his daughter, that his commands had been disregarded by his wife. It put him upon thinking, however.

After he had enjoyed a comfortable repast, at which Gertrude presided, they both returned to Emily's room; and now Mr. Graham's first inquiry was for the *Evening Transcript.*

"I will go for it," said Gertrude, rising.

"Ring!" said Mr. Graham, imperatively. He had observed at the tea-table that Gertrude's ring was disregarded, and wished to know the cause of so strange a piece of neglect. Gertrude rang several times, but obtained no answer to the bell. At last she heard Bridget's step in the entry, and, opening the door, said to her, "Bridget, won't you find the *Transcript,* and bring it to Miss Emily's room." Bridget soon returned, with the announcement that Miss Isabella was reading it, and declined to give it up.

A storm gathered on Mr. Graham's brow. "Such a message to *my daughter!*" he exclaimed. "Gertrude, go yourself, and tell the impertinent girl that *I* want the paper! What sort of behavior is this?" muttered he.

Gertrude entered the parlor with great composure, and, amid the stares and wonder of the company, spoke in a low tone to Belle, who immediately yielded up the paper, blushing and looking much confused as she did so. Belle was afraid of Mr. Graham; and, on her informing her aunt of his return, it was that lady's turn, also, to look disconcerted. She had fully calculated upon seeing her husband before he had access to Emily; she knew the importance of giving the desired bias to a man of his strong prejudices.

But it was too late now. She would not go to *seek* him; she must take her chance, and trust to fortune to befriend her. She used all her tact, however, to disperse her friends at an early hour, and then found Mr. Graham smoking in the dining-room.

He was in an unpleasant mood (as she told her niece afterwards, cross as a bear); but she contrived to conciliate rather than irritate him, avoided all discordant subjects, and was able the next morning to introduce to her friends an apparently affable and obliging host.

This serenity was disturbed, however, long before the Sabbath drew to a close. As he walked up the church-aisle, before morning service, with Emily, according to invariable custom, leaning upon his arm, his brow darkened at seeing Isabel complacently seated in that corner of the old-fashioned square pew which all the family were well aware had for years been sacred to his blind daughter. Mrs. Graham, who accompanied them, winked at her niece; but Isabel was mentally rather obtuse, and was, consequently, subjected to the mortification of having Mr. Graham deliberately take her hand and remove her from the seat, in which he immediately placed Emily, while the displaced occupant, who had been so mean as for the last three Sundays to purposely deprive Miss Graham of this old established right, was compelled to sit during the service in the only vacant place, beside Mr. Graham, with her back to the pulpit. And very angry was she at observing the smiles visible upon many countenances in the neighboring pews; and especially chagrined when Fanny Bruce, who was close to her in the next pew, giggled outright.

Emily would have been grieved if she had been in the least aware of the triumph she had unconsciously achieved. But her heart and thoughts were turned upward, and, as she had felt no pang of provocation at Isabel's past encroachment, so had she no consciousness of present satisfaction, except as the force of habit made her feel more at ease in her old seat.

Mr. Graham had not been at home a week before he understood plainly the existing state of feeling in the mind of his wife and Isabel, and the manner in which it was likely to act upon the happiness of the household. He saw that Emily was superior to complaint; he knew that she had never in her life complained; he observed, too, Gertrude's devotion to his much-loved child, and it stamped her in his mind as one who had a claim to his regard which should never be disputed. It is not, then, to be wondered at, that when, with much art and many plausible words, Mrs. Graham made her intended insinuations against his youthful protegée, Mr. Graham treated them with indifference and contempt.

He had known Gertrude from a child. She was high-spirited,—he had sometimes thought her wilful,—but *never* mean or false. It was no use to tell him all that nonsense;—he was glad, for his part, that it was all off between Kitty and Bruce; for Ben was an idle fellow, and would never make a good husband; and, as to Kitty, he thought her much improved of late, and if it were owing to Gertrude's influence, the more they saw of each other the better.

Mrs. Graham was in despair. "It is all settled," said she to Isabel. "It is no use to contest the point; Mr. Graham is firm as a rock, and as sure as *we* go to Europe, Emily and Gertrude will go *too*."

She was almost startled, therefore, by what she considered an excess of good luck, when informed, a few days afterwards, that the couple she had so dreaded to have of the party were in reality to be left behind, and that, too, at Miss Graham's special request. Emily's scruples with regard to mentioning to her father the little prospect of pleasure the tour was likely to afford her all vanished when she found that Gertrude, whose interest she ever had at heart, would be likely to prove a still greater sufferer from the society to which she would be subjected.

Blind as she was, Emily understood and perceived almost everything that was passing around her. Quick of perception, and with a hearing rendered doubly intense by her want of sight, the events of the summer were, perhaps, more familiar to her than to any other member of the family. She more than suspected the exact state of matters betwixt Mr. Bruce and Gertrude, though the latter had never spoken to her on the subject. She imagined the manner in which Kitty was involved in the affair (no very difficult thing to be conceived by one who enjoyed the confidences which the simple-hearted girl unconsciously, but continually, made during her late intercourse with her).

As Mrs. Graham's and Isabel's abuse of power became more open and decided, Mrs. Ellis and Mrs. Prime both considered the embargo upon free speech in Miss Graham's presence wholly removed; and any pain which the knowledge of their neglect might have caused her was more than compensated to Emily by the proofs it had called forth of devoted attachment and willing service on the part of her adopted child, as she loved to consider Gertrude.

Calmly, and without hesitation, as without excitement, did she resolve to adopt a course which should at once free Gertrude from her self-sacrificing service. That she encountered much opposition from her father may well be imagined; but he knew too well the impossibility of any pleasure to be derived to herself from a tour in which mental pain was added to outward deprivation, to persist in urging her to accompany the party; and, concluding at last that it was, after all, the only way to reconcile opposing interests, and that Emily's plan was, perhaps, the best that could be adopted under the circumstances, decided to resign himself to the long separation from his daughter, and permit her to be happy in her own way. He had seen, during the previous winter at the south, how entirely Emily's infirmity unfitted her for travelling, especially when deprived of Gertrude's attendant eyes; he now realized how totally contrary to her tastes and habits were the tastes and habits of his new wife and her nieces; and, unwilling to be convinced of the folly of his sudden choice, and the probable chance of unhappiness arising from it, he appreciated the wisdom of Emily's proposal, and felt a sense of relief in the adoption of a course which would satisfy all parties.

## Chapter XXXIV

*A course of days, composing happy months.*
WORDSWORTH

Mrs. Warren's pleasant boarding-house was the place chosen by Emily for her own and Gertrude's winter home; and one month from the time of Mr. Graham's return from New York his country-house was closed, he, with his wife, Isabel and Kitty, were on their way to Havre; Mrs. Ellis gone to enjoy a little rest from care with some cousins at the eastward; and Mrs. Prime established as cook in Mrs. Warren's household, where all the morning she grumbled at the increase of duty she was here called upon to perform, and all the evening blessed her stars that she was still under the same roof with her dear young ladies.

Although ample arrangements were made by Mr. Graham, and all-sufficient means provided for the support of both Emily and Gertrude, the

latter was anxious to be once more usefully employed, and, therefore, resumed a portion of her school duties at Mr. W.'s. Much as Emily loved
Gertrude's constant presence, she gladly resigned her for a few hours every
day, rejoiced in the spirit which prompted her exertions, and rewarded her
with her encouragement and praise. In the undisturbed enjoyment of
each other's society, and in their intercourse with a small but intelligent
circle of friends, they passed a season of sweet tranquillity. They read, walked
and communed, as in times long past. Together they attended lectures,
concerts, and galleries of art. As they stood before the works of a master's
hand, whether in the sculptured marble or the painted canvas, and Emily
listened while Gertrude, with glowing eyes and a face radiant with enthusiasm, described with minuteness and accuracy the subject of the pieces,
the manner in which the artist had expressed in his work the original conception of his mind,—the attitudes of figures, the expression of faces, the
coloring of landscapes, and the effect produced upon her mind and heart
by the thoughts which the work conveyed,—such was the eloquence of the
one, and the sympathizing attention of the other, that, as they stood there in
striking contrast, forgetful of all around, they were themselves a study, if
not for the artist, for the observer of human nature, as manifested in novel
forms and free from affectation and worldliness.

Then, too, as, in their daily walks, or gazing upon the glories of a brilliant
winter's night, Gertrude, enraptured at the work of the great Master of
the universe, poured out without reserve her soul's deep and earnest admiration, dilated upon the gorgeousness of a clear sunset, or in the sweet hour
of twilight sat watching the coming on of beautiful night, and lighting of
Heaven's lamps, then would Emily, from the secret fountains of her largely-
illumined nature, speak out such truths of the inner life as made it seem
that she alone were blessed with the true light, and all the seeing world sat
in comparative darkness.

It was a blissful and an improving winter which they thus passed together. They lived not for themselves alone; the poor blessed them, the
sorrowful came to them for sympathy, and the affection which they both
inspired in the family circle was boundless. Gertrude often recurred to it,
in her after life, as the time when she and Emily lived in a beautiful world
of their own. Spring came, and passed, and still they lingered there, loth
to leave a place where they had been so happy; and nothing at last
drove them from the city, but a sudden failure in Emily's health, and Dr.
Jeremy's peremptory command that they should at once seek the country
air, as the best restorative.

Added to her anxiety about Emily, Gertrude began to feel much troubled
at Willie Sullivan's long silence; no word from him for two or three months.
Willie could not have forgotten or meant to neglect her. That was impossible. But why this strange suspension to their correspondence? She tried,
however, not to feel disturbed about it, and gave all her care to Emily, who
now began indeed to require it.

They went to the sea-side for a few weeks; but the clear and bracing
atmosphere brought no strength to the blind girl's feeble frame. She was
obliged to give up her daily walks; a continued weariness robbed her step

of its elasticity, and her usually equal spirits were subject to an unwonted
depression, while her nervous temperament became so susceptible that the
utmost care was requisite to preserve her from all excitement.

The good doctor came frequently to see his favorite patient, but, finding
on every visit that she seemed worse instead of better, he at last ordered her
back to the city, declaring that Mrs. Jerry's front chamber was as cool and
comfortable as the little stived-up apartments of the crowded boarding-
house at Nahant, and there he should insist upon both her and Gertrude's
taking up their quarters, at least for a week or two; at the end of which time,
if Emily had not found her health, he hoped to have leisure to start off with
them in search of it.

Emily thought she was doing very well where she was; was afraid she
should be troublesome to Mrs. Jeremy.

"Don't talk about trouble, Emily. You ought to know Mrs. Jerry and me
better, by this time. Come up to-morrow; I'll meet you at the cars! Good-
by!" and he took his hat and was off.

Gertrude followed him. "I see, doctor, you think Emily is not so well."

"No; how should she be? What with the sea roaring on one side, and
Mrs. Fellows' babies on the other, it's enough to wear away her strength. I
won't have it so! This isn't the place for her, and do you bring her up to my
house to-morrow."

"The babies don't usually cry as much as they have to-day," said Gertrude,
smiling; "and as to the ocean, Emily loves dearly to hear the waves rolling in.
She sits and listens to them by the hour together."

"Knew she did!" said the doctor. "Shan't do it; bad for her; it makes her
sad, without her knowing why. Bring her up to Boston, as I tell you."

It was full three weeks after the arrival of his visitors before the popular
physician could steal away from his patients to enjoy a few weeks' recreation in travelling. For his own sake he would hardly have thought of
attempting so unusual a thing as a journey; and his wife, too, loved home
so much better than any other place, that she was loth to start for parts
unknown; but both were willing, and even anxious, to sacrifice their
long-indulged habits for what they considered the advantage of their young
friends.

Emily was decidedly better; so much so as to view with pleasure the prospect of visiting West Point, Catskill and Saratoga, even on her own account;
and when she reflected upon the probable enjoyment the trip would afford
Gertrude, she felt herself endowed with new strength for the undertaking.
Gertrude needed change of scene and diversion of mind almost as much
as Emily. The excessive heat of the last few weeks, and her constant attendance in the invalid's room, had paled the roses in her cheeks, while care
and anxiety had weighed upon her mind. The late improvement in Emily,
however, and the alacrity with which she entered into the doctor's plans,
relieved Gertrude of her fears, and, as she moved actively about to complete
the few preparations which were needed in her own and her friend's wardrobe, her step was as light, and her voice as gladsome, as her fingers were busy
and skilful.

New York was their first destination; but the heat and dust of the city were almost insufferable, and during the one day which they passed there Dr. Jeremy was the only member of the party who ventured out of the hotel, except on occasion of a short expedition which Mrs. Jeremy and Gertrude made in search of dress-caps, the former lady's stock being still limited to the old yellow and the lilac-and-pink, neither of which, she feared, would be just the thing for Saratoga.

The doctor, however, seemed quite insensible to the state of the weather, so much was he occupied with visits to some of his Aesculapian brethren, several of whom were college class-mates whom he had not seen for years. He passed the whole day in the revival of old acquaintances and associations; and, a number of these newly-found but warm-hearted friends having presented themselves at the hotel in the evening, to be introduced to Mrs. Jeremy and her travelling companions, their parlor was enlivened until a late hour by the happy and cheerful conversation of a group of elderly men, who, as they recalled the past and dwelt upon the scenes and incidents of their youthful days, seemed to renew their boyish spirits, so joyous was the laughter and excitement with which each anecdote of former times received as it fell from the lips of the spokesman,—an office which each filled by turns. Dr. Jeremy had been a great favorite among his circle, and almost every narrative of college days (save those which he himself detailed) bore reference to some exploit in which he had borne a spirited and honorable part; and the three female auditors, especially Gertrude, who was enthusiastic in her own appreciation of the doctor's merits, listened triumphantly to this corroborative testimony of his worth.

The conversation, however, was not of a character to exclude the ladies from participating in as well as enjoying it; and Gertrude, who always got on famously with elderly men, and whom the doctor loved dearly to draw out, contributed not a little to the mirth and good-humor of the company by her playful and amusing sallies, and the quickness of repartee with which she responded to the adroit, puzzling, and sometimes ironical questions and jokes of an old-bachelor physician, who, from the first, took a wonderful fancy to her.

Emily listened with delighted interest to a conversation which had for her such varied charms, and shared with Gertrude the admiration of the doctor's friends, who were all excited to the warmest sympathy for her misfortune; while Mrs. Jeremy, proud, smiling and happy, looked so complacent as she sat ensconced in an arm-chair, listening to the encomiums pronounced on her husband's boyhood, that Gertrude declared, as they separated for the night, that she had almost come to the conclusion that the old yellow was becoming to her, and her new caps altogether superfluous.

Upon hearing that Dr. Jeremy's party were going up the Hudson the next morning, Dr. Gryseworth, of Philadelphia, who had many years before been a student of our good doctor's, expressed his satisfaction in the prospect of meeting them on board the boat, and introducing to Gertrude his two daughters, whom he was about to accompany to Saratoga to meet their grandmother, already established at Congress Hall for the summer.

It was midnight before Gertrude could compose her mind, and so far quiet her imagination (which, always lively, was now keenly excited by the next day's promise of pleasure) as to think of the necessity of fortifying herself by sleep; and Emily was finally obliged to check her gayety and loquacity by positively refusing to join in another laugh, or listen to another word that night. Thus condemned to silence, she sunk at once to slumber, unconscious that Emily, usually an excellent sleeper, had, in this instance, acted soley for her benefit, being herself so strangely wakeful that morning found her unrefreshed, and uncertain whether she had once during the night been lulled into a perfect state of repose.

Gertrude, who slept soundly until wakened by Miss Graham, started up in astonishment on seeing her dressed and standing by the bed-side,—a most unusual circumstance, and one which reversed the customary order of things, as Gertrude's morning kiss was wont to be Emily's first intimation of daylight.

"Six o'clock, Gerty, and the boat starts at seven! The doctor has already been knocking at our door."

"How soundly I have slept!" exclaimed Gertrude. "I wonder if it's a pleasant day."

"Beautiful," replied Emily, "but very warm. The sun was shining in so brightly, that I had to close the blinds on account of the heat."

Gertrude made haste to repair for lost time, but was not quite dressed when they were summoned to the early breakfast prepared for travellers. She had, also, her own and Emily's trunks to lock, and therefore insisted upon the others preceeding her to the breakfast-hall, where she promised to join them in a few moments.

The company assembled at this early hour was small, consisting only of two parties beside Dr. Jeremy's, and a few gentlemen, most of them business men, who, having partaken of their food in a business-like manner, started off in haste for their different destinations. Of those who still lingered at the table when Gerty made her appearance, there was only one whom she particularly observed, during the few moments allowed her by Dr. Jeremy for the enjoyment of her breakfast.

This was a gentleman who sat at some distance from her, idly balancing his tea-spoon on the edge of his cup. He had concluded his own repast, but seemed quite at his leisure, and previous to Gertrude's entrance had won Mrs. Jeremy's animadversions by a slight propensity he had manifested to make a more critical survey of her party than she found wholly agreeable. "Do, pray," said she to the doctor, "send the waiter to ask that man to take something himself: I can't bear to have anybody looking at me so when I'm eating!"

"He isn't looking at you, wife; it's Emily that has taken his fancy. Emily, my dear, there's a gentleman, over opposite, who admires you exceedingly."

"Is there?" said Emily, smiling. "I am very much obliged to him. May I venture to return the compliment?"

"Yes. He's a fine-looking fellow, though wife, here, doesn't seem to like him very well."

At this moment Gertrude joined them, and, as she made her morning salutation to the doctor and his wife, and gayly apologized to the former for her tardiness, the fine color which mantled her countenance, and the deep brilliancy of her large dark eyes, drew glances of affectionate admiration from the kind old couple, and were, perhaps, the cause of the stranger's attention being at once transferred from the lovely and interesting face of Emily to the more youthful, beaming and eloquent features of Gertrude.

She had hardly taken her seat before she became aware of the notice she was attracting. It embarrassed her, and she was glad when, after a moment or two, the gentleman hastily dropped his tea-spoon, rose and left the room. As he passed out, she had an opportunity of observing him, which she had not ventured to do while he sat opposite to her.

He was a man considerably above the middle height, slender, but finely formed, and of a graceful and dignified bearing. His features were rather sharp, but expressive, and even handsome; his eyes, dark, keen and piercing, had a most penetrating look, while his firmly-compressed lips spoke of resolution and strength of will.

But the chief peculiarity of his appearance was his hair, which was deeply tinged with gray, and in the vicinity of his temples almost snowy white. This was so strikingly in contrast with the youthful fire of his eye, and the easy lightness of his step, that, instead of seeming the effect of age, and giving him a title to veneration, it rather enhanced the contradictory claims of his otherwise apparent youth and vigor.

"What a queer-looking man!" exclaimed Mrs. Jeremy, when he had passed out.

"An elegant-looking man, isn't he?" said Gertrude.

"Elegant?" rejoined Mrs. Jeremy. "What! with that gray head?"

"I think it's beautiful," said Gertrude; "but I wish he didn't look so melancholy; it makes me quite sad to see him."

"How old should you think he was?" asked Dr. Jeremy.

"About fifty," said Mrs. Jeremy.

"About thirty," said Gertrude, and both in the same breath.

"A wide difference," remarked Emily. "Doctor, you must decide the point."

"Impossible! I wouldn't venture to tell that man's age within ten years, at least. Wife has got him old enough, certainly: I'm not sure but I should set him as low even as Gertrude's mark. Age never turned *his* hair gray—that is certain."

Intimation was now given that passengers for the boat must be on the alert; and all speculation upon the probable age of the stranger (a fruitless kind of speculation, often indulged in, and, sometimes a source of vain and endless discussion) was suddenly and peremptorily suspended.

❀❀❀❀❀❀❀❀❀❀❀❀❀❀❀❀❀❀❀❀❀❀❀❀❀❀❀

# Chapter XXXV

*His mien is lofty, but his gaze*
*Too well a wandering soul betrays:*
*His full, dark eye at times is bright*
*With strange and momentary light,*
*And oft his features and his air*
*A shade of troubled mystery wear,—*
*A glance of hurried wildness, fraught*
*With some unfathomable thought.*

MRS. HEMANS

To most of our travelling public a little trip from Boston into New York State seems an every-day affair, scarce worth calling a journey; but to Dr. Jeremy it was a momentous event, calling the good physician out of a routine of daily professional visits, which, during a period of twenty years, had not been interrupted by a week's absence from home, and plunging him at once into that whirl of hurry, tumult and excitement, which exists on all our great routes, especially in the summer season, the time when the American populace takes its yearly pleasure excursion.

The doctor was by nature and habit a social being; never shrinking from intercourse with his fellow-men, but rather seeking and enjoying their companionship on all occasions. He knew how to adapt himself to the taste of young and old, rich and poor, and was well acquainted with city life in all its forms. In the art of travelling, however,—an art to be acquired by practice only,—he was totally unversed. He had yet to learn the adroit use of those many springs, which, touched at the right moment, and by a skilful hand, soften the obdurate hearts of landlords, win the devoted attendance of waiters, inspire railroad conductors and steamboat officials with a spirit of accommodation, and convert the clamorous, noisy hackmen into quiet, obedient and humble servants at command. In Dr. Jeremy's travelling days the stage-coach was the chief vehicle of convenience and speed; the driver was a civil fellow, each passenger a person of consequence, and each passenger's baggage a thing not to be despised. Now, on the contrary, people moved in masses; a single individual was a man of no influence, a mere unit in the great whole, and his much-valued luggage that which seemed in his eyes a mark for the heaviest knocks and bruises. Dr. Jeremy was appalled at this new state of things, and quite unable to reconcile to it either his taste or temper. To him the modern landlord resembled the keeper of an intelligence-office, who condescendingly glances at his books to see if he can furnish the humble suppliant with a situation, and often turns him away mortified and disappointed; the waiters, whom the honest and unsophisticated doctor scorned to bribe, were an impudent, lazy set of varlets; conductors and steamboat masters, lordly tyrants; and the hackmen, a swarm of hungry, buzzing, stinging wasps, let loose on wharves and in dépots for the torment of their victims.

Thus were these important members of society stigmatized, and loudly were they railed at by our traveller, who invariably, at the commencement and close of every trip, got wrought up to a high pitch of excitement at the wrongs and indignities to which he was subjected. It was astonishing, however, to see how quickly he cooled down, and grew comfortable and contented, when he was once established in car or steamboat, or had succeeded in obtaining suitable quarters at a hotel. He would then immediately subside into the obliging, friendly and sociable man of the world; would make acquaintance with everybody about him, and talk and behave with such careless unconcern, that one would have supposed he considered himself fixed for life, and was moreover perfectly satisfied with the fate that destiny had assigned to him.

Thankful, therefore, were the ladies of his party when they were safe on board the steamboat; a circumstance upon which they were still congratulating themselves and each other, while they piled up their heavy shawls and other extra garments in an out-of-the-way corner of the cabin, when the doctor's voice was again heard calling to them from the other end of the long saloon: "Come, come, wife,—Gertrude,—Emily! what are you staying down in this stived-up place for? you'll lose the best part of the view;" and, coming towards them, he took Gertrude's arm, and would have hurried her away, leaving Mrs. Jeremy and Emily to follow when they were ready; but Gertrude would not trust Emily to ascend the cabin-stairs under any guardianship but her own, and Mrs. Jeremy immediately engaged the doctor in an animated discussion as to the advisability of his adopting a straw hat, which the thoughtful wife had brought from home in her hand, and which she was eager to see enjoyed. By the time the question was settled, and Emily, at Gertrude's persuasion, had been induced to exchange her thin mantilla for a light travelling-cloak, which the latter was sure she would require, as there was a fresh breeze stirring on the river, the boat had proceeded some distance; and when our party finally gained the head of the stairs, and looked about them for seats on deck, not a single vacant bench or accommodation of any sort was to be seen. There was an unusually large number of passengers, nearly all of whom were collected at the stern of the boat. Dr. Jeremy was obliged to leave his ladies, and go off in search of chairs.

"Don't let us stay here!" whispered Mrs. Jeremy to Gertrude and Emily. "Let's go right back, before the doctor comes! There are beautiful great rocking-chairs down in the cabin, without a soul to sit in them, and I'm sure we an't wanted here to make up a company. I hate to stand with all these people staring at us, and crowing to think they've got such nice places; don't you, Emily?"

Mrs. Jeremy was one of the people who were constantly forgetting that Emily could not see.

But Gertrude was not—she never forgot it; and, as she stood with her arm lightly passed around her friend's waist, to prevent the motion of the boat from throwing her off her balance, it was no wonder they attracted attention; the one so bright, erect, and strong with youth and health, that she seemed a fit protector for the other, who, in her sweet and gentle helplessness, leaned upon her so trustingly.

"I think, when we get seated in the shade, we shall find it cooler here than it is below," said Emily, in reply to Mrs. Jeremy's urgent proposition that they should make their escape in the doctor's absence. "You always prefer the coolest place, I believe."

"So I do; but I noticed there was a good draught of air in the ladies' saloon, and—" Here the good woman's argument was interrupted by the cordial salutation of Dr. Gryseworth, who, previously seated with his back towards them, had turned at the sound of Emily's flute-like voice, which, once heard, invariably left an impression upon the memory. When he had finished shaking hands, he insisted upon giving up his seat to Mrs. Jeremy; and, at the same instant, another gentleman, who, owing to the throng of passengers, had hitherto been unnoticed by our party, rose, and bowing politely, placed his own chair for the accommodation of Emily, and then walked quickly away. It was the stranger whom they had seen at breakfast. Gertrude recognized his keen, dark eye, even before she perceived his singular hair; and, as she thanked him, and placed Emily in the offered seat, she felt herself color under his earnest glance. But Dr. Gryseworth immediately claimed her attention for the introduction to his daughters, and all thought of the retreating stranger was banished for the present.

The Miss Gryseworths were intelligent-looking girls; the eldest, lately returned from Europe, where she had been travelling with her father, was considered a very elegant and superior person, and Gertrude was charmed with the lady-like cordiality with which they both made her acquaintance, and still more with the amiable and sympathizing attentions which they paid to Emily.

By the time that Dr. Jeremy returned with the solitary chair which he had been able to obtain, he found Gertrude and Dr. Gryseworth comfortably accommodated, through the skilful agency of the latter, and was thus enabled to sink at once into his seat, and subside into that state of easy unconcern which admirably became his pleasant, genial temperament.

Long before the boat reached West Point, where the Jeremys were to go on shore, it was plain to be seen that an excellent understanding subsisted between Gertrude and the Miss Gryseworths, and that time only was wanting to ripen their acquaintance into friendship.

Gertrude was not one of those young persons who consider every girl of their own age entitled to their immediate intimacy and confidence. She had her decided preferences, and, though invariably civil and obliging, was rarely disposed to admit new members into her sacred circle of friends. She was quick, however, to recognize a congenial spirit; and such an one, once found, was claimed by her enthusiastic nature, and engrafted into her affections as something of kindred birth. Nor was the readily adopted tie easily loosened or broken. Whom Gertrude once loved, she loved long and well; faithful was she in her efforts to serve, and prompt in her sympathy to feel for those whose interest and happiness friendship made dear to her as her own.

Perhaps Ellen Gryseworth divined this trait of her character, and appreciated the value of so steady and truthful a regard; for she certainly tried hard to win it; and her father, who had heard Gertrude's history from Dr. Jeremy, smiled approvingly, as he witnessed the pains which his high-bred and somewhat aristocratic daughter was taking to render herself agreeable to one whose social position had in it nothing to excite her ambition, and whose person, mind and manners, constituted her sole recommendation.

They had been for about an hour engaged in the enjoyment of each other's society, and in the view of some of the most charming scenery in the world, when Netta Gryseworth touched her sister's arm, and, glancing towards another part of the boat, said, in an under tone, "Ellen, do invite Mr. Phillips to come back and be introduced to Miss Flint!—see how lonesome the poor man looks."

Gertrude followed the direction of Netta's eye, and saw the stranger of the morning at some distance from them, slowly pacing up and down, with a serious and abstracted air.

"He has not been near us for an hour," said Netta. "I am afraid he has got the blues."

"I hope we have not frightened your friend away," said Gertrude.

"O, no, indeed!" replied Ellen. "Although Mr. Phillips is but a recent acquaintance, we have found him so independent, and sometimes so whimsical, that I am never astonished at his proceedings, or mortified at being suddenly forsaken by him. There are some people, you know, for whom it is always sufficient excuse to say, *It is their way.* I wish he would condescend to join us again, however; I should like to introduce him to you, Miss Flint."

"You wouldn't like him," said Netta.

"Now, that is not fair, Netta!" exclaimed her sister; "to try and prejudice Miss Flint against my friend. You mustn't let her influence you," added she, addressing Gertrude. "She hasn't known him half as long as I have; and I do not dislike him, by any means. My little, straightforward sister never likes odd people, and I must confess that Mr. Phillips is somewhat eccentric; but he interests me all the more on that account, and I feel positive he and you would have many ideas and sentiments in common."

"How can you say so, Ellen?" said Netta. "I think they are totally different."

"You must consider Netta's remark very complimentary, Miss Flint," said Ellen, good-naturedly; "it would not be quite so much so, if it had come from me."

"But you wished me to become acquainted with your oddity," remarked Gertrude, addressing herself to Netta. "I suspect you act on the principle that one's misfortunes should be shared by one's friends."

Netta laughed. "Not exactly," said she; "it was compassion *for him* that moved me. I can't help pitying him when he looks so homesick, and I thought your society would brighten him up and do him good."

"Ah, Netta! Netta!" cried her sister; "he has excited your sympathy, I see. A few days more, and I shouldn't be surprised if you went beyond me in your admiration of him. If so, take care, you transparent creature, not to betray your inconsistency." Then, turning to Gertrude, she said, "Netta met Mr. Phillips yesterday for the first time, and has not seemed very favorably impressed. Father and I were passengers in the same steamer in which he came from Liverpool, a few weeks ago. He had an ill turn in the early part of the voyage, and it was in a professional way that father first made his acquaintance. I was surprised at seeing him on board the boat to-day, for he mentioned no such intention yesterday."

Gertrude suspected that the agreeable young lady might herself be the cause of his journey; but she did not say so,—her native delicacy and the slight knowledge she had of the parties forbade such an allusion,—and the conversation soon taking another turn, Mr. Phillips was not again adverted to, though Gertrude observed, just before the boat stopped at West Point, that Dr. Jeremy and Dr. Gryseworth, having left their party, had joined him, and that the trio were engaged in a colloquy which seemed to possess equal interest to them all.

At West Point Gertrude parted from her new friends, who expressed an earnest hope that they should again meet in Saratoga; and before the bustle of going on shore had subsided, and she had found on the narrow pier a safe place of refuge for Emily and herself, the boat was far up the river, and the Miss Gryseworths quite undistinguishable among the crowd that swarmed the deck.

Our travellers passed one night only at West Point. The weather continued extremely hot, and Dr. Jeremy, perceiving that Emily drooped under the oppressive atmosphere, was desirous to reach the summit of Catskill Mountain before the Sabbath, which was now near at hand.

One solitary moonlight evening, however, sufficed to give Gertrude some idea of the beauties of the place. She had no opportunity to observe it in detail; she saw it only as a whole; but, thus presented to her vision in all the dreamy loveliness of a summer's night, it left on her fresh and impressive mind a vague sentiment of wonder and delight at the surpassing sweetness of what seemed rather a glimpse of Paradise than an actual show of earth, so harmonious was the scene, so calm, so still, so peaceful. "Emily, darling," said she, as they stood together in a rustic arbor, commanding the most striking prospect both of the river and the shore, "It looks like you; you ought to live here, and be the priestess of such a temple!" and, locking her hand in that of Emily, she poured into her attentive ear the holy and elevated sentiments to which the time and the place gave birth. To pour out her thoughts to Emily was like whispering to her own heart, and the response to those thoughts was as sure and certain.

So passed the evening away, and an early hour in the morning found them again steaming up the river. Their first day's experience having convinced them of the danger of delay, they lost no time in securing places on deck, for the boat was as crowded as on the previous morning; but the shores of West Point were hardly passed from their view before Gertrude's watchful eye detected in Emilys countenance the well-known signs of weariness and debility. Sacrificing, without hesitation, the intense pleasure she was herself deriving from the beautiful scenes through which the boat was at the moment passing, she at once proposed that they should seek the cabin, where Miss Graham might rest in greater stillness and comfort.

Emily, however, would not listen to the proposal; would not think of depriving Gertrude of the rare pleasure she knew she must be experiencing.

"The prospect is all lost upon me now, Emily," said Gertrude. "I see only your tired face. Do go and lie down, if it be only to please me; you hardly slept at all last night."

"Are you talking of going below?" exclaimed Mrs. Jeremy. "I, for one, shall be thankful to; it's as comfortable again, and we can see all we want to from the cabin-windows; can't we, Emily?"

"Should you really prefer it?" inquired Emily.

"Indeed, I should!" said Mrs. Jeremy, with such emphasis that her sincerity could not be doubted.

"Then, if you will promise to stay here, Gertrude," said Emily, "I will go with Mrs. Jeremy."

Gertrude assented to the plan; but insisted upon first accompanying them, to find a vacant berth for Emily, and see her under circumstances which would promise repose.

Dr. Jeremy having, in the mean time, gone to inquire about dinner, they at once carried their plan into effect. Emily was really too weak to endure the noise and confusion on deck, and, after she had lain down in the quiet and nearly deserted saloon, Gertrude stood smoothing back her hair, and watching her pale countenance, until she was accused of violating the conditions of their agreement, and was at last driven away by the lively and good-natured doctor's lady, who declared herself perfectly well able to take care of Emily.

"You'd better make haste back," said she, "before you lose your seat; and mind, Gerty, don't let the doctor come near us; he'll be teasing us to go back again, and we've no idea of doing any such thing." Saying which, Mrs. Jeremy untied her bonnet-strings, put her feet up in the opposite chair, clapped her hands at Gertrude, and bade her be gone.

Gertrude ran off laughing, and a smile was still on her face when she reached the staircase. As she came up with her usual quick and light step, a tall figure moved aside to let her pass. It was Mr. Phillips. He bowed, and Gertrude, returning the salutation, passed on to the place she had left, wondering how he came to be again their travelling companion. He could not have been on board previously to her going below with Emily; she was sure she should have seen him; she should have known him among a thousand. He must have taken the boat at Newburgh; it stopped there while she was in the cabin.

As these reflections passed through her mind, she resumed her seat, which was placed at the very stern of the boat, and, with her back to most of the company, gazed out upon the river. She had sat thus for about five minutes, her thoughts divided between the scenery and the interesting countenance of the stranger, when a shadow passed before her, and, looking up, prepared to see and address Dr. Jeremy, she betrayed a little confusion at again encountering a pair of eyes whose earnest, magnetic gaze had the power to disconcert and bewilder her. She was turning away, somewhat abruptly, when the stranger spoke.

"Good-morning, young lady! our paths still lie in the same direction, I see. Will you honor me by making use of my guidebook?"

As he spoke, he offered her a little book containing a map of the river, and the shores on either side. Gertrude took it, and thanked him. As she unfolded the map, he stationed himself a few steps distant, and leaned over the railing, in an apparently absent state of mind; nor did he speak to her again for some minutes. Then, suddenly turning towards her, he said, "You like all this very much."

"Very much," said Gertrude.

"You have never seen anything so beautiful before in your life." He did not seem to question her; he spoke as if he knew.

"It is an old story to you, I suppose," said Gertrude.

"What makes you think so?" asked he, smiling.

Gertrude was disconcerted by his look, and still more by his smile; it changed his whole face so,—it made him look so handsome, and yet so melancholy. She blushed, and could not reply; he saved her the trouble.— "That is hardly a fair question, is it? You probably think you have as much reason for your opinion as I had for mine. You are wrong, however; I never was here before; but I am too old a traveller to carry my enthusiasm in my eyes—as you do," added he, after a moment's pause, during which he looked her full in the face. Then, seeming, for the first time, to perceive the embarrassment which his scrutiny of her features occasioned, he turned away, and a shadow passed over his fine countenance, lending it for a moment an expression of mingled bitterness and pathos, which served at once to disarm Gertrude's confusion at his self-introduction and subsequent remarks, and render her forgetful of everything but the strange interest with which this singular man inspired her.

Presently, taking a vacant chair next hers, he directed her attention to a beautiful country residence on their right, spoke of its former owner, whom he had met in a foreign land, and related some interesting anecdotes concerning an adventurous journey which they had taken together. This again introduced other topics, chiefly connected with wanderings in countries almost unknown, even in this exploring age; and so rich and varied was the stranger's conversation, so graphic were his descriptions, so exuberant and glowing his imagination, and so powerful his command of words and his gift at expressing and giving force to his thoughts, that his young and enthusiastic listener sat entranced with admiration and delight.

Her highly-wrought and intellectual nature sympathized fully with the fervor and poetry of a mind as sensitive as her own to the great and wonderful, whether in nature or art; and, her fancy and interest thus taken by storm, her calm and observant entertainer had soon the satisfaction of perceiving that he had succeeded in disarming her diffidence and embarrassment; for, as she listened to his words, and even met the occasional glance of his dark eyes, her animated and beaming countenance no longer showed signs of fear or distrust.

He took no advantage, however, of the apparent self-forgetfulness with which she enjoyed his society, but continued to enlarge upon such subjects as naturally presented themselves, and was careful not to disturb her equanimity by again bestowing upon her the keen and scrutinizing gaze which had proved so disconcerting. By the time, therefore, that Dr. Jeremy came in search of his young charge, conversation between her and the stranger had assumed so much ease and freedom from restraint that the doctor opened his eyes in astonishment, shrugged his shoulders, and exclaimed, "This is pretty well, I declare!"

Gertrude did not see the doctor approach, but looked up at the sound of his voice. Conscious of the surprise it must be to him to find her talking so familiarly with a complete stranger, she colored slightly at his abrupt remark; but, observing that her companion was quite unconcerned, and even received it with a smile, she felt herself rather amused than embarrassed; for, strangely enough, the latter feeling had almost entirely vanished, and she had come to feel confidence in her fellow-traveller, who rose, shook hands with Dr. Jeremy, to whom he had, the previous day, been introduced, and said, with perfect composure, "Will you have the kindness, sir, to present me to this young lady? We have already had some conversation together, but do not yet know by what name we may address each other."

Dr. Jeremy having performed the ceremony of introduction, Mr. Phillips bowed gracefully, and looked at Gertrude in such a benignant, fatherly way that she hesitated not to take his offered hand. He detained hers a moment while he said, "Do not be afraid of me when we meet again;" and then walked away, and paced slowly up and down the deck until passengers for Catskill were summoned to dinner, when he, as well as Dr. Jeremy and Gertrude, went below.

The doctor tried to rally Gertrude a little about her gray-headed beau, declaring that he was yet young and handsome, and that she could have his hair dyed any color she pleased. But he could not succeed in annoying her in that way, for her interest in him, which she did not deny, was quite independent of his personal appearance.

The bustle, however, of dinner, and going on shore at Catskill, banished from the good doctor's head all thought of everything except the safety of himself, his ladies, and their baggage; fit cause, indeed, for anxiety to a more experienced traveller than he. For, so short was the time allotted for the boat to stop at the landing and deposit the passengers, and such was the confusion attending the operation of pushing them on shore and flinging their baggage after them, that when the panting engine was again set in motion the little crowd collected on the wharf resembled rather a flock of frightened sheep than human beings with a free will of their own.

Emily, whose nervous system was somewhat disordered, clung tremblingly to Gertrude; and Gertrude found herself, she knew not how, leaning on the arm of Mr. Phillips, to whose silent exertions they were both indebted for their safety in disembarking. Mrs. Jeremy, in the mean time, was counting up the trunks, while her husband, with his foot upon one of them, and a carpet-bag in his left hand, was loudly denouncing the steamboat, its conductors, and the whole hurrying, skurrying Yankee nation.

Two stage-coaches were waiting at the wharf to take passengers up the mountain, and before Dr. Jeremy had turned his back upon the river Emily and Gertrude were placed in one of them by Mr. Phillips, who, without asking questions, or even speaking at all, took this office upon himself, and then went to inform the doctor of their whereabouts. The doctor and his wife soon joined them; a party of strangers occupied the other seats in the coach, and, after some delay, they commenced the afternoon's drive.

✿✿✿✿✿✿✿✿✿✿✿✿✿✿✿✿✿✿✿✿✿✿✿✿✿✿✿✿✿

# Chapter XXXVI

*Along thy soul morn's youth restored shall glow;*
*Believe in God as in the sun,—and, lo!*
*As rests the earth, so rest, O, troubled heart,*
*Rest, till the burden of the cloud depart!*
NEW TIMON

Before they had passed through the dusty village, and gained the road leading in the direction of the Mountain House, they became painfully conscious of the vast difference between the temperature of the river and that of the inland country, and, in being suddenly deprived of the refreshing breeze they had enjoyed on board the boat, they fully realized the extreme heat of the weather. For the first few miles Gertrude's whole attention was required to shield Emily and herself from the rays of a burning sun which shone into the coach full upon their faces, and it was a great relief when they at last reached the steep but smooth and beautifully-shaded road which led up the side of the mountain.

The atmosphere being perfectly clear, the gradually widening prospect was most beautiful, and Gertrude's delight and rapture were such that the restraint imposed by stage-coach decorum was almost insupportable. When, therefore, the ascent became so laborious that the gentlemen were invited to alight, and relieve the weary horses of a part of their burden, Gertrude gladly accepted Dr. Jeremy's proposal that she should accompany him on a walk of a mile or two.

Gertrude was an excellent walker, and she and the still active doctor soon left the coaches far behind them. At a sudden turn in the road they stopped to view the scene below, and, lost in silent admiration, stood enjoying the stillness and beauty of the spot, when they were startled by a voice close beside them saying, "A fine landscape, certainly!"

They looked around, and saw Mr. Phillips seated upon a moss-grown rock, against which Gertrude was at the moment leaning. His attitude was easy and careless, his broad-brimmed straw hat lay on the ground, where it had fallen, and his snow-besprinkled but wavy and still beautiful hair was tossed back from his high and expanded forehead. One would have thought, to look at him, leaning so idly and even boyishly upon his hand, that he had been sitting there for hours at least, and felt quite at home in the place. He rose to his feet, however, immediately upon being perceived, and joined Dr. Jeremy and Gertrude.

"You have got the start of us, sir," said the former.

"Yes; I have walked from the village,—my practice always when the roads are such that no time can be gained by riding."

As he spoke, he placed in Gertrude's hand, without looking at her, or seeming conscious what he was doing, a bouquet of rich laurel-blossoms, which he had probably gathered during his walk. She would have thanked him, but his absent manner was such that it afforded her no opportunity, especially as he went on talking with the doctor, as if she had not been present.

All three resumed their walk. Mr. Phillips and Dr. Jeremy conversed in an animated manner, and Gertrude, content to be a listener, soon perceived that she was not the only person to whom the stranger had power to render himself agreeable. Dr. Jeremy engaged him upon a variety of subjects, upon all of which he appeared equally well-informed; and Gertrude smiled to see her old friend more than once rub his hands together, according to his well-known manner of expressing boundless satisfaction.

Now, Gertrude thought their new acquaintance must be a botanist by profession, so versed was he in everything relating to that department of science. Then, again, she was equally sure that geology must have been with him an absorbing study, so intimate seemed his acquaintance with mother earth; and both of these impressions were in turn dispelled, when he talked of the ocean like a sailor, of the counting-room like a merchant, of Paris like a man of fashion and the world.

In the mean time, she walked beside him, silent but not forgotten or unnoticed; for, as they approached a rough and steep ascent, he offered his arm, and expressed a fear lest she should become fatigued. She assured him there was no danger of that. Dr. Jeremy declared it his belief that Gerty could out-walk them both; and, thus satisfied, Mr. Phillips resumed the broken thread of their discourse, into which, before long, Gertrude was drawn, almost unawares.

Mr. Phillips was a man who knew how to inspire awe, and even fear, when such was his pleasure. The reverse being the case, however, he had equal ability to dispel such sentiments, awaken confidence, and bid character unfold itself at his bidding. He no longer seemed in Gertrude's eyes a stranger;—he was a mystery, certainly, but not a forbidding one. She longed to know more of him; to learn the history of a life which many an incident of his own narrating proved to have been made up of strange and mingled experience; especially did her sympathetic nature desire to fathom the cause of that deep-seated melancholy which shadowed and darkened his noble countenance, and made his very smile a sorrowful thing.

Dr. Jeremy, who, in a degree, shared her curiosity, asked a few leading questions, in hopes to obtain some clue to his new friend's personal history; but in vain. Mr. Phillips' lips were either sealed on the subject, or opened only to baffle the curiosity of his interrogator.

At length the doctor was compelled to give way to a weariness which he could no longer disguise from himself or his companions, much as he disliked to acknowledge the fact; and, seating themselves by the road-side, they awaited the arrival of the coach.

There had been a short silence, when the doctor, looking at Gertrude, remarked, "There will be no church for us to-morrow, Gerty."

"No church!" exclaimed Gertrude, gazing about her with a look of reverence; "how *can* you say so?"

Mr. Phillips bestowed upon her a smile of interest and inquiry, and said, in a peculiar tone, "There is no Sunday here, Miss Flint; it doesn't come up so high."

He spoke lightly,—too lightly, Gertrude thought,—and she replied with some seriousness, and much sweetness, "I have often rejoiced that the Sabbath had been sent *down* into the *lower* earth; the higher we go, the nearer we come, I trust, to the eternal Sabbath."

Mr. Phillips bit his lip, and turned away without replying. There was an expression about his mouth which Gertrude did not exactly like; but she could not find it in her heart to reproach him for the slight sneer which his manner, rather than his look, implied, for, as he gazed a moment or two into vacancy, there was in his wild and absent countenance such a look of sorrow, that she could only pity and wonder. The coaches now came up, and, as he placed her in her former seat, he resumed his wonted serene and kindly expression, and she felt convinced that it was only doing justice to his frank and open face to believe that nothing was hid behind it that would not do honor to the man.

An hour more brought them to the Mountain House, and, greatly to their joy, they were at once shown to some of the most excellent rooms the hotel afforded. As Gertrude stood at the window of the chamber allotted to herself and Emily, and heard the loud murmurs of some of her fellow-travellers who were denied any tolerable accommodation, she could not but be astonished at Dr. Jeremy's unusual good fortune in being treated with such marked partiality.

Emily, being greatly fatigued with the toilsome journey, had supper brought to her own room, and Gertrude partaking of it with her, neither of them sought other society that night, but at an early hour betook themselves to rest.

The last thing that Gertrude heard, before falling asleep, was the voice of Dr. Jeremy, saying, as he passed their door, "Take care, Gerty, and be up in time to see the sun rise."

She was not up in time, however, nor was the doctor himself; neither of them had calculated upon the sun's being such an early riser; and though Gertrude, mindful of the caution, sprung up almost before her eyes were open, a flood of daylight was pouring in at the window, and a scene met her gaze which at once put to flight every regret at having overslept herself, since nothing, she thought, could be more solemnly glorious than that which now lay outspread before her.

From the surface of the rocky platform upon which the house was built, far out to the distant horizon, nothing was to be seen but a sea of snowy clouds, which wholly overshadowed the lower earth, and hid it from view. Vast, solid, and of the most perfect whiteness, they stretched on every side, forming, as they lay in thick masses, between which not a crevice was discernible, an unbroken curtain, dividing the heavens from the earth.

While most of the world, however, was thus shut out from the clear light of morning, the mountain-top was rejoicing in an unusually brilliant and glorious dawn, the beauty of which was greatly enhanced by those very clouds which were obscuring and shadowing the dwellings of men below. A fairy bark might have floated upon the undulating waves which glistened in the sunshine like new-fallen snow, and which, contrasted with the clear blue sky above, formed a picture of singular grandeur. The foliage of the oaks, the pines and the maples, which had found root in this lofty region, was rich, clear and polished, and tame and fearless birds of various note were singing in the branches. Gertrude gave one long look, then hastened to dress herself and go out upon the platform. The house was perfectly still; no one seemed yet to be stirring, and she stood for some time entranced, almost breathless, with awe and admiration.

At length she heard footsteps, and, looking up, saw Dr. and Mrs. Jeremy approaching; the former, as usual, full of life, and dragging forward his reluctant, sleepy partner, whose countenance proclaimed how unwillingly she had foregone her morning nap. The doctor rubbed his hands as they joined Gertrude. "Very fine this, Gerty! A touch beyond anything I had calculated upon."

Gertrude turned upon him her beaming eyes, but did not speak. Satisfied, however, with the expression of her face, which was sufficient, without words, to indicate her appreciation of the scene, the doctor stepped to the edge of the flat rock upon which they stood, placed his hands beneath his coat-tails, and indulged in a soliloquy, made up of short exclamations and interjectional phrases, expressive of his approbation, still further confirmed and emphasized by a quick, regular nodding of his head.

"Why, this looks queer, doesn't it?" said Mrs. Jeremy, rubbing her eyes, and gazing about her; "but I dare say it would be just so an hour or two hence. I don't see what the doctor would make me get up so early for." Then, catching sight of her husband's position, she darted forward, exclaiming, "Dr. Jerry, for mercy's sake, don't stand so near the edge of that precipice! Why, are you crazy, man? You frighten me to death! you'll fall over and break your neck, as sure as the world!"

Finding the doctor deaf to her entreaties, she caught hold of his coat, and tried to drag him backwards; upon which he turned about, inquired what was the matter, and, perceiving her anxiety, considerably retreated a few paces; the next moment, however, he was once more in the same precarious spot. The same scene was reënacted, and finally, after the poor woman's fears had been excited and relieved half a dozen times in succession, she grew so disturbed, that, looking most imploringly at Gertrude, she begged her to get the doctor away from that dangerous place, for the poor man was so venturesome he would surely be killed.

"Suppose we explore that little path at the right of the house," suggested Gertrude; "it looks attractive."

"So it does," said Mrs. Jeremy; "beautiful little shady path! Come, doctor, Gerty and I are going to walk up here,—come."

The doctor looked in the direction in which she pointed. "Ah!" said he, "that is the path the man at the office spoke about; it leads up to the pine gardens. We'll climb up, by all means, and see what sort of a place it is."

Gertrude led the way, Mrs. Jeremy followed, and the doctor brought up the rear,—all walking in single file, for the path was a mere foot-track. The ascent was very steep, and they had not proceeded far before Mrs. Jeremy, panting with heat and fatigue, stopped short, and declared her inability to reach the top; she would not have thought of coming, if she had known what a horrid hard hill she had got to climb. Encouraged and assisted, however, by her husband and Gertrude, she was induced to make a further attempt; and they had gone on some distance, when Gertrude, who happened for a moment to be some steps in advance, heard Mrs. Jeremy give a slight scream. She looked back; the doctor was laughing heartily, but his wife, who was the picture of consternation, was endeavoring to pass him, and retrace her steps down the hill, at the same time calling upon her to follow.

"What is the matter?" asked Gertrude.

"Matter!" cried Mrs. Jeremy; "why, this hill is covered with rattlesnakes, and here we are all going up to be bitten to death!"

"No such thing, Gerty!" said the doctor, still laughing. "I only told her there had been one killed here this summer, and now she's making it an excuse for turning back."

"I don't care!" said the good-natured lady, half-laughing herself, in spite of her fears; "if there's been one, there may be another, and I won't stay here a minute longer! I thought it was a bad enough place before, and now I'm going down faster than I came up."

Finding her determined, the doctor hastened to accompany her, calling to Gertrude as he went, however, assuring her there was no danger, and begging her to keep on and wait for him at the top of the hill, where he would join her after he had left his wife in safety at the hotel. Gertrude, therefore, went on alone. For the first few rods she looked carefully about her, and thought of rattlesnakes; but the path was so well worn that she felt sure it must be often trod and was probably safe, and the beauty of the place soon engrossed all her attention. After a few moments spent in active climbing, she reached the highest point of ground, and found herself once more on an elevated woody platform, from which she could look forth as before upon the unbroken sea of clouds.

She seated herself at the root of an immense pine-tree, removed her bonnet, for she was warm from recent exercise, and, as she inhaled the refreshing mountain breeze, gave herself up to the train of reflection which she had been indulging when disturbed by Dr. and Mrs. Jeremy.

She had sat thus but a moment when a slight rustling noise startled her; she remembered the rattlesnakes, and was springing to her feet, but, hearing a low sound, as of some one breathing, turned her eyes in the direction from which it came, and saw, only a few yards from her, the figure of a man stretched upon the ground, apparently asleep. She went towards it with a careful step, and before she could see the face the large straw hat, and the long, blanched, wavy hair, betrayed the identity of the individual. Mr. Phillips was, or appeared to be, sleeping; his head was pillowed upon his arm, his eyes were closed, and his attitude denoted perfect repose. Gertrude stood still and looked at him. As she did so, his countenance suddenly changed; the peaceful expression gave place to the same unhappy look which had at first excited her sympathy. His lips moved, and in his dreams he spoke, or rather shouted, "No! no! no!" each time that he repeated the word pronouncing it with more vehemence and emphasis; then, wildly throwing one arm above his head, he let it fall gradually and heavily upon the ground, and, the excitement subsiding from his face, he uttered the simple words, "O, dear!" much as a grieved and tired child might do, as he leans his head upon his mother's knee.

Gertrude was deeply touched. She forgot that he was a stranger; she saw only a sufferer. An insect lit upon his fair, open forehead; she leaned over him, brushed away the greedy creature, and, as she did so, one of the many tears that filled her eyes fell upon his cheek.

Quietly, then, without motion or warning, he awoke, and looked full in the face of the embarrassed girl, who started, and would have hastened away, but, leaning on his elbow, he caught her hand and detained her. He gazed at her for a moment without speaking; then said, in a grave voice, "My child, did you shed that tear for me?"

She did not reply, except by her eyes, which were still glistening with the dew of sympathy.

"I believe you *did*," said he, "and from my heart I bless you! But never again weep for a stranger; you will have woes enough of your own, if you live to be of my age."

"If I had not had sorrows already," said Gertrude, "I should not know how to feel for others; if I had not often wept for myself, I should not weep now for you."

"But you are happy?"

"Yes."

"Some find it easy to forget the past."

"*I* have not forgotten it."

"Children's griefs are trifles, and you are still scarce more than a child."

"I *never* was a child," said Gertrude.

"Strange girl!" soliloquized her companion. "Will you sit down and talk with me a few minutes?"

Gertrude hesitated.

"Do not refuse; I am an old man, and very harmless. Take a seat here under this tree, and tell me what you think of the prospect."

Gertrude smiled inwardly at the idea of his being such an old man, and calling her a child; but, old or young, she had it not in her heart to fear him, or refuse his request. She sat down, and he seated himself beside her, but did not speak of the prospect, or of anything, for a moment or two; then turning to her abruptly, he said, "So you never were unhappy in your life?"

"Never!" exclaimed Gertrude. "O, yes; often."

"But never long?"

"Yes, I can remember whole years when happiness was a thing I had never even dreamed of."

"But comfort came at last. What do you think of those to whom it never comes?"

"I know enough of sorrow to pity and wish to help them."

"What can you do for them?"

"*Hope* for them, *pray* for them!" said Gertrude, with a voice full of feeling.

"What if they be past hope?—beyond the influence of prayer?"

"There are no such," said Gertrude, with decision.

"Do you see," said Mr. Phillips, "this curtain of thick clouds, now over-shadowing the world? Even so many a heart is weighed down and over-shadowed by thick and impenetrable darkness."

"But the light shines brightly above the clouds," said Gertrude.

"Above! well, that may be; but what avails it to those who see it not?"

"It is sometimes a weary and toilsome road that leads to the mountain-top; but the pilgrim is well repaid for the trouble which brings him *above the clouds*," replied Gertrude, with enthusiasm.

"Few ever find the road that leads so high," responded her melancholy companion; "and those who do cannot live long in so elevated an atmos-phere. They must come down from their height, and again dwell among the common herd; again mingle in the warfare with the mean, the base and the cruel; thicker clouds will gather over their heads, and they will be buried in redoubled darkness."

"But they have seen the glory; they know that the light is ever burning on high, and will have faith to believe it will pierce the gloom at last. See, see!" said she, her eyes glowing with the fervor with which she spoke,—"even now the heaviest clouds are parting; the sun will soon light up the valley!"

She pointed, as she spoke, to a wide fissure which was gradually disclosing itself, as the hitherto solid mass of clouds separated on either side, and then turned to the stranger to see if he observed the change; but, with the same smile upon his unmoved countenance, he was watching, not the dis-play of nature in the distance, but that close at his side. He was gazing with intense interest upon the young and ardent worshipper of the beautiful and the true; and, in studying her features and observing the play of her countenance, he seemed so wholly absorbed, that Gertrude—believing he was not listening to her words, but had fallen into one of his absent moods—ceased speaking, rather abruptly, and was turning away, when he said,

"Go on, happy child! Teach *me*, if you can, to see the world tinged with the rosy coloring it wears for *you*; teach me to love and pity, as you do, that miserable thing called *man*. I warn you that you have a difficult task, but you seem to be very hopeful."

"Do you hate the world?" asked Gertrude, with straight-forward simplicity.

"Almost," was Mr. Phillips' answer.

"*I* did *once*," said Gertrude, musingly.

"And will again, perhaps."

"No, that would be impossible; it has been a good foster-mother to its orphan child, and now I love it dearly."

"Have they been kind to you?" asked he, with eagerness. "Have heartless strangers deserved the love you seem to feel for them?"

"Heartless strangers!" exclaimed Gertrude, the tears rushing to her eyes. "O, sir, I wish you could have known my Uncle True, and Emily, dear, blind Emily! You would think better of the world, for their sakes."

"Tell me about them," said he, in a low, unsteady voice, and looking fixedly down into the precipice which yawned at his feet.

"There is not much to tell, only that one was old and poor, and the other wholly blind; and yet they made everything rich, and bright, and beautiful, to me, a poor, desolate, injured child."

"Injured! Then you acknowledge that you had previously met with wrong and injustice?"

"I!" exclaimed Gertrude; "my earliest recollections are only of want, suffering, and much unkindness."

"And these friends took pity on you?"

"Yes. One became an earthly father to me, and the other taught me where to find a heavenly one."

"And ever since then you have been free and light as air, without a wish or care in the world?"

"No, indeed, I did not say so,—I do not mean so," said Gertrude. "I have had to part from Uncle True, and to give up other dear friends, some for years and some forever; I have had many trials, many lonely, solitary hours, and even now am oppressed by more than one subject of anxiety and dread."

"How, then, so cheerful and happy?" asked Mr. Phillips.

Gertrude had risen, for she saw Dr. Jeremy approaching, and stood with one hand resting upon a solid mass of stone, under whose protecting shadow she had been seated. She smiled a thoughtful smile at Mr. Phillips' question; and after casting her eyes a moment into the deep valley beneath her, turned them upon him with a look of holy faith, and said, in a low but fervent tone, "I see the gulf yawning beneath me, but I lean upon the Rock of ages."

Gertrude had spoken truly when she said that more than one anxiety and dread oppressed her; for, mingled with a daily increasing fear lest the time was fast approaching when Emily would be taken from her, she had of late been harassed and grieved by the thought that Willie Sullivan, towards whom her heart yearned with more than a sister's love, was fast forgetting the friend of his childhood, or, at least, ceasing to regard her with the love and tenderness of former years. It was now some months since she had received a letter from India; the last was short, and written in a haste which Willie apologized for on the score of business cares and duties, and Gertrude was compelled unwillingly to admit the chilling presentiment that now his mother and grandfather were no more the ties which bound the exile to his native home were sensibly weakened.

Nothing would have induced her to hint, even to Emily, a suspicion of neglect on Willie's part; nothing would have shocked her more than hearing such neglect imputed to him by another; but still, in the depths of her own heart, she sometimes mused with wonder upon his long silence, and the strange diminution of intercourse between herself and him. During several weeks in which she had received no tidings she had still continued to write as usual, and felt sure that such reminders must have reached him by every mail. What, then, but illness or indifference could excuse his never replying to her faithfully despatched missives? She often tried to banish from her mind any self-questioning upon a subject so involved in uncertainty; but at times a sadness came over her which could only be dispersed by turning her thoughts upward with that trusting faith and hope which had so often sustained her drooping spirits, and it was from one of these soaring reveries that she had turned with pitying looks and words to the fellow-sufferer whose moans had escaped him even in his dreams.

Dr. Jeremy's approach was the signal for hearty congratulations and good-mornings between himself and Mr. Phillips; the doctor began to converse in his animated manner, spoke with hearty delight of the beauty and peacefulness of that bright Sabbath morning in the mountains; and Mr. Phillips, compelled to exert himself, and conceal, if he could not dispel, the gloom which weighed upon his mind, talked with an ease, and even playfulness, which astonished Gertrude, who walked back to the house silently wondering at this strange and inconsistent man. She did not see him at breakfast, and at dinner he took a seat at some distance from Dr. Jeremy's party, and merely acknowledged their acquaintance by a graceful salutation to Gertrude as she left the dining-hall.

Still later in the day, he suddenly made his appearance upon the broad piazza where Emily and Gertrude were seated, one pair of eyes serving, as usual, to paint pictures for the minds of both. There had been a thunder-shower, but, as the sun went down, and the storm passed away, a brilliant bow, and its almost equally brilliant reflection, spanned the horizon, seemingly far beneath the height of the mountain-top, and the lights and shadows which were playing upon the valley and its shining river were brilliant and beautiful in the extreme. Gertrude hoped Mr. Phillips would join them; she knew that Emily would be charmed with his rich and varied conversation, and felt an instinctive hope that the sweet tones of the comfort-carrying voice which so many loved and blessed would speak to his heart a lesson of peace. But she hoped in vain; he started on seeing them, walked hastily away, and Gertrude soon after espied him toiling up the same steep path which had attracted them both in the morning,—nor did he make his appearance at the hotel again that night.

The Jeremys stayed two days longer at the Mountain House; the invigorating air benefited Emily, who appeared stronger than she had done for weeks past, and was able to take many a little stroll in the neighborhood of the house.

Gertrude was never weary of the glorious prospect, upon which she gazed with ever increasing delight; and an excursion which she and the doctor made on foot to the cleft in the heart of the mountain, where a narrow stream leaps a distance of two hundred feet into the valley below, furnished the theme for many a descriptive revery, of which Emily reaped a part of the enjoyment. They saw no more of their new acquaintance, who had disappeared without their knowledge. Dr. Jeremy inquired of their host concerning him, and learned that he left at an early hour on Monday, and took up a pedestrian course down the mountain.

The doctor was surprised and disappointed, for he liked Mr. Phillips exceedingly, and had flattered himself, from some particular inquiries he had made concerning their proposed route, that he had an idea of attaching himself to their party.

"Never mind, Gerty," said he, in a tone of mock condolence. "I daresay we shall come across him yet, some time when we least expect it."

## Chapter XXXVII

*Led by simplicity divine,*
*She pleased, and never tried to shine.*
HANNAH MORE

From Catskill Dr. Jeremy proceeded directly to Saratoga. The place was crowded with visitors, for the season was at its height, and the improvident traveller having neglected to secure rooms, they had no right to expect any accommodation.

"Where do you propose stopping?" inquired an acquaintance of the doctor's, whom they accidentally encountered in the cars.

"At Congress Hall," was the reply. "It will be a quiet place for us old folks, and more agreeable than any other house to Miss Graham, who is an invalid."

"You are expected, I conclude?"

"Expected?—No; who should be expecting us?"

"Your landlord. If you have not engaged rooms you will fare badly, for every hotel is crowded to overflowing."

"We must take our chance, then," said the doctor, with an indifference of manner which wholly forsook him upon his fairly arriving at his destination, and learning that his friend's words were true.

"I don't know what we are going to do," said he, as he joined the ladies, whom he had left for a few moments while he made inquiries;

"they say every house is full; and, if so, we'd better take the next train of cars and be off, for we can't sleep in the street."

"Carriage, sir?" shouted a hackman, leaning over a railing a few steps distant, and beckoning to the doctor with all his might, while another and still bolder aspirant for employment tapped his shoulder, and made a similar suggestion, in a most insinuating tone of voice.

"Carriage!" repeated the doctor, angrily. "What for? where would you carry us, for mercy's sake? There isn't a garret to be had in your town, for love or money."

"Well sir," said the last-mentioned petitioner (a sort of omnibus attaché, taking off his cap as he spoke, and wiping his forehead with a torn and soiled pocket-handkerchief), "the houses is pretty considerable full just now, to be sure, but may-be you can get colonized out."

"*Colonized out?*" said the doctor, still in a tone of extreme vexation. "That's what I think we are already; what I want is to get *in* somewhere. Where do you usually drive your coach?"

"To Congress Hall."

"Drive up, then, and let us get in; and, mind, if they don't take us at Congress Hall, we shall expect you to keep us until we find better accommodations."

Mrs. Jeremy, Emily and Gertrude, were consequently assisted into a small omnibus, and closely packed away among half a dozen ladies and children, who, tired, dusty and anxious, were schooling themselves to patience, or encouraging themselves with hope. The doctor took a seat upon the outside, and the moment the vehicle stopped hastened to present himself to the landlord. As he had anticipated, there was not a vacant corner in the house. Wishing to accommodate him, however, the office-keeper announced the possibility that he might be able before night to furnish him with one room in a house in the next street.

"One room! in the next street!" cried the doctor. "Ah, that's being colonized out, is it? Well, sir, it won't do for me; I must have a place to put my ladies in at once. Why in conscience don't you have hotels enough for your visitors?"

"It is the height of the season, sir, and—"

"Why, Dr. Jeremy!" exclaimed the youthful voice of Netta Gryseworth, who was passing through the hall with her grandmother, "how do you do, sir? Are Miss Graham and Miss Flint with you? Have you come to stay?"

Before the doctor could answer her questions, and pay his respects to Madam Gryseworth, a venerable old lady, whom he had known thirty years before, the landlord of the hotel accosted him.

"Dr. Jeremy?" said he. "Excuse me, I did not know you. Dr. Jeremy, of Boston?"

"The same," said the doctor, bowing.

"Ah! we are all right, then. Your rooms are reserved, and will be made ready in a few minutes; they were vacated two days ago, and have not been occupied since."

"What is all this?" exclaimed the honest doctor. "I engaged no rooms."

"A friend did it for you, then, sir; a fortunate circumstance, especially as you have ladies with you. Saratoga is very crowded at this season; there were seven thousand strangers in the town yesterday."

The doctor thanked his stars and his unknown friend, and summoned the ladies to enjoy their good fortune.

"Why, now, an't we lucky?" said Mrs. Jeremy, as she glanced round the comfortable room allotted to herself, and then, crossing the narrow entry, took a similar survey of Emily's and Gertrude's apartment. "After all the talk everybody made, too, about the crowd of folks there were here scrambling for places!"

The doctor, who had just come up stairs, having waited to give directions concerning his baggage, approached the door in time to hear his wife's last remark, and entering with his finger upon his lip, and a mock air of mystery, exclaimed, in a low voice, "Hush! hush! don't say too much about it! We are profiting by a glorious mistake on the part of our good landlord. These rooms were engaged for somebody, that's certain, but not for us. However, they can't do more than turn us out when the right folks come, and until then we have a prospect, I see, of very good lodgings."

But, if the Jeremys were not the right folks, the right folks never came, and, in the course of a week, our party not only ceased to be conscious of their precarious footing in the house, but even had the presumption to propose, and the good fortune to obtain, a favorable exchange for Emily to a bed-room upon the first floor, which opened directly into the drawing-room, and saved her the necessity of passing up and down the often crowded staircases.

It was nearly tea-time on the day of their arrival, and Emily and Gertrude had just completed their toilet, when there was a light rap upon their door. Gertrude hastened to open it, and to admit Ellen Gryseworth, who, while she saluted her with southern warmth of manner, hesitated at the threshold, saying, "I am afraid you will think me an intruder, but Netta told me you had arrived, and hearing accidentally from the chambermaid that you had the next room to mine, I could not forbear stopping a moment as I passed to tell you how very glad I am to see you again."

Gertrude and Emily expressed their pleasure at the meeting, thanked her for her want of ceremony, and urged her to come in and remain with them until the gong sounded for tea. She availed herself of the invitation, and taking a seat upon the nearest trunk, proceeded to inquire concerning their travels and Emily's health since they parted at West Point.

Among other adventures, Gertrude mentioned their having again encountered Mr. Phillips. "Indeed!" said Miss Gryseworth, "he seems to be a ubiquitous individual. He was in Saratoga a day or two ago, and sat opposite to me at our dinner-table, but I have not seen him since. Did you become acquainted with him, Miss Graham?"

"I am sorry to say, I did not," replied Emily; then, looking smilingly at Gertrude, she added, "Gerty was so anxious for an opportunity to introduce me, that I was quite grieved for her disappointment."

"Then you liked him!" said Miss Gryseworth, addressing herself to Gertrude, and speaking with great earnestness. "I knew you would."

"He interested me much," replied Gertrude. "He is very agreeable, very peculiar, and to me rather incomprehensible."

"Non-committal, I see," said Miss Gryseworth, archly. "I hope you will have a chance to make up your mind; it is more than I can do, I confess; for, every time I am in his company, I recognize some new and unexpected trait of character. He got so angry with one of the waiters, the day he dined with us in New York, that I was actually frightened. However, I believe my fears were groundless, for he is too much of a gentleman to bandy words with an inferior, and though his eyes flashed like coals of fire, he kept his temper from blazing forth. I will do him the justice to say that this great indignation did not spring from any neglect he had himself received, but from the man's gross inattention to two dowdy-looking women from the country, who had never thought of such a thing as feeing him, and therefore got nothing to eat until everybody else had finished, and looked all the time as disappointed and ashamed as if they were just out of the State Prison."

"Too bad!" exclaimed Gertrude, energetically. "I don't wonder Mr. Phillips felt provoked with the mercenary fellow. I like him for that."

"It *was* too bad," said Miss Gryseworth. "I couldn't help pitying them, myself. One of them—a young girl, fresh from the churn, who had worn her best white gown on purpose to make a figure in the city—looked just ready to burst out crying."

"I hope such instances of neglect are not very common," said Gertrude. "I am afraid, if they are, Emily and I shall be on the crying list, for Dr. Jeremy never will fee the waiters beforehand; he says it is a mean thing, and he should scorn to command attention in that way."

"O, you need have no such fear," said Miss Gryseworth. "Persons in the least accustomed to hotel life can always command a moderate share of attention, especially in so well-regulated an establishment as this. Grandmamma shares the doctor's views with regard to bargaining for it beforehand, but no one ever sees her neglected here. The case which occurred in New York was a gross instance of that partiality for which the public are partly to blame. The waiters can tell easily enough who will endure to be imposed upon, and the embarrassed faces of the two country ladies, who found so fierce an advocate in Mr. Phillips, were alone sufficient to lay them open to any degree of neglect."

Another light tap at the door, and this time it was Netta Gryseworth, who entered, exclaiming, "I hear Ellen's voice, so I suppose I may come in. I am provoked," added she, as she kissed Emily's hand, and shook Gertrude's with a freedom and vivacity which seemed to spring partly from girlish hoydenism and partly from high-bred independence of manner, "to think that while I have been watching about the drawing-room doors for this half-hour, so as to see you the first minute you came in, Ellen has been sitting here on a trunk, as sociable as all the world, enjoying your society, and telling you every bit of the news."

"Not every bit, Netta," said Ellen; "I have left several choice little morsels for you."

"Have you told Miss Flint about the Foxes and the Coxes that were here yesterday?—Has she, Miss Flint?"

"Not a word about them," said Gertrude.

"Nor about the fright we had on board the steamboat?"

"No."

"Nor about Mr. Phillips' being here?"

"O, yes! she told us that."

"Ah, she did!" exclaimed Netta, with an arch look, which called up her sister's blushes. "And did she tell you how he occupied this room, and how we heard him through the thin partition pacing up and down all night, and how it kept me from sleeping, and gave me a terrible headache all the next day?"

"No, she did not tell me that," said Gertrude.

"You don't either of you walk all night, do you?" asked Netta.

"Not often."

"O, how thankful we ought to be to have you for neighbors!" replied Netta. "If that horrible man had staid here and kept up that measured tread, there would have been a suicide either in his room or ours before many nights."

"Do you think he was ill?" inquired Gertrude.

"No, indeed," said Ellen; "it was nothing very remarkable,—not for him, at least,—all his habits are peculiar; but it kept Netta awake an hour or two, and made her fidgetty."

"An hour or two, Ellen?" cried Netta. "It was the whole night!"

"My dear sis," said Ellen, "you don't know what a whole night is. You never saw one."

A little sisterly discussion might have ensued about the length of Mr. Phillips' walk and Netta's consequent wakefulness, but, fortunately, the gong sounded, and Netta flew off to her own room to brush out her puffs before tea.

Saratoga is a queer place. One sees congregated there, at the height of the season, delegates from every part of our own and from many foreign countries. Fashion's ladder is transplanted thither, and all its rounds are filled. Beauty, wealth, pride and folly, are well represented; and so too are wit, genius and learning. Idleness reigns supreme, and no one, not even the most active, busy and industrious citizen of our working land, dares, in this her legitimate province, to dispute her temporary sway. Every rank of society, every profession, and almost every trade, meet each other on an easy and friendly footing. The acknowledged belle, the bearer of an aristocratic name, the owner of a well-filled purse, the renowned scholar, artist or poet, have all a conspicuous sphere to shine in. There are many counterfeits, too. The nobodies at home stand a chance to be considered somebodies here; and the *first people* of a distant city, accustomed to consider themselves somebodies, sit in corners and pout at suddenly finding themselves nobodies. All come, however, from a common motive; all are in pursuit of amusement, recreation and rest from labor; and, in this search after pleasure, a friendly and benevolent sentiment for the most part prevails. All are in motion, and the throngs of well-dressed people moving to and fro, on foot, on horseback, and in carriages, together with the gay assemblages crowded upon the piazzas of the hotels, constitute a lively and festive scene; and he who loves to observe human nature may study it here in its most animated form.

It was a wholly new experience to Gertrude; and although, in the comparative retirement and privacy of Congress Hall, she saw only the reflection of Saratoga gayety, and heard only the echo of its distant hum, there was enough of novelty and excitement to entertain, amuse and surprise one who was a complete novice in the ways of fashionable life. In the circle of high-bred, polished, literary and talented persons whom Madam Gryseworth drew about her, and into which Dr. Jeremy's party were at once admitted as honored members, Gertrude found much that was congenial to her cultivated and superior taste, and she herself soon came to be appreciated and admired as she deserved. Madam Gryseworth was a lady of the old school,—one who had all her life been accustomed to the best society, and who continued, in spite of her advanced years, to enjoy and to adorn it. She was still an elegant-looking woman, tall and stately; and, though a little proud, and to strangers a little reserved, she soon proved herself an agreeable companion to people of all ages. For the first day or two of their acquaintance, poor Mrs. Jeremy stood much in awe of her, and could not feel quite at ease in her presence; but this feeling wore off wonderfully quick, and the stout little doctor's lady soon became exceedingly confiding and chatty towards the august dame.

One evening, when the Jeremys had now been a week at Saratoga, as Emily and Gertrude were leaving the tea-table, they were joined by Netta Gryseworth, who, linking her arm in Gertrude's, exclaimed, in her usual gay manner, "Gertrude, I shall quarrel with you soon!"

"Indeed!" said Gertrude, "on what ground?"

"Jealousy."

Gertrude blushed slightly.

"O! you needn't turn so red; it is not on account of any gray-headed gentleman's staring at you all dinner-time, from the other end of the table. No; I'm indifferent on that score. Ellen and you may disagree about Mr. Phillips' attentions, but I'm jealous of those of another person."

"I hope Gertrude isn't interfering with your happiness in any way," said Emily, smiling.

"She is, though," replied Netta, "my happiness, my pride, my comfort. She is undermining them all; she would not dare to conduct so, Miss Graham, if you could see her behavior."

"Tell me all about it," said Emily, coaxingly, "and I will promise to interest myself for you."

"I doubt that," answered Netta; "I am not sure but you are a coädjutor with her. However, I will state my grievance. Do you not see how entirely she engrosses the attention of an important personage? Are you not aware that Peter has ceased to have eyes for any one else? For my own part, I can get nothing to eat or drink until Miss Flint is served, and I'm determined to ask papa to change our seats at the table. It isn't that I care about my food; but I feel insulted,—my pride is essentially wounded. A few days ago, I was a great favorite with Peter, and all my pet dishes were sure to be placed directly in front of me; but now the tune is changed, and, this very evening, I saw him pass Gertrude the blackberries, which the creature knows I delight in, while he pushed a dish of blues towards me in a contemptuous manner, which seemed to imply, 'Blueberries are good enough for *you*, miss!' "

"I have noticed that the waiters are very attentive to us," said Emily; "do you suppose Gertrude has been secretly bribing them?"

"She says not," replied Netta. "Didn't you tell me so yesterday, Gertrude, when I was drawing a similar comparison between their devotion to you and to our party? Didn't you tell me that neither the doctor nor any of you ever gave Peter a cent?"

"Certainly," answered Gertrude; "his attentions are all voluntary; but I attribute them entirely to Emily's influence, and his desire to serve her."

"It's no such thing!" said Netta, emphasizing her remark by a mysterious little shake of the head;—"it's sorcery, I'm sure of it; you've been practising the black art, Gertrude, and I'll warn Peter this very day."

As she spoke, they reached a corner of the drawing-room where the old ladies Gryseworth and Jeremy were sitting upon a sofa, engaged in earnest conversation, while Ellen, who had just returned from a drive with her father, stood talking with him and a Mr. Petrancourt, who had that evening arrived from New York.

The ladies on the sofa made room for Emily, and Netta and Gertrude seated themselves near by. Occasionally Madam Gryseworth cast glances of annoyance at a group of children on the other side of the room, who by their noisy shouts continually interrupted her remarks, and prevented her understanding those of her neighbor. Gertrude's attention soon became attracted by them also to such a degree that she did not hear more than half of the lively and gay sallies of wit and nonsense which Netta continued to pour forth.

"Do go and play with those children, Gertrude," said Netta, at last; "I know you're longing to."

"I'm longing to stop their play!" exclaimed Gertrude; an apparently ill-natured remark, which we are bound to explain. Some half-dozen gayly and fancifully-dressed children, whose mothers were scattered about on the piazzas, and whose nurses were at supper, had collected around a strange little new-comer, whom they were subjecting to every species of persecution. Her clothes, though of rich material, were most untidily arranged, and appeared somewhat soiled by travelling. Her little black silk frock (for the child was clad in mourning) seemed to be quite outgrown, being much shorter than some of her other garments, and her whole appearance denoted great negligence on the part of her parents or guardians. When Madam Gryseworth's evident disturbance first led Gertrude to notice the youthful group, this little girl was standing in their midst, looking wildly about her, as if for a chance to escape; but this the children prevented, and continued to ply her with questions, each of which called forth a derisive shout from all but the poor little object of attack, who, on her part, looked ready to burst into tears. Whether the scene reminded Gertrude of some of her own experiences, or merely touched the chord of a universal spirit of sympathy for the injured, she could not keep her eyes from the little party; and, just as Netta was fairly launched upon one of her favorite topics,—namely, Mr. Phillips and his unaccountable conduct,— she sprung from her seat, exclaiming, "They shan't torment that child so!" and hastily crossed the room to the rescue.

Netta burst into a hearty laugh at Gertrude's excited and enthusiastic manner of starting on her benevolent errand; and this, together with the unusual circumstance of her crossing the large and crowded room hastily and alone, drew the inquiries of all the circle whom she had left, and during her absence she unconsciously became the subject of discussion and remark.

"What is the matter, Netta?" asked Madam Gryseworth. "Where has Gertrude gone?"

"To offer herself as a champion, grandmamma, for that little rowdy-dowdy looking child."

"Is she the one who has been making all this noise?"

"No, indeed, but I believe she is the cause of it."

"It isn't every girl," remarked Ellen, "who could cross a great room like this so gracefully as Gertrude can."

"She has a remarkably good figure," said Madam Gryseworth, "and knows how to walk; a very rare accomplishment, now-a-days."

"She is a very well-formed girl," remarked Dr. Gryseworth, who had observed Gertrude attentively as she crossed the room, and now, hearing her commented upon, turned to take his part in the criticism; "but the true secret of her looking so completely the lady lies in her having uncommon dignity of character, being wholly unconscious of observation and independent of the wish to attract it, and therefore simply acting herself. She dresses well, too;— Ellen, I wish you would imitate Miss Flint's style of dress; nothing could be in better taste."

"Or a greater saving to your purse, papa," whispered Netta, "Gertrude dresses very simply."

"Miss Flint's style of dress would not become Miss Gryseworth," said the fashionable Mrs. Petrancourt, who approached in time to hear the doctor's remark. "Your daughter, sir, is a noble, showy-looking girl, and can carry off a great deal of dress."

"So can a milliner's doll, Mrs. Petrancourt. However, I suppose, in a certain sense, you are right. The two girls are not sufficiently alike to resemble each other, if their dresses were matched with Chinese exactness."

"Resemble each other!—You surely would not wish to see your beautiful daughter the counterpart of one who has not half her attractions."

"Are you much acquainted with Miss Flint?"

"Not at all; but Netta pointed her out to me at the tea-table as being a particular friend."

"Then you must excuse me, ma'am, if I remark that it is impossible you should have any idea of her attractions, as they certainly do not lie on the surface."

"You confess, then, that you do not think her handsome, sir?"

"To tell the truth, I never thought anything about it. Ask Petrancourt; he is an acknowledged judge;" and the doctor bowed in a flattering manner to the lady, who had been the belle of the season at the time her husband paid his addresses to her.

"I will, when I can get a chance; but he is standing too near the blind lady,—Miss Flint's aunt, is she not?"

"Particular friend; not her aunt."

This conversation had been carried on in a low voice, that Emily might not hear it. Others, however, were either more careless or more indifferent to her presence; for Madam Gryseworth began to speak of Gertrude without restraint, and she was at this moment saying, "One must see her under peculiar circumstances to be struck with her beauty at once;—for instance, as I did yesterday, when she had just returned from horseback-riding, and her face was in a glow from exercise and excitement; or as she looks when animated by her intense interest in some glowing and eloquent speaker, or when her feelings are suddenly touched, and the tears start into her eyes, and her whole soul shines out through them!"

"Why, grandmamma!" cried Netta, "you are really eloquent!"

"So is Gertrude, at such times as those I speak of. O! she is a girl after my own heart."

"She must be a very agreeable young lady, from your account," said Mr. Petrancourt. "We must know her."

"You will not find her at all the same stamp as most of the agreeable young ladies whom you meet in the gay circles. I must tell you what Horace Willard said of her. He is an accomplished man and a scholar,—his opinion is worth something. He had been staying a fortnight at the United States Hotel, and used to call here occasionally, to see us. The day he left, he came to me and said, 'Where is Miss Flint? I must have one more refreshing conversation with her before I go. It is a perfect *rest* to be in that young lady's society, for she never seems to be making the least effort to talk with me, or to expect any attempt on my part; she is one of the few girls who never speak unless they have something to say.'—How she has contrived to quiet those children!"

Mr. Petrancourt followed the direction of Madam Gryseworth's eyes. "Is that the young lady you are speaking of?" asked he. "The one with great, dark eyes, and such a splendid head of hair? I have been noticing her for some time."

"Yes, that is she, talking to the little girl in black."

"Madam Gryseworth," said Dr. Jeremy, through the long, open window, and stepping inside as he spoke, "I see you appreciate our Gerty; I did not say too much in praise of her good sense, did I?"

"Not half enough, doctor; she is a very bright girl, and a very good one, I believe."

"Good!" exclaimed the doctor; "I didn't know that goodness counted in these places; but, if goodness is worth speaking of, I should like to tell you a little of what I know of that girl;"—and, without going closely into particulars, he commenced dilating enthusiastically upon Gertrude's noble and disinterested conduct under trying circumstances, and, warming with his subject, had recounted, in a touching manner, her devotion to one old paralytic,—to another infirm, imbecile and ill-tempered old man and his slowly-declining daughter,—and would have proceeded, perhaps, to speak of her recent self-sacrificing labors in Emily's service; but Miss Graham touched his arm, spoke in a low voice, and interrupted him.

He stopped abruptly. "Emily, my dear," said he, "I beg your pardon; I didn't know you were here; but what you say is very true. Gertrude is a private character, and I have no right to bring her before the public. I am an old fool, certainly; but there, we are all friends." And he looked around the circle a little anxiously, cast a slightly suspicious glance at the Petrancourts, and finally rested his gaze upon a figure directly behind Ellen Gryseworth. The latter turned, not having been previously aware that any stranger was in the neighborhood, and, to her surprise, found herself face to face with Mr. Phillips!

"Good-evening, sir," said she, on recognizing him; but he did not seem to hear her. Madam Gryseworth, who had never seen him before, looked up inquiringly.

"Mr. Phillips," said Ellen, "shall I make you acquainted with Mrs. Gryseworth, my—" But, before she could complete the introduction, he had darted quickly through the window, and was walking across the piazza with hasty strides. He drew forth his handkerchief, wiped the moisture from his brow, and, unseen and unsuspected, brushed away a tear.

## Chapter XXXVIII

*It was not thus in other days we met:*
*Hath time, hath absence, taught thee to forget?*
                                        MRS. HEMANS

Later in the evening, when Gertrude, having resigned her little charge to the nurse who came to seek her, had again joined her party, the attention of every one assembled in the drawing-room was attracted by the entrance of a beautiful and showily-dressed young lady, attended by two or three gentlemen. After glancing round the room for the person whom she came to seek, she advanced towards Mrs. Petrancourt, who, on her part, rose to receive her young visitor. Unexpected as the meeting was to Gertrude, she at once recognized Isabel Clinton, who, however, passed both her and Emily without observing them, and, there being no vacant chair near at hand, seated herself with Mrs. Petrancourt on a couch a little further up the room, and entered into earnest and familiar conversation; nor did she change her position or look in the direction of Dr. Jeremy's party, until just as she was taking her leave. She would have passed them then without noticing their presence, but accidentally hearing Dr. Gryseworth address Miss Flint by name, she half turned, caught Gertrude's eye, spoke a careless "How do you do," with that sort of indifference with which one salutes a very slight acquaintance, cast a look back at Emily, surveyed with an impertinent air of curiosity the rest of the circle to which they belonged, and, without stopping to exchange words or inquiries, walked off whispering to her companions some satirical comments both upon the place and the company.

"O, what a beauty!" exclaimed Netta to Mrs. Petrancourt. "Who is she?"

Mrs. Petrancourt related what she knew of Miss Clinton; told how she had travelled with her in Switzerland, and met her afterwards in Paris, where she was universally admired; then, turning to Gertrude, she remarked, "You are acquainted with her, I see, Miss Flint."

Gertrude replied that she knew her before she went abroad, but had seen nothing of her since her return.

"She has but just arrived," said Mrs. Petrancourt; "she came with her father in the last steamer, and has been in Saratoga but a day or two. She is making a great sensation at the United States, I hear, and has troops of beaux."

"Most of whom are probably aware," remarked Mr. Petrancourt, "that she will have plenty of money one of these days."

Emily's attention was by this time attracted. She had been conversing with Ellen Gryseworth, but now turned to ask Gertrude if they were speaking of Isabel Clinton.

"Yes," said Dr. Jeremy, taking upon himself to reply, "and if she were not the rudest girl in the world, my dear, you would not have remained so long in ignorance of her having been here."

Emily forbore to make any comment. It did not surprise her to hear that the Clintons had returned home, as they had separated from the Grahams soon after the latter went abroad, and she had since heard nothing of their movements; nor was she astonished at any degree of incivility from one who sometimes seemed ignorant of the most common rules of politeness. Gertrude was silent also; but she burned inwardly, as she always did, at any slights being offered to the gentle Emily.

Gertrude and Dr. Jeremy were always among the earliest morning visitors at the spring. The doctor enjoyed drinking the water at this hour; and, as Gertrude was an early riser and fond of walking before breakfast, he made it a point that she should accompany him, partake of the beverage of which he was himself so fond, and afterwards join him in brisk pedestrian exercise until near the hour of the morning meal, which was as early as Mrs. Jeremy or Emily cared to have their slumbers disturbed.

On the morning succeeding the evening of which we have been speaking they had as usual presented themselves at the spring. Gertrude had gratified the doctor, and made a martyr of herself, by imbibing a tumbler-full of a water which she found very unpalatable; and he having quaffed his seventh glass, they had both proceeded some distance on one more walk around the grounds, when he suddenly missed his cane, and, believing that he had left it at the spring, declared his intention to return and look for it.

Gertrude would have gone back also, but, as there might be some difficulty and delay in recovering it, he insisted upon her continuing her walk in the direction of the circular railway, promising to come round the other way and meet her. She had proceeded some little distance, and was walking thoughtfully along, when, at an abrupt winding in the path, she observed a couple approaching her,—a young lady leaning on the arm of a gentleman. A straw hat partly concealed the face of the latter, but in the former she at once recognized Belle Clinton. It was equally evident, too, that Belle saw Gertrude, and knew her, but did not mean to acknowledge her acquaintance; for, after the first glance, she kept her eyes obstinately fixed either upon her companion or the ground. This conduct did not disturb Gertrude in the least; Belle could not feel more indifferent about the acquaintance than she did; but, being thus saved the necessity of awaiting and returning any salutation from that quarter, she naturally bestowed her passing glance upon the gentleman who accompanied Miss Clinton. He looked up at the same instant, fixed his full gray eyes upon her, with merely that careless look, however, with which one stranger regards another, then, turning as carelessly away, made some slight remark to his companion.

They pass on. They have gone some steps,—but Gertrude stands fixed to the spot. She feels a great throbbing at her heart. She knows that look, that voice, as well as if she had seen and heard them yesterday. Could Gertrude forget Willie Sullivan?

But he has forgotten her. Shall she run after him, and stop him, and catch both his hands in hers, and compel him to see, and know, and speak to her? She started one step forward in the direction he had taken, then suddenly paused and hesitated. A crowd of emotions choked, blinded, suffocated her, and while she wrestled with them and they with her, he turned the corner and passed out of sight. She covered her face with her hands (always her first impulse in moments of distress), and leaned against a tree.

It was Willie. There was no doubt of that; but not her Willie,—the *boy* Willie. It was true, time had added but little to his height or breadth of figure, for he was a well-grown youth when he went away. But six years of Eastern life, including no small amount of travel, care, exposure and suffering, had done the work that twice that time would ordinarily have accomplished.

The fresh complexion of the boy had given place to the paler, beard-darkened and somewhat sun-browned tints that mark a ripened manhood; the joyous eye had a deeper cast of thought, the elastic step a more firm and measured tread; while the beaming, sunny expression of countenance had given place to a certain grave and composed look, which marked his features when in repose.

The winning attractiveness of the boy, however, had but given place to equal, if not superior qualities in the man, who was still eminently handsome, and gifted with that inborn and natural grace and ease of deportment which win universal remark and commendation. The broad, open forehead, the lines of mild but firm decision about the mouth, the frank, fearless manner, were as marked as ever, and were alone sufficient to betray his identity to one upon whose memory these, and all his other characteristics, were indelibly stamped; and Gertrude needed not the sound of his well-known voice, though that, too, at the same moment fell upon her ear, to proclaim at once to her beating heart that Willie Sullivan had met her face to face, had passed on, and that she was left alone, unrecognized, unknown, and, to all appearance, unthought of and uncared for!

For a time, this bitter thought, "He does not know me," was alone present to her mind; it filled and engrossed her entire imagination, and sent a thrill of surprise and agony through her whole frame. She did not stop to reflect upon the fact that she was but a child when she parted from him, and that the change in her appearance must be immense. Far less did it occur to her to congratulate herself upon a transformation every shade of which had been to her a proportionate improvement and advantage. The one painful idea, that she was forgotten and lost, as it were, to the dear friend of her childhood, obliterated every other recollection. Had they both been children, as in the earlier days of their brother and sister hood, it would have been easy, and but natural, to dart forward, overtake, and claim him. But time, in the changes it had wrought, had built up a huge barrier between them. Gertrude was a woman now, with all a woman's pride; and delicacy and maiden modesty deterred her from the course which impulse and old affection prompted. Other feelings, too, soon crowded into her mind, in confused and mingled array. Why was Willie here, and with Isabel Clinton leaning on his arm? How came he on this side the ocean? and how happened it that he had not immediately sought herself, the earliest, and, as she had supposed, almost the only friend he had left to welcome him back to his native land? Why had he not written and warned her of his coming? How should she account for his strange silence, and the still stranger circumstance of his hurrying at once to the haunts of fashion, without once visiting the city of his birth, and the sister of his adoption?

Question after question, and doubt following doubt, rushed into her mind so confusedly, that she could not reflect, could not come to any conclusion in the matter. She could only feel and weep; and, giving way to her overpowering emotion, she burst into a flood of tears.

Poor child! It was so different a meeting from what she had imagined and expected! For the six years that she had been growing into womanhood, it had been the dream of her waking hours, and had come as a beautiful though transient reality to her happy sleep. He could hardly have presented himself at any hour of the day or night, scarcely in any disguise, that would not have been foreseen and anticipated. He could have used no form of greeting that had not already rung in the ears of her fancy; he could bestow upon her no look that would not be familiar. What Willie would say when he first saw her, what he would do to express his delight, the questions he would ask, the exclamations he would utter and the corresponding replies on her part, the happiness of them both (lately sobered and subdued to her imagination by the thought of the dear departed ones they had both loved so well),—all this had been rehearsed by Gertrude again and again, in every new instance taking some new form, or varied by some additional circumstance.

But, among all her visions, there had been none which in the least approached the reality of this painful experience that had suddenly plunged her into disappointment and sorrow. Her darkest dreams had never pictured a meeting so chilling; her most fearful forebodings (and she had of late had many) had never prefigured anything so heart-rending as this seemingly total annihilation of all the sweet and cherished relations that had subsisted between herself and the long-absent and exiled wanderer.

No wonder, then, that she forgot the place, the time, everything but her own overwhelming grief; and that, as she stood leaning against the old tree, her chest heaved with sobs too deep for utterance, and great tears trickled from her eyes, and between the little taper fingers that vainly sought to hide her disturbed countenance.

She was startled from her position by the sound of an approaching footstep. Hastily starting forward, without looking in the direction from which it came, and throwing a lace veil (which, as the day was warm, was the only protection she wore upon her head) in such a manner as to hide her face, she wiped away her fast-flowing tears, and hastened on, to avoid being overtaken and observed by any of the numerous strangers who frequented the grounds at this hour.

Half-blinded, however, by the thick folds of the veil, and her sight rendered still dimmer by the tears which continued to fill her eyes, she was scarcely conscious of the unsteady course she was pursuing, when suddenly a loud, whizzing noise, close to her ears, frightened and confused her so that she knew not which way to turn; nor had she time to take a single step; for, at the same instant, an arm was suddenly flung round her waist, she was forcibly lifted from her feet with as much ease and lightness as if she had been a little child, and, before she was conscious what was taking place, found herself detained and supported by the same strong arm, while just in front of her a little hand-car containing two persons was whirling by at full speed. One step more, and she would have reached the track of the miniature railway, and been exposed to serious, perhaps fatal injury, from the rapidly-moving vehicle. Flinging back her veil, she at once perceived her fortunate escape; and, being at the same moment released from the firm grasp of her rescuer, she turned upon him a half-confused, half-grateful face, whose disturbed expression was much enhanced by her previous excitement and tears.

Mr. Phillips—for it was he—looked upon her in the most tender and pitying manner. "Poor child!" said he, soothingly, at the same time drawing her arm through his, "you were very much frightened. Here, sit down upon this bench;" and he would have drawn her towards a seat, but she shook her head, and signified by a movement her wish to proceed towards the hotel. She could not speak; the kindness of his look and voice only served to increase her trouble, and rob her of the power to articulate.

So he walked on in perfect silence, supporting her, however, with the greatest care, and bestowing upon her many an anxious glance. At last, making a great effort to recover her calmness, she partially succeeded,—so much so that he ventured to speak again, and asked, "Did *I* frighten you?"

"You?" replied she, in a low, and somewhat unsteady voice. "O, no! you are very kind."

"I am sorry you are so disturbed," said he; "those little cars are troublesome things; I wish they'd put a stop to them."

"The car?" said Gertrude, in an absent way. "O, yes, I forgot."

"You are a little nervous, I fear; can't you get Dr. Jeremy to prescribe for you?"

"The doctor! He went back for his cane, I believe."

Mr. Phillips saw that she was bewildered, obtuse he knew she never was; for, within the last few days, his acquaintance with her had grown and ripened by frequent intercourse. He forbore any attempt at conversation, and they continued their walk to the hotel without another word. Just before leaving her, however, he said, in a tone of the deepest interest, as he held her hand for a moment at parting, "Can I do anything for you? Can I help you?"

Gertrude looked up at him. She saw at once, from his countenance, that he understood and realized that she was unhappy, not nervous. Her eyes thanked him as they again glistened behind a shower of tears. "No, no," gasped she, "but you are very good;" and she hastened into the house, leaving him standing for more than a minute in the spot where she had left him, gazing at the door by which she had disappeared, as if she were still in sight, and he were watching her.

Gertrude's first thought, after parting from Mr. Phillips and gaining the shelter of the hotel, was, how she might best conceal from all her friends, and especially from Miss Graham, any knowledge of the load of grief she was sustaining. That she would receive sympathy and comfort from Emily there could be no doubt; but, in proportion as she loved and respected her benefactress, did she shrink, with jealous sensitiveness, from any disclosure which was calculated to lessen Willie Sullivan in the estimation of one in whose opinion she was anxious that he should sustain the high place to which her own praises had exalted him.

The chief knowledge that Emily had of Willie was derived from Gertrude, and with a mingled feeling of tenderness for him and pride on her own account did the latter dread to disclose the fact that he had returned after so many years of absence, that she had met him in the public walks of Saratoga, and that he had passed her carelessly by.

The possibility naturally presented itself to her mind that he had indeed visited Boston, sought her, and, learning where she might be found, had come hither purposely to see her; nor, on calm reflection, did this supposition seem contradicted by his failing, on a mere casual glance, to recognize her; for she could not be ignorant or insensible of the vast change which had taken place both in her face and figure. But the ray of hope which this thought called up was quickly dissipated by the recollection of a letter received the previous evening from Mrs. Ellis (now acting as housekeeper at Dr. Jeremy's), which would certainly have mentioned the arrival of so important a visitor. There was, however, the still further possibility that this arrival might have taken place since the date of Mrs. Ellis' concise epistle, and that Willie might have but just reached his destination, and not yet had time to discover her temporary place of abode. Though the leisurely manner in which he was escorting Miss Clinton on her morning walk seemed to contradict the supposition, Gertrude, clinging fondly to this frail hope, and believing that the rest of the day would not pass without his presenting himself at the hotel, determined to concentrate all her energies in the effort to maintain her usual composure, at least until her fears should become certainties.

It was very hard for her to appear as usual, and elude the vigilance of the affectionate and careful Emily, who, always deeply conscious of her responsibility towards her young charge, and fearful lest, owing to her blindness, she might often be an insufficient protection to one of so ardent and excitable a temperament, was keenly alive to every sensation and emotion experienced by Gertrude, especially to any fluctuation in her usually cheerful spirits.

And Gertrude's spirits, even when she had armed herself with confidence and hope by the encouraging thought that Willie would yet prove faithful to his old friendship, could not but be sorely depressed by the consciousness now forced upon her that he could no longer be to her as he had once been; that they could never meet on the same footing on which they had parted; that he was a man of the world now, with new relations, new cares, new interests; and that she had been deceiving herself, and laboring under a fond delusion, in cherishing the belief that in their case the laws of nature would be suspended, and time have no power to alter or modify the nature and extent of their mutual affection. There was something in the very circumstance of her first meeting him in company with Isabel Clinton which tended to impress her with this conviction. Isabel, of all people, one so essentially worldly, and with whom she had so little sympathy or congeniality! True, she was the daughter of Willie's early and generous employer, now the senior partner in the mercantile house to which he belonged, and would not only be likely to form his acquaintance, but would have an undoubted claim to every polite attention he might have it in his power to pay her; but still Gertrude could not but feel a greater sense of estrangement, a chilling presentiment of sorrow, from seeing him thus familiarly associated with one who had invariably treated her with scorn and incivility.

There was but one thing for her to do, however; to call up all her self-command, bring pride even to her aid, and endeavor, in any event, to behave with serenity and composure. The very fear that one keen and searching pair of eyes had already penetrated her secret so far as to discover that she was afflicted in some form or other served to put her still more upon her guard; and she therefore compelled herself to enter the room where Emily was awaiting her, bid her a cheerful "good-morning," and assist, as usual, in the completion of her toilet. Her face still bore indications of recent tears; but that Emily could not see, and by breakfast-time even they were effectually removed.

Now, again, new trials awaited her; for Dr. Jeremy, according to his promise, had, after recovering the missing cane, gone to meet her in the direction agreed upon, and, finding her false to her appointment, and nowhere to be found among the grounds, was full of inquiries as to the path she had taken, and her reasons for giving him the slip.

Now, for the first time, she recollected the doctor's promise to rejoin her, and the stipulation that she should proceed in the path she was then following; but, having, until these questions were put to her, quite forgotten the old gentleman, she was unprepared for a reply, blushed, and became very much confused. The truth was that when Gertrude heard Mr. Phillips approaching in the direction she should have taken, she, in her eagerness to avoid meeting any one, took the contrary path to that she had been pursuing, and, after he joined her, retraced her steps to the hotel in the same way she had come, consequently eluding the search of the doctor.

But, before she could plead any excuse, Netta Gryseworth came running up, evidently full of pleasantry and fun, and, leaning over Gertrude's shoulder, said, in a whisper loud enough to be heard by all the little circle, who were being delayed on their way to breakfast by the doctor's demand for an explanation, "Gertrude, my dear, such affecting partings ought to be private; I wonder you allow them to take place directly at the door-step."

This remark did not lessen Gertrude's discomfiture, which became extreme on Dr. Jeremy's catching Netta by the arm, as she was about to run off, and insisting upon knowing her meaning, declaring that he already had suspicions of Gertrude, and wanted to know who she had been walking with.

"O, a certain tall young beau of hers, who stood gazing after her when she left him, until I began to fear the cruel creature had turned him into stone. What did you do to the poor man, Gertrude?"

"Nothing," replied Gertrude. "He saved me from being thrown down by the little rail-car, and afterwards walked home with me."

Gertrude answered seriously; she could have laughed and joked with Netta at any other time, but now her heart was too heavy. The doctor did not perceive her growing agitation, however, and pushed the matter still further.

"Quite romantic! imminent danger! providential rescue! tête-à-tête walk home, carefully avoiding the old doctor, who might prove an interruption!— I understand!"

Poor Gertrude, blushing scarlet and pitiably distressed, tried to offer some explanation, and stammered out, with a faltering voice, that she did not notice —she didn't remember.

Ellen Gryseworth gave her a scrutinizing glance,—Emily, an anxious one,— and Netta, half-pitying half-enjoying her confusion, dragged her off towards the breakfast-hall, saying, "Never mind, Gertrude; it's no such dreadful thing, after all."

She made a pretence of eating breakfast, but could not conceal her want of appetite, and was glad, when Emily had finished her light repast, to accompany her to their own room, where, after relating circumstantially her escape from accident, and Mr. Phillips' agency in that escape, she was permitted by her apparently satisfied hearer to sit down quietly and read aloud to her in a book lent them by that gentleman, to whom, however, owing to unfriendly fortune, no opportunity had ever yet occurred of introducing Emily.

The whole morning passed away, and nothing was heard from Willie. Every time a servant passed through the entry, Gertrude was on the tiptoe of expectation; and on occasion of a tap at the door, such as occurred several times before dinner, she trembled so that she could hardly lift the latch. There was no summons to the parlor, however, and by noon the feverish excitement of alternate expectation and disappointment had brought a deep flush into her face, and she experienced, what was very unusual, symptoms of a severe headache. Conscious, however, of the wrong construction which would be sure to be put upon her conduct, if, upon any plea whatever, she on this day absented herself from the dinner-table, she made the effort to dress with as much care as usual; and, as she passed up the hall to her seat, it was not strange that, though suffering herself, the rich glow that mantled her cheeks, and the brilliancy which excitement had given to her dark eyes, attracted the notice of others beside Mr. Phillips, who, seated at some distance, continued, during the short time that he remained at the table, to observe her attentively.

❀❀❀❀❀❀❀❀❀❀❀❀❀❀❀❀❀—❀❀❀❀❀❀❀❀❀❀❀❀❀❀

# Chapter XXXIX

*O'er the wrung heart, from midnight's breathless sky,*
*Lone looks the pity of the Eternal Eye.*
                                    NEW TIMON

When Gertrude went to her room after dinner, which she did as soon as she had seen Emily comfortably established in the drawing-room in conversation with Madam Gryseworth, she found there a beautiful bouquet of the choicest flowers, which the chamber-maid assured her she had been commissioned to deliver to herself. She rightly imagined the source from whence they came, divined at once the motives of kindness and sympathy which had prompted the donor of so sweet and acceptable a gift, and felt that, if she must accept pity from any quarter, Mr. Phillips was one from whom she could more easily bear to receive it than from almost any other.

Notwithstanding Netta's intimations, she did not for a moment suspect that any other motives than those of kindness and compassion had instigated the offering of the beautiful flowers. Nor had she reason to do so; Mr. Phillips' manner towards her was rather fatherly than lover-like, and though she began to look upon him as a valuable friend, that was the only light in which she had ever thought of viewing him, or believed that he ever regarded her. She placed the flowers in water, returned to the parlor, and constrained herself to talk on indifferent subjects, until she was happily relieved by the breaking up of their circle, part to ride on horseback, part to take a drive, and the rest a nap. Among these last was Gertrude, who availed herself of her headache as an excuse to Emily for this unwonted indulgence. But she could not sleep, and the day wore wearily on.

Evening came at last, and with it an urgent invitation to Gertrude to accompany Dr. Gryseworth, his daughters, and the Petrancourts, to a concert to be given at the United States Hotel. This she declined doing, and persisted in her refusal, in spite of every endeavor to shake her resolution. She felt that it would be impossible for her to undergo another such encounter as that of the morning,—she should be sure to betray herself; and now that the whole day had passed, and Willie had made no attempt to see her, she felt that she would not, for the world, put herself in his way, and run the risk of being discovered and recognized by him in a crowded concert-room. No,— she would wait; she should see him soon, at the latest, and under the present circumstances she should not know how to meet him; she would preserve her incognito a little longer.

So they all went without her, and many others from their hotel; and the parlor, being half-deserted, was very quiet,—a great relief to Gertrude's aching head and troubled mind. Later in the evening, an elderly man, a clergyman, had been introduced to Emily, and was talking with her; Madam Gryseworth and Dr. Jeremy were entertaining each other, Mrs. Jeremy was nodding, and Gertrude, believing that she should not be missed, was gliding out of the room to go and sit a while by herself in the moonlight, when she met Mr. Phillips in the hall.

"What are you here all alone for?" asked he. "Why didn't you go to the concert?"

"I have a headache."

"I saw you had, at dinner. Is it no better?"

"No. I believe not."

"Come and walk with me on the piazza a little while. It will do you good."

She went; and he talked very entertainingly to her, told her a great many amusing anecdotes, succeeded in making her smile, and even laugh, and seemed very much pleased at having done so. He related many amusing things he had seen and heard since he had been staying at Saratoga in the character of a spectator, and ended by asking her if she didn't think it was a heartless show.

The question took Gertrude by surprise. She asked his meaning.

"Don't you think there is something very ridiculous in so many thousand people coming here to enjoy themselves?"

"I don't know," answered Gertrude; "but it has not seemed so to me. I think it's an excellent thing for those who *do* enjoy themselves."

"And how many do?"

"The greater part, I suppose."

"Pshaw! no, they don't. More than half go away miserable, and nearly all the rest dissatisfied."

"Do you think so? Now, I thought the charm of the place was seeing so many happy faces; they have nearly all looked happy to me."

"O, that's all on the surface, and, if you'll notice, those who look happy one day are wretched enough the next. Yours was one of the happy faces yesterday, but it isn't to-day, my poor child."

Then, perceiving that his remark caused the hand which rested on his arm to tremble, while the eyes which had been attentively raised to his suddenly fell, and hid themselves under their long lashes, he continued. "However, we will trust soon to see it as bright as ever. But they should not have brought you here. Catskill Mountain was a fitter place for your lively imagination and reflecting mind; a sensitive nature should not be exposed to all the shafts of malice, envy and ill-will, it is sure to encounter in one of these crowded resorts of selfish, base and cruel humanity."

"O!" exclaimed Gertrude, at once comprehending that Mr. Phillips suspected her to be smarting under some neglect, feeling of wounded pride, or, perhaps, serious injury; "you speak harshly; all are not selfish, all are not unkind."

"Ah! you are young, and full of faith; trust whom you can, and as long as you can. *I* trust *no one.*"

"No one! Is there none, then, in the whole world, whom you love and confide in?"

"Scarcely; certainly not more than one. Whom should I trust?"

"The good, the pure, the truly great."

"And who are they? How shall we distinguish them? I tell you, my young friend, that in my experience—and it has been rich, ay, very rich,"—and he set his teeth and spoke with bitterness,—"the so-called good, the honorable, the upright man, has proved but the varnished hypocrite, the highly-finished and polished sinner. Yes," continued he, his voice growing deeper, his manner more excited as he spoke, "I can think of one, a respectable man, one of your *first* men, yes, and a church-member, whose hardness, injustice and cruelty, made my life what it has been—a desert, a blank, or worse than that; and I can think of another, an old, rough, intemperate sailor, over whose head a day never passed that he did not take the name of his God in vain, who had, nevertheless, at the bottom of his heart, a drop of such pure, unsullied essence of virtue as could not be distilled from the souls of ten thousand of your polished rogues. Which, then, shall I trust,—the good, religious men, or the low, profane and abject ones?"

"Trust in *goodness,* wherever it be found," answered Gertrude. "But, O, trust *all,* rather than *none.*"

"Your world, your religion, draws a closer line."

"Call it not *my* world, or *my* religion," said Gertrude. "I know of no such line. I know of no religion but that of the heart. Christ died for us all alike, and, since few souls are so sunk in sin that they do not retain some spark of virtue and truth, who shall say in how many a light will at last spring up, by aid of which they may find their way to God?"

"You are a good child, and full of hope and charity," said Mr. Phillips, pressing her arm closely to his side. "I will try and have faith in *you.* But, see! our friends have returned from the concert. Let us go and meet them."

They had had a delightful time; Alboni had excelled herself, and they were *so* sorry Gertrude did not go. "But perhaps," whispered Netta, "you have enjoyed yourself more at home." She half repented of the sly intimation, even before the words had escaped her; for Gertrude, as she stood leaning unconcernedly upon Mr. Phillips' arm, looked so innocent of confusion or embarrassment, that her very manner refuted Netta's suspicions.

"Miss Clinton was there," continued Netta, "and looked beautifully. She had a crowd of gentlemen about her; but didn't you notice (and she turned to Mrs. Petrancourt) that one seemed to meet with such marked favor that I wonder the rest were not discouraged. I mean that tall, handsome young man, who waited upon her into the hall, and went out soon after. She devoted herself to him while he stayed."

"It was the same one, was it not," asked Ellen, "who afterwards, towards the close of the concert, came in and stood leaning against the wall for some minutes?"

"Yes," answered Netta; "but he only waited for Alboni to finish singing, and then, approaching Miss Clinton, leaned over and whispered a word or two in her ear. After that she got up, left her seat, and they both went off, rather to the mortification of the other gentlemen. I noticed them pass by the window where we sat, and walk across the grounds together."

"Yes, just in the midst of that beautiful piece from Lucia," said Ellen. "How could they go away?"

"O, it is not strange, under the circumstances," said Mr. Petrancourt, "that

Miss Clinton should prefer a walk with Mr. Sullivan to the best music in the world."

"Why?" asked Netta. "Is he very agreeable? Is he supposed to be the favored one?"

"I should think there was no doubt of it," answered Mr. Petrancourt. "I believe it is generally thought to be an engagement. He was in Paris with them during the spring, and they all came home in the same steamer. Everybody knows it is the wish of Mr. Clinton's heart, and Miss Isabel makes no secret of her preference."

"O, certainly," interposed Mrs. Petrancourt; "it is an understood thing. I heard it spoken of by two or three persons this evening."

What became of Gertrude, all this time? Could she, who for six years had nursed the fond idea that to Willie she was and should still continue to be, all in all,—could she stand patiently by, and hear him thus disposed of and given to another?

She did do it; not consciously, however, for her head swam round, and she would have fallen but for the firm support of Mr. Phillips, who held her arm so tightly that though he felt, the rest could not see, how she trembled. Fortunately, too, none but he thought of noticing her blanched face; and, as she stood somewhat in the shadow, he alone, fully aware of her agitation, was watching the strained and eager eyes, the parted and rigid lips, the death-like pallor of her countenance.

Standing there with her heart beating like a heavy drum, and almost believing herself in a horrid dream, she listened attentively, heard and comprehended every word. She could not, however, have spoken or moved for her life, for in an instant more accident might have betrayed her excited and almost alarming condition. But Mr. Phillips acted, spoke and moved *for* her, and she was spared an exposure from which her delicate and sensitive spirit would have shrunk indeed.

"Mr. Sullivan!" said he. "Ah! a fine fellow; I know him. Miss Gertrude, I must tell you an anecdote about that young man;" and, moving forward in the direction in which they had been walking when they met the party from the concert, he made as if they were still intending to prolong their promenade —a promenade, however, in which he was the only walker, for Gertrude was literally borne upon his arm, until the rest of the company, who started at the same moment for the parlor, were hid within its shelter, and he and his companion were left the sole occupants of that portion of the piazza.

Until then he proceeded with his story, and went so far as to relate that he and Mr. Sullivan were, a few years previous, travelling together across an Arabian desert, when the latter proved of signal service in saving him from a sudden attack by a wandering tribe of Bedouins. By the time he had thus opened his narration, he perceived that all danger of observation was passed, and hesitated not to stop abruptly, and, without ceremony or apology, place her in an arm-chair which stood conveniently near. "Sit here," said he, "while I go and bring you a glass of water." He then wrapped her mantle tightly about her, and walked quickly away.

O, how Gertrude thanked him in her heart for thus considerately leaving her, and giving her time to recover herself! It was the most judicious thing he could have done, and the kindest. He saw that she would not faint, and knew that left alone she would soon rally her powers; perhaps be deceived by the idea that even he was only half aware of her agitation, and wholly ignorant of its cause.

He was gone some minutes, and when he returned she was perfectly calm. She tasted the water, but he did not urge her to drink it; he knew she did not require it. "I have kept you out too long," said he; "come, you had better go in now."

She rose; he put her arm once more through his, guided her feeble steps to a window which opened into hers and Emily's room, and then, pausing a moment, said, in a meaning tone, at the same time enforcing his words by the fixed glance of his piercing eye, "You exhort me, Miss Gertrude, to have faith in everybody; but I bid you, all inexperienced as you are, to beware lest you believe too much. Where you have good foundation for confidence, abide by it, if you can, firmly and bravely; but trust nothing which you have not fairly tested, and, especially, rest assured that the idle gossip of a place like this is utterly unworthy of credit. Good-night."

What an utter revulsion of feeling these words occasioned Gertrude! They came to her with all the force of a prophecy, and struck deep into her heart. Was there not wisdom in the stranger's counsel? It was true, she thought, that he spoke merely such simple axioms as a long experience of the world might dictate; but how forcible, in her case, was their application! Had not she, blindly yielding to her gloomy presentiments and fears, been willing to lend a too ready ear to the whisperings of her own jealous imagination, and a too credulous one to the idle reports of others, while in reality she had proved a traitor to a more noble trust? Who, during the many years she had known him, could have proved himself more worthy of confidence than Willie? Had he not, from his boyhood, been exemplary in every virtue, superior to every meanness and every form of vice? Had he not in his early youth forsaken all that he held most dear, to toil and labor beneath an Indian sun, that he might provide comforts and luxuries for those whose support he eagerly took upon himself? Had he not ever proved honorable, high-minded, sincere and warm of heart? Above all, had he not been imbued from his infancy with the highest and purest of Christian principles?

He had, indeed, been all this: and while Gertrude called it to mind, and dwelt upon each phase of his consistent course, she could not fail to remember, too, that Willie, whether as the generous, kind-hearted boy, the adventurous, energetic youth, the successful, respected, yet sorrow-tried man, had ever manifested towards herself the same deep, ardent, enthusiastic attachment. The love which he had shown for her in her childhood, and during that period when, though still a child, she labored under the full-grown care and sorrow entailed upon her by Uncle True's sickness and death, had seemed to grow and deepen in every successive day, month and year, of their separation.

During their long and regular correspondence, no letter had come from Willie that did not breathe the same spirit of devoted affection for Gertrude,— an exclusive affection, in which there could be no rivalship. All his thoughts of home and future happy days were inseparably associated with her; and although Mrs. Sullivan, with that instinctive reserve which was one of her characteristics, never broached the subject to Gertrude, her whole treatment of the latter sufficiently evinced that to her mind the event of her future union with her son was a thing certain. The bold declaration on Willie's part, conveyed in the letter received by Gertrude soon after his mother's death, that his hopes, his prayers, his labors, were now all for her, was not a more convincing proof of the tender light in which he regarded her than all their previous intercourse had been.

Should Gertrude, then, distrust him? Should she at once set aside all past evidences of his worth, and give ready credence to his prompt desertion of his early friend? No! she resolved immediately to banish the unworthy thought; to cherish still the firm belief that some explanation would shortly offer itself, which would yet satisfy her aching heart. Until then, she would trust him; bravely and firmly too would she trust, for her confidence was not without foundation.

As she made this heroic resolve, she lifted up her drooping head and gazed out into the night. The moon had gone down, and the sky was studded with stars, bright, clear and beautiful. Gertrude loved a starry night. It invigorated and strengthened her; and now, as she looked up, directly above her head stood the star she so much loved,—the star which she had once fondly fancied it was Uncle True's blessed privilege to light for her. And, as in times long past these heavenly lights had spoken of comfort to her soul, she seemed now to hear ringing in her ears the familiar saying of the dear old man, "Cheer up, birdie, for I'm of the 'pinion 't will all come out right at last."

Gertrude continued through the short remainder of the evening in an elevated frame of mind, which might almost be termed joyful; and, thus sustained, she was able to go back to the drawing-room for Emily, say good-night to her friends with a cheerful voice, and before midnight she sought her pillow and went quietly to sleep.

This composed state of mind, however, was partly the result of strong excitement, and therefore could not last. The next morning found her once more yielding to depressed spirits, and the effort which she made to rise, dress and go to breakfast, was almost mechanical. She excused herself from her customary walk with the doctor, for to that she felt quite unequal. Her first wish was to leave Saratoga; she longed to go home, to be in a quiet place, where so many eyes would not be upon her; and when the doctor came in with the letters which had arrived by the early mail, she looked at them so eagerly that he observed it, and said, smilingly, "None for you, Gerty; but one for Emily, which is the next best thing, I suppose."

To Gertrude this was the *very* best thing, for it was a long-expected letter from Mr. Graham, which would probably mention the time of his return from abroad, and consequently determine the continuance of her own and Emily's visit at Saratoga.

To their astonishment, he had already arrived in New York, and desired them to join him there the following day. Gertrude could hardly conceal her satisfaction, which was, however, if noticed by her friends, merely attributed to the pleasure she probably felt at the return of Mr. and Mrs. Graham; and Emily, really delighted at the prospect of so soon meeting her father, to whom she was fondly attached, was eager to commence preparations for leaving.

They therefore retired to their own room, and Gertrude's time until dinner was fully occupied in the business of packing. Throughout the whole of the previous day she had been anxiously hoping that Willie would make his appearance at their hotel; now, on the contrary, she as earnestly dreaded such an event. To meet him in so public a manner too as must here be inevitable, would, under her present state of feelings, be insupportable; she would infinitely prefer to be in Boston when he should first see and recognize her; and, if she tormented herself yesterday with the fear that he would not come, the dread that he might do so was a still greater cause of distress to her to-day.

She was therefore relieved when, after dinner, Mr. Phillips kindly proposed a drive to the lake. Dr. Gryseworth and one of his daughters had, he assured Gertrude, agreed to take seats in a carriage which he had provided, and he hoped she would not refuse to occupy the fourth. As it was an hour when Emily would not require her presence, and she would thus be sure to avoid Willie, she gladly consented to the arrangement.

They had been at the lake nearly an hour. Dr. Gryseworth and his daughter Ellen had been persuaded by a party whom they met there to engage in bowling. Mr. Phillips and Gertrude had declined taking part, but stood for some time looking on. The day, however, being warm, and the air in the building uncomfortably close, they had gone outside and seated themselves on a bench at a little distance, to wait until the game was concluded. As they sat thus, surveying the beautiful sheet of water, now rosy red with the rays of the descending sun, a couple approached and took up a position near them. Mr. Phillips was quite screened from their observation by the trunk of a huge tree, and Gertrude sufficiently so to be unnoticed, though the sudden paleness which overspread her face as they drew near was so marked as clearly to indicate that she saw and recognized William Sullivan and Isabel Clinton. The words which they spoke, also, fell distinctly upon her ear.

"Shall I, then, be so much missed?" asked Isabel, looking earnestly in the face of her companion, who, with a serious air, was gazing out upon the water.

"Missed!" replied he, turning towards her, and speaking in a slightly-reproachful voice. "How can it be otherwise? Who can supply your place?"

"But it will be only two days."

"A short time, under ordinary circumstances," said Willie, "but an eternity—" He here checked himself, and made a sudden motion to proceed on their walk.

Isabel followed him, saying, "But you will wait here until my return?"

He again turned to reply, and this time the reproachful look which overspread his features was visible to Gertrude, as he said, with great earnestness, "Certainly; can you doubt it?"

The strange, fixed, unnatural expression which took possession of Gertrude's countenance as she listened to this conversation, to her so deeply fraught with meaning, was fearful to witness.

"Gertrude!" exclaimed Mr. Phillips, after watching her for a moment. "Gertrude, for heaven's sake do not look so! Speak, Gertrude! What is the matter?"

But she did not turn her eyes, did not move a feature of that stony face; she evidently did not hear him. He took her hand. It was cold as marble. His face now wore an appearance of distress almost equal to her own;— great tears rushed to his eyes, and rolled down his cheeks. Once he stretched forth his arms, as if he would gladly clasp her to his bosom and soothe her like a little child, but with evident effort he repressed the emotion. "Gertrude," said he, at length, leaning forward and fixing his eyes full upon hers, "what have these people done to you? Why do you care for them? If that young man has injured you,—the rascal!—he shall answer for it;" and he sprung to his feet.

The words and the action brought Gertrude to herself. "No, no!" said she, "he is not that. I am better now. Do not speak of it; don't tell," and she looked anxiously in the direction of the bowling-alley. "I am a great deal better." And, to his astonishment,—for the fearful, rigid look upon her face had frightened him,—she rose with perfect composure, and proposed going home.

He accompanied her silently, and before they were half-way up the hill where they had left the carriage, they were over-taken by the rest of their party, and, in a few moments, were driving towards Saratoga.

During the whole drive and the evening which followed Gertrude preserved this same rigid, unnatural composure. Once or twice before they reached the hotel Dr. Gryseworth asked her if she felt ill, and Mr. Phillips turned many an anxious glance towards her. The very tones of her voice were constrained,—so much so that Emily, on her reaching the house, inquired, at once, "What is the matter, my dear child?"

But she declared herself quite well, and went through all the duties and proprieties of the evening, bidding farewell to many of her friends, and when she parted from the Gryseworths arranging to see them again in the morning.

To the careless eye, Emily was the more troubled of the two; for Emily could not be deceived, and reflected back, in her whole demeanor, the better-concealed sufferings of Gertrude. Gertrude neither knew at the time, nor could afterwards recall, one-half of the occurrences of that evening. She never could understand what it was that sustained her, and enabled her, half unconsciously, to perform her part in them. How she so successfully concealed the misery she was enduring she never could comprehend or explain. She remembered it only as if it had all been a dream.

Not until the still hours of the night, when Emily appeared to be soundly sleeping by her side, did she venture for an instant to loosen the iron bands of restraint which she had imposed upon herself; but then, the barrier removed, the pent-up torrent of her grief burst forth without check or hindrance. She rose from her bed, and, burying her face in the cushions of a low couch which stood near the window, gave herself up to blessed tears, every drop of which was a relief to her aching soul. Since her early childhood she had never indulged so long and unrestrained a fit of weeping;

and, the heaving of her chest, and the deep sobs she uttered, proved the depth of her agony. All other sorrows had found her in a great degree fortified and prepared, armed with religious trust and encouraged by a holy hope; but beneath this sudden and unlooked-for blow she bent, staggered and shrunk, as the sapling of a summer's growth heaves and trembles beneath the wintry blast.

That Willie was faithless to his first love she could not now feel a shadow of doubt; and with this conviction she realized that the prop and stay of her life had fallen. Uncle True and Mrs. Sullivan were both her benefactors, and Emily was still a dear and steadfast friend; but all of these had been more or less dependent upon Gertrude, and, although she could ever repose in the assurance of their love, two had long before they passed away come to lean wholly upon her youthful arm, and the other, the last one left, not only trusted to her to guide her uncertain steps, but those steps were evidently now tending downwards to the grave.

Upon whom, then, should Gertrude lean? To whom should she look as the staff of her young and inexperienced life? To whom could she, with confidence, turn for counsel, protection, support and love? To whom but Willie? And Willie had given his heart to another,—and Gertrude would soon be left alone!

No wonder, then, that she wept as the broken-hearted weep; wept until the fountain of her tears was dry, and she felt herself sick, faint and exhausted. And now she rose, approached the window, flung back from her forehead the heavy folds of her long hair, leaned out, and from the breath of the cool night-breeze drank in a refreshing influence. Her soul grew calmer, as, with her eyes fixed upon the bright lights which shone so sweetly and calmly down, she seemed to commune with holy things. Once more they seemed to compassionate her, and, as in the days of her lonely childhood, to whisper, "Gerty!—Gerty!—poor little Gerty!"

Softened and touched by their pitying glance, she gradually sunk upon her knees; her uplifted face, her clasped hands, the sweet expression of resignation now gradually creeping over her countenance, all gave evidence that, as on the occasion of her first silent prayer to the then unknown God, her now enlightened soul was holding deep communion with its Maker, and once more her spirit was uttering the simple words, "Here am I, Lord!"

O, blessed religion which can sustain the heart in such an hour as this! O, blessed faith and trust, which, when earthly support fails us, and our strongest earthly stay proves but a rope of sand, lifts the soul above all other need, and clasps it to the bosom of its God!

And now a gentle hand is laid upon her head. She turns and sees Emily, whom she had believed to be asleep, but from whom anxiety had effectually banished slumber, and who, with fears redoubled by the sobs which Gertrude could not wholly repress, is standing by her side.

"Gertrude," said she, in a grieved tone, "are you in trouble, and did you seek to hide it from me? Do not turn from me, Gertrude!" and, throwing her arms around her, she drew her head close to her bosom, and whispered, "Tell me all, my darling! What is the matter with my poor child?"

And Gertrude unburdened her heart to Emily, disclosing to her attentive ear the confession of the only secret she had ever kept from her; and Emily wept as she listened, and when Gertrude had finished she pressed her again and again to her heart, exclaiming, as she did so, with an excitement of tone and manner which Gertrude had never before witnessed in the usually calm and placid blind girl, "Strange, strange, that you, too, should be thus doomed! O, Gertrude, my darling, we may well weep together; but still, believe me, your sorrow is far less bitter than mine!"

And then, in the darkness of that midnight hour, was Gertrude's confidence rewarded by the revelation of that tale of grief and woe which twenty years before had blighted Emily's youth, and which, notwithstanding the flight of time, was still vivid to her recollection, casting over her life a dark shadow, of which her blindness was but a single feature.

## Chapter XL

*When, lo! arrayed in robes of light,*
*A nymph celestial came;*
*She cleared the mists that dimmed my sight—*
*Religion was her name.*
*She proved the chastisement divine,*
*And bade me kiss the rod;*
*She taught this rebel heart of mine*
*Submission to its God.*

HANNAH MORE

"I was younger than you, Gertrude," said she, "when my trial came, and hardly the same person in any respect that I have been since you first knew me. You are aware, perhaps, that my mother died when I was too young to retain any recollection of her; but my father soon married again, and in this step-parent, whom I remember with as much tenderness as if she had been my own mother, I found a love and care which fully compensated for my loss. I can recall her now as she looked towards the latter part of her life,—a tall, delicate, feeble woman, with a very sweet, but rather sad face. She was a widow when my father married her, and had one son, who became at once my sole companion, the partner of all my youthful pleasures. You told me, many years ago, that I could not imagine how much you loved Willie, and I was then on the point of confiding to you a part of my early history, and convincing you that my own experience might well have taught me how to understand such a love; but I checked myself, for you were too young then to be burdened with the knowledge of so sad a story as mine, and I kept silent. How dear my young playmate became to me, no words can express. The office which each filled, the influence which each of us exerted upon the other, was such as to create mutual dependence; for, though his was the leading spirit, the strong and determined will, and I was ever submissive to a rule which to my easily-influenced nature was never irksome, there was one respect in which my bold young protector and ruler ever looked to me for aid and support. It was to act as mediator between him and my father; for, while the boy was almost an idol to his mother, he was ever treated with coldness and distrust by my father, who never understood or appreciated his many noble qualities, but seemed always to regard him with an eye of suspicion and dislike. To my supplicating looks and entreating words, however, he ever lent a willing ear, and all my eloquence was sure to be at the service of my companion when he had a favor to obtain or an excuse to plead.

"That my father's sternness towards her son was a great cause of unhappiness to our mother, I can have no doubt; for I well remember the anxiety with which she strove to conceal his faults and misdemeanors, and the frequent occasions on which she herself instructed me how to propitiate the parent, who, for my sake, would often forgive the boy, whose bold, adventurous, independent disposition, was continually bringing him into collision with one of whose severity, when displeased, you have yourself had some opportunity to judge. My step-mother had been extremely poor in her widowhood, and her child, having inherited nothing which he could call his own, was wholly dependent upon my father's bounty. This was a stinging cause of mortification and trial to the pride of which even as a boy he had an unusual share; and often have I seen him chafed and irritated at the reception of favors which he well understood were far from being awarded by a paternal hand; my father, in the mean time, who did not understand this feeling, mentally accusing him of gross ingratitude.

"As long as our mother was spared to us we lived in comparative harmony; but at last, when I was just sixteen years old, she was stricken with sudden illness, and died. Well do I remember, the last night of her life, her calling me to the bedside, and saying, in a solemn voice, 'Emily, my dying prayer is that you will be a guardian-angel to my boy!' God forgive me," ejaculated the now tearful blind girl, "if I have been faithless to the trust!

"He of whom I am telling you (for Emily carefully forbore to mention his name) was then about eighteen. He had lately become a clerk in my father's counting-room, much against his will, for he earnestly desired a collegiate education; but my father was determined, and, at his mother's and my persuasion, he was induced to submit. My step-mother's death knit the tie between her son and myself more closely than ever. He still continued an inmate of our house, and we passed all the time that he could be spared from the office in the enjoyment of each other's society; for my father was much from home, and, when there, usually shut himself up in his library, leaving us to entertain each other. I was then a school-girl, fond of books, and an excellent student. How often, when you have spoken of the assistance Willie was to you in your studies, have I been reminded of the time when I, too, received similar encouragement and aid from my own youthful companion and friend, who was ever ready to exert hand and brain in my behalf! We were not invariably happy, however. Often did my father's face wear that stern expression which I most dreaded to see; while the excited, disturbed and occasionally angry countenance of his step-son, denoted plainly that some storm had occurred, probably at the counting-room, of which I had no knowledge, except from its after effects. My office of mediator, too, was suspended, from the fact that the difficulties which arose were usually concerning some real or supposed neglect or mis-management of business matters on the part of the young and inexperienced clerk; a species of faults with which my father, a most thorough merchant and exact accountant, had very little patience, and to which the careless and unbusiness-like delinquent was exceedingly prone. Matters went on thus for about six months, when it suddenly became evident that my father had either been powerfully influenced by insinuations from some foreign quarter, or had himself suddenly conceived a new and alarming idea. He is, as you are aware, a plain man, honest and straight-forward in his pur-poses, whatever they may be; and, even if it occurred to him to manoeuvre, incapable of carrying out successfully, or with tact, any species of artifice. Our eyes could not, therefore, long be closed to the fact that he was re-solved to put an immediate check upon the freedom of intercourse which had hitherto subsisted between the two youthful inmates of his house; to forward which purpose he immediately introduced into the family, in the position of housekeeper, Mrs. Ellis, who has continued with us ever since. The almost constant presence of this stranger, together with the sudden interference of my father with such of our long-established customs as favored his step-son's familiar intimacy with me, sufficiently proved his in-tention to uproot and destroy, if possible, the closeness of our friendship. Nor was it surprising, considering the circumstance that I had already reached the period of womanhood, and the attachment between us could no longer be considered a childish one, while any other might be expected to draw forth my father's disapproval, since his wife's idolized son was as far as ever from being a favorite with him.

"My distress at these proceedings was only equalled by the indignation of my companion in suffering, whom no previous conduct on my father's part had ever angered as this did; nor did the scheme succeed in separating him from me; for, while he on every possible occasion avoided the presence of that spy (as he termed Mrs. Ellis), his inventive genius continually con-trived opportunities of seeing and conversing with me in her absence,— a course of behavior calculated to give still greater coloring to my father's suspicions.

"I am convinced that he was mainly actuated to this course by a deep sense of unkindness and injustice, and a desire to manifest his independence of what he considered unwarrantable tyranny; nor have I reason to believe that the idea of romance, or even future marriage with myself, entered at all into his calculations; and I, who at that time knew, or, at least, was influenced by no higher law than his will, lent myself unhesitatingly to a species of petty deception, to elude the vigilance which would have kept us apart. My father, however, as is frequently the case with people of his unsocial temperament and apparent obtuseness of observation, saw more of our manoeuvring than we were aware of, and imagined far more than ever in reality existed. He watched us carefully, and, contrary to his usual course of proceeding, forbore for a time any interference. I have since been led to think that he designed to wean us from each other in a less unnatural manner than that which he had at first attempted, by availing himself of the earliest opportunity to transfer his step-son to a situation connected with his own mercantile establishment, either in a foreign country, or a distant part of our own; and forbore, until his plans were ripe, to distress and grieve me by giving way to the feelings of annoyance and displeasure which were burning within him,—for he was, and had ever been, as kind and indulgent toward his undeserving child as was consistent with a due maintenance of his authority.

"Before such a course could be carried out, however, circumstances occurred, and suspicions became aroused, which destroyed one of their victims, and plunged the other—"

Here Emily's voice failed her. She laid her head upon Gertrude's shoulder, and sobbed bitterly.

"Do not try to tell me the rest, dear Emily," said Gertrude. "It is enough for me to know that you are so unhappy. Do not make yourself wretched by dwelling, for my sake, upon sorrows that are past."

"Past!" replied Emily, recovering her voice, and wiping away her tears; "no, they are never past; it is only because I am so little wont to speak of them that they overcome me now. Nor am I unhappy, Gertrude. It is but rarely that my peace is shaken; nor would I now allow my weak nerves to be unstrung by imparting to another the secrets of that never-to-be-forgotten time of trial, were it not that, since you know so well how harmoniously and sweetly my life is passing on to its great and eternal awakening, I desire to prove to my darling child the power of that heavenly faith which has turned my darkness into marvellous light, and made afflictions such as mine the blessed harbingers of final joy.

"But I have not much more to tell, and that shall be in as few words as possible."

She then went on, in a firm though low and suppressed voice.

"I was suddenly taken ill with a fever. Mrs. Ellis, whom I had always treated with coldness, and often with disdain (for you must remember I was a spoiled child), nursed me by night and day with a care and devotion which I had no right to expect at her hands; and, under her watchful attendance, and the skilful treatment of our good Dr. Jeremy (even then the family physician), I began, after some weeks, to recover. One day, when I was sufficiently well to be up and dressed for several hours at a time, I went, for change of air and scene, into my father's library, the room next my own, and there quite alone lay half reclining upon the sofa. Mrs. Ellis had gone to attend to household duties, but, before she left me, she brought from the adjoining chamber and placed within my reach a small table, upon which were arranged various phials, glasses, etc., and among them every-thing which I could possibly require before her return. It was towards the latter part of an afternoon in June, and I lay watching the approach of sunset from an opposite window. I was oppressed with a sad sense of loneliness, for during the past six weeks I had enjoyed no society but that of my nurse, together with periodical visits from my father; and felt there-fore no common satisfaction and pleasure when my most congenial but now nearly forbidden associate unexpectedly entered the room. He had not seen me since my illness, and after this unusually protracted and painful separation our meeting was proportionately tender and affectionate. He had, with all the fire of a hot and ungoverned temper, a woman's depth of feeling, warmth of heart, and sympathizing sweetness of manner. Well do I remember the expression of his noble face, the manly tones of his voice, as, seated beside me on the wide couch, he bathed the temples of my aching head with cologne, which he took from the table near by, at the same time expressing again and again his joy at once more seeing me.

"How long we had sat thus I cannot tell, but the twilight was deepen-ing in the room, when we were suddenly interrupted by my father, who entered abruptly, came towards us with hasty steps, but, stopping short when within a yard or two, folded his arms and confronted his step-son with such a look of angry contempt as I had never before seen upon his face. The latter rose and stood before him with a glance of proud defiance, and then ensued a scene which I have neither the wish nor the power to describe.

"It is sufficient to say that in the double accusation which my excited parent now brought against the object of his wrath he urged the fact of his seeking (as he expressed it) by mean, base, and contemptible artifice to win the affections, and with them the expected fortune, of his only child, as a secondary and pardonable crime, compared with his deeper, darker, and but just detected guilt of forgery,—forgery of a large amount, and upon his benefactor's name.

"To this day, so far as I know," said Emily, with feeling, "that charge remains uncontradicted; but I did not then, I do not now, and I never *can* believe it. Whatever were his faults (and his impetuous temper betrayed him into many), of this dark crime (though I have not even his own word in attestation) I dare pronounce him innocent.

"You cannot wonder, Gertrude, that in my feeble and invalid condition I was hardly capable of realizing at the time, far less of retaining any dis-tinct recollection of the circumstances that followed my father's words. A few dim pictures, however, the last my poor eyes ever beheld, are still en-graved upon my memory, and visible to my imagination. My father stood with his back to the light, and from the first moment of his entering the room I never saw his face again; but the countenance of the other, the object of his accusation, illumined as it was by the last rays of the golden sunset, stands ever in the foreground of my recollection. His head was thrown proudly back; conscious but injured innocence proclaimed itself in his clear, calm eye, which shrunk not from the closest scrutiny; his hand was clenched, as if he were vainly striving to repress the passion which proclaimed itself in the compressed lips, the set teeth, the deep and angry indignation which overspread his face. He did not speak,—apparently he could not command voice to do so; but my father continued to upbraid him, in language, no doubt, cutting and severe, though I remember not a word of it. It was fearful to watch the working of the young man's face, while he stood there listening to taunts and enduring reproaches which were no doubt believed by him who uttered them to be just and merited, but which wrought the youth to a degree of frenzy which it was terrible indeed to witness. Suddenly he took one step forward, slowly lifting the clenched hand which had hitherto hung at his side. I know not whether he might then have intended to call Heaven to witness his innocence of the crime with which he was charged, or whether he might have designed to strike my father; for I sprang from my seat, prepared to rush between them, and implore them, for my sake, to desist; but my strength failed me, and with a shriek I sunk back in a fainting fit.

"O, the horror of my awakening! How shall I find words to tell it?— and yet I must! Listen, Gertrude. He—the poor, ruined boy—sprung to help me; and, maddened by injustice, he knew not what he did. Heaven is my witness, I never blamed him; and if, in my agony, I uttered words that seemed like a reproach, it was because I too was frantic, and knew not what I said!"

"What!" exclaimed Gertrude; "he did not—"

"No, no! he did not—he *did not* put out my eyes!" exclaimed Emily; "it was an accident. He reached forward for the cologne which he had just had in his hand. There were several bottles, and, in his haste, he seized one containing a powerful acid which Mrs. Ellis had found occasion to use in my sick room. It had a heavy glass stopper,—and he—his hand was unsteady, and he spilt it all—"

"On your eyes?" shrieked Gertrude.

Emily bowed her head.

"O, poor Emily!" cried Gertrude, "and wretched, wretched young man!"

"Wretched indeed!" ejaculated Emily. "Bestow all your pity on him, Gertrude, for his was the harder fate of the two."

"O, Emily! how intense must have been the pain you endured! How could you suffer so, and live?"

"Do you mean the pain from my eyes? That was severe indeed, but the mental agony was worse!"

"What became of him?" said Gertrude. "What did Mr. Graham do?"

"I cannot give you any exact account of what followed. I was in no state to know anything of my father's treatment of his step-son. You can imagine it, however. He banished him from his sight and knowledge forever; and it is easy to believe it was with no added gentleness, since he had now, beside the other crimes imputed to him, been the unhappy cause of his daughter's blindness."

"And did you never hear from him again?"

"Yes. Through the good doctor, who alone knew all the circumstances, I learned—after a long interval of suspense—that he had sailed for South America; and, in the hope of once more communicating with the poor exile, and assuring him of my continued love, I rallied from the wretched state of sickness, fever and blindness, into which I had fallen; the doctor had even some expectation of restoring sight to my eyes, which were in a much more hopeful condition. Several months passed away, and my kind friend, who was most diligent and persevering in his inquiries, having at length learned the actual residence and address of the ill-fated youth, I was commencing, through the aid of Mrs. Ellis (whom pity had now wholly won to my service), a letter of love, and an entreaty for his return, when a fatal seal was put to all my earthly hopes. He died, in a foreign land, alone, unnursed, untended, and uncared for; he died of that inhospitable southern disease, which takes the stranger for its victim; and I, on hearing the news of it, sunk back into a more pitiable malady; and—alas for the encouragement the good doctor had held out of my gradual restoration to sight!—I wept all his hopes away!"

Emily paused. Gertrude put her arms around her, and they clung closely to each other; grief and sorrow made the union between them dearer than ever.

"I was then, Gertrude," continued Emily, "a child of the world, eager for worldly pleasures, and ignorant of any other. For a time, therefore, I dwelt in utter darkness,—the darkness of despair. I began too again to feel my bodily strength restored, and to look forward to a useless and miserable life. You can form no idea of the utter wretchedness in which my days were passed. Often have I since reproached myself for the misery I must have caused my poor father, who, though he never spoke of it, was, I am sure, deeply pained by the recollection of the terrible scenes we had lately gone through, and who would, I am convinced, have given worlds to restore the past.

"But at last there came a dawn to my seemingly everlasting night. It came in the shape of a minister of Christ, our own dear Mr. Arnold; who opened the eyes of my understanding, lit the lamp of religion in my now softened soul, taught me the way to peace, and led my feeble steps into that blessed rest which even on earth remaineth to the people of God.

"In the eyes of the world, I am still the unfortunate blind girl; one who, by her sad fate, is cut off from every enjoyment; but so great is the awakening I have experienced, that to me it is far otherwise,—and I am ready to exclaim, like him who in old time experienced his Saviour's healing power, 'Once I was blind, but now I see!'"

Gertrude half forgot her own troubles while listening to Emily's sad story; and when the latter laid her hand upon her head, and prayed that she too might be fitted for a patient endurance of trial, and be made stronger and better thereby, she felt her heart penetrated with that deep love and trust which seldom come to us except in the hour of sorrow, and prove that it is through suffering only we are made perfect.

# Chapter XLI

*But in that hour of agony the maid*
*Deserted not herself; her very dread*
*Had calmed her; and her heart*
*Knew the whole horror, and its only part.*
SOUTHEY

As Mr. Graham had expressed in his letter the intention of being at the steamboat wharf in New York to meet his daughter and Gertrude on their arrival, Dr. Jeremy thought it unnecessary for him to accompany his charges further than Albany, where he could see them safely on their way, and then proceed to Boston with his wife over the Western Railroad; Mrs. Jeremy being now impatient to return home, and having, moreover, no disposition to revisit the great metropolis of New York during the warm weather.

"Good-by, Gerty," said the doctor, as he bade them farewell on the deck of one of the Hudson-river boats. "I'm afraid you've lost your heart in Saratoga; you don't look quite so bright as you did when we first arrived there. It can't have strayed far, however, I think, in such a place as that; so be sure and find it before I see you in Boston."

He had hardly gone, and it wanted a few minutes only of the time for the boat to start, when a gay group of fashionables made their appearance, talking and laughing too loud, as it seemed to Gertrude, to be well-bred; and conspicuous among them was Miss Clinton, whose companions were evidently making her the subject of a great deal of wit and pleasantry, by which, although she feigned to be teased and half-offended, her smiling, blushing face gave evidence that she felt flattered and pleased. At length, the significant gestures of some of the party, and a half-smothered hush-h! gave intimation of the approach of some one who must not overhear their remarks; and presently William Sullivan, with a travelling-bag in his hand, a heavy shawl thrown over one arm, and his countenance grave, as if he had not quite recovered from the chagrin of the previous evening, appeared in sight, passed Gertrude, whose veil was drawn over her face, and joined Isabel, placing his burden on a chair which stood near.

He had hardly commenced speaking to Miss Clinton, however, before the violent ringing of the bell gave notice to all but the passengers to quit the boat, and he was compelled to make a hasty movement to depart. As he did so, he drew a step nearer Gertrude, a step further from her whom he was addressing, and the former plainly distinguished the closing words of his remark: "Then, if you will do your best to return on Thursday, I will try not to be impatient in the mean time."

A moment more, and the boat was on its way; not, however, until a tall figure, who reached the landing just as she started, had, to the horror of the spectators, daringly leaped the gap that already divided her from the shore; after which, he sought the gentleman's saloon, threw himself upon a couch, drew a book from his pocket, and commenced reading.

As soon as the boat was fairly under way, and quiet prevailed in their neighborhood, Emily spoke softly to Gertrude, and said,

"Didn't I just now hear Isabel Clinton's voice?"

"She is here," replied Gertrude, "on the opposite side of the deck, but sitting with her back towards us."

"Didn't she see us?"

"I believe she did," answered Gertrude, "She stood looking this way while her party were arranging their seats."

"And then chose one which commanded a *different* view?"

"Yes."

"Perhaps she is going to New York to meet Mrs. Graham."

"Very possible," replied Gertrude. "I didn't think of it before."

There was then quite a pause. Emily appeared to be engaged in thought. Presently she asked, in the softest of whispers, "Who was the gentleman who came and spoke to her just before the boat started?"

"Willie," was the tremulous response.

Emily pressed Gertrude's hand, and was silent. She, too, had overheard his farewell remark, and felt its significance.

Several hours passed away, and they had proceeded some distance down the river; for the motion of the boat was rapid—too rapid, as it seemed to Gertrude, for safety. At first occupied by her own thoughts, and unable to enjoy the beautiful scenery, which a few weeks previously had caused her such keen delight, she had sat, inattentive to all around, gazing down into the deep blue water, and communing with her own heart. Gradually, however, she was led to observe several circumstances, which excited so much curiosity, and finally so much alarm, that, effectually aroused from the train of reflections she had been indulging, she had leisure only to take into view her own and Emily's present situation, and its probable consequences.

Several times, since they left Albany, had the boat in which they were passengers passed and repassed another of similar size, construction and speed, likewise responsibly charged with busy, living freight, and bound in the same direction. Occasionally, during their headlong and reckless course, the contiguity of the two boats was such as to excite the serious alarm of one sex, and the unmeasured censure of the other. The rumor began to be circulated that they were racing, and racing desperately. Some few, regardless of danger, and entering upon the interest of the chase with an insane and foolish excitement, watched with pleased eagerness the mad career of rival ambition; but by far the majority of the company, including all persons of reason and sense, looked on in indignation and fear. The usual stopping-places on the river were either recklessly passed by, or only paused at, while, with indecent haste, passengers were shuffled backwards and forwards, at the risk of life and limb, their baggage (or somebody's else) unceremoniously flung after them, the panting, snorting engine in the mean time bellowing with rage at the check thus unwillingly imposed upon its freedom. Towards noon the fever of agitation had reached its height, and could not be wholly quieted even by the assurance from head-quarters that there was no danger.

Gertrude sat with her hand locked in Emily's, anxiously watching every indication of terror, and endeavoring to judge from the countenances and words of her most intelligent-looking fellow-travellers the actual degree of their insecurity. Emily, shut out from the sight of all that was going on, but rendered, through her acute hearing, vividly conscious of the prevailing alarm, was perfectly calm, though very pale; and, from time to time, questioned Gertrude concerning the vicinity of the other boat, a collision with which was the principal cause of fear.

At length their boat for a few moments distanced its competitor; the assurance of perfect safety was impressively asserted, anxiety began to be relieved, and, most of the passengers being restored to their wonted composure, the various parties scattered about the deck resumed their newspapers or their conversation. The gay group to which Isabel Clinton belonged, several of whom had been the victims of nervous agitation and trembling, seemed reässured, and began once more to talk and laugh merrily. Emily, however, still looked pallid, and, as Gertrude fancied, a little faint. "Let us go below, Emily," said she; "it appears now to be very quiet and safe. There are sofas in the ladies' cabin, where you can lie down; and we can both get a glass of water."

Emily assented, and in a few minutes was comfortably reclining in a corner of the saloon, where she and Gertrude remained undisturbed until dinner-time. They did not go to the dinner-table; it was not their intention from the first, and, after the agitation of the morning, was far from being desirable. So they stayed quietly where they were, while the greater part of the passengers crowded from every part of the boat, to invigorate themselves, after their fright, by the enjoyment of a comfortable meal; which they had reason to expect, as the racing appeared to have ceased, and everything was orderly and peaceable.

Gertrude opened her travelling-basket, and took out the package which contained their luncheon. It was not one of those luncheons which careful mothers provide for their travelling families, choice in its material, and tempting in its arrangement; but consisted merely of such dry morsels as had been hastily collected and put up at their hotel, in Albany, by Dr. Jeremy's direction. Gertrude looked from the little withered slices of tongue and stale bread to the veteran sponge-cakes which completed the assortment, and was hesitating which she could most conscientiously recommend to Emily, when a civil-looking waiter appeared, bearing a huge tray of refreshments, which he placed upon a table close by, at the same time turning to Gertrude, and asking if there was anything else he could serve her with.

"This is not for us," said Gertrude. "You have made a mistake."

"No mistake," replied the man. "Orders was for de blind lady and hansum young miss. I only 'beys orders. Anyting furder, miss?"

Gertrude dismissed the man with the assurance that they wanted nothing more, and then, turning to Emily, asked, with an attempt at cheerfulness, what they should do with this Aladdin-like repast.

"Eat it, my dear, if you can," said Emily. "It is no doubt meant for us."

"But to whom are we indebted for it?"

"To my blindness and your beauty, I suppose," said Emily, smiling. She then continued, with wonderful simplicity, "Perhaps the chief steward, or master of ceremonies, took pity on our inability to come to dinner, and so sent the dinner to us. At any rate, my child, you must eat it before it is cold."

"I!" said Gertrude, conscious of her utter want of appetite; "I am not hungry; but I will select a nice bit for you."

The sable waiter, when he came to remove the dishes, really looked sad to see how little they had eaten. Gertrude drew out her purse, and, after bestowing a fee upon the man, inquired whom she should pay for the meal.

"Pay, miss!" said the man, grinning. "Bless my stars! de gentleman pays for all!"

"Who? What gentleman?" asked Gertrude, in surprise.

But before the man could give her any reply, another white-aproned individual appeared, and beckoned to his fellow-waiter, who, thereupon, snatched up his tray and trotted off, bending beneath its weight, and leaving Gertrude and Emily to wonder who the benevolent gentleman might be.

They finally came to the conclusion that this unexpected attention was due to the thoughtfulness of Dr. Jeremy, who must have given orders to that effect before he left the boat; and great was the unmerited praise and the undeserved gratitude which the doctor received that day, for an act of considerate politeness of which the old gentleman, with all his kindness of heart, would never have dreamed.

Dinner concluded, Emily again laid down, advised Gertrude to do the same, and, supposing that her advice was being followed, slept for an hour; while her companion sat by, watching the peaceful slumber of her friend, and carefully and noiselessly brushing away every fly that threatened to disturb a repose much needed by Miss Graham, who could, in her feeble state of health, ill afford to spare the rest she had been deprived of for one or two previous nights.

"What time is it?" asked she, on awaking.

"Nearly a quarter past three," replied Gertrude, glancing at her watch (a beautiful gift from a class of her former pupils).

Emily started up. "We can't be far from New York," said she; "where are we now?"

"I don't know exactly," replied Gertrude; "I think we must be near the Palisades; if you will stay here, I will go and see." She passed across the saloon, and was about ascending the staircase, when she was startled and alarmed by a rushing sound, mingled with the hurried tread of feet. She kept on, however, though once or twice jostled by persons with frightened faces, who crowded past and pressed forward to learn the cause of the commotion. She had just gained the head of the stairway, and was looking fearfully round her, when a man rushed past, gasping for breath, his face of an ashen paleness, and shrieking the horrid word of alarm—fire—fire!

A second more, and a scene of dismay and confusion ensued too terrible for description. Shrieks rose upon the air, groans and cries of despair burst forth from hearts that were breaking with fear for others, or maddened at the certainty of their own destruction. Each called upon each for help, when all were alike helpless. Those who had never prayed before poured out their souls in the fervent ejaculation, "O, my God!" Many a brain reeled in that time of darkness and peril. Many a brave spirit sickened and sunk under the fearfulness of the hour.

Gertrude straightened her slight figure, and, with her dark eyes almost starting from their sockets, gazed around her upon every side. All was alike tumult; but the destroyer was as yet discernible in one direction only. Towards the centre of the boat, where the machinery, heated to the last degree, had fired the parched and inflammable vessel, a huge volume of flame was already visible, darting out its fiery fangs, and causing the stoutest hearts to shrink and crouch in horror. She gave but one glance; then bounded down the stairs, bent solely on rejoining Emily. But she was arrested at the very onset. One step only had she taken when she felt herself encircled by a pair of powerful arms, and a movement made to again rush with her upon deck; while a familiar voice gasped forth the words, "Gertrude, my child! my own darling! Be quiet—be quiet!—I will save you!"

Well might he urge her to be quiet,—for she was struggling madly. "No, no!" shouted she; "Emily! Emily! Let me die! let me die! but I must find Emily!"

"Where is she?" asked Mr. Phillips; for it was he.

"There, there," pointed Gertrude,—"in the cabin. Let me go! let me go!"

He cast one look around him; then said, in a firm tone, "Be calm, my child! I can save you both; follow me closely!"

With a leap he cleared the staircase, and rushed into the cabin. In the farthest corner knelt Emily, her head thrown back, her hands clasped, and her face like the face of an angel.

Gertrude and Mr. Phillips were by her side in an instant. He stooped to lift her in his arms, Gertrude at the same time exclaiming, "Come, Emily, come! He will save us!"

But Emily resisted. "Leave me, Gertrude—leave me, and save yourselves! O!" said she, looking imploringly in the face of the stranger,—"leave me, and save my child." Ere the words had left her lips, however, she was borne half-way across the saloon, Gertrude following closely.

"If we can cross to the bows of the boat, we are safe!" said Mr. Phillips, in a husky voice.

To do so, however, proved impossible. The whole centre of the boat was now one sheet of flame. "Good Heavens!" exclaimed he, "we are too late! we must go back!"

A moment more, and they had with much difficulty regained the long saloon. And now the boat, which, as soon as the fire was discovered, had been turned towards the shore, struck upon the rocks, and parted in the middle. Her bows were consequently brought near to the land; near enough to almost insure the safety of such persons as were at that part of the vessel. But, alas for those near the stern! which was far out in the river, while the breeze which blew fresh from the shore fostered and spread the devouring flame in the very direction to place those who yet clung to the broken fragment between two equally fatal elements.

Mr. Phillips' first thought, on gaining the saloon, was to beat down a window-sash, spring upon the guards, and drag Emily and Gertrude after him. Some ropes hung upon the guards; he seized one, and, with the ease and skill of an old sailor, made it fast to the boat; then turned to Gertrude, who stood firm and unwavering by his side.

"Gertrude," said he, speaking distinctly and steadily, "I shall swim to the shore with Emily. If the fire comes too near, cling to the guards; as a last chance, hold on to the rope. Keep your veil flying; I shall return."

"No, no!" cried Emily. "Gertrude, go first!"

"Hush, Emily!" exclaimed Gertrude; "we shall both be saved."

"Cling to my shoulder in the water, Emily," said Mr. Phillips, utterly regardless of her protestations. He took her once more in his arms; there was a splash, and they were gone. At the same instant Gertrude was seized from behind. She turned, and found herself grasped by Isabel Clinton, who, kneeling upon the platform, and frantic with terror, was clinging so closely to her as utterly to disable them both; at the same time shrieking, in pitiable tones, "O, Gertrude! Gertrude! save me!"

Gertrude tried to lift her up, but she was immovable; and, without making the slightest effort to help herself, was madly winding Gertrude's thick travelling-dress around her person, as if for a protection from the flames; while ever, as they darted forth new and nearer lightnings, the frightened girl would cling more wildly to her companion in danger, at the same time praying, with piercing shrieks, that she would help and save her.

But so long as Gertrude stood thus imprisoned and restrained by the arms which were clasped entirely around her she was powerless to do anything for her own or Isabel's salvation. She looked forth in the direction Mr. Phillips had taken, and, to her joy, she saw him returning. He had deposited Emily on board a boat, which was fortunately at hand, and was now approaching to claim another burden. At the same instant, a volume of flame swept so near the spot where the two girls were stationed, that Gertrude, who was standing upright, felt the scorching heat, and both were almost suffocated with smoke.

And now a new and heroic resolution took possession of the mind of Gertrude. One of them could be saved; for Mr. Phillips was within a few rods of the wreck. It should be Isabel! She had called on her for protection, and it should not be denied her! Moreover, Willie loved Isabel. Willie would weep for her loss, and that must not be. He would not weep for Gertrude—at least not much; and, if one must die, it should be she.

With Gertrude, to resolve was to do. "Isabel," said she, in a tone of such severity as one might employ towards a refractory child, with whom, as in this instance, milder remonstrances had failed—"Isabel, do you hear me?

Stand up on your feet; do as I tell you, and you shall be saved. Do you hear me, Isabel?"

She heard, shuddered, but did not move.

Gertrude stooped down, and, forcibly wrenching apart the hands which were convulsively clenched, said, with a sternness which necessity alone extorted from her, "Isabel, if you do as I tell you, you will be on shore in five minutes, safe and well; but, if you stay there behaving like a foolish child, we shall both be burnt to death. For mercy's sake, get up quickly and listen to me!"

Isabel rose, fixed her eyes upon Gertrude's calm, steadfast face, and said, in a moaning tone, "What must I do? I will try."

"Do you see that person swimming this way?"

"Yes."

"He will come to this spot. Hold fast to that piece of rope, and I will let you gradually down to the water. But, stay!"—and, snatching the deep blue veil from her own head, she tied it round the neck and flung it over the fair hair of Isabel. Mr. Phillips was within a rod or two. "Now, Isabel, now!" exclaimed Gertrude, "or you will be too late!" Isabel took the rope between her hands, but shrunk back, appalled at the sight of the water. One more hot burst of fire, however, which issued forth through the window, gave her renewed courage to brave a mere seeming danger; and, aided by Gertrude, who helped her over the guards, she allowed herself to be let down to the water's edge. Mr. Phillips was fortunately just in time to receive her, for she was so utterly exhausted with fear that she could not have clung long to the rope. Gertrude had no opportunity to follow them with her eye; her own situation, it may well be believed, was now all-engrossing. The flames had reached her. She could hardly breathe, so enveloped was she in clouds of dark smoke, which had more than once been relieved by streaks of fire, which had darted out within a foot of her. She could hesitate no longer. She seized the piece of rope, now left vacant by Isabel, who was rapidly approaching a place of safety, and, grasping it with all her might, leaped over the side of the fast-consuming vessel. How long her strength would have enabled her thus to cling,—how long the guards, as yet unapproached by the fire, would have continued a sure support for the cable,—there was no opportunity to test; for, just as her feet touched the cold surface of the river, the huge wheel, which was but a little distance from where she hung, gave one sudden, expiring revolution, sounding like a death-dirge through the water, which came foaming and dashing up against the side of the boat, and, as it swept away again, bore with it the light form of Gertrude!

## Chapter XLII

*'Tis Reason's part
To govern and to guard the heart;
To lull the wayward soul to rest,
When hopes and fears distract the breast.*
                                    COTTON

Let us now revisit calmer scenes, and turn our eyes towards the quiet, familiar country-seat of Mr. Graham.

The old gentleman himself, wearied with travels, and society but little congenial to his years, is pacing up and down his garden-walks, stopping now and then to observe the growth of some favorite tree, or the overgrowth of some petted shrub, whose neglected, drooping twigs call for the master's pruning hand; his contented, satisfied countenance denoting plainly enough how rejoiced he is to find himself once more in his cherished homestead. Perhaps he would not like to acknowledge it, but it is nevertheless a fact, that no small part of his satisfaction arises from the circumstance that the repose and seclusion of his household is rendered complete and secure by the temporary absence of its bustling, excitable mistress, whom he has left behind him in New York. There is something pleasant, too, in being able to indulge his imagination so far as almost to deceive himself into the belief that the good old times have come back again when he was his own master; for, to tell the truth, Mrs. Graham takes advantage of his years and growing infirmities, and rules him with wonderful tact.

Emily and Gertrude, too, are closely associated with those good old times; and it adds greatly to the delusion of his fancy to dwell upon the certainty that they are both in the house, and that he shall see them at dinner; a cosey, comfortable dinner, at which Mrs. Ellis will preside with her wonted formality and precision, and which no noisy, intruding upstarts will venture to interrupt or disturb.

Yes, Gertrude is there, as well as the rest, saved (she hardly knew how) from the watery grave that threatened and almost engulfed her, and established once more in the peaceful, venerable spot, now the dearest to her on earth.

When, with some difficulty, restored to the consciousness which had utterly forsaken her in the protracted struggle between death and life, she was informed that she had been found and picked up by some humane individuals, who had hastily pushed a boat from the shore, and aided in the rescue of the sufferers; that she was clinging to a chair, which she had probably grasped when washed away by the sudden rushing of the water, and that her situation was such that, a moment more, and it would have been impossible to save her from the flames, close to which she was drifting.

But of all this she had herself no recollection. From the moment when she committed her light weight to the frail tenure of the rope, until she opened her eyes in a quiet spot, and saw Emily leaning anxiously over the bed upon which she lay, all had been a blank to her senses. A few hours from the time of the terrible catastrophe brought Mr. Graham to the scene, and the next day restored all three in safety to the long-deserted old mansion-house in D——.

This respectable, venerable habitation, and its adjoining grounds, wore nearly the same aspect as when they met the admiring eyes of Gerty on the first visit that she made Miss Graham in her early childhood,—that long-expected and keenly-enjoyed visit, which proved a lasting topic for her youthful enthusiasm to dwell upon.

The great elm-trees, casting their deep shade upon the green and velvety lawn in front; the neat, smooth gravel-walk, which led to the door-step, and then wound off in separate directions, into the mass of embowered shrubbery on the right, and the peach-orchard on the left; the old arbor, with its luxuriant growth of woodbine; the large summer-house, with its knotted, untrimmed, rustic pillars; the little fish-pond and fountain; and especially the flower-garden, during the last season nearly restored, by Gertrude's true friend George, to its original appearance when under her superintendence; all had the same friendly, familiar look as during the first happy summers, when Emily, sitting in her garden-chair beneath the wide-spreading tulip-tree, listened with delight to the cheerful voice, the merry laugh, and the light step of the joyous little gardener, who, as she moved about in her favorite element among the flowers, seemed to her affectionate, loving blind friend the sweetest Flora of them all.

Now and then, a stray robin, the last of the numerous throng that had flocked to the cherry-feast and departed long ago, came hopping across the paths, and over the neatly-trimmed box, lifting his head, and looking about him with an air that seemed to say, "It is time for me, too, to be off." A family of squirrels, on the other hand, old pets of Gertrude's, whom she loved to watch as they played in the willow-tree opposite her window, were just gathering in their harvest, and were busily journeying up and down, each with a nut in its mouth (for there were nut-trees in that garden, and quiet corners, such as squirrels love). Last year they did not come,—at least, they did not *stay*,—for Mrs. Graham and her new gardener voted them a nuisance; but this year they had had it all their own way, and were laying up rich stores for the coming winter.

The old house itself had a look of contentment and repose. The hall-door stood wide open. Mr. Graham's arm-chair was in its usual place; Gertrude's birds, of which Mrs. Ellis had taken excellent care, were hopping about on the slender perches of the great Indian cage which hung on the wide piazza. The old house-dog lay stretched in the sun, sure that nobody would molest him. Plenty of flowers once more graced the parlor, and all was very still, very quiet, and very comfortable; and Mr. Graham thought so, as he came up the steps, patted the dog, whistled to the birds, sat down in the arm-chair, and took the morning paper from the hand of the neat housemaid, who came bringing it across the hall.

The dear old place was the dear old place still. Time seemed only to lend it additional grace, to give it an air of greater peace, seclusion and repose.

But how is it with the inmates?

Mr. Graham, as we have already hinted, has been having new experiences; and although some features of his character are too closely inwrought to be ever wholly eradicated, he is, in many respects, a changed man. The time had once been when he would have resisted courageously every innovation upon his domestic prejudices and comforts; but old age and ill-health had somewhat broken his spirit, and subdued his hitherto invincible will. Just at this crisis, too, he united his fortunes with one who had sufficient energy of purpose, combined with just enough good-nature and tact, to gain her point on every occasion when she thought it material to do so. She indulged him, to be sure, in his favorite hobbies, allowed him to continue in the fond belief that his sway (when he chose to exercise it) was indisputable, and yet contrived to decide herself in all important matters, and had, at last, driven him to such extremity, that he had taken it for his maxim to get what comfort he could, and let things take their course.

No wonder, therefore, that he looked forward to a few weeks of old-fashioned enjoyment much as a school-boy does to his vacation.

Emily is sitting in her own room, carelessly clad in a loose wrapper. She is paler than ever, and her face has an anxious, troubled expression. Every time the door opens, she starts, trembles, a sudden flush overspreads her face, and twice already during the morning she has suddenly burst into tears. Every exertion, even that of dressing, seems a labor to her; she cannot listen to Gertrude's reading, but will constantly interrupt her, to ask questions concerning the burning boat, her own and others' rescue, and every circumstance connected with the terrible scene of agony and death. Her nervous system is evidently fearfully shattered, and Gertrude looks at her and weeps, and wonders to see how her wonted calmness and composure have forsaken her.

They have been together since breakfast, but Emily will not allow Gertrude to stay with her any longer. She must go away and walk, or, at least, change the scene. She may come back in an hour and help her dress for dinner,—a ceremony which Miss Graham will by no means omit, her chief desire seeming to be to maintain the appearance of health and happiness in the presence of her father. Gertrude feels that Emily is in earnest,—that she really wishes to be left alone; and, believing that, for the first time, *her* presence even is burdensome, she retires to her own room, leaving Emily to bow her head upon her hands, and, for the third time, utter a few hysterical sobs.

Gertrude is immediately followed by Mrs. Ellis, who shuts the door, seats herself, and, with a manner of her own, alone sufficient to excite alarm, adds to the poor girl's fear and distress by declaiming at length upon the dreadful effect the recollection of that shocking accident is having upon poor Emily. "She's completely upset," is the housekeeper's closing remark, "and if she don't begin to get better in a day or two, I don't hesitate to say there's no knowing what the consequences may be. Emily is feeble, and not fit to travel; I wish, for my part, she had staid at home. I don't approve of travelling, especially in these shocking dangerous times."

Fortunately for poor Gertrude, Mrs. Ellis is at length summoned to the kitchen, and she is left to reflect upon the strange circumstances of the last few days,—days fraught to her with matter of thought for years, if so long a time had been allowed her. A moment, however, and she is again interrupted. The housemaid who carried Mr. Graham his paper has something for her, too. A letter! With a trembling hand she receives it, scarcely daring to look at the writing or post-mark. Her first thought is of Willie; but before she could indulge either a hope or a fear on that score the illusion is dispelled, for, though the post-mark is New York, and he might be there, the handwriting is wholly strange. Another idea, of scarcely less moment, flashes into her mind, and, hardly able to breathe from the violence of the emotions by which she is oppressed, she breaks the seal and reads:

"MY DARLING GERTRUDE: My much-loved child,—for such you indeed are, though a father's agony of fear and despair alone wrung from me the words that claimed you. It was no madness that, in the dark hour of danger, compelled me to clasp you to my heart and call you mine. A dozen times before had I been seized by the same emotion, and as often had it been subdued and smothered. And even now I would crush the promptings of nature, and depart and weep my poor life away alone; but the voice within me has spoken once, and cannot again be silenced. Had I seen you happy, gay and light-hearted, I would not have asked to share your joy, far less would I have cast a shadow on your path; but you are sad and troubled, my poor child, and your grief unites the tie between us closer than that of kindred, and makes you a thousand times my daughter; for I am a wretched, weary man, and know how to feel for others' woe.

"You have a kind and a gentle heart, my child. You have wept once for the stranger's sorrows,—will you now refuse to pity, if you cannot love, the solitary parent, who, with a breaking heart and a trembling hand, writes the ill-fated word that dooms him, perhaps, to the hatred and contempt of the only being on earth with whom he can claim the fellowship of a natural tie? Twice before have I striven to utter it, and, laying down my pen, have shrunk from the cruel task. But, hard as it is to speak, I find it harder to still the beating of my restless heart; therefore listen to me, though it may be for the last time. Is there one being on earth whom you shudder to think of? Is there one associated only in your mind with deeds of darkness and of shame? Is there one name which you have from your childhood learned to abhor and hate; and, in proportion as you love your best friend, have you been taught to shrink from and despise her worst enemy?

It cannot be otherwise. Ah! I tremble to think how my child will recoil
from her father when she learns the secret, so long preserved, so sorrow-
fully revealed, that he is

"PHILLIP AMORY!"

As Gertrude looked up when she had finished reading this strange and
unintelligible letter, her countenance expressed only complete bewilderment,
—her eyes glistened with great tears, her face was flushed with wonder and
excitement; but she was evidently at a total loss to account for the meaning
of the stranger's words.

She sat for an instant wildly gazing into vacancy, then, springing suddenly up, with the letter grasped in one hand, ran across the entry towards
Emily's room, to share with her the wonderful contents, and eagerly ask
her opinion of their hidden meaning. She stopped, however, when her
hand was on the door-lock. Emily was already ill,—the victim of agitation
and excitement,—it would not do to distress or even disturb her; and, retreating to her own room as hastily as she had come, Gertrude once more
sat down, to reperuse the singular words, and endeavor to find some clue
to the mystery.

That Mr. Phillips and the letter-writer were identical she at once perceived. It was no slight impression that his exclamation and conduct during
the time of their imminent danger on board the boat had left upon the
mind of Gertrude. During the three days that had succeeded the accident,
the words "My child! my own darling!" had been continually ringing in
her ears and haunting her imagination. Now the blissful idea would flash
upon her that the noble, disinterested stranger, who had risked his life so
daringly in her own and Emily's cause, might indeed be her father; and
every fibre of her being had thrilled at the thought, while her head grew
dizzy and confused with the strong sensation of hope that agitated and
almost overwhelmed her brain. Then, again, she had repulsed the idea, as
suggesting only the height of impossibility and folly, and had compelled herself to take a more rational and probable view of the matter, and believe
that the stranger's words and conduct were merely the result of powerful
and overwhelming excitement, or possibly the indications of a somewhat
disordered and unsettled imagination,—a supposition which much of his
previous behavior seemed to warrant.

Her first inquiries, on recovering consciousness, had been for the preserver
of Emily and Isabel, but he had disappeared; no trace of him could be
obtained, and Mr. Graham soon arriving and hurrying them from the
neighborhood, she had been reluctantly compelled to abandon the hope of
seeing him again, and was consequently left entirely to her own vague and
unsatisfactory conjectures.

The same motives which now induced her to forbear consulting Emily
concerning the mysterious epistle had hitherto prevented her from imparting
the secret of Mr. Phillips' inexplicable language and manner; but she had
dwelt upon them none the less, and day and night had silently pondered,
not only upon recent events, but on the entire demeanor of this strange
man towards her, ever since the earliest moment of their acquaintance.

The first perusal of the letter served only to excite and alarm her. It neither called forth distinct ideas and impressions, nor added life and coloring to those she had already formed.

But, as she sat for more than an hour gazing upon the page, which she read and re-read until it was blistered and blotted with the great tears that fell upon it, the varying expression of her face denoted the emotions that, one after another, possessed her; and which, at last, snatching a sheet of paper, she committed to writing with a feverish rapidity, that betrayed how deeply, almost fearfully, her whole being, heart, mind and body, bent and staggered beneath the weight of contending hopes, anxieties, warmly-enkindled affections, and gloomy upstarting fears.

"MY DEAR, DEAR FATHER,—If I may dare to believe that you are so, and, if not that, my best of friends,—how shall I write to you, and what shall I say, since all your words are a mystery! Father! blessed word! O, that my noble friend were indeed my father! Yet tell me, tell me, how can this be? Alas! I feel a sad presentiment that the bright dream is all an illusion, an error. I never before remember to have heard the name of Philip Amory. My sweet, pure and gentle Emily has taught me to love all the world; and hatred and contempt are foreign to her nature, and, I trust, to my own. Moreover, she has not an enemy in the wide world; never had, or could have. One might as well war with an angel of Heaven as with a creature so holy and lovely as she.

"Nor bid me think of yourself as a man of sin and crime. It cannot be. It would be wronging a noble nature to believe it, and I say again it cannot be. Gladly would I trust myself to repose on the bosom of such a parent; gladly would I hail the sweet duty of consoling the sorrows of one so self-sacrificing, so kind, so generous; whose life has been so freely offered for me, and for others whose existence was dearer to me than my own. When you took me in your arms and called me your child, your darling child, I fancied that the excitement of that dreadful scene had for the moment disturbed your mind and brain so far as to invest me with a false identity,—perhaps confound my image with that of some loved and absent one. I now believe that it was no sudden madness, but rather that I have been all along mistaken for another, whose glad office it may perhaps be to cheer a father's saddened life, while I remain unrecognized, unsought,—the fatherless, motherless one I am accustomed to consider myself. If you have lost a daughter, God grant she may be restored to you, to love you as I would do, were I so blessed as to be that daughter! And I,—consider me not a stranger; let me be your child in heart; let me love, pray and weep for you; let me pour out my soul in thankfulness for the kind care and sympathy you have already given me. And yet, though I disclaim it all, and dare not, yes, dare not dwell for a moment on the thought that you are otherwise than deceived in believing me your child, my heart leaps up in spite of me, and I tremble and almost cease to breathe as there flashes upon me the possibility, the blissful, God-given hope! No, no! I will not think it, lest I could not bear to have it crushed! O, what am I writing? I know not. I cannot endure the suspense long; write quickly, or come to me, my father,—for I will call you so once, though perhaps never again.

"GERTRUDE."

Mr. Phillips—or rather Mr. Amory, for we will call him by his true name—had either forgotten or neglected to mention his address. Gertrude did not observe this circumstance until she had folded and was preparing to direct her letter. She then recollected the unfortunate omission, and for a moment experienced a severe pang in the thought that her communication would never reach him. She was reässured, however, on examining the post-mark, which was evidently New York, to which place she unhesitatingly addressed her missive; and then, unwilling to trust it to other hands, tied on her bonnet, caught up a veil with which to protect and conceal her agitated face, and hastened to deposit the letter herself in the village post-office.

To persons of an excitable and imaginative temperament there is, perhaps, no greater or more painful state of trial than that occasioned by severe and long-continued suspense. When we know precisely what we have to bear, we can usually call to our aid the needed strength and submission; but a more than ordinary patience and forbearance is necessary to enable us calmly and tranquilly to await the approach of an important crisis, big with events the nature of which we can have no means of foreseeing, but which will inevitably exercise an all-controlling influence upon the life. One moment hope usurps the mastery, and promises a happy issue; we smile, breathe freely, and banish care and anxiety; but an instant more, and some word, look, or even thought, changes the whole current of our feelings, clouds take the place of smiles, the chest heaves with a sudden oppression, fear starts up like a nightmare, and in proportion as we have cherished a confident joy are we plunged into the torture of doubt or the agony of despair.

Gertrude's case seemed a peculiarly trying one. She had been, already, for a week past, struggling with a degree of suspense and anxiety which agitated her almost beyond endurance; and now a new occasion of uncertainty and mystery had arisen, involving in its issues an almost equal amount of self-questioning and torture. It seemed almost beyond the power of so young, so sensitive, and so inexperienced a girl, to rally such self-command as would enable her to control her emotions, disguise them from observation, and compel herself to endure alone and in silence this cruel dispensation of her destiny.

But she did do it, and bravely, too. Whether the greatness of the emergency called forth, as it ever does in a true-hearted woman, a proportionate greatness of spirit; whether the complication of her web of destiny compelled her, with closed hands and a submissive will, to cease all efforts for its disentanglement; or, whether, with that humble trust, which ever grew more deep and ardent as the sense of her own helplessness pressed upon her, she turned for help to Him whose strength is made perfect in weakness,—it is certain that, as she took her way towards home after depositing the letter in the post-master's hand, the firmness of her step, the calm uplifting of her eye, gave token that she that moment conceived a brave resolve,—a resolve which, during the two days that intervened ere she received the expected reply, never for one moment deserted her.

And it was this. She would endeavor to suspend for the present those vain conjectures, that fruitless weighing of probabilities, which served only to harass her mind, puzzle her understanding, and destroy her peace; she would ponder no more on matters which concerned herself, but with a desperate effort turn all her mental and all her physical energy into some other and more disinterested channel, and patiently wait until the cloud which hung over her fate should be dissipated by the light of truth, and explanation triumph over mystery.

She was herself surprised, afterwards, when she called to mind and brought up in long array the numerous household, domestic and friendly duties which she almost unconsciously accomplished in those few days during which she was wrestling with thoughts that were ever struggling to be uppermost, and were only kept down by a force of will that was almost exhausting.

She dusted and reärranged every book in Mr. Graham's extensive library; unpacked and put in their appropriate places every article of her own and Emily's long-scattered wardrobe; aided Mrs. Ellis in her labors to restore order to the china-closet and the linen-press; and many other neglected or long-postponed duties now found a time for their fulfilment.

In these praiseworthy efforts to drive away such reflections as were fatal to her peace, and employ her hands, at least, if not her heart, in such services as might promote the comfort and well-being of others, let us leave her for the present.

## Chapter XLIII

*Thou neither dost persuade me to seek wealth*
*For empire's sake, nor empire to affect*
*For glory's sake, by all thy argument.*

MILTON

In a well-furnished private parlor of one of those first-class hotels in which New York city abounds, Philip Amory sat alone. It was evening. The window-curtains were drawn, the gas-lamps burning brightly, bringing out the gorgeous colors of the gayly-tinted carpet and draperies, and giving a cheerful glow to the room, the comfortable appearance of which contrasted strongly with the pale countenance and desponding attitude of its solitary inmate, who, with his head bowed upon his hands, leaned upon a table in the centre of the apartment.

He had sat for nearly an hour in precisely the same position, without once moving or looking up. With his left hand, upon which his forehead rested, he had thrust back the wavy masses of his silvered hair, as if their light weight were too oppressive for his heated brow; and the occasional movement of his fingers, as they were slowly passed to and fro beneath the graceful curls, alone gave evidence that he had not fallen asleep.

Suddenly he started up, straightened his commanding figure to its full height, and slowly commenced pacing the room. A light knock at the door arrested his measured steps; a look of nervous agitation and annoyance overspread his countenance; he again flung himself into his chair, and, in reply to the servant's announcing "a gentleman, sir," was preparing to say, "I cannot be interrupted,"—but it was too late; the visitor had already advanced within the door, which the waiter quietly closed and retreated.

The new comer—a young man—stepped quickly and eagerly forward, but checked himself, somewhat abashed at the unexpected coldness of the reception he met from his host, who rose slowly and deliberately to meet his guest, while the cloud upon his countenance and the frigid manner in which he touched the young man's cordially-offered hand seemed to imply that the latter's presence was unwelcome.

"Excuse me, Mr. Phillips," said William Sullivan, for it was he who had thus unintentionally forced an entrance to the secluded man. "I am afraid my visit is an intrusion."

"Do not speak of it," replied Mr. Amory. "I beg you will be seated;" and he politely handed a chair.

Willie availed himself of the offered seat no further than to lean lightly upon it with one hand, while he still remained standing. "You are changed, sir," continued he, "since I last saw you."

"Changed! Yes, I am," returned the other, absently.

"Your health, I fear, is not—"

"My health is excellent," said Mr. Amory, interrupting his unfinished remark. Then seeming for the first time to realize the necessity of exerting himself, in order to sustain the conversation, he added, "It is a long time, sir, since we met. I have not yet forgotten the debt I owe you for your timely interference between me and Ali, that Arab traitor, with his rascally army of Bedouin rogues."

"Do not name it, sir," replied Willie. "Our meeting was fortunate indeed; but the benefit was as mutual as the danger to which we were alike exposed."

"I cannot think so. You seemed to have a most excellent understanding with your own party of guides and attendants, Arabs though they were."

"True; I have had some experience in Eastern travel, and usually know how to manage these inflammable spirits of the desert. But at the time I joined you I was myself entering the neighborhood of hostile tribes, and might soon have found our party overawed, but for the advantage of having joined forces with yourself."

"You set but a modest value upon your conciliatory powers, my young man. To you, who are so well acquainted with the facts in the case, I can hardly claim the merit of frankness for the acknowledgment that it was only my own hot temper and stubborn will which exposed us both to the imminent danger which you were fortunately able to avert. No, no! you must not deprive me of the satisfaction of once more expressing my gratitude for your invaluable aid."

"You are making my visit, sir," said Willie, smiling, "the very reverse of what it was intended to be. I did not come here this evening to receive, but, to the best of my ability, to render thanks."

"For what, sir?" asked Mr. Amory, abruptly, almost roughly. "You owe me nothing!"

"The friends of Isabella Clinton, sir, owe you a debt of gratitude which it will be impossible for them ever to repay."

"You are mistaken, Mr. Sullivan; I have done nothing which places that young lady's friends under a particle of obligation to me."

"Did you not save her life?"

"Yes; but nothing was further from my intention."

Willie smiled; "It could have been no accident, I think, which led you to risk your own life to rescue a fellow-passenger."

"It was no accident, indeed, which led to Miss Clinton's safety from destruction. I am convinced of that. But you must not thank *me:* it is due to another than myself that she does not now sleep in death."

"May I ask to whom you refer? Your words are mysterious."

"I refer to a dear and noble girl whom I swam to that burning wreck to save. Her veil had been agreed upon as a signal between us. That veil, carefully thrown over the head of Miss Clinton, whom I found clinging to the spot assigned to—to her whom I was seeking, deceived me, and I bore in safety to the shore the burden which I had ignorantly seized from the gaping waters, leaving my own darling, who had offered her life as a sacrifice, to—"

"O, not to die!" exclaimed Willie.

"No; to be saved by a miracle. Go thank her for Miss Clinton's life."

"I thank God," said Willie, with fervor, "that the horrors of such scenes of destruction are half redeemed by heroism like that."

The hitherto stern countenance of Mr. Amory softened as he listened to the young man's enthusiastic outburst of admiration at Gertrude's noble self-devotion.

"Who is she? Where is she?" continued Willie.

"Ask me not!" replied Mr. Amory, with a gesture of impatience; "I cannot tell you, if I would. I have not seen her since that ill-fated day."

His manner, even more than his words, seemed to intimate an unwillingness to enter into any further explanation regarding Isabel's rescue, and Willie, perceiving it, stood for a moment silent and irresolute. Then, advancing a step nearer, he said,

"Though you so utterly disclaim, Mr. Phillips, any participation in Miss Clinton's happy escape, I feel that my errand here would be but imperfectly fulfilled if I should fail to deliver the message which I bring to one who was, at least, the final means, if not the original cause, of her safety. Mr.

Clinton, the young lady's father, desired me to tell you that, in saving the life of his only surviving child, the last of seven, all of whom but herself were doomed to an early death, you have prolonged his own days, and rendered him grateful to that degree which words on his part are powerless to express; but that, as long as his feeble life is spared, he shall never cease to bless your name, and pray to Heaven for its choicest gifts upon you and those who dwell next your heart."

There was a slight moisture in the clear, penetrating eye of Mr. Amory, but a bland and courteous smile upon his lip, as he said, in reply to Willie's words:

"All this from Mr. Clinton! Very gentlemanly, and equally sincere, I doubt not; but you surely do not mean to thank me wholly in his name, my young friend. Have you nothing to say for your own sake?"

Willie looked surprised at the question, but replied, unhesitatingly, "Certainly, sir; as one of a large circle of acquaintances and friends, whom Miss Clinton honors with her regard, you may rest assured that my admiration and gratitude for your disinterested exertions are unbounded; and, not only on her account, but on that of every other whom you had the noble satisfaction of rescuing from a most terrific form of death and destruction."

"Am I to understand, by your words, that you speak only as a friend of humanity, and that you felt no deep personal interest in any of my fellow-passengers?"

"I was unacquainted with nearly all of them. Miss Clinton was the only one whom I had known for any greater length of time than during two or three days of Saratoga intercourse; but I should certainly have felt deeply grieved at her death, since I was in the habit of meeting her familiarly in her childhood, have lately been continually in her society, and am aware that her father, my respected partner, an old and invaluable friend, who is now much enfeebled in health, could hardly have survived so severe a shock as the loss, under such harrowing circumstances, of an only child, whom he almost idolizes."

"You speak very coolly, Mr. Sullivan. Are you aware that the prevailing belief gives you credit for feeling more than a mere friendly interest in Miss Clinton?"

The gradual dilating of Willie's large gray eyes, as he fixed them inquiringly upon Mr. Amory,—the half-scrutinizing, half-astonished expression which crept over his face, as he deliberately seated himself in the chair, which, until then, he had not occupied,—were sufficient evidence of the effect of the question so unexpectedly put to him.

"Sir," said he, "I either misunderstood you, or the prevailing belief is a most mistaken one."

"Then you never before heard of your own engagement?"

"Never, I assure you. Is it possible that so idle a report has obtained an extensive circulation among Miss Clinton's friends?"

"Sufficiently extensive for me, a mere spectator of Saratoga life, to hear it not only whispered from ear to ear, but openly proclaimed as a fact worthy of credit."

"I am exceedingly surprised and vexed at what you tell me," said

Willie, looking really disturbed and chagrined. "Nonsensical and false as such a rumor is, it will very naturally, if it should reach Miss Clinton, be a source of indignation and annoyance to her; and it is on that account, far more than my own, that I regret the circumstances which have probably given rise to it."

"Do you refer to considerations of delicacy on the lady's part, or have you the modesty to believe that her pride would be wounded by having her name thus coupled with that of her father's junior partner, a young man hitherto unknown to fashionable circles? But, excuse me; perhaps I am stepping on dangerous ground, and your own pride may shrink from the frankness of my speech."

"By no means, sir; you wrong me if you believe my pride to be of such a nature. But, in answer to your question, I have not only reference to both the motives you name, but to many others, when I assert my opinion of the resentment Miss Clinton would probably cherish, if the foolish and unwarranted remarks you mention should chance to reach her ears."

"Mr. Sullivan," said Mr. Amory, drawing his chair nearer to Willie's, and speaking in a tone of great interest, "are you sure you are not standing in your own light? Are you aware that undue modesty, coupled with false and overstrained notions of refinement, has before now stood in the way of many a man's good fortune, and is likely to interfere largely with your own?"

"How so, sir? You speak in riddles, and I am ignorant of your meaning."

"Handsome young fellows, like you," continued Mr. Amory, "can, I know, often command almost any amount of property for the asking; but many such chances rarely occur to one individual; and the world will laugh at you, if you waste so fair an opportunity as that which you now enjoy."

"Opportunity for what? You surely do not mean to advise me—"

"I do, though. I am older than you are, and I know something of the world. A fortune is not made in a day, nor is money a thing to be despised. Mr. Clinton's life is, I dare say, enfeebled and almost worn out in toiling after that wealth which will soon be the inheritance of his daughter. She is young, beautiful, and the pride of that high circle in which she moves. Both father and daughter smile upon you;—you need not look disconcerted, —I speak as between friends, and you know the truth of that which strangers have observed, and which I have frequently heard mentioned as beyond doubt. Why, then, do you hesitate? I trust you are not deterred from taking advantage of your position by any romantic and chivalrous sense of inferiority on your part, or unworthiness to obtain so fair a prize."

"Mr. Phillips," said Willie, with hesitation, and evident embarrassment, "the comments of mere casual acquaintances, such as the greater part of those with whom Miss Clinton associated in Saratoga, are not in the least to be depended upon. The peculiar relations in which I stand towards Mr. Clinton have been such as of late to draw me into constant intercourse both with himself and his daughter. He is almost entirely without relatives, has scarcely any trustworthy friend at command, and therefore appears, perhaps, to the world more favorably disposed towards me than would be found to be the case should I aspire to his daughter's hand. The lady herself, too, has so many admirers, that it would be the height of vanity in me to believe—"

"Pooh, pooh!" exclaimed Mr. Phillips, springing from his chair, and, as he commenced pacing the room, clapping the young man heartily upon the shoulder, "tell that, Sullivan, to a greater novice, a more unsophisticated individual, than I am! It is very becoming in you to say so; but (though I hate to flatter) a few slight reminders will hardly harm a youth who has such a very low opinion of his own merits. Pray, who was the gentleman for whose society Miss Clinton was, a few nights since, so ready to forego the music of Alboni, the brilliancy of the well-lighted and crowded hall, and the smiles and compliments of a whole train of adorers? With whom, I say, did she, in comparison with all this, prefer a quiet moonlight walk in the garden of the United States Hotel?"

Willie hesitated a moment, while endeavoring to rally his recollection; then, as if the circumstance and its consequences had just flashed upon him, he exclaimed, "I remember!—That, then, was one of the causes of suspicion. I was, on that occasion, a messenger merely, to summon Miss Isabel to the bed-side of her father, by whom I had been anxiously watching for hours, and who, on awakening from a long-protracted and almost lethargic sleep, which had excited the alarm of the physician, inquired for his daughter with such eagerness, that I did not hesitate to interrupt the pleasure of the evening, and call her to the post of duty, which awaited her in the cottage occupied by Mr. Clinton, at the further extremity of the grounds, to which I accompanied her by moonlight."

Mr. Amory almost laughed outright, cast upon Willie, for the first time, that look of sweet benignity which, though rare, well became his fine countenance, and exclaimed, "So much for watering-place gossip! I believe I must forbear speaking of any further evidences of a tender interest manifested by either of you. But, these things apart, and there is every reason to believe, my dear Sullivan, that though the young lady's heart be still, like her fortune, in the united keeping of herself and her father, there is nothing easier than for you to win and claim them both. You are a rising young man, and possess business talent indispensable, I hear, to the elder party; if, with your handsome face, figure and accomplishments, you cannot render yourself equally so to the younger, there is no one to blame but yourself."

Willie laughed. "If I had that object in view, I know of no one to whom I would so soon come for encouragement as to you, sir; but the flattering prospect you hold out is quite wasted upon me."

"Not if you are the man I think you," replied Mr. Amory. "I cannot believe you will be such a fool (I beg your pardon for using so strong a term) as to allow yourself to be blinded to the opportunity you see held out before you of making that appearance in society, and taking that stand in life, to which your birth, your education and your personal qualities, entitle you. Your father was a respectable clergyman (always an honorable profession); you enjoyed and profited by every advantage in your youth, and have done yourself such credit in India as would enable you, with plenty of capital at command, to take the lead in a few years among mercantile men. All this, indeed, might not, probably would not, give you an opportunity to mingle freely and at once in the highest ranks of our aristocracy; but a union with Miss Clinton would entitle you immediately to such a position as years of assiduous effort could hardly win, and you would find yourself at twenty-five at the highest point in every respect to which you could possibly aspire; nor have you, I will venture to say, lived for six years utterly deprived of female society, without becoming proportionately susceptible to such uncommon grace and beauty as Miss Clinton's.

"A man just returned from a long residence abroad is usually thought to be an easy prey to the charms of the first of his fair countrywomen into whose society he may chance to be thrown; and it can scarcely then be wondered at, if you are subdued by such winning attractions as are rarely to be met with in this land of beautiful women. Nor can it be possible that you have for six years toiled beneath an Indian sun without learning to appreciate as it deserves the unlooked-for but happy and honorable termination of your toils, the easily-attained rest from labor, whose crowning blessing will be the possession of your beautiful bride."

A moment's pause ensued, during which Mr. Amory sat watching the countenance of Willie, while he awaited his reply. He was not kept long in ignorance of the effect his glowing picture had produced.

"Mr. Phillips," said Willie, speaking with prompt decision, and a nervous energy which proved how heart-felt were the words he uttered, "I have not, indeed, spent many of the best years of my life toiling beneath a burning sun, and in a protracted exile from all that I held most dear, without being sustained and encouraged by high hopes, aims and aspirations. But you misjudge me greatly, if you believe that the ambition that has hitherto spurred me on can find its gratification in those rewards which you have so vividly presented to my imagination. No, sir! believe me, though these advantages may seem beyond the grasp of most men, I aspire to something higher yet, and should think my best endeavors wasted indeed, if my hopes and wishes tended not to a still more glorious good."

"And to what quarter do you look for the fulfilment of such flattering prospects?" asked Mr. Amory, in an ironical tone of voice.

"Not to the gay circles of fashion," replied Willie, "nor yet to that moneyed aristocracy which awards to each man his position in life. I do not depreciate an honorable standing in the eyes of my fellow-men; I am not blind to the advantages of wealth, or insensible to the claims of grace and beauty; but these were not the things for which I left my home, and it is not to claim them that I have now returned. Young as I am, I have lived long enough, and seen enough of trial, to lay to heart the belief that the only blessings worth striving for are something more enduring, more satisfying, than doubtful honors, precarious wealth, or fleeting smiles."

"To what, then, may I ask, do you look forward?"

"To a *home,* and that, not so much for myself—though I have long pined for such a rest—as for another, with whom I hope to share it. A year since," —and Willie's lip trembled, his voice shook with emotion, as he spoke,— "and there were others, beside that dear one whose image now entirely fills my heart, whom I had fondly hoped, and should deeply have rejoiced, to see reaping the fruits of my exertions. But we were not permitted to meet again; and now,—but pardon me, sir; I did not mean to intrude upon you my private affairs."

"Go on," said Mr. Amory; "go on; I deserve some degree of confidence, in return for the disinterested advice I have been giving you. Speak to me as to an old friend; I am much interested in what you say."

"It is long since I have spoken freely of myself," said Willie; "but frankness is natural to me, and, since you profess a desire to learn something of my aim in life, I know of no motive I have for reserve or concealment. But my position, sir, even as a child, was singular; and you must excuse me if I refer to it for a moment. I could not have been more than twelve or fourteen years of age when I began to realize the necessity which rested upon me. My widowed mother and her aged father were the only relatives, almost the only friends, I knew. One was feeble delicate, and quite unequal to active exertion; the other was old and poor, being wholly dependent upon the small salary he received for officiating as sexton of a neighboring church. You are aware, for I have mentioned it in our earlier acquaintance abroad, that, in spite of these circumstances, they maintained me for several years in comfort and decency, and gave me an excellent education.

"At an age when kites and marbles are wont to be all-engrossing I became possessed with an earnest desire to relieve my mother and grandfather of a part of their burden of care and labor; and, with this purpose in view, sought and obtained a situation, in which I was well treated and well paid, and which I retained until the death of my excellent master. Then, for a time, I felt bitterly the want of employment, became desponding and unhappy; a state of mind which was fostered by constant association with one of so melancholy and despairing a temperament as my grandfather, who, having met with great disappointment in life, held out no encouragement to me, but was forever hinting at the probability of my utterly failing in every scheme for success and advancement.

"I bitterly regretted, at the time, the depressing influence of the old man's innuendoes; but I have since thought they answered a good purpose; for nothing so urged me on to ever-increasing efforts as the indomitable desire to prove the mistaken nature of his gloomy predictions, and few things have given me more satisfaction than the assurances I have frequently received during the few past years that he came at last to a full conviction that my prosperity was established beyond a doubt, and that one of his ill-fated family was destined to escape the trials and evils of poverty.

"My mother was a quiet, gentle woman, small in person, with great simplicity and some reserve of manner. She loved me like her own soul; she taught me everything I know of goodness; there is no sacrifice I would not have made for her happiness. I would have died to save her life; but we shall never meet again in this world, and I—I—am learning to be resigned!

"For these two, and one other, whom I shall speak of presently, I was ready to go away, and strive, and suffer, and be patient. The opportunity came, and I embraced it. And soon one great object of my ambition was won. I was able to earn a competency for myself and for them. In the course of time, luxuries even were within my means, and I had begun to look forward to a not very distant day, when my long-looked-for return should render our happiness perfect and complete. I little thought, then, that the sad tidings of my grandfather's death were on their way, and the news of my mother's slow but equally sure decline so soon to follow.

"It is true, however, they are both gone; and I should now be so solitary as almost to long to follow them, but for one other, whose love will bind me to earth so long as she is spared."

"And she?" exclaimed Mr. Amory, with an eagerness which Willie, engrossed with his own thoughts, did not observe.

"Is a young girl," continued Willie, "without family, wealth or beauty; but with a spirit so elevated as to make her great, a heart so noble as to make her rich, a soul so pure as to make her beautiful."

Mr. Amory's attitude of fixed attention, his evident waiting to hear more, emboldened Willie to speak still further.

"There lived in the same house which my grandfather occupied an old man, a city lamplighter. He was poor, poorer even than we were, but, I will venture to say, there never was a better or a kinder-hearted person in the world. One evening, when engaged in his round of duty, he picked up and brought home a little ragged child, whom a cruel woman had just thrust into the street to perish with cold, or die a more lingering death in the alms-house; for nothing but such devoted care as she received from my mother and Uncle True (so we always called our old friend) could have saved the feeble, half-starved creature from the consequences of long-continued exposure and ill-treatment. Through their unwearied watching and efforts she was spared, to repay in after years all, and more than all, the love bestowed upon her. She was at that time miserably thin and attenuated, sallow, and extremely plain in her appearance, besides being possessed of a violent temper, which she had never been taught to restrain, and a stubbornness of will, which undoubtedly resulted from her having long lived in opposition to all the world.

"All this, however, did not repel Uncle True, under whose loving influence new and hitherto undeveloped virtues and capacities soon began to manifest themselves. In the atmosphere of love in which she now lived, she soon became a changed being; and when, in addition to the example and precepts taught her at home, a divine light was shed upon her life by one who, herself sitting in darkness, casts a halo forth from her own spirit to illumine those of all who are blessed with her presence, she became, what she has ever since been, a being to love and trust for a lifetime. For myself, there were no bounds to the affection I soon came to cherish for the little girl, to whom I was first attracted by compassion merely.

"We were constantly together; we had no thoughts, no studies, no pleasures, sorrows or interests, that were not shared. I was her teacher, her protector, the partner of all her childish amusements; and she, on her part, was by turns an advising, consoling, sympathizing and encouraging friend. In this latter character she was indispensable to me, for she had a hopeful nature, and a buoyancy of spirit which often imparted itself to me. I well remember, when my kind employer died, and I was plunged in boyish grief and despair, the confidence and energy with which she, then very young, inspired me. The relation between her and Uncle True was beautiful. Boy as I was, I could not but view with admiration the old man's devoted love for the adopted darling of his latter years (his birdie, as he always called her), and the deep and grateful affection which she bore him in return.

"During the first few years she was wholly dependent upon him, and seemed only a fond, affectionate child; but a time came, at last, when the case was reversed, and the old man, stricken with disease, became infirm and helpless. It was then that the beauty of her woman's nature shone forth triumphant; and, O! how gently, child as she was, she guided his steps as he descended to the grave! Often have I gone to his room at midnight, fearing lest he might be in need of care which she, in her youth and inexperience, would be unable to render; and never shall I forget the little figure, seated calmly by his bed-side, at an hour when many of her years would be shrinking from fears conjured up by the night and the darkness, with a lamp dimly burning on a table before her, and she herself, with his hand in hers, sweetly soothing his wakefulness by her loving words, or with her eyes bent upon her little Bible, reading to him holy lessons.

"But all her care could not prolong his life; and, shortly before I went to India, he died, blessing God for the peace imparted to him through his gentle nurse.

"It was my task to soothe our little Gerty's sorrows, and do what I could to comfort her; an office which, before I left the country, I was rejoiced to transfer to the willing hands of the excellent blind lady who had long befriended both her and Uncle True. Before I went away, I solemnly committed to Gerty, who had in one instance proved herself both willing and able, the care of my mother and grandfather. She promised to be faithful to the trust; and nobly was that promise kept. In spite of the unkindness and deep displeasure of Mr. Graham (the blind lady's father), upon whose bounty she had for a long time been dependent, she devoted herself heart and hand to the fulfilment of duties which in her eyes were sacred and holy. In spite of suffering, labor, watching and privation, she voluntarily forsook case and pleasure, and spent day and night in the patient service of friends whom she loved with a greater love than a daughter's, for it was that of a saint.

"With all my earnestness of purpose, I could never have done half that she did; I might have loved as much, but none but a woman's heart could have conceived and planned, none but a woman's hand could have patiently executed, the deeds that Gertrude wrought. She was more than a sister to me before; she was my constant correspondent, my dearest friend: now she is bound to me by ties that are not of earth nor of time."

❀❀❀❀❀❀❀❀❀❀❀❀❀❀❀❀❀❀❀❀❀❀❀❀❀❀❀❀

# Chapter XLIV

*And opportunity I here have had*
*To try thee, sift thee, and confess have found thee*
*Proof against all temptation.*

MILTON

"Certainly," said Mr. Amory, who had waited patiently for the conclusion of Willie's story, "I can well understand that. A man of a generous spirit could hardly fail to cherish a deep and lasting gratitude for one who devoted herself so disinterestedly to a trying and toilsome attendance upon the last hours of beloved friends, to whose wants he himself was prevented from ministering; and the warmth with which you eulogize this girl does you credit, Sullivan. She must, too, be a young person of great excellence, to have fulfilled so faithfully and well a promise of such remote date that it would probably have been ignored by a less disinterested friend. But do not let any enthusiastic sense of honor induce you to sacrifice yourself on the shrine of gratitude.

"I shall find it hard to believe that a young man who has had the ambition to mark out, and the energy to pursue, such a course on the road to fortune as you have thus far successfully followed, can, in his sober senses, have made a serious resolve to unite himself and his prospects with an insignificant little playmate, of unacknowledged birth, without beauty or fortune, unless there is already a standing engagement, by which he is unwillingly bound, or he allows himself to be drawn on to matrimony by the belief that the highest compliment he can pay (namely, the offer of himself) will alone cancel the immense obligations under which he labors. May I ask if you are already shackled by promises?"

"I am not," replied Willie.

"Then listen to me a moment. My motives are friendly when I beg you not to act rashly in a matter which will affect the happiness of your whole life; and to hear,—with patience, too, if you can," for Willie already gave symptoms of restlessness,—"the few words which I have to say on the subject.

"You are much mistaken, my young friend, if you believe that the happiness of Gerty, as you call her (a very ugly name, by the way), can be insured, any more than your own, by an ill-assorted union, of which you will both find occasion to repent. You have not seen her for six years; think, then, of all that has happened in the mean time, and beware how you act with precipitation.

"You have all this time been living abroad, engaged in active life, growing in knowledge of the world, and its various phases of society. In India, to be sure, you witnessed a mode of life wholly different from that which prevails with us, or in European cities; but the independence, both of character and manner, which you there acquired, fitted you admirably for the polished sphere of Parisian life, to which you were so suddenly introduced, and in which, I may say without flattery, you met with such marked success.

"Notwithstanding the privilege you enjoyed of being presented in polite circles as the friend of a man so well known and so much respected as Mr. Clinton, you cannot have been insensible to the marked attentions bestowed upon you by American residents abroad, or unaware of the advantage you enjoyed, on your return home, from having been known as the object of such favor. Though not so fortunate as to meet you in Paris, I was there at the same time with yourself, and had some opportunity of being acquainted with facts which I am sure you would have too much modesty to acknowledge.

"That you were not wholly devoid of taste for choice society it is easy to infer; since, otherwise, you would never have been able to render yourself an ornament to it, or even maintain a place within its precincts. It is also equally evident that your pride must have been flattered, and your views in life somewhat biased, by the favorable reception you have met, both abroad and at home, not only from your own sex, but especially from the young, fair, and beautiful women who have honored you with their smiles, and among whom she whose name the crowd already associates with your own stands preëminent.

"When I think of all this, and of those pecuniary hopes you may so reasonably indulge, and on which I have already dilated, and then imagine you suddenly flinging all these aside, to chivalrously throw yourself at the feet of your mother's little nurse, I confess I find it impossible to keep silent, and avoid reminding you of the reäction that must come, the disappointment that must ensue, on finding yourself at once and forever shut out from participation in pleasures which have been within your reach, and voluntarily discarded.

"You must remember that much of the consideration which is paid to a young bachelor of growing prospects ceases to be awarded to him after marriage, and is never extended to his bride, unless she be chosen from the select circles to which he aspires. This unportioned orphan, with whom you propose to share your fate,—this little patient school-mistress—"

"I did not tell you she had ever been a teacher!" exclaimed Willie, stopping short in his walk up and down the room, which latterly he had been, in his turn, pacing impatiently, while he listened to Mr. Amory's words,—"I did not tell you anything of the sort! How did you know it?"

Mr. Amory, who by his negligence had thus betrayed more knowledge than he had been supposed to possess, hesitated a moment, but, quickly recovering himself, answered, with apparent frankness. "To tell the truth, Sullivan, I have seen the girl, in company with an old doctor."

"Dr. Jeremy?" asked Willie, quickly.

"The same."

"When did you see her? How did it happen?"

"Do not question me!" said Mr. Amory, petulantly, as if the matter were of little consequence, and he did not choose to be interrogated. "I happened to see the old gentleman in the course of my travels, and this Gertrude Flint was with him. He told me a few facts concerning her;—nothing to her disadvantage, however; in warning you against a mis-alliance, I speak only in general terms."

Willie looked at Mr. Amory in a half-scrutinizing, half-wondering manner, and appeared on the point of persisting in his attempt to learn further particulars; but Mr. Amory, taking up the thread of his previous conversation, went on, without giving him a chance to speak.

"This Gerty, as I was saying, Sullivan, will be a dead weight upon your hands; a constant drawback to all your efforts for the attainment of fashionable society, in which it is hardly to be expected she can be exactly fitted to shine. You yourself pronounce her to be without wealth or beauty; of her family you know nothing, and have certainly little reason to expect that, if discovered, it would do her any credit. I believe, then, that I only speak from the dictates of common sense, when I bid you beware how you make, in the disposal of yourself, such a very unequal bargain."

"I am very willing to believe, sir," said Willie, resuming his seat and settling himself into a composed attitude, "that the arguments you have so powerfully brought to bear upon a question most important to my welfare are grounded upon calm reasoning, and a disinterested desire to promote my prosperity. I confess you are the last man, judging from our short, but, for the length of time, intimate acquaintance, from whom I should have expected such advice; for I had believed you so independent of the opinion and so indifferent to the applause of the world that they would weigh but little with you in forming estimates for the guidance of others.

"Still, though your suggestions have failed to influence or in the least degree change my sentiments or intentions, I fully appreciate and thank you for the sincerity and earnestness with which you have sought to mould my judgment by your own; and will reply to your arguments with such frankness as will, I think, persuade you that, so far from following the impulses of a blind enthusiasm, to plunge with haste and precipitation into a course of action hereafter to be deplored, I am actuated by feelings which reason approves, and which have already stood the test of experience.

"You speak truly when you impute to me a natural taste for good society; a taste which poverty, and the retirement in which my boyhood was passed, gave me little opportunity to manifest, but which had, nevertheless, no small influence in determining my aims and ambition in life. The fine houses, equipages, and clothes of the rich, had far less charm to my fancy than the high-bred ease, refinement, and elegance of manner, which distinguished some few of their owners who chanced to come under my observation; and, much as I desired the attainment of wealth for the sake of its own intrinsic advantages, and the means it would afford of contributing to the comfort and happiness of others, it would have seemed to me divested of half its value, should it fail to secure to its possessor a free admittance to the polite and polished circles upon which I looked with admiring eyes.

"I needed not, therefore, the social deprivations I experienced in India to prepare me to enter with eager zest into the excitement and pleasure of

recovered from the dazzling, blinding effect which the glitter and show of Fashion imposed upon the clearness of my perceptions. My suspicions of its falsehood and vanity were based upon instances of selfishness, folly and cold-heartedness, which, one after another, came to my knowledge. I could relate to you the thousand mean deceits, the contemptible rivalries, the gross neglect of sacred duties, which came under my immediate observation; but I will not betray the secrets of individuals, or weary you with their recital.

"Especially was I astonished at the effect of an uninterrupted pursuit of pleasure upon the sensibilities, the tempers, and the domestic affections, of women. Though bearing within my heart an image of female goodness and purity, this sweet remembrance, this living ideal, might possibly have been driven from its throne, and supplanted by some one of the lovely faces which, at first, bewildered me by their beauty, had these last been the index to souls of equal perfection. There may be—I have no doubt that there are—noble and excellent women, moving in the highest walks of life, whose beauty, grace and other outward adornments, are less admirable than their own high natures; but among those with whom I became familiarly acquainted there was not one who could in the least compare with her who was continually present to my memory, who is still, and ever must be, a model to her sex.

"It is no wonder that others failed to come up to my conception of all that is lovely in woman, since the character of Gertrude Flint was the standard by which each in my mind was measured. How could I help contrasting the folly, the worldliness, and the cold-heartedness around me, with the cultivated mind, the self-sacrificing and affectionate disposition, of one who possesses every quality that can adorn life, whether at home or abroad? You have indeed failed to convince me that Gertrude can in any way be a drawback or disadvantage to the man who shall be so fortunate as to call her his. For my own part, I desire no better, no more truly aristocratic position in life, than that to which she is so well entitled, and to which she would be one of the brightest ornaments,—the aristocracy of true refinement, knowledge, grace and beauty. You talk to me of wealth. Gertrude has no money in her purse, but her soul is the pure gold, tried in the furnace of sorrow and affliction, and thence come forth bright and unalloyed. You speak of family, and an honorable birth. She has no family, and her birth is shrouded in mystery; but the blood that courses in her veins would never disgrace the race from which she sprung, and every throb of her unselfish heart allies her to all that is noble.

"You are eloquent on the subject of beauty. When I parted from Gertrude, she was, in all but character, a mere child, being only twelve or thirteen years of age. Though much altered and improved since the time when she first came among us, I scarcely think she could have been said to possess much of what the world calls beauty. For myself, it was a matter of which I seldom thought or cared; and, had I been less indifferent on the subject she was so dear to me that I should have been utterly unable to form an impartial judgment of her claims in this respect.

"I well remember, however, the indignation I once felt at hearing a fellow-clerk, who had accidentally met her in one of our walks, sneeringly contrast her personal appearance with that of our mutual employer's handsome daughter, the same Miss Clinton of whom we have been speaking; and the proportionate rapture with which I listened to the excellent teacher, Miss Browne, when on a certain occasion, being present at a school-examination, I overheard her commenting to a lady upon Gertrude's wonderful promise in person as well as in mind. Whether the first part of this promise has been fulfilled, I have no means of judging; but, as I recall her dignified and graceful little figure, her large, intelligent, sparkling eyes, the glow of feeling that lit up her whole countenance, and the peaceful, almost majestic expression which purity of soul imparted to her yet childish features, she stands forth to my remembrance the embodiment of all that I hold most dear.

"Six years may have outwardly changed her much; but they cannot have robbed her of what I prize the most. She has charms over which time can have no power, a grace that is a gift of Heaven, a beauty that is eternal. Could I ask for more?

"Do not believe, then," continued he, after a short pause, "that my fidelity to my early playmate is an emotion of gratitude merely. It is true I owe her much,—far more than I can ever repay; but the honest warmth of my affection for the noble girl springs from the truest love of a purity of character and singleness of heart which I have never seen equalled.

"What is there in the wearisome and foolish walks of Fashion, the glitter and show of wealth, the homage of an idle crowd, that could so fill my heart, elevate my spirit, and inspire my exertions, as the thought of a peaceful, happy home, blessed by a presiding spirit so formed for confidence, love, and a communion that time can never dissolve, and eternity will but render more secure and unbroken?"

"And she whom you loved so well?—are you sure—" asked Mr. Phillips, speaking with visible effort, and faltering ere he had completed his sentence.

"No," answered Willie, anticipating the question. "I know what you would ask.—I am *not* sure. I have no reason to indulge the hopes I have been dwelling upon so fondly; but I do not regret having spoken with such openness and candor; for, should she grieve my heart by her coldness, I should still be proud to have loved her. Until this time, ever since I gained my native land, I have been shackled with duties, which, sacred as they were, have chafed a spirit longing for freedom to follow its own impulses. In this visit to you, sir (and, as he spoke, he rose to depart), I have fulfilled the last obligation imposed upon me by my excellent friend, and to-morrow I shall be at liberty to go where duty alone prevented me from at once hastening."

He offered his hand to Mr. Amory, who grasped it with a cordiality very different from the feeble greeting he had given him on his entrance. "Good-by," said he. "You carry with you my best wishes for a success which you seem to have so much at heart; but some day or other I feel sure you will be reminded of all I have said to you this evening."

"Strange man!" thought Willie, as he walked towards his own hotel.

"How warmly he shook my hand at parting! and with what a friendly manner he bade me farewell, notwithstanding the coldness of the reception he gave me, and the pertinacity with which, throughout my whole visit, I rejected his opinions and repelled his advice!"

## Chapter XLV

*Yet 't is a weary task to school the heart,*
*Ere years of griefs have tamed its fiery spirit*
*Into that still and passive fortitude*
*Which is but learned from suffering.*

HEMANS

"Miss Gertrude," said Mrs. Prime, opening the parlor-door, putting her head cautiously in, looking round, and then advancing with a stealthy pace, like that of a favorite family cat which is venturing to step a little beyond its usual limits,—"my! how busy you are! Lor's sakes alive, if you an't rippin' up them great curtains of Miss Graham's for the wash! I wouldn't be botherin' with 'em, Miss Gertrude; she won't be here for this fortnight, and Miss Ellis will have time enough."

"O, I have nothing else to do, Mrs. Prime; it's no trouble." Then, looking up pleasantly at the old cook, she added, "It seems very cosey for us all to be at home again; doesn't it?"

"It seems beautiful!" answered Mrs. Prime, with emphasis; "and—I hope there's no harm in sayin' it—I can't help thinkin' how nice it would be, if we could all live on jist as we are now, without no more intrusions."

Gertrude smiled, and said, "Everything looks as it used to in old times, when I first came here. I was quite a child then," continued she, with a sigh.

"Gracious me! What are you now?" said Mrs. Prime. "For mercy's sake, Miss Gertrude, don't you begin to think about growin' old! There's nothin' like feelin' young, to keep young. There's Miss Patty Pace, now—"

"I have been meaning to ask after her," exclaimed Gertrude, resuming her scissors, and commencing to rip another window-curtain. "Is she alive and well yet?"

"She!" replied Mrs. Prime; "Lor, she won't never die! Old women like her, that feels themselves young gals, allers live forever; but I came a purpose to speak to you about her. The baker's boy that fetched the loaves, this mornin', brought an arrant from her, and she wants to see you the first chance she can get; but I wouldn't hurry, either, about goin' there, or anywhere, Miss Gertrude, till I got rested; for I believe you an't well, you look so spent and kind o' tired out."

"Did she wish to see me?" asked Gertrude. "Poor old thing! I'll go and see her, this very afternoon; and you needn't feel anxious about me, Mrs. Prime,—I am quite well."

And Gertrude went. It was now her second day of suspense; and this, like every other motive for action, was eagerly hailed.

She found Miss Patty nearly bent double with rheumatism, dressed with less than her usual care, and crouching over a miserable fire, built of a few chips and shavings. She appeared, however, to be in tolerable spirits, and hailed Gertrude's entrance by a cordial greeting.

The curiosity for which she was always remarkable seemed to have increased, rather than diminished, with the infirmities of age. Innumerable were the questions she put to Gertrude regarding her own personal experiences during the past year, and the movements of the circles in which she had been living. She showed a special interest in Saratoga life, the latest fashions exhibited there, and the opportunities which the place afforded for forming advantageous matrimonial connections.

"So you have not yet chosen a companion," said she, after Gertrude had patiently and good-naturedly responded to all her queries. "That is a circumstance to be regretted. Not," continued she, with a little smirk, and a slight wave of the hand, "that it is ever too late in life for one to meditate the conjugal tie, which is often assumed with advantage by persons of fifty or more; and certainly you, who are still in the bloom of your days, need not despair of a youthful swain. However, existence, I may say, is two-fold when it is shared with a congenial partner; and I had hoped that before now, Miss Gertrude, both you and myself would have formed such an alliance. Experience prompts me, when I declare the protection of the matrimonial union one of its greatest advantages."

"I hope you have not suffered from the want of it." said Gertrude.

"I have, Miss Gertrude, suffered incalculably. Let me impress upon you, however, that the keenest pangs have been those of the sensibilities; yes, the sensibilities,—the finest part of our nature, and that which will least bear wounding."

"I am sorry to hear that you have been thus grieved," said Gertrude. "I should have supposed that, living quite alone, you might have been spared this trial."

"O, Miss Gertrude!" exclaimed the old lady, lifting up both hands, and speaking in such a pitiable tone as would have excited the compassion of her listener, if it had been one grain less ridiculous,—"O, that I had the wings of a dove, wherewith to flee away from my kindred! I fondly thought to have distanced them, but within the last revolving year they have discovered my retreat, and I can no longer elude their vigilance. Hardly can I recover from the shock of one visitation,—made, as I am convinced, for the sole purpose of taking an inventory of my possessions, and measuring the length of my days,—before the vultures are again seen hovering round my dwelling. But," exclaimed the old lady, raising her voice and inwardly chuckling as she spoke, "they shall fall into their own snare; for I will dupe every one of them, yet!"

"I was not aware that you had any relations," said Gertrude; "and it seems they are such only in name."

"Name!" said Miss Pace, emphatically. "I am animated with gladness at the thought that they are not honored with a cognomen which not one of them is worthy to bear. No, they pass by a different name; a name as plebian as their own coarse souls. There are three of them, who stand to each other in a fraternal relation, and all are alike hateful to me. One, a contemptible coxcomb, comes here to overawe me with his presence, which he conceives to be imposing; calls me aunt—aunt; thus testifying by his speech to a consanguinity which he blindly fancies makes him nearer akin to my property!" The old lady, excited to wrath, almost shrieked the last word. "And the other two," continued she, with equal heat, "are beggars! always were,—always will be,—let 'em be,—I'm glad of it!

"You hear me, Miss Gertrude; you are a young lady of quick comprehension, and I avail myself of your contiguity; which, although you deny the charge, may shortly be interrupted by some eager lover, to request at your hands a favor, such as I little thought once I should ever feel compelled to seek. I want you—I sent for you to write (Miss Patty lowered her voice to a whisper) the last will and testament of Miss Patty Pace."

The poor woman's trembling voice evidenced a deep compassion for herself, which Gertrude could not help sharing; and she expressed a willingness to comply with her wishes as far as was in her power, at the same time declaring her utter ignorance of all the forms of law.

To Gertrude's astonishment, Miss Patty announced her own perfect acquaintance with all the legal knowledge which the case demanded; and in so complete and faultless a manner did she dictate the words of the important instrument, that, being afterwards properly witnessed, signed and sealed, it was found at the end of a few months,—at which time Miss Patty was called upon to give up her earthly trust,—free from imperfection and flaw, and proved a satisfactory direction for the disposal of the inheritance.

It may be as well to state here, however, that he who was pronounced sole heir to her really valuable property never availed himself of the bequest, otherwise than to make a careful bestowal of it among the most needy and worthy of her relatives. Notwithstanding the protestations of several respectable individuals who were present at the attestation of the document, all of whom pronounced Miss Patty sane and collected to her last moments, he never would believe that a sound mind could have made so wild and erratic a disposal of the hardly-earned and carefully-preserved savings of years.

This sole inheritor of her estates was William Sullivan, the knight of the rosy countenance; and the same chivalrous spirit which won Miss Patty's virgin heart, and gained for him her lasting favor, prompted him to disclaim and utterly refuse the acceptance of a reward so wholly disproportioned to the slight service he had rendered the old lady.

Though he could not fail to be amused, he was nevertheless deeply touched, by the preamble to the will, in which Miss Patty set forth in a most characteristic manner the feelings and motives which had influenced her in the choice of an heir to her possessions.

"A gentlewoman, of advanced years, who has clung to life and its hopes, and, in spite of many vexatious vicissitudes, feels something loth to depart, has been forcibly reminded by her relations that ere another smiling spring-time she may have a call to join the deceased line of Paces,—a family which will, on her departure, here become extinct. With the most polite of courtesies, and a passing wave of the hand, Miss Patty acknowledges the forethought of her relations of the other branch, in reminding her, before it be too late, of the propriety of naming the individual for whose benefit it is her desire to make a testamentary provision.

"She has looked about the world, viewed all her fellows in the glass of memory, and made her final election. The youth himself—the most gallant young gentleman of his day—will open his eyes in astonishment, and declare, 'Madam, I know you not!' But, sir, Miss Patty, old, ugly and infirm, has a heart which feels as keenly as it did in youth. She has not forgotten— she means now to signify, by her last deeds, how vividly she remembers— the rosy-cheeked youth who once raised her from the frosty earth, took her withered hand, placed it within his vigorous young arm, and, with sunny smiles and cheering words, escorted the rheumatic old woman to a refuge from the wintry elements. Miss Patty has a natural love of courtesy and the deference offered by gay and beautiful youth to helpless and despised old age has touched a sensitive chord. Miss Patty—it is no secret— has some little hoarded treasures; and, since she cannot be on the spot to superintend their expenditure, she has, after some struggles, resolved to secure them from pollution by awarding these savings of years to one possessed of such true gentility as Master William Sullivan, confidently assured that he will never disgrace the former owner of the property, or permit her wealth to flow into vulgar channels."

Then followed an inventory of the estate,—a most remarkable estate, consisting of odds and ends of everything; and finally a carefully and legally worded document, assigning the whole of the strange medley, without legacies or encumbrances, to the sole use and disposal of the appointed heir.

Gertrude found it no easy task to gather and transfix in writing the exact idea which the old woman's rambling dictation was intended to convey; and it was two or three hours before the manuscript was completed, and the patient and diligent scribe permitted to depart.

The sky was overcast, and a drizzling rain beginning to fall, as she commenced walking towards home; but the distance was not great, and the only damage she sustained was a slight dampness to her garments. Emily perceived it at once, however. "Your dress is quite wet," said she. "You must go and sit by the parlor-fire. I shall not go down until tea-time, but father is there, and will be glad of your company; he has been alone all the afternoon."

Gertrude found Mr. Graham sitting in front of a pleasant wood-fire, half dozing, half reading. She took a book and a low chair, and joined him. Finding the heat too great, however, she soon retreated to a sofa, at the opposite side of the room.

Hardly had she done so when there was a ring at the front-door bell. The housemaid, who was passing by the door, opened it, and immediately ushered in a visitor.

It was Willie!

Gertrude rose, but trembling from head to foot, so that she dared not trust herself to take a step forward. Willie advanced into the centre of the room, then looked at Gertrude, bowed, hesitated, and said, "Miss Flint! —is she here?"

The color rushed into Gertrude's face. She attempted to speak, but failed.

It was not necessary. The blush was enough. Willie recognized her, and, starting forward, eagerly seized her hand.

"Gerty! is it possible?"

The perfect naturalness and ease of his manner, the warmth and earnestness with which he took and retained her hand, reässured the agitated girl. The spell seemed partially removed. For a moment he became in her eyes the Willie of old, her dear friend and playmate, and she found voice to exclaim, "O, Willie! you have come at last! I am so glad to see you!"

The sound of their voices disturbed Mr. Graham, who had fallen into a nap, from which the ringing of the door-bell and the entrance of a strange step had failed to arouse him. He turned round in his easy-chair, then rose. Willie dropped Gertrude's hand, and stepped towards him. "Mr. Sullivan," said Gertrude, with a feeble attempt at a suitable introduction.

They shook hands, and then all three sat down.

And now all Gertrude's embarrassment returned. It is not unfrequently the case that when the best of friends meet after a long separation they salute or embrace each other, and then, notwithstanding the weight of matter pressing on the mind of each,—sufficient, perhaps, to furnish subjects of conversation for weeks to come,—nothing of importance presents itself at once, and a pause ensues, which is finally filled up by some most trivial and unimportant question concerning the journey of the newly-arrived party, or the safety of his baggage. But to these latter questions, or any of a similar nature, Gertrude required no answer. She had seen Willie before; she was aware of his arrival; knew even the steamer in which he had come; but was anxious to conceal from him this knowledge. She could not tell him, since he seemed so ignorant of the fact himself, that they had met before; and it may well be imagined that she was at an utter loss what to do or say, under the circumstances. Her embarrassment soon communicated itself to Willie; and Mr. Graham's presence, which was a restraint to both, made matters worse.

Willie, however, first broke the momentary silence. "I should hardly have known you, Gertrude. I did not know you. How—"

"How did you come?" asked Mr. Graham, abruptly, apparently unconscious that he was interrupting Willie's remark.

"In the Europa," replied Willie. "She got into New York about a week ago."

"Out here, I meant," said Mr. Graham, rather stiffly. "Did you come out in the coach?"

"O, excuse me, sir," rejoined Willie; "I misunderstood you. No, I drove out from Boston in a chaise."

"Did any one take your horse?"

"I fastened him in front of the house."

Willie glanced out of the window (it was now nearly dusk) to see that the animal was still where he had left him. Mr. Graham settled himself in his easy-chair, and looked into the fire. There was another pause, more painful than the first.

"You are changed, too," said Gertrude, at last, in reply to Willie's unfinished comment. Then, fearing he might feel hurt at what he must know to be true in more ways than one, the color, which had retreated, mounted once more to her cheeks.

He did not seem to feel hurt, however, but replied, "Yes, an Eastern climate makes great changes; but I think I can hardly have altered more than you have. Why, only think, Gerty, you were a child when I went away! I suppose I must have known I should have found you a young lady, but I begin to think I never fully realized it."

"When did you leave Calcutta?"

"The latter part of February. I passed the spring months in Paris."

"You did not write," said Gertrude, in a faltering voice.

"No, I was expecting to come across by every steamer, and wanted to surprise you."

Conscious that she had probably seemed far less surprised than he expected, she looked confused, but replied, "I was disappointed about the letters, but I am very glad to see you again, Willie."

"You can't be so glad as I am," said he, lowering his voice, and looking at her with great tenderness. "You seem more and more like yourself to me every minute that I see you. I begin to think, however, that I ought to have written, and told you I was coming."

Gertrude smiled. Willie's manner was so unchanged, his words so affectionate, that it seemed unkind to doubt his friendliness, although to his undivided love she felt she could have no claim.

"No," said she, "I like surprises. Don't you remember, I always did?"

"Remember?—Certainly," replied he; "I have never forgotten anything that you liked."

Just at this moment, Gertrude's birds, whose cage hung in the window at which Willie sat, commenced a little twittering noise, which they always made just at night. He looked up. "Your birds," said Gertrude; "the birds you sent me."

"Are they all alive, and well?" asked he.

"Yes, all of them."

"You have been a kind mistress to the little things. They are very tender."

"I am very fond of them."

"You take such care of those you love, dear Gerty, that you are sure to preserve their lives as long as may be."

His tone, still more than his words, betrayed the deep meaning with which he spoke. Gertrude was silent.

"Is Miss Graham well?" asked Willie.

Gertrude related, in reply, that her nerves had been recently much disturbed by the terrible experiences through which she had passed; and this led to the subject of the recent disaster, at which Gertrude forbore to mention her having been herself present.

Willie spoke with feeling of the sad catastrophe, and with severity of the reckless carelessness which had been the cause of it; and ended by remarking that he had valued friends on board the boat, but was unaware that Miss Graham, whom he loved for Gertrude's sake, was among them.

Conversation between Gertrude and Willie had by this time assumed a footing of ease, and something of their former familiarity. The latter had taken a seat near her, on the sofa, that they might talk more unrestrainedly; for, although Mr. Graham might have dropped asleep again, for anything they knew to the contrary, it was not easy wholly to forget his presence. There were many subjects, however, on which it would have seemed natural for them to speak, had not Gertrude purposely avoided them. The causes of Willie's sudden return, his probable stay, his future plans in life, and especially his reasons for having postponed his visit to herself until he had been in the country more than a week;—all these were inquiries which even ordinary interest and curiosity would have suggested; but to Gertrude they all lay under embargo. She neither felt prepared to receive nor willing to force his confidence on matters which must inevitably be influenced by his engagement with Miss Clinton; and therefore preserved utter silence on these topics, even taking pains to avoid them. And Willie, deeply grieved at this strange want of sympathy on her part, forbore to thrust upon her notice these seemingly forgotten or neglected circumstances.

They talked of Calcutta life, of Parisian novelties, of Gertrude's school-keeping, and many other things, but spoke not a word of matters which lay nearest to the hearts of both. At length a servant appeared at the door, and, not observing that there was company, announced tea. Mr. Graham rose, and stood with his back to the fire. Willie rose also, and prepared to take leave. Mr. Graham, with frigid civility, invited him to remain, and Gertrude hesitated not to urge him to do so; but he declined with such decision that the latter understood plainly that he perceived and felt the neglect with which Mr. Graham had treated him and his visit. In addition to the fact that the old gentleman disliked young men as a class, and that Willie had intruded upon the rare and sacred privacy in which he was indulging, there was the bitter and still rankling recollection that Gertrude had once forsaken himself and Emily (for so he, in his own mind, styled her conscientious choice between conflicting duties) for the very family of which their visitor was the only remaining member; a recollection which did not tend to soften or conciliate the easily-prejudiced and obstinate-minded man.

Gertrude accompanied Willie to the door. The rain had ceased, but the wind whistled across the piazza. It seemed to be growing cold. Willie buttoned his coat, while he promised to see Gertrude on the following day.

"You have no overcoat," said she; "the night is chilly, and you are accustomed to a hot climate. You had better take this shawl;" and she took from the hat-tree a heavy Scotch plaid, which always hung there to be used on occasions like the present.

He thanked her, and threw it over his arm; then, taking both her hands in his, looked her steadily in the face for a moment, as if he would fain have spoken. Seeing, however, that she shrank from his mild and affectionate gaze, he dropped her hands, and, with a troubled expression, bade her good-night, and ran down the door-steps.

Gertrude stood with the handle of the door in her hand until she heard the sound of his horse's hoofs as he drove down the road; then, hastily shutting it, ran and hid herself in her own room. Well as she had borne up during the longed-for and yet much-dreaded meeting, calmly and naturally as she had sustained her part, her courage all forsook her now, and in looking forward to days, weeks and months, of frequent intercourse, she felt that the most trying part of the struggle was yet to come.

Had Willie been wholly changed,—had he seemed the thoughtless worldling, the fashionable man of society, the cold-hearted devotee of business or of gain,—in one of which characters she had lately half-fancied he would appear,—had he greeted her with chilling formality, with heartless indifference, or with awkward restraint, she might, while she despised, pitied or blamed, have learned to love him less. But he had come back as he went, open-hearted, generous, manly and affectionate. He had manifested the same unaffected warmth of feeling, the same thoughtful tenderness, he had ever shown. In short, he was the Willie she had thought of, dreamed of, imagined and loved. It was evident that in giving his heart to another he had never wholly forgotten her; while he loved Isabel, he would still feel a friendly, almost a brotherly regard for Gertrude. More than that it had never occurred to him to bestow.

And she must school herself to the cruel task of seeing him day by day, hearing the story of his love for another, and wishing him all joy, as a sister might do a kind and affectionate brother. She must learn to subdue the love whose depth and intensity she had scarcely known until now, and mould it into friendship. As she thought of all this, she found it impossible to still the wildly-beating waves that swelled against her aching, throbbing heart. She threw herself upon the bed, buried her face in pillows, and wept.

Presently there was a light tap at her door. Believing it to be a summons to the tea-table, she said, without rising, "Jane, is that you? I do not wish for any supper."

"It isn't that, miss," said the girl; "but I have brought you a letter."

Gertrude sprung up, and opened the door.

"A little boy handed it to me, and then ran off as fast as he could," said the girl, placing a package in her hand. "He told me to give it to you straight away."

"Bring me a light," said Gertrude.

The girl went for a lamp, Gertrude, in the mean time, endeavoring to judge what a package of such unusual size and thickness could contain. She thought it impossible that any letter could so soon arrive from Mr. Amory. The next morning was the earliest time at which she had expected one. Who, then, could it be from? And, while she was wondering, Jane brought a lamp, by the light of which she at once detected his handwriting; and, breaking the seal, she drew from the envelope several closely-written pages, whose contents she perused with all the eagerness and excitement which the weight, import, and intense interest of the subject, might well demand.

## Chapter XLVI

*There are swift hours in life,—strong, rushing hours,*
*That do the work of tempests in their might!*
HEMANS

It ran as follows:

"MY DAUGHTER,—My loving, tender-hearted girl. Now that your own words encourage me with the assurance that my worst fear was unfounded (the fear that my name was already blasted to your young ears, and your father doomed by your young heart to infamy),—now that I can appeal to you as to an impartial witness, I will disclose the story of my life, and, while I prove to you your parentage, will hope that my unprejudiced child, at least, will believe, love and trust her father, in spite of a world's injustice.

"I will conceal nothing. I will plunge at once into those disclosures which I most dread to utter, and trust to after explanation to palliate the darkness of my tale.

"Mr. Graham is my step-father, and my blessed mother, long since dead, was, in all but the tie of nature, a true mother to Emily. Thus allied, however, to those whom you love best, I am parted from them by a heavy curse; for, not only was mine the ill-fated hand (O, hate me not yet, Gertrude!) which locked poor Emily up in darkness, but, in addition to that horrid deed, I stand accused in the eyes of my fellow-men of another crime, deep, dark and disgraceful. And yet, though living under a ban, wandering up and down the world a doomed and a broken-hearted man, I am innocent as a child of all intentional wrong, as you will learn, if you can trust to the truth of the tale I am about to tell.

"Nature gave and education fostered in me a rebellious spirit. I was the idol of my invalid mother, who, though she loved me with a love for which I bless her memory, had not the energy to tame and subdue the passionate and wilful nature of her boy. Though ungoverned, however, I was neither cruelly nor viciously disposed, and though my sway at home and among my school-fellows was alike indisputable, I made many friends, and not a single enemy. But a sudden check was at length put to my freedom. My mother married, and I soon came to feel, and feel bitterly, the check which her husband, Mr. Graham, was likely to impose upon my boyish independence. Had he treated me with kindness, had he won my affection (which he might easily have done, for my sensitive and impassioned nature disposed me to every tender and grateful emotion), it is impossible to measure the influence he might have had in moulding my yet unformed character.

"But the reverse was the case. His behavior towards me was that of chilling coldness and reserve. He repelled with scorn the first advance on my part, which led me, at my mother's instigation, to address him by the paternal title,—an offence of which I never again was guilty. And yet, while he seemed to ignore the relationship, he assumed its privileges and authority, thus wounding my feelings and my pride, and exciting a spirit of rebellious opposition to his commands.

"Two things served to embitter my sentiments and strengthen my growing dislike for my overbearing step-father. One was the consciousness of my utter dependence upon his bounty; the other, a hint, which I received through the mistaken kindness of a domestic who had always known the family, that Mr. Graham's dislike to me had its origin in an old enmity between himself and my own father,—an honorable and high-minded man, whom it was ever my greatest pride to be told that I resembled.

"Great, however, as was the warfare in my heart, power rested with Mr. Graham; for I was yet but a child, and necessarily subject to government. Nor could I be deaf to my mother's entreaties that, for her sake, I would learn submission. It was only occasionally, therefore, when I had been, as I considered, most unjustly thwarted, that I broke forth into direct rebellion; and even then there were influences ever at work to preserve at least outward harmony in our household. Thus years passed on, and, though I did not learn to love Mr. Graham more, the force of habit, the intense interest afforded by my studies, and a growing capability of self-control, rendered my mode of life far less obnoxious to me than it had once been.

"There was one great compensation for my trials, and that was the love I cherished for Emily, who responded to it with equal warmth on her part. It was not because she stood between me and her father, a mediator and a friend; it was not because she submitted patiently to my dictation, and aided me in all my plans. It was because our natures were made for each other, and, as they grew and expanded, were bound together by ties which a rude hand only could snap and rend asunder. I pause not to dwell upon the tenderness and depth of this affection; it is enough to say that it became the life of my life.

"At length my mother died. I was at that time—sorely against my will—employed in Mr. Graham's counting-house, and still continued an inmate of his family. And now, without excuse or even warning, my step-father commenced a course of policy as unwise as it was cruel; and so irritating to my pride, so torturing to my feelings, and so maddening to my hot nature, that it excited and angered me almost to frenzy. He tried to rob me of the only thing that sweetened and blessed my existence—the love of Emily. I will not here recount the motives I imputed to him, nor the means he employed. It is sufficient to say that they were such as to change my former dislike into bitter hatred,—my unwilling obedience to his will into open and deliberate opposition.

"Instead of submitting to what I considered his tyrannical interference, I sought Emily's society on all occasions, and persuaded the gentle girl to lend herself to my schemes for thwarting her father's purposes. I did not speak to her of love; I did not seek to bind her to me by promises; I hinted not at marriage; a sense of honor forbade it. But, with a boyish independence, which I have since feared was the height of folly and imprudence, I sought every occasion, even in her father's presence, to manifest my determination to maintain that constant freedom and familiarity of intercourse which had been the growth of circumstances, and could not, without force, be restrained.

"At length Emily was taken ill, and for six weeks I was debarred her presence. As soon as she was sufficiently recovered to leave her room, I constantly sought and at last obtained an opportunity to see and speak with her. We had been together in the library more than an hour when Mr. Graham suddenly entered, and came towards us with a face whose harshness and severity I shall not soon forget. I did not heed an interruption, for the probable consequences of which I believed myself prepared. I was little prepared, however, for the nature of the attack actually made upon me.

"That he would accuse me of disobedience to wishes which he had hinted in every possible way, and even intimate more plainly than before his resolve to place barriers between Emily and myself, I fully expected, and was ready with my replies; but when he burst forth with a torrent of unqualified and ungentlemanly abuse,—when he stormed and raved, imputing to me mean, selfish and contemptible motives, which had never for a moment influenced me, or even occurred to my mind,—I was struck dumb with surprise, impatience and anger.

"But this was not all. It was then, in the presence of the pure-minded girl whom I worshipped, that he charged me with a dark and horrid crime, —the crime of forgery,—asserting my guilt as recently discovered, but positive and undoubted. My spirit had raged before,—now it was on fire. I lifted my hand, and clenched my fist. What I would have done I know not. Whether I should have found words to assert my innocence, fling back the lie, and refute a charge as unexpected as it was false,—or whether, my voice failing me from passion, I should have swept Mr. Graham from my path, perhaps felled him to the floor, while I strode away to rally my calmness in the open air,—I cannot now conjecture; for a wild shriek from Emily recalled me to myself, and, turning, I saw her fall fainting upon the sofa.

Forgetting everything then but the apparently dying condition into which the horror of the scene had thrown her, I sprung forward to her relief. There was a table beside her, and some bottles upon it. I hastily snatched what I believed to be a simple restorative, and, in my agitation, emptied the contents of the phial in her face. I know not what the exact character of the mixture could have been; but it matters not,—its effect was too awfully evident. The deed was done,—the fatal deed,—and mine was the hand that did it!

"Brought suddenly to consciousness by the intolerable torture that succeeded, the poor girl sprung screaming from the sofa, flung her arms wildly above her head, rushed in a frantic manner through the room, and finally crouched in a corner. I followed, in an agony scarce less than her own; but she repelled me with her hands, at the same time uttering piercing shrieks. Mr. Graham, who for an instant had looked like one paralyzed by the scene, now rushed forward like a madman. Instead of aiding me in my efforts to lift poor Emily from the floor, and so far from compassionating my situation, which was only less pitiable than hers, he, with a fierceness redoubled at my being, as he considered, the sole cause of the disaster, attacked me with a storm of jeering taunts and cruel reproaches, declaring that I had killed his child. With words like these, which are still ringing in my ears, he drove me from the room and the house; a repulsion which I, overpowered by the misery of contrition and remorse, had neither the wish nor the strength to resist.

"O! the terrible night and day that succeeded! I can give you no idea how they were passed. I wandered out into the country, spent the whole night walking beneath the open sky, endeavoring to collect my thoughts and compose my mind, and still morning found me with a fevered pulse and excited brain. With the returning light, however, I began to realize the necessity of forming some future plan of action.

"Emily's sad situation, and my intense anxiety to learn the worst effects of the fatal accident, gave me the strongest motives for hastening, with the earliest morning, either openly or by stealth, to Mr. Graham's house. Everything also which I possessed,—all my money, consisting merely of the residue of my last quarter's allowance, my clothing, and a few valuable gifts from my mother,—were in the chamber which I had there occupied. There seemed, therefore, to be no other course for me than to return thither once more, at least; and having thus resolved, I retraced my steps to the city, determined, if it were necessary in order to gain the desired particulars concerning Emily, to meet her father face to face. As I drew near the house, however, I hesitated, and dared not proceed. Mr. Graham had exhausted upon me already every angry word, had threatened even deeds of violence, should I ever again cross his threshold: and I feared to trust my own fiery spirit to a collision in which, might be led on to an open resistance of the man whom I had already sufficiently injured.

"In the terrible work I had but yesterday done,—a work of whose fatal effect I had even then a gloomy foreshadowing,—I had blighted the existence of his worshipped child, and drawn a dark pall over his dearest hopes. It was enough. I would not, for worlds, be guilty of the added sin of lifting my hand against the man who, unjust as he had been towards an innocent youth, had met a retaliation far, far too severe.

"Still, I knew his wrath to be unmitigated, was well aware of his power to excite my hot nature to frenzy, and resolved to beware how I crossed his path. Meet him I must, to refute the false charges he had brought against me; but not within the walls of his dwelling, the home of his suffering daughter. In the counting-house, where the crime of forgery was said to have been committed, and in the presence of my fellow-clerks, I would publicly deny the deed, and dare him to its proof. But first I must either see or hear from Emily; before I met the father at all, I must learn the exact nature and extent of the wrong I had done him in the person of his child. For this, however, I must wait, until, under cover of the next night's darkness, I could enter the house unperceived.

"So I wandered about all day in torment, without tasting or even desiring food or rest, the thought of my poor, darling, tortured Emily ever present to my wretched thoughts. The hours seemed interminable. I remember that day of suspense as if it had been a whole year of misery. But night came at last, cloudy, and the air thickened with a heavy fog, which, as I approached the street where Mr. Graham lived, enveloped the neighborhood, and concealed the house until I was directly opposite to it. I shuddered at the sight of the physician's chaise standing before the door; for I knew that Dr. Jeremy had closed his visits to Emily more than a week previously, and must have been summoned to attend her since the accident. Finding him there, and thinking it probable Mr. Graham was also in the house at this hour, I forbore to enter, but stood effectually concealed by the cloud of mist, and watching my opportunity.

"Once or twice Mrs. Ellis, the housekeeper, passed up and down the staircase, as I could distinctly see through the side-lights of the door, which afforded me a full view of the entry-way; and presently Dr. Jeremy descended slowly, followed by Mr. Graham. The doctor would have passed hastily out; but Mr. Graham detained him, to question him regarding his patient, as I judged from the deep anxiety depicted on my step-father's countenance, while, with one hand resting on the shoulder of this old friend of the family, he sought to read his opinion in his face. The doctor's back was towards me, and I could only judge of his replies by the effect they produced on the questioner, whose haggard, worn appearance became more fearfully distressed at every syllable that fell from the honest and truthful lips of the medical man, whose words were oracles to all who knew his skill.

"I needed, therefore, no further testimony to force upon me the conviction that Emily's fate was sealed; and, as I looked with pity upon the afflicted parent, and shudderingly thought how immediate had been my agency in the work of destruction, I felt that the unhappy father could not curse me more bitterly than I cursed myself. Deeply, however, as I mourned, and have never ceased to repent, my share in the exciting of that storm wherein the poor girl had been so cruelly shipwrecked, I could not forget the part that Mr. Graham had borne in the transaction, or forgive the wicked injustice and insults which had so unnerved and unmanned me as to render my hand a fit instrument only of ruin; and as, immediately after the doctor's departure, I watched my step-father also come down the steps and walk away, and saw, by a street-lamp, that the look of pain had passed from his face, giving place to his usual composed, self-complacent and arrogant expression, and understood, by the loud and measured manner in which he struck his cane upon the pavement, that he was far from sharing my humble, penitent mood, I ceased to waste upon him a compassion which he seemed so little to require or deserve; and, pitying myself only, I looked upon his stern face with a soul which cherished for him no other sentiment than that of unmitigated hatred.

"Do not shrink from me, Gertrude, as you read this frank confession of my passionate, and, at that moment, deeply-stirred nature. You know not, perhaps, what it is to hate; but have you ever been tried as I was?

"As Mr. Graham turned the corner of the street, I approached his house, drew forth a pass-key of my own, by means of which I opened the door, and went in. It was perfectly quiet within, and no person was to be seen in any of the lower rooms. I then passed noiselessly up stairs, and entered a little chamber at the head of the passage which communicated with Emily's room. I waited here a long time, hearing no sound and seeing no one. At length, fearing that Mr. Graham would shortly return, I determined to ascend to my own room, which was in the next story, collect my money, and a few articles of value, which I was unwilling to leave behind, and then make my way to the kitchen, and gain what news I could of Emily from Mrs. Prime, the cook, a kind-hearted woman, who would, I felt sure, befriend me.

"The first part of my object was accomplished, and I had descended the back staircase to gain Mrs. Prime's premises, when I suddenly encountered Mrs. Ellis coming from the kitchen, with a bowl of gruel in her hand. This woman was a recent addition to the household, introduced there a few weeks before as a spy upon my actions, and intolerable to me on that account. She was well acquainted with all the particulars of the accident, and had been a witness to my expulsion from the house. She stopped short on seeing me, gave a slight scream, dropped the bowl of gruel, and prepared to make her escape, as if from a wild beast, which I doubt not that I resembled; since wretchedness, fasting, suffering and desperation, must all have been depicted in my features.

"I placed myself in her path, and compelled her to stop and listen to me. But before my eager questions could find utterance, an outburst from her confirmed my worst fears.

"'Let me go!' she exclaimed. 'You villain! you will be putting my eyes out, next!'

"'Where is Emily?' I cried. 'Let me see her!'

"'See her!' replied she. 'You horrid wretch! No! she has suffered enough from you. She is satisfied herself now; so let her alone.'

"'What do you mean?' shouted I, shaking the housekeeper violently by the shoulder, for her words scared my very soul, and I was frantic.

"'Mean?' continued she. 'I mean that Emily will never see anybody again; and, if she had a thousand eyes, you are the last person upon whom she would wish to look!'

"'Does Emily hate me, too?' burst from me then, in the form of a soliloquy rather than a question.

"The reply was ready, however. 'Hate you? Yes,—more than that; she cannot find words that are bad enough for you! She mutters, even in her pain, "cruel!—wicked!" and so on. She even shudders at the sound of your name; and we are all forbidden to speak it in her presence.'

"I waited to hear no more, but, turning, rushed out of the house.

"That moment was the crisis of my life. The thunderbolt had fallen upon and crushed me. My hopes, my happiness, my fortune, my good name, had gone before; but one solitary light had, until now, glimmered in the darkness. It was Emily's love. I had trusted in that,—that only. It had passed away, and with it my youth, my faith, my hope of heaven. I was a blank on the earth, and cared not whither I went, or what became of me.

"From that moment I ceased to be myself. Then fell upon me the cloud in which I have ever since been shrouded, and under the shadow of which you have seen and known me. In that instant the blight had come, under the gnawing influence of which my happy laugh changed to the bitter smile; my frank and pleasant speech to tones of ill-concealed irony and sarcasm; my hair became prematurely gray, my features sharp, and oftentimes severe; my fellow-men, to whom it had been my noblest hope to prove some day a benefactor, were henceforth the armed hosts of antagonists, with whom I would wage endless war; and the God whom I had worshipped,—whom I had believed in, as a just and faithful friend and avenger,—who was He?—where was He?—and why did He not right my cause? What direful and premeditated deed of darkness had I been guilty of, that He should thus desert me? Alas!—greatest of all misfortunes,—I lost my faith in Heaven!

"I know not what direction I took on leaving Mr. Graham's house. I have no recollection of any of the streets through which I passed, though doubtless they were all familiar; but I paused not, until, having reached the end of a wharf, I found myself gazing down into the deep water, longing to take one mad leap, and lose myself in everlasting oblivion!

"But for this final blow, beneath which my manhood had fallen, I would have cherished my life, at least until I could vindicate its fair fame; I would never have left a blackened memory for men to dwell upon, and for Emily to weep over. But now what cared I for my fellow-men? And Emily!—she had ceased to love, and would not mourn; and I longed for nothingness and the grave.

"There are moments in human life when a word, a look, or a thought, may weigh down the balance in the scales of fate, and decide a destiny.

"So was it with me now. I was incapable of forming any plan for myself; but accident, as it were, decided for me. I was startled from the apathy into which I had fallen by the sudden splashing of oars in the water beneath, and in a moment a little boat was moored to a pier within a rod of the spot where I stood. At the same instant I heard quick footsteps on the wharf, and, turning, saw by the light of the moon, which was just appearing from behind a heavy cloud, a stout, sea-faring man, with a heavy pea-jacket under one arm, and an old-fashioned carpet-bag in his left hand. He had a ruddy, good-humored face, and as he approached, and was about to pass me and leap into the boat, where two sailors, with their oars dipped and ready for motion, were awaiting him, he slapped me heartily on the shoulder, and exclaimed, 'Well, my fine fellow, will you ship with us?'

"I answered as readily in the affirmative; and, with one look in my face, and a glance at my dress, which seemed to assure him of my station in life, and probable ability to make compensation for the passage, he said, in a laughing tone, 'In with you, then!'

"To his astonishment,—for he had scarcely believed me in earnest,—I sprang into the boat, and in a few moments was on board of a fine bark, bound I knew not whither.

"The vessel's destination proved to be Rio Janeiro; a fact which I did not learn, however, till we had been two or three days at sea, and to which, even then, I felt wholly indifferent. There was one other passenger beside myself,—the captain's daughter, Lucy Grey, whom, during the first week, I scarcely noticed, but who appeared to be as much at home, whether in the cabin or on deck, as if she had passed her whole life at sea. I might, perhaps, have made the entire passage without giving another thought to this young girl,—half child, half woman,—had not my strange and mysterious behavior led her to conduct in a manner which at first surprised, and finally interested me. My wild and excited countenance, my constant restlessness, avoidance of food, and apparent indifference to everything that went on about me, excited her wonder and sympathy to the utmost. She at first believed me partially deranged, and treated me accordingly. She would take a seat on deck directly opposite mine, look in my face for an hour, either ignorant or regardless of my observing her, and then walk away with a heavy sigh. Occasionally she would come and offer me some little delicacy, begging that I would try and eat; and as, touched by her kindness, I took food more readily from her hand than any other, these little attentions became at last habitual. As my manners and looks grew calmer, however, and I settled into a melancholy, which, though equally deep, was less fearful than the feverish torment under which I had labored, she became proportionately reserved; and when, at last, I began to appear somewhat like my fellow-men, went regularly to the table, and, instead of pacing the deck all night, spent a part of it, at least, quietly in my state-room, Lucy absented herself wholly from that part of the vessel where I passed the greater portion of the day, and I seldom exchanged a word with her, unless I purposely sought her society.

"We experienced much stormy weather, however, which drove me to the cabin, where she usually sat on the transom, reading, or watching the troubled waves; and, as the voyage was very long, we were necessarily thrown much in each other's way, especially as Captain Grey, the same individual who had invited me to ship with him, and who seemed still to take an interest in my welfare, good-naturedly encouraged an intercourse by which he probably hoped I might be won from a state of melancholy that seemed to astonish and grieve the jolly ship-master almost as much as it did his kind-hearted, sensitive child.

"Lucy's shyness, therefore, wore gradually away, and before our tedious passage was completed I ceased to be a restraint upon her. She talked freely with, or rather to me; for while, notwithstanding her occasional intimations of curiosity, I maintained a rigid silence concerning my own past experiences, of which I could scarcely endure to *think,* much less to *speak,* she exerted herself freely for my entertainment, and related, with simple frankness, almost every circumstance of her past life. Sometimes I listened attentively; sometimes, absorbed in my own painful reflections, I would be deaf to her voice, and forgetful of her presence. In the latter case, I would often observe, however, that she had suddenly ceased speaking, and, starting from my revery, and looking quickly up, would find her eyes fixed upon me so reproachfully that, rallying my self-command, I would endeavor to appear, and not unfrequently really became, seriously interested in the artless narratives of my little entertainer. She told me that until she was fourteen years old she lived with her mother in a little cottage on Cape Cod, their home being only occasionally enlivened by the return of her father from his long absences at sea. They would then usually make a visit to the city where his vessel lay, pass a few weeks in uninterrupted enjoyment, and at length return home to mourn the departure of the cheerful, light-hearted sea-captain, and patiently count the weeks and months until he would come back again.

"She told me how her mother died at last; how bitterly she mourned her loss; and how her father wept when he came home and heard the news; how she had lived on ship-board ever since; and how sad and lonely she felt in time of storms, when, the master at his post of duty, she sat alone in the cabin, listening to the roar of the winds and waves.

"Tears would come into her eyes when she spoke of these things, and I would look upon her with pity, as one whom sorrow made my sister. Trial, however, had not yet robbed her of an elastic, buoyant spirit; and when, five minutes after the completion of some eloquent little tale of early grief, the captain would approach unseen, and surprise her by a sudden joke, exclamation, or sly piece of mischief, thus provoking her to retaliate, she was always ready and alert for a war of wits, a laughing frolic, or even a game of romps. Her sorrow forgotten, and her tears dried up, her merry voice and her playful words would delight her father, and the cabin or the deck would ring with his joyous peals of laughter; while I, shrinking from a mirth and gayety sadly at variance with my own unhappiness, and the sound of which was discordant to my sensitive nerves, would retire to brood over miseries for which it was hopeless to expect sympathy, which could not be shared, and with which I must dwell alone.

"Such a misanthrope had my misfortunes made me that the sportive raillery between the captain and his merry daughter, and the musical laugh with which she would respond to the occasional witticisms of one or two old and privileged sailors, grated upon my ears like something scarce less than personal injuries; nor could I have believed it possible that one so little able as Lucy to comprehend the depth of my sufferings could feel any sincere compassion for them, had I not once or twice been touched to see how her innocent mirth would give place to sudden gravity and sadness of countenance, if she chanced unexpectedly to encounter my woe-begone face, rendered doubly gloomy when contrasted with the gayety of herself and her companions.

"But I must not linger too long upon the details of our life on shipboard; for I have to relate events which occupied many years, and must confine myself, as far as possible, to a concise statement of facts. I must forbear giving any account of a terrific gale that we encountered, during which, for two days and a night, poor Lucy was half-frantic with fear, while I, careless of outward discomforts, and indifferent to personal danger, was afforded an opportunity to requite her kindness by such protection and encouragement as I was able to render. But this, and various other incidents of the voyage, all bore a part in inspiring her with a degree of confidence in me, which, by the time we arrived in port, was put to a severe and somewhat embarrassing test.

## Chapter XLVII

*Do not spurn me*
*In my prayer!*
*For this wandering, ever longer, evermore,*
*Hath overworn me,*
*And I know not on what shore*
*I may rest from my despair.*

E. B. BROWNING

"Captain Grey died. We were within a week's sail of our destination when he was taken ill, and three days before we were safely anchored in the harbor of Rio he breathed his last. I shared with Lucy the office of ministering to the suffering man, closed his eyes at last, and carried the fainting girl in my arms to another part of the vessel. With kind words and persuasions I restored her to her senses; and then, as the full consciousness of her desolation rushed upon her, she sunk at once into a state of hopeless despondency, more painful to witness than her previous condition of utter insensibility. Captain Grey had made no provision for his daughter; indeed, it would have been impossible for him to do so, as the state of his affairs afterwards proved. Well might the poor girl lament her sad fate! for she was without a relative in the world, penniless, and approaching a strange shore, which afforded no refuge to the orphan. We buried her father in the sea; and, that sad office fulfilled, I sought Lucy, and endeavored, as I had several times tried to do without success, to arouse her to a sense of her situation, and advise with her concerning the future; for we were now so near our port that in a few hours we might be compelled to leave the vessel and seek quarters in the city. She listened to me without replying.

"At length I hinted at the necessity of my leaving her, and begged to know if she had any plans for the future. She answered me only by a burst of tears.

"I expressed the deepest sympathy for her grief, and begged her not to weep.

"And then, with many sobs, and interrupting herself by frequent outbreaks and exclamations of vehement sorrow, she threw herself upon my compassion, and, with unaffected simplicity and child-like artlessness, entreated me not to leave, or, as she termed it, to desert her. She reminded me that she was all alone in the world; that the moment she stepped foot on shore she should be in a land of strangers; and, appealing to my mercy, besought me not to forsake and leave her to die alone.

"What could I do? I had nothing on earth to live for. We were both alike orphaned and desolate. There was but one point of difference. I could work and protect her; she could do neither for herself. It would be something for *me* to live for; and for *her,* though but a refuge of poverty and want, it was better than the exposure and suffering that must otherwise await her. I told her plainly how little I had to offer; that my heart even was crushed and broken; but that I was ready to labor in her behalf, to guard her from danger, to pity, and, perhaps, in time, learn to love her.

"The unsophisticated girl had never thought of marriage; she had sought the protection of a friend, not a husband; but I explained to her that the latter tie only would obviate the necessity of our parting; and, in the humility of sorrow, she finally accepted my unflattering offer.

"The only confidant to our sudden engagement, the only witness of the marriage, which, within a few hours, ensued, was a veteran mariner, an old, weather-beaten sailor, who had known and loved Lucy from her childhood, and whose name will be, perhaps, familiar to you,—Ben Grant. He accompanied us on shore, and to the church, which was our first destination. He followed us to the humble lodgings with which we contrived for the present to be contented, and devoted himself to Lucy with self-sacrificing, but in one instance, alas! (as you will soon learn) with mistaken and fatal zeal.

"After much difficulty, I obtained employment from a man in whom I accidentally recognized an old and valued friend of my father. He had been in Rio several years, was actively engaged in trade, willingly employed me as clerk, occasionally despatching me from home to transact business at a distance. My duties being regular and profitable, we were soon not only raised above want, but I was enabled to place my young wife in a situation that insured comfort, if not luxury.

"The sweetness of her disposition, the cheerfulness with which she endured privation, the earnestness with which she strove to make me happy, were not without effect. I perseveringly rallied from my gloom; I succeeded in banishing the frown from my brow; and the premature wrinkles, which her little hand would softly sweep away, finally ceased to return. The few months that I passed with your mother, Gertrude, form a sweet epistle in the memory of my stormy life. I came to love her much,—not as I loved Emily; that could not be expected,—but, as the solitary flower that bloomed on the grave of all my early hopes, she cast a fragrance round my path; and her child is not more dear to me because a part of myself than as the memento of the cherished blossom, snatched hastily from my hand, and rarely crushed.

"About two months after your birth, my child, and before your eyes had ever learned to brighten at the sight of your father, who was necessarily much from home, the business in which I was engaged called me, in the capacity of an agent, to a station of some distance from Rio. I had been absent nearly a month, had extended my journey beyond my original intentions, and had written regularly to Lucy, informing her of all my movements (though I have since believed that the letters never reached her, when the neighborhood in which I was stationed became infected with a fatal malaria. For the sake of my family, I took every measure to ward off contagion, but failed. I was seized with the terrible fever, and lay for weeks at the point of death. I was cruelly neglected during my illness; for I had no friends near me, and my slender purse held out little inducement for mercenary service, but my sufferings and forebodings on account of Lucy and yourself were far greater than any which I endured from my bodily torments, although the latter were great indeed. I conjured up every fear that the imagination could conceive; but nothing, alas! which could compare with the reality that awaited me, when, after an almost interminable illness, I made my way, destitute, ragged and emaciated, back to Rio. I sought my former home. It was deserted, and I was warned to flee from its vicinity, as the fearful disease of which I had already been the prey had nearly depopulated that and the neighboring streets. I made every inquiry, but could obtain no intelligence of my wife and child. I hastened to the horrible charnel-house where, during the raging of the pestilence, the unrecognized dead were exposed; but, among the disfigured and mouldering remains, it was impossible to distinguish friends from strangers. I lingered about the city for weeks, in hopes to gain some information concerning Lucy; but could find no one who had ever heard of her. All day I wandered about the streets and on the wharves,—the latter being places which Ben Grant (in whose faithful charge I had left your mother and yourself) was in the habit of frequenting,—but not a syllable could I learn of any persons that answered my description.

"My first thought had been that they would naturally seek my employer, to learn, if possible, the cause of my prolonged absence; and, on finding my home empty, I had hastened in search of him. But he too had, within a recent period, fallen a victim to the prevailing distemper. His place of business was closed, and the establishment broken up. I prolonged my search and continued my inquiries until hope died within me. I was assured that scarce an inmate of the fatal neighborhood where I had left my family had escaped the withering blast; and convinced, finally, that my fate was still pursuing me with an unmitigated wrath, of which this last blow was but a single expression, that I might have foreseen and expected, I madly agreed to work my passage in the first vessel which promised me an escape from scenes so fraught with harrowing recollections.

"And now commenced in truth that course of wretched wandering, which, knowing neither pause nor cessation, has made up the sum of my existence. With varied ends in view, following strongly-contrasted employments, and with fluctuating fortune, I have travelled over the world. My feet have trodden almost every land; I have sailed upon every sea, and breathed the air of every clime. I am familiar with the city and the wilderness, the civilized man and the savage. I have learned the sad lesson that peace is nowhere, and friendship for the most part but a name. If I have taught myself to hate, shun and despise humanity, it is because I know it well.

"Once, during my wanderings, I visited the home of my boyhood. Unseen and unknown I trod familiar ground, and gazed on familiar though time-worn faces. I stood at the window of Mr. Graham's library; saw the contented, happy countenance of Emily,—happy in her blindness and her forgetfulness of the past. A young girl sat near the fire, endeavoring to read by its flickering light. I knew not then what gave such a charm to her thoughtful features, nor why my eyes dwelt upon them with a rare pleasure; for there was no voice to proclaim to the father's heart that he looked on the face of his child. I am not sure that the strong impulse which prompted me then to enter, acknowledge my identity, and beg Emily to speak to me a word of forgiveness, might not have prevailed over the dread of her displeasure; but Mr. Graham at the moment made his appearance, cold and implacable as ever; I looked upon him an instant, then fled from the house, and the next day departed for other lands.

"Although, in the various labors which I was compelled to undertake, to earn for myself a decent maintenance, I had more than once met with such success as to give me temporary independence, and enable me to indulge myself in expensive travelling, I had never amassed a fortune; indeed, I had not cared to do so, since I had no use for money, except to employ it in the gratification of my immediate wants. Accident, however, at last thrust upon me a wealth which I could scarcely be said to have sought.

"After a year spent in the wilderness of the west, amid adventures the relation of which would seem to you almost incredible, I gradually continued my retreat across the country, and, after encountering innumerable hardships in a solitary journey, which had in it no other object than the indulgence of my vagrant habits, I found myself in that land which has recently been termed the land of promise, but which has proved to many a greedy emigrant a land of falsehood and deceit. For me, however, who sought it not, it showered gold. I was among the earliest discoverers of its treasure-vaults,—one of the most successful, though the least laborious of the seekers after gain. Nor was it merely, or indeed chiefly, at the mines that fortune favored me. With the first results of my labors I chanced to purchase an immense tract of land, little dreaming at the time that those desert acres were destined to become the streets and squares of a great and prosperous city.

"So it was, however; and without effort, almost without my own knowledge, I achieved the greatness which springs from untold wealth.

"But this was not all. The blessed accident which led me to this golden land was the means of disclosing a pearl of price, a treasure in comparison with which California and all its mines shrink to my mind into insignificance. You know how the war-cry went forth to all lands, and men of every name and nation brought their arms to the field of fortune. Famine came next, with disease and death in its train; and many a man, hurrying on to reap the golden harvest, fell by the way-side, without once seeing the waving of the yellow grain.

"Half scorning the greedy rabble, I could not refuse, in this my time of prosperity, to minister to the wants of such as fell in my way; and now, for once, my humanity found its own reward.

"A miserable, ragged, half-starved and apparently dying man crept to the door of my tent (for these were the primitive days, when that land afforded no better habitation), and asked in a feeble voice for charity. I did not refuse to admit him into my narrow domicile, and to the extent of my ability relieve his suffering condition. He proved to be the victim of want rather than disease, and, his hunger appeased, the savage brutality of his coarse nature soon manifested itself in the dogged indifference with which he received a stranger's bounty, and the gross ingratitude with which he abused my hospitality. A few days sufficed to restore him to his full strength; and then, anxious to dismiss my visitor, whose conduct had already excited suspicions of his good faith, I gave him warning that he must depart; at the same time placing in his hands a sufficient amount of gold to insure his support until he could reach the mines, which were his professed destination.

"He appeared dissatisfied, and begged permission to remain until the next morning, as the night was near, and he had no shelter provided. To this I made no objection, little imagining how base a serpent I was harboring. At midnight I was awakened from my light and easily-disturbed sleep, to find my lodger busily engaged in rifling my property, and preparing to take an unceremonious leave of my dwelling. Nor did his villany end here. Upon my seizing and charging him with the theft, he snatched a weapon which lay near at hand, and attempted the life of his benefactor. I was prepared, however, to ward off the stroke, and by means of my superior strength succeeded in a few moments in subduing and mastering my desperate antagonist. He now crouched at my feet in such abject and mean submission as might have been expected from so contemptible a knave. Well might he tremble with fear; for the lynch-law was then in full force, and summary in its execution of justice upon criminals like him. I should probably have handed the traitor over to his fate, but, ere I had time to do so, he by chance held out to my cupidity a bribe so tempting, that I forgot the deservings of my knavish guest in the eagerness with which I bartered his freedom as the price of its possession.

"He freely emptied his pockets at my bidding, and restored to me the gold, for the loss of which I never should have repined. As the base metal rolled at my feet, however, there glittered among the coins a jewel as truly *mine* as any of the rest, but which, as it met my sight, filled me with greater surprise and rapture than if it had been a new-fallen star.

"It was a ring of peculiar design and workmanship, which had once been the property of my father, and after his death had been worn by my mother until the time of her marriage with Mr. Graham, when it was transferred to myself. I had ever prized it as a precious heirloom, and it was one of the few valuables which I took with me when I fled from my stepfather's house. This ring, with a watch and some other trinkets, had been left in the possession of Lucy when I parted with her at Rio, and the sight of it once more seemed to me like a voice from the grave. I eagerly sought to learn from my prisoner the source whence it had been obtained, but he maintained an obstinate silence. It was now my turn to plead, and at length the promise of instant permission to depart, 'unwhipped by justice,' at the conclusion of his tale, wrung from him a secret fraught to me with vital interest. What I learned from him, in disjointed and often incoherent phrases, I will relate to you in few words.

"This man was Stephen Grant, the son of my old friend Ben. He had heard from his father's lips the story of your mother's misfortunes; and the circumstance of a violent quarrel, which arose between Ben and his vixen wife, at the young stranger's introduction to their household, impressed the tale upon his recollection. From his account, it appeared that my long-continued absence from Lucy, during the time of my illness, was construed by her honest but distrustful counsellor and friend into voluntary and cruel desertion. The poor girl, to whom my early life was all a mystery which she had never shared, and to whom much of my character and conduct was consequently inexplicable, began soon to feel convinced of the correctness of the old sailor's suspicions and fears. She had already applied to my employer for information concerning me; but he, who had heard of the pestilence to which I was exposed, and fully believed me to be among the dead, forbore to distress her by a communication of his belief, and replied to her questionings with an obscurity which served to give new force to her hitherto vague and uncertain surmises. She positively refused, however, to leave our home; and, clinging to the hope of my final return thither, remained where I had left her until the terrible fever began its ravages. Her small stock of money was by this time consumed; her strength both of mind and body gave way; and Ben, becoming every day more confident that the simple-hearted Lucy had been betrayed and forsaken, persuaded her at last to sell her furniture, and with the sum thus raised flee the infected country before it should be too late. She sailed for Boston in the same vessel in which Ben shipped before the mast; and on reaching that port her humble protector took her immediately to the only home he had to offer.

"There your mother's sad fate found a mournful termination, and you, her infant child, were left to the mercy of the cruel woman, who, but for her consciousness of guilt and her fear of its betrayal, would doubtless have thrust you at once from the miserable shelter her dwelling afforded. This guilt consisted in a foul robbery committed by Nan and her already infamous son upon your innocent and hapless mother, now rendered, through her feebleness, an easy prey to their rapacity. The fruits of this vile theft, however, were never participated in by Nan, whose promising son so far exceeded her in duplicity and craft, that, having obtained possession of the jewels for the alleged purpose of bartering them away, he reserved such as he thought proper, and appropriated to his own use the proceeds of the remainder.

"The antique ring which I now hold in my possession, the priceless relic of a mournful tragedy, would have shared the fate of the rest, but for its apparent worthlessness. To the luckless Stephen, however, it proved at last a temporary salvation from the felon's doom which must finally await that hardened sinner; and to me—ah! to *me*—it remains to be proved whether the knowledge of the secrets to which it has been the key will bless my future life, or darken it with a heavier curse! Notwithstanding the information thus gained, and the exciting idea to which it gave rise, that my child might be still living and finally restored to me, I could not yet feel any security that these daring hopes were not destined to be crushed in their infancy, and that my newly-found treasure might not again elude my eager search. To my inquiries concerning you, Gertrude, Stephen, who had no longer any motives for concealing the truth, declared his inability to acquaint me with any particulars of a later period than the time of your residence with Trueman Flint. He knew that the lamplighter had taken you to his home, and was accidentally made aware, a few months later, of your continuance in that place of refuge, from the old man's being (to use my informant's expression) such a confounded fool as to call upon his mother and voluntarily make compensation for injury done to her windows in your outburst of childish revenge.

"Further than this I could learn nothing; but it was enough to inspire all my energies, and fill me with one desire only,—the recovery of my child. I hastened to Boston, had no difficulty in tracing your benefactor, and, though he had been long since dead, found many a truthful witness to his well-known virtues. Nor, when I asked for his adopted child, did I find her forgotten in the quarter of the city where she had passed her childhood. More than one grateful voice was ready to respond to my questioning, and to proclaim the cause they had to remember the girl who, having experienced the trials of poverty, made it both the duty and the pleasure of her prosperity to administer to the wants of a neighborhood whose sufferings she had aforetime both witnessed and shared.

"But, alas! to complete the sum of sad vicissitudes with which my unhappy destiny was already crowded, at the very moment when I was assured of my daughter's safety, and my ears were drinking in the sweet praises that accompanied the mention of her name, there fell upon me like a thunder-bolt the startling words, 'She is now the adopted child of sweet Emily Graham, the blind girl.'

"O, strange coincidence! O, righteous retribution! which, at the very moment when I was picturing to myself the consummation of my cherished hopes, crushed me once more beneath the iron hand of a destiny that would not be cheated of its victim!

"My child, my only child, bound by the gratitude and love of years to one in whose face I scarcely dared to look, lest my soul should be withered by the expression of condemnation which the consciousness of my presence would inspire!

"The seas and lands, which had hitherto divided us, seemed not to my tortured fancy so insurmountable a barrier between myself and my long-lost daughter, as the dreadful reflection that the only earthly being whose love I had hoped in time to win had been reared from her infancy in a household where my very name was a thing abhorred.

"Stung to the quick by the harrowing thought that all my prayers, entreaties and explanations, could never undo her early impressions, and that all my labors and all my love could never call forth other than a cold and formal recognition of my claims, or, worse still, a feigned and hypocritical pretence of filial affection, I half resolved to leave my child in ignorance of her birth, and never seek to look upon her face, rather than subject her to the terrible necessity of choosing between the friend whom she loved and the father from whose crimes she had learned to shrink with horror and dread.

"After wrestling and struggling long with contending and warring emotions, I resolved to make one endeavor to see and recognize you, Gertrude, and at the same time guard myself from discovery. I trusted (and, as it proved, not without reason) to the immense change which time had wrought in my appearance, to conceal me effectually from all eyes but those which had known me intimately; and therefore approached Mr. Graham's house without the slightest fear of betrayal. I found it empty, and apparently deserted.

"I now directed my steps to the well-remembered counting-room, and here learned, from a clerk (who was, as it proved, but ill-informed concerning the movements of his master's family), that the whole household, including yourself, had been passing the winter in Paris, and were at present at a German watering-place. Without hesitation, or further inquiry, I took the steamer to Liverpool, and from thence hastened to Baden-Baden,—a trifling excursion in the eyes of a traveller of my experience.

"Without risking myself in the presence of my step-father, I took an early opportunity to obtain an introduction to Mrs. Graham, and, thanks to her unreserved conversation, made myself master of the fact that Emily and yourself were left in Boston, and were, at that time, under the care of Dr. Jeremy.

"It was on my return voyage, which was immediately undertaken, that I made the acquaintance of Dr. Gryseworth and his daughter,—an acquaintance which accidentally proved of great value in facilitating my intercourse with yourself.

"Once more arrived in Boston, Dr. Jeremy's house also wore a desolate appearance, and looked as if closed for the season. There was a man, however, making some repairs about the door-steps, who informed me that the family were absent from town. He was not himself aware of the direction they had taken; but the servants were at home, and could, no doubt, acquaint me with their route. Upon this, I boldly rung the door-bell. It was answered by Mrs. Ellis, the woman who, nearly twenty years before, had cruelly and unpityingly sounded in my ears the death-knell of all my hopes in life. I saw at once that my incognito was secure, as she met my keen and piercing glance without quailing, shrinking or taking flight, as I fully expected she would do at sight of the ghost of my former self.

"She replied to my queries as coolly and collectedly as she had probably done during the day to some dozen of the doctor's disappointed patients,—telling me that he had left that very morning for New York, and would not be back for two or three weeks.

"Nothing could have been more favorable to my wishes than the chance thus afforded of overtaking your party, and, in the character of a travelling companion, introducing myself gradually to your notice.

"You know how this purpose was effected; how, now in the rear and now in advance, I nevertheless maintained a constant proximity to your footsteps. To add one particle to the comfort of yourself and Emily,—to learn your plans, forestall your wishes, secure to your use the best of rooms, and bribe to your service the most devoted of attendants,—I spared myself neither pains, fatigue, trouble, nor expense.

"For much of the freedom with which I approached you, and made myself an occasional member of your circle, I was indebted to Emily's blindness; for I could not doubt that otherwise time and its changes would fail to conceal from her my identity, and I should meet with a premature recognition. Nor, until the final act of the drama, when death stared us all in the face, and concealment became impossible, did I once trust my voice to her hearing.

"How closely, during those few weeks, I watched and weighed your every word and action, seeking even to read your thoughts in your face, none can tell whose acuteness is not sharpened and vivified by motives so all-engrossing as mine; and who can measure the anguish of the fond father, who, day by day, learned to worship his child with a more absorbing idolatry, and yet dared not clasp her to his heart!

"Especially when I saw you the victim of grief and trouble did I long to assert a claim to your confidence; and more than once my self-control would have given way, but for the dread inspired by the gentle Emily—gentle to all but me. I could not brook the thought that with my confession I should cease to be the trusted friend, and become the abhorred parent. I preferred to maintain my distant and unacknowledged guardianship of my child, rather than that she should behold in me the dreaded tyrant who might tear her from the home from which he had himself been driven, and the hearts which, though warm with love for *her*, were ice and stone to *him*.

"And so I kept silent; and, sometimes present to your sight, but still oftener hid from view, I hovered around your path, until that dreadful day, which you will long remember, when, everything forgotten but the safety of yourself and Emily, my heart spoke out, and betrayed my secret.

"And now you know all,—my follies, misfortunes, sufferings and sins!

"Can you love me, Gertrude? It is all I ask. I seek not to steal you from your present home—to rob poor Emily of a child whom she values perhaps as much as I. The only balm my wounded spirit seeks is the simple, guileless confession that you will at least *try* to love your father.

"I have no hope in this world, and none, alas! beyond, but in yourself. Could you feel my heart now beating against its prison-bars, you would realize, as I do, that unless soothed it will burst ere long. Will you soothe it by your pity, my sweet, my darling child? Will you bless it by your love? If so, come, clasp your arms around me, and whisper to me words of peace. Within sight of your window, in the old summer-house at the end of the garden, with straining ear, I wait listening for your footsteps."

## Chapter XLVIII

*Around her path a vision's glow is cast,*
*Back, back her lost one comes in hues of morn!*
*For her the gulf is filled, the dark night fled,*
*Whose mystery parts the living and the dead.*

HEMANS

As Gertrude's eyes, after greedily devouring the manuscript, fell upon its closing words, she sprung to her feet, and the next instant her little room (the floor strewed with the scattered sheets, which had dropped from her lap as she rose) is left vacant. She has flown down the staircase, escaped through the hall-door, and, bounding over a lawn at the back of the house, now wet with the evening dew, she approaches the summer-house from the opposite entrance to that at which Mr. Amory, with folded arms and a fixed countenance, is watching for her coming.

So noiseless is her light step, that, before he is conscious of her presence, she has thrown herself upon his bosom, and, her whole frame trembling with the vehemence of long-suppressed and now uncontrolled agitation, she bursts into a torrent of passionate tears, interrupted only by frequent sobs, so deep and so exhausting that her father, with his arms folded tightly around her, and clasping her so closely to his heart that she feels its irregular beating, endeavors to still the tempest of her grief, whispering softly, as to an infant, "Hush! hush, my child! you frighten me!"

And, gradually soothed by his gentle caresses, her excitement subsides, and she is able to lift her face to his, and smile upon him through her tears. They stand thus for many minutes, in a silence that speaks far more than words. Wrapped in the folds of his heavy cloak to preserve her from the evening air, and still encircled in his strong embrace, Gertrude feels that their union of spirit is not less complete; while the long-banished man, who for years has never felt the sweet influence of a kindly smile, glows with a melting tenderness which hardening solitude has not had the power to subdue.

Again and again the moon retires behind a cloud, and peeps out to find them still in the attitude in which she saw them last. At length, as she gains a broad and open expanse, and looks clearly down, Mr. Amory, lifting his daughter's face, and gazing into her glistening eyes, while he gently strokes the disordered hair from her forehead, asks, in an accent of touching appeal, "You will love me, then?"

"O, I do! I do!" exclaimed Gertrude, sealing his lips with kisses.

His hitherto unmoved countenance relaxes at this fervent assurance. He bows his head upon her shoulder, and the strong man weeps.

Not long, however. Her self-possession all restored at seeing him thus overcome, Gertrude places her hand in his, and startles him from his position by the firm and decided tone with which she whispers, "Come!"

"Whither?" exclaims he, looking up in surprise.

"To Emily."

With a half shudder, and a mournful shake of the head, he retreats, instead of advancing in the direction in which she would lead him.—"I cannot."

"But she waits for you. She, too, weeps and longs and prays for your coming."

"Emily!—you know not what you are saying, my child!"

"Indeed, indeed, my father, it is you who are deceived. Emily does not hate you; she never did. She believed you dead long ago; but your voice, though heard but once, has half robbed her of her reason, so wholly, so entirely does she love you still. Come, and she will tell you, better than I can, what a wretched mistake has made martyrs of you both."

Emily, who had heard the voice of Willie Sullivan, as he bade Gertrude farewell on the door-step, and rightly conjectured that it was he, forbore making any inquiries for the absent girl at the tea-table, and, thinking it probable that she preferred to remain undisturbed, retired to the sitting-room at the conclusion of the meal, where (as Mr. Graham sought the library) she remained alone for more than an hour.

It was a delightful, social-looking room. The fire still burned brightly, sending forth a ruddy glow, and (as the evening was unusually chilly for the season) rendering the temperature of the great old-fashioned parlor highly agreeable. There were candles under the mirror, but they did not give light enough to destroy the pleasant effect of the shadows which the fire-light made upon the wall and about the couch where Emily was reclining.

The invalid girl, if we may call her such (for, in spite of ill health, she still retained much of the freshness and all the loveliness of her girlhood), had, by chance, chosen such a position, opposite to the cheerful blaze, that its flickering light played about her face, and brought to view the rich and unwonted bloom which inward excitement had called up in her usually pale countenance. The exquisite and refined taste which always made Emily's dress an index to the soft purity of her character was never more strikingly developed than when she wore, as on the present occasion, a flowing robe of white cashmere, fastened at the waist with a silken girdle, and with full, drapery sleeves, whose lining and border of snowy silk could only have been rivalled by the delicate hand and wrist which had escaped from beneath their folds, and somewhat nervously played with the heavy crimson fringe of a shawl, worn in the chilly dining-room, and now thrown carelessly over the arm of the sofa.

Supporting herself upon her elbow, she sat with her head bent forward, and, as she watched the images reflected in the glass of memory, one who knew her not, and was unaware of her want of sight, might have believed that, looking forth from her long, drooping eyelashes, she were tracing imaginary forms among the shining embers, so intently was her face bent in that direction.

Occasionally, as the summer wind sighed among the branches of the trees, causing them to beat lightly against the window-pane, she would lift her head from the hand on which it rested, and, gracefully arching her slender throat, incline in a listening attitude; and then, as the trifling nature of the sound betrayed itself, she would sink, with a low sigh, into her former somewhat listless position. Once Mrs. Prime opened the door, looked around the room in search of the housekeeper, and, not finding her, retreated across the passage, saying to herself, as she did so, "Law! dear sakes alive! I wish she only had eyes now, to see how like a picter she looks!"

At length a low, quick bark from the house-dog once more attracted her attention, and in a moment steps were heard crossing the piazza.

Before they had gained the door, Emily was standing upright, straining her ear to catch the sound of every foot-fall; and, when Gertrude and Mr. Amory entered, she looked more like a statue than a living figure, as, with clasped hands, parted lips, and one foot slightly advanced, she silently awaited their approach.

One glance at Emily's face, another at that of her agitated father, and Gertrude was gone. She saw the completeness of their mutual recognition, and, with instinctive delicacy, forbore to mar by her presence the sacredness of so holy an interview.

As the door closed upon her retreating figure, Emily parted her clasped hands, stretched them forth into the dim vacancy, and murmured "Philip!"

He seized them between both of his, and, with one step forward, fell upon his knees. As he did so, the half-fainting girl dropped upon the seat behind her. Mr. Amory bowed his head upon the hands, which, still held tightly between his own, now rested on her lap; and, hiding his face upon her slender fingers, tremblingly uttered her name.

"The grave has given up its dead!" exclaimed Emily. "My God, I thank thee!" and, extricating her hands from his convulsive grasp, she flung her arms around his neck, rested her head upon his bosom, and whispered, in a voice half choked with emotion, "Philip!—dear, dear Philip! am I dreaming, or have you come back again?"

The conventional rules, the enforced restrictions, which often set limits to the outbursts of natural feeling, had no existence for one so wholly the child of nature as Emily. She and Philip had loved each other in their childhood; before that childhood was fully past, they had parted; and as children they met again. During the lapse of many years, in which, shut out from the world, she had lived among the cherished memories of the past, she had been safe from worldly contagion, and had retained all the guileless simplicity of girlhood,—all the freshness of her spring-time; and Philip, who had never willingly bound himself by any ties save those imposed upon him by circumstance and necessity, felt his boyhood come rushing upon him once more, as, with Emily's soft hand resting on his head, she blessed Heaven for his safe return. She could not see how time had silvered his hair, and sobered and shaded the face that she loved. Whether he came in the shape of the fiery-eyed youth that she saw him last, the middle-aged man, with hoary hair, whose years the curious found it hard to determine, or the glorified angel which she had pictured to herself in every dream of heaven, it was all alike to one whose world was a world of spirits.

And to him, as he beheld the face he had half dreaded to encounter beaming with the holy light of sympathy and love, the blind girl's countenance seemed encircled with a halo not of earth. And, therefore, this union had in it less of earth than heaven. Had they wakened on the other side the grave, and soul met soul in that happy land where the long-parted meet, their rapture could scarcely have been more pure, their happiness more unalloyed.

Not until, seated beside each other, with their hands still fondly clasped, Philip had heard from Emily's lips the history of her hopes, her fears, her prayers and her despair, and she, while listening to the sad incidents of his life, had dropped upon the hand she held many a kiss and tear of sympathy, did either fully realize the mercy, so long delayed, so fully accorded now, which promised even on earth to crown their days.

Emily wept at the tale of Lucy's trials and her early death; and when she learned that it was hers and Philip's child whom she had taken to her heart, and fostered with the truest affection, she sent up a silent prayer of gratitude that it had been allotted to her apparently bereaved and darkened destiny to fulfil so blest a mission.

"If I could love her more, dear Philip," exclaimed she, while the tears trickled down her cheeks, "I would do so, for your sake, and that of her sweet, innocent, suffering mother."

"And you forgive me, then, Emily?" said Philip, as, both having finished their sad recitals of the past, they gave themselves up to the sweet reflection of their present joy.

"Forgive?—O, Philip! what have I to forgive?"

"The deed that locked you in prison darkness," he mournfully replied.

"Philip!" exclaimed Emily, in a reproachful tone, "could you for one moment believe that I attributed that to you?—that I blamed you, for an instant, even in my secret thought?"

"Not willingly, I am sure, dear Emily. But, O, you have forgotten what I can never forget,—that in your time of anguish, not only the obtruding thought, but the lip that gave utterance to it, proclaimed how your soul refused to pity and forgive the cruel hand that wrought you so much woe!"

"You cruel, Philip! Never, even in my wild frenzy, did I so abuse and wrong you. If my unfilial heart sinfully railed against the cruel injustice of my father, it was never guilty of such treachery towards you."

"That fiendish woman lied, then, when she told me that you shuddered at my very name?"

"If I shuddered, Philip, it was because my whole nature recoiled at the thought of the wrong that you had sustained; and O, believe me, if she gave you any other assurance than of my continued love, it was because she labored under a sad and unhappy error."

"Good heavens!" ejaculated Philip. "How wickedly have I been deceived!"

"Not wickedly," replied Emily. "Mrs. Ellis, with all her stern formality, was, in that instance, the victim of circumstances. She was a stranger among us, and believed you other than you were; but, had you seen her a few weeks later, sobbing over her share in the unhappy transaction which drove you to desperation, and, as we then supposed, to death, you would have felt, as I did, that we had greatly misjudged her in return, and that she carried a heart of flesh beneath a stony disguise. The bitterness of her grief astonished me at the time; for I never until now had reason to suspect that it was mingled with remorse at the recollection of her own harshness. Let us forget, however, the sad events of the past, and trust that the loving hand which has thus far shaped our course has but afflicted us in mercy."

"In mercy?" exclaimed Philip. "What mercy does my past experience give evidence of, or your life of everlasting darkness? Can you believe it a loving hand which made me the ill-fated instrument, and you the life-long sufferer, from one of the dreariest misfortunes that can afflict humanity?"

"Speak not of my blindness as a misfortune," answered Emily; "I have long ceased to think it such. It is only through the darkness of the night that we discern the lights of heaven, and only when shut out from earth that we enter the gates of Paradise. With eyes to see the wonderful working of nature and nature's God, I nevertheless closed them to the evidences of almighty love that were around me on every side. While enjoying the beautiful and glorious gifts that were showered on my pathway, I forgot to thank and praise the Giver; but, with an ungrateful heart, walked sinfully and selfishly on, little dreaming of the beguiling and deceitful snares which entangle the footsteps of youth.

"And therefore did He, who is ever over us for good, arrest with fatherly hand the child who was wandering from the only road that leads to peace; and, though the discipline of his chastening rod was sudden and severe, mercy still tempered justice. From the tomb of my buried joys sprang hopes that will bloom in immortality. From the clouds and the darkness broke forth a glorious light. What was hidden from my outer sight became manifest to my awakened soul, and even on earth my troubled spirit gained its eternal rest. Then grieve not, dear Philip, over the fate that, in reality, is far from sad; but rejoice with me in the thought of that blessed and not far distant awakening, when, with restored and beautified vision, I shall stand before God's throne, in full view of that glorious Presence, from which, but for the guiding light which has burst upon my spirit through the veil of earthly darkness, I might have been eternally shut out."

As Emily finished speaking, and Philip, gazing with awe upon the rapt expression of her soul-illumined face, beheld the triumph of an immortal mind, and pondered on the might, the majesty and power, of the influence wrought by simple piety, the door of the room opened abruptly, and Mr. Graham entered.

The sound of the well-known footstep disturbed the soaring thoughts of both, and the flush of excitement which had mounted into Emily's cheeks subsided into more than her wonted paleness, as Philip, rising slowly and deliberately from his seat at her side, stood face to face with her father.

Mr. Graham approached with the puzzled and scrutinizing air of one who finds himself called upon in the character of a host to greet a visitor who, though an apparent stranger, may possibly have claims to recognition, and glanced at his daughter as if hoping she would relieve the awkwardness by an introduction. But the agitated Emily maintained perfect silence, and every feature of Philip's countenance remained immovable as Mr. Graham slowly came forward.

He had advanced within one step of the spot where Philip stood waiting to receive him, when, struck by the stern look and attitude of the latter, he stopped short, gazed one moment into the eagle eyes of his step-son, then staggered, grasped at the mantel-piece, and would have fallen; but Philip, starting forward, helped him to his arm-chair, which stood opposite to the sofa.

And yet no word was spoken. At length Mr. Graham, who, having fallen into the seat, sat still gazing into the face of Mr. Amory, ejaculated, in a tone of wondering excitement, "Philip Amory! O, my God!"

"Yes, father," exclaimed Emily, suddenly rising and grasping her father's arm. "It is Philip; he, whom we have so long believed among the dead, restored to us in health and safety!"

Mr. Graham rose from his chair, and, leaning heavily on Emily's shoulder, again approached Mr. Amory, who, with folded arms, stood fixed as marble. His step tottered with a feebleness never before observable in the sturdy frame of the old man, and the hand which he extended to Philip was marked by an unusual tremulousness.

But Philip did not offer to receive the proffered hand, or reply by word to the rejected salutation.

Mr. Graham turned towards Emily, and, forgetting that this neglect was shut from her sight, exclaimed, half-bitterly, half-sadly, "I cannot blame him! God knows I wronged the boy!"

"Wronged him!" cried Philip, in a voice so deep as to be almost fearful. "Yes, wronged him, indeed! Blighted his life, crushed his youth, half-broke his heart, and wholly blasted his reputation!"

"No," exclaimed Mr. Graham, who had quailed beneath these accusations, until he reached the final one. "Not that, Philip! not that! I never harmed you there. I discovered my error before I had doomed you to infamy in the eyes of one of your fellow-men."

"You acknowledge, then, the error?"

"I do, I do! I imputed to you the deed which proved to have been accomplished through the agency of my most confidential clerk. I learned the truth almost immediately; but too late, alas! to recall you. Then came the news of your death, and I felt that the injury had been irreparable. But it was not strange, Philip; you must allow that. Archer had been in my employment more than twenty years. I had a right to believe him trustworthy."

"No! O, no!" replied Philip. "It was nothing strange that, a crime committed, you should have readily ascribed it to me. You thought me capable only of evil."

"I was unjust, Philip," answered Mr. Graham, with an attempt to rally his dignity, "but I had some cause,—I had some cause."

"Perhaps so," responded Philip; "I am willing to grant that."

"Let us shake hands upon it, then," said Mr. Graham, "and endeavor to forget the past."

Philip did not again refuse to accede to this request, though there was but little warmth or eagerness in the manner of his compliance.

Mr. Graham, seeming now to think the matter quite ended, looked relieved, and as if he had shaken off a burden which had been weighing upon his conscience for years (for he had a conscience, though not a very tender one); and, subsiding into his arm-chair, begged to learn the particulars of Philip's experience during the last twenty years.

The outline of the story was soon told; Mr. Graham listening to it with attention, and inquiring into its particulars with an interest which proved that, during a lengthened period of regret and remorse, his feelings had sensibly softened towards the step-son with every memory of whom there had come to his heart a pang of self-reproach.

Mr. Amory was unable to afford any satisfactory explanation of the report of his own death, which had been confidently affirmed by Dr. Jeremy's correspondent at Rio. Upon a comparison of dates, however, it seemed probable that the doctor's agent had obtained this information from Philip's employer, who, for some weeks previous to his own death, had every reason to believe that the young man had perished of the infection prevailing in the low and unhealthy region to which he had been despatched.

To Philip himself it was an almost equal matter of wonder that his friends should ever have obtained knowledge of his flight and destination. But this was more easily accounted for, since the vessel in which he had embarked returned directly to Boston, and there were among her crew and officers those who had ample means of replying to the inquiries which the benevolent doctor had set on foot some months before, and which, being accompanied by the offer of a liberal reward, had not yet ceased to attract the attention of the public.

Notwithstanding the many strange and romantic incidents which were unfolding themselves, none seemed to produce so great an impression upon Mr. Graham's mind as the singular circumstance that the child who had been reared under his roof, and endeared herself to him, in spite of some clashing of interests and opinions, should prove to be Philip's daughter. As he left the room, at the conclusion of the tale, and again sought the solitude of his library, he muttered to himself more than once, "Singular coincidence! Very singular! Very!"

Hardly had he departed, before another door was timidly opened, and Gertrude looked cautiously in.

Her father went quickly towards her, and, passing his arm around her waist, drew her towards Emily, and clasped them both in a long and silent embrace.

"Philip," exclaimed Emily, "can you still doubt the mercy and love which have spared us for such a meeting?"

"O, Emily!" replied he, "I am deeply grateful. Teach me how and where to bestow my tribute of praise."

On the hour of sweet communion which succeeded we forbear to dwell;—the silent rapture of Emily, the passionately-expressed joy of Philip, or the trusting, loving glances which Gertrude cast upon both.

It was nearly midnight when Mr. Amory rose, and announced his intention to depart. Emily, who had not thought of his leaving the spot which she hoped he would now consider his home, entreated him to remain; and Gertrude, with her eyes, joined in the eager petition. But he persisted in his resolution with a firmness and seriousness which proved how vain would be the attempt to shake it.

"Philip," said Emily, at length, laying her hand upon his arm, "you have not yet forgiven my father."

She had divined his thoughts. He shrank under her reproachful tones, and made no answer.

"But you *will*, dear Philip,—you *will*," continued she, in a pleading voice.

He hesitated, then glanced at her once more, and replied, "I will, dearest Emily, I will—in time."

When he had gone, Gertrude lingered a moment at the door, to watch his retreating figure, just visible in the light of the waning moon; then returned to the parlor, drawing a long breath and saying, "O, what a day this has been!" but checked herself, at the sight of Emily, who, kneeling by the sofa, with clasped hands, uplifted face, and with her white garments sweeping the floor, looked the very impersonation of purity and prayer.

Throwing one arm around her neck, Gertrude knelt on the floor beside her, and together they sent up to the throne of God the incense of thanksgiving and praise!

❀❀❀❀❀❀❀❀❀❀❀❀❀❀❀❀❀❀❀❀❀❀❀❀❀❀❀❀

## Chapter XLIX

*Thee have I loved, thou gentlest, from a child,*
*And borne thine image with me o'er the sea,—*
*Thy soft voice in my soul,—speak! O, yet live for me!*
                                                    HEMANS

When Uncle True died, Mr. Cooper reverently buried his old friend in the ancient grave-yard which adjoined the church where he had long officiated as sexton. It was a dilapidated-looking place, whose half-fallen and moss-grown stones proclaimed its recent neglect and disuse. But long before the adjacent and time-worn building gave place to a modern and more imposing structure the hallowed remains of Uncle True had found a quieter resting-place.

With that good taste and good feeling which, in latter days, has dedicated to the sacred dead some of the fairest spots on earth, a beautiful piece of undulating woodland in the neighborhood of Mr. Graham's country residence had been consecrated as a rural cemetery, and in the loveliest nook of this sweet and venerated spot the ashes of the good old lamplighter found their final repose.

This lot of land, which had been purchased through Willie's thoughtful liberality, selected by Gertrude, and by her made fragrant and beautiful with summer rose and winter ivy, now enclosed also the forms of Mr. Cooper and Mrs. Sullivan; and over these three graves Gertrude had planted many a flower, and watered it with her tears. Especially did she view it as a sacred duty and privilege to mark the anniversary of the death of each by a tribute of fresh garlands; and, with this pious purpose in view, she left Mr. Graham's house one beautiful afternoon, about a week after the events took place which are narrated in the previous chapter.

She carried on her arm a basket, which contained her offering of flowers; and, as she had a long walk before her, started at a rapid pace. Let us follow her, and briefly pursue the train of thought which accompanied her on her way.

She had left her father with Emily. She would not ask him to join her in her walk, though he had once expressed a desire to visit the grave of Uncle True; for he and Emily were talking together so contentedly, it would have been a pity to disturb them; and for a few moments Gertrude's reflections were engrossed by the thought of their calm and tranquil happiness. She thought of herself, too, as associated with them both; of the deep and long-tried love of Emily, and of the fond outpourings of affection daily and hourly lavished upon her by her newly-found parent, and felt that she could scarcely repay their kindness by the devotion of a lifetime.

Now and then, as she dwelt in her musings upon the sweet tie between herself and Emily, which had gained strength with every succeeding year, and the equally close and kindred union between father and child, which, though recent in its origin, was scarcely capable of being more firmly cemented by time, her thoughts would, in spite of herself, wander to that earlier-formed and not less tender friendship, now, alas! sadly ruptured and wounded, if not wholly uprooted and destroyed. She tried to banish the remembrance of Willie's faithlessness and desertion, deeming it the part of an ungrateful spirit to mourn over past hopes, regardless of the blessings that yet remained. She tried to keep in mind the resolutions lately formed to forget the most painful feature in her past life, and consecrate the remainder of her days to the happiness of her father and Emily.

But it would not do. The obtruding and painful recollection presented itself continually, notwithstanding her utmost efforts to repress it, and at last, ceasing the struggle, she gave herself up for the time to a deep and saddening revery.

She had received two visits from Willie since the one already mentioned; but the second meeting had been in its character very similar to the first, and on the succeeding occasion the constraint had increased, instead of diminishing. Several times Willie had made an apparent effort to break through this unnatural barrier, and speak and act with the freedom of former days; but a sudden blush, or sign of confusion and distress, on Gertrude's part, deterred him from any further attempt to put to flight the reserve and want of confidence which subsisted in their intercourse. Again, Gertrude, who had resolved, previous to his last visit, to meet him with the frankness and cordiality which he might reasonably expect, smiled upon him affectionately at his coming, and offered her hand with such sisterly freedom, that he was emboldened to take and retain it in his grasp, and was evidently on the point of unburdening his mind of some weighty secret, when she turned abruptly away, took up some trivial piece of work, and, while she seemed wholly absorbed in it, addressed to him an unimportant question;—a course of conduct which put to flight all his ideas, and disconcerted him for the remainder of his stay.

As Gertrude pondered the awkward and distressing results of every visit he had made her, she half hoped he would discontinue them altogether; believing that the feelings of both would be less wounded by a total separation than by interviews which must leave on the mind of each a still greater sense of estrangement.

Strange as it may seem, she had not yet acquainted him with the event so deep in its interest to herself,—the discovery of her dearly-loved father. Once she tried to speak of it, but found herself so overcome, at the very idea of imparting to the confidant of her childhood an experience of which she could scarcely yet think without emotion, that she paused in the attempt, fearing that, should she, on any topic, give way to her sensibilities, she should lose all restraint over her feelings, and lay open her whole heart to Willie.

But there was one thing that distressed her more than all others. In his first vain attempt to throw off all disguise, Willie had more than intimated to her his own unhappiness; and, ere she could find an opportunity to change the subject, and repel a confidence for which she still felt herself unprepared, he had gone so far as to speak mournfully of his future prospects in life.

The only construction which Gertrude could give to this confession was that it had reference to his engagement with Isabel; and it gave rise at once to the suspicion that, infatuated by her beauty, he had impulsively and heedlessly bound himself to one who could never make him wholly happy. The little scenes to which she had herself been a witness corroborated this idea, as, on both occasions of her seeing the lovers and overhearing their words, some cause of vexation seemed to exist on Willie's part.

"He loves her," thought Gertrude, "and is also bound to her in honor; but he sees already the want of harmony in their natures. Poor Willie! It is impossible he should ever be happy with Isabel."

And Gertrude's sympathizing heart mourned not more deeply over her own grief than over the disappointment that Willie must be experiencing, if he had ever hoped to find peace in a union with so overbearing, ill-humored and unreasonable a girl.

Wholly occupied with these and similar musings, she walked on with a pace of whose quickness she was scarcely herself aware, and soon gained the shelter of the heavy pines which bordered the entrance to the cemetery. Here she paused for a moment to enjoy the refreshing breeze that played beneath the branches; and then, passing through the gateway, entered a carriage-road at the right, and proceeded slowly up the gradual ascent. The place, always quiet and peaceful, seemed unusually still and secluded, and, save the occasional carol of a bird, there was no sound to disturb the perfect silence and repose. As Gertrude gazed upon the familiar beauties of those sacred grounds, which had been her frequent resort during several years,—as she walked between beds of flowers, inhaled the fragrant and balmy air, and felt the solemn appeal, the spiritual breathings, that haunted the holy place,—every emotion that was not in harmony with the scene gradually took its flight, and she experienced only that sensation of sweet and half-joyful melancholy which was awakened by the thought of the happy dead.

After a while, she left the broad road which she had been following, and turned into a little by-path. This she pursued for some distance; and then, again diverging through another and still narrower foot-track, gained the shady and retired spot which, partly from its remoteness to the public walks, and partly from its own natural beauty, had attracted her attention and recommended itself to her choice. It was situated on the slope of a little hill; a huge rock protected it on one side from the observation of the passer-by, and a fine old oak overshadowed it upon the other. The iron enclosure, of simple workmanship, was nearly overgrown by the green ivy, which had been planted there by Gertrude's hand, and the moss-grown rock also was festooned by its graceful and clinging tendrils. Upon a jutting piece of stone, directly beside the grave of Uncle True, Gertrude seated herself, as was her wont, and after a few moments of contemplation, during which she sat with her elbow upon her knee and her head resting upon her hand, she straightened her slight figure, sighed heavily, and then, lifting the cover of her basket, emptied her flowers upon the grass, and with skilful fingers commenced weaving a graceful chaplet, which, when completed, she placed upon the grave at her feet. With the remainder of the blossoms she strewed the other mounds; and then, drawing forth a pair of gardening-gloves and a little trowel, she employed herself for nearly an hour among the flowers and vines with which she had embowered the spot.

Her work at last being finished, she again placed herself at the foot of the old rock, removed her gloves, pushed back from her forehead the simple but heavy braids of her hair, and appeared to be resting from her labors.

It was seven years that day since Uncle True died, but the time had not yet come for Gertrude to forget the simple, kind old man. Often did his pleasant smile and cheering words come to her in her dreams; and both by day and night did the image of him who had gladdened and blessed her childhood encourage her to the imitation of his humble and patient virtue. As she gazed upon the grassy mound that covered him, and scene after scene rose up before her in which that earliest friend and herself had whiled away the happy hours, there came, to embitter the otherwise cherished remembrance, the recollection of that third and seldom absent one, who completed and made perfect the memory of their fireside joys; and Gertrude, while yielding to the inward reflection, unconsciously exclaimed aloud, "O, Uncle True! you and I are not parted yet; but Willie is not of us!"

"O, Gertrude," said a reproachful voice close at her side; "is Willie to blame for that?"

She started, turned, saw the object of her thoughts with his mild sad eyes fixed inquiringly upon her, and, without replying to his question, buried her face in her hands.

He threw himself upon the ground at her feet, and, as on the occasion of their first childish interview, gently lifted her bowed head from the hands upon which it had fallen, and compelled her to look him in the face, saying, at the same time, in the most imploring accents, "Tell me, Gerty, in pity tell me why am I excluded from your sympathy?"

But still she made no reply, except by the tears that coursed down her cheeks.

"You make me miserable," continued he, vehemently. "What have I done that you have so shut me out from your affection? Why do you look so coldly upon me,—and even shrink from my sight?" added he, as Gertrude, unable to endure his steadfast, searching look, turned her eyes in another direction, and strove to free her hands from his grasp.

"I am not cold,—I do not mean to be," said she, her voice half-choked with emotion.

"O, Gertrude," replied he, relinquishing her hands, and turning away, "I see you have wholly ceased to love me. I trembled when I first beheld you, so lovely, so beautiful, and so beloved by all, and feared lest some fortunate rival had stolen your heart from its boyish keeper. But even then I did not dream that you would refuse me, at least, a *brother's* claim to your affection."

"I will not," exclaimed Gertrude eagerly. "O, Willie, you must not be angry with me! Let me be your sister!"

He smiled a most mournful smile. "I was right, then," continued he; "you feared lest I should claim too much, and discouraged my presumption by awarding me nothing. Be it so. Perhaps your prudence was for the best; but O, Gertrude, it has made me heart-broken!"

"Willie," exclaimed Gertrude, with excitement, "do you know how strangely you are speaking?"

"Strangely?" responded Willie, in a half-offended tone. "Is it so strange that I should love you? Have I not for years cherished the remembrance of our past affection, and looked forward to our reünion as my only hope of happiness? Has not this fond expectation inspired my labors, and cheered my toils, and endeared to me my life, in spite of its bereavements? And can you, in the very sight of these cold mounds, beneath which lie buried all else that I held dear on earth, crush and destroy, without compassion, this solitary but all engrossing—"

"Willie," interrupted Gertrude, her calmness suddenly restored, and speaking in a kind but serious tone, "is it honorable for you to address me thus? Have you forgotten—"

"No, I have *not* forgotten," exclaimed he, vehemently. "I have not forgotten that I have no right to distress or annoy you, and I will do so no more. But, O, Gerty! my sister Gerty (since all hope of a nearer tie is at an end), blame me not, and wonder not, if I fail at present to perform a brother's part. I cannot stay in this neighborhood. I cannot be the patient witness of another's happiness. My services, my time, my life, you may command, and in my far-distant home I will never cease to pray that the husband you have chosen, whoever he be, may prove himself worthy of my noble Gertrude, and love her one-half as well as I do!"

"Willie," said Gertrude, "what madness is this? I am bound by no such tie as you describe; but what shall I think of your treachery to Isabel?"

"To Isabel?" cried Willie, starting up, as if seized with a new idea. "And has that silly rumor reached *you* too? and did you put faith in the falsehood?"

"Falsehood!" exclaimed Gertrude, lifting her hitherto drooping eyelids, and casting upon him, through their wet lashes, a look of earnest scrutiny.

Calmly returning a glance which he had neither avoided nor quailed under, Willie responded, unhesitatingly, and with a tone of astonishment not unmingled with reproach, "Falsehood?—Yes. With the knowledge you have both of her and myself, could you doubt its being such for a moment?"

"O, Willie!" cried Gertrude, "could I doubt the evidence of my own eyes and ears? Had I trusted to less faithful witnesses, I might have been deceived. Do not attempt to conceal from me the truth to which my own observation can testify. Treat me with frankness, Willie!—Indeed, indeed, I deserve it at your hands!"

"Frankness, Gertrude! It is you only who are mysterious. Could I lay my whole soul bare to your gaze, you would be convinced of its truth, its perfect truth, to its first affection. And as to Isabel Clinton, if it is to her that you have reference, your eyes and your ears have both played you false, if—"

"O, Willie! Willie!" exclaimed Gertrude, interrupting him, "have you so soon forgotten your devotion to the belle of Saratoga; your unwillingness to sanction her temporary absence from your sight; the pain which the mere suggestion of the journey caused you, and the fond impatience which threatened to render those few days an eternity?"

"Stop! stop!" cried Willie, a new light breaking in upon him, "and tell me where you learned all this."

"In the very spot where you spoke and acted. Mr. Graham's parlor did not witness our first meeting. In the public promenade-ground, on the shore of Saratoga lake, and on board the steamboat at Albany, did I both see and recognize you—myself unknown. There too did your own words serve to convince me of the truth of that which from other lips I had refused to believe."

The sunshine which gilds the morning is scarcely more bright and glad-some than the glow of rekindled hope which now animated the face of Willie.

"Listen to me, Gertrude," said he, in a fervent and almost solemn tone, "and believe that in sight of my mother's grave, and in the presence of that pure spirit (and he looked reverently upward) who taught me the love of truth, I speak with such sincerity and candor as are fitting for the ears of angels. I do not question the accuracy with which you overheard my expostulations and entreaties on the subject of Miss Clinton's proposed journey, or the impatience I expressed at parting for her speedy return. I will not pause, either, to inquire where the object of all my thoughts could have been at the time, that, notwithstanding the changes of years, she escaped my eager eyes. Let me first clear myself of the imputation under which I labor, and then there will be room for all further explanations.

"I did, indeed, feel deep pain at Miss Clinton's sudden departure for New York, under a pretext which ought not to have weighed with her for a moment. I did indeed employ every argument to dissuade her from her purpose; and when my eloquence had failed to induce the abandonment of the scheme, I availed myself of every suggestion and motive which might possibly influence her to shorten her absence. Not because the society of the selfish girl was essential, or even conducive, to my own happiness,—far from it,—but because her excellent father, who so worshipped and idolized his only child that he would have thought no sacrifice too great by means of which he could add one particle to her enjoyment, was, at that very time, amid all the noise and discomfort of a crowded watering-place, hovering between life and death, and I was disgusted at the heartlessness which voluntarily left the fondest of parents deprived of all female tending, to the charge of a hired nurse, and an unskilful though willing youth like myself. That eternity might, in Miss Clinton's absence, set a seal to the life of her father, was a thought which, in my indignation, I was on the point of uttering; but I checked myself, unwilling to interfere too far in a matter which came not within my rightful province, and perhaps excite unnecessary alarm in Isabel. If selfishness mingled at all in my views, dear Gerty, and made me over-impatient for the return of the daughter to her post of duty, it was that I might be released from almost constant attendance upon my invalid friend, and hasten to her from whom I hoped such warmth of greeting as I was only too eager to bestow. Can you wonder, then, that your reception struck cold upon my throbbing heart?"

"But you understand the cause of that coldness now," said Gertrude, looking up at him through a rain of tears, which, like a summer sun-shower, reflected itself in rainbow smiles upon her happy countenance. "You know now why I dared not let my heart speak out."

"And this was all, then?" cried Willie; "and you are free, and I may love you still?"

"Free from all bonds, dear Willie, but those which you yourself clasped around me, and which have encircled me from my childhood."

And now, with heart pressed to heart, they pour in each other's ear the tale of a mutual affection, planted in infancy, nourished in youth, fostered and strengthened amid separation and absence, and perfected through trial, to bless and sanctify every year of their after life.

"But, Gerty," exclaimed Willie, as, confidence restored, they sat side by side, conversing freely of the past, "how could you think, for an instant, that Isabel Clinton would have power to displace you in my regard? I was not guilty of so great an injustice towards you; for, even when I believed myself supplanted by another, I fancied that other some hero of such shining qualities as could scarcely be surpassed."

"And who could surpass Isabel?" inquired Gerty. "Can you wonder that I trembled for your allegiance, when I thought of her beauty, her fashion, her family and her wealth, and remembered the forcible manner in which all these were presented to your sight and knowledge?"

"But what are all these, Gerty, to one who knows her as we do? Do not a proud eye and a scornful lip destroy the effect of beauty? Can fashion excuse rudeness, or noble birth cover natural deficiencies? And, as to money, what did I ever want of that, except to employ it for the happiness of yourself—and them?"—and he glanced at the graves of his mother and grandfather.

"O, Willie! You are so disinterested!"

"Not in this case. Had Isabel possessed the beauty of a Venus and the wisdom of a Minerva, I could not have forgotten how little happiness there could be with one who, while devoting herself to the pursuit of pleasure, had become dead to natural affections, and indifferent to the holiest of duties. Could I see her flee from the bed-side of her father to engage in the frivolities and drink in the flatteries of an idle crowd,—or, when unwillingly summoned thither, shrink from the toils and the watchings imposed by his feebleness,—and still imagine that such a woman could bless and adorn a fireside? Could I fail to contrast her unfeeling neglect, ill-concealed petulance, flagrant levity and irreverence of spirit, with the sweet and loving devotion, the saintly patience, and the deep and fervent piety, of my own Gertrude? I should have been false to myself, as well as to you, dearest, if such traits of character as Miss Clinton constantly evinced could have weakened my love and admiration for yourself. And now, to see the little playmate whose image I cherished so fondly matured into the lovely and graceful woman, her sweet attractions crowned by so much beauty as almost to place her beyond recognition, and still her heart as much my own as ever!—O, Gerty, it is too much happiness! Would that I could impart a share of it to those who loved us both so well!"

And who can say that they did not share it?—that the spirit of Uncle True was not there, to witness the completion of his many hopeful prophecies? that the old grandfather was not there, to see all his doubts and fears giving place to joyful certainties? and that the soul of the gentle mother, whose rapt slumbers had, even in life, foreshadowed such a meeting, and who, by the lessons she had given her child in his boyhood, the warnings spoken to his later years, and the ministering guidance of her disembodied spirit, had fitted him for the struggle with temptation, sustained him through its trials, and restored him triumphant to the sweet friend of his infancy,—who shall say that, even now, she hovered not over them with parted wings, realizing the joy prefigured in that dreamy vision which pictured to her sight the union between the son and daughter of her love, when the one, shielded by her fond care from every danger, and snatched from the power of temptation, should be restored to the arms of the other, who, by long and patient continuance in well-doing, had earned so full a recompense, so all-sufficient a reward?

## Chapter L

*"Through night to light—in every stage,*
*From childhood's morn to hoary age,*
*What shall illume the pilgrimage*
*By mortals trod?*

*"There is a pure and heavenly ray,*
*That brightest shines in darkest day,*
*When earthly beams are quenched for aye;*
*'T is lit by God."*

The sun was casting long shadows, and the sunset hour was near, when Gertrude and Willie rose to depart. They left the cemetery by a different gateway, and in the opposite direction to that by which Gertrude had entered. Here Willie found the chaise in which he had come, though the horse had contrived to loosen the bridle by which he was fastened; had strayed to the side of the road, eaten as much grass as he wished, or the place afforded, and was now sniffing the air, looking up and down the road, and, despairing of his master's return, seemed on the point of taking his departure.

He was reclaimed, however, without difficulty, and, as if glad after his long rest to be again in motion, brought them in half an hour to Mr. Graham's door.

As soon as they came in sight of the house, Gertrude, familiar with the customary ways of the family, perceived that something unusual was going forward. Lamps were moving about in every direction; the front-door stood wide open; there was, what she had never seen before, the blaze of a bright fire discernible through the windows of the best chamber; and, as they drew still nearer, she observed that the piazza was half covered with trunks.

All these appearances, as she rightly conjectured, betokened the arrival of Mrs. Graham, and possibly of other company. She might, perhaps, have regretted the ill-timed coming of this bustling lady, at the very moment when she was eager for a quiet opportunity to present Willie to Emily and her father, and communicate to them her own happiness; but, if such a thought presented itself, it vanished in a moment. Her joy was too complete to be marred by so trifling a disappointment.

"Let us drive up the avenue, Willie," said she, "to the side-door, so that George may see us, and take your horse to the stable."

"No," said Willie, as he stopped opposite the front gate; "I can't come in now—there seems to be a house full of company; and, besides, I have an appointment in town at eight o'clock, and promised to be punctual;"—he glanced at his watch as he spoke, and added, "it is near that already. I did not think of its being so late; but I shall see you to-morrow morning, may I not?" She looked her assent, and, with a warm grasp of the hand, as he helped her from the chaise, and a mutual smile of confidence and love, they separated.

He drove rapidly towards Boston, and she, opening the gate, found herself in the arms of Fanny Bruce, who had been impatiently awaiting the departure of Willie to seize her dear Miss Gertrude, and, between tears and kisses, pour out her congratulations and thanks for her happy escape from that horrid steamboat; for this was the first time they had met since the accident.

"Has Mrs. Graham come, Fanny?" asked Gertrude, as, the first excitement of the meeting over, they walked up to the house together.

"Yes, indeed, Mrs. Graham, and Kitty, and Isabel, and a little girl, and a sick gentleman,—Mr. Clinton, I believe; and another gentleman,—but *he's* gone."

"Who has gone?"

"O, a tall, dignified-looking man, with black eyes, and a beautiful face, and hair as white as if he were old,—and he isn't old, either."

"And do you say he has gone?"

"Yes; he didn't come with the rest. He was here when I came, and he went away about an hour ago. I heard him tell Miss Emily that he had agreed to meet a friend in Boston, but perhaps he'd come back this evening. I hope he will, Miss Gertrude; you ought to see him."

They had now reached the house, and, through the open door, Gertrude could plainly distinguish the loud tones of Mrs. Graham's voice, proceeding from the parlor on the right. She was talking to her husband and Emily, and was just saying, as Gertrude entered, "O, it was the most *awful* thing I ever heard of in my life! and to think, Emily, of your being on board, and our Isabel! Poor child! she hasn't got her color back yet, after her fright. And Gertrude Flint, too! By the way, they say Gertrude behaved very well. Where is the child?"

Turning round, she now saw Gertrude, who was just entering the room, and, going towards her, she kissed her with considerable heartiness and sincerity; for Mrs. Graham, though somewhat coarse and blunt, was not without good feelings when the occasion was such as to awaken them.

Gertrude's entrance having served to interrupt the stream of exclamatory remarks in which the excitable lady had been indulging for ten minutes or more, she now bethought herself of the necessity of removing her bonnet and outside garments, a part of which, being loosed from their fastenings, she had been dragging after her about the floor.

"Well!" exclaimed she, "I suppose I had better follow the girls' example, and go and get some of the dust off from me! I'm half buried, I believe! But, there, that's better than coming on in the horrid steamboat, last night, as my brother Clinton was so crazy as to propose. Where's Bridget? I want her to take up some of my things."

"I will assist you," said Gertrude, taking up a little carpet-bag, throwing a scarf which had been stretching across the room over her arm, and then following Mrs. Graham closely, in order to support the heavy travelling-shawl which was hanging half off that lady's shoulders. At the first landing-place, however, she found herself suddenly encircled in Kitty's warm embrace, and, laying down her burdens, gave herself up for a few moments to the hugging and kissing that succeeded.

At the head of the staircase she met Isabel, wrapped in a dressing-gown, with a large pitcher in her hand, and a most discontented and dissatisfied expression of countenance. She set the pitcher on the floor, however, and saluted Gertrude with a good grace. "I'm glad to see you alive," said she, "though I can't look at you without shuddering, it reminds me so of that dreadful day when we were in such frightful danger. How lucky we were to be saved, when there were so many drowned! I've wondered, ever since, Gertrude, how you could be so calm; I'm sure I shouldn't have known what to do, if you hadn't been there to suggest. But, O, dear! don't let us speak of it; it's a thing I can't bear to think of!" and, with a shudder and shrug of the shoulders, Isabel dismissed the subject, and called somewhat petishly to Kitty,—"Kitty, I thought you went to get our pitcher filled!"

Kitty, who, in obedience to a loud call and demand from her aunt, had hastily run to her room with the little travelling-bag which Gertrude had dropped on the staircase, now came back quite out of breath, saying, "I did ring the bell, twice. Hasn't anybody come?"

"No!" replied Belle; "and I should like to wash my face and curl my hair before tea, if I could."

"Let me take the pitcher," said Gertrude; "I am going down stairs, and will send Jane up with the water."

"Thank you," said Belle, rather feebly; while Kitty exclaimed, "No, no, Gertrude; I'll go myself."

But it was too late; Gertrude had gone.

Gertrude found Mrs. Ellis full of troubles and perplexities. "Only think," said the astonished housekeeper, "of their coming, five of them, without the least warning in the world; and here I've nothing in the house fit for tea;—not a bit of rich cake, not a scrap of cold ham! And, of course, they're hungry after their long journey, and will want something nice!"

"O, if they are very hungry, Mrs. Ellis, they can eat dried beef, and fresh biscuit, and plain cake; and, if you will give me the keys, I will get out the preserves, and the best silver, and see that the table is set properly."

Nothing was a trouble to Gertrude, that night. Everything that she touched went right. Jane caught her spirit, and became astonishingly active; and when the really bountiful table was spread, and Mrs. Ellis, after glancing around, and seeing that all was as it should be, looked into the beaming eyes and observed the glowing cheek and sunny smile of the happy girl, she exclaimed, in her ignorance, "Good gracious, Gertrude! anybody would think you were overjoyed to see all these folks back again!"

It wanted but a few moments to tea-time, and Gertrude was selecting fresh napkins from a drawer in the china-closet, when Kitty Ray peeped in at the door, and finally entered, leading by the hand a little girl, neatly dressed in black. Her face was, at first, full of smiles; but, the moment she attempted to speak, she burst into tears, and, throwing her arms round Gertrude's neck, whispered in her ear, "O, Gertrude, I'm so happy! I came to tell you!"

"Happy?" replied Gertrude; "then you mustn't cry."

Upon this, Kitty laughed, and then cried again, and then laughed once more, and, in the intervals, explained to Gertrude that she was engaged,—had been engaged a week, to the best man in the world,—and that the child she held by the hand was his orphan niece, and just like a daughter to him. "And, only think," continued she, "it's all owing to you!"

"To me?" said the astonished Gertrude.

"Yes; because I was so vain and silly, you know, and liked folks that were not worth liking, and didn't care much for anybody's comfort but my own; and, if you hadn't taught me to be something better than that, and set me a good example, which I've tried to follow ever since, he never would have thought of looking at me, much less loving me, and believing I should be a fit mother for little Gracie, here," and she looked down affectionately at the child, who was clinging fondly to her. "He is a minister, Gertrude, and very good. Only think of such a childish creature as I am being a minister's wife!"

The sympathy which Kitty came to claim was not denied her, and Gertrude, with her own eyes brimming with tears, assured her of her full participation in her joy.

In the mean time, little Grace, who still clung to Kitty with one hand, had gently inserted the other within that of Gertrude, who, looking down upon her for the first time, recognized the child whom she had rescued from persecution in the drawing-room at Saratoga.

Kitty was charmed with the coïncidence, and Gertrude, as she remarked the happy transformation which had already been effected in the countenance and dress of the little girl who had been so sadly in want of female superintendence, felt an added conviction of the wisdom of the young clergyman's choice.

Kitty was eager to give Gertrude a description of her lover, but a summons to the tea-table compelled her to postpone all further communications.

Mr. Graham's cheerful parlor had never looked so cheerful as on that evening. The weather was mild, but a light fire, which had been kindled on Mr. Clinton's account, did not render the room too warm. It had, however, driven the young people into a remote corner, leaving the neighborhood of the fireplace to Mrs. Graham and Emily, who occupied the sofa, and Mr. Clinton and Mr. Graham, whose arm-chairs were placed on the opposite side.

This arrangement enabled Mr. Graham to converse freely and uninterruptedly with his guest upon some grave topic of interest, while his talkative wife entertained herself and Emily by a recapitulation of her travels and adventures. On a table, at the further extremity of the room, was placed a huge portfolio of beautiful engravings, recently purchased and brought home by Mr. Graham, and representing a series of European views. Gertrude and Kitty were turning them carefully over; and little Grace, who was sitting in Kitty's lap, and Fanny, who was leaning over Gertrude's shoulder, were listening eagerly to the young ladies' explanations and comments.

Occasionally Isabel, the only restless or unoccupied person present, would lean over the table to glance at the likeness of some familiar spot, and exclaim, "Kitty, there's the shop where I bought my blue silk!" or, "Kitty, there's the waterfall that we visited in company with the Russian officers!"

While the assembled company were thus occupied, the door opened, and, without any announcement, Mr. Amory and William Sullivan entered.

Had either made his appearance singly, he would have been looked upon with astonishment by the majority of the company; but coming, as they did, together, and with an apparently good understanding existing between them, there was no countenance present (save the children's) which expressed any emotion but that of utter surprise.

Mr. and Mrs. Graham, however, were too much accustomed to society to betray any further evidence of that sentiment than was contained in a momentary glance, and, rising, received their visitors with due politeness and propriety. The former nodded carelessly to Mr. Amory, whom he had seen in the morning, presented him to Mr. Clinton (without, however, mentioning the existing connection with himself), and was preparing to go through the same ceremony to Mrs. Graham, but was saved the trouble, as she had not forgotten the acquaintance formed at Baden-Baden.

Willie's knowledge of the company also spared the necessity of introduction to all but Emily; and that being accidentally omitted, he gave an arch glance at Gertrude, and, taking an offered seat near Isabel, entered into conversation with her; Mr. Amory being in like manner engrossed by Mrs. Graham.

"Miss Gertrude," whispered Fanny, as soon as the interrupted composure of the party was once more restored, and glancing at Willie, as she spoke, "that's the gentleman you were out driving with, this afternoon. I know it is," continued she, as she observed Gertrude change color, and endeavor to hush her, while she looked anxiously round, as if fearful the remark had been overheard; "is it Willie, Gertrude?—is it Mr. Sullivan?"

Gertrude became more and more embarrassed, while the mischievous Fanny continued to ply her with questions; and Isabel, who had jealously noticed that Willie's eyes wandered more than once to the table, turned on her such a scrutinizing look as rendered her confusion distressing.

Accident came to her relief, however. The housemaid, with the evening paper, endeavored to open the door, against which her chair was placed; thus giving her an opportunity to rise, receive the paper, and, at the same time, an unimportant message. While she was thus engaged, Mr. Clinton left his chair, with the feeble step of an invalid, crossed the room, addressed a question in a low voice to Willie, and, receiving an affirmatory reply, took Isabel by the hand, and, approaching Mr. Amory, exclaimed, with deep emotion, "Sir, Mr. Sullivan tells me that you are the person who saved the life of my daughter; and here she is to thank you."

Mr. Amory rose and flung his arm over the shoulder and around the waist of Gertrude, who was passing on her way to hand the newspaper to Mr. Graham, and who, not having heard the remark of Mr. Clinton, received the caress with a sweet smile and an upturned face. "Here," said he, "Mr. Clinton is the person who saved the life of your daughter. It is true that I swam with her to the shore; but it was under the mistaken impression that I was bearing to a place of safety my own darling child, whom I little suspected then of having voluntarily relinquished to another her only apparent chance of rescue."

"Just like you, Gertrude! Just like you!" shouted Kitty and Fanny in a breath, each struggling to obtain a foremost place in the little circle that had gathered round her.

"My own noble Gertrude!" whispered Emily, as, leaning on Mr. Amory's arm, she pressed Gertrude's hand to her lips.

"O, Gertrude!" exclaimed Isabel, with tears in her eyes, "I didn't know. I never thought—"

"Your child?" cried Mrs. Graham's loud voice, interrupting Isabel's unfinished exclamation.

"Yes, my child, thank God!" said Mr. Amory, reverently; "restored, at last, to her unworthy father, and—you have no secrets here, my darling?"— Gertrude shook her head, and glanced at Willie, who now stood at her side, —"and gladly bestowed by him upon her faithful and far more deserving lover." And he placed her hand in Willie's.

There was a moment's pause. All were impressed with the solemnity of the action. Then Mr. Graham came forward, shook each of the young couple heartily by the hand, and, passing his sleeve hastily across his eyes, sought his customary refuge in the library.

"Gertrude," said Fanny, pulling Gertrude's dress to attract her attention, and speaking in a loud whisper, "are you engaged?—are you engaged to him?"

"Yes," whispered Gertrude, anxious, if possible, to gratify Fanny's curiosity, and silence her questioning.

"O! I'm so glad! I'm so glad!" shouted Fanny, dancing round the room, and flinging up her arms.

"And I'm glad, too!" said Gracie, catching the tone of congratulation, and putting her mouth up to Gertrude for a kiss.

"And *I* am glad," said Mr. Clinton, placing his hands upon those of Willie and Gertrude, which were still clasped together, "that the noble and self-sacrificing girl, whom I have no words to thank, and no power to repay, has reaped a worthy reward in the love of one of the few men with whom a fond father may venture wholly to trust the happiness of his child."

Exhausted by so much excitement, Mr. Clinton now complained of sudden faintness, and was assisted to his room by Willie, who, after waiting to see him fully restored, returned to receive the blessing of Emily upon his new hopes, and hear with wonder and delight the circumstances which attended the discovery of Gertrude's parentage.

For, although it was an appointment to meet Mr. Amory which had summoned him back to Boston, and he had in the course of their interview acquainted him with the happy termination of a lover's doubts, he had not, until the disclosure took place in Mr. Graham's parlor, received in return the slightest hint of the great surprise which awaited him. He had felt a little astonishment at his friend's expressed desire to join him at once in a visit to Mr. Graham's; but, on being informed that he had made the acquaintance of Mrs. Graham in Germany, he concluded that a desire to renew his intercourse with the family, and possibly a slight curiosity to see the lady of his own choice, were the only motives which had influenced him.

And now, amid retrospections of the past, thanksgiving for the present, and hopes and aspirations for the future, the evening passed rapidly away.

\*      \*      \*      \*      \*

"Come here, Gerty!" said Willie; "come to the window, and see what a beautiful night it is."

It was indeed a glorious night. Snow lay on the ground. The air was intensely cold without, as might be judged from the quick movements of pedestrians, and the brilliant icicles with which everything that had an edge was fringed. The stars were glittering, too, as they never glitter, except on the most intense of winter nights. The moon was just peeping above an old brown building,—the same old corner building which had been visible from the door-step where Willie and Gerty were wont to sit in their childhood, and from behind which they had often watched the coming of that same round moon.

Leaning on Willie's shoulder, Gertrude stood gazing until the full circle was visible in a space of clear and cloudless ether. Neither of them spoke, but their hearts throbbed with the same emotion, as they thought of the days that were past.

Just then, the gas-man came quickly up the street, lit, as by an electric touch, the bright burners that in close ranks lined either side-walk, and in a moment more was out of sight.

Gertrude sighed. "It was no such easy task for poor old Uncle True," said she; "there have been great improvements since his time."

"There have, indeed!" said Willie, glancing round the well-lit, warm and pleasantly-furnished parlor of his own and Gertrude's home, and resting his eyes, at last, upon the beloved one by his side, whose beaming face but reflected back his own happiness,—"such improvements, Gerty, as we only dreamt of once! I wish the dear old man could be here to see and share them!"

A tear started to Gertrude's eye; but, pressing Willie's arm, she pointed reverently upward to a beautiful, bright star, just breaking forth from a silvery film, which had hitherto half-overshadowed it; the star through which Gertrude had ever fancied she could discern the smile of the kind old man.

"Dear Uncle True!" said she; "his lamp still burns brightly in heaven, Willie; and its light is not yet gone out on earth!"

\* \* \* \* \*

In a beautiful town about thirty miles from Boston, and on the shore of one of those hill-embosomed ponds which would be immortalized by the poet in a country less rich than ours with such sheets of blue, transparent water, there stood a mansion-house of solid though ancient architecture. It had been the property of Philip Amory's paternal grand-parents, and the early home and sole inheritance of his father, who so cherished the spot that it was only with great reluctance, and when driven to the act by the spur of poverty, that he was induced to part with the much-valued estate.

To reclaim the venerable homestead, repair and judiciously modernize the house, and fertilize and adorn the grounds, was a favorite scheme with Philip. His ample means now rendering it practicable, he lost no time in putting it into execution, and, the spring after he returned from his wanderings, saw the work in a fair way to be speedily completed.

In the mean time, Gertrude's marriage had taken place, the Grahams had removed to their house in town (which, out of compliment to Isabel, who was passing the winter with her aunt, was more than ever crowded with gay company), and the bustling mistress was already projecting changes in her husband's country-seat.

And Emily, who had parted with her greatest treasure, and found herself in an atmosphere which was little in harmony with her spirit, murmured not; but, contented with her lot, neither dreamed of nor asked for outward change, until Philip came to her one day, and, taking her hand, said, gently,

"This is no home for you, Emily. You are as much alone as I in my solitary farm-house. We loved each other in childhood, our hearts became one in youth, and have continued so until now. Why should we be longer parted? Your father will not oppose our wishes; and will you, dearest, refuse to bless and gladden the lonely life of your gray-haired lover?"

But Emily shook her head, while she answered, with her smile of ineffable sweetness,

"O, no, Philip! do not speak of it! Think of my frail health and my helplessness!"

"Your health, dear Emily, is improving. The roses are already coming back to your cheeks; and, for your helplessness, what task can be so sweet to me as teaching you, through my devotion, to forget it? O, do not send me away disappointed, Emily! A cruel fate divided us for years; do not by your own act prolong that separation! Believe me, a union with my early love is my brightest, my only hope of happiness!"

And she did not withdraw the hand which he held, but yielded the other also to his fervent clasp.

"My only thought had been, dear Philip," said she, "that ere this I should have been called to my Father's home; and even now I feel many a warning that I cannot be very long for earth; but while I stay, be it longer or shorter, it shall be as you wish. No word of mine shall part hearts so truly one, and your home shall be mine."

And when the grass turned green, and the flowers sent up their fragrance, and the birds sang in the branches, and the spring gales blew soft and made a gentle ripple on the water, Emily came to live on the hill-side with Philip. And Mrs. Ellis came too, to superintend all things, and especially the dairy, which became henceforth her pride. She had long since tearfully implored, and easily obtained, the forgiveness of the much-wronged Philip; and proved, by the humility of her voluntary confession, that she was not without a woman's heart.

Mrs. Prime pleaded hard for the cook's situation at the farm; but Emily kindly expostulated with her, saying,

"We cannot all leave my father, Mrs. Prime. Who would see to his hot toast, and the fire in the library?" and the good old woman saw the matter in the right light, and submitted.

And is the long-wandering, much-suffering, and deeply-sorrowing exile happy now? He is; but his peace springs not from his beautiful home, his wide possessions, an honorable repute among his fellow-men, or even the love of the gentle Emily.

All these are blessings that he well knows how to prize; but his world-tried soul has found a deeper anchor yet,—a surer refuge from the tempest and the storm; for, through the power of a living faith, he has laid hold on eternal life. The blind girl's prayers are answered; her last, best work is done; she has cast a ray from her blessed spirit into his darkened soul; and, should her call to depart soon come, she will leave behind one to follow in her footsteps, fulfil her charities, and do good on earth, until such time as he be summoned to join her again in heaven.

As they go forth in the summer evening, to breathe the balmy air, listen to the winged songster of the grove, and drink in the refreshing influences of a summer sunset, all things speak a holy peace to the new-born heart of him who has so long been a man of sorrow.

As the sun sinks among gorgeous clouds, as the western light grows dim, and the moon and the stars come forth in their solemn beauty, they utter a lesson to his awakened soul; and the voice of nature around, and the still, small voice within, whisper, in gentlest, holiest accents,

"The sun shall be no more thy light by day, neither for brightness shall the moon give light unto thee; but the Lord shall be unto thee an everlasting light, and thy God thy glory."

"Thy sun shall no more go down, neither shall thy moon withdraw itself; for the Lord shall be thine everlasting light, and the days of thy mourning shall be ended."